WHAT DID THESE MEN
WANT OF THEM?

As Meryt stepped from the royal barge that had borne her in splendor down the Nile, she shivered at the sight of the great palace of Akhenaten, the heretic Pharaoh of Egypt. What use did this fearfully warped yet awesomely brilliant ruler have for her, a woman he claimed to desire yet clearly despised?

Aimee trembled as she waited in her Victorian bridal bed for her husband, Lord Edward, to join her for their wedding night. She knew nothing of men, yet what she knew of this man filled her with dread. It was not love she had read in his gaze, not even lust, but a menace too monstrous to conceive.

Both of these women had so much to learn—and only one had a chance to survive. . . .

WINE OF THE DREAMERS

Big Bestsellers from SIGNET

WINE OF THE DREAMERS

SUSANNAH LEIGH

A SIGNET BOOK
NEW AMERICAN LIBRARY
TIMES MIRROR
PUBLISHED BY
THE NEW AMERICAN LIBRARY
OF CANADA LIMITED

NAL BOOKS ARE AVAILABLE AT QUANTITY DISCOUNTS
WHEN USED TO PROMOTE PRODUCTS OR SERVICES. FOR
INFORMATION PLEASE WRITE TO PREMIUM MARKETING
DIVISION, THE NEW AMERICAN LIBRARY, INC.,
1633 BROADWAY, NEW YORK, NEW YORK 10019.

Copyright © 1980 by Susannah Leigh

First Printing, April, 1980

1 2 3 4 5 6 7 8 9

SIGNET TRADEMARK REG. U.S. PAT. OFF. AND FOREIGN COUNTRIES
REGISTERED TRADEMARK - MARCA REGISTRADA
HECHO EN WINNIPEG, CANADA

SIGNET, SIGNET CLASSICS, MENTOR, PLUME, MERIDIAN
and NAL BOOKS are published in Canada by The New American
Library of Canada, Limited, Scarborough, Ontario

PRINTED IN CANADA

COVER PRINTED IN U.S.A.

ONE

The River Is Like Wine

☾☾ Meryt

> Seven days I have not seen my sister,
> And sickness has overcome me;
> My limbs are grown heavy,
> And I cannot feel my body.
> Let the physicians come to me,
> My heart takes no comfort in their cures.

The voice of the scribe Senmut was deep and earthy, lingering on the plaintive notes of his melody until the haunting words seemed to float across the swollen brown waters of the Nile. It was the month of Thoth, the first month of Inundation, and the whitewashed walls of the shining new city of Ahket-Aten sparkled in the midday sun. Up and down the river, the people of Kemet, the rich, fertile realm of the pharaohs and their powerful gods, raised their voices in raucous jubilation, celebrating once again the annual renewal of the earth by the life-giving Nile. But beside the royal docks, isolated in their splendor from the teeming life of the city, all the excitement and noise seemed far away.

> Better for me is my sister than all the physicians,
> Better my beloved than all their remedies.
> Her coming is my salvation;
> When I see her, I am whole.

The princess Meryt-Ankh-Re, seated quietly beside the cool water, glanced up at the scribe. Her straight black hair drifted softly to her shoulders, forming a dark halo for delicate features.

Senmut saw her look up at him. Skillfully he ran his fingers across the strings of his lyre, bringing a new sweetness to the song.

> She turns her eyes upon me, I am young again;
> She speaks to me, I am strong,

> She embraces me, my body is free of evil.
> But I have not seen her seven days.

He let his voice soften provocatively on the closing words. The lyre lay mutely beneath his fingers for a moment. Then slowly he lifted it, setting it gently on the sandy earth beside him. He made no attempt to hide his admiration as he gazed at the beautiful form only a few yards away from him.

He did not think he had ever seen anything so lovely. Meryt had been only a child last year when he came as a scribe to her father Ramose's house, a little girl of thirteen—dazzling, charming, pretty, but a little girl for all that. Now, for the first time she showed hints of the woman she was about to become. Her dark, haunting eyes, touched not with the black of her people, but a deep, alien blue, as rich as the midnight sky, were beginning to hold subtle, mysterious promises in their depths, promises her ripening body could understand better than her youthful mind. Senmut felt his own body begin to ache in response, swelling with a kind of hunger he knew no man had the right to feel for a woman who was not his.

Meryt did not fail to sense his longing, and it tore her heart apart. Only yesterday, that same longing had excited her, making her tingle with new, unfamiliar emotions, intriguing and frightening both—but yesterday she had still dared to hope that a young scribe, clever and ambitious, might one day aspire to the hand of a princess. Today she felt only an uneasy sense of foreboding.

Abruptly she turned her head away, fixing her gaze on the sunlit waters of the Nile. As she did, she caught sight of a tiny boat, an elaborately carved and painted toy, darting boldly in and out among the tall, gilded barques that lined the docks. It was an exquisitely pretty thing, its small square sail barely catching a trace of wind, its curved prow cutting through the current as if it were fighting high, angry waves to push its way out into the sea. In the center, between two ranks of tiny carved oarsmen, stood a single figure, a miniature man formed from faience, like the little ushabti figures dead men carried into their tombs to serve them in the afterworld.

Senmut smiled as he watched her. The sudden concentration on her features did not fool him for a minute. He knew she was still intensely aware of him, just as he was aware of her. Leaning back, he rested one elbow on the sand, taking

3

advantage of the moment to study her frankly. He was enchanted by what he saw.

The girl's body, though still slim and childlike, already had begun to develop, calling out to his own youthful masculinity. Softly rounded hips flowed into a slender waist, not even as large as the span of his hands. Sheer white linen, fastened fashionably over a single shoulder, only half-concealed the firm contours of one breast, leaving the other free to glow, sensuous and golden brown, in the warm rays of the sun.

Would she be shocked, he wondered, if he picked up his lyre again, singing to her of the hunger in his body to linger against hers, the thirst in his lips to suck the sweet, warm honey of her breast? Somehow, he did not think she would. It seemed to him the Princess Meryt had been more than a little aware of him recently—and more than a little eager to let her own body respond to his.

Even without turning, Meryt was keenly conscious of the intensity of Senmut's gaze. She longed to rise and go to him, not for the caresses he seemed to offer, but simply for the comfort her heart needed so desperately that day. It was hard to keep her eyes riveted on the shimmering water.

The little boat bounced up and down on the current, but Meryt barely saw it through the sudden spate of tears that rose in her eyes. She did not even notice when the swirling waters clutched at the prow of the miniature vessel, drawing it away from the haven of the shore. Only when a sharp stone gouged suddenly into the soft wood, did she break out of her reverie at last. For an instant she could not figure out what had happened. All she could do was watch with fascination as the little faience figure slipped from the deck and sunk into the murky water.

Curiously, Meryt turned to scan the shore. She was just in time to catch sight of a small boy, no more than eight or nine years old, his pretty features twisted into a petulant expression as he watched his toy drift farther and farther away from him. Sensing Meryt's presence, he looked up abruptly. The instant he saw the surprised look in her eyes, his anger melted away, disappearing in a burst of boyish laughter.

"Gone to Osiris," he shouted. Still laughing, he turned and began to race down the banks of the river. The sound of his merriment grew fainter and fainter as he sprinted away, lost in a world of his own.

Gone to Osiris.

The words filled Meryt with dread. Gone to Osiris, the god

4

of the dead, the lord of all the dark, empty places they must one day walk.

A sudden loud howling jolted Meryt out of her own thoughts. Turning, she saw her baby brother, Tuti, standing at the edge of the river, his plump toddler's legs stomping up and down. Tears glistened on his cheeks as he pointed a trembling finger toward the little boat.

Meryt laughed, holding her arms out to the boy. She was only half-surprised when he insisted on holding his ground. Already, though he was less than three years old, Tuti was showing a will of his own.

Meryt was tempted to wade out into the river, trying to retrieve the boat and its fallen helmsman for Tuti. Common sense warned her she would be too late. The little craft had already drifted far out into the river, and the tiny ushabti figure no doubt would be lost in the mud at the bottom.

"Its no good, Tuti," she called out soothingly, "The little helmsman has gone to Osiris."

Gone to Osiris. The second time in minutes she had heard those fateful words—only now they were on her own lips.

Gone to Osiris. She had meant the words lightly, teasingly—merely as a comfort for her baby brother. Now they seemed light no longer. Forgetting Tuti and his tears, she pulled her knees up, clasping her arms tightly around them as she stared at the subtle, twisting patterns of the current.

Gone to Osiris.

How many men would go to Osiris that day? How many good men would moor their boats to the western shore that night?

Angrily she pushed the thought away from her. She could not let herself dwell on such things. Not now . . . not yet. Soon enough she would have to face them. Soon there would no longer be any escape. Until then, for the few hours she had left, she wanted her heart to feel only the sunlight.

Pulling herself to her feet, she turned her back on the river and all the bright, gilded craft that waited to sail out and greet the pharaoh when he returned. She could bear the place no longer. It was intolerable sitting, staring at the water, watching, waiting—not even knowing what to pray for. Silently she followed the wide, covered portico that led away from the docks, making her way toward the gentle hillside beyond. She was aware of Senmut's quizzical look as he followed her, but she did not try to turn back. She knew if she did, the tears that glistened on her lashes would slip warmly down her cheeks, betraying her at last.

The hillside lay deserted in the golden afternoon sun. It seemed to Meryt that everyone in the city was down at the waterfront, laughing and shouting and drinking, singing at the top of their lungs as they waited for pharaoh to come back to them, returning as he had returned every year in splendor from the solemn ceremonies up the river. She did not mind the solitude. She had always loved the quiet, open temple her uncle built for the Aten, high on a hilltop overlooking the shores of his shining new city. She was glad to have it to herself today.

Slowly, surprised at her own weariness, Meryt sank down in the shade of one of the tall columns. Tucking her knees into her arms once more, she let her eyes drift down the slopes, lingering on the same royal fleet she had promised herself she would not look at again. As she did, she was surprised to find her thoughts dwelling not on the strong, vital father who had always dominated her life, but rather on the one man he despised more than any other man on earth.

And yet, Meryt thought, smiling a little at the idea, all her father's anger, all his hatred, had never quite been enough to keep her from liking her strange, moody uncle. Even when he was only young Amenhotep, son of the great pharaoh Amenhotep III, Meryt's own grandfather, the girl had been drawn toward him, feeling in her heart a strong empathy for the very ugliness that caused everyone else to scorn him. Now that he was pharaoh, now that the sun rose and set in his being—now that he was no longer Amenhotep, but Akhenaten, the rebel, the fanatic—Meryt found the secret habits of her heart too strong to break.

They had called Akhenaten a heretic when he cast out the old gods, setting up the Aten, the one true god, in their place. They whispered the word in the dark corners of their houses, reviling the man who was both ruler and deity, daring even to speak it aloud on the streets of the city he had raised from the barren sand. But he wasn't a heretic, Meryt thought pensively. Not really. He was only a dreamer, a madman perhaps, but a madman with a vision of beauty and love and freedom from fear. It saddened her to realize the world was not ready for him.

Meryt was surprised to see a shadow cross the range of her vision, dulling the sandy hillside in front of her. Silently, she glanced up.

Senmut's lips were smiling as he looked down at her, but his eyes were solemn.

"The princess is sad today."

6

Meryt started awkwardly at the sound of his words. It made her uncomfortable to realize how transparent she was.

"Not sad," she retorted hastily. "Just bored. I am tired of all this ostentation my uncle is so fond of."

Her answer was not fair, and she knew it. It was not Akhenaten who doted on ceremony, but rather her grandfather, the late Amenhotep III. Yes, and if she was going to be honest about it, her father, too. Ramose was an ambitious man, bitter at the fate that made him the son of a minor wife, while his younger—and to his eyes lesser—half-brother inherited the throne. All the pomp of today's rites could serve only to rankle his soul, eating away at it until there was nothing left but envy.

Senmut dropped to one knee beside her. He reached out his hand, as if to lay it on her arm. Then, remembering she was a princess and he only her father's scribe, he let it drop limply to his side.

"The daughter of the pharaoh is very beautiful."

All the longing he had not dared in the touch of his hand trembled in his voice. He was sure she could not fail to recognize and respond to it.

The daughter of the pharaoh? Meryt felt her body shiver, not with the passion he had intended, but only cold apprehension. Anxiously she looked up to see if he understood what he had said. She was relieved to realize he did not.

No, Senmut intended the words only generally. A princess, a granddaughter of the pharaoh, inheritor of the blood royal—that was all he meant.

But if her father had his way today . . .

"Sing me another song, Senmut," she cried out suddenly. She could not bear her sadness another minute.

Senmut laughed softly. "I didn't bring my lyre with me."

"It doesn't matter." She tried to keep her tone light and teasing. "You know you sing well without it."

Senmut sat beside her. His voice was low and deliberately sensuous as he began to sing:

I sail north in the ferry.
I am going to Memphis;
I will say to Ptah, the Lord of the Truth.
Give me my sister tonight.

The words were more explicit than anything he had dared to sing to her before. Leaning back against the warm sand, Meryt closed her eyes, blocking out the sunlight on the hillside, the shadows of the temple, even the sparkling river below.

Give me my sister tonight.

How sweet it would be to belong to this man, to go into his arms tonight and feel his lips against hers, to have her body satisfied at last.

> The river is like wine;
> The golden goddess is my joy,
> The sun rises in her beauty.
> I will say to Ptah, the Lord of the Truth,
> Give me my sister tonight.

Give me my sister tonight.

If only she could be his sister, his beloved, and he her brother, her husband. If only she could spend eternity in the safety of his arms.

Give me my sister tonight.

How strange their language was, she mused dreamily, questioning the words she had always taken for granted. *Brother* was this man whose strong arms were made to embrace her, whose lips cried out to the yearning in her own lips and breast, whose body she longed to feel beside hers through the long, honeyed, sleepless hours of darkness. And yet *brother* was the baby on the bank, the fat little toddler whose bare feet stomped angrily at the edges of the water as he wept for a toy that was not even his.

Yet not so strange, she sighed, opening her eyes to stare down into the fertile river valley. In a land where heredity passed through the female line, where many a man had to marry his sister—or even his daughter—to secure his inheritance, brother and husband were often the same thing.

Meryt found herself shivering at the thought. It was a thing that had never seemed to touch her before. Her father did not approve of close marriages, and as the granddaughter of only a minor wife of pharaoh, she had expected to be able to marry the man of her choice—even a humble scribe.

But if her father had his way today . . .

She blocked the implications from her mind. It was incomprehensible, impossible even to imagine, that one day she might be forced into a marriage bed with the toddler on the riverbank, or worse yet . . .

"Isn't my uncle's temple pretty?" she said hastily, eager to find some sort of diversion.

Senmut turned away from her, letting his eyes scan the

sunlit columns. He could understand why the girl would call the place pretty. The old temples, the temples to Amon, the Hidden One, had been dark, secret structures accessible only to rich men and the corrupt priests who both served and used them. By contrast, the temples of the Aten should have seemed bright and free—and enticing. It was one of the stranger whims of fate that the people did not enjoy them.

His eyes were troubled as he turned back to her. "Your uncle is a fool," he said softly.

Meryt's jaw tightened at his frankness, but she did not argue with him. Instinct warned her he was right. She had always found her uncle's faith beautiful and serene, free from darkness and fear, but she knew it was unpopular.

"I don't understand, Senmut. The Aten is good and pure. Why do the people turn away from him?"

"Because they don't want him. It doesn't matter how good a god is, or how pure, if the people don't want him. You can't force faith down their throats."

"But they don't even try. They just cling to the old gods, refusing to let go of them."

Senmut laughed as he watched her brow tighten into a scowl of concentration. "Just like you, my little one."

"What do you mean?" She felt herself bristle with indignation. "You know I worship the Aten, Senmut. With all my heart."

"As the one true god? With no false gods to diminish his power?"

"Of course."

Senmut leaned forward, peering into her eyes. Meryt had the feeling he was laughing at her.

"Can you honestly tell me, pretty little Meryt-Ankh-Re, that you would be willing to give up your love for Isis?"

Unconsciously Meryt's hand slipped up to the heavy jeweled pectoral that circled her shoulders and dangled onto her breast. She did not need to glance down to remember what it looked like. Long, sweeping wings—gold set with carnelian, turquoise, and lapis lazuli—wrapped themselves around her neck, and in the center, in place of the hawk or vulture that would have been more common, her father had had the goldsmith mold an exquisite figure of the goddess Isis, her long golden arms stretching gracefully over her wings. It was an expensive piece, a costly fancy, but one that Ramose, who still held to the old gods, had been only too happy to provide for his daughter.

"But Isis is different," Meryt protested uncomfortably.

9

And Isis *was* different. Isis was her own personal emblem of womanhood, the epitome of courage and fidelity . . . and love. It was Isis, the perfect sister, who wept for Osiris when he was slain by their jealous brother, Seth; Isis, the perfect wife, who searched patiently for the scattered pieces of his body so they could be restored to life by the sacrifice of her son, Horus. If it weren't for Isis, there would be no Osiris, no god to open the gates of the underworld to man, no dream of immortality reaching out forever and ever. There would be no love.

"No," she said softly. "I would not give up Isis."

"Nor will the people give up the gods they love—and need. Don't you see, Meryt? They want to be buried in the west with the setting sun, as men have been buried since the beginning of time. They want to carry the Book of the Dead as a talisman into the tomb with them. They want the dark, hidden temples and the solemn rites, the cleansing catharsis of fear. They even want the corruption. Remember, it is easier for a rich, powerful man to buy immortality than to earn it."

A rich, powerful man. Meryt shuddered at the words. Rich and powerful, like her father. And ambitious.

Slowly she turned her eyes toward the Nile.

Two men had sailed up the river with the rising sun. One man would return in the blood red sunset. One man would stand alone beneath the canopy of the royal barge, resplendent in his jewels, tall in the crown of the two lands.

Only one man could be the Living Horus, the Son of the Sun—the pharaoh of all Kemet.

The red gold of the late-afternoon sun burnished the approaching boats, creating the illusion of an unearthly fire glowing upon the cool waters of the Nile. Red and blue banners shimmered above the small fleet, signaling the return of the royal party, and the long wail of trumpets punctuated the air. The far-off cries of the helmsmen were bare echoes in the distance.

A single boat, taller and more splendid than the others, drifted in the lead, its huge square sail furled in the windless air. A long row of gold and ebony oars caught the sunlight as they dipped into the water, then rose rhythmically, in and out, in and out again. A solitary figure stood alone beneath a gilded canopy in the center.

Meryt squinted into the light, trying desperately to catch a glimpse of the man's face, veiled by the shadows of the canopy. She did not know if she was relieved or frightened when she could not make them out. She only knew that no matter what had happened that day, no matter who had proved victorious in the bitter struggle that was now at an end, all the happiness she had ever known, all the dreams in her youthful heart, had been shattered forever.

Turning away from the water, she let herself look one last time at the tall bronzed man beside her. Long black hair emphasized the strength of sharply molded features, and black eyes danced with a thousand lights of laughter and exhilaration. Meryt was tempted to reach out and touch him. Her hand trembled as she held it back.

Yesterday she had been an insignificant princess, far from the throne and its demands. Today . . .

Today, if her father had won his desperate gamble, she would be pharaoh's daughter, the only girl child of his chief wife, the beautiful foreign princess whose dark blue eyes she had inherited.

At last she dared, let her hand rest lightly on the arm of the man she sensed she would never see again. Feeling her touch, Senmut glanced down. The slow smile that formed at the corners of his mouth told Meryt he did not understand the pain that had prompted her gesture.

And if her father had lost . . .

She felt her body stiffen. She knew she could not think about it, she could not dwell on the fate that would be hers if her father had not triumphed that afternoon. Turning back to the water, she forced her eyes to study the boat once again.

She was terrified to see how much nearer it had drawn. The figure in the center, deceptively tall in the double crown, was so much larger now, so much more tangible. It would only be a minute, a brief, fleeting minute, before his features were recognizable.

Meryt was conscious of small hands tugging at the sheer linen of her skirt. Baby whimpers rang in her ears as Tuti demanded to be lifted up so he could see better. Usually her little brother amused her. Today she had no patience with him.

"Hush, Tuti," she cried, startling the child as she pushed him away from her.

The boy howled his disappointment, reaching up stubbornly to pull at her skirts once again. When Meryt felt him let go suddenly, his protests melting into a stream of giggles, she could not resist turning. She had to smile as she saw him perched smugly on Senmut's strong shoulders, his fingers locked securely in the scribe's long hair. His face was shining with eagerness as he watched the tall ships approach.

It broke Meryt's heart to see him. He had never looked so small and vulnerable, or so full of vitality and joy. She wondered if she would ever see laughter in his eyes again. In these last few minutes, he was still baby Tuti, just like all the other children shouting with excitement as the ships drew near. But when they landed, he would be little Tuti no longer. From that time on, he would either be the son of a pharaoh—the Crown Prince Tutankhaten, heir to cares and responsibilities that would crush even a mature heart—or he would be the mortal enemy of a pharaoh.

Meryt was keenly aware that the moment had arrived at last, the moment that would decide her fate as well as her brother's. Even if the oarsmen had been sluggish in their task, even if they had not moved half as swiftly as on other days, the ship must still be near enough to discern the face of the man who wore the double crown. She was only a little surprised when she could not force herself to look at him. Instead she let her eyes search Senmut's face. One glance was enough to tell her everything she needed to know.

There was no surprise in the scribe's eyes as he gazed at the pharaoh. The face beneath the double crown was the face he had expected to see.

Slowly Meryt turned.

Akhenaten stood alone in the center of the boat, his head bent, as if the crown had grown too heavy for him to bear. The sun touched his sallow complexion with hints of golden pink, hiding the deathlike pallor of his skin. It seemed to Meryt she had never seen anyone so grotesquely ugly.

The deformed, elongated lines of the pharaoh's head, only partially concealed beneath the tall crown, stretched the sharp contours of his cheekbones out into a jutting chin. Taut skin, drawn across crude features, made his eyes look like narrow slits, glinting like cat's eyes over arrogant, sensuous lips. His body, clumsy and misshapen, was dominated by its feminine characteristics, the belly swollen and distended, the hips wide and rounded, the breasts as soft and pendulous as an old woman's.

When the ship finally stopped, Akhenaten was slow to move, as if he had become so weary he could barely force his body forward. It was several minutes before his feet touched the shore.

Meryt slipped quietly out of the anonymity of the crowd. Her body moved automatically, her feet taking the steps they were expected to take, but she could not make her mind focus on what she was doing. She felt as if she were walking in a dream, a hazy nightmare where everything was illusory and unreal and she could not determine where she was.

Coolly, with an outward calm she had not known she possessed, she sank to her knees before the pharaoh.

"Uncle."

Her voice was low and steady, offering the word as if it were a routine greeting. Only a slight quiver of her hands gave her away, and she was careful to keep them clenched at her sides. It was a long time before she could bring herself to raise her eyes from the earth.

The haunted look that greeted her gaze sent a chill through her heart. If her uncle had stared down at her with hatred, or even dread, she would have been able to understand it. Instead she saw only pain, a slow, twisting pain that seemed to burn into his soul. Dully she wondered which hurt him most, the betrayal of a brother whose love he had never been able to win, or the savage need to extend to a man's heirs the bloodbath he himself had begun.

Then, without warning, Meryt saw her uncle thrust his hand stiffly toward her, the gesture unmistakable and commanding. There was nothing in his tense controlled expression to tell her what he was thinking. Slowly she raised her own hand, slipping it into the cold flesh of waiting fingers. Her heart was numb as she felt him pull her to her feet.

She did not try to protest as firm hands urged her forward, drawing her away from the riverbank. Even when her uncle ignored the waiting chariots, moving instead on foot toward the long avenue that led to the royal palace, she did not question him. She knew only too well the fate that must be hers. She did not need confirmation from his lips.

An expectant roar rose when they emerged from the private wharf, as if even the masses, half drunk with beer and celebration, sensed something out of the ordinary and could barely control their excitement. Meryt scarcely noticed them. Somewhere in that crowd, she knew, Senmut would be pushing his way anxiously along the side of the avenue, Tuti still safe on his shoulders, but she could not bring herself to look at him. There was nothing they could say to each other now, even with their eyes.

Akhenaten did not hurry toward the palace, strolling instead at a cool, leisurely pace down the broad, stone-paved avenue. Only when they finally reached the tall gates, did he begin to move with nervous haste, rushing his niece toward

13

the Window of Appearances, high in one of the outer walls. Meryt wondered if he was truly impatient to get to the place, hungry for the cries and cheers that offered him his only reassurance, or if he, like she, was simply eager to get the thing over with.

The Window of Appearances was a recent innovation, an unusual custom initiated by her uncle as much in response to his own narcissistic needs as to please the people. It seemed to excite him to stand there, high above his subjects, tossing down gifts from his lofty vantage point—a golden chalice for one favorite, a jeweled collar for another—reminding himself as much as them that he was a living deity, a god on earth. The roar that ran through the crowd when he stepped out on the balcony now, proud and tall in his crown, his pretty niece fragile and childlike beside him, was charged with anticipation.

Akhenaten did not attempt to rush the moment, moving instead with the same deliberation that had marked their promenade down the avenue leading to the palace. The sun was already beginning to set, staining the streets and whitewashed walls with scarlet before he raised his hands, coaxing his subjects to silence. Meryt shivered as she watched him. She was certain he had done it on purpose, timing his melodramatic announcement to coincide with the moment the world seemed to be bathed in blood. If she had any lingering doubts about her fate, they vanished.

"My beloved people."

Akhenaten's voice, usually thin and strained, seemed to have deepened with emotion. The muscles of his face were drawn, pulling his full lips into a sharp line. The crowd, sensing his mood, fell silent.

"I tell you, I Akhenaten, Lord of the Two Lands, Son of the Sun, He Who Lives in Truth, I tell you that today my heart is heavy with sorrow. Today my brother, Ramose, son of my father, Amenhotep—may his *ka* live forever—has gone to dwell with his ancestors in the lands beyond the realm of mortal men. I shall see him no more."

Meryt felt a sickening wave of faintness sweep over her. She had known her father was dead—reason warned her it could be no other way—but still the words were hard to bear. It was all she could do to keep from crying out in grief and fear.

For an instant, a quick treacherous instant, she let herself hope there was some way she could escape her father's fate.

Perhaps if she pleaded with her uncle, if she reminded him of the fondness he had always felt for her . . .

Angrily she pushed the thought away. Neither pleas nor tears would move her uncle. All they would bring was one last moment of shame and regret.

It would not be so bad, she reminded herself, trying frantically to still the rapid beating of her heart. A moment of terror, a quick flash of pain, and then it would all be over.

Tonight she would be with her father, standing beside him on the western shores of the river that flowed on forever. Tonight the jackal god Annubis would place her heart in his scales, weighing it against the lightness of a feather. And tomorrow, with the rising sun, her *ba* would be free of her body, taking the form of a bird to soar through the air with a freedom she had never known on earth.

She was surprised to feel her uncle's hand against hers, cold fingers tightening around her own. It was almost as if he wanted to give her comfort . . . or to take it from her.

Akhenaten's voice was hesitant as he continued. He stammered slightly on the words, half-whispering them, as though it was hard to speak them aloud.

"Know you all, for the love I bore my brother, and the love I still bear the beautiful young woman who is the child of his loins, I shall not leave her alone in the world with none to care or provide for her."

Meryt listened to his words in silence, trying to understand what they meant. These were not the words she had expected to hear on her uncle's lips, the words she had steeled herself against. Puzzled, she pulled away from him. His grasp was surprisingly strong as he closed his fingers around hers again, forcing her body against his.

"From this day forth, the Princess Meryt-Ankh-Re, daughter of my brother, Ramose, will be my wife, second only to my chief wife, Nefertiti. From her body will come the sons of my loins who will one day rule all Kemet."

Meyrt gasped aloud at his boldness. Too late she realized what she should have known all along, that her uncle had outwitted them all.

She would not die that day, but neither would she be allowed to live again.

The crowd, ignorant of the realities of the political game being played out in front of them, roared their approval. Meryt, with her exotic eyes and dazzling beauty, had always been a favorite. It delighted them now to have her for a queen.

Reluctantly the girl forced herself to admit how clever her uncle had been. With one swift, clean stroke he had defeated all his enemies at once. By the mercy of his act, by sparing his rival's issue, he had shamed even the most rabid of his critics into grudging silence. As for her father's supporters, weakened as they were by their loss that day, which of them would move against the man who had guaranteed their leader's heir, the son of his own daughter, the throne of Kemet?

Meryt was cold in her sheer linen gown as the sun slipped at last beneath the horizon. She was intensely aware of the man at her side, but she could not force herself to turn.

And yet he was her husband, she told herself with a dull finality. In the space of a few seconds he had bound her to him, not just for life, but for all eternity. There were no rites, no ceremonies, no celebration. Just the simple words from pharaoh's lips—"From this day forth, the princess Meryt-Ankh-Re . . . will be my wife"—and she belonged to him.

The wild jubilation of the crowd rang in her ears, but Meryt barely heard it above the sharp, heavy beating of her own heart. Somewhere in that alien sea of faces was the one face she longed to see, somewhere among all those dark, anonymous eyes, the pair of eyes she would never dare to meet again.

She had known that afternoon she must lose him. She had not known how much it would hurt.

She felt the pressure of a hand on her arm, light and gentle, yet subtly commanding. Her eyes still averted, she turned slowly, following her new husband into the palace.

∞ Aimée

1

Bright rays of spring sunshine glinted on the waters of the Seine, teasing the surface with golden fire. A pair of barges drifted by, silhouetted black against the current as they idled their way toward the busy docks of Paris. In a moment they had passed, leaving the water still and unbroken once again on this lazy Sunday afternoon. Near the embankment a tiny craft hugged the shore, its bow and mast barely larger than the childish hands that had fashioned it from an odd assortment of bark and twigs and leaves.

Aimée LeClare, leaning against a railing high above the river, stared down at the miniature bateau with mingled amusement and contentment. It seemed to her there could be no more perfect place than Paris in these last years of the nineteenth century, and she felt a vague sense of pity for anyone who had never known the sound of laughter echoing off the water or the pungent scent of horse chestnuts sprouting new bonnets of green along wide avenues. Even the child's boat, far below in the water, had a sense of Parisian spring about it, for it had been laden with a cargo of newly opened blossoms before being turned adrift in the Seine.

"Bang! Bang! Bang!"

High-pitched boyish shouts broke the serenity of the afternoon. A lone fisherman, tending his pole at the water's edge, turned to cast a disapproving eye on the small boy who raced along the embankment, a bent branch clutched in his hand. He stared at the child for a long, critical moment, then shrugging his shoulders, he turned back to his pole.

"Bang! Bang! Bang!"

With quick, sharp jabs the boy lunged at the boat, thrusting his stick forward again and again with a single-mindedness that shut out everything else in the world. Oblivious of Aimée's watching eyes, he stepped up his assault, acting out the part of an entire army bombarding the vessel from the shore—or perhaps, Aimée thought with a smile, a whole band of pirates waiting to board it the instant it surrendered.

The vessel held out valiantly, but only for a moment. It was obvious, even from the beginning, that the strength of the attacking army was too much for it. Giving one quick, almost audible quiver, the makeshift craft collapsed into a shapeless assortment of dead twigs and dying leaves. Its flowery cargo, tossed rudely into the current, gave a last burst of color as the blossoms separated and began to drift away, each touched with tiny beads of moisture like a dewy garden in the early morning.

With a cry of triumph the boy cast his stick into the water, watching as it floated beside the scattering remnants of his boat. Then suddenly, shouting in answer to a call Aimée had not even heard, he raced up the steps of the embankment, taking them two and three at a time. As he passed, Aimée caught a glimpse of his determined expression. She realized that she had forgotten how serious it was to be a child—how serious and full of magic the world of make-believe could be. The realization surprised her. Until that moment it had not really occurred to her that she was anything more than a child herself.

On a sudden impulse she tugged at the sheer linen of her skirt, pulling it high above her ankles as she raced down the steep flight of steps. Bending gracefully, still careful to keep the fragile fabric from trailing on the wet stones, she reached out toward a bright bit of color swirling swiftly through the dark river. Her own cry of triumph was every bit as exultant as the child's when she caught a broken blossom in her fingers. Rising swiftly, her skirts forgotten at last, she cupped the tiny treasure in her hands. She was laughing softly to herself as she made her way back up the embankment.

She did not even notice the tall, dark man who had taken her place beside the railing. She became aware of him only when she saw a shadow cross her own on the pavement. She was not surprised by his presence, for she assumed that he, too, had been watching the child at play and, like herself, had been delighted by the sight. Spontaneously, she raised the flower in her hand, eager to share her own pleasure with the stranger.

The gesture died in midair as she caught sight of the man's face. His expression was dark and brooding—so potent and intent it was almost frightening. Feeling awkward and unsure, she hesitated, letting her hand drop to her side.

The man was quick to notice her confusion. He found it both amusing and enchanting, though he was careful to let only the amusement show. From the first moment he had seen the girl racing down the embankment to capture a hint of childish make-believe from the currents of the Seine, he had been aware of the ambiguity of his reaction to her. The girl was a beauty, he could not deny that, small and dainty and touchingly childlike, hovering tentatively just on the threshold of her own womanhood. There was a porcelain-fragile loveliness about her that appealed to him, from the raven black of her tresses, shimmering against milk-white skin, to the striking blue of her eyes, so dark they turned to jet in the shadows. But it was a loveliness he knew would never last.

Already, he sensed, the aura of enchantment that surrounded the girl had begun to dissolve in a sea of studied manner-isms and expensive, affected fashions. He let his eyes linger with unconcealed frankness on her, slipping from the soft, embroidered linen of her shirt, modishly bustled at the back, to the gracefully contrived arrangement of flowers and lace perched on her curls; from the pinched toes of dainty, stylish slippers to long, slender, perfectly manicured fingers. He made no effort to conceal his disdain.

Aimée could not fail to sense his scorn. It made her feel uncomfortable, and even, in some inexplicable way, ashamed. She almost felt she ought to apologize for herself—and yet she had no idea what she was supposed to apologize for.

Irritably she shook her feeling of awkwardness. Really, the man was impossible, she told herself angrily. And she was even worse! What on earth was she doing, reading all kinds of accusative meanings into a stranger's gaze? Why, it was obvious he was no different from all the other vulgar old lechers who lined the riverbank on sunny afternoons, leering disgustingly at every young girl who wandered by.

Yet the man was not that old, she had to admit as she scrutinized him more carefully. He could not have been more than thirty or thirty-five, perhaps even younger, and if it were not for that uncomfortable disdain in his eyes, he would not be totally unappealing. Not that he was handsome, she told herself objectively. He was hardly that, or even stylish. His narrow trousers were fashionably cut, and his coat and vest modishly casual, but their effect was marred by an untamed, almost shaggy mass of black hair spilling down onto his fore-head and setting off his dark eyes. Then, too, the lines of his face were too rugged to suit her tastes. Still, for all that, there was something about him . . .

Aimée broke off her thoughts, warmth racing into her cheeks as she realized she had been staring at the man and that he had not failed to notice it. She was glad her mother had moved away from her side, wandering farther down the riverbank, so she could not see the frank glances her carefully brought-up young daughter had just exchanged with a total stranger.

The man seemed to know what she was thinking, for his lips turned up slowly, joining his eyes in mirth. Aimée sensed a challenge in his laughter. It was a challenge they both knew she was too unsophisticated to answer.

Too late the girl realized what she had done. Realizing the compromising position she had placed herself in, she whirled away, resisting the impulse to cast a swift glance over her shoulder to see if he was still watching her.

She was surprised to find that her legs were shaking, as much from embarrassment as anger. Aimée stood still for a moment, scanning the open bookstalls beside the railing, searching for the tall figure of her cousin Franz. Wait until the stranger saw her with Franz, she thought with sudden satisfaction. Wait until he saw her on her handsome cousin's arm. Then it would be he who would feel like a fool, trying to catch the eye of a young woman who already had a more suitable—and attractive—escort.

Aimée found her cousin quickly, riffling through a book at one of the colorful little stalls. She was grateful to feel his protective familiarity beside her as she linked her arm through his. Glancing down at the worn, dog-eared pages of the volume in his hand, she felt herself begin to relax.

"A tome in French, Franz?" She laughed. French was a language her Viennese cousin had never mastered well enough to completely comprehend the heavy philosophical treatises he favored. "Are you really going to read that, or is it just going to molder on your shelves like the rest of your French library?"

Franz took her teasing good-naturedly. Flipping back the cover so she could make out the scratched, faded letters of the title, he replied amiably, "I've always meant to get *Candide* in French. And really, Aimée, it is a superb copy—just look at it."

Aimée watched him with amused tolerance. Franz had once tried to explain to her why he loved books that had been cherished by someone else—books that had a sense of the past about them—but she could not even begin to understand. To her, old books were just that. Old and shabby and not particularly appealing. She was wise enough not to tell him so.

"A good choice," she agreed tactfully. "Monsieur Voltaire's use of language is simple enough, even for an Austrian."

She had the grace to blush at the curious look that met her words. How Franz would have loved the copy of *Candide* she had read that winter when she was fourteen. Passed around surreptitiously each night through dark convent corridors, it was at least as cherished as any book he had ever seen.

Not that Voltaire's philosophy held any appeal for the girls, Aimée reminded herself, nearly laughing again at the thought. After all, any man who had been dead over a century was of little interest to modern young ladies. Still, there were a few facets of Candide's education that could hardly fail to capture the attention of sheltered, convent-bred girls, just beginning to be curious about the mysterious things that went on between men and women.

Dear, foolish Papa. How he had insisted on sending her to that dreadful, stifling convent, even above her gentle mother's protests. What would he think, she wondered, if he knew some of the things she had really learned there?

After a moment Franz pulled out a handful of coins, buying the volume as Aimée had known he would, for he could never let go of a book once it caught his eye. Impatiently she tugged his arm, eager to distract him from the tempting stall. When at last she urged him away, she did not let herself turn and see if the stranger was still there—and if he was still staring at her.

And what did it matter if he was? she asked herself. The man had nothing to do with her, or she with him. What did she care for someone like that when she had her handsome cousin all to herself at last. Through carefully lowered lashes she studied Franz's classically perfect features.

To Aimée, Franz was the most attractive man she had ever seen. Tall and slender, he moved with an easy grace that made him look even more elegant and sophisticated than he was. His hair, once highlighted with copper, had mellowed to a deep auburn, and his clear blue-gray eyes gave his face a dreamy, romantic quality. As long as she could remember, Aimée had adored her handsome older cousin.

No, not cousin, she reminded herself with a smug little smile, *second* cousin. She could still remember the thrill she had felt the first time she realized there was a difference. Even when she was a little girl, all her romantic fantasies had centered on Franz, by that time already an eligible young widower. Now that she was eighteen, now that her body had begun to mature at last, and her cousin had started to look at her not as a child but as a beautiful young woman, she dared to hope her day dreams had not been idle longings after all. Clinging to Franz, she let her hand squeeze his arm a little more tightly.

She was more obvious than she had realized. Franz stiffened, pulling his arm away.

"Don't you think we ought to join your father?"

A single cloud, a solitary bit of white fluff in the clear blue sky, drifted across the sun, bathing the riverside in a veil of gray. Aimée shivered in the unexpected chill. Sighing, she turned from her cousin to search for the conservative, dark-clad form of her father. Even without seeing him, she knew the expression she would find on his face.

For the life of her, she had never been able to figure out why her father was so unreasonable about Franz—or about the rest of her mother's family, for that matter. *Le bon Dieu* only knew, they had never been anything but kind to him, at least as far as she could see. And now with Franz's latest visit to Paris, her father's coldness, or so it seemed to Aimée at least, had erupted into open hostility.

"Come along, Aimée." Franz's voice was patient, but Aimée sensed an undercurrent of tension. She glanced at him in sympathy. It could not be easy for Franz to maintain his courtesy in the face of her father's growing rudeness.

"Don't be so stuffy, Franz," she teased, trying to lighten his mood. She dragged her feet, hoping to prolong the confrontation with her father. "There's no need to hurry."

Even as she spoke, she knew it was no use. Franz was stubborn, every bit as stubborn in his own way as her father. Already she sensed it would be his stubbornness that would provide the most serious obstacle to her dreams. Fanciful as she sometimes was, it was impossible to imagine Franz courting any woman—especially his cousin's child—without her father's consent.

"There you are, Papa," she cried out, forcing gaiety into her voice as she caught sight of his scowling face. "We've been looking for you everywhere." Flashing Franz a quick smile—a smile she was careful to hide from her father—she flitted to his side, looping her arm through his.

Etienne LeClare glowered at his daughter. The man was no fool. He saw what Aimée was doing, just as he had seen the smile she took such pains to hide, and he was determined not to let her get away with it.

But Aimée was a match for her father. Ignoring his frown, she pulled his arm, drawing him closer.

"You should have seen it, Papa," Her voice was as cheerful as if he were smiling back at her. "There was a boy with a boat, a funny little thing he made out of leaves and twigs, all loaded with flowers. When they called him to go back home, he couldn't bear to leave it behind, so he attacked it, quite ferociously, until there was nothing left of it at all. Really, you should have seen it. I swear, he thought he was a whole band of pirates—at the very least."

Even when her father did not respond, Aimée refused to give up. Since her prattle was not working, she changed her approach. Lowering her lashes with a deliberately wistful look, she drew her lips together with a mock pout.

"What a grouch you are today." She reached up with impish fingers to catch at a drooping corner of his graying blond mustache, giving it a sudden nimble tug. Etienne held out for a moment, his lips trembling stubbornly against his mirth, then gave in to the spontaneity of his daughter's affection.

"So you've been watching the children, have you?" The gruffness in his voice could not conceal the depth of his affection. Aimée hoped she had eased the tension. But as soon as Franz joined them, she knew she had underestimated the depth of her father's antipathy.

Warily Etienne eyed the worn volume in Franz's hand.

"More books?" He made an effort to keep his tone jovial, but disapproval bristled through his voice. "One of those interminable philosophies you're so fond of, I suppose."

Aimée cringed at his words. She could not help wishing Franz had been able to resist, just this once, adding another book to his already bulging library. Surely he must know how her father felt about it. Etienne had never attempted to hide his disapproval, muttering often enough that Franz, like the rest of his family, lived with his head in the clouds and his nose in a book.

"No such luck, sir," Franz replied easily, deliberately ignoring the challenge. "Just an old *roman* I thought might amuse me."

To Aimée's relief, he did not show the book to her father. He must have sensed, as she did, that it would only irritate him all the more to see Monsieur Voltaire's bawdy little tale in Franz's hand—especially in front of his impressionable daughter.

"Now, don't turn into a grouch again, Papa," she scolded. "I suppose you're worried about business, but it's too nice an afternoon to fuss about something like that."

As soon as the words were out of her mouth she regretted

them. She had intended them only as a distraction, a ruse to disguise her father's rudeness, but now she realized they were at least partly true.

Silently she chided herself for her lack of consideration. She knew her father was worried about the small import business he founded and carried on alone, but she was so wrapped up in herself that she had barely given it a moment's thought.

For the first time in months, Aimée turned objective eyes toward her father's face. It hurt her to see how deep the creases in his brow and cheeks had grown, and how old and tired he looked. To her child's eyes, her father had always seemed tall and invincibly strong. It came as a shock now to realize he was barely above average height, his stocky figure grown surprisingly frail, his thinning dark blond hair turned half to gray.

Dear Papa, she thought, giving his arm an extra squeeze. Somehow, when she had not been watching, he had grown old. Old and terribly worried.

Not that his worries weren't well-grounded, Aimée had to admit. Etienne LeClare had three young sons to educate and place, hardly an easy task, especially with a small business that could support only one of them, and a pampered daughter to find a husband for, a husband who would not only be good to her but also would give her the luxuries a doting father had raised her to expect.

Yet perhaps, she reminded herself, forcing her chin upward, that was all for the best. If her father was really worried about her future, at least that was one worry he could solve easily enough, even if the solution was an unpalatable one for him. Franz was not rich, but he had a comfortable income and a handsome estate on the outskirts of Vienna. Besides, he was the one man her father knew who would not demand an extravagant dowry for her.

She stood silently beside Etienne, watching as her cousin returned to the river, seeking out the place where her mother waited patiently at the railing. The beginnings of a plan were already taking shape in her mind. She waited until Franz had moved beyond the range of her voice. Then, standing on tiptoe, she pressed her lips against her father's ear.

She was surprised to feel the sharp pressure of her own heart pumping against her chest. She realized she was awed by the boldness of the thing she was about to do, but it was an awe that was based on excitement, not fear. There was no way she could lose the game she was about to begin, no way she could savor the bitter taste of defeat. All the logic, all the arguments, were on her side.

"Come, Papa, we both know what I want, and we both know I am right."

Etienne made no attempt to speak or even to move. Only the tension in his body indicated he had heard her. Aimée feared she had gone too far. She knew her father's moodiness well, perhaps better than anyone else. As long as she could remember, she had always been closest to him. It was her father she had taken her broken toys to, her father who had bandaged her bleeding knees and kissed away the pain—always her father, never the pale, pretty mother who seemed too ethereal to be truly real.

But even then, she reminded herself with belated clarity, even when she was a small child, she had known better than to pester him when one of his dark moods was on him. Why had she chosen today of all days to forget that simple fact?

She was careful to avoid his gaze as they continued wordlessly down the wide walkway that lined the riverbank. Only when they reached the hired carriage waiting at the corner did she at last pluck up the courage to look at him. When she did, she was surprised to see not the stubbornness she had expected, but only a look of sheer, naked pain. The starkness of it took her breath away.

It was a long time before she understood what it meant. When she did, even when the slow realization settled at last over her heart, she could hardly believe it was true.

There was nothing in her father's expression of the proud, inflexible man she had always known and loved. Today, she saw only the anguish of a man who knows he has been badly defeated. Stunned, Aimée realized that, without even knowing it, she had won. She felt no triumph, but only a deep sadness.

Did it really hurt so much? she asked herself, bewildered by her father's pain. Was it really so hard for him to give his only daughter to a man he did not like, even if it was the man she had chosen for herself? She wanted to reach out to him, to tell him that it did not matter, that she would give up Franz if it meant that much to him. It tore her apart to realize she could not do it.

Was this what it was like to grow up? she wondered. Was this the tantalizing world that had seemed so fascinating and full of excitement all those long years of childhood? And would it always be like this? Would every decision she made involve pain for someone else, and every dream come true mean a corresponding loss for someone she loved?

In the end, it was her father who reached out to her. Instead of grasping her fingers tightly in his own, he laid a tentative hand on her arm.

"It's time you were married," he conceded.

By the time Franz arrived at the carriage, escorting her mother across the avenue, Aimée had already come to terms with the conditions of her own victory. The scent of it was beginning to smell as sweet as the spring breeze. The smile she offered to the man she loved was disarming, filled with sadness and promises both. It was obvious from Franz's confusion that he did not understand what was happening. Aimée made no effort to enlighten him. There would be time enough to tell him later. Time enough to let him know he dared ask her father for her hand—and he would not be refused.

The flowery scent of her mother's perfume filled the air as she climbed into the carriage, taking her place opposite her daughter. Slowly Aimée turned from Franz to her mother. She had the uncanny feeling, as she so often did, that she was looking into a mirror—only it was a mirror that paled and distorted reality, giving back a blurred image that was only half the truth.

Hélène LeClare was still a beautiful woman, her smooth skin untouched by age, her figure as youthful as her daughter's. But it was her face that struck Aimée with such startling familiarity, for in its delicate perfectly chiseled loveliness, the girl recognized an almost exact duplicate of herself. Only their coloring was different, with Aimée's dark vitality eclipsing the graying gold of her mother's hair and the pale ice blue of her eyes.

It was like seeing a ghost, Aimée thought—a ghost of herself.

At her daughter's intensity Hélène looked up for an instant, smiling with gentle warmth. Aimée wondered if her mother had guessed what she was thinking. Sometimes, when she was a little girl, it had seemed to her that nothing ever escaped those veiled eyes. Now she wondered if Hélène really saw anything at all or if she lived in some dream world of her own, untouched by all the hurts of life.

The long ride home was slow and pleasant. Aimée felt all the while as if she were wrapped in the warm, soft mantle of her own secret dreams. It was a happy hour, she was often to remind herself later—the last purely happy hour of her life.

Perhaps it was simply because her dreams were so lovely and uncomplicated then, so childishly perfect in their simplicity. It had not yet occurred to her that life would not always be so simple.

The mood was shattered when they pulled into the spacious courtyard of their home on the outskirts of Paris. Aimée was aware of a subtle tension in the carriage, though she could not figure out where it came from or even what it was. It seemed to her that her mother was more nervous than usual, her hands fidgeting with the folds of her skirt, but that was only an intangible feeling. As for her father—well, if her father seemed edgy and distracted, that was only natural after what had just passed between them.

She did not even see the strange carriage standing silently at the edge of the courtyard until she had begun to climb down from their own vehicle. Even then she did not associate it with the tension in the air only a moment before. True, it was unusual to find a carriage waiting when they returned from their Sunday drive, but beyond that there was nothing startling in its presence. It was a perfectly ordinary carriage, more opulent than the hired cab that had brought them from the river, but somber and black, with only a few ornate gold curlicues to relieve its sobriety. Aimée stared at the crest on the door, trying to find something in the unfamiliar markings that would tell her who their visitor was, but beyond the fact that it seemed English, she could make out nothing.

A soft hissing like a sudden intake of breath caught her ear. Aimée whirled around and was surprised to see her mother's face only inches from her own, the color so drained it was completely ashen.

Anxiously Aimée turned back to the strange carriage, studying it this time with more concentration. The tension had already mounted, almost unbearably, before the door at last began to swing slowly open. Aimée leaned forward, straining to catch a glimpse of the man still half-hidden in the darkness of the interior.

When at last he emerged, Aimée was aware of a keen disappointment. The man who stepped out into the spring sunlight was quite ordinary. There was nothing of the threatening power her mother's reaction had hinted at, or even of the elegance she might have expected from the expensive carriage.

He was a young man, but there was nothing appealing about him. His features were dominated by a hawklike nose, too strong and sharply chiseled for the puffy flesh that surrounded it, and his chin receded somewhat beneath full, rather pendulous lips. His eyes were set too close together, and brown curls carefully brushed over a receding hairline gave him a foolish, rather foppish appearance.

Even his youthfulness was an illusion, Aimée realized after a moment. The man could hardly be younger than thirty-eight or forty, for deep creases had begun to settle around his eyes, and touches of gray were visible in his carefully coiffed hair. It was only his clothes, garb more suited for an adolescent than a mature man, that made him seem younger at first glance—his clothes and an air of childishness.

"Lord Edward, we are honored."

Etienne's voice was almost fawning as he bent over the man's casually proffered hand. It startled Aimée to watch him. Never had she seen her father grovel before anyone.

Etienne turned slowly, his eyes seeking his wife. There was a commanding urgency in their depths.

"Lord Edward Ellingham, my dear."

His voice was controlled, but Aimée sensed an underlying tremor as he introduced Hélène and Franz to the English lord. Only as his eyes rested on Aimée did he falter. His lips opened, but for an instant he could not force any sound out of them. It was only with a visible effort that he managed to continue, "My daughter, Aimée."

The words were a whisper. It was almost as if he were afraid or ashamed to speak them aloud.

For a moment Aimée did not understand. Bewildered and frightened, she turned toward her mother for help, but Hélène's eyes were averted. Slowly she sought out Franz, but he too could not meet her gaze. Then at last she knew.

It's time you were married.

Mon Dieu, and she thought that meant she had won. She thought her father's pain was nothing more than the token of a stubborn man's surrender.

It's time you were married.

Married not to the man she had loved as long as she could remember, but to the man her father had chosen—the man who stood before her now, his eyes warning her the bargain had already been made.

But how could it be? How could this stranger take her without even knowing her, without having heard her utter so much as a single word? Was physical beauty all he cared about, had he no appreciation of intelligence or humor or charm? *Juste ciel*, to be married to a man like that would be living hell. Why, she would as soon be courted by the crass stranger who had challenged her on the riverbank that afternoon. No, she would *sooner* be courted by him, for at least behind his arrogance she had sensed cleverness and vitality and even a certain animal magnetism. Behind this man's arrogance, there was only self-centered pettiness.

"You have not greeted our guest, daughter."

Etienne's voice was stiff and awkward. For the first time in Aimée's memory, he sounded unsure of himself.

"No, I haven't."

Aimée was surprised at her own calmness. She did not look up at her father, knowing the anger she would see but she held her ground. This was her life they were bargaining away between them, her father and this wealthy, unattractive stranger, and she would not let it go without a fight. They could do what they wanted to her—they could argue, they could cajole, they could threaten—but they could never, *never* force her to marry a man she did not want.

Her father had told her often enough she was stubborn, she thought, raising her chin high.

He would find out now he was right.

2

By God, the girl was a beauty, Lord Edward told himself for the hundredth time that day. His eyes drifted toward the miniature of Aimée set in a gilded frame on the ornate inlaid top of his writing desk. What exquisite luck that he happened to spy her at the opera, a tedious event he almost never forced himself to endure, and what an extraordinary coincidence that her father should be in serious enough straits to consider parting with such a jewel to a perfect stranger.

That the girl was a jewel, he had no doubt. He could not remember ever having seen such delicate features or such striking coloring. The raven black of her hair was a perfect foil for pale skin, touched only with the faintest hint of pink, and her blue eyes were as dark as the midnight sky. God, with those eyes and her lovely slender figure, dainty and fragile as that of a Dresden shepherdess and not vulgar like the modishly plump women with their swollen hips and bosoms, she was the perfect mate for him. He could already see her in the salon of his London house—or better yet, his country manor—her beauty outshining even the expensive crystal chandeliers. How they would envy him then, all the hundreds of friends and acquaintances who would never believe he could have had captured such a treasure.

His thoughts were interrupted by the sound of the door as it swung open. Nervously, like a small boy caught in an embarrassing prank, he turned away from the miniature. The look on the intruder's face warned him he had not been quick enough.

"Stop snickering, Buffy," he snapped, "It doesn't become you at all. It makes you look like a simpering schoolboy."

Buffy Montmorency stepped calmly into the room, untouched by Edward's rancor. He bore a striking resemblance to the man who was his patron, but it was a resemblance that had been tempered by the gentler whims of fate. Where Edward was ugly, he was handsome in an earthy, almost provocative way. His nose was a trifle finer, his eyes larger, his chin more definite, his lips full instead of pendulous.

"Really, the girl is lovely, a perfect asset for you, Eddie."

He noted Edward's scowl at the sound of his words. It amused him—just as he knew the whole business was going to amuse him. The two times he had seen the girl, he had not failed to notice her grace and beauty—nor the desire for possession in Edward's eyes every time he looked at her. But he had seen something else, too, something his patron had evidently decided to overlook. Obviously, the little baggage had a will of her own.

He made no attempt to hide his malice as he pondered the thought. Yes, it would amuse him, he told himself delightedly; it would amuse him greatly. He would enjoy watching Edward try to come to terms with his new bride, fighting with that steel will in a vain effort to dominate it. It would be rather like watching a superb production of *The Taming of the Shrew*—or would it be the other way around? If he were a gambling man, and Buffy was too shrewd for that, he rather thought he would put his money on the shrew.

"Of course we may be rushing things a bit," he added quickly, running his words together to mask the snicker he knew would add to Edward's annoyance. "After all, the girl hasn't yet agreed to have you."

Edward turned cold eyes on Buffy's face. His fingers played nervously with his cravat, but he did not reply for a moment. When he spoke, his face was cool and indifferent.

"You ought to take better care of yourself, Buffy. Really, you're beginning to get quite puffy around the eyes."

Buffy forced a quick smirk to his lips. He was aware that it was unconvincing. His eyes *were* getting puffy, and he knew it—and he knew that Edward knew it.

Buffy had no illusions about himself. He knew he appealed to his patron for one reason, and one only—because he resembled him. In that softened version of his own features, Edward could pretend he was holding a flattering mirror up to nature. When the mirror ceased to flatter, he would have little use for the secretary-companion who no longer soothed his ego. Buffy had nightmares about it sometimes, cold, sweaty nightmares that would not let him sleep for nights on end. He remembered only too well what it was like to be plain Bobbie More, a poor man in the midst of thousands of other poor men in the heart of London's slums. He had no desire to go back there again.

"Well, I suppose she'll have you," he conceded. He could not keep the malice out of his voice, even to appease his protector. "After all, you've plenty of money . . . and money can buy anything."

Edward ignored the biting sarcasm of his words. "Of course she'll have me. She'd be a fool to turn me down."

It was one thing for Edward to put on a show of confidence for the man he forced to grovel in front of him. It was quite something else, he discovered the next day, to sit in her father's drawing room and face a coolly aloof Aimée.

That the girl was there only at her father's bidding was painfully obvious. Edward sensed she was conscious of it every moment she sat on the soft velvet divan, pointedly looking downward to ignore him, just as he sensed she was deliberately making him conscious of it. There was a thinly veiled hostility in everything she did. He could see it in the rigidity of her movements and hear it in the indifferent monosyllables that were her only response to his attempts at small talk.

And yet she was beautiful—exquisitely beautiful. He could not help responding to her beauty as he stared at her, his eyes running up and down her slender figure with bold possessiveness. Everything about her was perfect, from the elegance of her coiffure to the little gold crucifix that hung around her neck; from the arrogant tilt of her chin to the easy grace of her manicured fingers as she poured steaming tea into a fragile china cup. It seemed to him that everything he had ever wanted was embodied in her beauty. He longed for her with an ardor that burned beyond anything he had ever known.

Damn the little minx anyway. Why was she making things so hard for him? She knew why he was there—her father must have told her—and she knew she had to accept him. Why not give in now and make things easier on both of them?

It took him well over an hour to bring himself to utter the words they both knew he had come to speak. By that time he could already feel an unpleasant dampness beneath the stifling wool of his coat.

"It is my understanding . . . that is, your father has led me to believe . . ."

Dammit, why was it so hard? He was not used to coming as a suitor, the image of his heart pinned ludicrously to his sleeve. Always before, everything had come without effort. Just the flick of a hand or a signature on a bank draft.

"Your father has told me I can . . . I might . . . ask for your hand."

Aimée felt hollow as she listened to his faltering words. Had she been less frightened, she might perhaps have found his clumsiness touching. As it was, she felt nothing.

She did not try to answer at once. The silence had an oppressive quality. Aimée sensed it as an ally, a potent, invisible force that drained away the last ounces of his confidence even as it steadied her own nerve. It was a long time before she finally ended the suspense with carefully rehearsed words.

"I am sorry, sir. I cannot accept your . . . your kind proposal."

Stunned, Edward leaned back in his chair. The cup in his hand tilted, spilling hot tea over the edge. Embarrassed, he righted it in the saucer. His hand was shaking as he set it on the long, low table between them.

"You cannot . . . accept?"

By God, what could the girl mean by her insolence? He knew it was fashionable for modern young ladies to play coy at marriage proposals, but that was stupid, and he loathed it—he had made that perfectly clear to her father. Surely the man had had the wit to instruct his daughter. Damn the little chit, anyway. He would tolerate none of her girlish games.

A smile touched Aimée's lips at the man's discomfort. He was unsure of himself, and she was not. That, she sensed, would give her the upper hand.

"I cannot marry you for two reasons, sir. In the first place, I fear you are far too old for me."

She uttered the conventional words with barely repressed laughter. It seemed a delightful private joke, rejecting this man for his age when he was scarcely older than the cousin she intended to have.

"In the second place—and let me be frank about this, sir—I do not find you pleasing in any way."

She saw him wince and was sorry she had gone so far. It had not occurred to her until that very moment that the man, odious as he was, might have feelings, too, perhaps as deep as her own. And yet she knew if she had it to do all over again, she would not change a word of what she had said. Nothing short of brutal truth would dissuade him.

A soft choking sound came from the doorway and Aimée saw Buffy Montmorency standing there. It took her a minute to realize the choking sound was his laughter.

She had seen the man only twice before, but she had developed an immediate antipathy toward him. She was surprised to see him now, although she knew she should not be. She had noticed that Edward seemed to take his secretary everywhere with him, as if he could not manage without him.

"You must forgive Eddie's gaucheness, *mademoiselle*." The man's voice, like his appearance, was deceptively attractive. "You see, he's used to getting his own way. People never say no to him."

At Buffy's taunt anger began to well up in Edward. Aimée sensed that something in his friend's mockery had restored her unwelcome suitor's confidence. It was as if he could not let himself fail in front of the other man, as if he feared his disdain even more than that of the girl he had come to court.

"I *am* used to getting my own way," he admitted slowly. To Aimée's horror, his eyes were filled with a new resolution and firmness. "I *always* get what I want."

Looking from one face to another, Aimée felt her foreboding increase. There was something between these two men, she realized, some kind of conscious rivalry that made them deliberately belittle and taunt each other. And she was caught in the middle of it.

She could only stare mutely at Edward with growing despair. God help her, the man's will was stronger than she had thought, perhaps even stronger than her own. She could only pray that he did not see her weakness. The brightness in his eyes warned her that he did.

Her father found her hours later, seated quietly before the window of the morning room, absently staring out at the miniature pond in the formal garden. The late-afternoon sun touched her face with a warm caress. She felt the unfamiliar sting of salt tears, and desperately fought to hold them back. Never, as long as she could remember, had she cried, not even in the privacy of her room. It had always been a point of pride with her, especially in front of her younger brothers, to be the "bravest little soldier" of them all. Now, for the first time, her bravery threatened to fail her.

Etienne saw the tears that glistened unshed in her eyes. He stood beside her, helpless and awkward, frightened by the show of weakness he had never before seen in his pretty, stubborn daughter. He wished he could relent, take her in his arms and dry away her tears, offering her anything, even the man she loved, if it would make her happy.

"I can't see why you're being so stubborn," he muttered awkwardly. He was conscious that his voice was far less forceful than he had intended. "Any other girl would be dancing with joy right now. Why, the man is incredibly rich, and titled, too. It's nothing short of a miracle that he's so set on you."

Aimée turned her face away. She could not bear her father's callousness and lack of understanding. It was a long time before she could bring herself to speak. When she did, her voice was so low it was almost inaudible.

"I can never love him."

"Bah, love!" Etienne snorted with impatience. If he needed proof that his daughter was only being stubborn, he had it now. He was glad he hadn't given in to his weakness a moment ago. "And what do you know about love, my pretty little innocent? Listen to me, love is not something that bursts full blown. It is something that grows slowly, cautiously, nurtured by years of a good marriage."

Aimée turned back to him, sensing something in his tone that made her examine his face.

"Does it?"

She found herself wondering about her parents' marriage, that same marriage she and her brothers had always taken for granted. Did they really love each other, her father and mother? Had they ever felt the same sweet longing for each other that she felt for Franz?

That her father doted on her mother, treating her like a pampered child, was something Aimée had always taken for granted. But was that love? Was that part of the shared passion that made two people grow closer and closer as the years passed? And her mother—did she love her father? Did she really see him as she looked out from the secret world that lay beyond the veiled mystery of her pale eyes?

His daughter's steady gaze unnerved Etienne. He moved down the long, windowed wall, stopping only when he reached the end. It seemed to him that the sunlit garden was strangely at variance with the darkness that had settled over the room.

God give him strength, how he hated forcing his cherished daughter into a marriage she did not want! How he hated the tears she struggled to hide. If only it were not necessary. If only there were some other way.

But there was no other way, nothing else he could do. He had to see his daughter safe and well provided for, no matter what it cost him. He would force her if he had to. He would even lie to her to get her to agree.

"I have not told you the whole truth, Aimée." He turned from the window to face her once again. Aimée felt her heart leap into her throat when she saw how ashen his face had become.

"What do you mean?"

Etienne heard the anxiety in his daughter's voice. He realized it was at least half for him. It did not make it any easier to go on.

"Do you remember Sunday when we walked by the river? You chided me then for worrying about business. Your words were far more accurate than you knew."

There, he told himself with relief. It had not been nearly as hard as he had thought. He had managed to tell her, and he had not had to lie after all.

"Oh, please, Papa . . ." She whispered urgently, her own fears forgotten at last in her concern for him. "Please tell me what is wrong."

"I wish I didn't have to. You are far too young to worry about such things."

"I am eighteen," she retorted quickly. "I am old enough to know."

Etienne almost smiled in spite of himself. Thank God there were some things that never changed. He had always been able to count on his daughter's stubbornness.

He moved slowly toward his favorite chair, easing his weary body into the cushions. He was careful to measure his breath so she could not see how badly even that little bit of exertion had tired him. Leaning back, he closed his eyes, shutting out the sunlight that slanted through the window.

"You don't know much about the import business, *ma jolie*. And I suppose you won't ever have to. But even you must know that all those things, pretty as they are—all those trinkets from India and Palestine, Egypt and Syria—are not very valuable. There is a profit to be made from them, but not enough to maintain an expensive house like this."

He opened his eyes to see if she understood what he was trying to tell her. It only added to his tension to realize she did not.

"Credit, my dear." Raising his hand with effort, he let it sweep through the air in a broad gesture, taking in not only the room itself but the wide windows that opened onto the gardens as well. "All credit."

He paused for a moment, gauging her reaction before he continued.

"Now the credit has come to an end."

The room seemed unbearably stifling, and for a moment Etienne thought he would not be able to breathe. He struggled to continue, trying to find some way to make her understand without having to actually speak the words. Gulping air painfully into his lungs, he admitted at last that was impossible.

"Unless I can find some new creditor," he explained starkly, determined not to spare himself now, "unless I can find someone to pay my debts and lend me enough money to salvage the business, everything will be lost. The house, the gardens, all your mother's hopes and yours . . . and your brothers'. It will all be lost."

For a time Aimée still did not understand. When at last comprehension dawned in her eyes, it was twisted by a gleam of horror.

"You mean . . . you would *sell* me?"

"*Mon Dieu, non!* Sell you, *ma petite?* Never!"

Yet that must be how it looked to her—and God help him, there was nothing he could do about it. At all costs, he dared not tell her the truth.

"I am not proposing to sell you into slavery, Aimée," he said with a forced lightness, trying to twist the ugliness of the thing around into a joke. "You do me wrong if you think that of me. Lord Edward is an honorable man, and he has made you an honorable proposal of marriage. Good God, child, the man has offered to share his life with you. Surely you cannot treat that as an insult."

Aimée's voice was contrite and thoughtful.

"I did not mean to do that." Her quiet dignity tore at him. He remembered the way she had looked at him when she was a little girl, her eyes so bright and full of trust. How easy it had been then to heal all the hurts and heartaches. "I do not treat the honor lightly, but I cannot marry a man I loathe."

"No, of course not." Etienne was careful not to push her. He had made an ally of her stubbornness once that afternoon. He did not intend to make an enemy of it now. "I would not ask such a thing of you. But surely . . . if you will not think of yourself, at least consider your brothers."

It was a shabby trick, and he knew it. Aimée had always been fiercely protective of the younger children, especially the baby, Edouard. She could not turn away from their needs now.

"At least think about it," he urged gently. "Promise me you'll think about it. Then perhaps you will find you do not loathe the man so much after all."

The sun was already setting when Aimée left the room. Its dying rays touched the waters of the pond with a breathtaking splash of crimson. Etienne sat alone for a long time, watching the deep reds turn slowly to gray and remembering the image of his daughter's face as she left him.

How he hated deceiving her. He rose and faced the window again. The twilight darkness had already begun to hide the garden in a veil of mystery. How he hated having to trick her into this marriage.

Not that it was wholly a trick, he told his aching conscience. He had not lied to her, not really. His business *was* finished, unless Lord Edward stepped in to save it. It *was* all over for the elegant house and the extravagant life-style they had all enjoyed.

But that was not the whole truth. The business was ruined, but it was not the boys he worried about. Whatever happened, they would be all right. If only out of kindness—or charity, he thought, wincing at the word—Hélène's family would see that they got an education and a good start in life.

But Aimée—oh, God, yes, he feared for Aimée. She was too beautiful, and too innocent. She did not know what beauty could mean in a world used to corrupting loveliness, twisting it around to meet its own foul ends. He had to see her safely settled into a life of her own, and he had to see it soon.

Que le bon Dieu l'aide, the girl was too much like her mother—yes, and like her father, too, if he was going to be honest about it. He felt pain contract his chest at the thought. Beneath her laughter and vitality, beneath the very coquettishness she was just beginning to learn, there lay a kind of wildness, a hint of that same untamed passion of the spirit that had . . .

He broke off his thoughts, disturbed at where they were taking him. Someday, he warned himself, perhaps someday soon, those passions might lead his daughter in directions she had never dreamed of. What would happen to her then if she had no doting father to protect her?

The familiar pain pressed again at his chest, expanding until it barely left him room to breathe. Groping almost blindly through the darkness, he worked his way back to the chair, sinking into the cushions until it eased.

They had been honest with him, all those doctors—he had forced them to be. Oh, they had hemmed and hawed, trying to talk their way around it, but in the end they had told him the truth. A few years, they had said—if he was lucky. If not, a few months.

A few months, and then his family would be alone and unprotected.

He could not let that happen, not to Aimée. She was too vulnerable. No matter how she felt about it, even if she hated him to her dying day, he had to find a way to leave her safe. He had to find a way to protect her—as he had never been able to protect the beautiful woman who was her mother.

He did not even notice when Hélène slipped into the room. She moved so silently that the touch of her hand on his arm startled him. Looking up, he was stunned to catch a glimpse of silver on her cheeks. Like her daughter, Hélène LeClare never cried. He had seen her tears only once, and that was long ago. Now they flowed free and unashamed down her cheeks.

The sight of them frightened him. All the security in the world, all the comfort and stability he had ever known, was slipping away between his fingers, and he was powerless to stop it.

"I have to see her settled," he said with the same gruffness he had used with Aimée. "Don't you see, it's for her sake. I have to do it."

He had not told his wife about the doctors, but she seemed to understand, for she did not argue with him. She gave his arm a gentle caress. It was the first time he could remember that she had reached out to him. Always before it had been he who reached toward her.

"Does it have to be this man?" she asked softly.

Etienne was startled by her words. He had never known her to question him before. No, that was not true, he reminded himself. She had questioned him once, when he insisted on sending Aimée to that confounded convent school. Well, she had been right about that. Those rigid confines had not been good for Aimée's high spirits and vitality. But she was not right now.

"There is no one else."

That was the simple truth. There was no one else. In all the years he had struggled to provide for his family, he had failed miserably. In the end, he could offer them nothing, not wealth for his sons or security for his wife, not even the prospect of a suitable husband for his beautiful, impetuous daughter.

Hélène hesitated for a moment.

"What about Franz?"

Etienne half-rose out of his chair, sputtering in anger and amazement. Ignoring the pain in his chest, he gaped at his wife. In all the years they had been married, she had never once defied him so openly. She knew how he felt about Franz, knew how he felt about all of her family, yet still she dared . . .

"Do you think I'd let that faint-hearted weakling have my Aimée?" he cried out, half in fury, half in pain. "What kind of husband would he make, with his nose buried in a book all the time? Why, he'd sooner read one of those philosophies of his than talk to a real person. Where do you think he'd be when she needed him? I'll tell you where—hidden away in his own world of daydreams, that's where!"

No, dammit, he would not let the man have his daughter. Aimée needed someone strong and dominant, not a weakling or a dreamer. She needed a man who was her match, a man as strong-willed as herself, one who would know how to control and guide her.

Hélène did not try to speak again. The tears had already begun to dry on her cheeks, but her eyes still glowed with the echoes of her plea. It was an expression Etienne found both poignant and disturbing. He wondered if his wife knew the effect it had on him, if she knew he could deny her nothing as long as she looked at him like that. He hoped she didn't.

In the end, she seemed to misjudge him as badly as he had misjudged her. Surrendering to the will she thought was inflexible, she let the light dim in her eyes, leaving them lifeless once again. Etienne could only watch her helplessly. He wondered if he would ever see passion in her eyes again.

Without another word, without even a gesture to show she remembered he was in the room, Hélène rose and glided toward the door, melting into the gray haze of the twilight like some shadowy figure from the netherworld.

No, dammit, Etienne told himself again as he sat alone in the darkness, he would not let that man get his hands on Aimée—not him or any of his blasted family. Hélène was already a ghost in her own life. He would not let that happen to her daughter.

Aimée smiled as she watched her little brother push his new boat into the pond. His feet danced dangerously close to the water that rippled against the gravel shore. She was surprised to see how earnest his eyes looked as the craft made its way toward the center of the pond. How earnest and solemn.

Just like the little boy on the banks of the Seine, she remembered with a laugh. Only, that boy's boat had been a simple craft, while Edouard's was an expensive plaything, the best money could buy.

The boy sensed his sister's eyes on him. Turning excitedly, he thrust out his arm, pointing with pride.

"Look at it, Aimée. Isn't it pretty? Isn't it the prettiest thing you've ever seen?"

Darling, pampered Edouard, she thought with a sudden rush of mingled affection and doubt. What would it be like for him when they could no longer buy him expensive toys? What would it be like . . . ?

But it would not be like that at all, she reminded herself. It would never be like that for Edouard—not now.

She realized she had not given up until that moment. She had been determined—so determined—to hold out against her father, even when she knew what the cost of her defiance would be. Now that would be impossible.

She had made one last move to secure her future, but even as she had done it, she knew it was doomed to failure. She could still see Franz's face when, swallowing her pride, she had gone to him and begged him to run away with her. She was not surprised when he refused.

"Not without your father's permission, Aimée." It seemed to her his voice held regret. She wondered later if she had heard it only because she longed so desperately for it to be there.

How very like Franz, she thought, unable to feel angry with

him, even in her disappointment. How like him to be so stuffy and proper and so unyieldingly stubborn. And yet, if he had been anything else, if he were even slightly more willing to let go of everything he held honorable and decent, then he would not be Franz anymore, and she would not love him.

"Don't mind so much," he had whispered softly. She was sure then that she caught a hint of his own disappointment. "It's really for the best, you know. Even though you don't believe it now, your father is right. I am not the man for you. There is too much exhilaration, too much passion for life, in your heart. You could never be happy sharing a world of dreams and books."

But if they were *your* dreams and books, she had wanted to cry out, if they were the things *you* loved . . .

But she stilled the words before they could reach her lips, just as she stilled them now in her heart. She knew she would never be able to persuade Franz to marry her without her father's permission. It would be better to accept her defeat graciously, with as much dignity as she could still salvage, than to tarnish the image of her he would carry forever in his memory.

Besides, perhaps he was right after all. Perhaps it was all for the best—though hardly in the way he had meant it.

"You are not watching, Aimée." The childish eagerness of Edouard's scolding broke into her thoughts. "See how well I am sailing it."

Like the little boat on the Seine, she thought again. How delighted she had been when she rescued one of the blossoms from the wreckage, telling herself she had secretly recaptured a moment of her own youthful make-believe. She wondered if she would ever feel like a child again.

"Be careful, *petit*," she teased, her voice surprisingly light now that she was free of the burden at last. "Take good care of it. It's too pretty to lose."

3

Brilliant streaks of crimson and gold, emerald and azure, streamed through the ancient windows of the tall cathedral, touching the haloes of a thousand candles with a trembling splash of color. To the hundreds of spectators crowded into row upon row of uncomfortable pews, it was the event of the season, a fairy tale come true. But for the beautiful girl who stood poised on the edge of the circle of light, the real-life Cinderella, it was a moment that drew her out of herself, giving her the illusion that she was somehow unreal.

That she had never looked more beautiful, Aimée knew only too well. And never had she cared less. Only a few minutes earlier, she had stared dispassionately at the image in the glass they held up to her. The girl who gazed back at her, her skin blending into the iridescent sheen of milky satin, seemed almost a stranger. Nowhere in the sapphire depths of those eyes could Aimée see the anguish in her own heart.

Aimée was barely conscious of the touch of her father's hand, though his fingers dug deep into her arm, just as she barely heard the swell of music that marked her cue to move into the vast depths of the cathedral. All her senses were concentrated on the long aisle stretching endlessly before her, its finite limits obscured by the shimmering brilliance of light. A sea of faces closed in around it, undulating in flickering rays of the candles, until it melted into a single mass, all individual features drowned in a wave of anonymity. Nowhere in that vast montage of light and color could she find anything familiar, anything comfortable, to focus on.

And yet they must be there, she knew, all the people she loved and needed to feel around her. Their faces must be hidden somewhere in that huge, empty mass. Her mother, her features pale but composed—if only she knew where to find her. And her brothers, Claude and Jean-Pierre and the baby, Edouard—how their eyes must be shining with excitement.

And Franz. Somewhere, even though her own eyes could not pick him out, his eyes must be following her. Aimée wondered, if she could see them now, if she would catch a reflection of her own despair in their cool blue-gray depths, an echo of the broken dreams she must leave behind her forever.

The aisle that had seemed so long when she first set foot on it suddenly grew terrifyingly short. Then the altar had been a blur of light and color far in the distance; now it was frighteningly clear, every line of it sharp and distinct to her eyes. With a last hint of rebellion she slowed her pace deliberately, barely creeping the last few yards toward the altar. It did her no good. No matter how slowly she moved, she reached the end at last.

As she drew her eyes up from her white satin slippers, taking in the dark-clad man who was so soon to become her husband, Aimée was startled to see that his face was even paler than her own. For a moment she almost felt sorry for him, sensing in their shared nervousness a surprising kinship. It was so solemn, this thing they were about to do, so irreversible. She wondered if he, too, longed for one last pause, one last chance to feel free before he committed himself forever.

Beside Lord Edward, Buffy Montmorency looked incredibly young and innocent, the puffy lines of his face settled into an illusion of baby fat, the malice in his dark eyes quelled for once by the solemnity of the occasion. For an instant Aimée was tempted to burst into a fit of nervous giggles. How preposterous the man was, how pompous, and how always, unceasingly there! Did he ever leave his master's side, she wondered, or would he follow them everywhere, from their wedding to their wedding supper, even into the bedchamber when they closed the doors behind themselves at night?

Then suddenly, just as quickly as it had come, the temptation to laugh died away. In its place she felt only an urge to burst into tears. Frantically she fought against it.

I can't cry, she told herself desperately, mouthing the words until she almost whispered them aloud. I can't, I can't, I *can't!*

Not she, who had always been a brave little soldier. She couldn't stand it if she made a fool of herself now.

She was aware of her father's hand only when he released her arm at last. He had held on a moment longer than necessary. Did he have doubts, too, she wondered, second thoughts that made him question his own decision? She sensed that he did, just as she sensed he would never be able to admit them to her.

The priest's voice was loud and monotonous chanting the words that would bind her for life to the stranger who stood beside her. Her own voice, by contrast, was muted, almost inaudible, as she repeated the sacred vows that could never be broken. The fingers of one hand played with the tiny diamond cross at her throat, a cross Edward had given her. The other hand was captive in Edward's sweaty grip.

Then miraculously, it was over, and she was turning to confront a sea of faces. Suddenly she was Aimée LeClare no longer. From that moment on, she would be Lady Ellingham, the wife of one of Europe's wealthiest, most influential men.

Slowly she turned to face Lord Edward. If she had been capable of feeling anything, it would have amused her to see that this man, for all his power and influence, seemed every bit as relieved as she that the ceremony was finally over.

She was surprised at her total lack of emotion. She had not

expected to feel so little, not even a sense of loathing or anger at what had been forced on her. It seemed strange that, despite the intimacy of the vows they had exchanged, she and this man were still strangers, existing in their own private worlds, shut off from each other by both circumstance and inclination.

And yet he was her husband. She felt a dull surprise flood through her at the thought. This was the man she had promised to honor and obey for the rest of her life, the man she had promised to love.

She scanned the harsh, unpleasant face. At least she could obey him, she reminded herself slowly. She could keep that much of her vow. And someday, if she was lucky, perhaps she could learn to honor him as well.

The gala dinner that followed the late-afternoon ceremony had a festive air, as if to make up for the solemnity of the marriage rite. Candles flickered in crystal chandeliers, and vintage champagne bubbled in tall gleaming glasses. Soon the sound of laughter filled the air, driving away even the shadows in the farthest corners of the long hall.

Etienne LeClare drank deeply of the sparkling liquid, gulping down glassful after glassful with a kind of quiet desperation, until at last the haunted look in his eyes began to melt away and his laughter boomed out over the other sounds in the room. Aimée stared at him in wonder, for she had never seen him in such a state, but she said nothing. She did not begrudge him his moments of gaiety, forced though they seemed to her. She sensed that the day had been almost as hard on him as on her.

Of all the guests, Hélène alone did not savor the champagne, leaving it untouched in her glass as she stared in abstract silence at the festivities. Her solemnity unnerved Aimée, for she had never seen her mother quite so withdrawn. It frightened her to realize she could do nothing about it. It was almost as if, with her wedding, she had somehow slipped away from her parents, moving into a world she could not share with them. Her mother with her aloofness, her father with his forced, drunken gaiety—it was all the same thing. They had both erected shields around themselves. She wondered if she would ever be able to break through to them again.

Why did you let this happen to me, Mother? she longed to cry out, piercing the armor Hélène had created to hide from her daughter's pain. Why did you shelter me from reality, letting me believe in childish dreams of love and romance,

44

dreams you knew were bound to be shattered? She was not surprised when she could not force her mother to meet her eyes. She knew Hélène could not face the accusation she would see there.

And yet she should face it, Aimée told herself bitterly, feeling anger and indignation rush into her heart for the first time that day. She should have faced it long ago. She should have told her daughter the truth, preparing her for a marriage based not on love but practical convenience, she should have prepared her for life.

It was only later that Aimée found how truly unprepared she was, not only for life, but for marriage as well. As she sat alone on the edge of the bed in the chamber that was to be hers in her husband's elegant town house, she felt her chest contract with fear. She was surprised at the intensity of the sensation. If her mother had been there at that moment, Aimée's accusations would no longer have been mute.

Why didn't you prepare me, Mother? she would have cried out. Why didn't you tell me what was going to happen tonight?

Giggling serving maids hovered just outside the doorway, finding a dozen excuses to linger in the bright lights of the hallway. The sound of their laughter made Aimée feel intensely lonely, left out, denied even the merriment and gaiety of her own wedding festivities. She hated the stifling confines of the room, the dimness relieved only by the light of a single candle.

What would her new husband think of her, she wondered, if she were to ask him to leave her alone that night? Would he be furious with her, raging at her for denying her wifely duties so soon, or would he be as relieved as she?

But that was nonsense, she reminded herself. Lord Edward would not be frightened or uncomfortable. He was a man, and men were never afraid of such things.

Odd little snatches of conversation, words and meaningless phrases, drifted with the laughter through the open doorway.

"Poor little thing."

Aimée started at the sound. The voice was Maria's, Edward's kindly German housekeeper, but the words were nonsense. She must have misunderstood them. She had thought the woman called her a "poor little thing," but she was hardly a "poor thing" at all. Why, she was the bride of one of the wealthiest men in Europe, and the envy that night of all of Paris.

45

"Does she even know what's going to happen to her, do you think?"

This time Aimée knew she had not misheard. The voice was soft, barely audible, but the words were clear enough. She felt her cheeks grow crimson, as if she had been caught in some secret sin.

"Does it matter?" Aimée recognized the vibrant voice of Suzanne, a sharp-tongued maid she had only met the day before. Somehow it did not surprise her that the girl made no attempt to lower her voice. "With the man she's getting, I don't think she has anything to worry about."

The loud burst of laughter that met Suzanne's caustic quip died away suddenly. The silence that followed was so heavy and unnatural it was frightening. Aimée rose from the bed and tiptoed to the doorway, peeking out cautiously.

There, to her horror, less than halfway down the long hall, stood her husband. His face was a bright scarlet, the flush of too much wine deepened by anger. God help me now, Aimée thought, her heartbeat quickening. Even if she got up the nerve to ask him to leave her alone that night, he would never be able to do it—not after the mocking challenge in Suzanne's voice.

Lord Edward did not speak at first. When he did, his voice was harsh.

"Get her ready for me."

If he saw his bride hovering on the threshold of her room, he did not acknowledge it. Turning, he strode with long, brisk steps down the hallway. His footsteps echoed eerily through the silence.

The maids hurried Aimée back into the room, removing the expensive satin and lace that still covered her slender body. Her sheer silk nightdress was cool as they slid it over her body, arranging its translucent whiteness in artful folds against the snowy white of the bedsheets. It was all over in a few minutes.

Silently, the maids scurried from the room, leaving her alone and perfumed to wait for her husband. Only Suzanne paused on the threshold, her dark eyes sending back a mute message. Aimée realized that the girl was saying good-bye to her. No doubt she knew, as Aimée herself did, that they would never see each other again. Aimée thought she saw sadness in the girl's eyes—or was it pity?

Alone at last, with only the light of the candle to comfort her, Aimée suddenly felt very small and very young. It was like all the terrifying dreams of her childhood, dreams in which she was alone and lost, trapped in a darkening woods at twilight, crying for the mother who never came.

"Oh, Mother, why didn't you tell me?" she thought again, this time daring to speak the words aloud in her fear. "Why didn't you tell me what was going to happen to me?"

Mon Dieu, why hadn't they been cleverer at figuring it out, all those little girls in the convent that year she had turned fourteen and was beginning to feel an urgent curiosity about the ways of life. A handful of pages in a risqué book, a tantalizing hint about illicit rendezvous in the bushes—that was not enough.

And yet they had tried, she remembered, almost smiling through her fears at their eagerness, still vivid through the haze of memory. They had tried, but their attempts had been so futile, so childish. A few awkward fumblings with their own ripening bodies, a few fantasies of the ecstasy and pain to come—that was all.

Still, there was that girl—what was her name . . . ? Oh, yes, Elise—Elise, with the innocent eyes and the face of a little angel. How scandalized the nuns had been when they discovered her thickening waistline.

The girls had talked of nothing else for weeks. Elise had "done it," they whispered, half scandalized, half excited and filled with awe. Elise had "done it," but Elise was gone, and they still did not know what "it" was.

Then there had been that gardener from the village, the one who crept over the walls and tried to lure one of the novitiates into his arms—or was it the other way around? Aimée wondered now, remembering how quickly the young woman had been hustled out of the convent. How they had loved gossiping about that, too, speculating on every lurid detail of the story told by two girls who had stumbled across the scene, before the horrified nuns could rush them away. But it had been a preposterous story, so incredible it was impossible to believe.

Aimée could still remember it as clearly as if she had heard it only yesterday. The man's trousers had been unfastened, the girls had said, and some strange, ugly growth projected out of the front of them. He had pulled up the girl's skirt and . . .

But of course that was ridiculous. Even at that time Aimée had known it could not possibly be true. The whole thing was too unromantic, too . . . too undignified. It was obvious that the girls were incorrigible liars.

The sound of the door banging heavily against the wall

broke abruptly into Aimée's thoughts. Startled, she whirled to face it, disarranging the artful folds of her gown as she looked anxiously at her husband.

For a moment Edward stood silently in the doorway, staring in at her. He was clad in a wine-colored silk dressing gown. As he watched Aimée's hands gripping the soft folds of her nightdress, he recognized both her fear of him and his mastery over her. It steadied him. There would be no more of the stupid games that had marked the beginning of their courtship, he told himself angrily, no more of that air of superiority she loved to assume, pretending that her breeding was as good as his.

Aimée saw the bitterness in his eyes instantly. It probably reflected Suzanne's idle chatter more than anything she herself had done, but she would be the one to bear the brunt of it. Her body stiffened.

It was a moment before she noticed the bottle in his hand. The instant she did, she felt her whole body begin to relax. What a fool she had been to be so terrified of him. In her mind she had been making him into some kind of monster, while in reality he was obviously a kind man, remembering even in his anger to bring a glass of champagne to soothe his bride's nervousness.

Perhaps she had not been fair to him after all, she thought, questioning herself for the first time since they had begun their awkward courtship. She had scorned him for judging her solely on the basis of her appearance, calling him crass and unfeeling when he looked for beauty in lieu of character. Now she began to wonder if she hadn't done the same thing with him, looking only at the unfortunate ugliness of his features and making no effort to see through to the soul beneath.

Only as Edward stepped forward, reaching out with his arm to steady himself against the doorjamb, the champagne glasses rattling precariously in his hand, did Aimée realize the bottle was more for himself than for her. Moving with exaggerated slowness, he inched his way into the room. Aimée shivered as she caught sight of his eyes. They were glowing, not with the lust she had expected, but only a latently violent anger. It was almost as if he found her distasteful, she thought with mounting fear, almost as if he had used that moment in the doorway to assess her beauty—and found it wanting.

He set the glasses awkwardly on the table beside the bed. The silence in the room was so deep Aimée could almost hear her heart beating. It was broken only by the bubbling sound of the champagne falling into the delicate crystal glasses and spilling out onto the table beneath.

Aimée lifted her glass slowly, raising it to her lips with a surprisingly steady hand. Edward's hand, by contrast, trembled so badly he spilled half of the champagne out of his glass. He seemed startled as he looked down at the widening stain that marred the deep burgundy carpet. Then he raised his glass again, using both hands to steady it as he eased it to his lips, and gulped the liquid down.

Aimée sipped her champagne. The sensation of tiny bubbles playing against her lips was light and teasing, a stark contrast to the tension surrounding her. The liquid seemed to glow in her throat and stomach as she drained the glass. She wished the warmth it created were enough to thaw the chill in her heart.

"Lord Edward," she said softly, unable to bear the silence any longer, "thank you for bringing the champagne to me. I am sure you sensed my nervousness tonight, and that is why you were so thoughtful."

His face relaxed in surprise at her words, easing into a cautious kind of softness. Aimée trembled with relief at the change. She did not think she could have borne the anger in his eyes, or the distaste, a moment longer.

And yet that look was her own fault, she reminded herself. If she had not treated him with such coldness, perhaps his disdain for her would not have grown to such proportions.

"Come, my lord." She extended her hand toward him in an impulsive gesture. The touch of his palm was cold against hers as she pulled him beside her on the bed. Whatever was going to be done to her that night, she sensed, it would be easier if it was done not with anger but with kindness.

Edward could only stare at her blankly, confusion written on his features. He found it hard to believe that the sacred vows she had been forced to utter could already have instilled such a sense of wifely devotion in her. Yet he could think of no other explanation.

Unless . . .

Oh, God, could it be? Could it possibly be that?

Appalled, he pulled his hand away from her. Could this cool, fragile-looking girl actually be looking forward to the disgusting things that were about to be done to her?

Aimée noticed the change in his expression. She knew she had done something to anger him, but she could not for the life of her figure out what it might be. Nervously she let her eyes plead with him.

Please, they begged mutely, *please* tell me what to do, and I will do it gladly. I will do anything to make this easier for me . . . and for you.

When his eyes did not respond, she felt despair flood her heart.

God help her, what did he want of her? What was it he expected? And why, in heaven's name, *why* had they let her come to this so ignorant?

Then, remembering the hint of warmth in his eyes when she had taken the initiative, holding out her hand to welcome him into her bed, she sensed she must do the same thing again. Perhaps that was all that was wrong, she told herself hopefully. Perhaps the disgust in his eyes was only for the false modesty she paraded in front of him.

"Would you . . ." she whispered softly, barely able to say the words, "would you like me to undress for you?"

When he did not reply, she sensed she must be bolder. Slowly, with fingers so stiff and rigid she could hardly force them to do her bidding, she moved her hand upward, unfastening the front of her gown. The stifling air in the room felt suddenly frigid as the sheer silk slipped away from her shoulders.

With cold fascination Edward watched the gossamer veil float away from her flesh. He was unable to move or even to glance away from her. At first she seemed small and slightly built, her body trembling with a childlike fragility that was oddly appealing, even while it repelled him. Only after his eyes had darted curiously up and down her body, did he realize how wrong he had been. The girl was slender, but her body was more developed, far more feminine, than he had realized. Her breasts, though small, were high and softly rounded, their ivory pallor highlighted by the glowing pink of surprisingly large nipples. Her hips had already begun to curve with a hint of womanly maturity, sweeping gracefully around the black curls that nestled between her legs.

He had been right about her after all, he told himself with a wave of revulsion. The thought gave him a tight feeling in the pit of his stomach. For a minute he thought he was going to vomit. The girl was a tramp, nothing better than a common whore.

And she was his wife!

Fighting back his nausea, Edward reached out, grasping a handful of thick black hair as he pulled her head toward him. The heavy scent of her perfume invaded his nostrils.

Dammit, if she was a whore, he was going to treat her like

one! He closed his eyes to block out the vision of moist, sensuous lips, already parted as if in lust. Forcing his own head downward, he clamped his mouth on hers. The whimper that rose from her throat seemed to him a moan of passion. Angered almost beyond reason, he pushed his tongue brutally into the depths of her mouth.

With a strangled cry, as much of defeat as rage, he pressed his body downward, forcing her back into the bed until he could feel her flesh through his dressing gown. His body began to writhe uncontrollably as the firm muscles of her leg and thigh pressed against him, issuing invitations his own flesh was ashamed to answer. Finally, after what seemed forever, he felt his body begin to respond, swelling at last to a masculine hardness. With a grunt of triumph he pulled himself to a sitting position.

As he drew away from her, Aimée felt an intense relief flood her body. Somehow, though she could hardly believe it, the thing was over—and it had been accomplished without all the pain she had feared. Only when she saw him reach toward his sash, tearing at it as he struggled to unfasten his robe, did she realize the truth. It was not over—not over at all. It had just begun.

What if it was true? she asked herself, gaping at him in horror and disbelief. What if those horrible girls at school had been right after all? What if there really was some monstrous, threatening growth . . . ?

Even as the thought crossed her mind, the robe fell away from Edward's body, revealing the half-rigid beginnings of his erection.

"Oh, no," she gasped, too startled and frightened to realize what she was doing. "Oh, no."

To her horror, she began to giggle nervously, softly at first, then louder and louder.

Edward could only gape at her in amazement and growing anger. The sound of her laughter ran through his body like an electric shock. The early, promising traces of his erection melted away until his penis curled back into a shapeless mass of pink flesh nestling harmlessly in the dark, scraggly hair that surrounded it.

Damn the girl, he thought furiously. She was laughing at him, just like all the others had laughed at him.

Just like the little bitch in the hallway.

With the man she's getting, she doesn't have anything to worry about.

Just like *all* the little bitches in the hallway, their smug

51

faces pink with mirth. They would still be laughing, he knew, wherever they were—huddled beside the stove in the kitchen perhaps, or all curled up together in one disgusting mass of gossip and laughter on one of the beds in the servants' quarters.

How they must be looking forward to the morning, relishing the moment they would come into the bedroom to search for the telltale traces of blood they were so sure they would not find.

"Dammit," he cried out. Damn the little bitches! They would never laugh at him again.

His eyes searched the room feverishly lighting at last on the empty champagne bottle on the bedside table. Grasping it in sweaty fingers, he raised it over his head. The sound of laughter still echoed in his ears, driving the last traces of reason from his mind.

Laugh at him, would they? He would show them.

Reaching down with his free hand, he clamped his fingers tightly around Aimée's leg. He felt a surging sense of triumph at the cry of pain and fear that escaped her lips. Wedging the other leg firmly beneath his knees, he forced her thighs farther and farther apart. He could think of nothing but the childish giggles he had heard on her lips only moments before.

She had laughed at him. He had exposed his own barely firm flesh to her eyes, and she had laughed.

Clutching the neck of the bottle in his hands, he brought it down sharply on the edge of the table. The marble top quivered for an instant, resisting the force of the thick glass, as the bottle broke in half. The jagged edges glinted in the candlelight as Edward brought it forward swiftly, cutting into the side of her leg in a single deft movement. The girl squirmed in terror, and he cut her deeper than he had intended, but the act gave him no remorse. Grimly he turned his eyes toward her face, waiting for the tears that would mark both her humiliation and her subjugation to him. He was disappointed when they did not come.

So they wanted blood, did they? Well, they would have it now—and plenty of it.

He eyed the bleeding wound on the side of her leg, assessing it with satisfaction. No more than an inch or two in length, it lay close to the dark edges of her pubic hair, so close that no one would ever notice it, not even the maids when they came in to dress her in the morning.

Unless, of course, she told someone about it. Somehow, he didn't think she would.

The tension had almost left his body when he turned away from her, moving with deliberation toward the door.

The sound of laughter echoed in Aimée's ears as she lay alone in the wide bed. At first it seemed distorted and unreal, as if she were only imagining it. Only after a moment did she realize that the sound was real—harsh and penetrating and full of malice.

Bitterly she reminded herself that she was a bride and that this was her wedding night. She still did not know what should have happened to her that night, or what she had done to fail so miserably in her first hours as a wife. She only knew that it could not be right for a bride to lie alone through the long hours of the night, her heart crying out in despair.

The laughter continued, magnified and echoing, until it seemed to have been absorbed into the walls of her room. Yet it was an ugly sound, rough and at the same time curiously high-pitched and girlish. Even the pillows wrapped around her ears could not shut it out.

Sadly she let her mind turn backward, remembering a lovely afternoon by the Seine, when she had been at least part child. She was astonished at how vivid the memory was. She could almost smell the river, feel the fragile flower petals in her fingers. For the first time she was glad her parents had not prepared her for the bitter reality of life. She would not have liked to know that afternoon what lay ahead for her.

The tiny candle sputtered for a moment, flickering with one last flash of glory. Aimée lay watching helplessly as it went out, leaving her alone in the darkness.

Still the laughter did not fade.

4

Aimée was not surprised when she did not recognize the maid who appeared at her door the next morning. She had not expected to see any of the girls who served her the night before, but she was surprised at the maid's downcast eyes and the nervous twitching of her features. It took her a moment to remember that news of last night's fiasco must have spread through the servants' quarters, striking fear into every heart.

"I will have breakfast in my room," Aimée told the girl.

"On a tray." She was careful to inject enough confidence into her tone to make sure the girl would not question her. She did not think she could bear to see Edward again so soon.

The girl paled. She took an awkward step backward, but she did not attempt to leave the room.

"I am sorry, miss . . . madam," she stammered clumsily. "But the master said, I mean the master has ordered . . . well, you are to join him in the breakfast room whether . . . whether you like it or not."

Whether she liked it or not! For the first time since her wedding, Aimée felt rebellious. Whether she liked it or not? What did he think she was, some kind of servant to be ordered about at whim? Furious, she was about to offer an indignant retort when the look of terror on the girl's face stopped her.

Bitterly she realized there was no way she could defy her husband. She *was* a servant—no, worse than a servant, for at least they could seek a new position if they wanted. When her father had placed her hand in Edward's at the altar, he had turned her over to him, completely and utterly. She belonged to him now. There was not a thing she could do—or not do—without his permission.

It was a quiet but composed Aimée who entered the breakfast room half an hour later, slipping into one of the empty chairs at the side of the long table. She had chosen her plainest dress, a slate-gray silk, and her hair was piled simply on top of her head. If Edward noticed the sudden drabness of the spectacularly beautiful girl his money had bought for him, he did not choose to remark on it.

"How thoughtful of you to join us." His biting sarcasm was not lost on Aimée. "We would not like to be deprived of the loveliness of your presence on such a chilly morning."

Aimée was startled by his use of the word "we." Except for herself, he was alone in the room.

Bon Dieu, what kind of a man had she married? she asked herself with mounting despair. Was he so imperious, so haughty, that he had to use "we" and "us" like the ruler of some petty kingdom, as if the word "I" were inadequate for a man of his importance.

Aimée let her eyes drift up to his face, and was startled to see that he was still a stranger. Even with the intimacies they had shared—or not quite shared—the night before, they were still no closer than they had been before they exchanged their vows. Was this all there was to it, she asked herself bitterly, all she could expect of marriage? Not the growing, shared af-

54

fection and sense of purpose her father had promised her, but simply the constant passing of two strangers in the same house?

The icy look Edward gave her warned Aimée she was as much a stranger to him as he was to her. She was startled that he seemed reconciled to the fact. Whatever he had attempted in her bedroom the night before, she sensed he would not try it again.

She was appalled by the relief that surged through her at the realization. Only the day before, not twenty-four hours ago, she had promised in front of God and his priest that she would be a good wife to this man. Now, barely a day later, she was ready, even eager, to break those sacred vows.

Edward made no attempt at conversation, but turned to his food, attacking it with a crudity more like a peasant's than a wealthy lord's. He did not look up again until the doors to the room burst open, slamming against the wall with a dull thud.

Aimée was only mildly surprised to see Buffy Montmorency standing in the doorway. Somehow, it seemed right to have him there since she had rarely seen Edward without him. Perhaps, she realized, it had been Buffy in the next room the night before, laughing at their awkward fumbling. No wonder Edward said "we." For Edward, there was no such thing as "I." He seemed to have no life of his own, outside the one he shared with Buffy.

Buffy cast a benign look in Aimée's direction. He was surprisingly cheerful as he took his place opposite her at the table. Although he could not have failed to see her tension, he was tactful enough not to call attention to it, smiling instead as he wished her good morning. If she had not known better, Aimée would have thought he was trying to be kind to her.

Edward did not attempt to match his good humor. "You're late, Buffy. You and my charming bride both. You know I insist on punctuality."

Buffy hardly noticed Edward's irritation. "Really, Eddie," he retorted, popping a bite of buttered croissant into his mouth, "I'm terribly sorry and all that, but after all, I expected to have the breakfast room to myself this morning. I mean, aren't you supposed to be lingering late in your bride's arms, savoring the sweet taste of love?"

Edward's face deepened to crimson, but Buffy paid him scant attention. Balancing a dab of marmalade on the end of his knife with impeccable manners, he spread it generously onto a piece of croissant.

Aimée shuddered at the man's callousness. She had been right about him all along. It *was* his laughter she had heard the night before. He must have had his ear pressed against the wall—or more probably, his eye to the keyhole.

Edward was quick to see Aimée's reaction. For a minute a fragile bond flickered between them, a kind of rapport that had never been there before. It was almost as if Buffy's blatant cruelty gave them a common enemy to unite against.

"Really, you are a toad, Buffy."

Buffy only smiled, twisting his lips into an innocuous grin. It was a moment before he spoke. When he did, he addressed himself not to Edward but to Aimée.

"I understand your father sells trinkets from Egypt." The words seemed casual, a simple attempt at polite conversation. Only his tone of voice hinted that they held more than their surface meaning.

"Egypt?" Aimée stared at him curiously. She did not know why, but even the name of a land she had never seen filled her with a sudden apprehension. She was determined not to let him see it. "Among other things. He runs a small import business—as I am sure you already know."

"Ah!" Buffy's face lit up with mock seriousness. "I thought perhaps that was an Egyptian cross around your neck."

Aimée's hand jerked upward, clutching at her gold crucifix. She realized instantly it had been a mistake to wear it in lieu of the expensive diamond cross her husband had given her as a wedding gift.

"It is French, *monsieur*," she replied, determined to salvage whatever she could from the unfortunate incident. "I wear it as a token of my faith—a thing *you* no doubt would never understand."

The flush that met her words told her her impudent barb had struck home. To her amazement, Edward seemed to approve.

"I think you'd better trot around the garden, Buffy," he said dryly. "If you don't work off some of those rolls you've eaten, you'll get so fat no one will be able to look at you."

If he expected a sharp retort, he was disappointed. Buffy rose amiably, pausing only long enough to wrap a pair of brioches in his napkin before he turned and made his way to the door.

The instant he was gone, Edward changed abruptly, losing both his composure and his sense of amusement. A scowl

56

darkened his features as he toyed with the eggs and sausages cooling on his plate. Aimée was startled to see how quickly the rapport between them vanished, as if it had been held together only by the man who antagonized them both. She was relieved when Edward's valet, Antoine, appeared at the door.

She was puzzled to see her husband rise, moving toward the servant instead of waiting for the man to come to him. Only when she heard the whispered conversation did she realize he had not wanted her to make out what they were saying. She caught only a little of it, a single name—Raoul Villière. It was a name that meant nothing to her. She watched as her husband turned on his heels and hurried out into the hallway, without so much as a perfunctory farewell.

Half an hour later, Aimée wrapped a shawl tightly around her shoulders and went outside to explore the gardens of her husband's spacious Paris home. At first she was careful to stay in the sunshine, for the wind had a biting edge to it in the shade, but she found herself lingering close to the formal clipped hedges that bordered the graveled paths. She wanted to be close enough to duck behind them if she had to. She was not at all sure Buffy would not take her husband's command literally, and she had no intention of subjecting herself to the unpleasantness of running into him.

She discovered a large lake at the back of the garden, its serene surface dotted with white swans. Eagerly she hurried toward it, wishing she had thought to steal a few crumbs from the breakfast table to lure the graceful creatures closer to the shore. She had nearly reached the water's edge before she realized she was not alone.

She stopped abruptly as she saw two men ahead of her. Although their backs were turned toward her, she was sure one of them was Buffy Montmorency. Quickly she went back down the path, taking care not to stumble or make any noise to attract his attention. Only then did she dare pause long enough to look at him carefully. When she did, she saw rounded shoulders and thinning hair, and to her amazement, realized that she had stumbled across, not Buffy, but rather her own husband.

She had not expected to see Edward in the gardens, and yet she realized she should have. He had been so secretive, so careful not to let her hear anything about his caller. She should have known that he would not want anyone to see or hear him with the stranger. Where better to hold their rendezvous than by the lake?

57

Inching back into the cover of the hedge, Aimée allowed herself one last look at her husband. This time she was careful to note the stranger who stood beside him. His face, like Edward's, was still turned away from her.

He was a tall man, his body lean and strongly built, his shoulders straining against the dark fabric of his coat. There was a grace and power about him, a magnetism that projected even across the distance of the garden. She had an uncanny sensation, as she stared at him, that she had seen him somewhere before.

Forgetting caution, Aimée allowed herself to stare at him openly. She wondered what there was about him—the arrogance of his bearing, perhaps, or the way the wind whipped his dark hair out behind him—that made him so familiar. Perhaps she had not actually seen the man before, she told herself, for where in her limited experience would she have met the kind of man Edward could not invite openly to his home? Perhaps it was simply that he reminded her of someone—someone she still could not place.

"So you're curious about the famous Raoul Villière?"

Aimée whirled around. She was appalled to see Buffy Montmorency, so close she could feel his breath on her cheek.

"Famous?" She tried to hide the curiosity in her voice. She did not want him to think she had been spying on her husband. She could just imagine what it would sound like when he ran to Edward with the tale.

"Don't tell me you don't know who he is?"

Aimée was relieved by the whispered tone of his question. It was obvious that Buffy was every bit as anxious as she to keep Edward from turning and catching them. Slowly she moved away, easing around the corner of the hedge until she was sure they were hidden from sight.

"Really, Buffy, I don't believe he's really famous; I think you're making the whole thing up. It makes you feel important to pretend you know something no one else does."

Her ploy worked. Buffy pouted for a minute, his disappointment evident as he realized she was not going to coax him, but he could not keep from telling her anyway.

"He's an archaeologist. You mean you really haven't heard of him? He's a famous Egyptologist."

Aimée was disappointed. Buffy's hints had led her to expect something glamorous, perhaps even a little sinister. If not a pirate or a mass murderer, then surely an infamous gambler or a smuggler—or at least a dashing cavalier noted for his notorious way with the ladies. But an Egyptologist . . . ?

It was a moment before Aimée remembered she had heard the word "Egypt" once before that morning. Then as now it had given her an unpleasant feeling. Shivering, she wrapped her shawl tightly around her shoulders.

Buffy did not miss the gesture. Yes, he told himself contentedly, the girl was going to be amusing—every bit as amusing as he had hoped.

"You'll hear the name Raoul Villière again," he said meaningfully. Without waiting to see her reaction, he turned away, hurrying down the path until he disappeared into the maze of hedges.

Bewildered, Aimée stared down the empty paths, trying to sort out the pieces of the puzzle Buffy had laid out for her. He had told her the man was an Egyptologist, but what did that mean? He could be anything from a musty old scholar, his fingernails caked with dirt and his nose buried in broken clay tablets and rotting scrolls of papyrus, to an unscrupulous soldier of fortune, fully prepared to steal or even kill as he plundered ancient graves of their treasure. From the little she knew of her new husband, Aimée could only assume Monsieur Villière fell into the latter category.

But more specifically, what did his presence mean to her? For it did mean something, of that she was sure. Otherwise, Buffy would never have looked at her with such smugness.

Raoul Villière. She turned the name over and over in her mind in the days that followed. Raoul Villière—and Egypt. But what could they have to do with her? And why did it frighten her to think of them?

I thought perhaps that was an Egyptian cross.

An Egyptian cross? Without realizing it, she let her hand slip up to her neck, closing around the simple crucifix. What a strange idea. Why, she didn't even know what an Egyptian cross looked like. Closing her eyes, she ran her fingertips along the cool metal, trying to call up alien pictures in her imagination.

The images she formed were not visual ones. Sensory impressions, so strong she could barely believe they did not exist, began to take over her body. Heat. She could feel the heat, heavy and prickly, until the sweat oozed out of her pores in response to it. And the smell of the sand. No, not sand, really. Dust. But a dust so dry and clean she had never experienced it before. And warm river water. And exotic flowers, rich with perfume.

Even the cross. At last she could see it, the shape that had eluded her. An Egyptian cross. Thick and gold and ornate. Hanging on a plain mudbrick wall in a room she could almost recognize.

She snapped her eyes open. Suddenly, the vision had become real—too real. It was almost as if she had seen it with her own eyes. As if it were a memory she could not quite remember. A feeling she could not feel.

But she was being idiotic, she told herself sharply. She knew nothing about Egypt. She had never been there, and her father had never told a single story about the place. Besides, all this was absurd anyhow. She would know what Egypt—and Raoul Villière—meant to her when Edward decided to tell her and not a moment before. Anything else was the silliest kind of speculation.

It was nearly two weeks before she finally learned the truth. Edward had invited her parents to join them at a fashionable restaurant for their midday meal. It was a gesture that made Aimée uncomfortable. In the short time she had been married, she had already recognized her husband's stinginess. Not that he couldn't be remarkably free with his money when he wanted something. He thought nothing of spending a king's ransom for a prized painting, even when it was a stolen piece that had to be hidden away in his vaults, or at the other extreme, an expensive jewel to adorn a beautiful wife, as long as she took care to wear it in public where everyone could see and envy it. But for anything else—for food for his private table or necessities for the servants' quarters—he would haggle over every penny. The idea of spending an extravagant sum on her parents, especially now that he already had their daughter and no longer needed to bribe them, was totally out of character.

It was almost as if he had done it on purpose, Aimée told herself nervously. As if he had picked an expensive public restaurant simply because it was expensive . . . because the subdued elegance of the place would discourage anything but polite small talk.

When Aimée greeted her father she sensed that he, too, was uncomfortable. She did not miss the scent of whiskey on his breath, nor could she fail to see how swiftly he gulped down the first drink Edward offered him, and how willingly he accepted another. Eyeing him carefully Aimée wondered if his anxiety might not prove to be well-founded.

No matter how hard she tried, Aimée could not shake off a sense of trepidation. All through the meal she studied Edward's expression, then Buffy's, searching for some kind of sign. But nowhere in the face of either man and nowhere in the idle talk that accompanied their meal, could she find even a hint to justify her suspicions.

It was only when they had finished their coffee, and glasses of brandy were placed before the men, that Aimée at last detected a trace of strain in Edward's manner. As he leaned forward, turning toward her father, she was sure she caught an unnatural gleam in his eyes. She found her palms were sweating and she nervously wiped them against her skirt as she waited for him to speak.

"You have traveled extensively in Egypt, I suppose." His voice was low and polite.

Egypt? The question might have been innocent if it weren't for the repetition of that one word—and the startling effect it had.

Her father began to choke, reaching up with his hand to catch at his throat. Aimée watched him struggle to compose himself, fighting as he forced an even breath of air into his lungs. He made no effort to pretend that nothing had happened—or that he had simply choked on a swig of brandy.

Her mother's reaction, though subtler, was even more telling. The glass of sherry—the only intoxicant she allowed herself—seemed to float in her hands, as if it were suspended in the air. Her eyes were fixed not on her husband, but on Lord Edward. It seemed to Aimée that in some strange way she had expected his question.

Furiously Aimée turned to her husband. "My father has been to Egypt several times—though not for many years. He has agents to handle that kind of thing now."

Edward barely glanced at her. He continued to stare at her father.

"Then you have heard of Raoul Villière, I am sure."

The question sounded casual, but the effect was no less dramatic than before. Hélène LeClare lowered her glass slowly to the table, her hand trembling visibly. Her husband did just the opposite. Lifting his own glass, he drained it in one rapid gulp.

"The man is an Egyptologist," Etienne acknowledged at last. " A *respected* one." The emphatic way he said it made it plain that he did not expect Edward to have anything to do with such a man. Aimée wondered what could have hap-

61

pened in the two short weeks since her wedding to turn her father against the son-in-law he himself had chosen.

Edward ignored the implied criticism. "Villière has been digging near the Valley of the Kings. He thinks he has a lead to an unplundered tomb belonging to one of the princes of the eighteenth dynasty." His eyes shone at the thought. "Think of it! An unplundered tomb! Why, there might be thousands . . . millions, in undiscovered treasure. I've hired Villière to help me find it."

"No!"

Aimée was amazed at the violence of her father's cry. Diners at nearby tables turned to stare, but Etienne did not notice them.

"I will not have it! Tomb-robbing and smuggling and God knows what else. I will not have it, do you hear me?"

"*You* will not have it?" Edward was as amused as he was irritated. "Who do you think you are, trying to tell me what to do? Do you seriously believe I would listen to advice— much less commands—from a man who made such a mess of his own affairs he couldn't get out of it without selling his own daughter?"

Etienne recoiled as if he had been struck, but he did not try to defend himself. Aimée could see that he believed he had earned his own pain. She could not bear to watch him, but there was nothing she could do to help him.

"Do what you want," Etienne agreed, weary and defeated. "I cannot stop you. Just leave my daughter out of it."

Edward only smiled at his words. "Aimée is mine now," he said with deceptive quietness. "If you think I'll leave her behind, you don't know the first thing about me."

Aimée was stunned by his words. For the first time she felt the real impact of what had happened. She had been so absorbed in her father's reaction that she had not stopped to ask herself if the situation also concerned her.

Hélène LeClare said nothing as she reached out to clutch at the glass in front of her. Raising it to her lips, she emptied it as swiftly as her husband had drained his own only a moment before. Setting it on the tablecloth, she laid her hand on her son-in-law's arm.

"But surely, my dear, you don't expect Aimée to accompany you." Her voice was soft and coaxing. "Not to a place like Egypt."

Aimée stared at her in amazement. Could this be her mother? Her own gentle mother, who always let her father take the initiative?

"And what do you know of Egypt, madam? Have you been there?"

Hélène turned white, but she did not draw back. "I know enough to realize it is a foul, filthy place, ridden with poverty and violence and disease. I know it is no place for a woman, especially one of childbearing age."

She whispered the last words temptingly, sensing his vanity would be roused by the thought of the son who would one day be his. She could not know how badly she had miscalculated. Aimée glanced at her husband, shivering at the anger in his face. She knew she had been right about him, that morning after the wedding; whatever he had attempted with her the night before, he would not try it again.

Quickly, as much to relieve her own tension as Hélène's, Aimée grasped her mother's hand. "Don't worry," she told her warmly. "It's all right."

And it was all right. It really was. All those premonitions she had had about the place were only foolish fancies. Besides, she knew her mother was wrong. Egypt might be filthy and disease ridden, but Edward was rich and they would live in comfort and cleanliness. And if it was far away from her parents—well, wouldn't they miss her just as much if she were only across the channel in England?

Mon Dieu, why was it so hard for them? She was impatient at the intensity of their distress. Was it always like this? Did parents always find it so painful to face the fact that their children were growing up and drifting into lives of their own? Would it be the same for her, too, someday when her own . . . ?

But there would be no children of her own. The realization was so sudden it took her breath away. In all her thoughts of Edward, in the pity and contempt she had felt for his inability to father a child, it somehow had not occurred to her that the barrenness of his life was something she would be forced to share. Suddenly the years ahead of her seemed long and stifling, filled with nothing but regret and loneliness.

She let her gaze drift toward Edward. At that moment she hated him doubly, both for the unhappiness he had already caused and for the pain that lay ahead. His amusement as he sensed the suffering she could not conceal was enough to draw her out of herself, prompting a burst of anger.

"Really, you mustn't mind," she said brightly, turning toward her parents with a new composure. "Actually, I think it will be exciting—like a great adventure." Her smile as she

63

turned back to her husband was as artificial as any of Buffy's. It had the same effect.

Petulantly Edward turned away from her. For the first time that afternoon, he looked toward Buffy, who had been sitting by his side.

"I've asked Villière to join us here." He half-whispered the words, as if they were meant for Buffy's ears alone. "I know you've been dying to meet him." He slipped an arm around the younger man's shoulders, giving him an affectionate squeeze.

Aimée could hardly believe the sudden benevolence in his manner. Never before had she seen Edward treat Buffy with such kindness. Even more startling was the tinge of pink that rose to Buffy's cheeks in response.

Why, he adores Edward, she thought with surprise. The artificiality of Buffy's mannerisms, just like the coyness of her own smile a moment before, was nothing but a carefully built-up defense, a shield against Edward's cruelty. What a fool her husband was. He had, in the secretary his money had bought for him, the one human being in the world who would be completely devoted to him. All he had to do was throw the man a scrap of affection now and then—just a scrap, that was all—and he could have anything he wanted from him.

Lost in her thoughts, Aimée barely noticed the tall man who worked his way confidently across the crowded restaurant. Even when he reached their table, she did not look up. She knew this must be the man she had been wondering about for days, but she could not find it in her heart to care about him now. He had to be a soldier of fortune, as she thought earlier. If he were the reputable scientist Etienne claimed, he would never have sold himself to Edward.

Reluctantly she let her gaze drift upward, certain of what she would see. The instant she caught sight of the man's face, her eyes widened with astonishment.

His eyes revealed an astonishment no less than her own. Only when Edward introduced her as his wife did the expression fade, merging slowly into deliberate disdain. He did not bother to acknowledge Edward's introduction.

"I hope you realize, Ellingham, it will be impossible to bring your wife on a trip like this."

Aimée bristled with indignation. "You forget yourself, *monsieur*," she retorted, covering her confusion with an icy arrogance that matched his own. "My husband is paying for this expedition. *He* will decide who is to go and who is to stay behind."

Too late she realized the trap she had fallen into. Only a moment ago she herself had not wanted to go. Now she was committed to the venture.

As she saw the answering flash of anger in Villière's eyes, she found she was unrepentant of her folly. The man was furious—she could see that only too well—but she could also see there was nothing he could do about it. The realization gave her intense satisfaction.

There had been a challenge in his eyes the first time she had seen him, that sunny afternoon as she strolled along the banks of the Seine on her cousin's arm, enjoying the last hours of her childhood. It was a challenge they had both known she could not answer.

Today, she sensed, she had answered that challenge with one of her own. Now it was he who was helpless to reply.

Slowly she let her lips turn up in the hint of a smile. She was Edward's wife now, like it or not, and she would play the part well. It was all that was left for her.

"I am sure we will all have a pleasant association, Monsieur Villière," she said coolly. "I for one look forward to it."

5

The wind tugged at the cashmere of Aimée's shawl, tearing it off her head and whipping her long black tresses dramatically in the icy air. Frantically she clutched at it with the fingers of one hand, fighting to hold it around her shoulders. With the other she clung to the ship's railing, terrified that the wind would catch her up as easily as it had her shawl, dashing her into the churning waves beneath.

It was frightening to stand alone on the deck, watching the rage of the gathering storm, but it was exciting, too. She turned her head deliberately into the wind, reveling in its sting, relishing the taste of salt on her lips. It was wonderful to stand up to the violence of nature and know she could hold her own against it. Nothing in her sheltered life in Paris had prepared her for this.

How far away that seemed now, she thought. And how different she was from the spoiled little girl who had once dared to open her arms spontaneously to life, dreaming dreams of love.

Now when she thought of the past, only one image came to mind, the last image she would ever have of a life that was already gone. If she closed her eyes, she could still see her mother's face, as vivid as if it were before her at that very moment, vanishing into a crowd of faces on the dock at Marseilles. How strange it seemed, even now, that it was her mother who had made that painful, gallant voyage with her, her mother whose lips had parted at the last moment, as if to say all the things she had never dared say before, then whispered only, "God keep you." Always before, it had been her father's strength she had relied on, his sturdy good sense she had looked to in time of need. But always before, life had been carefree and easy. Now that the easy days were gone, she realized perhaps it was her mother who had been the strong one all the time.

Raoul Villière stood back from the railing, half-hidden in the shadows. The collar of his jacket was turned up against the wind. As he watched, the moonlight peeked from beneath heavy clouds, touching the hair of the girl who stood by the rail. Even from a distance, he could see that her eyes were glowing. God, she was beautiful, he told himself, responding to her sensuality and hating himself for it at the same time. Beautiful and exciting, with a half-tamed passion only partially concealed beneath her perfectly groomed surface.

He could not help remembering how lovely she had looked that first day by the Seine. The deep blue of her eyes had been touched with hints of fire, mocking the childlike ingenuousness of her laughter. At last he forced himself to acknowledge what he had refused to admit that day—that even then he had longed to run up to her and tear the pins from her hair, rumpling her fashionable dress in an urgent search for the passion and vitality her eyes seemed to promise. She had been a little girl that day, all decked out in the finery of the trivial lady of fashion she was apprenticing to become. Today, for the first time, she showed signs of the woman she could be, free and unfettered, eager for a taste of real life. It was an image he found both provocative and disturbing.

He stepped out of the shadows, making his way slowly toward the railing.

"You shouldn't be here," he said gruffly. He was conscious of her perfume as the wind swept silken strands of jet-black hair across his cheek. "There's a storm brewing. You'd better get inside."

"But it's so . . ." she protested, faltering over the words as

66

she struggled with the wayward wisps of hair, trying to catch them back from his face, ". . . so exciting!"

She raised her eyes to meet his. He could see that they were filled with a tentative, awkward questioning. It almost seemed to him that the girl was afraid of him.

And why shouldn't she be? he asked himself. What had he ever done to lead her to expect kindness or even fairness at his hands? He had been antagonistic toward her from the very beginning, deciding in those first few moments in an elegant Parisian restaurant to declare all-out war on her. He was uncomfortably aware that it was a war in which he had made all the rules—and not even had the courtesy to explain them to her.

Well, she had put him in his place smartly enough, he thought, laughing at himself as he recalled the haughty efficiency with which she had met her first rude outburst. What a surprising little bitch she had turned out to be, all fire and arrogance and spirit. He had felt the beginnings of a grudging admiration for her then, an admiration he took pains to conceal.

"Why are you looking at me like that?"

Her voice startled Raoul. "I was just remembering," he said quickly. Then, fearing he had admitted too much, he turned away, staring into the vast emptiness of the wind-tossed waves. "I was remembering my first storm at sea. I didn't want to go inside either, but believe me, it's much safer."

Aimée felt herself relax at the sudden kindness in his voice. Daring to look at him, she studied his profile as he gazed out at the moon-drenched sea. His face was surprisingly handsome—no, not handsome really, she reminded herself, for his eyes burned with too much fire and his features were too rugged. Exciting—that was the word for him. Exciting and bold, filled with a passion for life she was just beginning to understand.

"You don't like me, do you?" she asked softly.

Caught off guard by her frankness, Raoul whirled back to face her.

"I don't dislike you, Aimée," he said slowly. He had the unpleasant sensation that he was being forced into words he did not want to say. "I think you're a lovely young woman, and in another time, another place, I might admire you ardently. But here . . . well, we've months of long, strenuous work ahead of us, and barely tolerable living conditions. It will be bad enough catering to a self-indulgent nobleman and that simpering parasite of a secretary. I don't need to add a pampered female to the lot."

To his surprise, Aimée laughed at his words. "Have I really been so bad?" Her voice issued a teasing challenge.

The question unnerved Raoul. If he was going to be honest, he realized, he would have to admit she had not created any of the problems he expected—at least not yet. The ship her husband had chosen, with the consummate thrift only a wealthy man could perfect so superbly, was a filthy, vermin-infested tub, the cheapest thing afloat, and the ugliest. But even with all the complaining, all the whining that persisted day and night, not a word of protest had passed Aimée's lips.

Raoul was spared the awkwardness of answering by a sudden violent gust of wind. It was almost as if the storm, recognizing in him another tempestuous being, had decided to come to his aid. Snatching the shawl from Aimée's shoulders, the wind whipped it away. Raoul barely had time to reach out and retrieve it before it was swept into the ocean.

Wordlessly he wrapped the shawl around her body, laughing with her as the wind struggled to pull it away again. Damn, she was beautiful, he thought with a pang of regret—superbly beautiful. Far too beautiful for that swine Ellingham.

He was acutely conscious of the warmth of her shoulders under his fingers. God help him, she felt so smooth, so young, so tantalizingly soft beneath the work-hardened calluses of his hands. He had the almost frightening sensation that if he did not pull away now, he would never be able to free himself from her.

For Aimée, the touch of Raoul's fingers was electric, and sent a tingling shock coursing through her entire body. Never before had the touch of a man felt like that. Not with the fumbling boys who had contrived transparent excuses to press their bodies against hers, not even with her cousin Franz when he had taken her arm in a gentle show of affection, and certainly not with her husband the one time he had laid possessive hands on her. It was a feeling that was both terrifying and exhilarating—like the storm itself.

"You are right," she said, pulling away from him with the instinct of self-preservation. She had liked the way his hand felt on her arm, just as she liked the warm glow in his eyes when he looked down at her. She was not at all sure she would like whatever followed. "I should go inside, out of the storm."

She turned quickly, fighting the wind as she worked her way toward the door. Only when she reached it did she turn to see if he were staring after her. She smiled when she saw that he was.

Raoul leaned back against the railing, wrapping his fingers around the cold metal. He had to laugh at himself as he watched her disappear into the passageway.

What a little minx she was, he thought with admiration and amusement, and how neatly she had handled him.

Who the hell did he think he was, trying to lay his hands on another man's wife—and the wife of his own rich patron at that? Grudgingly he had to admit that the girl had behaved perfectly. A cool smile, a quick exit, nothing could have been smoother or less embarrassing for both of them.

In the long days that followed, Raoul's tentative admiration for Aimée had ample opportunity to grow, as he continued the reassessment of her character that began that tempestuous night. The storm that had threatened came on them full force, and in the violence of tossing, angry waves, the already uncomfortable vessel became a virtual hellhole. For the first few days Aimée was as sick as the other passengers, barely able to crawl out on deck for a breath of fresh air, but uncomfortable as she was, she never once complained. That was something Raoul could not say about the man who had brought her there, or the sniveling, whining companion who was always at his side.

Later, as the storm began to abate and Aimée felt more like herself at last, she began to do what little she could to ease the discomfort of the others, especially those few children on the voyage whose mothers were too ill to tend them. To Raoul, who had never expected to see a spoiled young Parisienne patiently spoon mouthfuls of broth down the throats of whimpering children, unmindful of the spills that stained her expensive gown, much less mop up the vomit by their bedsides, it was a revelation. Ruefully he had to admit it was a lesson in the reliability of his stubborn prejudices.

"Perhaps," he admitted when at last the water was smooth again, "you are not quite as pampered as I thought."

It was the closest he could come to an apology, and Aimée recognized it as such. She rewarded him with a bright flash of laughter.

"I *am* pampered," she admitted easily. "But that doesn't mean I can't learn—if I have to."

They were nearly alone in the large dining hall. Although the sea was now as calm as glass, most of the passengers had not recovered sufficiently to rouse themselves for dinner. Edward and Buffy, still moaning in unison in their adjoining cabins, had not been able to bear the thought of moving, so Aimée and Raoul had the large table in the center of the room to themselves.

Raoul poured a generous portion of champagne into Aimée's glass. He smiled as he watched her raise it to her lips, congratulating himself that he had been clever enough to bribe the captain for it. Although he noticed she barely touched the greasy food on her plate, it was obvious that she enjoyed champagne with a childlike delight.

Impetuously he reached for her hand.

"Truce?" he asked, thinking of the ugly sparring that had marked their first meetings.

"Truce," she agreed softly. Her eyes were as serious as his own.

Acutely conscious of the warmth of her hand beneath his, Raoul finally admitted to himself that somehow, without his even knowing it, his feelings for her had slipped beyond the bonds of simple attraction. It was a sobering thought, and a confusing one. He had never been so vitally aware of a woman before, not merely of her physical presence, but the essence of her spirit as well. Not even with Thea. . . .

The thought of Thea troubled him, making him uncomfortable in a way he did not want to consider. Conscious of a new awkwardness between himself and the girl who sat across from him, he lowered his eyes. But he made no attempt to drop her hand.

The intensity of his emotions seemed to echo in Aimée's heart, as if they had passed from him directly into her. These feelings were even more unnerving to her than they had been to him. All the heat, the passion just beneath the surface of this man she had once thought so cold and calculating brought with it not only an enticing sense of danger but also an almost unbearable sense of loneliness. Never in her life had a man looked at her or touched her with that kind of feeling. And never, she sensed, would it happen again. For the rest of her days she would have to content herself with the fading memory of one fleeting hint of passion. She sensed it would not be enough as she watched herself grow old—old and ugly and bitter—beside a man who had not even a trace of love in his soul.

Slowly, with a strong reluctance, she pulled her hand away.

"You've never told me about this mysterious tomb you're

looking for. Don't you think it's time you shared your secret with me?"

Raoul smiled at her words. Raising his glass, he offered her a salute before he lifted it to his lips. As before, Aimée had had to extricate them from his clumsy, ill-advised advances. Again she had done it with grace and tact.

"What do you want to know?"

"Lord Edward said you were on the track of it. That sounds mysterious—like a detective tracking down clues."

"I suppose it does," he agreed, laughing. "But it isn't as glamorous as it sounds. Still, I imagine being a detective isn't glamorous either. Just a lot of hard work and constant, petty routine."

"But you have found clues?"

"You might call them clues. In a barren area near the Valley of the Kings, we found a cache of funerary jars from one of the most exciting periods in Egyptian history. They are inscribed with the name Ramose—a prince no one has ever heard of before."

Aimée looked puzzled. "But what are funerary jars?"

Raoul smiled as he realized how little she knew of the sun-baked land they had come to study. "The ancient Egyptians did not consider their burial places tombs," he explained patiently. "They called them 'Houses of Eternity.' A man of means would spend many years constructing this last house for himself, making it as rich and large as he could possibly afford. When he died, he wanted to be sure all his favorite possessions would be piled around him: his furnishings and jewels, his clothes and favorite games, even models of his servants to tend his needs in the afterlife."

Aimée burst out laughing. "And you called me pampered!" She felt suddenly giddy, as if the bubbles from the champagne had raced directly to her head.

"I thought we had a truce," Raoul told her with mock sternness. "Are you going to taunt me forever for my rudeness?"

"Perhaps," she teased. "But not now—not if you tell me more about these mysterious jars of yours. Whose funeral were they used for—Ramose's? And what kind of function did they have?"

"We don't know." He was surprised at the astuteness of her questions. "They may have been used in the embalming process, or perhaps in the ceremony of sealing the burial chamber. But whatever their use, they were buried separately, probably not far from the tomb itself."

Aimée looked at him expectantly. It was obvious she did not quite understand what he was trying to tell her.

"Don't you see?" he prompted. "If the tomb exists—and it must, otherwise why would those jars exist?—then it must be somewhere in that area. If it had been plundered, the tomb's contents would have shown up somewhere, and the name Ramose would not be totally unknown to us."

He was surprised to see her eyes darken with a shadow he could not understand. Thinking he had not explained things clearly, or perhaps she was not as quick to catch on as he had thought, he hastened to continue.

"Of course, there are many gaps in Egyptian history. Many names and dates are unknown to us. I suppose it is possible that everything from a plundered tomb might have been irretrievably lost and the name of its occupant—"

"No, no," She brushed aside his explanations with a casual hand. "I understand all that. It's just that this tomb—if there is such a tomb . . ." She hesitated for a moment, trying to pick out the words she wanted. "If you find this tomb and it has gone through all those centuries unplundered, then what are you going to do? Plunder it yourself?"

"Good God, no! I am an archaeologist. It's my job to save things from plunderers."

Her expression warned him she did not believe him. At first he was irritated by her stubbornness. Then, calming a little, he forced himself to consider her point of view. It made him uncomfortable to admit she was not totally wrong.

To her, Ramose would be a fairy-tale prince, young and handsome, tragically dead before his time, not a paunchy old man ending a lifetime of wealth and indulgence. The violation of his tomb would be the violation of a dream, her own as well as his. What did it matter ultimately, to either of them, if their dreams were destroyed by thieves or by archaeologists?

"I suppose it must seem that way," he conceded. "But you have to remember, Ramose's tomb is part of the heritage of all mankind. It belongs as much to us as it does to the man who is buried in it. Without that tomb, without careful scientific excavation and cataloging of every detail, a little bit of the past will be lost to us forever."

She did not seem convinced. It bothered him to see that the troubled look had not left her eyes. He wondered why it disturbed him so. Disapproval had never hurt him before.

"Is that what my husband is after?" she asked softly. "A scientific excavation of the tomb?"

So that was what was disturbing her, he thought with relief. She was worried about her husband's motives. He was tempted to lie to her, telling her Lord Edward's intentions were as unselfish as his own. Instinct warned him it would be a foolish move. Young as she was, she was far too intelligent to be taken in so easily.

"No, of course not," he told her honestly. "Ellingham is interested in the gold, though perhaps that's only fair, since it's his money we're risking in the search. We have an agreement, your husband and I. Whatever we find, I will excavate it and record it properly. After that, the gold and the jewels will be his to dispose of as he likes."

He did not tell her that he had already begun to suspect Lord Edward's promise was more easily given than honored. He did not have to. Her veiled expression told him she already knew this.

Then suddenly, with a lightness he had not expected, Aimée raised the half-empty champagne glass to her lips.

"I may be naive, but I can't help wondering what makes you so sure, with only these meager clues, that you can find the tomb at all."

"Naive?" He burst into laughter. "No, *ma petite*, I am the one who is naive—and arrogant and smug to boot. But I seem to have a sixth sense about these things, fostered no doubt by years of study. Besides, I have been digging in the area for two seasons. I've got it pretty well narrowed down by now."

"So we'll find it this year?"

Her eyes were glowing. He wondered if it was from the champagne or if she was thinking of the discovery to come. Or if perhaps . . .

"This year," he promised, lifting his glass in a hurried toast to interrupt thoughts he did not dare pursue.

Aimée did not speak, but simply raised her own glass, touching it against his. He felt the vibration run through his flesh as keenly as if her hand had actually touched his.

Dammit, he thought, irritated that he was so aware of her presence. Why was it no other girl had ever listened to him with such rapt attention? Or looked up at him with such soft, melting eyes?

Even Thea. God help him, Thea had never looked at him like that. With warmth and affection, yes; amused tolerance for his long discourses, yes; but passionate interest? A nameless yearning that set his heart on fire?

73

Abruptly he pushed his chair away from the table. The girl seemed to understand, for she did not question him.

"I have some work to do," he said awkwardly. "I'd better get at it."

Still she did not question him, but simply bid him good night. He was insanely tempted to ask her to come out and walk with him on the deck, letting the wind brush through her hair again, as it had the night the storm began. Reminding himself he was a fool, he hurried from the room.

The night air was cool and refreshing. He felt his body relax as he leaned against the railing, staring down into the blue-green water eerily lighted by the full moon. Dammit, what had he been thinking of anyhow? he chided himself angrily. Only a fool would let himself get involved with a married woman, even one as lovely as Aimée—especially when his entire future depended on that woman's husband.

It seemed he had been outside only a moment when he sensed someone in the darkness behind him. He did not know if some barely detectable sound had warned him, or if he had caught a hint of motion. Or perhaps he had known she was there simply because he wanted it so much. He felt no surprise when he turned around and saw her, only a sense of destiny.

She stood by the doorway for a long time staring at him with a solemnity that tore at his heart. Then, just as he had known she would, she began to walk slowly toward him. She moved like a sleepwalker drifting through a dream. His arms were already open before she reached him.

At first his embrace was cautious, protective, as much an impulse to warm as to possess. Then slowly, as she trembled beneath his hands, his arms began to tighten around her. God help them both, he thought with a swift fatalism—there was nothing he could do to stop himself.

Aimée felt his strong arms sweep her up, pressing her against his chest. The gesture neither startled nor frightened her. She accepted it as something that was only right and natural. It was almost as if she had expected it all the time.

Perhaps she *had* expected it, she told herself with a flash of realization. Perhaps she had known, even as she calmly searched for a wrap in her cabin, that she would find him on deck waiting for her—and what would happen when she did.

When at last he lowered his lips to hers, it was as tender and tantalizing a kiss as she had ever imagined. It was just as she had always dreamed, she thought with a sweet thrill of pleasure, remembering the thousand childish fantasies in which she had raised her mouth at last to meet the warm, gentle lips of her handsome cousin.

Only this time the lips that pressed down on hers were not her affectionate cousin's. This time they were firmer, hungrier, and more and more demanding with each passing second. Slowly, patiently, taking care not to frighten her with his aggressiveness, Raoul forced Aimée's lips apart, half teasingly at first, then with mounting passion. Only when, with a yearning he could no longer disguise, he tried to press his tongue into her mouth did Aimée stiffen with fright, remembering with searing clarity what Edward had done to her on their wedding night. But then, as Raoul's hands grew bolder, moving with daring intimacy, her resistance began to melt away. When he reached downward, grasping her buttocks in the strong sweep of his hands and pressing her hips against his, she felt her body surge forward until it seemed her flesh must merge into his. Eagerly, with a hot passion she had not known she possessed, she accepted his tongue.

Heaven help her, there was nothing she could do to save herself from him—no way she could salvage the last traces of her honor and dignity.

Sensing her acquiescence, Raoul grew even bolder, caressing her with a hunger he had neither the power nor the will to control. His hands were strong, eager, demanding, unleashing powerful answering passions that could no longer be denied. It seemed to her that every ounce of her concentration, every last nerve ending in her body, was centered on the flesh beneath his burning fingertips as he traced a slow, deliberate path toward her breasts.

Only when she felt his hands slip up to her neck, groping at the fastenings of her dress, did the cool powers of reason return, rushing at her with violent urgency. Gasping with shock and fear, she pushed Raoul's hands away.

"*Mon Dieu*, what are we doing?" she cried out in horror.

Urgently, with a despair he could not control, Raoul caught her hands in his, holding them so tightly she could not get away.

"Ah, my sweet, my beauty, don't pull away. God help me, I want you as I've never wanted any other woman."

His voice grew soft and low. His hands were tempting as he tried to draw her back toward him.

"Come, *ma chère*, come back to my arms. I want you so much . . . I *need* you so much."

The yearning in his voice seemed to cut through Aimée, leaving a raw wound in its wake. The loneliness and longing in her heart cried out to her to go back to him, to surrender at last to the need they shared. Only the icy kiss of the tiny cross around her neck held her back, reminding her of the sacred vows that could never be broken.

"I cannot," she whispered. "Oh, forgive me. I cannot."

The pain that flashed through his eyes at the sound of her words slowly turned into simmering anger. The sight tore Aimée's heart in two. She knew she could not stand there and watch him an instant longer. She could not bear to see the hurt of her rejection in his eyes. Whirling suddenly, without allowing herself even a backward glance, she raced toward the inside doorway.

God damn her, Raoul thought, channeling his frustration into a mounting surge of fury. He turned to face the ocean again, scowling at the placid surface that seemed a deliberate mockery of the turmoil in his heart. What a calculating bitch she had turned out to be after all. He had been right about her, right from the first. She was nothing but a spoiled little brat. He had been a fool to let her beauty blind him to her faults. Well, he had fallen into her trap, all right. He had played her stupid games, and she had gotten exactly what she wanted. He had admitted that he needed her, needed her more than any other woman he had ever known. God, how her ego must have swelled at that. Angrily he gripped the railing, barely noticing the icy bite of cold metal against his hand.

And yet he was not being fair, he had to admit, as the anger at last began to fade, leaving in its place only a tormenting loneliness and frustration. The girl was pious—any idiot could tell that—and no doubt innocent in the ways of the world. God knows, whatever awkward fumblings that boor of a husband had forced on her could only have aroused her disgust. She must have been terrified tonight, feeling the sudden awakening of passions she had never known before. And he hadn't helped things much, he reminded himself with a wry smile, rushing at her like a wild animal, not even taking the time to court her tenderly.

What a bastard he was, what a clumsy, arrogant bastard. Once again it was Aimée who had to save them from his reckless passion. Once again it was she who had to remember for both of them that she was a woman bound by holy vows to another man.

Dammit, Villière, he cursed himself sharply. Get back to your books and your clay tablets and your endless decipherings of dead languages. That's all you're good for. You

haven't the tact or the decency to deal in human relation-
ships.

The wind began to rise, twisting into bitter gusts that tore
at his hair and whipped his jacket out behind him. Still he
did not move.

6

The shoreline of Alexandria shimmered in the distance
green and full of promise. Aimée leaned against the ship'
railing, her shawl half pushed off her shoulders in the warmth
of the midday sun. It would be good to land at last, she told
herself, daring to let hope into her heart for the first time in
weeks. Already she anticipated the solidity of the earth
beneath her feet and the fresh, clean air that would drive the
stench of the ship from her nostrils. Soon she would be free
of the cramped walls that had closed in around her, penning
her in with emotions she could neither control nor understand.

The last few days had been a torture. Ever since that
moonlit night on deck—the night she had been forced to
recognize the longings of her heart—Aimée had felt like a
prisoner in the confines of the ship. Every time she stepped
into the salon, Raoul seemed to have entered only a moment
before; every time she stood by the railing, she sensed his
presence behind her. And every time she saw him, she was
reminded all over again of the doubt and conflict that
wracked her soul.

To Raoul, standing only a few feet away from her at the
railing, the torment in her eyes was obvious. He wished there
were something he could do to comfort her, some way he
could reach out and take her hand in his, could talk quietly
about their shared guilt—about the pain that was his as much
as hers. How much easier it would be if he could only say to
her, "I understand how you feel—believe me, I understand.
You have a husband, but I have a fiancée, a lovely, gentle
Englishwoman I betray in my heart every time I look at
you." If only they could be honest with each other, open and
free and unafraid of the truth. It tore him apart to realize
they could not.

The oasis-green shores of Alexandria, so tantalizing from a
distance, were disappointing at closer view. The tall palms,
swaying in far-off breezes, were in reality sharp and jagged

and oddly devoid of grace, and the lush green grasses of the delta were barely more than an illusion, ending abruptly at the dirty hovels that marked the edge of town. The crowds that thronged the dock were even more appalling, a grotesque mockery, as if they were part of a gigantic montage put together by some mad artist—a sea of twisted, toothless faces pasted onto a background of rags and sweat and sand. Aimée drew back from the railing, some primal fear deep inside her body awakened by the sight.

Egypt is a foul, filthy place, ridden with poverty and violence and disease. It is no place for a woman.

Hélène LeClare's words echoed in her daughter's ears. Fleetingly Aimée wondered if her mother had ever been to Egypt, if she had perhaps accompanied her father on one of his earlier trips, in the years before the children had come to tie her down. What a fool she had been to dismiss her fears so cavalierly, assuming they were nothing more than a woman's natural reluctance at having to let go of her child. What a smug, self-complacent little fool!

She drew her skirts tightly around her body as she stepped at last onto the sandy soil of Egypt. She was surprised as her husband moved protectively toward her, hovering so close he was only inches away. A heavily scented handkerchief was pressed against his nostrils to block out the strong odors that seemed to come from the very soil. Uncomfortably Aimée realized that only her stubbornness, her strong need to hide her fear from the others, kept her from doing the same thing.

Of them all, only Buffy seemed unconcerned by their surroundings. Moved by neither the excitement of the place nor its grotesque squalor, he worked his way calmly through the masses that swarmed around the dock, with an air of indifference and even nonchalance. Only his nostrils, tautened slightly to block out the stench, betrayed his disgust. To him the crowded streets were oddly familiar, calling back memories of the London slums of his childhood. They were a little poorer perhaps, a little filthier and fouler-smelling, but in their very strangeness he could find a sense of security. In these streets it was easy to remember he was just a foreigner passing through.

The house Edward had found for them was in the European sector of town. With the same thrift that marked his choice of a vessel, he had managed to find the smallest, shabbiest house in the area, but even so, Aimée had to admit the place was not uncomfortable. A wide veranda swept across the front of the house, catching cool northern breezes from

78

the sea, and the small courtyard in the center, onto which most of the rooms opened, was a miniature tropical garden teeming with exotic greenery and sun-drenched color.

The heavy perfume of the garden followed Aimée as she stepped into the cool dark room that had been set aside for her. She sank gratefully onto the straight-backed chair by the bed and warily let her eyes scan the room, discovering to her surprise that the place seemed reasonably clean and free from vermin, though she was careful not to peer too closely into the corners. The large double bed, set against the longest wall, looked lumpy and uncomfortable, but at least the linen was immaculate, so snowy white it almost glowed in the perpetual twilight of the shuttered room.

They were to remain only a few days in Alexandria, four or five at most, Raoul told her. As soon as they had collected their supplies and arranged to transport them to the arid valley across the river from Luxor where they were planning to dig, they would move on to Cairo, staying there only long enough to arrange for the necessary permits. After the tension and discomfort on board ship, Aimée was certain those few days in Alexandria would be pleasant. She quickly discovered she was wrong.

She had expected the heat that turned the afternoon sky into a gigantic furnace, and she did not complain as she searched out meager patches of shade in the garden, sitting quietly while the servants fanned her or wiped away her perspiration with a cool, scented cloth. She had even expected the dust that clung to the inside of her nostrils, so that the entire world seemed to be permeated with a stale, dry odor. What she had not expected was the monotony of the place, the utter boredom. Without a soul to talk to, without so much as a single servant who spoke more than a few words of her own language, the minutes dragged by with a wearying languor.

Enviously she strolled through the early twilight shadows, peering around the corner at the veranda where Edward had settled himself in a comfortable chair with the perennially faithful Buffy at his side. Broad parasols shaded them from the last traces of the sun, and tall, cool glasses of English gin stood within their reach. For a moment Aimée was tempted to join them, pretending to be relaxed enough in her husband's company to share an hour or two of amusement with him. She was angry that she could not force herself to do it.

When she saw Raoul round the corner at the end of the street, making his way back toward the house after a day in the local markets, she envied the masculine freedom that allowed him to roam fearlessly through the streets of Alexandria while she was confined to the house and yard. She recalled bitterly the camaraderie that seemed to have grown between them in the days before she had been foolish enough to spend a few passionate moments in his arms. She wondered now, if she had been strong enough to resist that one blazing surge of desire, if he would have taken her with him on his forays into town.

Raoul did not see her until he had stepped into the garden. He paused to greet her with the same guarded smile she had come to know only too well.

"Wherever have you been?" she asked quickly. In spite of everything, Raoul was her only friend there, the only person she could speak to with any degree of warmth or pleasure. She could not let him go so easily. "What on earth are you looking for on all these mysterious trips into town?"

His expression was guarded as he looked at her. Then suddenly, as if he understood how important a moment of conversation was to her, he relaxed.

"Would you believe I don't even know?" he admitted with amusement. "Being an archaeologist is like that—like being a detective, remember? Only, archaeologists are at a disadvantage. You don't know what kind of clues you're looking for, or even where you expect them to lead you. All you can do is go into the market and nose around a little, ask a few questions here and there, and wait for someone to offer you something. And then, like as not, it turns out to be nothing but a worthless forgery."

He paused to laugh at himself. It was a light, easy laugh that took neither himself nor his work too seriously. But when he continued, although his voice was still deceptively soft, there was a sudden vibrant light in his eyes.

"But sometimes—just sometimes—you find something that makes it all worthwhile."

Aimée's heart contracted as she witnessed this flash of excitement. Somehow it made her feel lonely and left out. Once, aboard the ship, she had thought he was going to share his enthusiasm with her. Now she sensed she would never have that chance again.

Yet, to her surprise, only the next day, almost as if it were an answer to her own needs and dreams, Raoul seemed ready to open his world to her again.

It was shortly after the scorching heat of the noon hour. Aimée had already opened and closed her door at least a dozen times, trying by turns to catch a faint breeze from outside and to block the searing rays of the sun. Neither ploy seemed to make the least bit of difference. She had just opened the door again in one last weary attempt, knowing it would be as futile as all the others, when she caught sight of Raoul. He was hurrying across the garden, a large bundle of filthy rags cradled in his arms.

Puzzled, Aimée stepped across the threshold, staring out at him. She had never seen Raoul come home so early before.

Catching sight of her, Raoul turned and at almost the same moment, lowered the bundle gingerly onto a large stone table at the side of the garden. He moved slowly, as if the thing were both heavy and fragile.

"Come see what I've got," he called out. To Aimée's delight, the excitement in his voice completely masked his usual caution toward her.

"What is it?" she asked, beginning to feel a trace of his enthusiasm.

Raoul made no attempt to answer, but turning back to the bundle, began to peel the rags away with careful movements. He was so engrossed in his task that he seemed to have forgotten Aimée was there. Finally, after what seemed an hour to her, the bundle had been diminished to less than half its original size. Cautiously Raoul stripped the last rag away.

Aimée drew closer, a sense of excitement and suspense mounting. Peering down eagerly, she saw a handful of broken clay tablets.

"Is that all?" She could not keep the disappointment out of her voice. "I thought it was something special."

Raoul glanced up sharply, startled, then broke out in laughter.

"What did you expect?" he teased. "Gold or jewels? The treasures of the pharaohs?" His laughter died away slowly, and his voice grew serious again. "These *are* treasures, Aimée, although they do not glitter, as you would have them do. They are the past, and the past does not always glitter— not to the naked eye, at least."

"The past?" Aimée reached out toward the tablets. Raoul reproved her gently, pushing her hand away with his own. She could only suppose the things were rarer, more delicate than they looked.

"Well, they do look old," she admitted hesitantly.

He smiled at her. "More than three thousand years old."

"Three thousand years!" She could only stare at him in amazement. She had known the ancient Egyptian civilization was old—but three thousand years? Why, the number was so large it didn't mean anything to her. No wonder Raoul had not let her touch the tablets with a careless hand, and no wonder he had taken so much time to unwrap them. "But where did you find them, Raoul?"

"I didn't find them. An old peasant woman did. She was plowing the soil in an area the ancients called Akhet-Aten— the Horizon of Aten. Her plow turned up a cache of tablets, perhaps the entire library of the pharaoh Akhenaten."

"Akhenaten." Aimée repeated the alien syllables, letting them roll off her tongue slowly to savor their strangeness. "And the city—the city was called . . ."

"Akhet-Aten." He enunciated the word carefully so she could hear and understand it.

"How funny," she mused. "Was he named after the city . . . or did he call it after himself?" She smiled at the thought. It was a vanity that suited her concept of an ancient pharaoh.

"Neither one, I suspect," Raoul smiled at her enthusiasm. "He must have chosen his own name and the name of his city at much the same time. He was born with the name Amenhotep, and he was the son of another great pharaoh, Amenhotep III. But somewhere early in his reign he turned away from the worship of the chief deity of Egypt, the sun god Amon, and began to worship the Aten, another form of the sun. He took the name Akhenaten to honor his god, and he built his city for the same reason."

To Aimée, the idea of choosing between gods—of turning from one god to another—was alien, exotic. It was an idea that satisfied her visions of the heathen arrogance that must have been ancient Egypt.

"Was it a very great city?" She imagined long gilded streets paved with semiprecious stones, and thousands of slaves pulling golden chariots down their length or piling masses of stones into pyramids marking the eternal glory of the men who were both gods and rulers to them.

"It must have been," Raoul was careful to do nothing to shatter her fantasy. "It was a royal city and no doubt a beautiful one, for it was the center of a kind of artistic excitement that was unique in Egyptian history. But it was an ephemeral city, too, lasting no longer than the man who dared to dream it."

"Akhenaten?" she whispered, repeating the name to memorize it.

Raoul nodded agreement. "The man was a fanatic, perhaps

even a madman, but he was a man of vision and dreams and had the courage to try to make them come true. His reign was a short one, but it must have been vital and exciting. I daresay, when more has been learned about it, the era of Akhenaten will go down as one of the most fascinating in Egyptian history, though it lasted a scant twenty years."

"Twenty years?"

Aimée found the numbers confusing. First three thousand years—impossible even to imagine—and then a mere twenty years. Twenty years! Why, it was barely longer than her own life, and yet it had been the life span of an entire city.

Raoul saw the wonder in her eyes and smiled. It reminded him of the awe and amazement he had felt when he was a small boy and the wonders of history had just begun to unfold for him.

"And nearly all the records of that city," he reminded her, "were turned up by an old woman with a crude wooden plow in her hand—the same kind of plow those other Egyptians used more than three thousand years ago."

At his words Aimée's eyes clouded with indignation and then horror.

"But those tablets," she said slowly. "They're made of clay. Weren't they damaged by the plow?"

It only reinforced her anger to see him burst into laughter. "Damaged? Why, they were half ruined, first by the plow, then by a long, rough trip into town on the backs of donkeys. And when they arrived, those that weren't already broken were chopped into pieces so they would bring in more money."

Aimée was indignant. "How can you laugh, Raoul?" she cried out furiously. "You're an archaeologist. You're supposed to protect things, not laugh when they are destroyed."

"You think so?" Aimée was surprised at the bitterness in his voice. "Even more damage is done by archaeologists, those so-called 'experts' who spend more time collecting spectacular treasures for their museums than studying the sites they claim to be interested in. Take these tablets, for instance. By the time the experts get around to examining them so they can decide whether they're 'genuine' or not, most of them will have been cut into pieces for souvenir-hunting tourists or lost somewhere in the shuffle. I was lucky to rescue the few I did."

Then, seeing the effect his anger had on her, he softened his voice, letting himself smile again.

"Besides, the damage the peasants did was not really intentional, nor was it incomprehensible. Sometimes when I think of the way those scoundrels rob tombs or break things apart so they have more to sell, I go half-mad with rage. But then I remember how poor these people are. The treasures they find can mean the difference between life and death for them, between sickness and salvation. When a man does not have food to feed his family that day, it is hard for him to care about a world three thousand years away."

Aimée was silent. The image he had presented was sobering. She was every bit as incapable of imagining what it was like to have no food—absolutely none at all—as a poor peasant was of imagining the excitement she felt at bringing a piece of the past to life again.

Raoul saw her confusion, and it touched him deeply. He sensed that she understood, even better than she realized, the feelings in his own heart, the excitement and the doubt . . . and the yearning. It seemed to him at that moment there was a light in her eyes, intensifying the dark luster of her beauty until it took his breath away. It was all he could do to keep from throwing caution to the desert winds, reaching out his arms and drawing her into them so tightly she could never get away.

Raoul had always believed in fate, accepting it as neither friend nor foe, but merely as an entity that could not be altered. He was painfully aware that fate had touched him now.

He stared searchingly at the girl, scanning the strange midnight depths of her eyes to see if it had touched her too. It seemed to him it had, though she was only half-conscious of the fact. He thought he saw fear in her eyes, and wonder.

And a kind of hunger that nearly matched his own.

What a fool he had been to think he could turn away from her so casually, to think that lips once touched by her passion, however briefly, could ever be satisfied with less again. What a fool to bury his head in the sand, making believe his life was still in his own hands.

And the fool he had already been was nothing to the fool he was about to become.

Glistening waves touched with hints of sunset fire washed onto the lonely beach. Raoul sat on the warm sand, unlacing his shoes, then tucking his socks tidily into them. Rolling his pants up to his knees, he wandered out into the water, feeling the sand ooze between his toes and the waves lap sensuously around his shins. He tried to keep his mind a blank, tried not to think of what had happened to him only hours ago, but it was no use.

She was so beautiful, he told himself with despair, beautiful and warm and filled with a vitality he had never known before.

But she was another man's wife.

She was exciting . . . but she belonged to someone else. She set his blood on fire . . . but . . .

"Yes, dammit," he exploded angrily. She *did* belong to someone else, but surely she could not have gone to him of her own choice. There was no way he could believe she would have accepted a swine like that if she had not been forced into it, by a grasping father perhaps, or an ambitious mother, eager to see her daughter settled with a title and a fortune. She may have uttered the sacred vows that bound her eternally to another, but they were vows that had been pressed on her by others.

And vows not freely given could never be binding.

Yet he *was* being a fool. What did he have to offer the girl? A cheap affair? But he knew already she would refuse that, just as he knew he would refuse it for her. Marriage? But that was out of the question. She was bound by law to another man, a man just spiteful enough to hold on to her if he knew it would thwart her happiness.

But what was left? His undying devotion? He had to laugh at the thought. His undying devotion indeed! What would that compensate for the wealth and comfort he was asking her to leave behind? Or the honor?

And yet she was beautiful. Beautiful in body and beautiful in spirit. He had never seen that kind of light in a woman's eyes before, not even in Thea's eyes—not even dear, generous Thea, whom he was about to betray forever. He knew if he let Aimée go now, he would never see that light again.

But if he didn't let her go, if he didn't end it now . . .

Dammit, everything he had ever worked for was at stake. Everything he had built his life around. The woman he had courted so long, the excavation he had worked so hard to organize, the ambitions of a lifetime. Could he let them all go in one single, impulsive act?

And in their place, what? What would he have to show for it all? Loveliness, yes—but was that enough? Loveliness and vitality and the sense that for the first time in his life he was sharing, sharing not just his passions but his dreams as well;

not merely the physical touch of his body, but the essence of his soul.

He had been lonely—he had to admit that. All his life he had lived with an unexpressed loneliness, a sense of solitude that was the secret harvest of his private dreams. It had always been hidden, never acknowledged even to himself, but it had been there, dark and brooding, forming a basis for his life. If he let the girl go now, he would never be able to deny that loneliness again.

The sun dipped into the water with one last graceful plunge, bathing the world in a sudden chill of gray. The water felt warm against Raoul's ankles, but he did not notice as he gazed out at the fading streaks of pink easing their way slowly into the horizon. He was not even aware that he was laughing softly to himself. He knew only that all the time he was standing there, pretending he had great, earth-shaking decisions to make, the matter was already out of his hands. The choice, if indeed there had truly been a choice, was long since made.

The cool night air felt like a caress against her skin which was still warm from the heat of the day. Aimée sat at the small vanity table in her room, untwisting her long hair until it fell in billows onto the translucent silk of her dressing gown. The night was quiet, so deceptively quiet the sounds of the desert melted away in the darkness. Closing her eyes, she could almost imagine she was back in her room in Paris, listening to the comfortable sound of her father's footsteps in the hall, or laughing at the boisterous squabbling of her younger brothers, audible halfway across the house.

A sharp knock on her door broke abruptly into Aimée's reverie, reminding her where she was. She felt a surge of fear as she laid down the silver-handled brush and forced herself slowly to her feet. Her legs were trembling as she made her way toward the door.

Le bon Dieu protect her. She had been sure—_so_ sure —he would not come to her room again.

She opened the door slowly, her fingers hesitating. Nervously she peered out into the shadows of the garden. For a moment she was too startled to speak.

"You!" she whispered hoarsely when at last she found her voice again. "What do you want?"

"What do you think I want, my dear?"

Buffy Montmorency's handsome, boyish features twisted into a grin as he forced his way into the room. Aimée made a frantic effort to push him back, trying to slam the door in his face, but he was too quick. Sailing past her, he strutted into the center of the room.

As she whirled to face him, Aimée's eyes flashed with anger. Only when she saw the smug smile spreading across his features did her anger change to alarm. He was clad in a long, expensive dressing gown, a twin to the deep wine robe Edward had worn to her room on their wedding night.

Buffy saw her nervousness instantly. He did not hesitate to laugh at it.

"Can you be so naive?" he said, answering the unspoken question in her eyes. "Really, my dear, I thought a sophisticated young Parisienne would understand instantly."

"Understand what?"

Aimée had the hideous feeling that she did indeed understand what he meant, but she could not bring herself to believe it. Desperately she searched for a way to handle the situation.

"Must I spell it out?" The mockery in Buffy's voice only accented his amusement. "Very well, pretty wife of my friend. I am here to make up for the aborted ecstasy of your wedding night."

Aimée could only gasp in shock. Even from Buffy she had never expected such coarse bluntness. She was bitterly aware that she would have to move, and move quickly. If she allowed the man to stay there even another minute, she would be in danger.

"Leave my room at once," she ordered. "If you do not, I will call my husband." It was a desperate threat, and she knew it. Buffy was her husband's favorite. She wondered which one of them Edward would blame most when he discovered the man had been in her room.

To her horror, Buffy only laughed at her words.

"You really *are* naive." He chuckled. "Come, my dear, do you think I'm reckless enough to defy Eddie so boldly? Oh, no, I assure you, I know only too well which side of my bread has a nice fat layer of butter on it, and I intend to keep it that way. I would never dare to come here—except at your husband's invitation."

Aimée was too stunned to speak. She could only shake her head slowly, aware of a growing sense of fear and disbelief. Finally she forced a faint protest to her lips.

"No . . . no, it can't be . . ."

But even as she whispered the words, she sensed that he

was telling the truth. Buffy's face was too calm, too sure. He was not lying to her.

"Oh, *mon Dieu* . . . no!"

Buffy's expression changed. All the smug complacency that had frightened her so badly was replaced by an expression of unconcealed disgust.

"You don't think Eddie ever wanted you, do you?"

Aimée felt her stomach begin to knot, but she could not find the words to answer him. All she could do was stand and gape at him.

"You still haven't caught on, have you?" The amusement in Buffy's eyes masked the naked revulsion for a moment. "Your husband is one of those men who does not like women, my dear. You thought he married you for your beauty, and in a way of course you were right. But he wanted your beauty as a showpiece to dazzle all his envious friends. He didn't want your body at all. Oh, no, my vain little beauty. It was not *you* your husband wanted, not ever. It was *me*."

Aimée gave a cry of horror. God help her, it all seemed so obvious now, so clear. She wondered why she hadn't realized it before. He had always been there, this man she now knew was her husband's lover. He had hidden around every corner during their courtship, stood at the altar with them on the day of their wedding, pale and solemn and perhaps a little nervous, had gloated and mocked them the morning after. He had even been there on their wedding night, listening no doubt in the next room to everything that passed between them, laughing with malice—and relief—at the lover who was forced to crawl back to him in failure.

"Oh, dear God," she cried out, horrified. "But why . . . ?"

Buffy only laughed at the question she could not bring herself to finish. "Why did he marry you—or why did he come to your room? For the same reason, my dear. Because he wanted a mask for his 'sordid' activities, something that would make him respectable in the eyes of the world. For that, he needed a wife—and a child."

A child? Aimée felt the warmth drain from her body. A wife and a child. God help her, he had the wife now, for whatever that was worth. But the child . . . ?

Buffy continued to laugh. "He said he could do it. He said he had done it once before, with a prostitute. He probably had, otherwise he would never have had the nerve to try with you. But I knew it wouldn't work. You were too fiery, too independent. I knew he would be afraid of you."

His laughter gave Aimée a cold, sick feeling. She remembered the sound of her own laughter that night. How terrible it must have been for him, coming to her afraid and insecure, only to have her burst into a fit of giggles the instant he exposed his body to her. For just a minute she almost felt sorry for him.

Buffy eyed her coldly. "He still wants the child."

Aimée gazed at him tensely. "I don't understand."

"Don't you?" His eyes were brittle, mocking.

Yes, she had to admit, she did understand. She understood only too well.

"I'm sure you can see the beauty of it. I resemble him in many ways. When the child comes, no one will question that it's his."

Aimée still found the thought too brutal to bear. "But you . . . How could you . . . ?" This man was her husband's lover. Surely if Edward could not . . .

Buffy laughed unpleasantly. "Don't worry about me. I can do it, all right—if I have to."

His eyes glowed with excitement and disgust at the same time. With despair Aimée forced herself to admit he was telling the truth. His body would respond to her beauty and the softness of her femininity, but he would despise himself for it. It would seem a weakness to him, a weakness he would never be able to tolerate in himself. Bitterly she realized he would find a way to punish her for it. Her initiation into the mysterious rites of love—those same rites she had dreamed of when she was barely more than a child—would not be a gentle one.

Sick with dread, she watched as he loosened his robe, exposing his body to her terrified eyes.

The moon was a full, pale disk in the sky. Raoul watched as it touched the waves, dancing off them with reflections of midnight blue. It reminded him of the eyes of the woman he had finally dared to admit he loved. It was time at last to leave the security of the shore and keep his rendezvous with destiny.

He was keenly aware of the irony of the situation as he retraced his steps to the house where they were both staying. He knew now what he had to do, but he had no idea how the girl would respond. By God, it would serve him right if she slammed the door in his face, or worse yet, called her husband to come and protect her against this intrusion in the middle of the night.

And even if she didn't, even if her eyes were filled with

more longing than he dared hope, did he really have the right to ask her to give up everything for him? Her honor, her home, her wealth, the respect of her family and friends—what did he have to offer in exchange for all that? A near-penniless existence with an archaeologist who had given up his one big chance? An endless series of furnished rooms without so much as a single respectable person who would dare—or want—to call her friend? God help him, even by his standards that was a shoddy existence. He would not blame the girl for tossing his love back in his face.

The shadows were deep when he reached the garden outside her door. At first he did not see a dim figure in the moonlight. When he did, he realized with a start that he had no right to be there. Turning, he began to move away, pretending he had been heading for his own room all along.

God damn that pig of a husband of hers. His fists were clenched at his sides to remind him he dared not cry out in rage. He had forgotten that the man still had a right to visit his wife in her room. Dammit, he could not stand that. Anything else. He would put up with anything, but not that. Somehow, he didn't know how, but *somehow*, he had to convince her. No matter what happened, he couldn't let her submit to that again.

It wasn't until the man had moved away from Aimée's door that the moon illuminated his face. Startled, Raoul stopped to stare at him.

Buffy Montmorency! Not Ellingham at all. What on earth was that puffed-up popinjay doing in Aimée's room? And at that hour?

For an instant his mind rebelled against reality. Only the self-satisfied smile on Buffy's face warned him there were things that could not be denied—or misunderstood. As if in emphasis, Buffy reached down to tighten the belt of his dressing gown. Raoul felt dread and revulsion flood into his chest, expanding until he could barely breathe.

Buffy stepped closer, his eyes sparkling with malice.

"Are you shocked?"

Raoul tightened the muscles of his face into a mask of unconcern. "Should I be?" he snapped, turning on his heels before his eyes could betray his confusion. He stumbled awkwardly as he made his way through the garden, tripping on the stones that lined the paths, but Buffy was already gone. There was no one left to see his weakness.

So that was how it was. He had been an even bigger fool

than he had thought. A pretty face, a sensuous smile—and he had been so blinded to the truth he could not even see the most obvious things.

She had been forced to marry that toad, he had told himself over and over again. She would never have done a thing like that of her own free will. Yet that was absurd, of course. No one could have forced her to utter those vows if she didn't want to. She had married the swine because she wanted his money. Nothing more—and nothing less.

As for her willingness to run into his own arms, all sweet and pious and innocent in the moonlight—had he really thought that meant she sensed the beginning of a deep and honest love between them? Or had he thought, perhaps, that she had simply found him too attractive to resist?

Attractive, hell! He had just been available. How it must have amused her to play her little games with him, leading him on as she must have done with many a man in the past. Why had she really come to his arms? Because she was a cheap little tramp, that was why—and a goddamn cock-tease in the bargain.

God, how she must have laughed, watching the passion he could not control. Perhaps she had even laughed at him that very night while she lay in the arms of another lover. No wonder the man's eyes had been filled with smugness just now. He knew how Raoul felt, and he enjoyed his pain. He actually enjoyed it.

Well, thank God he had discovered the truth in time. He did not like to think of the way she would have laughed as he bared his heart to her. He would take it as a lesson, a reminder that the ways of the heart were painful and traitorous. He had come close to making a mockery of his own emotions that night. He would never let it happen again.

Aimée lay silently on clean cool sheets in the darkened room. She was grateful that Buffy had insisted on taking away the soiled linen so the servants would never guess the truth. The unfamiliar feel of tears stung the inside of her eyelids. Desperately she fought against them, holding their soothing balm back from the flushed warmth of her cheeks.

"I will not cry," she whispered hoarsely, forcing an anger into her voice she could not make herself feel. "I will not . . . I will not."

Brave little soldiers never cried.

Look at your sister, Claude, her father had cried on that day long ago when the boat overturned at the landing and the three of them fell into the icy waters of the lake. *She doesn't cry. Look at your sister, Jean-Pierre. She is the bravest little soldier of them all.*

"I won't cry, Papa," she whispered into the darkness. "I am still your brave little soldier, Papa. I will always be the bravest soldier of them all."

TWO

Let Not Your Heart Be Troubled

∞ Meryt

The long cry of a single trumpet lay like a mournful wail on the sultry morning air. The silence in its wake was broken only by the whispers of the current as it lapped against the sides of a wooden boat tied securely to the dock. Meryt shivered as the sound was repeated. She had not seen her uncle in the seventy long days of mourning for her father. She had hoped she would not have to face him today.

A golden chariot hurtled suddenly into the deserted square in front of the docks, glittering in the bright rays of the sun. A pair of spirited Eastern steeds snorted rebelliously, pawing at the earth as their royal driver pulled them to a stop. Meryt watched with a sense of detached curiosity, fascinated by the energy that caused the beasts to toss their shining manes in the slight breeze. It seemed to her they were strangely out of place in the empty silence of the square.

Awkwardly the girl hesitated in the center of the boat, her eyes drifting down to the stylized effigy that graced the coffin at her feet. The gilded and painted, glassed and jeweled image that stared back at her offered no comfort. At last, realizing she could put it off no longer, she forced herself to slip quietly to the edge of the boat to greet her uncle.

Akhenaten did not hurry toward her, but moved slowly across the square, his shoulders more stooped than usual. His eyes were cast down, even when he paused in front of the dock. It was a long time before he raised them to her face.

"I have come to bid my brother a last farewell."

The words were stilted, as if they came hard to him.

"It was kind of you to come, Uncle."

Meryt wondered if he noticed she could not bring herself to utter the word "husband." If he did, he was generous enough not to correct her.

For a long time he stood silently before her, his body as tense and rigid as her own. Meryt had the uneasy sense, watching him, that much lay unspoken in his heart, heavy matters awaiting only the right words to express them. It seemed to anger him that he could not find them. Moving awkwardly, he turned away from her, striding with determination toward the waiting chariot. He was halfway there when he whirled to face her again.

"I wish my brother a safe journey to the Land of the West." His voice was hoarse, the words lying deep in his throat as if they had the power to strangle him. "May his *ka* live forever."

To the Land of the West?

For a moment Meryt could only stare at her uncle, sadness sweeping her heart. The West was the land of the setting sun, the domain of the ancient gods Akhenaten had forsaken forever. She knew only too well the pain it cost a proud man to bid farewell to his brother—and rival—on his own terms.

"Thank you, Uncle."

The words were soft, half-whispered, but her voice vibrated with emotion. She was conscious of a strong, compelling bond between her and this strange man who was now her husband. It was a bond she had never felt before.

The moment was shattered by a sudden burst of laughter echoing out of the shadows at the far side of the square. Startled, Meryt faced the chariot her uncle had left beside one of the tall whitewashed walls surrounding the dock area. She was surprised to see it was not empty. She had not even noticed a slender, tanned form beside Akhenaten when he raced into the square. Catching sight of the man now, she shivered with revulsion.

She had always disliked her young uncle, Smenkhkare, half-brother to both Akhenaten and her father. Now, letting her eyes run coolly up and down the surface prettiness of his body, it seemed to her he had grown even more loathsome than ever.

Smenkhkare was quick to sense her antipathy. Too clever to attempt to meet it with hostility of his own, he turned dark, cool eyes on her face, letting his lips twist in a mocking parody of a smile.

Staring back at him, Meryt had to admit that Smenkhkare had at least the outward semblance of beauty, his face and body glowing with a vain, affected kind of comeliness. She was startled as she had been so often in the past, by how remarkably he resembled his brother.

But it was an eerie, distorted resemblance, almost as if the gods had played a malicious joke on the pair, elongating and deforming the skull of one brother to contrast with the exotically interesting bone structure of the other; sharpening the features of the pharaoh until they were coarse and repugnant, blunting and softening the prince's until he looked pretty and delicate; giving Akhenaten only a grotesque, feminine body, while his sibling was allowed to stand with all the regal arrogance, all the strength and vitality and kingly power that should have been his.

Was that why her uncle insisted on keeping his younger brother at his side? Meryt asked herself suddenly, surprised that the thought had never occurred to her before. Was that why he spent more and more time with Smenkhkare, avoiding everyone else, even his chief wife, the beautiful Nefertiti? Did he see in his brother an image of himself, not as he was, but as he might have been had the gods been kinder to him?

The thought saddened Meryt. It was a sadness she did not understand—or want to. Turning slowly, she moved toward the center of the boat, kneeling gracefully beside the long gilded case that rested alone on a shallow platform. It was her signal that she was ready to leave, accompanying her father at last on his final solemn journey through the lands of men. She did not know if her uncle would understand the gesture, or if his kingly vanity would allow her so bold a move, but she was determined to stand her ground. She was relieved when she felt the gentle motion of the boat drifting slowly away from the dock.

The sound of the oars dipping into cool water was clean and rhythmic, echoing in her ears like the faraway strains of a wordless melody. The steersman, high on the stern, manipulated his paddle with deft hands, raising his eyes every now and then to study the passing craft. The riverbank was strangely silent, with only a handful of tanned, naked bodies silhouetted against the fertile green of the earth.

Meryt felt a sense of loss as they pulled out into the river, a deep, passionate yearning for the shore they were leaving behind. She was painfully aware that the last of her memories were wrapped up in that place. It was there that she had bid her father a final tense farewell, watching with tears in her eyes as he disappeared, tall and proud, into the shimmering lights of the river. It was there, too, that she had watched Senmut's bronzed fingers play over the strings of his lyre, making his music vibrate through her body with longing she knew could never be answered. There that she had watched the tall ships sail back down the river, their gaudy pennants and blaring trumpets heralding the end of all her dreams.

Keenly aware of the dull ache in her heart, Meryt turned

to catch one last haunting glimpse of the world she was leaving behind. She was surprised to see a solitary form, still standing in the deserted square, staring after her. Even from that distance she could have sworn she saw the look of pain in his eyes.

I have come to wish my brother a safe journey to the Land of the West.

The Land of the West. The land of the ancient gods. Far from the faith of Akhenaten, far from all his dreams.

May his ka live forever.

How strange her uncle was, Meryt told herself, only half-surprised at the thought. Strange and, even after all these years, unpredictable. Who would have thought he could be so generous or so forgiving?

Her eyes slipped down to the gilded features on the coffin beside her. She could not help imagining what it would have been like if her father, and not his brother, had emerged victorious seventy days ago. The anonymous artist, whoever he was, had captured Ramose's features well, the strength of his jaw, the brightness of his eyes, the forcefulness of his personality. All he had missed was his anger and arrogance—and his ambition.

No, Akhenaten would not have fared well at her father's hands. Meryt told herself coolly. There would have been no elaborate embalming process for him, no seventy-day ritual of preservation for the body his *ka* needed for all eternity. There would have been no tomb on the slopes favored by his gods, no memorials bearing his name in elaborate hieroglyphs, setting it before the eyes of living men so it would stay on their lips forever. Had Akhenaten died seventy days ago, he would have been truly dead, not just for today but for all eternity.

"That was a cruel fate, Father," she whispered. She could not keep a hint of reproach from her voice.

It *was* a cruel fate, cruel and vindictive. It was Ramose's good fortune that those were not traits he shared with his brother.

Thick papyrus swamps lined the riverbanks, offering cooling sights of green in the hot, sunny afternoon. Leaning against the side of the boat, Meryt rested her head on her arm, watching as they drifted past.

It seemed strange that there was no hatred, no vengeance in her uncle's heart. Somewhere beneath that ugly, twisted body lay a captive soul that cried out, unheard, for all the softness and beauty that could never be his, all the love he would never know.

Perhaps, Meryt thought, life with a man like that would not be the torture she had imagined. She could not pretend it was the life she had planned for herself, the life that had filled all her youthful dreams and fantasies, but at least it was not the dark world of her nightmares. If her days would be void of gaiety and passion, of all the soft, lovely moments her feminine heart yearned for, at least she would never lack for kindness and understanding. Already she sensed there were far worse fates to be feared.

Slowly she closed her eyes, letting the warm sun lull her nearly to sleep.

The slender silver barque of the moon god Khons was high in the heavens when the flat-bottomed boat bearing the coffin of Prince Ramose moored at last on the western shore. On the opposite bank, the buildings of the former capital loomed in the moonlight, silent and abandoned, like a legion of ghosts come to bid him farewell.

Meryt sat alone on the deck, keeping one last vigil beside her father before he began his solitary journey through the twelve dark hours of the night. Lifting her eyes, she let them linger on the deep blue sky, punctuated by thousands of silver stars. Each of them, she knew, marked a separate soul, the essence and the spirit of someone who had gone before. Fascinated by the thought, she began to search for a new star, one that had not been there before, one that even now must bear the name Ramose. She smiled a little at her disappointment when she could not find it.

One day there would be another star in the heavens, she told herself. A small star called Meryt-Ankh-Re. She found that the thought did not frighten her. Tucking her knees up to her chin, she wrapped her arms tightly around her legs, trying to drive away the desert chill.

They came for her father at sunrise. Meryt would have liked them to wait for twilight, the symbolic moment of the death of the sun, but she knew her uncle had insisted on haste, not wanting to give Ramose's supporters any clue to his burial place. Even in her grief Meryt could not blame him for his caution. Slowly she rose, her muscles still aching from the long vigil as she made her way to the bank of the Nile.

As she glanced up, she saw a slender white line moving slowly out of the distant hills toward the shore. It had been years since she had seen the priests of Amon, arrogant in their snowy robes. It touched her deeply to see them now.

It was well over an hour before the slaves could unload the boats, piling the ebony furnishings and the tall alabaster urns, the jeweled shrines and the painted, inlaid funerary chests high on the golden sleighs that would carry them to Ramose's House of Eternity. Meryt could only gasp as she watched them. Generous as her uncle had been, she had never expected to see such a show of wealth.

At last the procession was ready to form. First the mourners stepped into line, the women who had been hired especially for the occasion, their pale blue robes torn and stained in a ritual show of grief. Meryt watched with a kind of morbid fascination as they let out the first melancholy keening sounds. She wondered if they sensed these would be the last false tears they would ever weep. Determined as her uncle was to keep the location of his brother's tomb a secret, he would hardly be likely to leave any idle tongues to wag in the morning.

Next the sleighs began to move, inching slowly forward, their heavy burdens making them clumsy and unwieldy. Only the last was sparsely laden, bearing nothing more than the four canopic jars that held the prince's viscera.

At last it was time for the coffin. Four massive oxen, red as the fertile earth, were hitched to the flat-bottomed boat, dragging it laboriously onto the shore. The priests of Amon grouped themselves slowly around its flanks, forming long protective lines on either side. A pair of them, separating from the rest, slipped in front of the coffin to sprinkle the soil with the milk that would ensure the prince's eternal renewal of life.

As they moved forward, Meryt joined the procession, taking her place behind her father's coffin. Her own robe was clean and white, touched neither with mourning blue or stains and rents. All she had to show her grief was a single funeral necklace, cornflowers mingling with blue lotus, olive leaves twined around bright blue varnished beads. She did not want anything else. She needed no outward tokens to remind her of her pain.

The hot sand burned into the soles of her bare feet, but Meryt barely noticed as she moved slowly forward. It was a moment before she could bring herself to raise her eyes, focusing them at last on her father's coffin.

"Everything is the way you would have wanted it, Father."

She whispered the words, uttering them so softly even the

priests could not hear her above the keening of the women. She was aware of the sting of tears against her lids.

And it *was* the way he would have wanted. The ceremony was not as ostentatious as he might have hoped, not as elaborate. There were no bronze trumpets mingling with the shrill cries of the women, no metallic, rhythmic sistrums in the hands of the priestesses of Amon, but at least the rituals had been fulfilled—the rituals that would guarantee his immortality forever.

The rituals had begun seventy days before. In silence and stealth, the embalmers had crept to the riverbank, claiming the body of the fallen prince and carrying it under cover of darkness to their chambers. There, the elaborate rites of preservation could begin. First, the most perishable parts of the body were removed, the brains drawn out through the nose with long sharp hooks, the lungs and intestines extracted through an incision in the flank made with a blade of Ethiopian flint. Only the heart remained, waiting for the dark night hour it would be placed on the scales of the jackal-god Annubis, weighed against the lightness of a feather.

At last the body was ready for its long ritual soaking in a bath of natron. Only then, perfumed with myrrh and cassia, skin colored with cedar oil, lips and nails painted, could it be molded into the mummiform image of Osiris, the god who himself had died, yet been renewed. Each toe was bound individually in long linen strips; each finger, ringed and sheathed in gold, had its own tight bandages. Even the penis was wrapped separately, molded strong and erect, a symbol of the power and vitality of a man. Amulets were carefully tucked between the layers of linen, a sacred scarab carved of lapis lazuli laid over the heart.

A scarab over his heart?

In spite of herself, Meryt could not help smiling at the thought. A busy little beetle, pushing a roll of dung along the earth, as bustling and important as if he were the sun god himself rolling his fiery burden through the heavens. What a whimsical, strangely human conceit of the gods to pick such an odd little creature as their emblem. Meryt let her eyes scan the side of the path, hoping to spot one of the scurrying insects, outlined against the blazing gold of the sand. She was disappointed when she did not. It would have been an omen, she knew, a happy omen, both for her father and herself.

The sun had already begun to dip toward the western horizon when they reached the tomb Ramose had begun to build for himself a generation ago. There was another tomb that bore his name now, a larger, grander tomb on the eastern slopes of Akhet-Aten. By rights, he should have been laid there, beside the coffin of the beautiful foreign princess who was his wife. That he was not, that her uncle had chosen to bury his brother instead in the valley of the ancient gods, was a thing that surprised Meryt. She wondered if it was an act of love—a hunger to atone for all the hatred and hostility that had scarred their lives—or if it was merely an act of fear, brought on by the need to keep Ramose's burial place a secret from his fanatical supporters.

Meryt lingered outside in the sunlight while the priests finished their preparations in the tomb. Only when the heavy boxes and the furnishings, the adornments and the gilded shrines, had been carefully arranged did she at last force her feet between the tall, polished sheets of bronze that flanked the doorway.

The interior of the tomb glowed with the reflected light of the bronze mirrors. Meryt stood silently for a moment, just inside the doorway. She had never seen her father's tomb before, for she had been a small child when they left the old city, moving to the new capital Akhenaten had raised in the desert. One glance was enough to tell her that everything must have been left as it was. Only a single painting by the doorway, a brightly sketched portrait of the pharaoh followed by the family of the man he mourned—the pretty daughter who was now the pharaoh's wife, the baby son who would never be the pharaoh of his father's dreams—bore witness to the new regime.

Only three chambers had been gouged out of the rock, for the tomb was far from finished when it had been abandoned. A large antechamber in the center led to two smaller rooms, one at the side, the other behind the back wall. It took Meryt only a moment to see that most of the furnishings had been placed in the side room, leaving ample space in the antechamber for a wide aisle leading to the room in the rear. Two tall statues, black as the underworld in which they would dwell forever, flanked the doorway, their features chiseled in an eerie reminiscence of Ramose, in the days when he had been young and strong. The gold of their tunics and sandals was unnaturally bright in the warm rays reflected through the doorway.

The small inner chamber, by contrast, was bathed in heavy shadows. Meryt faltered for a moment on the threshold. There was a brooding silence inside that penetrated through her bones. It was all she could do to force herself to enter.

Her eyes were riveted on the massive stone sarcophagus in the center of the room.

"Come in peace to the West."

The voice of the priest was low and impersonal as he droned the words of Ramose's last farewell to the land of the living.

"Come in peace, you who are praised and adored. When this day becomes eternity, then we shall see you again. Walk in peace in the land where men become as one."

Meryt watched him step toward the coffin, his body tall and lean beneath the leopard tunic that covered his white robe, his upraised arms casting shadows on the wall. She knew he was performing the last rite her father would ever need, the Ceremony of Opening the Mouth and Eyes, ensuring his survival in the afterworld, but she could not make herself believe it was truly happening. She became supremely conscious that moment, for the first time, that she, too, like her father, had reached an ending. That she, like he, was leaving behind the only life she had ever known.

At last the long incantations stopped. Stepping forward, Meryt lifted the blue garland from her neck, placing it on the lid of her father's coffin. Slowly she turned away, slipping into the light again.

Cool darkness lingered along the banks of the Nile, hugging the red-golden firelight in its velvet embrace. There was no massive tent by the shore that night, no raucous group of mourners casting off their grief at last, no lithe, naked dancers swaying to the notes of the musicians. Only a handful of paid professional mourners gathered around the fire, their laughter shrill and boisterous.

Meryt sat apart from the others, her knees drawn up against her chin. She could find no comfort in the circle of faces that reflected the flickering flames. Not one among them was anything but a stranger. Not one had known—or loved—her father.

Generations pass away, others come in their place; yea,
    from the dawn of the world.
Re rises in the morning and sets in the west.
Men beget, women bear, and every life draws breath,
    but in the dawning, their children come in their
    place.

The tremulous voice of the harper seemed to float on the

dying wind on the chill night. Meryt turned to see the delicately chiseled lines of the man's face, half-hidden in the shadows. His sightless eyes stared into the darkness, picking up hazy visions no one else could see; his hands moved effortlessly across the strings of his instrument.

Follow your desires, let not your heart be troubled, until
    the day of mourning comes at last.
Be happy in thy days, and weary not of them; for none
    may take his goods with him, and none that has
    gone may ever return again.

For none may take his goods with him . . .
But they tried. O Isis, how they tried!
Meryt's eyes filled with tears as she thought of her father. All the gold and electrum and jewels, all the furnishings and statues and shrines, all the accumulated ostentation of a lifetime, crammed into three little rooms in an unfinished tomb. And for what? For the same end that met all men, great and small. For the last vanity, the last conceit.

Wearily she pulled herself to her feet, making her way through the darkness toward the riverbank. No one noticed her slip away. The song of the blind harper echoed in her ears as she clapped for the ferryman.

For none may take his goods with him, and none that has
    gone may ever return again.

"Take me across the river."
Her voice was so low the ferryman had to bend toward her to hear it. He did not recognize the sad-eyed girl who stood before him. It did not occur to him to equate her with the merry, laughing little princess who had left the old capital many years ago.

Meryt sank gratefully onto the hard wooden seat, leaning her head against the rough side of the boat. She had not realized how exhausted she was. It would be good to reach the far shore, she told herself drowsily, good to climb into her own bed, feeling the cool linen against her tired body. Closing her eyes, she let herself succumb to the lullaby of the current as it caressed the side of the boat. She was half-asleep when the grating sound of wood against sand jolted her back to reality.

Stumbling onto the shore, she barely noticed a tall barge, dark and heavy against the moonlit background of the sky.

Only when she had nearly passed it and had started down the long walkway that led to the royal palace, did the first recognition penetrate her consciousness. Cautiously, feeling a kind of trepidation she could not understand, she turned to face it directly.

The instant she saw it, a wave of horror flooded her body.

The red and blue banners that dangled from its mast were limp and still in the night air, the dazzling electrum that plated its sides dull in the pale moonlight, but she recognized it instantly. It was the royal barge.

Isis help her, what a fool she had been!

Had she really believed her uncle, kind as he had been, would leave her alone forever? Had she forgotten that a ruler with only daughters must long for a son?

She was surprised at how heavy her feet had grown, their weight making them almost impossible to lift as she dragged them, one after another, down the dark path. Her heart was pounding against the wall of her chest as she approached the gate.

If only he were not so ugly, she thought with despair, struggling to drive away the unwanted vision of her uncle's malformed features.

"Oh, Isis, help me find the strength," she whispered as her fingers moved to clutch the heavy pectoral on her breast.

If only it did not make her skin crawl to look at him.

The gatekeeper glanced up as she approached, studying her face for an instant before he stepped aside to let her pass. The image in their depths was all too clear.

He did not see a lovely young queen as he gazed at her, no sweetly dutiful wife going to her husband. To him she was just a frightened little girl forcing herself to meet a fate she could not even understand. It only added to Meryt's terror to realize he was right.

The gods help her, if only the rumors had been true, those ugly rumors that added such a fillip to the servants' gossip—and brought tears of sadness to her gentle mother's eyes. If only the disease that had warped her uncle's body, malforming him until sometimes he seemed more woman than man, had continued to run its course, robbing him of the final vestiges of his masculinity. If only he were not capable of the act he intended to perform tonight.

The door to her suite of rooms was ajar as she approached it. She was surprised to find she was tiptoeing, pretending, like the little girl the gatekeeper had seen in her, that she could somehow escape if only she could keep him from hearing her.

Her hand was surprisingly steady as she laid it on the door. She had no sensation of the cold wood beneath her fingers. The heavy door began to swing noiselessly into the room.

At first Meryt did not see the shadowy figure against the far wall. Even when she did, she hesitated on the threshold. It was a long time before he stirred at last, shifting his weight as he swung toward her. The instant she saw his face, she gasped.

"You!"

Smenkhkare's boyish features twisted into a grin of amusement.

"You didn't really expect to see my brother here?"

Meryt felt a wave of revulsion as she stared back at him. So it was true, she told herself with despair. All the malicious, pitying gossip was true. Akhenaten was no longer a man. Now even the daughters that were useless to him had to be fathered by someone else.

"No, I did not expect him."

And she had prayed to Isis, only a moment before, to be spared the ugliness of a man who was at least kind. Isis had answered her prayer with more justice than mercy.

Smenkhkare extended his hand. Rigid with fear, Meryt knew she dared not resist. Everything in his expression warned her he would take pleasure in her pain and humiliation.

She remembered a sad, lonely morning, so long ago and yet so close in time. She had told herself that morning there were far worse fates than an alliance with her uncle. She knew now she had been right.

Slowly she reached out. Smenkhkare's fingers were hot and feverish, searing into her skin like a hated brand.

∞ Aimée

1

The minarets of Cairo rose out of the distant haze like jeweled fingers stretching toward the heavens. To Aimée, riding in a closed carriage, the early-morning mists had an unearthly quality about them, as if they were part of a half-remembered dream. There was a chill in the air, a deceptive desert cold that robbed the earth of its heat in the early hours before the sun turned it into an inferno again. The strangeness of the atmosphere seemed to Aimée both alien and hauntingly familiar. The sensation was not pleasant. She did not want to dwell on it.

As they drew closer to the narrow, crowded streets of the city, the mists grew thicker, rising like a heavy fog from the earth. It was a moment before Aimée realized the increased density was caused by the accumulated smoke of dozens of fires glowing dully through the darkness.

Her eyes began to tear from the sting of smoke as she stared into the dim gray light. Slowly she became aware of figures that seemed to materialize from nowhere: a man in a long, filthy robe nearly as gray as the air, leading a small, scraggly herd of sheep; a solitary woman, her features half-concealed beneath the black robe that made her look like a silent shadow; a handful of skittering urchins, crawling like maggots over a heap of garbage, fighting a scrawny cat for a rotting fish head; a little boy crouching in the doorway of a filthy hovel, a crust of moldy bread clutched in his fingers, his dark eyes coated with a layer of flies so dense they looked like kohl.

The pyramids, however, were clean and pure in the distance, their steep sides glowing blue in the morning light. Rising from the earth, strong and eternal, they stood aloof from the slums and squalor at their feet. They were the past, the essence of a life thousands of years removed, completely untouched by the present.

It seemed to Aimée as she stared at them in the distance, remote from the mundane ugliness of the present, that the past must indeed have been a glorious, exciting time. She could understand why it held such a powerful lure for Raoul.

Cautiously she let her eyes drift toward the man seated opposite her in the carriage. She was disappointed to find that he was looking straight ahead. His expression was blank and rigidly fixed, as if he were determined not to look in her direction. The coldness in his manner would have kept her silent even had she had the courage to speak warmly to him in front of her husband and the man who was his lover.

There had been a time, one sunny afternoon a few days before, in Alexandria, when she had thought Raoul was going to forgive her the indiscretion of her one moment of honest emotion aboard the ship and offer her his friendship again. Now she realized she had been a fool to hope. The fleeting rush of excitement, the discovery of tablets that meant so much to him, had robbed him of his caution—but only for a short time. Now it seemed to her he was even more remote than before.

And yet he was right, she had to admit. God help them both, he was right to stay away from her. And the worst of it was, it was all her own stupid fault. That one impetuous moment of self-indulgence had cost her a friendship she valued highly, and she had no one but herself to blame. Wearily she let her head rest against the window and pulled her shawl more closely around her shoulders.

Raoul caught the gesture out of the corner of his eye. Misinterpreting it, he said, his lips tight with disapproval, "Cairo is not to your liking, madam?"

The sharpness in his voice cut through Aimée with an almost physical force. For a minute she did not know if she would be able to bear it.

"What did you expect, sir?" she snapped, determined to hide her pain from him. "There's nothing but squalor and poverty here, and no one cares enough to do anything about it. The poor fight in the streets like packs of filthy animals for a rotting crust of bread, while the rich dine like kings in their castles, and little children go blind from the flies in their eyes and no one tries to brush them away. Not to my liking, you say? By God, could any human being with even half a heart find conditions like that to his liking?"

Aimée was surprised to catch a flicker of response in Raoul's eyes. At first she thought he was angry at the sharpness of her retort. Then it seemed to her it was something else, something darker that she could not begin to understand.

Buffy Montmorency, seated beside Raoul in the carriage, did not fail to notice the conflict between them. A calculated smile began to play at the corners of his mouth.

"I think our esteemed archaeologist does not approve of you, my dear," he said dryly. He leaned back as far as he could in the cramped seat, stretching his legs in front of him. Since the night Edward had forced him to begin visiting Aimée in her chamber, he had been ill-at-ease with her. He was pleased to feel his detached amusement beginning to return. "I think he can hardly wait to show you how a proper young lady behaves."

"A proper young lady?" she replied acidly. What could he mean? Her eyes did not leave Raoul's face.

Raoul was conscious of his own discomfort. Damn it, did Edward tell his friend everything? And why the hell did the man have to bring it up now? The girl was nothing but a little minx, a tease who had flirted with him to boost her own ego. What the devil did he care what she thought of him?

"I've invited my fiancée to join us," he said, avoiding her eyes. "As long as we're going to be burdened with women, I thought I'd like to have one of my own."

His fiancée? For a moment, Aimée could only stare at him in disbelief. Even in the days they had seemed close to each other, he had never mentioned a fiancée to her.

And yet, she reminded herself bitterly, she had no right to be surprised. Raoul was a virile, attractive man, likely to excite the interest of women and be excited by them. To assume he had formed no serious attachment was the height of self-deception. She turned her head away, anxious to keep him from seeing the hurt in her eyes.

She was not quick enough. Raoul could not help seeing her pain—or responding to it. Angrily he warned himself it was nothing more than her wounded ego crying out in discomfort at his indifference. He would be a fool to read anything deeper into it, to try to pretend her anguish was real and profound, a response to the passion in her soul. Turning away, he stared out the window again.

Aimée did not miss the deliberate rejection of his gesture. Retreating farther into her own corner, she tugged the shawl tighter around her shoulders, as if it had the power to provide the warmth to drive away her inner chill as well. She felt suddenly isolated and alone.

I have invited my fiancée to join us. Why did those words keep ringing in her ears? *I wanted to have a woman of my own.*

A woman of his own.

Mon Dieu, how that hurt. A woman to touch, a woman to caress, a woman to look at with longing.

A woman to share all the hopes and dreams of the rest of his life.

And she would be beautiful, Aimée knew. Raoul would never settle for anything less. His fiancée would be tall and statuesque, her womanly curves making Aimée's slender body seem childlike and insignificant. She would be gentle and golden, with fair curls and wide pale eyes, a perfect foil for Raoul's dark good looks. And there would be a softness in her manner, a kind of graceful femininity that allowed neither frivolity nor stubbornness, neither dark moods of despair nor sudden volatile flashes of temperament.

Aimée was intelligent enough to know that the picture of Raoul's fiancée she had formed in her mind was unreal, a fantasy shaped more out of her own fears than her sense of Raoul's taste, but the knowledge did not alleviate her pain. Slowly, she let her head drop once again against the cool glass of the windowpane. She barely felt the clumsy jolting of the carriage as it twisted through the winding streets of town.

The long sunlit days they spent in Cairo were pleasanter than Aimée had expected. The house Edward rented for them proved surprisingly large and comfortable. Although it was made of mud brick, like all the other buildings on the street, its carved wooden balconies had been painted a crisp white, matching both the railing on the veranda and the prim picket fence that circled bright patches of African daisies in the front. There was a safe, familiar feeling about the place, cutting it off from the alien city surrounding it as surely as the high wooden gates at the end of the street that were locked and bolted each night at sunset. If it had not been for Raoul, Aimée sensed she would almost have been happy there.

By the time they had been in Cairo a week, Aimée at last felt her pain begin to ease a little. For the first time she dared to hope she had finally found enough inner strength to accept the necessity—and the wisdom—for Raoul's coolness toward her. As she sat beside a small artificial lake in the garden, she was almost content. There was a hint of crispness in the early-afternoon air, presaging the winter breezes that would soon bathe the desert city in a mantle of cold. The surface of the lake looked like a black sheet of glass. Aimée found herself staring at the still waters, half-hypnotized by their serenity. She was so engrossed in her thoughts she did not even hear the sound of approaching footsteps. Glancing up, she was startled to see Raoul crossing the garden toward her. As she rose to greet him, her heart was beating rapidly.

Raoul stopped abruptly as he caught sight of her, then hesitated, as if he were unsure of himself. Aimée realized she was longing for him to stop and talk to her, if only to exchange a few words of polite conversation. She was destined to be disappointed, however. His face cool and indifferent, Raoul turned on his heel and vanished around the corner of the house without so much as a single word.

The pain that shot through Aimée's body was so sharp it took her breath away. She was dismayed to find that Raoul's aloofness still had so much power to hurt her. She had been so sure she was becoming reconciled to it. Wearily she leaned against the trunk of an ancient gnarled tree at the water's edge. The rough bark felt warm against her cheek. She was tempted to throw her arms around its stout bulk and weep for all the doubts and loneliness and despair that tore her heart apart.

It would be good to cry, she told herself—good to wallow in the self-pity that she had been battling for weeks. Good to stop pretending she was the bravest little soldier of them all.

Instead, she pulled herself together, and turned slowly toward the house. As she did, she became aware of a stooped figure lingering in the shadows.

"Ibrahim, come here," she called out impetuously, suddenly eager for company. She remembered how relieved she had been when she first learned the servants all spoke at least a little French or English.

The old man moved toward her with a careless shuffle. The long galabiya that rustled faintly as he moved was worn and faded, barely touched now with hints of the blue it had once been, but it was carefully mended and immaculately clean. The man's mouth was set in a broad toothless grin. In spite of herself, Aimée began to smile.

Ibrahim always had that effect on her, drawing her out of her depression and loneliness for a few precious moments of laughter. The old servant was almost a caricature of everything she had expected to find in Egypt; he was strident and grasping, utterly transparent in his greed—yet somehow so charming and ingenuous she could never quite bring herself to mind.

He had taught her her first word in Arabic, "baksheesh." It

was a word she was often to hear on his lips. Baksheesh was a present, Ibrahim explained to her solemnly, a token between friends to express their devotion to each other. His presents to her took the form of small services, or perhaps an occasional story to help her laugh away the lonely hours. Her presents, she quickly learned—her baksheesh—were always expected to take the form of small silver coins. It was amazing to see how many ways he could find to coax and wheedle them out of her.

"I am bored in the garden today, Ibrahim," she called out, not even waiting until he had reached her side. Suddenly she felt a burst of anger at herself, an impatience for all the pain and self-pity that seemed to be engulfing her. She could do nothing about Raoul and his coldness—just as she could do nothing to remedy the mistakes of the past. But she could keep herself from brooding about it. "I want to go into town to the market."

Clearly Ibrahim had not anticipated her words. "The marketplace, lady?" he asked clumsily, his expression slowly changing to one of horror. "Oh, no, lady. The lordship will be very angry."

Aimée did not try to tell him "the lordship" would not even notice she was gone. She knew Ibrahim would not believe her. It would be impossible for him to imagine any husband being so careless of his wife's whereabouts.

"Come, Ibrahim," she coaxed, dropping her hand pointedly into her pocket. "I will be perfectly safe if you are with me."

For once the ploy did not work. "No, lady, not safe," he insisted, his sallow features paling at the thought. "Not good. A lady cannot go to market—only with her husband."

"With her husband?" Aimée cried out in frustration. "But Edward would never do that. You know that, Ibrahim. Edward is too . . . too fussy. He might get his clothes dirty."

Impishly she began to mince around the garden in an imitation of Edward, her skirts drawn close to her body, her nose pinched together in an expression of disdain. The old servant was obviously shocked by her blatant disrespect, but despite his strong disapproval he could not keep the corners of his mouth from twitching at her clever mimicry.

"You will do it for me, won't you?" she cried out in delight. "You will, I know you will."

In the end, Aimée realized, it was more the lure of generous baksheesh than the compelling force of her enthusiasm that prompted the old man to submit. But submit he did, and Aimée felt her heart lighten as she raced back to her room to get a heavy damask shawl to protect her dress from the dust of the marketplace. It seemed to her, in those few brief moments, that she had rediscovered her love of adventure. It was the first time she had felt like that since the day her father had brought Lord Edward Ellingham to her as a suitor.

To her delight, the market justified all her hopes. The bright midday sun streamed down on faces not unlike those that had stared out at her from the dense mist the morning they had arrived, but this time their gaunt, harsh lines had been softened by golden light, as if some kindly artist, ashamed of the pain and poverty he had depicted, had touched up the scene, painting out all the shadows with a few swift strokes of the brush. Aimée was still aware of the squalor and filth of the narrow streets, but in the sunlight she was no longer afraid of them. The city was not unlike the poorer areas of Paris and London. The children were dark-skinned and strangely dressed, but they played games that were familiar to her, and their laughter was the laughter of children everywhere. The peasants and shopkeepers, haggling vigorously with each other, spoke in a tongue she could not understand, but the tones of their bargaining were universal.

Ibrahim translated the cries of the vendors for her. "Figs, fruits of the sultans!" the men called out, their turbans reflecting the bright sunlight. "Scents of paradise!" the flower girls cried, holding out armfuls of dark Persian roses, anemones, gladioli, and African daisies. To Aimée their whining and cajoling was no more exotic than French farmers selling their chickens and onions, or pretty *mademoiselles* trying to peddle pots of bright red geraniums.

In an odd way, the whole scene seemed familiar to Aimée as she stood in the center of one of the widest squares and turned around slowly, trying to take in all the sights and sounds at once. Once past her fear of its strangeness, she could imagine that the market was set not in the streets of Cairo, but in the lanes and alleyways of her own beloved Paris, as if she had found precious, half-forgotten memories and laid them out in the bright light of the sun.

She was glad she had coaxed Ibrahim to bring her here, glad she had not based all her impressions of Cairo on one dark, smoky morning. She told herself, with a little surge of excitement, that dark, intimidating scenes should always be examined again in the bright light of day.

She spent an enticing afternoon trudging through the narrow, cluttered streets of the city. As she poked her nose into one little souk after another, she became aware that an increasingly disgruntled Ibrahim was lagging farther and farther behind.

"Come on, slowpoke," she called out gaily, tossing the remark over her shoulder. She relented a little as she saw how tired he was, reminding herself that he was, after all, an old man. But to her relief, the promise of a little more baksheesh was all that was needed to put a jaunty eagerness back into his step. Aimée hurried on breathlessly. She wanted to look at everything, touch everything, smell everything before the sun went down and they had to return to the house.

It was truly a fairy-tale world—an Arabian-nights dream come true. Never in her life had she seen so many strange, fascinating things in one place. Silversmiths stood in the dark recesses of their stalls, their glistening brown bodies drenched with sweat while little boys fanned the fires with bellows that looked as if they had been made from goatskins. Basket weavers worked patiently in the bright sunlight, their bleeding hands twisting sharp reeds in and out, in and out. Peasants carried squawking geese under their arms as they pushed their way past old sheikhs hobbling on their sticks, and sheep and goats mingled in the narrow streets with old men leading their donkeys, dark veiled women, and half-naked laborers.

Even the smell of the place was potent and exciting. There was something primal about it, something earthy and basic, yet, again, familiar. It was almost as if there was a universality in strangeness, Aimée told herself with surprise—a kind of common human bond that reached across the chasms of space and culture.

It was a peculiar smell, she admitted, but one that was not at all unpleasant. The scent of cooking meat and exotically spiced Eastern food from the native cafés mingled with the odors of the marketplace: the perfume of sandalwood and cinnamon, the sweet stench of sweat, fresh coffee beans and Persian roses, dust and jasmine. It was the smells that affected her most, giving her a deep, abiding sense of the place. She knew the sensation would linger long after the sights and sounds had faded from her memory.

The afternoon shadows began to lengthen, until they covered half her path. Reluctantly she turned back to seek out Ibrahim, lingering halfway down the street. She smiled indulgently as she watched him sink gratefully onto a stool in front of the stall of a friendly shopkeeper.

Twenty minutes more, she promised herself. Just twenty minutes of this exotic, wonderful world, and then she would turn back and let the old man lead her home. He would be all right where he was for a few more minutes, and besides, she did not really need him. She would be perfectly safe without him, at least for a little while.

A dramatic burst of color at the end of the street drew her toward a stand of vivid, fragrant flowers. Nearby, barely halfway down the next short lane, dark figs, their flesh plump and tender beneath their leathery brown skins, lay next to piles of pungent tangerines, while persimmons made a bright contrast to mounds of prickly green pears and sweet white grapes.

Mon Dieu, it was exciting, she told herself, hardly able to believe her good fortune in being able to see it all. Entrancing and excitingly exotic. She wished her mother could see her now, wandering safely through the Egyptian streets they had both feared so much. She would have liked to laugh with her as she told her how foolish—and groundless—those fears had been.

Only when the sun dipped beneath an ornately carved arch, blanketing the marketplace in gray, did Aimée realize how late it was and how long she had lingered. Feeling guilty, she turned quickly, scanning the emptying streets for Ibrahim's familiar form. When she did not see him right away, she was not alarmed.

She retraced her steps slowly, moving back toward the little square she had just left. Her eyes scanned the dark interior of each souk she passed, but still she did not find him. Stepping into the center of the square, she began to feel apprehensive. She had moved so quickly, flitting from one stall to another, while he had lingered to gossip and rest. What if she had gone too fast for him to follow?

But that was nonsense, she reminded herself sternly. Of course she had not gone too fast for him. Pausing for a minute, she took a deep calming breath. Ibrahim must have followed her, she told herself with a certainty that was beginning to feel forced. He was too kind and diligent—and much too afraid of her husband—to leave her alone. Coolly, methodically she began to scan the square, watching as the shopkeepers wrapped up their wares and closed their souks for the night. It was several minutes before she could admit to herself that he was not there.

She felt a sudden tightening in her chest at the thought. Heaven help her, she was alone, alone and unprotected, and night was coming on. There was nothing she could do, no way she could get home without Ibrahim's help. Even if she found someone who spoke enough French or English to understand what she wanted, she would never be able to bribe him to lead her safely home. She had given her last coin to Ibrahim to guide her into the market. It had not occurred to her she might have to buy her way out, too.

Pressing her hand against her chest in a vain attempt to steady her heartbeat, Aimée took another long, deep breath. She knew she dared not let herself panic now. Besides, she was probably being foolish about the whole thing. No doubt Ibrahim was still where she had left him, enjoying a tall glass of sweet mint tea with a friend, unaware that she had slipped away from him. All she had to do was work her way back to the street where she had lost him, and everything would be all right.

But, oh, *bon Dieu*, how was she to do that? she asked herself, her panic rising. Every street, every narrow lane and alleyway, looked so exactly alike, she did not know how to begin. How could she hope to make her way out of that dark maze when she couldn't find so much as a single landmark, a single stall she could even remember passing by?

Where was the little flower stand? she asked herself desperately. The flowers were all sold and gone. And the fruit stand with the tempting tangerines? But there were a dozen fruit stands, and they all had tempting tangerines. And, oh, God help her, they all seemed to be closing their stalls, packing up their wares, and slipping away into the shadows.

Frantically she spun around, trying to find something, *anything*, that would give her a clue. In despair she realized there was nothing. Finally, acting more from need than reason, she forced herself to pick a street, heading down it with a grim show of determination. She knew only too well she might be going the wrong way, but she dared not stay where she was. Already people were beginning to stare at her with strange expressions on their faces. It was better to keep moving, better to look like she knew what she was doing, than to hesitate in confusion, attracting the wrong kind of attention. Besides, if she was lucky she might stumble onto something she recognized. She might even work her way by accident into the European sector of the town.

Aimée lost all sense of time as she stumbled through the darkening streets, her eyes constantly flitting from one spot to another in a futile search for something she recognized. She did not know how late it was or even how long she had been wandering. She only knew that the shadows were deepening and the streets were emptier, far too empty to feel safe anymore. She clutched at the tiny cross around her neck, praying as she had never prayed before to a God who suddenly seemed terrifyingly remote and faraway.

"Please," she whispered softly. "Please help me find my way out of here."

The words were mechanical, filled with doubt and despair. It was a prayer she did not expect to have answered, but she prayed because she did not know what else to do. She could barely feel the cold metal of the cross beneath her fingertips.

She had already forgotten her own urgent words when, barely a few minutes later, she stumbled across a street she recognized. At first she could only stop and gape at it in wonder. She had been so frightened, so filled with despair, she had not even dared to hope anymore. Now it seemed her prayers had been answered.

She did not know what there was about the street that made it seem right to her. It was a narrow, dirty street, just like all the other narrow, dirty streets she had walked down, without so much as a single stall or shop left open on it. But there was something familiar about it, something so hauntingly reminiscent that there was no doubt in her mind that she had been there before.

Sensing she had already lingered too long at the mouth of the street, gaping like the vulnerable foreigner she was, Aimée began to hurry forward. Her feet moved with a new lightness, nearly skipping as they carried her past doorway after darkened doorway, moving deeper and deeper into the shadows. She could barely control her excitement as she raced toward the end of the street.

When she rounded a corner and saw the alien architecture of an Eastern church rising in front of her, it did not surprise her. She could not consciously remember having seen a church in this city of mosques, but she knew as she looked at it that it had a comfortable, familiar quality. It must have been there all the time, covered over by vegetable stalls and flower stands until it was barely visible behind them.

It was not a very big church nor an elegant one. Certainly nothing in its humble lines reminded her of the graceful mosques she had seen, or the tall, solemn churches of Europe. And yet, as she stared at it, she found something almost awesome about the building. It was as if the very simplicity of its plain mud bricks suggested a holiness the richest cathedral could not hope to match.

Barely realizing what she was doing, Aimée began to move toward the tall wooden doorway. Something about the little church appealed to her, sending out an enticing welcome. She could not leave without seeing the inside of it. Besides, she felt safe enough to linger for a few minutes. Now that she knew where she was at last, she was not afraid of getting lost again.

The interior of the church was dark. Dim rays of twilight slipped in through narrow windows high in the unpainted walls, and the hazy gold of a candle flickered in the distance. Aimée squinted, waiting for her eyes to adjust to the darkness before she moved slowly away from the door, letting it slide noiselessly shut behind her. She pulled her shawl over her head, wrapping a corner of it around her face to hide her features from anyone who might be lurking in the shadows. It was several minutes before she realized she was alone in the church. Even then she did not feel comfortable enough to remove the shawl from her head.

The church seemed to be divided into two rooms, each equal in size. The room she was standing in was small and dingy, with plain mud-brick walls and a dirt floor packed down by the pressure of countless feet. But even in the midst of all the poverty and emptiness, Aimée sensed an aura of quiet, confident faith. She could not help recalling the strong emotions that had swept over her as she stood outside the church staring up at its high walls. God was in that little room, she told herself with a certainty she had never felt before. He was there in a way he had never been there for her in all the churches and cathedrals of Europe.

She stepped forward slowly, moving toward the light that seemed to come from the other room. As she neared the dividing wall, she saw that it was not a wall at all, but a tall, delicately carved wooden screen. Pausing to stare at it for a moment, she marveled at its lacy perfection. The gossamer intricacy was highlighted by the hints of candlelight behind it, making it look as fragile and ephemeral as a spiderweb stretched across a dusty corner.

When she reached the small, low doorway in the center of the screen, Aimée hesitated, sensing she was an intruder, an uninvited visitor in someone else's faith. She regarded the inner room as she lingered awkwardly on the threshold.

The pale golden light came from a pair of tapers rising out of tall candlesticks at the side of the room. The only decoration in the church, a single painted image, was hanging on the wall between the candles. Aimée stared at it with almost hypnotized curiosity. There was something compelling about the face of the man in the portrait; his dark beard and swarthy skin were a sharp contrast to the drab surface of the wall. Forgetting her reluctance, Aimée stepped slowly forward.

As she drew nearer, the portrait became more distinct. From the man's garb, Aimée realized he was some kind of holy man or Eastern monk, but his features, powerful and magnetic though they were, still seemed obscure, as if the artist had deliberately chosen to hide them in the shadows. It was only when she stood directly before the portrait that she could see them clearly at last. When she did, she gasped in surprise.

The man, dark and Eastern though he was, had eyes as blue as her own.

Aimée felt a strong sense of affinity with the stranger in the portrait. No, not affinity, she told herself with a sense of wonder—something stronger, far deeper than that. It was almost as if she and the stranger were part of the same entity, as if it were her own midnight-blue eyes staring back at her from the painted board on the wall. It was a ridiculous feeling, she knew, but it was one she could not shake.

Slowly, her hand trembling, Aimée ran her fingers along the surface of the portrait. She was surprised to find the wood warm to her touch, almost as if the painted flesh were real and alive.

She smiled a little at her fancy. The flesh was not real, of course—the heat she felt was simply from the candles in front of the wood. And no doubt the man's eyes were not that deep, peculiar color at all. It was an artist's fancy perhaps, or just an artist's inadequacy, a failure to find the proper shade on his palette.

Yet, did it really matter? she asked herself. Even if the man's eyes were nothing more than a common blue-gray, they would still be unusual in a land of dark people—every bit as unusual as her own deep eyes were in the country of her birth. They would have set him subtly apart from the others, making him always a little bit of a stranger, an alien among his own people.

So that was it, she told herself with a burst of recognition. That was the sense of affinity she had felt for this man the instant she saw his portrait hanging on the wall. Not the compelling power that seemed to radiate from his features, not even the strange, piercing color of his eyes—nothing more than a simple sense of his aloofness, his unique quality of being totally, utterly alone.

It was something Aimée could understand. All her life she had felt the same way. There was an aloofness in her, too, a sense of being different from the others, even in the midst of a large, loving family. It was a feeling that had been strengthened by an unwanted marriage that cut her off irrevocably from everything she had ever known or held dear. Now she saw the same feeling clearly depicted in the eyes of this man.

A sudden touch on her arm jolted her back to reality. Whirling nervously, she saw an old woman standing behind her. The lower part of her face was covered with a black veil, but her dark eyes were blazing with rage. Too late Aimée remembered her first feeling that she was an intruder in this holy place. Awkwardly she opened her lips to explain her presence, hoping that words spoken in a foreign tongue would somehow be understood. She did not even get a chance to try. The change that came over the woman's face as she stared back at her was enough to startle her into silence.

It was almost as if, looking at Aimée's delicate foreign features, the woman saw a resemblance to something she feared, perhaps an evil spirit. Her expression of utter horror seemed unreal to Aimée. She could have sworn when she first whirled around there had been only anger in those dark eyes. Now they widened with fear, dilating until they seemed to grow even blacker in the shadows.

Suddenly, without warning, the old woman threw back her head, letting a deep animal wail build up in her throat, rising until it seemed to fill every corner of the room. It was an eerie sound, halfway between the howling of a beast in pain and the keening of the peasant women for their dead.

Juste ciel, she must be mad, Aimée thought, as her own fear began to mount. The woman was mad . . . and she was alone with her.

She began to back away from her. She could find no rational cause to be afraid of such a frail old woman, but she could not help herself. It was almost as if there were something else she was afraid of, some kind of power beyond the woman herself. It took a moment to realize what that power was. When she did, cold terror flooded her body.

The old woman might not have the strength to hurt her, but her cries would draw those who did. Shivering, Aimée imagined what it would be like for her if she was still there when they came. If one old woman had looked at her with fear and hatred, how would a whole mob react? What would they do to her, a helpless woman completely in their power?

Terrified, she turned and began to race toward the outer door.

She had gone only a few steps when she felt sharp fingers clutching at her back, grasping the fabric of her dress so tightly she could not get away. Her terror rising, she struggled to free herself, pulling away from the clawlike hands that seemed to have dug right through the cloth and into her flesh. Desperately she realized it was no use. She had been a fool to underrate the woman so badly. She had heard that rage could give a person an almost superhuman strength. Now she knew it was true.

Redoubling her efforts, she struggled even more urgently, sensing that she might be fighting for her very life. When she heard the silk of her dress give, she almost sobbed with relief. Now at last she was free.

But the respite was only an illusion. She quickly discovered that the old woman had no intention of letting her get away so easily. Dropping the torn fabric, she lunged forward again, clutching at her bare skin. The pain was excruciating, but Aimée barely noticed it. She was too terrified to care about anything but the need to get away. In an attempt to catch the old woman off balance, she whirled swiftly and began to flail her arms, hoping to deflect her, if only for a moment. Too late she realized she had miscalculated. The woman lashed out so fiercely it was Aimée who was thrown off balance. Terrified, she felt the ground slip away under her feet.

She cried out sharply as her legs twisted under her, hurling her roughly to the packed earthen floor. The woman did not relent for a moment. Sensing her quarry's helplessness, she stepped up the fury of her attack. Her gnarled, bent fingers swooped down on Aimée, their sharp nails searching for her face.

No, not her face, Aimée realized with sudden horror. Not her face at all. Those ugly, twisted talons were reaching for her eyes.

All she could do was raise her hands in an instinctive shield across her face.

2

Terrified, Aimée held her hands tightly over her face. She was agonizingly conscious of sharp nails clawing into her fingers, trying to gouge their way through to her eyes, but there was nothing she could do. It was as if the woman were some gigantic vindictive bird of prey acting out some private malice with angry talons aimed unerringly at her victim's most vulnerable point—her eyes.

Aimée did not dare pull her hands away from her face, not even for an instant, but without them she could not defend herself. All she could do was crouch there helplessly, praying the woman would finally exhaust herself, spending her strength in the wild fury of her assault. In the end, the terror of it proved too much. Forsaking reason, a low wail began to rise in her throat, increasing slowly until it became a prolonged scream, piercing the air.

She knew her cry was foolish. Whoever responded to it would hardly be disposed to help her, but she was beyond caring. She knew only that somehow, in one terrifying moment, control of her life had slipped from her and there was no way she could regain it. Her reaction was one of pure terror. All she could do was scream and scream—and keep on screaming.

The sound of her anguish filled her ears, blocking out everything else. She did not hear the creak of the door as it swung slowly open. Even the twilight that flooded into the room was denied her, for her hands were clasped too securely over her eyes to let in a trace of it. She sensed another presence in the room only when the talons pulled away from her at last. She was conscious for the first time of the pain from deep scratches on her hands. A moist sensation, like a warm coursing of blood, ran down her arms, but she was only dimly aware of it. All she could feel was intense relief. The ordeal was over at last.

It was a moment before reason returned to her, but it was closely followed by renewed fear. She had been rescued, she knew—but by whom? And what would they do to her when they found out that she, a foreigner and an unveiled woman, had violated the sanctity of their shrine? It was a full minute before she could force herself to pull her hands away from her face. When she did, she raised her eyes cautiously.

She had expected dark Eastern faces in a ring around her, their eyes flashing with anger and accusation. Instead she saw only a single man, dressed in European clothes. His back was half-turned toward her as he grappled with the old woman, still fighting to subdue the amazing wildness of her strength. At first Aimée did not recognize him, but when she did, she let out a cry of surprise.

"Raoul!"

Her body gave one vast sigh of relief. Raoul was there. Everything would be all right.

Raoul paid no attention to her as he continued to struggle with the flailing bundle of bones and claws in his arms. Only as he finally began to subdue her, pulling her tightly against his own body, did Aimée get a close look at the woman's face. The veil had been torn from her features so they were clearly visible in the dim twilight that filtered through the open doorway.

Aimée could only gape at her in horror. Her skin was so brittle and lined, it looked like a piece of rotting parchment, and her eyes were set like two burning coals in its surface. Her only expression was a potent, malignant hatred that twisted her features until they were barely recognizable as human. It had never occurred to Aimée that it was possible to hate a stranger so much, or that religious zeal could be so strong it totally banished reason.

With the woman subdued, Raoul turned to Aimée at last. There was no softness in his expression as he looked down at her.

"Get her out of here!"

For the first time, Aimée realized Raoul was not alone. Turning toward the doorway, she caught sight of a reluctant figure faltering on the threshold.

Dear, faithful Ibrahim, she thought, trying to manage a faint smile of gratitude. He must have run all the way back to the house to get help for her. Thank God Raoul had been there when he arrived. And thank God the terror of her own loud screams had drawn them to her.

She offered no protest as the old man stepped toward her, urging her to her feet. She felt the trembling in his hands as he picked up her fallen shawl, easing it around her raw, bleeding shoulders. Gratefully she wrapped it tightly around her.

The carriage that waited in the street outside was a welcome sight. Aimée clambered into it eagerly, not even waiting for Ibrahim to help her up. Once inside, she huddled into a corner, trying to hide her shame.

If only Raoul would come, she thought desperately, nearly breaking down at last. If only he would draw her into his arms, soothing away her fear with the strength of his embrace. If only he would tell her it was all right to cry at last, all right to admit the weaknesses she had been hiding all her life.

But the instant Raoul stepped out of the church, Aimée

knew she was bound to be disappointed. Whatever comfort she had expected from him, his expression warned her she would not get it. The rift that had formed between them was as deep as ever.

Hurrying forward, Raoul leaped into the carriage, not even pausing as he shouted out a quick command in Arabic to the driver. The carriage jolted to a start even before he could pull the door shut behind him. It seemed to Aimée he was taking care not to look at her, staring instead into the darkening streets. Only when they had rounded the corner did he turn to face her.

"What the devil did you think you were doing?"

Aimée shivered at the harshness of his tone, but she could find no words to answer him. All she could do was stare at him helplessly.

Raoul was aware of her pain, but he did everything he could to hide his feelings. God help him if Aimée saw how deeply she had touched the protective instincts in his heart, he warned himself grimly. She had already tormented him enough as it was. He couldn't let her have a weapon like that to use against him.

He reached up with deliberate nonchalance to straighten the jacket of his suit, which had been badly rumpled in the fray. He was acutely conscious that his hand was trembling. He hoped if the girl noticed it, she would attribute it to his anger. He dared not let her see how frightened he had been, how utterly terrified when Ibrahim had come tearing back to the house, crying out in awkward, broken phrases that his mistress was lost in the marketplace. He didn't ever want to live through those dark moments again, racing blindly through twisting streets, not knowing where to go or where to turn, not even knowing if she was still all right.

"Haven't you learned yet that women have a place in this country?" He knew he was using his anger to cover his confusion. "And that place isn't in someone else's church—especially without a veil."

Aimée felt as if he had reached out to strike her. "I'm sorry. It's just that I was lost . . . and frightened."

Raoul realized how desperately she needed to hear even a single word of kindness from him. In spite of himself, he felt his anger begin to soften, easing away until he could barely remember it at all. Damn the appealing helplessness in her eyes, he told himself irritably—her seeming fragility and vulnerability. It would be his downfall yet if he didn't guard against it.

"That was a Christian church," he explained, trying unsuccessfully to keep his voice cold and noncommittal. "Egyptian Christian—Copts, we call them. They are direct descendants of the first Egyptians, a breed apart from the Moslem invaders who come at a later time. They are a proud and ancient people. You cannot expect them to take it kindly when some frivolous tourist violates one of their holy places."

He did not add that he had been alarmed by the violence of the woman's reaction, so out of keeping with the magnitude of Aimée's sin. He sensed he did not have to. The terror on Aimée's face told him she would not be so foolish again.

Then Aimée heard Raoul begin to laugh. Warily she glanced up, searching for a hint of derision in his eyes. She did not find it.

"By all that's sacred, Aimée," he said at last, shaking his head in disbelief, "what made you choose *that* church?"

The question confused her. "I didn't *choose* it, Raoul. It was just there."

"I know, I know." He brushed aside her protests impatiently. "But dammit, Aimée, that's the shrine of Tadrus the Martyr. He died there on the street. His mother kept on going there for years, lighting candles in front of his picture and keeping his memory alive. For all I know, that might have been her you encountered today, though I doubt it. I imagine she's long dead by now. But it's still one of the most revered churches in Cairo. Tadrus died for his people, or so they believed at least. Everyone old enough to remember him adores him with a passion that borders on fanaticism. Try to imagine how that old woman felt, seeing a heathen—for that's what you are to her, you know—standing in front of his sacred picture."

Standing in front of it? Aimée felt a cold shiver run up her spine as she remembered the moment. She had not merely stood in front of the picture, she had actually reached up and touched it with corrupt, profane fingers.

"It was his eyes," she whispered, trying to explain actions she knew were unforgivable. "I couldn't help looking at them. They were so . . . so . . ."

"Oh, my God, I had forgotten," Raoul cried out. "Tadrus was famous for his eyes, deep and penetrating, and the color of the midnight sky. No wonder the woman went half-crazy when she saw you. An infidel with those eyes? She must have thought you were the devil incarnate—or at least some evil jinn come to torment her. It would have terrified her half out of her wits."

Of course it would, Aimée realized, her self-disgust growing with each passing minute. Her rude disregard of other people's customs, to say nothing of their faith, had been not only thoughtless, but cruel as well. Why, the poor woman must have thought she was fighting for her life as she grappled with Aimée in the shadowy shrine, clawing away at the eyes that were the symbol of all her superstitious terror.

"I won't do anything like that again," she whispered contritely.

"I know goddamn well you won't. We'll be leaving Cairo in a day or two. Until then, you stay in the house. Is that understood?"

Mutely she nodded her agreement. She looked at him in her unhappiness, begging silently for compassion, but she did not dare repeat the plea with her lips.

Raoul did not try to speak again, but turning away slowly, stared into the darkness. He hoped she did not realize he was deliberately hiding his eyes from her. He would not have liked her to guess at the pain in their depths.

Raoul still felt the same pain hours later as he sat in the deep night shadows, watching the reflection of a full moon in the placid waters of the lake in the garden. The sight fascinated him, holding him with a hypnotic lure he was powerless to resist. It seemed to him he had never seen water that color before.

Midnight blue, he thought, disturbed by the image it conjured up in his heart. Midnight blue. The color of moonlight reflected in deep night waters. The color of a dead man's eyes, a martyr who sold his life for a moment of glory and a handful of fading memories.

Or the color of eyes that would haunt his dreams forever.

Once a fool, always a fool, he told himself with a short, dry laugh. Had he really thought he could forget her so easily—just blot her out of his mind? That he could sit in the darkness and watch the full moon touch the clear waters of the lake and not think of her?

A few cold looks, biting sarcasm, a mask of indifference—was he really fool enough to think that was all it took? An overt show of scorn, and then he would be able to forget her forever.

Or was he being honest with himself? He had tried to tell himself he didn't want the girl anymore, didn't want to have anything to do with the deceitful games she played, but was that really the truth? Was it honor that made him cling to the memory of the woman he had promised his life to? Self-protectiveness that made him shield himself from the union he knew would be disastrous? Or was it something simpler, something more basic than that? Was it perhaps nothing more complex than a need to hurt her, to punish her for not wanting him?

Dammit, he owed Aimée an apology, he told himself irritably. He had been unfair to her, brutally unfair. Besides, she had been terrified out of her wits that afternoon. What would it hurt to offer a word of comfort? If he couldn't give her an explanation, at least he could let her know he was sorry.

He was aware as he rose from the lake and began to move toward her door that his feet had followed a similar course once before. It was a painful memory, one his mind did not want to dwell on. At least this time there would be no nasty surprises. Lord Edward and Buffy had both gone out for the evening. He would find Aimée alone.

He would stay only five minutes, he promised himself. Five minutes and no more. Not long enough to be threatening to her—or to feel threatened himself. All he would do was offer her a few belated words of sympathy. Then he would leave.

The soft rapping at the door startled Aimée, giving her an uneasy sense of apprehension. She had expected Buffy to visit her that night, for he had not been there for the past three days, but she had not expected him to knock. Rising, she made her way toward the door and inched it open cautiously.

She was amazed to see the tall figure of Raoul Villière standing on the threshold. At first she was too startled to move; then, remembering the sheer translucence of her dressing gown, she clutched at the garment, pulling it tighter around her.

"May I come in?" His voice was low and surprisingly soft.

"Raoul? What are you doing here? *Mon Dieu*, if Edward should see you . . ."

But it was not Edward she feared. God help her, what if Buffy should decide to come to her now?

She didn't know which she feared most, Buffy's malicious tongue as he hurried to tell her husband or the look of scorn on Raoul's face when he saw him there.

Raoul saw her turmoil and he understood it.

"Lord Edward has gone out for the evening," he said coldly. "And so has his charming little friend, if that's what you're worried about."

Aimée stood aside, startled and confused, as he stepped into the room. Closing the door behind him, he strode over to the windows, pulling the heavy shutters inward until the moonlight was completely blocked from the room. He did not himself understand why he was being so secretive, fearing servants who would almost certainly not pass by that side of the house. He only knew he had to do it.

His confusion mounted as he turned to face her again. How lovely she was, how soft and vulnerably feminine. He had not expected her dark hair to hang free and shimmering down her back, or her gown to be so white and innocent, faintly diaphanous in the golden candlelight.

"I was a little hard on you this afternoon," he said quickly, eager to cover his confusion. He was aware that his voice was too loud, too sharp. He wanted to add, "I'm sorry," but the words came hard to him, and he was afraid they would sound stilted and insincere.

"I suppose I deserved it." She spoke with slow caution, as if she were more than a little afraid of the man who stood before her. It only made her more vulnerable in his eyes.

God, she was lovely, he told himself with despair. Her hair was so soft, so silky, circling her face in a gentle frame of darkness. He longed to reach out and touch it, to bury his fingers in its rich warmth. It was all he could do to hold himself back.

"You were foolish," he admitted. They weren't the words he wanted, but he couldn't seem to find the right ones. "But I know you didn't mean any harm."

Dammit, that didn't help at all, he told himself furiously. The girl was still frightened, still hurt by his seeming indifference. What the hell was wrong with him anyhow? Why couldn't he, just once in his life, swallow his stubborn pride and admit to caring for someone—even if she didn't care for him?

Her next words startled him.

"Who was he, Raoul? Can you tell me about him?"

"Him?" For a moment Raoul could remember only the old woman and the violence of her attack. It took him a few seconds to recall the portrait in the shrine and grasp the fact that Aimée was curious about it. "You mean Tadrus—Tadrus the Martyr?"

She did not answer him. At the word "martyr," sadness crept into her heart. It was hard to think of the man in the portrait as dead. He had been so alive to her that afternoon.

Raoul saw her distress and it annoyed him. Damn the girl anyhow. What right did she have to look like an innocent schoolgirl, all caught up in tales of saints who died before their time? It was an obscenity as far as he was concerned. God knows, there was nothing innocent about her anymore.

"Save your pity; the man may have been a saint, but he was far from holy."

Aimée heard his words with disbelief. She could not accept what he was saying. She had seen the man's portrait herself, seen the haunting loneliness and sorrow in his eyes. She could not believe the pain was only for himself.

"Tadrus was a monk," Raoul explained harshly. He was surprised at his need to take every hint of romance out of the man's story, but he could not help himself. "He was locked away for years in one of those barren desert cells the Copts are so fond of. Only, he was not a very good monk, you see—he was much too human to be holy. As the years passed, he found himself lonely, hungering as a man does for the touch of a woman's flesh. It was not too long before he found one. I don't know if she was some pathetic waif, as lonely as he, or if she was a calculating little bitch who found it amusing to separate a man from his faith. But whoever she was, they carried on secretly for months, so secretly that news of his shame didn't leak out until years after his death. By that time, he was so 'holy' no one would believe it."

Raoul searched Aimée's face, expecting to see shock and disillusionment. When he did not, he found it was he himself who was shocked. Good God, had she sunk so far into her own debauchery, this young girl who had once been sheltered in a convent, that she could actually find such an unwholesome union appealing?

"Damn your warped sense of romanticism. Do you really think this is a sad, pretty story? Well, let me tell you how pretty it really is. Your Tadrus the Martyr, your revered holy man, got the stupid girl pregnant, and the first thing he did was abandon her."

"Abandon her?"

At last the reaction Raoul had wanted began to flood across Aimée's face. Common sense told her Raoul had no reason to lie, yet she found the story hard to accept. She could not bring herself to think of Tadrus in that way. She had formed a different image of him in her heart.

Raoul did not miss her pain. It told him he had accomplished his purpose all too well, but the realization gave him no satisfaction. He wished it were not too late to call the words back.

Who the hell did he think he was anyway? What gave him the right to tear away the last remnants of innocence from this girl's heart? Slowly he leaned forward, burying his hand at last in her hair. He was careful to keep the gesture light and casual, more comforting than provocative.

"Perhaps he didn't mean to hurt her. It couldn't have been easy for him, you know. To acknowledge her, to accept his responsibilities, would have meant giving up everything he ever worked for or dreamed of. It's not easy for a man to give up his dreams."

"What happened to her?" Aimée asked softly, her eyes troubled. "The girl?"

Raoul saw her unhappiness. He did not fail to understand it. She was putting herself in that other girl's place, wondering what would happen to her one day when she, too, was abandoned by the men who had used her.

"Don't worry about her. She proved strong in the end, far stronger than he. Though he had abandoned her, she refused to leave him, sensing he might one day need her. It was only years later, after his death, that she agreed to leave Cairo. Some say a relative came to claim her, a cousin, others that she found a man to marry her. But whatever happened to her, I'm sure she's all right."

Bitterly Raoul realized his words had accomplished nothing. Once again he cursed himself for his roughness. He wondered if he would ever be able to stop punishing her for the one thing she could not help—not loving him. Slowly, so gently he was barely aware of it himself, he let his hand slide through her hair, running his fingers through the silken strands. Candlelight shimmered behind the fragile fabric of her gown, outlining her breasts.

Dammit, he was being a fool again, he told himself in despair, but his body still ached for her. He was a fool, but he wanted her more than ever.

"You are so beautiful," he whispered hoarsely. His hand tangling in her hair, he gripped the back of her head, tilting it upward until her face was turned toward his. He laid his other hand on her cheek, drawing it softly across her skin. The intensity of his longing grew until he could no longer control it. Slowly he let his lips sink down on hers.

Aimée's body quivered as he touched her. The sensation of his lips against hers was sweetly tender and drew her toward him with a yearning beyond anything she had ever known. Her own lips parted in eagerness to taste his kiss.

Raoul sensed her response, full and complete for the first time, without a hint of caution. He was careful to keep his mouth gentle and undemanding, careful not to push her any faster than she was willing to go.

Perhaps this was how *he* had won her, he thought with surprise, the man he had been so shocked to find was her lover. Perhaps it was not his handsome face at all, or his flippant artificial manners. Perhaps it was simply that he had been careful enough—and wise enough—not to frighten her off with a burst of unbridled passion.

Aimée's heart responded to the gentleness of Raoul's kiss, just as her body was drawn toward the leashed passion that strained his muscles until they were taut with longing. Her own passions soared to meet his. Gone at last were all the inhibitions that had held her back from him before, all the doubts and questioning and fears. She knew only that her body yearned for him, crying out with a hunger she had never felt before. Her arms longed to reach up to him, pulling him down against her.

"Oh, Raoul," she whispered, feeling her body shiver as his lips raced along her cheek and neck, tantalizing them with tender kisses. "I have missed you so much."

The yearning in her voice raced through his body like an electric current. The hard, swelling pressure in his groin was a stabbing, burning pain. It took all his strength to control his fingers, forcing them to move slowly, carefully toward the delicate laces that held her sheer gown together. He was acutely conscious of the heightened feeling in his fingertips, and he sensed every thread in the fabric as he pulled it gently away from her skin, slipping it lightly from her shoulders.

God help him, she was so beautiful he did not know if he could bear it. He laid his hands on the soft curls that spilled over her shoulders, not daring yet to rest them on her flesh.

He wondered a little at himself as he pulled back from her for a moment, staring at her with a hunger so deep he thought it would tear him in two. She was not like any of the other women he had ever touched—or wanted. He had always liked soft, fluffy, feminine creatures, all golden and gossamer and lace, but this woman was fire and luster, a burning challenge to match his own searing pain. He had dreamed of full voluptuous bodies, with breasts that tempted him to bury his head in their warmth, but she was slender and fragile, her touching vulnerability calling out to his every protective instinct. Her breasts were small and delicate, but perfectly formed, their large pink nipples a teasing invitation to his lips and tongue. Slowly, barely daring to move, he let his hands reach out at last, cupping their softness in his fingers.

Aimée felt as if her skin were burning beneath his hands, the heat spreading through her body. So this was how it was between a man and a woman, she thought with a sense of wonder. This was the excitement her dreams had only hinted at. The excitement she no longer had the strength or will to resist.

"Oh, my dear, this is wrong," she cried out, her words more a sigh of longing than a protest. "So wrong."

And it was wrong. It was a sin, a violation of all she held sacred. But the rest of her life lay ahead of her, long and empty. She did not think she could face the loneliness without tasting the joys of love just once.

She felt Raoul stiffen suddenly, drawing abruptly away from her. She could not understand the angry look that flashed in his eyes.

The impact of her words cut through his body as painfully as if she held a knife in her hands. He trembled as he looked down on her, trembled with pent-up longing and frustration—and a deep anger. Furiously he turned away from her, unwilling to let her see his pain. He caught a glimpse of his own face in the mirror above her dressing table. He was shocked to see how grim it looked.

Dammit, what the hell was he doing? Was he punishing himself as well as her because she could offer him only lust and not love? With any other woman, especially one as beautiful as Aimée, lust was a thing he could have accepted gladly.

It is wrong, she had whispered, quivering with that hypocritical self-righteousness of hers. *It is wrong*—as if she had not done it time and again with other men. Damn her anyway, why should it matter how many times she had done it before—and with whom?

He turned slowly to face her.

"Well, if it is wrong, then we should not do it."

And it *was* wrong, he had to admit, wrong for himself and for her. It would be nothing more than a single moment of love, a trifle that could not last, and they would pay for it dearly if they were caught, he with the love of a good woman and the dreams of a lifetime, she with the marriage that must already have cost her more than she could admit, even to herself. Let her stick with her own kind. She would be happier with the likes of Buffy Montmorency. He was a man who could accept the dalliance she offered on her own terms, without trying to inject hypocritical moral values into the thing—and forcing her to do the same.

As he turned one last time at the door, he was startled by the intense pain and anger in her eyes.

She still wanted him, he realized with a mingling of satisfaction and anguish. Her pride was hurt, just as his own pride had been hurt that night on board ship when she ran away from him, but the hurt would pass all too soon. Only the longing would remain.

It would happen again, he told himself with a sense of destiny. And next time . . .

"In two days we leave for Luxor."

Things would be better in Luxor, he promised himself. There, in a valley on the sunset side of the river, they would have less privacy. It would be difficult for him to go to her there, even if pride and caution betrayed him again.

Difficult . . .

But not impossible.

Yearning blazed out of her eyes, matching the urgent need in his own body. He wondered if, even in Luxor, he would be able to keep away from her—or she from him. It terrified him to find that he doubted it.

He closed the door silently behind him, slipping out into the darkness of the garden.

3

The once proud city of Thebes, home of the ancient gods and the powerful pharaohs who were their images on earth, had become in the end an empty place. The tall pillars were broken, and heads of massive idols lay in desolation along the earth. The sands of centuries touched the scattered stones, pitting and burying them until they seemed to fade into the desert itself.

To Aimée the wasted ruins of the temple of Amon, once the mightiest of the gods, looked like a gigantic broken skeleton, its bleached bones picked clean by scavengers. She felt as if she could almost hear them, the hyenas and jackals, the pariah dogs of the desert, their high-pitched, ululating wails echoing off the rocks of the distant mountains. It seemed to her they were out there somewhere, watching, waiting with the patience of centuries, knowing that someday yet another civilization must fall.

It must have been glorious once, Aimée thought, trying to hear in her imagination the blare of music from instruments long forgotten or to see the bright light and color of processions moving down a broad avenue of sphinxes toward the Nile. But now the sphinxes were buried beneath the earth, with only an occasional piece of eroded stone to show where they stood, and the instruments were decayed and gone. Nothing was left of the city the ancients had called No-Amon, the Place of Amon. Nothing but sand and ruins.

Aimée stared at the emptiness that stretched out in front of her, seemingly into eternity itself. She wished Raoul were there beside her to explain it all. Then the walls would rise once more before her eyes. The tall columns would rival the grace of swaying palms, and the brightly painted decorations challenge even the brilliance of the sun. Then, for a few brief moments, the city would live again. The people would laugh as they had once laughed thousands of years ago, and dream, and love.

But that of course was impossible, she reminded herself, shifting the parasol over her head to shield her from the glaring rays of the midday sun. Since that night in Cairo, Raoul had grown colder toward her than ever, making it perfectly clear he had no intention of exposing himself to temptation again. Sighing, Aimée had to admit he was right. She was bound by vows to the man who was now her husband, just as Raoul was promised to another woman. Slowly she let her eyes drift toward the dark, slightly stooped figure by her side.

It seemed strange to her to have Edward there. In the months that had passed since their marriage, he had spent less and less time in her presence. She did not know if his aloofness was a natural reaction to the embarrassment of sharing a lover with his own wife, or if, more simply, he had decided he did not like her very much. She did not truly care. She only knew it was more comfortable for her this way. She couldn't help wondering what had made him break the pattern that day.

That he did not enjoy her company was all too clear. His expression was irritable as he walked beside her, brushing tiny beads of perspiration away from his forehead with a handkerchief dipped in rosewater.

"Isn't it fascinating?" Aimée said lightly, trying to sustain at least the semblance of a conversation with him. "Do you suppose that's the avenue of sphinxes Raoul told us about? Didn't he say it was over a mile long, lined with human-headed beasts all the way?"

Aimée realized she was chattering. The sullen expression that darkened Edward's features, pulling his full lips into a

133

childish pout, warned her that the sound of her voice irritated him. In fact, she told herself, gazing up at him through lowered lashes, everything about the excursion seemed to irritate him. She wondered why he had come at all. It seemed to her he would have been happier in the camp with Buffy, lolling in the meager shade of his tent, a tall glass of sherbet in his hand.

She had been surprised when Buffy had not come with them. It was so completely out of character for him to decide to remain behind today.

Or *had* he decided to remain behind? she asked herself suddenly. Was that, perhaps, what this whole expedition was about, this excursion to a place Edward was not interested in, with a woman he did not care about? Was it nothing more than a need to thwart Buffy? To punish him for some real or imagined fault?

The image of Buffy's features, plump and peevishly sensuous, rose up, chilling the warmth of the bright desert sun. It had been nearly two months since Edward first sent Buffy to her room. As the second month drew to a close she did not know which she dreaded more, the possibility of discovering life growing within her body or the prospect of bearing more of Buffy's attentions.

"Do you suppose that's Ramses?" she asked quickly, pointing at a statue half-hidden by the shifting yellow sands. She was determined to push away thoughts too painful to dwell on. "Every time we see a statue, Raoul always says it's Ramses, so now I am beginning to think all the statues are of him."

She was chattering again, and she knew it. One glance at Edward was enough to tell her he was aware of it, too.

"Really, my dear, I have no way of knowing." The irritation in his voice made it clear he had no desire to pursue the subject. "Frankly, I can't understand why anyone would be interested in this old junk."

Aimée did not reply, knowing her continued chatter would only add to her husband's annoyance and boredom. It was a painful realization for her. All her life had been spent in an enchanted circle of love and attention. It was frightening to think of sharing the rest of her days with a man who was completely and utterly bored by her.

And yet if she was going to be honest about it, she had to admit she was every bit as bored with him. God help them both, was that what their life was to be like? Meeting occasionally in the common rooms of a series of houses, each a little more ostentatious and expensive than the last, and finding they had absolutely nothing to say to each other?

The donkey-drawn arabiya that took them back to the riverbank rambled through the narrow streets of the city. Aimée looked eagerly this way and that, enjoying the bustling excitement that vibrated all around her. How she would love to have been a part of it. She could think of nothing more pleasant than wandering with a guide through the lively streets, then returning home to lounge on one of the hotel verandas with the other ladies in their cotton dresses, sipping iced lemonade or sherbet and enjoying the roses that crept untamed through hedges of jasmine white with blossoms.

When Raoul had decided to stay on the other side of the river, giving up the comfort of a hotel to be near the excavation, Aimée had not been surprised. But when Edward, who had nothing to do with the actual work, insited on staying with him, she was appalled. It was the first concrete hint she had that the two men did not trust each other. The thought gave her a sense of foreboding.

As the carriage pulled up to the landing on the eastern bank of the Nile, the old boatman, Aziz, who had been lounging in the little dahabiya they rented for the season, leaped up to greet them. His filthy yellow robe glimmered in the sun as he hurried toward them. His lips were fixed in a permanent toothless grin, reminding her of old Ibrahim, their servant in Cairo.

In the shadow of the boat, a small figure stirred, jumping up belatedly to stare at them with solemn eyes. Aimée recognized the boy as young Ahmed, one of the more aggressive little urchins who flocked around the tourists in the marketplace and at the landing docks. With his thousand transparent ploys to wheedle an extra bit of baksheesh out of her, he, too, reminded her of Ibrahim, making her suddenly homesick for Cairo, a city she barely knew.

The lad, with one quick glance at Edward, called out a word of farewell to the old boatman, then turned to race along the riverbank. He was a shrewd judge of character, Aimée told herself grimly. Young as he was, even he sensed there was no generosity to be found at Edward's hands.

The late-afternoon sunlight turned the waters of the Nile dark gold as the dahabiya slid silently across its surface. The rich green of the far bank sparkled in the distance, an echo of the lush vegetation they were leaving behind. It seemed to Aimée that Egypt was divided into two separate and distinct lands: a narrow, verdant strip bordering both sides of the river, created by the fertile earth that spilled out of the Nile each flooding season; and the desolate wastes that lay on either side, as different from the river valley as night from day—or dreams from nightmares.

Only when they disembarked on the far side of the river did it become apparent that the resemblance between the two banks was a superficial one. To the ancient Egyptians, the land of the setting sun had been the realm of Osiris, their god of the underworld, and the barren deserts and desolate hillsides of the west were reserved for their Houses of Eternity. Surprisingly, modern men had followed the heathen customs, shunning the valleys of the dead for their homes and mosques, their bustling marketplaces and shops and profitable tourist hotels, leaving them as the centuries had left them, empty and alone, the domain only of Osiris and Annubis, the jackal god of the dead.

The scent of sugarcane and burseem was heavy in the air as they mounted the donkeys that were to carry them on the long journey inland. As often as she followed that path, it never ceased to fascinate her. There was a timeless, inviolate wonder about it that took her breath away. The long-robed fellahin broke the soil with the same crude plows the ancients had used, and the shadoofs—clumsy buckets swinging on long poles, balanced with a counterweight on the other end—had not changed since the time of Christ and before. Aimée reined in her donkey for a moment, marveling at the patience of the peasant who dipped a heavy bucket again and again into the water, swinging it around slowly to tilt its precious contents into one of the long irrigation canals.

The fertile belt of green ended abruptly, changing into an endless stretch of golden ochre as they passed the last of the fields and began to head into the desert hills. The dividing line between the greenery and the desert was sharp and dramatic, more stark than anything Aimée had ever seen before.

On the one side, everything was lush and green. On the other, there was nothing—absolutely nothing as far as she could see, only a dull, lifeless brown. The heat from the valley floor seemed to pick up the desert sand as it rose, drawing it upward until it distorted the color of the atmosphere itself. To Aimée it almost looked as if the yellow desert and the stark blue sky had blended into each other until she could no longer tell where one left off and the other began.

The pathway ahead led through a dry wadi to the Biban El-Malouk, the Valley of the Kings, where many of the mighty pharaohs had been laid to rest, their secret tombs only half-hidden from thieves of time by the shifting sands of the desert. The princes and the princesses, the lesser nobles and the queens, had their own Houses of Eternity carved out of the rocks in the surrounding foothills and valleys. It was in one of these areas that Raoul had chosen to dig.

A breeze had already begun to blow by the time they arrived at the camp, but it did not offer even a touch of coolness at the end of a sweltering day. The boy, Ahmed, had once told Aimée the Arabs hated the wind. Feeling its sultry touch against her skin, she could understand why. The breezes that sometimes came from the north were cooling and welcome, but the khamsin, the hot wind of the south, brought with it only arid heat as it whipped up the sand, driving it into their skin with stinging force.

As she dismounted, Aimée scanned the area where the men were working, curious to see if they had discovered anything that afternoon. She saw nothing more than routine late-afternoon activities. Mohammed Reis, Raoul's trusted foreman, assisted by the youngest of his three sons, Hassan, was methodically supervising the packing up of tools and equipment. Raoul himself was nowhere in sight.

Aimée was acutely conscious of a new pair of ghaffirs, lounging with deceptive nonchalance beside the steps that led down into an abandoned tomb Raoul had fitted out as a workshop. The sun glinted off the metal of their rifles, slung carelessly over their shoulders, and the blue fabric of their long galabiyas was crisscrossed with the dark lines of bandoliers. Aimée knew the men must have been hired by Raoul that morning, provided out of his own funds to counterbalance the other guards Edward had already taken on. Their presence was another reminder of the atmosphere of distrust that existed in the camp.

The tent that served Aimée as both sitting room and bedchamber was spacious and even elegant, but the late-afternoon heat made it unbearably stifling and close. Outside, in the shade of the flap that had been raised before the doorway, Aimée found breathing a little more tolerable, but the air was still heavy, and the wind blew the sand against her lips until they grated dryly across her teeth. Black flies clung to her eyelids as if they had been glued in place, resisting her as she reached up time and again with a weary hand to brush them away. She could not help casting long, envious glances at the shaded stairway that led deep into the tomb Raoul had chosen to occupy instead of a tent.

She smiled a little at herself, remembering how horrified she had been when Raoul said that he, together with the few workmen who would be staying with them in the valley, were actually going to live in the burial chambers. It seemed to her unthinkable. Even if they had been empty for thousands of years, they were still, after all, tombs, dark and filled with the odor of death.

Raoul had only laughed at her disgust. "Don't worry, my fine lady," he had assured her, making no effort to hide his sarcasm, "We'll put up elaborate tents for you and your party. But don't forget, the people of the desert have been taking refuge in these artificial caves for centuries. Perhaps one day you will understand why."

In a way, Aimée was forced to admit, Raoul had been right. She could never have lived in a tomb herself, not with all the ghosts that must linger in the darkness, but she could not deny they were infinitely more comfortable than her own tent. The air within them proved surprisingly dry and crisp, and the thick underground walls were protective, shutting out the blazing heat of the sun and the chill of the night, as well as the stinging force of the wind-blown sand.

Aimée was surprised at the dull pain that filled her heart when she thought of Raoul. She had hoped she would have forgotten him by now—forgotten her need both for the touch of his hand and for the warmth of his friendship. She closed her eyes for an instant, capturing an image of his face, the power of his dark, burning eyes. The pain in her heart expanded until she could barely catch her breath.

She understood that honor and reason both held him away from her, but even as she understood it, she knew she could never accept it. That she could not have his love, if indeed love had ever entered into what was between them, was a fact she did not question. She did not even hope for the physical semblance of love that had once almost been hers, for that, too, she sensed, was beyond her reach. But friendship, companionship, the ability to reach out her hand and know someone was there—surely that was not too much to ask. Even the strict tenets of her own faith did not deny that.

She felt her heart begin to beat faster, as if something in her own thoughts had frightened her. At first, she could not understand. When she did, she was startled by her audacity.

She was going to him. It was as simple as that. She was going to get up from her tent and walk slowly toward the stairway that led down into the tomb where he was working. She did not know when she had made that decision. She did not even know when it had first occurred to her as a possibility. She only knew she must do it.

Perhaps that was all it would take, she told herself nervously. Perhaps she only needed to go to him and tell him what was in her heart—well, not everything that was in her heart, of course, she would never dare to do that—and things would be all right between them again. Perhaps he only needed to know that she was asking for his friendship, not the physical solace they had nearly stolen with each other, that she would never do anything to put him in a compromising position with either his financial backer or the woman he had given his heart to. Perhaps then . . .

She was surprised to discover that she was not trembling as she rose and moved toward the stairway. The cold sweat in the palms of her hands was the only outward sign of her inner turmoil, and Raoul would never be able to see that.

Raoul had moved his worktable out of the crowded interior of the tomb, setting it up at the base of the steps where it could catch the last fading rays of afternoon light. His head was bent over the sheet in front of him, his pen poised in his hand. He did not even notice Aimée slip silently down the dark steps.

Aimée was acutely aware of his physical presence, just as she knew he had not yet felt hers. She found it strangely exciting to realize she still had time to change her mind, to turn around and slip away without ever letting him know she had been there. It gave her the heady sensation of being master of her own destiny. She did not know if it was courage that kept her there or the strength of her need for him—or simply the fear that she would not be able to get up the steps without stumbling.

"Raoul. . . ."

He glanced up from his work. In that instant, his eyes were frank and unguarded, giving Aimée a glimpse of remembered warmth. He caught himself quickly, tightening his expression into a mask of wary aloofness.

"What are you doing here?"

For a moment Aimée could not bring herself to answer. His tone was every bit as harsh as she had feared. When at last she spoke, she decided on a bold move.

"Why are you so angry with me, Raoul?" She made no effort to hide the hurt in her voice. "What have I done to make you despise me so much?"

His startled look told her he was taken aback by her question.

"I don't despise you, Aimée," he said quickly. She had put him on the defensive, and he didn't like it. "I just don't have time to coddle pampered females here. I warned you about that before, remember? I told you living here would be difficult and uncomfortable."

Aimée ignored his words, sensing he was using them as a screen to hide his true feelings.

"I thought once we were friends, Raoul," She almost smiled as she saw the look of confusion in his eyes. She had never seen him so unsure before.

"What do you mean?" He was even more aware of his own awkwardness than she was. "If you're remembering the vulgarity of my behavior that last time we were alone—"

"*Mon Dieu*, no," she gasped. It had never occurred to her he would misinterpret her words so grossly. "I don't mean *that*. I was just remembering the way you used to talk to me, as if you really enjoyed being with me and explaining things to me. That's all I'm asking for now, don't you understand? To be friends again—just to be friends."

Raoul's expression seemed to soften as he looked at her. Aimée hoped she was not imagining it simply because she wanted it to be there so much.

"Do you really think we can be friends, Aimée?" he asked gently. "Just friends?"

Aimée sensed that the moment had come to be truthful with one another. She was surprised to find how hard it was.

"I don't ask for you as a lover, Raoul," she whispered, half-choking on the shame of the words. "I have not forgotten that I am another man's wife, for all it may seem that way to you, nor that you are pledged to another woman. But I do ask for you as a friend, or if not as a friend, at least as someone I can talk to with a degree of amiability."

Raoul stared at her in admiration. How lovely she looked, and how wonderfully ingenuous. Did she really believe that little speech of hers? Did she really think they would just be friends, sitting down and talking to each other every now and then like two civilized human beings? Or was it another ploy, a clever trick to help her move close to him again? And did it really matter? Did he really think he could resist her, one way or the other?

"If we were to talk to each other," he said slowly, trying to keep all hint of surrender out of his voice, "what would you want to talk about?"

His coolness did not fool her. A surge of relief flooded through her body.

"Oh, Raoul," she cried out, her voice tremulous. "Everything! I want to talk about everything. There's so much I want you to explain to me, so much I want to know."

In spite of himself, Raoul could not help smiling at her enthusiasm. "And where does 'everything' begin, *petite*?"

Anxiously Aimée gazed around the small area in front of the tomb, searching for something to question him about. She sensed the good humor in his tone and did not want to give him time to change his mind.

"This," she cried eagerly, her eyes lighting on a wide sheet of paper spread on top of the worktable. "Tell me what on earth it is, and what you're doing with it."

Raoul turned the bulky paper around so she could see the dark lines that had been drawn across its surface in the pattern of a grid. "It's like a map," he explained patiently. "A picture of the area, but it's been marked off in squares so we can keep track of our progress. See these—the squares colored in with gray? They're the places we've dug already and haven't found anything. Only by doing this, by checking everything off methodically on a chart, can we be sure we haven't missed even the smallest area."

He watched the concentrated look on her face as she stared down at the grid, trying to make some sense out of it. After a moment, he burst out laughing.

"I did warn you, you know," he teased. "Archaeology is just routine hard work. It isn't glamorous at all."

"I never expected it to be," she replied quietly. Raoul, catching a hint of reproof in her tone, was painfully aware that his delight in her loveliness was beginning to grow again. It made him uncomfortable to realize there was nothing he could do about it.

"And there," he said, trying to cover his confusion by pointing at a small square in the corner of the grid, "that's where I found the funerary jars. Ramose's tomb, if it still exists, must be somewhere near there."

"Here?" Aimée leaned forward to brush her fingers against a cluster of unmarked squares. "In this place?"

Raoul felt his resistance melt at her eagerness. "Come on," he said impulsively, catching her hand and pulling her toward the stairway that led to the surface. He knew he was being a fool again, but he knew, too, there was no way he could stop himself. He needed desperately to communicate his enthusiasm for his work, almost as desperately as he needed to revel in the loveliness of the exotic, mockingly ingenuous child-woman who had enchanted him.

"Look around you," he told her eagerly, pulling her toward the area the workmen had been digging in that afternoon. "Do you see how much higher the land is here? How much rougher? It looks natural, and in a way it is now, for the sands of centuries have covered it, but once it was a dumping ground, an area where the debris from hollowed-out tombs was cast. If Ramose's tomb is here—and if for some reason its existence was unknown to ancient robbers—then that same debris might have acted as a natural shield, protecting it from later discovery."

All vestiges of his caution gone, Raoul took advantage of the last of the sunlight to show Aimée around the site, pointing out the places the workers had already excavated and those they still planned to dig. As they strolled along, Aimée felt as if she were wandering through a dream. It hardly seemed possible that she was walking beside Raoul, listening to him describe the many tombs, long since robbed and empty, that nestled into the dunes and hillsides. She was careful not to chatter or ask too many questions, fearing if she made herself too obtrusive she would break the friendship between them.

Mohammed Reis followed several steps behind them, waiting beside one of the tombs as Raoul guided her into the interior. Stooping low to keep from hitting her head on the entrance, Aimée squinted into an overwhelming void. She wished she had the courage to reach out and grasp Raoul's hand, for she was terrified she would stumble in the darkness, but she knew she did not dare. Thick dust coated the inside of her mouth and nose with every breath she took, burning her lungs until it was all she could do to keep from coughing. She choked it back, desperately afraid that Raoul would interpret her weakness as a sign of frivolity or a lack of determination.

A welcome beam of light suddenly illuminated the inside of the tomb. Startled, Aimée glanced toward the entrance. Mohammed was standing in the shadows, a mirror shining in his hand. It took her a minute to see what he was doing. He had turned the mirror toward the late-afternoon sun, catching its rays and reflecting them into the interior of the tomb.

Aimée was delighted. "How clever!" she cried out, forgetting she had vowed to be quiet and unobtrusive. "How did you ever think of that?"

Raoul only laughed. "It's appropriate that you should see the tomb this way," he explained. "Not with a torch or a lantern. Only, I didn't think of it at all. The technique is thousands of years old. This is much the way tombs were illuminated in ancient days."

The dust was still heavy in her throat and nostrils, a constant, nagging irritation, but Aimée barely noticed it after the first few minutes. The tomb was too fascinating to allow room in her mind for anything else.

Raoul had chosen the place well. Although it had obviously been used as a dwelling place, perhaps for centuries, and many of the walls and ceilings had been blackened by soot, there was a single chamber deep in the interior where the decorations had been preserved intact, their colors as sharp and vivid as the day they had been painted thousands of years before. The walls in this tiny room were crowded with hundreds of strange, bright, two-dimensional forms. Aimée stood gaping at them in wonder.

The dominant painting was that of a woman, her body distorted and elongated until it stretched all the way across the black background of the ceiling. She was the goddess Nut, Raoul explained, the deity of the sky, and the stars that decorated her form represented her kingdom at night. The golden ball that seemed to skim across the ceiling was in reality the sun. The Egyptians believed that Nut swallowed the sun every evening at twilight, letting it pass through her torso so she could give birth to it again every morning in a constant renewal of the miracle of life.

The paintings on the walls were even more complex, representing scenes from the Egyptian Book of the Dead. Aimée watched in fascination as Raoul pointed out figure after figure from the strange tableaux. Although she could not understand all the unfamiliar names, much less remember them, some of the personalities caught her fancy. There was Annubis, the god with the head of a sharp-eared jackal, calmly adjusting the scales that would weigh the dead man's heart against a feather. Behind him crouched an odd, humorous figure, a creature with a crocodile's head and a body that seemed a composite of several African animals. Raoul called it the devouress.

"In case the man fails the test," he told her impishly.

She shivered at the thought. The painting no longer seemed quite so quaint and charming. Two-dimensional as the creature was, Aimée caught a hungry glint in its eye, as if it were only too eager to gobble up the heart of a dead man, denying him his immortality.

But the figure that stood out most was the tall white form of Osiris, the powerful god of the underworld. Slender and immobile, it seemed to Aimée he had been wrapped up in long linen tapes, like the mummies whose eternity he dominated. She amused herself by walking around the small chamber, trying to pick out his shape from among the various scenes painted on the walls. She was amazed and delighted when she spotted one image painted in a vivid green.

"How incongruous," she cried out, laughing aloud at the sight. It looked like something from a child's book, boldly colored without the least regard for nature or reality.

"Incongruous?" Raoul asked with a smile. "Not really. You see, Osiris was not only the god of the underworld, but of vegetation as well."

"Death and vegetation at the same time?" Aimée was horrified. "But that . . . that's disgusting!"

"Not *death*," Raoul explained gently. "The ancient Egyptians did not believe in death—only a continuation of life. The pharaohs were earthly incarnations of the sun, swallowed each night by the sky and born again each morning. To them, the moment of death was but a single night, followed by a continual cycle of rebirth throughout eternity. The whole earth was part of that cycle, dying a little each winter, only to come alive in the spring as bright green seedlings burst forth from fertile soil."

Raoul was keenly aware of Mohammed's presence as he led Aimée out into the sunlight again. He was intensely grateful that the man was there, making it impossible for him to lay even a protective hand on her arm. He was not sure he would have been able to react to her so calmly if they had been alone.

They had time to explore just one more tomb. Aimée found it even more intriguing than the first. The pictures on these walls were less somber, less symbolic, and infinitely more human. They were typical, Raoul told her, of the paintings in many of the tombs, a celebration not of the ritual of death but of the extension of life it symbolized. Painted workers toiled in painted fields, cutting the grain and carrying it to granaries where it could be counted by the scribes, and vineyard laborers trampled dark red grapes beneath their feet, sampling their yield until they could barely keep from bursting into song. Household servants busied themselves plucking geese and bottling beer, and wealthy ladies of leisure, ornate in jeweled collars and rings and bracelets, sipped wine at banquets while little cones of wax melted slowly on their heavy black wigs, releasing a sweet fragrance into the air.

They were not without whimsy either, Aimée noticed, these artists of ancient times. They seemed to have stamped their own individual humor into their work, capturing two little girls in a corner, furiously tugging each other's hair, or a scroungy yellow cat hiding under his master's chair to enjoy the fish he had stolen from the table—even a tipsy lady, unashamed of having enjoyed herself a little too much, relieving her discomfort into the basin held out to her by a slave girl.

"Oh, Raoul," Aimée cried, as twilight forced them out into the darkness at last. "It is all so fascinating, so exciting. I hope we find Ramose's tomb soon—tomorrow!"

"Perhaps we will," he replied lightly. His heart was aching as he looked down at her, watching the last rays of the sun paint her cheeks a becoming shade of pink. "Perhaps it will be tomorrow."

But the next day proved uneventful, as did the day after that. It was fully a week before there was any break in their routine. By that time, tempers were already running short. Buffy was whining about the heat, and Edward had begun to make ominous noises about giving the whole thing up as a bad business. Even Aimée was discouraged, feeling perhaps that their task was a hopeless one. Only Raoul remained calm and unperturbed, as if he had long since learned to accept drudgery and disappointment as a routine part of his work.

It was midmorning, and Raoul was working in the large tomb he had chosen for a workshop, fitting a last heavy wooden shelf into the wall in anticipation of the treasures he hoped to find. Aimée had drifted in to watch him, taking care to sit quietly in a shadowy corner so her presence would not disturb him. She had no premonition that anything was about to happen, no sense that that day was to be any different from the rest. Even when Mohammed Reis hurried into the tomb, stumbling in his eagerness, she barely turned her head to look at him.

"Quick, *monsieur*," Mohammed gasped, choking on the words as he struggled to catch his breath. "Come quick!"

Raoul let the board he was working on fall noisily to the ground as he turned to his foreman.

"What is it?"

"A step, *monsier*. The workmen have found a stone step leading into the earth."

Aimée's heart skipped a beat. Could this be it? Could this really be the moment they had been waiting for? Anxiously she looked at Raoul. He shook his head disapprovingly.

145

"Is that all, Mohammed? You know better than to get worked up over a thing like that. There are dozens of empty tombs in this area, and all of them have steps."

Aimée could hardly believe her ears. After all the weeks of preparation, all the long, hard days of searching, how could Raoul dismiss his foreman's announcement so cavalierly?

Mohammed looked abashed. "I am sorry, *monsier*. You are right, of course. We have been foolish. I will tell the men."

Only after he had left did Raoul turn toward Aimée, noting her bitter disappointment.

"We'll look at it tomorrow, *petite*," he promised. But I don't want you to get your hopes up. No doubt it's just another dead end."

Aimée let herself sink wearily onto a large stone that stood in a corner of the workshop. It seemed to her she had never been so tired or so discouraged in her life. She knew Raoul was right. She knew there was only a chance in a thousand, maybe a chance in a million, that this was what they were looking for. But it had felt so good, so exciting, to be able to hope for a moment. She could hardly bear to let go of that hope now.

Slowly she let her eyes drift upward to meet Raoul's. She caught a hint of laughter in their depths.

4

Raoul promised Aimée they would investigate the stone steps the next day. What he did not tell her was that he planned to take his own sweet time about it. She could hardly believe it the next morning as she watched him amble nonchalantly toward the area where the workmen had begun to gather, drawing out stakes and ropes to mark off another square of his grid, across the site from the step. It almost seemed that he had completely forgotten about its discovery.

The sun was already high in the sky before anyone moved toward the single stone step that had been uncovered the day before. Even then, it was not Raoul but Mohammed who approached the place with his tools, accompanied first by his eldest son, Daoud, then by the youngest, Hassan. To Aimée, standing in the hot sun beside the shallow pit, watching as the steps began to emerge slowly from the sand, the men seemed uninterested, almost bored with their task. Realistically, she had to admit they were right. If there were any reason to hope for anything—anything at all—Raoul would never have been able to stand aside so calmly.

Aimée remembered the words she had heard only the day before. *Don't get your hopes up*, petite. But, fool that she was, she had refused to believe him, dwelling instead on that small glint of laughter she caught in his expression, pretending to herself all the time he was only teasing her. Now at last she had to admit the truth. Raoul had told her not to get her hopes up for one reason, and one only—he did not want her to be disappointed.

There would be nothing at the bottom of those steps. Nothing but a black gaping hole where a sealed door should have been. Nothing but another card in Raoul's files, inked in with the discouraging words so familiar to archaeologists: "Robbed in antiquity."

Mohammed and his sons had already gouged a deep hole into the earth before Raoul finally joined them. When he did, Aimée sensed a subtle change in the character of the dig, an undercurrent of excitement that had not been there before. The pit was now almost as deep as the height of a man, effectively screening their stooped forms from watching eyes.

"They'll find it, you know."

The whispered tones, hissed into her ear, startled Aimée. Turning her head, she saw Buffy Montmorency crouching on the sand at the edge of the steps. She had been so engrossed in the work she had not even heard him approach. His eyes danced with fiery highlights.

"What do you mean?"

In spite of herself, Aimée's hopes began to rise. Something in Buffy's excitement eyes was contagious.

"I have ways of knowing," Buffy replied slowly, staring at the workmen. "You forget, I am a child of the streets. You can't survive on the streets if you don't develop a sixth sense."

Aimée stared at him, surprised at his words. Buffy had never talked about himself before, at least not in front of her. It unnerved her to think of him as a human being with fears and feelings, just like herself. She was glad his attention was concentrated on the men. She would not have liked him to see her confusion.

Slowly she turned back toward the steps. The men were digging much faster now, and had gone much deeper. There was a new urgency in their work; they no longer seemed careless or nonchalant. Curious, Aimée began to ease her way down the steps, hesitating for a moment at the bottom. Then, gathering up her courage, she touched Raoul lightly on the arm.

He spun around to face her, almost as if he had forgotten she was there.

"What on earth are you doing?" she asked, "I mean, why all this secrecy . . . this pretense?"

Raoul paused, leaning on the handle of his shovel. The corners of his eyes crinkled up.

"Surely you didn't expect us to advertise our discovery, *petite*. If the men found out what was happening, word would be all over town before we finished digging. The authorities would be here in no time."

"But what difference does that make? You have a permit to dig, don't you?"

"To dig, yes," he agreed, laughing. "But not to take things away. We would have to give everything we find to the government. That would hardly suit your husband—or me."

Aimée could hardly believe her ears. The sound of his laughter only reinforced her mounting horror.

"Don't look so shocked, *petite*," he told her, still laughing. "We are not quite the despicable blackguards you seem to think. Or at least I am not. I don't give a damn who gets the things in the end. I just don't want a lot of incompetents stomping all over the place, trampling things under their clumsy feet and taking them away before they have been properly assessed and recorded. I promise you, they would not be above selling trinkets to the tourists . . . or requisitioning more important pieces to bribe high officials."

He was silent for a moment. When he continued, his voice was light and teasing. "Besides, all this is just conjecture. There's probably nothing down there but an empty hole."

They were not to learn the truth that afternoon, for despite their redoubled efforts it was obvious they could not reach the bottom before nightfall. To Aimée's amazement, Raoul insisted on refilling the pit halfway to the top, a deterrent, he told her with a wry smile, against any curious workmen who might be tempted to come back and see what they had been doing all afternoon.

When work recommenced in the morning, again with Mohammed and two of his sons, the men continued at the same slow pace, playing their little game of secrecy as long as they were still visible to watching eyes. But this time their work went faster, for the earth was already loose and easy to move. By early afternoon they had reached the bottom, but Raoul, with the same caution that had marked all his moves, would not let them go on. Aimée could see by the tension in all their faces—Mohammed and his sons, her own husband and his lover—that they were all as anxious as she to see what lay beyond that last shallow layer of sand, but Raoul was adamant. To Aimée's surprise, even Edward did not try to dissuade him.

Twilight had already begun to lay a soft mantle of gray over the desert before Raoul at last decided it was safe to return to the steps. Aimée stood breathlessly behind him as he cleared the last of the sand away with a soft brush. As she watched him, she knew he was thinking the same thing they were all thinking, praying the same thing they were praying.

If only there was a sealed door in the doorway. If only it was not a dark, empty space.

It was a moment before Raoul could work through the sand. When at last he managed to push his hand through, it came in contact with cold, hard stone. He tried to control his exhilaration as he turned to tell the others, for he was well aware that there were other pitfalls to come.

He worked slowly, taking care not to let his eagerness cause thoughtless damage as he brushed the sand away from the heavy rectangular stones that sealed the doorway. It was at least an hour before the entire area was uncovered. Anxiously his eyes scanned its broad surface. In the dim twilight he could find no telltale signs of tampering.

"Get me a lantern."

It was Hassan, his eyes almost as bright as Raoul's, who raced up the steps, returning only a moment later with a lantern in his hand. Raoul reached out slowly to take it from him. Even more slowly he turned back to the doorway, raising the light, then lowering it again as he studied every inch of the thick stone blocks.

Aimée barely dared to breathe as she watched him. She saw him lean forward, squinting into the dim light as he examined the edge of the doorway. Carefully he raised his hand to run it lightly across the surface. It was a while before Aimée realized what he was doing. When she did, she felt as if her heart had stopped beating.

It must be the seal—the seal that marked the final closing of the tomb. If it was intact, so was Raoul's dream. If it was not . . .

Slowly, with visible effort, Raoul rose and turned to face

them. Aimée did not need to hear his words. His expression was enough to tell her what he had seen.

"The seal has been broken."

Broken! *Mon Dieu*, all their hopes, all their dreams, gone in the brief space of a single word. The seal had been broken, and the tomb opened.

"Then it has been plundered?"

Raoul did not attempt a reply. Stepping aside, he made room for her to move up to the door and examine it herself. One glance was enough to tell her there could be no mistake. The seal had been so badly crushed and mangled it was barely recognizable. She ran her fingers across the surface, as Raoul had done only a moment before. The edges of the hieroglyphs felt strange beneath her skin.

"What does it say?" she asked softly. "Can you read it?"

"I'm not sure. It's been so badly damaged it's hard to tell, but I think . . . Yes, I'm positive. It's the seal of the pharaoh Akhenaten."

Aimée's heart caught in her throat. Raoul had told her the tomb they were seeking, the last resting place of the prince Ramose, belonged to the era of Akhenaten. There could be little doubt now that they had found it.

But they were three thousand years too late!

Bitterly she glanced back at the doorway, letting her eyes drift up and down the dark stones. She was barely aware of what she was doing. She knew only that she could not bring herself to turn and face Raoul's disappointment. Suddenly, she caught sight of something unexpected on the lower part of the door. She leaned down to examine it more closely.

"Look at that, Raoul. Doesn't that look like another seal?"

She did not add that this seal seemed to be in better condition than the first. She did not need to. Raoul had already stooped to examine it, pushing the lantern toward it so he could see better. It was a long time before he rose. When he did, there was a new, cautious note in his voice.

"It seems to be intact."

"Akhenaten again?"

Raoul shook his head slowly. "Not Akhenaten . . . Tutankhamon."

"Tutan . . ." Aimée stumbled over the unfamiliar word.

Raoul repeated it slowly. "Tut-ankh-amon. The pharaoh who followed Akhenaten. We know little about him except that he came to the throne as a young boy and ruled only a few years."

"But what does it mean?" she asked, still puzzled. "Why would there be two seals?"

"I'm afraid it can mean only one thing, the tomb was originally sealed in the time of Akhenaten. Sometime after that—probably during the reign of Tutankhamon—it must have been opened and plundered. When the damage was discovered, it was resealed by the boy king or his agents."

Aimée felt her heart sink. "But why?" she asked, feeling a sudden burst of anger at the tantalizing hopes the seal had seemed to offer. "Why shut the thing up again if it was already plundered? Unless . . ."

She left the thought unspoken, not even daring to speak the words aloud. She did not need to. One look at Raoul was enough to tell her he was thinking the same thing.

If the tomb was already empty, there would have been no point resealing it. The fact that the boy king went to all that trouble could only mean there was something left in there worth protecting.

Wordlessly Raoul turned back to the doorway. Placing the lantern on the ground, he began to gouge with a small pick at the edges of one of the stones. It was nearly an hour before he could work it loose. In all that time, not a single word was spoken. There was not a sound, not even a harsh breath to break the heavy silence.

Finally Raoul managed to ease the stone out of position. Pulling it away from the doorway, he turned to place it in the waiting hands of Mohammed Reis. The space it left was black and impenetrable.

"Give me a candle," Raoul said quietly, not even glancing toward the blazing lantern at his feet. Daoud, Mohammed's oldest son, reached into the heavy folds of his galabiya, pulling out a slender taper. Raoul's hands were steady as he grasped it, striking a light and touching it to the wick. Aimée marveled at his self-control. She had expected to see him press his face eagerly against the dark hole. Instead, he stood back from it, easing the candle cautiously inside. She watched as it flickered, then slowly died away.

Mohammed nodded knowingly. "Gases."

"Perhaps," Raoul agreed. "Or perhaps just the breeze caused by too anxious a hand. "Let's try again."

Moving with slow deliberation, he struck another light, fumbling awkwardly as it went out in his hand. Lighting still another, he finally managed to coax the wick into a tiny golden glow. This time he moved even more carefully as he pushed the candle through the hole. The flame did not waver.

Taking care not to extinguish the flame, Raoul moved closer to the darkness. His body was immobile as he stood and stared at a sight he had waited years to see. To the watchers in the shadows behind him the suspense was agonizing. It was Edward who broke under the strain first.

"What is it?" he cried out anxiously. "Dammit, what do you see?"

Raoul's face was deathly pale as he turned back to them. His eyes burned like two dark embers.

"You wouldn't believe it if I told you." His voice was so soft it was barely audible. "By God, I don't even believe it myself."

Edward reached out abruptly, his hand shaking as he struggled to wrench the candle from Raoul's grasp. Raoul, jolted suddenly back to reality, turned to face him. His icy anger was enough to stay Edward's hand in midair.

"Your wife first," Raoul said coldly. With a surprisingly gentle hand he touched Aimée's waist, guiding her toward the provocatively murky hole. He pressed the candle into her hand.

Edward's body trembled with anger at Raoul's arrogant assumption of command, but he was careful to make no overt objections. He was not in a position to defy the expert he had hired to help him satisfy his greed, and he knew it. He forced himself to take a step backward, leaving the area free for his wife.

The hot wax dripping down the side of the candle burned Aimée's skin, but she barely noticed it. She was intensely aware of the suspense of the moment. Years later, when she remembered the events of that day, she could not recall what she had expected to see, but certainly not the sight that met her eyes. Nothing had prepared her for anything like it.

Everywhere she looked, her eyes fell on gold—a bright, burnished fire out of the darkness of three thousand years ago. It took her a few seconds to distinguish individual forms amid the glittering mass: a heavy, curiously graceful cow's head with gilded horns; an oversized black dog, its paws outstretched, its pointed ears touched with the same gold that lingered everywhere in the chamber; piles of delicately painted boxes on gilded sleighs, and long etched horns leaning against the walls, and gleaming jeweled shrines; and dominating everything, two massive black statues guarding the single door on the far side of the room like a pair of gigantic African slaves.

Aimée scarcely breathed the whole time she was staring at

152

the treasures. She barely managed to catch her breath when at last she stepped back, relinquishing the candle to Edward's waiting hand. In a daze of wonder and disbelief, she watched as, one after another, the men peered into the secrets of the tomb. She sensed from the expressions on their faces as they pulled back again that the things they saw were beyond even their wildest dreams.

She had expected the men to set to work immediately, tearing at the walls in their eagerness to get at the treasures. She was amazed when they showed no inclination to do anything of the kind. Even Edward, frantic as he was to get a return on his investment, did not press them to hurry.

Instead, they began almost immediately to cover the traces of everything they had already done, working through the night to seal the tomb as thoroughly as the ancients had sealed it thousands of years before. First they rigged up a hurried, makeshift shell of timbers and loose boards around the doorway, creating a protective antechamber in front of the entrance; then, turning to their shovels once again, they began to fill in the stairway with earth, tamping it down and covering it with loose sand until it could barely be distinguished from the landscape around it. They did not leave until it was nearly dawn. When they did, it was almost impossible to tell they had been there at all.

The next morning, Aimée stood beside Raoul, surveying the site with astonishment. Looking at it, she could barely believe the place had ever been touched by human hands. It was almost as if the whole thing had never happened, as if it were all part of an extravagant dream.

"But this is crazy, Raoul," she protested, thinking of all the work that had been undone when they blocked the stairway up again. "If we cover everything like that, how will we get at it again?"

Raoul glanced down at her, trying to pretend that he did not notice the way the sun shone on her dark hair or picked up the fiery highlights in her deep blue eyes.

"The same way the other robbers did," he told her. "They needed secrecy even more than we do. The ancient priests would have had them put to death if they caught them robbing the royal tombs."

Aimée soon learned that Raoul meant his words literally. The robbers of ancient times had devised ingenious systems to get at the wealth in the tombs. The complex network of tunnels they had built, crisscrossing the hills and valleys of the dead, had grown until it was a vast labyrinth of hidden passageways beneath the earth. It was these tunnels Raoul was planning to use.

The scheme was not quite as simple as it seemed when Raoul first explained it to Aimée. The tunnels were extensive, but they led only to tombs the robbers had known about, not to the last secret resting place of a prince even the past seemed to have overlooked. To reach that tomb, Raoul had to calculate the nearest spot in the existing network, then branch off with a tunnel of his own, aiming for the small, crude antechamber he himself had made. It would be arduous work, complicated by the fact that he could trust no one except Mohammed and his three sons.

Raoul was not surprised when Edward, eager as he was to get at the treasures his money had procured for him, did not offer to take his turn with a pick and shovel. Nor did he expect anything more from Buffy Montmorency. When on the second day of the digging Buffy suddenly offered to help, Raoul was taken aback. One glance at the man's hands was enough to tell him he would be of little use, but common sense warned him not to refuse. There would be enough friction with Lord Edward in the days that lay ahead. He dared not antagonize him now by insulting the man who seemed as much his protégé as his employee.

Buffy saw Raoul's disdain. It amused him, as everything else on the dig had amused him. He knew it would be even more amusing to watch that same expression fade into surprise.

Buffy had no doubt about his ability to keep up with the others. For all of the softness of his last few years, he was still a child of the slums, conditioned to fight for a crust of bread—or to kill if need be for a scrap of meat. A few blisters on his hands would not stop him. He was at least the match of any man in those tunnels.

Besides, it was exhilarating, he told himself as he crawled through the darkness, stooping in the low passages to drag out bags of dirt and dump them in abandoned tunnels. It was exhilarating and exciting. With a pick in his hand he could be part of the dig, truly a part of it, in a way Eddie with all his wealth and power could never hope to be.

As the hours passed into days in the loneliness of the long, silent passages, Buffy began to think of the tomb they were struggling toward as something that was exclusively his. It was not Raoul's discovery, though his expertise had led them to it, and certainly not Edward's, for all that his money had bought it, but his, Buffy's—his alone. It gave him a heady sense of power to think of all those golden treasures as his own private possessions.

It was two weeks before they stood again in front of the doorway that led to the tomb. Once again it was twilight, for even though they had broken into the antechamber early in the morning, Raoul refused to arouse the workmen's suspicion by pulling everyone away from the excavation at the same time. It seemed to Aimée that the tension in the small cramped room was even greater than before.

Dammit," Edward cried out, his patience snapping at last, "break the door down. There's no need for caution now. No one can see us."

Raoul whirled to face him, his eyes blazing with barely controlled anger. "We have an agreement, Ellingham. I excavate the tomb as I see fit—*then* you lay your filthy hands on the treasure. Is that perfectly clear?"

Edward's face turned ashen, but he did not speak. Even had he been a physical match for Raoul, it was obvious that he was outnumbered by the other man's supporters. But his eyes flashed an angry challenge. Both he and Raoul knew it was a challenge that would never be stilled again.

For the moment, Raoul chose to ignore it. Moving coolly and casually, as if there were no tension in the room—as if all the treasure did not lie only yards away from their grasp—he began to set up his equipment. The tight confines of the area made it too dangerous to explode chemicals to illuminate the place for photography, but he did not let that discourage him. Drawing out his notebook, he made quick sketches of the doorway from every angle, supplementing them with pages of notes in his own shorthand, notes he would copy out later in more legible form. Then there were paper squeezes to be taken of each of the seals—the one that was broken as well as the one still intact—and dozens of measurements to be made with tapes and plumb lines and leveling instruments. It seemed to Aimée as she watched him, working with such painful precision, that her own patience would soon grow as thin as Edward's.

Only once did Raoul come out of his absorption for an instant to glance up at her. His eyes danced with hints of laughter when he saw the expression on her face.

"I warned you, *petite*," he reminded her. "Archaeology isn't glamorous at all—just plain hard work."

Aimée refrained from retorting sharply that she was beginning to see what he meant. She sensed that, beneath all that cool composure, he was just as impatient as she, just as eager to break through the wall and see what lay beyond it.

It was nearly midnight before Raoul was at last ready to begin removing the stones that blocked the doorway. Even then the task did not proceed swiftly. Each individual stone had to be numbered, its precise position recorded meticulously in Raoul's notebook, before he would let Mohammed help him ease it out of the wall. Then Daoud or one of his younger brothers would reach out with waiting hands, piling the stones neatly in a corner of the antechamber.

Finally, after at least an hour of effort, the doorway was open. Golden highlights shone in the darkness, startling in their intensity. For a moment, no one moved or spoke.

Then at last Raoul reached down, gripping the handle of the lantern tightly and slowly stepped forward. Automatically Aimée began to follow him. She did not even notice that the others had remained behind, hesitating on the threshold. She and Raoul were alone in the narrow aisle that led halfway to the shallow wall at the side of the tomb.

The instant Aimée stepped into the dark chamber, she felt the cold begin to seep into her flesh. There was an illusion of icy dampness, even in the arid atmosphere of the tomb, and the dust that stung her nostrils was heavy and choking, catching in her throat and filling her lungs. The smell of the place was sweet and stale. It was a smell that was hauntingly familiar. It took her a moment to realize what it was.

It was the smell of an old attic, filled with the decaying fabrics of a previous time. The smell of dried corsages, fragile and crumbling, rotting away.

It was the smell of death.

Aimée caught her breath at the thought. She wondered how she could have forgotten it. In the excitement of the moment, in the greed that surrounded the gold she had glimpsed for just an instant, it had not occurred to her to remember where she was. Perhaps it was Raoul's fault. He had made it all sound so intriguing, so exotic. Now she was forced to remember that a House of Eternity was in reality a tomb.

And somewhere in that tomb, somewhere in those dark, hidden depths, there lay a man, a man who had once lived and breathed and laughed, a man whose limbs were now wrapped in long white strips of linen. She closed her eyes, suddenly faint at the thought.

Raoul sensed her hesitation. Turning, he took her hand securely in his.

His grip was strong and comforting, making Aimée forget

everything else. There was no tomb around her, taunting her with eerie sensations, no husband lingering in the doorway staring at her, there was not even a beautiful English fiancée, threatening to arrive at any instant to mar her happiness. There was only Raoul standing beside her, his hand warm in hers.

Gently he drew her closer. With the warmth of his body next to hers, Aimée at last let herself look up. She was no longer frightened or awed to gaze on the last earthly vanity of a man who had lived—and died—three thousand years ago.

The treasures looked no different now than they had when she dared only to peek at them through a narrow opening in the doorway. She could see more of the details, but in reality the details did not make any difference, The cow's head, one of the first things she had noticed, was attached to a full figure, completely visible now, but the impact of its shimmering profusion of gold was no more—or less—stunning than it had been before. The sharp-eared black dog, seen at closer view, looked more like an ebony jackal, its dark body half-covered by a fraying linen cloth, but there was still an aura of fantasy about it.

Perhaps that was the problem, she told herself, surprised at the thought. Perhaps it was all too splendid, too glittering and awesome. Perhaps later, as they began to open the boxes, bringing to light the clothing and the jewels, the utensils and the games, all the thousand and one little everyday items that had been part of this man's life and were now his private stake in eternity—perhaps then she would be able to feel the full impact. Now she could not even comprehend it.

She turned back to the doorway, content at last to leave the place. Raoul's hand was still in hers as he followed her toward the spot where the others were waiting. Only when they had nearly reached the threshold did he stop abruptly, his whole body taking on a sudden tautness. Curiously, she looked up at him.

He was staring not at the doorway they were approaching but at the wall to the side of it. The entire space was taken up with a single painting, but as Aimée turned toward it, she saw nothing that could have caused his reaction. It appeared to be a family grouping, a tall man followed by the smaller figures of a woman and a boy. The style was oddly childlike and two-dimensional, much like the paintings she had seen in the other tombs. But even to her untutored eyes it seemed to be marked by a crude, unique fluidity, as if it were intended more as a caricature than a portrait.

Only as she studied the figure of the man who dominated the painting did Aimée catch a hint of what Raoul must have felt. There was a powerful, commanding force to his presence, though she could not for the life of her figure out what it was. The man wore the double crowns of Upper and Lower Egypt, marking him as a pharaoh, but aside from that there was nothing regal about his appearance. His body was awkward, almost deformed, with distended belly and wide, feminine hips; and his face, accented by a strange, elongated head, was narrow and unpleasant, with pendulous lips. He was, Aimée thought, the ugliest man she had ever seen in her life.

She turned back to Raoul. Sensing her gaze, he glanced down for an instant. His lips formed a single word.

"Akhenaten."

Akhenaten! At last Aimée understood. Akhenaten, the pharaoh who had defied the gods—the mad dreamer Raoul longed to study. Akhenaten, the ruler whose era was one of the most fascinating in Egyptian history. She knew the triumph that was Raoul's at that moment.

Even more curious now, Aimée let her gaze drift back toward the painting. This time she found her eyes focusing not on the pharaoh himself but on the lithe form lingering a few paces behind him. It seemed to her, even in those stylized lines, that the woman was incredibly lovely—dark and child-like and so fragile it looked as if she would break if anyone reached up to touch her. There was an air of sadness about her, a hint of loss and mourning as poignant as it was timeless.

"Who is she?" she asked softly.

Raoul turned his gaze to the girl. "We don't know," he replied gently. "Perhaps we never will. Archaeology is like that. Often these people are never anything more than an anonymous painting on a tomb."

Aimée continued to stare at the girl. She felt a renewal of the same cold foreboding that had swept over her when she entered the tomb.

This time as she began to cross the threshold, Aimée knew she would not look back. She had caught a sense of death and sorrow in the young woman's bearing. It was an emotion she did not want to face. Slipping her hand out of Raoul's, she pushed past the others, making her way out into the fresher air of the antechamber.

Suddenly she was no longer sure she was going to enjoy the days that lay ahead, browsing through the boxes and jars and shrines that filled the tomb. It was not going to be the fun she had imagined—not the childish game of rifling through old trunks in someone's attic, dressing up in quaint gowns and giggling at absurd outdated hats. It would not be trunks her hands would violate in this place, but the secret recesses of a man's private life; and it would not be old-fashioned hats and dresses she would find, but all the grief and loneliness and personal tragedy that made up the sum total of his life.

The memory of Raoul's words echoed in her ears. *Archaeology is not glamorous* he had told her, *not glamorous at all.* It was proving a painful lesson to learn how right he was.

She watched the men set a wooden grille across the doorway, locking it securely into place. The swaying light of the lantern cast dark, undulating shadows along the floor.

The next evening at sunset Aimée lingered on the steps of the workshop, hesitating to make her way through the labyrinth of tunnels to the tomb where the men would soon be working. In the deep crimson of twilight, the desert was a majestic place, its sands stretching toward the eternity the ancients had yearned for, its mountains reaching upward for the last rays of the sun.

A single black form cut through the cloudless red of the sky, winging its way in long, sweeping arcs toward the arid valleys of the dead. As it drew near, Aimée recognized it as a solitary raven, its lonely path strangely far from the cool waters and fertile green banks of the Nile. Hugging her arms around her knees, she stared at the bird, watching as it drew closer and closer to the spot where she sat.

She was so engrossed in the raven she did not even notice Raoul approach. The sound of his voice startled her.

"Perhaps it is the *ba* of Prince Ramose."

The sudden intensity of the quizzical glance she threw him made Raoul regret his words instantly. Too late he remembered how deeply she had been affected by the tomb the night before. He sensed he had made a mistake reminding her now of the mysticism of the ancient world.

"The Egyptians believed a man has two spirits," he explained reluctantly, trying to keep the words as dry and academic as he could. "The *ka* is a separate entity, created at the moment of a man's creation to guide him through the treacheries of life and the dark realms of death. But the *ba* is different. The *ba* is an integral part of a man's essence, tied to his physical being throughout his life. Only after death can the *ba* at last leave the body, taking the form of a bird to revisit earthly haunts. But at sunset it must return to the tomb, reuniting the spiritual and physical man for the long night's journey through the underworld."

Aimée listened to his words in silence. Turning away from him, she scanned the skies for the dark form that had already begun to mingle with the darkening shadows of twilight. She had been deeply moved by Raoul's words. She could not truly believe the raven was the essence of the man who lay in the tomb, a living incarnation in an eternity that had already reached through centuries; yet in a strange way, she found herself drawn to the story. She had sensed a sadness in that tomb the night before, a kind of lonely pain that was too much to bear. It eased her heart to equate it now with the graceful freedom of the bird's flight.

Squinting into the last blazing bursts of color that still touched the edge of the horizon, Aimée continued to search for the dark, solitary form. It had vanished.

Turning back to Raoul, she saw that he, too, had disappeared, slipping away while she had searched the heavens for a raven that was no longer there.

The twilight air suddenly felt chilly against her skin. She had never been so alone in her life.

5

Two factors had marked the opening of the tomb—stealth and meticulousness. Aimée soon learned they were to be the keynotes for the entire excavation.

Each morning, as he had done since the day they arrived in the valley, Raoul would set off with his tools, joining Mohammed and his sons in the corner of the site where the workers were fruitlessly digging. There he would remain for the bulk of the morning, slipping away only when he was sure he had stayed long enough not to arouse suspicion. Even then he was careful to leave Mohammed and at least one of his older sons behind, cautioning them to remain in full sight of the men at all times. Only Hassan, because he was the youngest and had the least responsibility, dared absent himself for long periods of time.

As a result, the work progressed slowly. The effect was

only heightened by Raoul's compulsive attention to every detail, no matter how minute or insignificant it might seem.

He dared risk the use of dangerous chemicals only a few times to photograph the outer chamber of the tomb exactly as it had been discovered, but he did not overlook anything else. Every piece that was touched or moved had to be sketched and recorded first, its exact position measured from every conceivable angle. Even Aimée, although she was beginning to understand how important it was for archaeologists to know where each piece had been found, and what its relationship was to every other piece in the tomb, found herself growing impatient as she watched the calculated slowness of his pace.

The tension of waiting proved too much for Edward. "Dammit, Villière," he cried out furiously from the doorway. "What the devil is taking so long?" He was furious to discover that the work had not progressed visibly since the last time he had looked in, well over an hour before. "At this rate you won't have the place cleared out before the end of the century."

Irritably he let his eyes sweep across the small chamber. It seemed to him that Raoul had made not even a dent in the disorderly heaps of sleighs and boxes, statues and jars that were piled so high they nearly touched the ceiling in places. And that was only the first room. God alone knew what lay behind that tempting door on the far wall, guarded as effectively by the profusion of treasure strewn in front of it as by the massive black-and-gilt figures that flanked its sides.

Raoul glanced up, annoyed at the rasping sound of Edward's voice. He had been bent over a cluster of colored glass beads, still in the shape of a stunning pectoral even though the cord that originally held them together had rotted away centuries ago. He wasted only a second studying his investor's petulant features. Turning back to his work, he continued to melt a steady stream of wax onto the beads, letting it form a hard, protective case around them. He paused only long enough to reach up with his hand and wipe away the sweat that dripped from his thick dark hair into his eyes.

Edward glowered at him angrily. Tugging a soft linen handkerchief out of his pocket, he began to daub at his own brow. The man infuriated him—and there was nothing he could do about it. It was bad enough when he barked out arrogant commands, pushing Edward around as if it were not his money that had paid for the whole thing, but to completely ignore him . . . That was an insult he could never forgive.

Aimée was aware of her husband's rage as he pushed past her in the small antechamber, making his way back into the cooler air of the tunnels. She was not naive enough to misinterpret it.

"Should you antagonize him like that?" she asked tentatively, half-expecting Raoul to be angry with her for questioning him. "Don't you think it could be dangerous?"

"Dangerous, *petite*?" Raoul's amusement was evident in his voice. "I rather suspect your husband has bitten off more than he can chew. He never expected a discovery like this when he agreed to let me excavate completely before taking anything away. I have no doubt he'd go back on his word now if he could. But it would take him weeks, months, to get everything out of here. Long before then, I'd have called the authorities."

"But you said you didn't want the authorities—"

"I said I didn't want anyone trampling things underfoot, spiriting away half the treasures for their own private use. But I'd risk that any day before I'd let the whole thing be carted out of here in wagons by a pack of thieves and scoundrels—and your husband knows it."

He paused awkwardly, realizing what he had said. The man *was* a thief and a scoundrel, but he was still Aimée's husband. Illogical as it seemed, she might feel some bond of affection for him. It had been thoughtless to speak that way in front of her. Clumsily he turned back to his work, noting with satisfaction that the wax had solidified enough to let him slip a thin sheet of paper cautiously under the beads.

The methodical precision required for the task engrossed him for the next few minutes. When he looked up again, Aimée had turned away from him, fixing her concentration on her own work. In spite of himself, he paused to watch her.

He had given her one of the sturdier artifacts to tie onto a wide slab of wood, teaching her how to lash it securely with gauze tape so one of Mohammed's sons could carry it to the workshop. She was completely absorbed in the undertaking, her lips puckered in intense concentration. Raoul smiled as he watched her. She looked to him like a little girl learning to buckle her shoe for the first time, solemnly intent at the grown-up importance of her task.

She looked so pretty, he thought helplessly. With her hair caught back in a kerchief, and another knotted loosely around her neck, ready to tie over her mouth and nose if the

162

dust grew unbearable; with her nails chipped and broken and a smudge of dirt on the end of her nose, she seemed to him the loveliest thing he had ever seen in his life.

As he stared at her, his mind drifted back in time, remembering another lovely face. He realized the image it evoked was a painful one.

Thea. He could not remember how long it had been since he had dreamed of her. Thea. Soft and fragile, golden, warm and generous. Try as he would, he could not imagine Thea seated opposite him on the floor, the skirt of her immaculate dress filthy with dust, her hair tied back in disarray.

And why the hell should she look like that? He was going to make Thea his wife, not one of his workmen. Wives were supposed to be soft and fragile and golden. Angry at the irrationality of his own thoughts, he forced himself to turn back to his work.

Aimée was only half-conscious of Raoul beside her in the tomb. Struggling with the unwieldy tapes and board, she finally managed to tie down a single slender alabaster cosmetic jar, its stopper in the form of a miniature lion's head caked with unguents that had dried centuries ago. It gave her intense satisfaction to finish the task. Leaning back, she closed her eyes for a moment, stretching her arms to relieve her strained, cramped muscles.

Her whole body relaxed with the easing of her muscles, and a slow, quiet peace flooded her consciousness. It was an uncanny sensation. For an instant she could not figure out why. Then she realized she had not felt such contentment since before she agreed to become Edward's bride.

And yet, why shouldn't she feel contented? she thought with a secret smile. Why shouldn't she let herself relax for the first time in months? Fate, in the form of a rich unplundered tomb, had touched her kindly at last.

Her eyes still closed, she reached up with her hands to massage the muscles at the back of her neck. If they hadn't discovered the tomb, Edward would probably never have been able to free her from the one burden she could no longer bear. But now, with the lure of gold, with the dazzling treasures of the ancient gods—all the accumulated wealth that would make him a god himself in the salons of London and Paris—he had suddenly discovered he no longer needed her or the child she could offer him.

Actually, in a grotesque way, Edward seemed to have enjoyed the failure of his paramour to father a child. She would never forget the way his mouth had twisted in a harsh smile when he told Buffy, making a point to do it in front of her, that his "services" would no longer be required.

Hastily she forced her eyes open, determined to dispel the ugly memory. She was keenly aware of Raoul's presence only a few feet away from her in the narrow aisle that seemed to lead only to a blank wall. His eyes were cast downward in concentration on the beads he had just managed to slide onto a sturdy board.

Off guard and unprotected, his features held a softness Aimée had never seen before. She wondered as she watched him how she could ever have thought he was not really handsome. His rugged features, accented by jet-black hair spilling down onto his forehead, bespoke masculinity. She knew it was madness to let herself look at him like that, to let her body hunger for the passion she would never know, but there was no way she could stop herself, nor did she want to. The rest of her life seemed to stretch out in front of her, as endless and barren as the desert that surrounded them. She could not deny herself the only memories that would make it endurable.

And it was good, she told herself, struggling to compromise with her own uncompromising sense of reality. It was good to work beside this man in the long lantern-lit hours, sharing a link of silent communication as provocative and fulfilling in its own way as the kisses they denied themselves. She smiled to herself as she remembered how frightened she had once been to work in the tomb, how eerie and morbid it seemed the night they broke into it. Now it was the only place on earth where she dared, even for a moment, to let herself relax. It seemed to her it would be perfect if only . . .

If only . . .

The words tore at her heart. *If only* it could last forever. *If only* this man she wanted so desperately could really be hers.

If only the image that had haunted her dreams for weeks were not true.

And yet, she knew it was true. She knew the woman she had never seen would be tall and stately, if only because she herself was always "*petite*" to Raoul; she would be voluptuous and womanly, not slender and childlike; fair, not dark. She would be everything Aimée could never hope to be.

I have invited my fiancée to join us.

Mon Dieu, it was weeks since he had uttered those words—weeks! Even now the woman must be on her way. Any day, any hour, she might arrive to shatter the last happiness Aimée would ever know.

Aimée rose to her feet, tripping as her ankle twisted beneath her. She was aware of the quizzical look in Raoul's eyes.

"It's so cramped in here," she stammered quickly, determined not to let him catch a glimpse of her turmoil. "How can you work for hours like this without even moving?"

"I'm sorry, *petite*," he said lightly. He heard the affection in his voice and admitted that "*petite*" had become for him an endearment, a substitute for the loving words he would never dare speak to her. "Why don't you go outside and walk around for a while?"

Aimée shook her head silently. She had only a few days, perhaps a few hours, to share with him. She could not bring herself to waste them.

Instead she moved a few steps down the narrow aisle, pausing by the doorway to study the painting that had intrigued Raoul so much the first time he saw it. The sheer ugliness of the man portrayed fascinated her.

"Tell me about him, Raoul."

"Him?" Raoul followed her gaze. "Oh, Akhenaten. I've already told you about him. He was a dreamer, a visionary . . . a madman perhaps, but one of the most interesting characters ancient Egypt ever produced."

Aimée barely heard his words.

"But he was so ugly," she said, staring at the unflattering portrait. "Why?"

Raoul laughed softly. "I am not God, my sweet. I cannot tell you why one man is ugly and another is not, any more than I can tell you why one woman is beautiful and another is not."

"But there must have been other ugly pharaohs. Yet in their pictures they all look so noble, so strong, so perfectly formed. Why didn't Akhenaten have himself painted like that?"

Raoul was startled by her perceptiveness. "I can't tell you that, Aimée. The man believed in truth—that which the ancients called *ma'at*—but why he found the courage or the need to extend it to himself, I do not know."

Aimée turned back to the painting. This time she studied the figure more carefully. For the first time she saw defiance in that warped form—defiance and anger. She wondered if it could be those same emotions that prompted him to flaunt his ugliness, even in front of the very gods who had created it. It was a strange, anguished gesture, but one she could understand.

After a moment she let her gaze drift idly toward the girl a few paces behind the pharaoh. A poignant sadness emanated from that lovely figure, but it was a sadness that no longer frightened her. Perhaps simply because she had known pain herself, she felt a kinship with the girl. Picking up one of the lanterns from the floor, she raised it to examine the delicate features more closely.

Delighted and astonished by what she saw, she cried out, "Look, Raoul . . . she has blue eyes—as blue as mine."

Raoul rose abruptly, hastening to her side. Taking the lantern from her hand, he leaned forward, peering closely at the girl's face. When he finally drew back again, he was laughing.

"What an imagination you have, *petite*," he told her, shaking his head incredulously. "The eyes have a bluish tone, I will admit, but that's not unnatural. You must remember there's no such thing as pure black pigment. Black always has a hint of violet or blue or brown in certain light."

"I suppose you're right," she conceded reluctantly. "I imagine blue eyes were unheard of in ancient Egypt."

"Not unheard of. There was foreign blood in Egypt, often from alien princesses sent as second or third wives to the pharaohs. But they would have been extremely rare."

Too late he caught her disappointment. He was sorry he had spoken so quickly, spoiling the illusion that had obviously enchanted her. Seeking to distract her, he turned toward the pharaoh again.

"Akhenaten was an intriguing man, as fascinating as he was revolutionary. The religion he created was unique, the first in history to replace an elaborate hierarchy of gods with the concept of one universal god—a true god with no false gods before him."

He paused for an instant to see if he had captured her interest. When she seemed to be listening, he went on.

"Even this god's places of worship were different. The temples to Amon-Re, the Hidden One, had always been dark and secret, buried away beneath piles of rock, accessible only to the rich and influential. But with the coming of the Aten, the temples were opened, freed to the touch of the wind and the sun. At last everyone could come to worship, naked and unashamed—"

"Naked?" Aimée was sure he was teasing her.

"I told you he was revolutionary." Raoul laughed. "Though in truth nudity was an accepted practice in ancient Egypt, and quite practical, too—don't you think?—considering the heat. Besides, I suspect we could use a touch of that same

166

freedom to liven up our own stuffy services. How about a bunch of little altar boys running like cherubs down the aisles to light the candles, and perhaps a fat archbishop or two celebrating Mass. As for the nuns—"

"Raoul!" Aimée was horrified not so much by his words as by her own barely controllable urge to giggle. "That's . . . that's profane."

"Is it?" His eyes were dancing with laughter. "Perhaps it is . . . and yet I think our own churches are nothing but a composite of those two temples of ancient Egypt. Like the great hidden halls of Amon, our cathedrals are dark and vast, with thick walls to keep out the warmth of the sun, and high vaulted ceilings to remind us of our own insignificance. And yet, like Akhenaten, I think there is a yearning for freedom in all of us. You can see it in the tall stained windows that let in touches of light and color, and the heavy wooden doors that push inward, inviting even the poorest Christian to seek his solace there—though perhaps not in the front pews."

"How can you say that, Raoul?" Aimée's fingers slipped upward, clutching superstitiously at the crucifix around her neck. "How can you compare our faith with theirs? Why, the Egyptians were nothing but . . . but pagans!"

"I suppose they were, *petite*," he admitted. "But you forget, to those 'pagans' Osiris was every bit as real as your Christ is to you."

Aimée was stunned by his words. Seeing her confusion, Raoul relented.

"Don't think too harshly of me, pretty little Aimée." He laid his hand gently on her arm. "And don't remember me in your prayers tonight. I am not quite the heathen you think. I am just a man who has come close enough to the faith of others to understand and respect it, as I would have them understand and respect mine."

His hand was warm against her skin, reminding Aimée that she dared not leave it there. Still, she did not move. In the end, it was Raoul who pulled away from her. With an apologetic smile he turned back to his work.

Aimée did not remember Raoul in her prayers. She did not say her prayers—that night or any night that followed. It was almost as if she thought that by silencing her lips she could somehow keep God from seeing into her heart. The loss of her prayers left her with an empty feeling. In its place she felt a strange primitive urge to pray to the same pagan gods she had scorned—to Isis, who had known love, rather than

Christ, who had known forgiveness. It was an absurd idea, she knew, and a blasphemous one, but she had the eerie sense that Isis would understand better.

And yet it had all begun so innocently. The afternoon had drifted toward its close with a quiet serenity. The air was cool, the sky so clear and blue the horizon stood out sharply in the distance. Edward and Buffy had not yet returned from an excursion across the river, and the picks and spades of the workmen, all the way on the other side of the site, were muted and faraway. To Aimée, relaxing for a few minutes on the workshop steps, the loneliness of the desert gave an illusion of isolation, as if the whole place were exclusively and privately hers.

Then suddenly, without so much as a warning, everything began to change. Within minutes the cool air had grown hot, and the wind began to drive tiny grains of sand against her face. Even as she watched, the sky darkened visibly, taking on a distorted, unnatural yellow tinge.

The khamsin, she thought apprehensively. The dreaded wind of the south. This time, it seemed determined to rage into a full-fledged storm. Anxiously she rose and hurried toward her tent, one hand clutching at her skirts to keep them from whipping up in the wind, the other shielding her face from the stinging sand. Reaching her tent, she pulled the flap over the doorway, tying it in place. Exhausted, she sank down onto the bed.

The storm worsened rapidly, darkening the sky until Aimée could barely see anything in the tent. She longed for light, but she dared not touch a flame to the oil lamp for fear the force of the wind would hurl it to the earth, setting the whole tent ablaze. The angry howling increased as the temperamental storm tugged at the corners of the tent, threatening to rip it away from the stakes that bound it to the earth. Aimée ruefully considered her aloneness. Edward and Buffy, stranded no doubt in comfortable rooms in Luxor, would not attempt to return. The workmen would long since have made their way to mud-brick hovels, and Raoul and the ghaffirs would be safely sheltered in the tombs.

Aimée forced herself to lie down on the bed, wrapping a blanket around her dress to ward off the sand that oozed through the cracks and openings in the tent, but she was too restless to stay still for more than a few minutes. The storm was increasing, growing more and more violent every second, until the whole tent vibrated and shivered with the force of it.

What if the tent didn't hold? she asked herself with a sud-

168

den burst of fear. What if the whole thing ripped away, blowing off in gales of wind, leaving her exposed and helpless to the rage of the storm?

But that was ridiculous, she told herself, furious at her fears. The tent was not going to blow away. It couldn't. If there were any danger of that—any danger at all—Raoul would never . . .

But what if Raoul didn't know where she was?

The thought was terrifying. What if Raoul thought she was still in the workshop? What if he assumed she had had the sense to remain inside its strong walls once she saw the storm threatening?

The workshop! Aimée gasped at the thought of it. Of course! The workshop—that's where she belonged. That's where she would be safe. She had been a fool to leave it, but it was not too late. She could still get back if she really wanted to.

Her fingers were awkward as she tugged at the knot that held the tent flap in place. The force of the wind had driven grains of sand into the cords until they seemed to be cemented together. It took her several minutes, but at last she worked them free. When she finished, she felt the wind tear the fabric from her fingers, whipping it savagely against the wall of the tent. It was all she could do to keep her balance as she stepped outside.

She was terrified to see how dark the sky had grown in the brief time she had been inside. Twilight and the storm had contrived to hang a heavy gray-yellow veil over the earth, blocking out familiar landmarks. With mounting fear Aimée realized she could not even pick out Edward's tent, barely a few yards from her own. If she wanted to get to the workshop, she would have to grope her way through the swirling sands, with nothing but memory to guide her.

It took her a moment to work up the courage to push away from the side of the tent. Raising her hands to shield her face, she inched her way slowly through the darkness. If only she could make it to Edward's tent, if only she could feel its smooth surface beneath her fingers, she would be all right. From Edward's tent it was only a short distance to Buffy's; then she could aim for the workshop itself.

It seemed a hopeless task. The harder she pushed forward, the more the wind buffeted her about, tossing her backward and sideways until she could barely keep her feet on the course she had set. At first she struggled single-mindedly, concentrating on the fierce battle with the raging khamsin. But after a few minutes had gone by and she had still not reached Edward's tent, she became alarmed.

Edward's tent was not that far away. It should have taken seconds, perhaps a minute or two in the raging storm, to reach it. But still she was not there.

Aimée peered into the darkness, trying to pick out something—anything—that would show her where she was. Instead she saw only twilight. The howling wind drowned out her cry of pain as the sand cut into her cheeks and neck.

There was nothing she could do, she realized in despair, thrusting her hands upward to protect her face as best she could. Nothing but force herself forward again, stumbling blindly through the darkness, praying for something that would help her. It was a slim hope, one that grew slimmer with each passing minute, but she knew there was nothing else she could do. She was so turned around she no longer even knew where the workshop lay. She could no more find her way to it than she could hope to stumble back to the tent she had left behind.

Suddenly she let out a sharp cry, feeling her ankle twist painfully beneath her. Staggering awkwardly, she touched a sharp edge of stone.

Steps! Thank God there were steps beneath her feet. Somehow in the darkness she had stumbled onto one of the tombs. Now, if only it was the workshop . . .

Anxiously she groped with her fingers, trying to make out the shape of the steps. The sand had grown so thick she could not see an inch in front of her face. She almost cried with disappointment when she realized the sharp stones were cut in a deep, narrow line, far too narrow to be the steps that led to the workshop.

Yet if it wasn't the workshop, then what . . .?

Even before she could finish forming the question, she knew the answer. If it wasn't the workshop, there was only one other place it could be.

It was the tomb Raoul had chosen for his own lodging.

Aimée was horrified at the thought. She couldn't go down there—she didn't dare. If Raoul saw her come into his chamber in the middle of the night, what would he think?

And yet what else could she do? Angry gusts of sandy wind swirled around her, gouging into her skin, reminding her she dared not stay where she was. It was an agonizing decision, but one quickly made. Even as she decided she could not go inside, she knew she had to. There was no other choice.

The light from a single lantern touched the glossy black of Raoul's hair as he leaned over a worktable in the center of the room, poring over the books that covered its surface. A heavy blanket was draped across the doorway, blocking out the drifting sand so effectively that he completely forgot the storm. His mind had drifted backward, moving into pagan centuries of the past, dwelling on the life and death of people who had nothing to do with today's wind or sand or darkness. It was a satisfying world, one that pleased him, and he was oblivious of everything else.

A sharp gust of sand swept through the room, bringing him back into the present. Impatiently he rose and moved toward the doorway. He thought he had secured the blanket better than that. Why the hell—?

He stopped in his tracks as he saw her. She stepped awkwardly into the room, her dark hair encrusted with sand. The midnight blue of her eyes had turned almost black with fear.

"My God, Aimée. What on earth made you come out on a night like this?"

She mistook the anxiety in his voice for anger.

"I'm sorry, Raoul, I didn't mean . . . It's just that I was . . . well, I was afraid."

Dammit, what a bastard he'd been, Raoul thought irritably. What else had he expected? He knew the girl would be alone. That fool of a husband of hers would never have the gumption to make it through the storm. Her tent was secure enough—he had seen to that himself—but he should have known she'd be terrified. He should have taken better care of her.

"It's all right, Aimée." His voice was gentle and reassuring. His arms opened automatically, reaching out with instincts too powerful to resist.

Aimée relaxed into his embrace. Sighing, she let her head drop onto his chest. She had been so frightened, so alone. It was good not to be alone anymore.

"Shhh, *petite*," he whispered. His hands caressed her lightly, tenderly, stilling the violent trembling of her body. "Shhh, it's all right now." He let his hands drift upward, tugging at the pins that held her hair, until it fell thick and free down her back. His fingers were gentle as he ran them through the dark tresses, brushing away the sand that marred their silken surface.

Aimée thrilled to his touch, even through the abundance of her hair. She longed to cry out to him, begging him to press those same strong, gentle hands into the soft flesh of her body, setting her afire with the contagious heat of their passion. For the first time, she was not afraid with him. It was almost as if, in some strange, inexplicable way, what was happening between them had been ordained centuries ago by destiny. As if her entire life had been but a preparation, a time of waiting for this moment.

His hands were both rough and tender as he laid them on her cheeks, tilting her face upward until her lips were only inches from his own.

"Don't you know you're a fool? Don't you know you'd be safer out there in the storm than here with me?"

"I don't care," she cried recklessly, feeling her cheeks burn beneath his fingers. "I've never known anything like this in my life, and I never will again. I'm not going to run away from it now."

He was startled by the cry that came from his own lips as he brought them harshly down on hers, his hunger undisguised at last. It was a cry of surrender, and he recognized it as such. Damn her for the little witch she was, he told himself, half in anger, half in longing, as he explored her mouth with untamed passion. He had the terrifying, exhilarating sensation that this time she was demanding not only his passion but also the love he had once been all too willing to give.

He tore his lips from hers, pressing his face deep into her hair. His arms tightened ravenously around her. He could feel the painful swelling of his body surging toward her, crying out to him to bury it at last in the soft, pliant moisture of her flesh. God help him now . . . God help them both. If she tried to pull away from him again, he knew he would force her.

With a last show of will, the final resistance his longing body would allow, he drew away from her. Steadying his fingers with almost superhuman effort, he reached out slowly. Gently, with a tenderness he had not known he possessed, he began to undress her. This time it seemed to him her dark blue eyes were filled more with trust than fear. He could feel her trembling, but she did not try to pull away.

What had she meant? he asked himself, daring at last to question the words he had tried to drive out of his consciousness. What had she meant—she had never known anything like this before?

Oh, God, why did women have to wear so many absurd layers of clothes? His fingers fumbled awkwardly with the hooks of her corset. Was it only vanity that made them contort their bodies into shapes they thought becoming, or were they trying to shield themselves from the lusty hands of men? Well, it wasn't going to work this time. Nothing—nothing—could protect her from him now.

And had she meant it? Had there never been anything for her before him? A husband whose clumsy advances brought only disgust. A lover, taken in desperation, equally unsatisfactory. Was that all there was?

And why should it matter . . . why should it matter?

At last the camisole fell from her shoulders, revealing the soft slender flesh that had haunted his dreams for weeks. Aimée felt the cool air of the underground chamber sweep over her skin like a welcome caress, freeing her from the stiff confines of her gown. Outside, the noise of the storm seemed subdued and faraway.

Aimée was strangely unafraid as she gazed at him, this man who would so soon be her lover. She sensed his longing, his longing and his anguish. She understood only the longing. She reached out her arms to him.

With a cry of impatience he drew away from her. Tearing at his clothes, he half-ripped the seams apart as he jerked them savagely from his body. It was only a moment before he stood, tall and naked, before her. The swollen proof of his longing seemed to thrust itself toward her in a gesture of arrogant defiance.

Aimée could only stare at him, half-enticed, half-bewildered by the bold challenge of his throbbing flesh. God help her, this man, though his body was harder and more masculine, his chest matted with dark hair, and his shoulders strong and virile, was in essence no different from the other men who had touched her. Why should it be his body alone that had the power to exhilarate her?

She was acutely aware of his physical presence as he stepped toward her, his arms reaching out, slowly, cautiously, as if he were afraid to lose her even now. With a quivering sigh, she slipped into his embrace, feeling as if she had come at last to the place where she belonged. This time, as his mouth closed on hers, she knew the passions of their bodies would not be denied.

She felt him push her slowly, demandingly down onto the bed. Oh, God, it was so narrow, so narrow and confining, like a prison cell from which there was no escape. She felt as if she were falling—a sickening, terrifying, helpless flight through space—and there was nothing she could grasp, nothing she could cling to.

"Oh, Raoul, hold me, my dearest. Oh, hold me, hold me, hold me."

And then it was too late. Then suddenly she was no longer falling. Suddenly her body was rising, arching upward with an urgency beyond understanding. Her arms were around him, drawing him toward her, even as her hips pressed upward, welcoming the hard flesh that thrust down to meet her.

How good it felt, how perfect and complete, beyond anything she had ever dreamed. The pain of it swelled to agony, a sweet, yearning agony that filled her body until she was sure she would burst from it. With a cry of longing, she let her teeth sink into his shoulder, marking him with the intensity of her passion.

He grunted in response to the pain, but he did not slacken his assault for an instant. Instead, the tearing pressure of her teeth seemed to excite him more, urging his body to thrash with a new wildness, up and down, up and down, forcing her hips into his rhythm, a wanton captive of his lust. Aimée felt her body writhe beneath his, surrendering to the sweet, tormenting violence of his lovemaking.

And then suddenly it was over, sweetly, exhilaratingly over. A blinding flash of yearning that vibrated through her veins, bursting her body as if it had the power to tear her apart, and then at last, a slow, swelling wave of peace. But ah, what a peace, she thought as she clung to Raoul's sweating body, pressing him tighter against her, clamping her legs around him to hold him inside her just a second longer. It was a peace the likes of which she had never known before.

Raoul eased himself gently away from her body, taking care not to pull away from her too suddenly. Drawing her into his arms, he held her body against him, struggling to find room for both of them on the narrow cot.

His eyes lingered on her face, fascinated with the beauty and the passion he saw there. Never had he dreamed such fire mingled with the blood in her veins. God help him, he had hoped this one time with her would cure him forever of his obsessive longing. Now he knew he would never be able to let go of her.

"You have bewitched me." His voice was filled as much with admiration as reproach.

Aimée gazed up at him, struck by the tenderness in his tone. She had never heard lover's words from his lips before.

"Have I?" she asked with a soft laugh, drawing her lips

forward to trace a line of kisses along the side of his face. "Oh my darling, I hope so."

And she had, he thought, his heart filled with a resignation that was more sweet than bitter. It did not matter any longer how many lovers she had had—or would have. She was in his blood now, as much a part of him as any other part of his flesh.

Slowly, with an urgent tenderness he could not understand, he lowered his lips to her face, touching her cheeks, her forehead, the tip of her nose, resting at last for a breathless moment on her eyelids, closed in pleasure. She was so beautiful, so warm, so passionate—and so painfully, agonizingly his, if only for that night.

He lowered his lips to her breast. His hands following, he cupped the soft flesh between his fingers, pointing her nipples upward so he could tease them lightly with his teeth. How delicate she was, he told himself with a sense of wonder, how small and fragile, her body barely developed. There was a childlike essence about her, a lovely innocence and delicacy that made him long to gather her up in his arms, drawing her toward him in an instinctive gesture of protectiveness.

With a slow, languishing warmth, he felt his body begin to swell again, answering the renewing hunger in his heart. Letting his lips sink lower, he traced a course of kisses down the smooth, flat flesh of her stomach, resting at last on the silken curls at its base, still warm and wet from their lovemaking. Gently, tantalizingly, teasing her with the trembling desire he could already feel in her body, he began to spread her legs apart. His lips burned with an intense longing for her flesh; his tongue yearned to touch her, driving her to new peaks of ecstasy.

He drew his head back for an instant, letting his hand slide downward, following the same path his lips had taken. He was conscious of trying to prolong the moment. He wanted to make it beautiful for her, to give her something more perfect than anyone had given her before. As he gazed down at her, he saw the rays of the lantern flicker on an angry red scar at the side of her leg. Idly he ran his finger along the edge of it.

Her body tensed at the gesture. He could not know the sudden pain it had recreated in her heart.

"An old battle scar," she said quickly, trying to make light of it.

His body recoiled at her words. A battle scar? The awkward tension in her voice made it only too clear what sort of field that battle had been fought on.

And yet, dammit, he reminded himself impatiently, what business was it of his? Whatever fiendish things other men had done to her in other beds, whatever things she had done to them, it was no concern of his. He had no right to question or judge her.

Still, he could not help it. He could no more regulate the angry pain that racked his body at the thought of it than he could control the urge of his lungs to draw in fresh gulps of air.

Slowly, Raoul forced his lips upward again. He was careful to retrace the same course along her flesh, touching her in a kind of mirror image of his half-tamed passion of a moment before. He did not let her see his confusion or his pain. His pride would not let him acknowledge them in front of her.

Aimée felt his lips, soft and tender and provocative, filling her with a new, sweet yearning. She reached down, cradling his head in her hands. Drawing him slowly upward, she eased his lips toward the hungry cavern of her mouth.

"Oh, *mon coeur*," she whispered softly, her voice filled as much with yearning as contentment. "It is so beautiful . . . so beautiful. I never dreamed it could be like this."

He felt her lips against his, parting, probing, searching for the tongue it longed to draw into its depths, and his body responded once more, swelling toward her. With a violent burst of passion he worked his hands beneath her body, forcing her hips upward until they were pressed so tightly against his own he had the eerie sensation her bones would shatter with the pressure. Half his heart longed to cry out in rage: Liar, hypocrite, do you think I am such a fool? But the other half longed to be that very fool, believing her, trusting her, loving her once again.

He released the pressure of his arms, drawing away from her for an instant. He could see by the startled expression on her face that she had been caught off guard by the suddenness of his assault. Yet she had not been frightened by it. The longing in her eyes had not diminished.

He admitted then what he had known all along. That his need for her was too great to be denied.

"Stay with me tonight. Don't leave me."

Her eyes danced with little lights of blue fire.

"And where would I go, my sweet?"

He laughed a little at her words. The sound was light and gentle.

"The storm," he whispered lightly. "I had forgotten the storm."

How he loved the storm. He had always loved storms. Now he understood why.

"I want you," he whispered hoarsely. He was surprised at the tension in his voice. He was bitterly aware that the words "I want you" were a substitute for the words he really longed to say: "I love you."

Her body shivered as his hands raced along her flesh, provoking, tempting, resting at last on the moist hair between her thighs. She needed no urging from him to pull her legs apart, raising them ravenously to draw him back into the warmth of her body.

"*Mon Dieu*, it is good," he hear her sigh. "So good."

And it was good. God help him, it was good. It was wrong, it was foolish—but oh, God, it was good.

THREE

She Turns Her Eyes Upon Me

⦾ Meryt

Bright morning sunlight trickled through the quivering leaves of the acacia, breaking up dark patches of shade with dancing patterns of gold. Spring cornflowers, cheerful in their bonnets of morning blue, nestled in the tall green grasses of the garden, and lotuses and mandrakes, lapping up the cool waters of a small, still pond, added their own touches of blue and white and purple to the peaceful scene. It was the month of Epiphy, the season of the harvest, nearly a year from the day a young princess had stood breathlessly by the riverbank, her heart still alive to love and hope as she watched a tall ship sail out of the dying rays of the sun. It seemed to Meryt, as she looked back on that day, that the girl by the dock must have been someone else, some vivacious young stranger she did not even know. There was nothing in her to call to mind the sad young queen who lingered today in the shadows of her uncle's garden.

The shade of the acacia was like a cool caress, a welcome respite from the heat of the sun. A little slave girl, twelve or thirteen years old, scurried around the corner of the house, half-running, half-skipping toward the massive water barrel beside the pond. Realizing the girl was planning to fill a heavy clay jar with water, a soothing balm to pour over her mistress's sweating arms and hands, Meryt waved her back. It was cool enough in the shade. Besides, she had no intention of letting herself get trapped by the idle chatter of the slaves. Today, of all days, she wanted to be alone with her thoughts.

She let her hand rest on the surface of her belly, warm and smooth beneath the translucent veil of her gown. Funny, she thought, the flesh was not even rounded yet. There was still no hint of the secret it held.

"Ah, there you are, cousin."

The words were sharp and unpleasantly shrill. Jolted out of the privacy of her thoughts, Meryt glanced up, meeting the eyes of her uncle Akhenaten's oldest daughter.

"I'm usually here in the morning, Meritaten," she replied shortly. "Were you looking for me?"

"Was I?" The other girl laughed lightly, as if her own enigmatic riposte amused her. "May I sit beside you?"

Her body was sleekly feline as she lowered herself to the grass, her movements as sensuous and controlled as a preying leopard's. Even her eyes were cat's eyes, glittering and predatory, their dark surface glowing almost yellow in the warm sun.

"Did you want something?"

She knew it was foolhardy to snap at Meritaten, but she could not help herself. The girl was Akhenaten's favorite, the darling of the palace now that her father was formally estranged from Nefertiti, but that did not keep Meryt from disliking her. It seemed to her Meritaten had grown almost unbearably smug since she had married her father's own favorite, Smenkhkare, a man she would have detested were he not the closest male heir to the throne.

Meryt let her fingers play across the smooth, flat flesh of her belly. What would Meritaten say, she wondered, if she knew her husband would not be Akhenaten's heir much longer? She felt a certain satisfaction at the thought. She knew how desperately Meritaten wanted to be queen.

Meritaten's sharp cat's eyes did not fail to pick up the gesture. Narrowing, they turned into dark slits.

"So you think you'll bear him a son?" The words were a low hiss on the sultry air. "Bah, you are a fool! It will be nothing but a worthless daughter—like all the rest."

Meryt glanced at her cousin sharply, startled at the pain in her voice. In her distaste for Meritaten, it was all too easy to forget that she, too, had once fallen victim to her father's desperate desire for a male heir. Shuddering, Meryt wondered who had sired the tiny girl child that lived so short a time, Akhenaten's loathsome surrogate, Smenkhkare, or Akhenaten himself?

"So far it doesn't look as if I'm going to bear anything," Meryt retorted. She was surprised at the coolness of her lie. She knew Meritaten had guessed her secret, but she could not bear the thought of sparring with her now. "Perhaps I will prove to be barren."

Meritaten's eyes glowed with suspicion as they scanned her cousin's slender form. Noting the tight, pinched look on the older girl's features, Meryt almost felt sorry for her. Meritaten had been a child herself, all those years ago, when she had been forced into childbirth. Her body would never recover from the abuse.

Meritaten leaned back, her pursed lips full but tense.

"Do you think so?" Her voice was soft, almost soothing, but suspicion still blazed in her eyes. "If you are, all the better for you."

The darkness in her eyes sent a long, penetrating shiver down Meryt's spine. Pulling her knees up instinctively, she locked her arms around them, pressing them against her belly as if she could shut out the force of her cousin's hatred.

Meritaten did not miss the gesture, nor did she misunderstand it. Leaping to her feet, she glowered down at the girl, her eyes flashing with jealousy and rage.

"You *are* a fool," she cried out bitterly. "But then, so was I—as foolish and ambitious as you."

Her eyes clouded over for an instant, taking on emotions Meryt could not even begin to understand. Slowly her lips curled in the trace of a smile.

"If I had it to do all over again," she said softly, "I would go to my mother. You are twice the fool if you don't learn from my mistakes."

Then suddenly, breaking the darkness of her own mood, Meritaten tossed her head back, letting an unexpected trill of laughter pour through her lips. The sound was frothy and bubbling, as carefree and infectious as the laughter of the little girl she had been only a few years before. Her eyes were sparkling with mirth as she flitted across the garden with the effortless grace of a golden butterfly. Meryt stared after her, intrigued and puzzled, as she disappeared into the shadows that bordered the wall of the palace.

Now, what on earth was that about? the girl asked herself, bewildered and oddly frightened by her cousin's mercurial changes in mood. Why had Meritaten come to a distant corner of the garden to seek her out, and why were her eyes dancing when she left?

Strolling slowly toward the edge of the pond, Meryt turned the question over and over in her mind. Meritaten's last words had been blunt and simple, yet frustratingly enigmatic. I would go to my mother, she had said, and yet in the end that made no sense at all. Stooping, Meryt plucked a newly opened lotus from its stem, wrapping her fingers around the pale blue petals, still wet with beads of moisture.

I would go to my mother . . .

But Meritaten hadn't seen her mother for months, not since the day Nefertiti had moved into her own palace at the northern end of the city. Even before that, in the long years that had passed since the loss of the baby, the two had not been close. Besides, what could Nefertiti have to do with her daughter's child, Meryt asked herself, puzzled, or with the unborn babe that lay beneath her own heart?

It was a long moment before Meryt at last understood. When she did, she felt a bitter chill seep into her veins. Unconsciously her fingers tightened around the blossom in her hand, pressing it against the warmth of her body. The dewy beads of moisture felt like tears against her breast.

I would go to my mother . . .

So that was why Meritaten had come to the garden. Sly and catlike, she had crept in to put an end to her rival's dreams.

Nefertiti. Of course, Nefertiti. If her mind had been working clearly, Meryt would have thought of her at once. Akhenaten's queen was as clever as she was beautiful, as wise and worldly as she was serene. If anyone would know what to do about an unwanted child . . .

But was it unwanted?

Meryt was startled at the thought. For an instant it gave her a helpless, sickening feeling, as if she were about to fall and could not protect herself. Instinctively she thrust out her hand, reaching toward a tall tree to steady herself. She glanced down at the flower still in her fingers. The fragile petals, once so lovely and vibrant, were now crushed and broken, lying like pale ghosts against her fingers.

She had thought if she got pregnant it would all be so simple and uncomplicated. All she would remember was the twisted smile on her young uncle's face, the dark laughter in his eyes, as he forced indignity after indignity on her unwilling body. All she would feel for the tiny life growing inside her—that parasitic extension of the man she loathed—would be a single-minded hatred.

Well, it hadn't turned out to be that simple. Not that simple at all. That fragile little life, still unseen, unnamed, untouched, was as much a part of her as of the man who had fathered it. No, it was more hers, she corrected herself, for she would love and cherish it, and he was a man incapable of any warm, generous emotion. It was she who would hold the baby in her arms, nestling it warm and soft and dependent against her breast, she who would cradle and fondle it, wiping the damp hair from its brow on hot afternoons, laughing as she felt its tiny hand curl around her finger.

Slowly, forcing her breath through the tightness of her

throat, Meryt eased her clenched fist open. The sun touched the pieces of broken petals on her palm. Lifting her arm in a graceful arc, the girl tossed them away from her, watching as they floated downward, drifting onto the glassy surface of the pond. Her hand felt strangely empty without them.

Her cousin was a sly little cat, vindictive and jealous and mean of spirit, but this time Meryt knew she was right. If she let herself bear the child she carried inside her, there would never be anything but pain for her—the pain of her youthful body as it was ripped apart by the process of birth, the pain of her woman's heart as it wept for the child torn too soon from her arms.

And for what? she asked herself bitterly. For what all that pain, all the weeping and the raw, bleeding emotions? For a son she would rarely be allowed to see because the duties of his royal upbringing consumed all his time and passion? A husband she barely knew or cared to know? Servants who peeked up at her through carefully lowered lashes, watching her, pitying her, weeping for her perhaps until she grew old and they were bored with it all? A long, empty, tedious life that would make her in the end as brittle and transparent—and vindictive—as her spiteful cousin?

"But the child," she whispered. What about the child? In the end, after everything had been said and thought and tallied up, wasn't the child the only thing that really counted? No matter what the pain, the sacrifice, no matter how cruelly her own life might be destroyed, surely the child had a right to live.

To live?

Harsh laughter erupted from her lips. If she had not known better, she would have sworn the sound came from Meritaten, not from herself.

To live? Was she really naive enough to believe her child would be allowed to have a life of his own? Even as a baby, he would be protected—and watched. Guards would walk before him as he crawled through the garden; slaves would taste each bit of food the nurses mashed up for him. But one day, despite all those precautions, one of the trusted guards would turn his head away for a moment, or one of the slaves would be bribed to . . .

"No!"

No, she could not let that happen, not to her child, not to herself. But oh, Isis, the choice was an agonizing one. Blindly, unable to see through the haze of her own tears, Meryt reached out, letting her arms circle the sturdy trunk of the tree at the water's edge. The bark felt rough against her skin, like the imagined touch of a man's cheek on hers, evoking the memory of yearnings that would be satisfied only in her dreams.

She made no attempt to stem the tears that flooded down her cheeks. She knew they were selfish tears, more for herself than the child she would never see, but she did not care. She was weeping for arms that would never rock a baby to sleep, lips that would never croon the lullabies mothers had sung since the world was young and the great god Re had just risen from the lotus. She was weeping for ears that would never know the sound of baby laughter, hands that would never brush away baby tears. She was weeping for all the long, lonely, empty days of her life.

The North Palace was dark and cool and lonely. Meryt's footsteps echoed on the cold stones of the long corridor that led to her aunt's private apartment. She paused for a moment at the end, hesitating on the threshold of the reception chamber. She felt small and vulnerable when she finally forced herself into the room.

It took a moment in the dim light for her to realize she was alone. Cautiously, daring to breathe for the first time since she stepped through the doorway, Meryt let her eyes sweep across the chamber, studying it with detached curiosity. She had not been in the room for years, but she remembered it well. She had always been fond of it when she was a little girl, delighting in the floor that was decorated to look like a papyrus swamp, with marsh birds pushing out of green reeds to fly up painted walls, and multicolored fish swimming in sparkling blue tanks. She wished it had the same power to intrigue and amuse her now.

Nefertiti slipped silently into the room. Meryt was aware of her aunt's presence only when she saw her shadow on the wall. Turning, she raised her eyes to the woman's face.

Nefertiti had always been beautiful. It took Meryt only a moment to realize the passing years had only made her lovelier. Sheer white linen veiled a form still slender and graceful, and the strong lines of a tall blue headdress accented her high cheekbones and dark, clear eyes. Standing in the doorway, with golden light behind her, she looked more like the statue of a goddess than a living human being.

Meryt took a step toward her, then hesitated, pulling herself abruptly to a stop. She had not seen her aunt since the day she had been forced into wedlock with her husband. It occurred to her now that there had always been, in those years so long in the past, a strong bond of affection between Nefertiti and Akhenaten. She was not sure how the woman would receive her now.

Nefertiti was quick to sense Meryt's discomfort. With a cool, studied grace she lifted her hands, extending them toward her.

"Aunt . . ."

Meryt's voice broke on the word. Hurrying forward, she clasped the woman's hands in her own. She was surprised to feel how cold and lifeless they were.

"I did not think . . . I did not want . . ."

"Shhhh." Nefertiti's voice was soothing as she silenced the girl. "Don't try to explain. I understand. Believe me, I understand."

"Do you?"

Meryt's voice was tremulous, unsure. For the first time, she wondered just how much her aunt knew. She had no idea how long Akhenaten's wasting disease had robbed him of his powers of masculinity, or how long Nefertiti had been estranged from his affections.

But the woman quickly eased her fears.

"Yes," she said slowly, her voice soft but solemn. "I *do* understand." As she looked down at the girl, her smile was warmer.

Meryt felt a flood of relief. It was idiotic, she knew, but she could not stand the idea her aunt might think she had lain beside her husband—or wanted to.

Nefertiti's touch was still cool as she pressed the girl's fingers in her own for a moment, then slowly drew away from her. Her hands were white and limp as she dropped them loosely to her side.

"You must not mind so much, you know. The kingdom must have an heir."

"The kingdom?" Meryt shouted the words in a rush of fury and frustration. All her aunt's kindness, all her warmth, had given her hope for a moment. Now she was talking like everyone else. "And what will the kingdom do for its little heir, pray tell? Will it shelter him, care for him, keep him safe and happy? Will it even let him live to be an adult?

Stepping back, Nefertiti ran a practiced eye up and down her niece's body, spotting the hints of pregnancy she had missed before. She understood the girl's heart, understood it even better than the child herself. She knew only too well what Meryt was about to ask her—and what her only answer could be. She could not meet the girl's gaze any longer.

"You must not think of yourself. You must think of the good of the kingdom."

"But, Aunt . . ."

Nefertiti listened as Meryt's voice trailed away, leaving the rest of her plea mute. Still she did not look up. She knew she had arrived at a moment of choice. It was a choice that was excruciating in its simplicity—the despair of a man trying to hold his world together balanced against the pain of a young girl on the threshold of maturity. It tore her heart apart to realize what that choice must be.

Still unable to raise her eyes, the woman shook her head.

"But Meritaten said I should come to you."

Meryt did not even know why she cried out those words, so futile and inane even to her own ears. She only knew they were a product of her own anguish, a dying call for help. It could do her no good. Nefertiti had been estranged from her daughter for a long time now. She could not possibly be interested in what the girl had to say.

Yet the mother's eyes were sharp as she raised them.

"Meritaten?"

Her voice was hesitant, touched with a tremor Meryt had never heard before. A troubled pain filled her eyes. For an instant the girl was tempted to stop, sensing that whatever she said could only hurt the woman more. Then, remembering how desperately she needed her help, no matter what the cost, she forced herself to go on.

"Meritaten said *she* should have come to you."

Nefertiti turned away, walking with calm, measured steps down the length of the room. Her eyes were clear but sightless as she stared at the colorful rainbow of fish, gliding mysteriously through the shimmering blue of their private world. If there was pain for the daughter she had not been able to help, she did not turn to let Meryt see it now.

The moment of choice had come again, she realized. Only, this time it was more complicated. This time she must balance the husband she had loved against the daughter she had loved—the man she had failed against the child she had failed.

"Meritaten was so pretty when she was a little girl." Her voice was so low it was barely audible. She spoke the words to herself, as if she had forgotten Meryt was in the room. "So pretty and vivacious and full of laughter."

Her eyes were shining as she turned. Meryt could not tell in the dim light if they were filled with tears.

"So were you."

This time, as she saw her aunt open her arms to her, Meryt knew the woman would not fail her. Gratefully she raced across the room letting herself sink against the warm, maternal comfort of a shoulder stronger than her own. She did not know if it was her own tears or Nefertiti's that stained the snowy surface of her gown.

Cool water rippled gently from long, deep canals into a large artificial lake behind the gardens of the old palace. The city of No-Amon, once the proud domain of the ancient gods, was quiet now, its neglected avenues strolled only by the old and weary, those too stubborn to give up the gods of the past or too near death to fear the consequences. Beyond the private gardens, bronzed naked peasants, untouched by the battles of the gods, worked the timeworn shadoofs, patiently tilting pail after pail of water into the tall, cumbersome devices that sustained the irrigation system. The air was warm and heavy, rich with the scent of flowers.

Meryt had not seen the lake since she was a little girl. Even now, after a whole night in the old palace, she found it hard to believe she was actually here at last, following the same garden paths where she had spent so many happy childhood hours. Here she would grow old, aging until she was just a dim shadow in the long, empty corridors, like her grandmother and all those other graying ghosts of an era already dead. Here, too, she would raise her baby brother, Tuti, teaching him to forget the pain of the past, just as she must teach herself to forget its dreams.

Nefertiti had arranged it all, as she had arranged everything since that fateful afternoon Meryt went to her for help. After the long, debilitating illness, after the loss of the unborn baby and the pain that left her body unfit for further childbearing, after her usefulness to her uncle and his compulsive dreams of a royal heir had ended at last, it had been a simple matter to have her banished to a gentler setting, a place where her heart could rest at last, a place where she could find, if not excitement, at least serenity, if not passion, then peace. It was an exile Meryt had been grateful to accept.

Impulsively Meryt kicked off her sandals, hiking her skirt up to her knees as she waded into the water, letting it splash, cool and refreshing, against her legs. She felt like a little girl again—a little girl who had somehow managed to bridge the gap of years and sorrows to return to the days when she had been happy. Glancing over her shoulder, she drank in the half-tamed garden and the bright palace walls with the thirst of a desert nomad at a long-awaited oasis. She had not realized how much she loved this place, how much she had hungered to see it again.

Suddenly Meryt felt her foot twist beneath her, caught in one of the invisible weeds that curled along the lake floor. With a cry of surprise she dropped her skirt, thrusting her hands out to steady herself as she slid into the water. The surface broke her fall, easing her gently to the bottom, but she could do nothing to save her freshly laundered gown. Her gasp of dismay as she pulled herself to her feet, gaping at the dripping pleats that clung to her torso and limbs, dissolved into a spate of giggles.

Now she felt even more like a little girl than ever. What was she doing anyhow, playing at being sedate and very, very grown-up, when all she wanted was to be a child again, if only for a morning? She tugged the sodden linen gown from her body and cast it on the sandy earth.

The water was icy against her legs, her thighs, her belly, as she waded out, letting herself sink at last into its cool embrace. She began to swim out toward the center of the lake, drawing herself with swift, practiced skill through the water. Only when she was far from shore did she allow herself the luxury of pausing, drifting onto her back to float through the current. Arching her back, she eased her head deeper into the water as she stared up at the clear, scintillating blue of the sky. The feel of the lake against her nakedness was refreshing and clean. There had been a time, not long ago, when she had thought she would never feel clean again.

Those had been long troubled days filled with pain and shame. Long, lonely hours mourning the loss of a child she would never know, children she would never bear. Long, terrifying nights when she dared not even pray to Isis, because Isis was a mother, and a mother could never forgive what she had done.

Angrily Meryt pushed the thought away. It was over. Right or wrong, it was over, and all her doubts, all her tears, could not change it now. Turning, she began to thrash through the water with all the pain and frustration buried deep inside her. She did not return to the shore until she was exhausted.

The sound of her breathing was hoarse and rhythmic as she lay on the banks of the lake, her body still resting in the shallow edges of the water. Tiny waves, barely perceptible, lapped against her skin, brushing long, dark strands of hair lightly against her cheek. Wearily she closed her eyes, daring to relax again. She had come home, she told herself, surprised at the sound of the word, for it had been many years since she thought of the old palace as home. She had come home at last.

The touch of the water had the sensuous feel of a lover's fingers, exploring her body with a tenderness she had never known. The sensation was poignant, setting her heart afire with half-submerged yearnings, calling them up from the hidden depths of her memory. Barely conscious of what she was doing, Meryt let her fingertips play across her flesh, retracing the loving course other fingers had followed a thousand times in her dreams.

God, how it hurt! Once there was a man whose hands she longed to feel touching her where her own hands rested now. Once there was a man whose kisses haunted her dreams. Now there was no one.

She did not try to hold back the tears that caressed her cheeks with a warmth that took away the chill of the water.

The sound of a lyre, faraway and dreamlike, fell lightly on the air, mingling with the whisper of the water as it lapped against her cheek. At first Meryt thought she was only imagining it, letting it drift out of her memory as a sort of bittersweet accompaniment to her own longing. Only as the sound drew nearer, its haunting melody trilling somewhere in the garden itself, did she realize it was genuine.

There was music, but it was not for her; dreams of love, but they were not her dreams. The young man whose fingers caressed the strings was not her lover, the girl who watched him, her lips curling in the half-smile she tried so hard to hide, would never be her again.

Seven days I have not seen my sister,
And sickness has overcome me.

The melody was one Meryt remembered well. She could almost hear the words, as if a loved, remembered voice was singing them in her ears at that very moment.

Slowly she opened her own lips, letting the words pour out, half in a whisper, half in the lyrical tones of a song.

Better for me is my sister than all the physicians,
Better my beloved than all the remedies.

Oh, Isis, it was sweet . . . so sweet. She could hear his rich voice, mingling with her own.

> Her coming is my salvation;
> When I see her, I am whole.

Breathlessly she raised her fingers, catching at her throat as she stilled her own voice. The other voice, pure and clear and strong now, continued on alone.

> She turns her eyes upon me, I am young again;
> She speaks to me, I am strong;
> She embraces me, my body is free of evil.

The voice drifted away, dying with the last words. Only the sound of the lyre remained, sweet in the heavy air.

She was mad, she knew she was mad—the voice was as real to her as if he were sitting beside her at that very moment, gazing down at her where she lay in the water, smiling at her in the sunlight. She was mad, but she did not care anymore. Madness was so much better than sanity.

Slowly she opened her eyes, pulling her body upward. Even the heat of the sun did not warm her wet skin. She steeled herself, preparing for the moment she would raise her gaze from the sandy earth, staring at last into the silent emptiness that marked the bitter finale of all her dreams.

She was startled to see a shadow on the ground in front of her, dark gray against the green-gold of the garden. For a moment she could not understand what it meant. Her body was trembling as she slowly lifted her eyes.

The eyes that stared back at her were filled with laughter.

"You look like you've seen a ghost, pretty little Meryt. Did you think you were only dreaming?"

It was a moment before she could find her voice.

"Senmut?"

She flushed under the heat of his gaze. She did not know if she was embarrassed by the water that tangled dark strands of hair across her face, or the tears that lingered on her cheeks, or the fact that he had caught her with her fingers on her own body.

"None other," he agreed good-naturedly. "But why do you look so surprised? Where else did you think I had gone?"

Meryt was amazed at her own naiveté. She had heard that many of her father's retainers, those who were untouched by the taint of his crime at least, had been allowed to move quietly to the old palace. Where else, indeed, could he have gone?

"But you don't look surprised at all," she said quickly, trying to cover her confusion. "You look as if you expected to see me here."

"I did," he told her laughingly. "Surely you don't think I just happened to be wandering through the garden, my lyre tucked under my arm."

"But how . . .?"

"Nefertiti," he said quietly, suddenly growing solemn. "She sent word."

"To you?" Meryt let her bewilderment show. That her aunt would send word to her grandmother was hardly a surprise, or even to one of the household staff—but to a scribe? "But why?"

Senmut leaned forward, daring at last to take her hand. "Because, my dove, she knows."

"She knows?"

Meryt was troubled. How could her aunt know how she felt about Senmut? How could anyone know?

Senmut smiled again. "You are not very subtle, you know, my adorable one. You carry your heart in your eyes."

But if her aunt knew, the aunt who had not even seen her in the long months her love for Senmut had been growing, then everyone must know. Then even . . .

"Then my uncle must know."

Senmut tightened his hand protectively around her fingers. He laid the other lightly on her cheek, brushing away the wet strands of hair from her skin.

"Be careful," Meryt told him, her voice a hoarse, low whisper. "The servants will see us."

"Then they will see."

Senmut's voice was calm as he drew her toward him, his hands strong and tender, urging her body against his. Meryt felt herself tremble with the sweet passion she had only dared to dream of before. The yearning in her body swelled. Desperately she fought against it. For his sake, if not for her own, she dared not give in to it.

"I am still pharaoh's wife," she cried out, pain cutting through her voice. "No matter that I have been cast aside. His pride will never let him forgive this."

Senmut did not seem to hear her protests. Tightening his embrace he pressed her against him, easing her head down with his hands until it rested against the warmth of his chest. His heart beat a tattoo as wild and violent as her own.

So this is what it is like, she thought, giving in at last to the power of his embrace. This is the love of a man and a woman.

And what is the love of a man and a woman?

Odd little snatches of old lessons echoed in her ears. The same words, copied again and again so laboriously on broken shards of pottery. Words that meant so little then.

And what is the love of a man and a woman? It is but a moment, a trifle, the likeness of a dream . . .

". . . and death will come as the end."

She felt Senmut pull away from her, his hand still resting on the back of her head as he urged her face upward, forcing her eyes to meet his own. He did not ask her to repeat her words. Meryt sensed he did not have to. He knew them as well as she.

"I have waited a long time for you," he told her, his voice hoarse with desire. "I will wait no longer." His lips were hard and firm as he lowered them on hers.

He did not lead her into the coolness of the palace, but took her instead on the shore of the lake, letting the water cool their bodies as they answered at last the yearnings of their separate dreams. The sound of peasants' voices, far in the distance, the light whistling of the north wind through the trees, the dark words of a warning uttered only moments before—none of these existed for them. They were alone with each other, lost in a world where only lovers could go.

At last, exhausted and satisfied, Meryt lay in her lover's arms. She knew the price for the act they had just committed—just as she knew he knew it—but she was no longer afraid.

It is but a moment, a trifle, the likeness of a dream . . .

But, oh, what a moment . . . what a dream. It was a dream worth risking everything for.

. . . and death will come as the end.

∞ Aimée

1

"Damn."

Raoul's voice was harsh as he pulled himself out of bed, grabbing for the clothes he had scattered on the floor. Beside him, Aimée stirred sleepily, reaching out to hold him back.

"Don't go, Raoul. Not yet."

Raoul paused, shrugging his shirt casually onto his shoulders as he gazed down at her. It seemed to him he had never seen anything so lovely as this woman who lay before him, black hair spilling across the pillow. He was tempted to throw caution to the devil, tossing his shirt back on the floor as he crawled in beside her again.

"I don't think you'd like it if I stayed, *petite*. I really don't think so."

Slowly Aimée opened her eyes. She was horrified to see the first gray light of dawn seeping through the cracks of the tent.

"Oh, *mon Dieu*." Sitting up, she pulled the sheet around her. "It's morning already. What are we going to do?"

Raoul's eyes hardened as he watched her. In the few nights he had come to her, in all the dark hours they had writhed against each other, stifling the lovers' cries that rose to their lips, they had never once dared fall asleep in each other's arms. Somehow he had deluded himself into thinking that would be the final intimacy, the closeness she would welcome as much as he, despite the danger.

"What's the matter, my dear? Are you afraid your husband will rise early and come to bid you a sweet good morning? That would put you in an unpleasant spot, wouldn't it?"

His coldness cut her deeply. Would it always be like this? she wondered. An hour of passion, a moment of tenderness, and then the inevitable recriminations and regret?

"That's not fair, Raoul. I wasn't thinking of myself, only of you."

Raoul hesitated, his fingers resting on his belt buckle as he studied her face. After all she had done, after all they had done together, she still looked like an innocent young girl, her eyes brimming over with unshed tears. For an instant he had the urge to pull her into his arms and kiss away the pain.

"You really do that very well, my sweet. You missed your calling—you should have gone on the stage. If I were less worldly, I might believe all that pretty concern was for me—and not the fat fortune you'll lose if Lord Edward finds out what a two-timing bitch you are."

"Raoul!" She recoiled as if he had slapped her. "You have no right to say that—and you know it. I'm not the only one who spends Edward's money."

The color drained from Raoul's face, but he did not speak. Aimée knew she had gone too far, but she was too angry and too hurt to stop.

"You're not ashamed of being caught with another man's wife. You're not even embarrassed. All you're worried about is what you stand to lose. Edward's patronage, for one thing. And your . . . your . . ."

"My what, my dear?"

"Your . . ." Why was it so hard to say? Why couldn't she just spit out the word "fiancée" and be done with it? "Your . . . your . . . That woman who's coming here, whatever her name is."

"Thea," he replied automatically. "Lady Theodora Welles."

It made him uncomfortable to say her name aloud. He had invited Thea to join them in a fit of pique—a retaliation against Aimée for daring to take another lover. He was already beginning to have second thoughts about it.

"Is she . . . is she pretty?"

He was at the doorway, his fingers struggling with the ties that held the flap. As he turned back to her, his features were carefully controlled.

"Does it matter?" he asked coolly. "I won't have any fiancée, pretty or not, if I don't get out of here—and fast."

Aimée pressed the pillow against her body, trying to make up for the closeness of the lover who had left her. Why did she always have to quarrel with him? she thought desperately. Why did she lose her temper when she only wanted to reach out to him, to stroke him with gentle fingers, to cover his body with tender kisses? Why, no matter what she did, no matter how hard she tried, did their meetings always end in bitterness?

The first morning light brought with it a stifling heat that would soon fill the entire tent. Aimée turned over on her side, hugging the pillow tightly. A familiar sensation of nausea accompanied the warmth that prickled her skin with sweat.

Raoul had not answered her question. She would not ask him again. His silence told her all she needed to know. Thea would be pretty, even prettier than she had feared.

Little beads of moisture worked their way down the cleavage of her breasts as she pushed the pillow away, struggling to pull herself up. A new wave of nausea rose from her stomach, constricting her chest and throat until she could barely breathe.

Damn the heat, she thought rebelliously. If it weren't for the heat, constantly sapping her strength, she would never have lost her temper with Raoul that morning. They would never have parted in anger.

The nausea returned, worse than before. Retching painfully, Aimée clamped her hand over her mouth, determined not to let the heat get the best of her. It did her no good. Admitting defeat at last, she reached for a basin beside the bed. The heat was already unbearable as she bent uncomfortably over it.

Is she pretty? The words echoed in Raoul's ears as he walked toward the workshop. *Is she pretty?* It startled him to realize he did not even remember. Somewhere in the last weeks, in the last months perhaps, he had lost his vision of Thea, and no matter how he tried, he could not call it back again. The thought troubled him more than he cared to admit, even to himself.

The workshop was silent as he stepped inside. Long rows of artifacts, each draped with its own white cloth, rested in cases in the back. Soon he would have to turn carpenter again, building another tier of shelves and yet another to hold all the treasures he would take from the tomb.

He raised his lantern, running a practiced eye along each shelf, checking to make sure everything was in place. It was a routine task, one he performed each morning. He did not expect it to take more than a few minutes.

But this time it was different.

"What the hell?"

Striding forward, he pulled the cover from a squat object in the center of one of the shelves. The instant he saw it, he let out a hiss of annoyance.

The basket he had uncovered was not an unusual piece, nor a particularly important one, but Raoul had always been fond of it. When he found it, it had been fragile and broken, its slender reeds so ravaged by time that even a light breath threatened to disintegrate them. He had worked over it for hours, gluing it together with bits of molten wax, waiting patiently for it to solidify so he could move it at last. It had been an especially satisfying moment when at last he had placed it on the shelf, positioning it securely in the back.

Now it rested at the front, jutting precariously over the edge.

Who could have moved it? he asked himself furiously. Aimée? But Aimée knew better than to touch fragile artifacts. And no one else was allowed near them.

Half a dozen visions raced through Raoul's mind, each uglier than the last. Edward, frustrated and thwarted, longing to possess the gold and jewels his money had purchased. Buffy, sweltering in envy and spite, hungering, as the covetous always hungered, for the things that could never be his. Mohammed's three sons, trapped in the poverty of today, surrounded by the wealth of the past. Even Mohammed himself, an old and trusted friend. . . .

Grimly Raoul turned back to the shelves. Uncovering each of the pieces, one by one, he examined them carefully, checking them off on long, detailed inventory lists. The fragile basket was not the only thing that had been touched. At least a dozen, perhaps two dozen, of the other objects showed visible signs of tampering.

When he finished the task, two hours later, Raoul had to admit he was confused. Someone had been in the workshop, there was no doubt about that, but he had done relatively little harm. There was some minor damage, a chip knocked out of a painted inlaid chest, reeds torn from a pair of baskets, but nothing had been seriously disturbed. And nothing was missing.

Puzzled, Raoul sank down on a packing case in the corner. What the devil did it mean? he asked himself over and over. Who had been there? And what did he want?

It was a minute before his sense of humor returned enough to let him laugh at himself.

"Dammit, Villière. You're behaving like a melodramatic schoolboy." What was he looking for? Thieves—when nothing was stolen? Vandals—when the damage was slight?

Thieves, hell! He was magnifying it out of all proportion. It was a simple matter of curiosity, perhaps even childish spite on Edward's part, that was all. A little tightening of the reins, an effort to clamp down on security, and the thing could be forgotten. There was no point letting his imagination run away with him.

The whole place was getting on his nerves, he told himself irritably, dropping his head into his hands to massage his throbbing temples. This was the site he had dreamed of for years, the glory that was supposed to be the high point of his life, and he had begun to hate it like the plague.

Dammit, he was an archaeologist, not a thief. Archaeologists didn't skulk through hidden tunnels, looking over their shoulders every minute to see if someone was watching them. They worked in the open, digging things up, restoring them—bringing them to light, not concealing them. Small wonder he couldn't think straight anymore, with the stealth and tension that had become a part of his daily life.

Or was it the tension? he asked himself coldly. Was that really what was bothering him, or was it something simpler? Something more personal and human?

Is she pretty?

Why couldn't he remember? Why were dark golden tresses so elusive to his imagination, and jet-black curls, peeking rebelliously from beneath a blue kerchief, so real? Why did soft gray eyes always darken, taking on bewitching hints of the midnight sky?

Aimée. It always came back to Aimée.

He liked the woman. He didn't love her—he couldn't love someone like Aimée no matter how passionately he was attracted to her—but he liked her. He liked being with her, sharing his work with her, his dreams . . . his bed. And when Thea came, all that would change.

Is she pretty?

He hoped so. Oh, God, he hoped so. He was close to Aimée, far closer than he had a right to be to any other man's wife. If Thea could not captivate him, as she had once long ago, nothing would keep him from his darkly lovely mistress in the end.

It was not his dark mistress, or even his golden fiancée, that captured Raoul's imagination later that day as he dipped his oar in the placid surface of the Nile. He had room in his thoughts at that moment for only one woman—a mysterious beauty from centuries past.

Hassan had raced into camp early that afternoon, his face flushed with excitement as he gasped out a tale so incredible Raoul could barely believe it.

"I saw it with my own eyes, *monsieur*. In a little village

not far from here. An ancient piece, I swear it—the head of a woman, all carved from wood and painted. Only, this one is not stiff and rigid like the others. She is so beautiful, so perfect and lifelike, she will take your breath away. And the villagers say she is for sale."

Raoul was skeptical. He knew the sort of villagers Hassan was talking about, thieves and cutthroats every last one of them, all too eager to lure a naive archaeologist—and his money—into some lonely village. But Hassan had seen the head himself, and he had worked in the tomb long enough to know the difference. If it was a forgery, it was a good one. Raoul was determined to see it with his own eyes.

Impatiently he pulled the oars, urging the boat out into the center of the river. Twisting his head, he caught a glimpse of the man behind him. His body tensed at the reminder.

He had wanted to make the hazardous trip alone. With dark hair and sun-bronzed skin half-hidden beneath a coarse galabiya, Raoul might have been able to slip unnoticed through narrow village streets. But Edward, with his fair complexion and foppish Western garb, would stand out wherever they went.

The patched triangular sail of the time-worn felucca hung limp in the still air, but the current was strong and Raoul guided the craft easily downstream. The last warm rays of sunset faded into dusk, and a solitary star shone white against the deep blue sky.

It was the time of day Raoul loved best. The eerie half-light that bathed the riverbanks gave the land an aura of timelessness, as if the pharaohs and slaves of ancient days would step out at any moment for an evening walk. Shepherds in long robes guided their flocks beside muddy canals, moving slowly, languidly, as if they knew the centuries had passed them by. A wooden plow rested idly on the soil, calling back memories of tools dropped by careless hands three thousand years before. Sorghum grew beside the native flax, maize and sugarcane beside the barley, but the fields were still the fields of Akhenaten and his heretic faith, of Cheops and his pyramids, Ramses and his massive temples—of Moses and his captive people crying out to their god for deliverance.

Raoul wished that Edward were a different kind of man. It would have been good to turn to him now, talking of the things they passed.

A tall, graceful woman bent to dip her water jar in the Nile. Did Edward even notice her? he wondered. Did he see her slip a dark veil over her face when she saw their boat drifting close to shore? When they were gone, when there were no longer men in sight, she would pull it down again, enjoying the cool night air on her skin.

A pair of men cut slowly across a distant field, their produce borne in large coarsely woven baskets on their heads. When Napoleon came to Egypt, he had brought wheelbarrows with him, but the Egyptians turned them over and made shelters out of them, and put their baskets on top of their heads again.

It was already dark when Raoul caught sight of a flash of light repeated at rhythmic intervals from the shore. Aiming toward it, he guided the boat deftly, waiting until he heard it scrape against the sand. The hem of his robe trailed in the water as he leaped out, tugging the craft onto the bank.

Mohammed was waiting for him. Thin streaks of gold trickled from the covered lantern in his hand. He hesitated when he saw Edward climb out of the boat.

"It would have been better to come alone, *monsieur*."

Edward bristled at his words. "It's my money. I have a right to be here."

Mohammed eyed him suspiciously. "You have it with you?"

"Of course not," Raoul snapped, answering for him. "You know better than that. I would never allow anything so careless. We'll only look at the bust tonight. If we like it, we'll arrange a transfer later."

Mohammed seemed pacified. Extinguishing his lantern, he wrapped it in a blanket, tucking it under the seat of the boat.

"We'd better go quickly. You do not know these people like I do. It is dangerous to linger, even here."

The village was typical. Set back from the fertile soil of the riverbank, its walls and crowded hovels were built of the sun-baked brick of the Exodus. It could have been a modern village or one as old as time, Raoul could not tell which. The buildings, shabby as they were, would have been occupied continuously, for decades or for centuries. As garbage accumulated, on the floors of the huts as well as on the streets outside, it was packed down with dirt until at last the ceilings were so low a man could no longer stand erect. Then the roofs were removed, another tier or two of bricks added, and the roofs replaced, until a new village stood on the remains of the old, preserving a vital link in the continuity that was Egypt.

Mohammed led the way, slipping through the dark, twisting streets as if he had known them all his life. He did not falter or hesitate. They had agreed on their plan in advance. A labyrinth of narrow alleyways, each stemming from the other, led to a small square that formed the center of the town. This was the way they would go. Later, if they refused the piece—or if the villagers thought they had brought cash with them—they might have need of stealth. Now they could afford to be direct.

Only when they reached the square did Mohammed pause. Slowly he turned his head, as if he were trying to pierce the darkness with his eyes. At last he nodded.

"There. That is the street. I am sure of it."

Raoul was dubious. To him the blackened pathway that led off the square looked no different from all the others. But he had known Mohammed long enough to trust him.

"Let's go."

The hut they stopped in front of was foul and dingy. Even in the dim light they could see filthy mud-brick walls coated with refuse and slime from the street. A chicken clucked sharply on a nearby roof, a dog snarled ominously somewhere in the darkness; then there was silence.

As Raoul stepped inside the doorway, groping to feel the way, the stench of urine and decay was suffocating. He was tempted to use his hand to block it out of his mouth and nostrils. It took an effort to force himself to move toward the faint, flickering light at the end of the deep entryway.

Inside, the hovel was even more disgusting. Raoul stood on the threshold, staring in at the garbage strewn across the floor. Chicken bones, picked nearly clean, mingled with bits of decaying vegetables, alive with maggots. Dried cattle dung, an ample supply of fuel, was stacked sloppily in one corner.

Raoul did not even see the man who hovered in a doorway at the end of the room. His sandals crunched on the debris as he stepped slyly forward.

He was a short man, a little past middle age, his sallow face sharp and lined. The coarse woolen robe that hung on his thin body was a filthy gray, streaked with dark brown tobacco stains. Raoul was grateful when he did not extend his hand. He would not have liked to touch him.

"I am Raoul Villière," he said shortly, addressing the man in Arabic. "I believe you have something to sell."

The man was startled by his directness. His eyes grew shifty, darting from Raoul's face to Mohammed's, then back again. They stopped when he caught sight of Edward. A slow grin began to cross his features. A flash of gold showed in his mouth as he spoke.

"You wish to buy, heh?"

"We wish to see what you're selling. Then we'll decide."

If the man heard Raoul, he gave no sign of it. He was still staring at Edward, assessing his plump, pampered features and the expensive cut of his suit Raoul knew he would have to move sharply to establish his authority.

"Well, do you have it or don't you?"

Reluctantly the man turned away from Edward. "Yes, I have it. It is inside. I will get it."

He took his time as he shuffled across the room, heading for the doorway in the rear. Left alone, the three men did not speak. Faint sounds drifted through the darkness: a woman's voice, shrill in the distance, crying out complaints they could not hear; a child's long, wailing whine; a loud burst of laughter from somewhere nearby. Lonely sounds that only hinted at life behind high walls where it could not be seen.

It was several minutes before the man returned. When he did, he had a package in his arms.

Raoul reached out to take it from him, his hands trembling as he peeled away the filthy rags that bound it. He turned aside so the man would not notice.

He knew it was insane to let himself get worked up like that. He was bound to be disappointed. The thing had to be a forgery, just like all the other forgeries he had followed up over the years.

But if it wasn't . . . If everything Hassan said about it was true . . .

The last layer of rags tangled unexpectedly, catching as if they had been tied deliberately into knots. It was all Raoul could do to keep from ripping them away. Forcing himself to work patiently, he finally managed to ease them apart.

One look was enough to tell him his efforts had not been in vain.

She is beautiful, Hassan had said. *So perfect and lifelike she will take your breath away*. He had not been wrong.

Raoul held the miniature head delicately in his hands, staring at it in wonder. He had never seen anything quite like it. Even the deep cracks that ran through the aging wood, chipping the subtly shaded paint, could not detract from the loveliness of the feminine features that stared back at him. Fluid of line, natural in both form and color, the bust was as rare as it was exquisite. And there was no doubt in his mind that it was genuine.

"Bring the light closer."

Leaning forward he let dark gold rays play on the softer

gold of the woman's features. High cheekbones accented a strong, straight nose, and dark brows hovered over deep-set eyes, reminding him of a sweetness that was hauntingly familiar. For a moment he could not place it. When he did, he sucked in his breath with astonishment.

It was the girl in the painting on the wall of the tomb. And unless he was very much mistaken, her eyes were blue, painted with pigment made from powdered lapis lazuli.

His mind reeled with the implications. If this was the girl in the painting, then the bust could only have come from Ramose's tomb—and Ramose's tomb had been sealed for more than three thousand years!

"Where did you get this?"

The sudden touch of Mohammed's hand on his arm warned him he had made a mistake. If the head had been taken after they had opened the tomb—and he was sure it had—then the man was a thief. He would not want his actions scrutinized.

But the man did not try to protest. He could see that the foreigner was interested, and that was all he cared about.

"I have it. That is what matters, is it not?"

"How much do you want for it?"

Raoul glanced up to see that the man was looking not at him, but at Edward. It was easy to see why. Greed and longing were written plainly on his features.

"Two thousand English pounds."

Raoul laughed harshly. Even with Edward's idiotic behavior, the price was ridiculous. "I'll give you two hundred."

"Two thousand," the man repeated calmly, picking up the head with one hand, the dingy rags that had bound it with the other.

Raoul, anticipating his tactics, relinquished the piece easily. But Edward was frantic with despair.

"What is it?" he cried out shrilly. "What does he want? Why is he wrapping it up like that?"

Raoul spun around to face him. "Be quiet, you fool. You've already driven up the price enough as it is. He wants two thousand pounds for it, and that's highway robbery."

"Well, give it to him, then. My God, man, didn't you see it? Haven't you got eyes? It's worth twice that much."

Raoul glared at him, disgusted. How could anyone as tight-fisted as Edward be so naive about money? He turned back to the man.

"Two hundred and fifty pounds—and that's my best price."

But the man was no fool. Without understanding a word of

English, he knew exactly what they had said. He did not try to speak, but finished wrapping the bust, securing it in its filthy veils again. When he was done, he turned away calmly.

That was too much for Edward.

"No!" he shouted frantically. "I want it. Do you hear me? I want it! Give it to me!"

The man faced Edward again. His eyes were shining in the lantern light, but his face was placid. He stared at Edward, then slowly shook his head.

Desperately Edward reached in his pocket. He could not speak Arabic, but he knew the language all men understood. Pulling out a roll of bills, he began to peel off twenty one-hundred-pound notes. His fingers were shaking so badly he could barely move them.

"You fool!"

Raoul's voice was hoarse as he glared at Edward. Dammit, he had told the man not to bring money with him. Didn't he know he was endangering all their lives?

Fool, was he? Edward thought furiously. Well, they'd see who the fool was. They wanted him to leave his money at home, did they? Well, if he had, the magnificent little sculpture would have gotten away from them.

Hands still shaking, he held out the money. He could tell by the look on the man's face—the sheer greed that nearly made him drool as he gaped at the worn, dirty notes—that he would not refuse them.

Raoul saw the look, too, but unlike Edward, he did not misread it. The man had seen the rest of the roll Edward put back in his pocket, and he knew a great deal more than two thousand pounds was at stake that night.

"Throw the money at him." Raoul's voice was a sharp command. "Toss it up high. Scatter it all over the place."

Edward looked confused for a minute, then obeyed automatically. Notes fluttered noisily in the air, floating down to the rubbish on the floor. Raoul strode forward, ripping the package abruptly from the man's hands.

"Let's get the hell out of here."

The night air was dark and impenetrable, but Raoul did not stop to get his bearings. Even a second's pause might be fatal. The man inside would not be alone. Somewhere in the back rooms, his cronies would be lurking, waiting to leap out at the first cry of alarm. They would pause for a few seconds, squabbling over the money on the floor—but only a few seconds.

"Hsst!"

Mohammed's voice came out of the darkness. Horrified, Raoul realized his foreman was already well ahead of him. Blindly he stumbled toward the sound, sliding his feet through the filth so his sandals would not clatter against the earth. Only at the last minute did he remember to reach out and grasp Edward's coat, pulling the man after him. He could lose himself in that garbage pit of a village for all Raoul cared, but not now. Not when his clumsy lingering could give them all away.

They followed the plan they had set up in advance, choosing a twisting, circuitous route to take them out of town. The thieves would expect them to use the same direct path that had brought them in. If they had already plotted an ambush, it would be staged somewhere on those streets.

As his eyes adjusted to the dark, Raoul looked around him. He took no comfort in what he saw. The street Mohammed had picked for them was so narrow they could not have gone two abreast, even had they wanted to. The houses were packed together, one doorway following close upon another. And each of those doorways was a deep, anonymous pit, sheltering things he could only guess at.

A sudden noise behind him made him whirl in alarm. Grimly he realized they had been fools to count on their own cleverness. A single noise, a single shadow, would have been enough to tell the thieves which way they had gone.

He searched the darkness. When he saw nothing, it only increased his tension. If he could see them, if he could count and assess them, at least he would know what he was up against.

Then the sound was repeated, a low rustle, like a careless foot brushing against a pile of trash. It was so near, it made his blood run cold. He paused, motionless, waiting for it to come again.

Instead, all he heard was the low, plaintive meow of a cat.

For a second he could not believe his ears. Then suddenly, so suddenly he could not control it, a wave of relief flooded his body. Weakly he thrust out his hand, steadying himself. As he watched, a scrawny yellow cat sidled out of the darkness, rubbing itself against the wall. It did not even notice Raoul as it continued its solitary prowl down the street.

Raoul pulled himself together quickly. He had already fallen too far behind the others. He had to catch up with them, and he had to do it now. If they were ever going to get out of that hellhole, they had to stick together.

He did not even see the man in the doorway ahead. All his

concentration was centered on the street behind him and the pursuers he was certain would catch up with him at any second. He had not expected to be attacked from the front.

By the time he saw the man, it was too late to retreat. One minute, he was nothing but a shadow lingering in the doorway; the next, he was a bold figure striding out to cut off Raoul's path. A long, curved blade gleamed in his fingers.

Reacting instinctively, Raoul thrust out his hand, twisting out of the way as the blade darted forward. Swifter than his assailant, he managed to elude the blow, bringing his hand up to clamp around the man's wrist. He heard a sharp grunt of pain, but he could not make him loosen his grip on the weapon.

Dammit, he had been waiting for them. Deliberately waiting. As if he had known in advance what path they would take. And he had let Edward and Mohammed go ahead, waiting until he saw the rag-swathed sculpture in Raoul's arms.

Raoul clenched his teeth as he struggled with his opponent, trying to wrench his arm sharply enough to throw him off balance. He knew he was at a disadvantage, clutching a bulky parcel in one hand, but there was nothing he could do about it. He could not bring himself to toss it aside and risk damage to the fragile wood.

The man was stronger than he had expected. Raoul managed to hold a grip on his arm, but there was no way he could throw him. For the moment, it was a stalemate, but Raoul sensed it would not last. There was a youthful vigor in the other man, a kind of power that would outlast his own. If he was going to do anything to save himself, he had to do it quickly.

Then suddenly he felt something at his throat, like a sturdy forearm, closing him in a vise so relentless he could barely breathe. Instantly he realized what had happened. There had been another assailant, a second man, hiding in the shadows behind him, biding his time until he could leap out to attack from behind.

Raoul was tempted to shout for help, but he did not dare. Any cry that brought Mohammed would bring a dozen thieves as well. Bracing himself for the fight—a fight that might be his last—he planted his feet firmly.

He tensed his body. Then abruptly, without warning, he gave in to the strength of the man behind. Swinging back, he let his right foot jab into the air. Clinging urgently to the first man's wrist, he landed a perfectly timed kick on his jaw. The combination was too much for his assailant. With his arm pulled roughly forward and his head snapping back, he could no longer hold his balance. The knife flew from his hand as he fell.

Now it was one to one again. Writhing urgently, Raoul tried to take advantage of the second man's surprise to work his way free. He had almost succeeded when he caught sight of another hooded figure hurtling through the night, with still another looming in the darkness behind him.

Damn them, he thought with a surge of rage. Another second and he would have been free. Now it was all over.

With a last rally of strength, as much in anger as self-defense, Raoul doubled up his arms. Thrusting his elbows back, he aimed a sharp blow at the pit of the man's stomach. It would do him no good, he knew. He could not win, but at least he would give them a run for it.

The blow was effective. Raoul felt the soft flesh of the man's belly give beneath his elbow. A startled burst of air grunted in his ear, and the arms loosened at last. Whirling, he raised the package in his hands, praying the delicate bust would be strong enough to sustain the force of a man's skull.

He never had a chance to use it.

One look at the savage fury in Raoul's face, and the man turned and fled. He did not even wait for his companion, groping through the dirt as he crawled past Raoul.

"What the devil . . .?"

Turning, Raoul found himself staring into the face of his foreman, Mohammed. Behind him, Edward, pale with fear, gaped at him with wide eyes.

So that was it. Mohammed, alarmed when he did not catch up, had come to look for him. No wonder the men had run away.

Glancing back, Raoul searched the darkness behind him. The man he had kicked was already stumbling to his feet. The blow had made him groggy, and he could not move well.

Dammit, he was not going to get away like that, Raoul thought furiously. Too many things had happened, too many questions were unanswered. He was going to catch the man and grill him soundly. Thrusting the package into Edward's hands, he began to hurry after him.

He had gone only a few steps when Mohammed stopped him, his hand firm on his arm. "I want the man as much as you, but it is too dangerous. If we go back now, they will all be on us."

Raoul tensed, but he did not argue. He hated to admit it,

but Mohammed was right. Reluctantly he turned back, reaching to take the bust from Edward's arms.

But Edward pulled away, his eyes defiant as he clutched it to his breast. He was frightened, desperately frightened, but the thing was his, and he would not give it up.

Disgusted, Raoul saw he would have another fight on his hands if he tried to take it from him. Well, let him keep it for now, he told himself. It would be safe enough in Edward's arms. No one could pull it out of that death grip he held it in. Time enough later to remind him it was part of the treasures of the tomb, to be kept in the workshop until everything had been properly excavated and recorded.

Raoul was still trembling when they reached the boat, as much from anger and fatigue as the aftermath of fear. Every muscle of his body ached as he pushed Edward into the crude wooden vessel, then helped Mohammed shove it out into the water. Both men jumped in at the same time, grabbing the oars as they steered toward the center of the river.

It was not until they moved upstream, well out of range of the thieves, that Raoul felt his tension relax at last. Pulling in the oars, he leaned back, stretching his aching muscles. After a moment, he threw back his head and roared with laughter.

He knew Mohammed was staring at him as if he were a madman, but he did not care. He had never felt so exhilarated in his life.

They had pulled it off. They had actually pulled it off. Edward, that damned fool, had nearly cost them their lives, carrying cash into a den of thieves, but what did that matter now? They had the sculpture, a perfect little gem of a sculpture, the loveliest piece of art he had ever seen, and they had not spilled a drop of their own blood to get it.

He was still in a buoyant mood when they pulled the boat onto the shore, mounting the horses that would take them back to the site. It was a false elation, he knew, a kind of euphoria following fear, but he had done battle with the worst elements in a primitive land, and he had won.

Aimée was waiting when they returned. Standing quietly on the steps of the workshop, she watched the horses approach. Raoul caught sight of her from the edge of the camp. With a burst of laughter he galloped toward her, reining in his horse so abruptly a cloud of sand flew up from its hooves.

She had never looked so beautiful to him. An intriguing study in colors—the deep gold of the sand and the black of her hair, blue eyes reflecting the mystery of the night sky. And he had never wanted her so badly.

He leaned down, not even turning to make sure Edward was safely in his tent. Cupping her chin in his hands, he tilted her face toward his.

"Are you waiting for me? My own private love goddess, offering me her passion?" He had never spoken so frankly before, but he was drunk with his own excitement. "Well, fear not, goddess, I will not deny what both you and I want. You will have your way with me—and now. I think your husband is too tired to set foot out of his tent."

He was surprised when she pulled away from him, taking a step backward. Swinging from the saddle, he stood before her. Tenderness mingled with the longing in his heart as he gazed at her.

"What is it, Aimée? You look so pale. Is something wrong?"

"Is it?"

Even as she spoke, she knew the words were empty. Her question was not meant for him. It was a question she alone could answer.

Something *was* wrong—for her. But it was right for him.

It took her a moment to work up the courage to speak. When she did, she tried to make her voice warm and generous.

"Thea is here."

2

Aimée leaned forward, elbows resting on the dirty marble tabletop. The small native café, the first she had ventured into, was one of the most fascinating places she had ever seen. The strong aroma of Turkish coffee was a perfect foil for the cloying scent of oleander, carried on cooling northern breezes through the open patio. The flowering shrub climbed tall stone columns and worked its way across high trellises to shade the diners from the searing sun. Waiters in long, grease-stained galabiyas and dirty white turbans strolled casually among the tables, setting steaming pots of tea beside plates of rice vivid with Eastern spices. The constant clatter of trictrac tiles joined with the murmur of conversation to form a backdrop for the sad tones of a tarabookah, drifting in from somewhere down the street.

Seeing the bright red oleander sparkling against deep green leaves peeking temptingly around the columns that rimmed the café, Aimée caught a branch in her hands, snapping it sharply with her fingers. The blossoms looked delicate against her skin.

"Aren't they lovely?" she said softly, raising her eyes to look at the woman seated across from her.

Lady Theodora Welles had been a surprise. Aimée had expected a far different sort of person. Someone tall and regal perhaps, graceful and willowy, the epitome of an aloof British aristocrat. Or a more fragile beauty, a kind of Meissen shepherdess with platinum hair and milky skin setting off forget-me-not eyes.

Yet in reality Thea was none of these things. Petite and feminine, she had a childlike air about her as she perched on the edge of her stool. The fine India muslin of her skirt, snowy and immaculate, had been pulled a discreet inch above her ankle so its delicate blue lace trim would not trail on the floor. Matching echoes of blue touched her bodice, daringly low-cut to show off plump young breasts. Her hair, the color of dark honey, was twisted into artful curls; her eyes were soft and gray and enormous.

"They are pretty," she agreed, catching the flowers in her own fingers and lifting them to her nose. "And the smell is certainly an improvement over most in this country."

Aimée did not try to respond. She enjoyed the smells of Egypt—the dust of the road, the burning grease from the brazier set up in the entryway, even the sweat of bodies hot in the afternoon sun—but she knew Thea would have been more comfortable on the wide, shaded veranda of one of the tourist hotels.

A waiter moved slowly past their table, stepping carelessly around the parcels piled on the floor beside them. Heaping plates of rice, rich with almonds and raisins, were balanced on his arms. The smell of cloves and cardamom lingered in Aimée's nostrils after he had gone.

"Doesn't that look delicious? I could order a whole plateful, I'm so ravenous."

"Ravenous?" Thea stared at her in amazement. "After that enormous lunch we had?"

"But that was hours ago. Besides, shopping always makes me hungry."

"Well, not me. I'm exhausted in all this heat. I don't want anything but a cup of tea and a chance to relax for a few minutes."

Aimée shook her head as she watched Thea lift the cup to her lips. How could anyone resist the tempting foods of the

East? Chicken roasted in lemon until it was crisp and brown; little kebabs of beef and lamb grilled over an open flame; coarse chunks of flat peasant bread dipped in garbanzo paste, heavy with oil and seasonings; savory little sweetmeats rich with the taste of honey and sesame.

"Come on, Thea," she coaxed. "Not the rice. That would be too much, I admit. But couldn't we have one of those little skewers of meat?"

Thea wrinkled up her nose. "Get one for yourself—if you have room. They look perfectly dreadful to me."

"All right, if you're sure you won't change your mind." Aimée jumped up eagerly. "I'll be back in a minute."

The heat was more intense at the entrance to the café, but for once Aimée did not mind. The bustling activity on the street outside was so intriguing, she could have stood and watched it for hours. Shielding her eyes with her hands, she squinted into the glaring sun.

The narrow dirt roads that crisscrossed the small town were different from the hectic excitement of the marketplace in Cairo, but they had a fascination all their own. Peddlers were more relaxed here, breaking their whining cries to squat beside friends in the open coffeehouses, laughing with raucous good humor at their own bawdy jokes. A little boy elbowed his way through the crowds, a huge bunch of African daisies balanced in arms that could barely reach around them. A tall, bony peasant, struggling with a squawking goose, laughed good-naturedly as he stopped to get a tighter hold on it, grasping it firmly by the wings.

Water vendors winked as they tapped pointedly on heavy earthenware jars, sweating in the sun. A massive black man, grinning a wide, toothless grin, lowered a tray of sweets from his head, tempting Aimée with parched peas and sugar. Fruit sellers hawked ne black bananas and bits of sweet melon, their flesh glistening beneath a layer of flies. A little boy sidled up, his voice low and urgent—"Hsst, lady! Hsst! Genuine scarabs from the tomb of the pharaoh"—as if he really believed his clumsy forgeries were stolen treasures of the ancient kings.

A solitary woman squatted in the doorway of a coffeehouse across the street, the hem of her long black malaya trailing in the dust. Her eyes were closed, her hands folded patiently in her lap. Beside her a beggar rested in the shade of the wall. Sightless eyes glazed white with trachoma seemed to be peering into the distance as he listened for the sound of alms.

"Allah will reward you," he cried again and again in the

same monotonous tone. "Every man who loves the poor will go to Paradise. Allah will ask of him nothing more."

Aimée was touched by his words. She reminded herself to slip a small coin out of her bag later when they left the café. She liked this alien concept of a charitable Paradise.

A burst of laughter from inside the café jolted her back to reality. Guiltily she turned toward the brazier. Thea had been a good sport to come there with her. It was not fair to leave her alone.

She picked out a few scraps of mutton from an open pile, trying to ignore the black flies that swarmed across its surface.

"Be sure it's well-done," she admonished the cook. Raoul had warned her to eat nothing unless it was well-cooked. No rare meats, no fresh fruits or unpeeled vegetables, not even a glass of lemonade unless she was sure the water had been boiled first. "Very black on the outside. Okay?"

"Okay lady," the man agreed cheerfully. "Sure. Okay."

Aimée studied his face, wondering if he really understood or if he was just being accommodating. There was no way to tell. She stood beside him for a minute, watching him thread the meat deftly on a pair of skewers, then hurried back inside, slipping into her place at the table.

"I'm sorry I took so long."

Thea looked up eagerly. She had opened one of her parcels, letting a length of fabric spill out on the table.

"Isn't it perfect, Aimée? I could never find anything this lovely in England. I'm going to have a dress made of it right away."

Aimée ran her fingers across the fabric. It was a sheer Egyptian cotton, delicately embroidered in powder blue, a perfect compliment for Thea's eyes.

"Not very practical for the desert, but pretty."

"Oh, I know." Thea sighed. "I meant to get something sensible, truly I did. A nice sturdy length of muslin for a blouse and skirt, just like yours. But then I saw this fabric, and . . . oh, Aimée, it looked so lovely. How could I let it go?"

In spite of herself, Aimée was amused. Thea sometimes seemed a silly creature, vain and capricious, helpless to the point of absurdity, but there was a warmth and spontaneity about her that was hard to resist.

"Keep your pretty fabric," she advised. "And all your lovely lacy dresses."

Thea might be frivolous, but she had the right idea. Aimée had given up her own corsets and petticoats and dainty lace-trimmed frocks, trading elegance for smudges and tatters so she could work beside Raoul in the tomb, but it was Thea—pretty, ladylike, perfectly groomed Thea—who had won his heart.

Thea did not notice her distraction. "Come to town with me tomorrow, will you, Aimée? I'm sure Raoul won't miss you if you're gone one more afternoon, and we could look for a good dressmaker . . ."

Aimée was surprised to hear Thea's voice trail off in the middle of a sentence. Her gray eyes had widened until they seemed to fill her entire face.

Curiously Aimée turned around. At first she saw nothing out of the ordinary. The men were concentrating on their trictrac games as they had been all afternoon, while waiters moved nonchalantly past the tables. A few Europeans were scattered around the room, their Western tailoring a striking contrast to the ancient robes of the East. In the entryway, an old woman paused, her black robe nearly brown with dust, a veil hiding all but her eyes.

Only when she concentrated on the woman's eyes did Aimée realize what Thea had seen. Black and intense, vibrating with power, they seemed to glow with a passion as violent as it was single-minded.

And she was looking right at Aimée!

Aimée did not even realize she had risen to her feet. Her hands moved upward, but she could not feel the protective fingers against her cheeks. The room was deathly silent.

The woman's hands were raised, her fingers pointing accusingly at Aimée. They were like the talons of a bird of prey, twisted and gnarled, the nails sharp and predatory as claws.

They were the same hands that had gouged at her eyes in the church in Cairo.

Every instinct in Aimée's body cried out to her to run. Furiously she fought the impulse. She was safe here. She knew she was safe. There were dozens of people around her. What could the old woman do to her?

"What . . . what do you want of me?"

Her voice seemed to anger the woman. Throwing her head back, as she had on that other, terrifying afternoon when Aimée first saw her, she let out a long, piercing cry, as eerie and penetrating as a wail for the dead.

Instantly the room, so hushed and silent only a moment before, exploded with excitement. Waiters sprang to life, hurrying forward, and men swept trictrac tiles to the floor with careless sleeves as they pushed back their stools. Women peeked in from the street in curiosity. It was only a matter of seconds before the old woman was surrounded.

Aimée stood in the center of the room, too dazed to do anything but stare after the men as they hustled the woman noisily out to the street. Then suddenly, just as suddenly as she had appeared, she was gone again, and the room was silent once more.

Had it really happened? Aimée asked herself, amazed at the sense of unreality that swept over her. She felt strangely alone, abandoned in the midst of empty tables. Had the old woman really been there, or had she imagined it all?

The silence was shattered when the men began to crowd back into the café, laughing and joking as they scrambled for trictrac tiles on the floor. Focusing her mind with effort, Aimée returned to her seat.

Thea leaned forward, concerned. "What on earth got into you, Aimée? What made you stand up like that? Why, I thought that old woman was going to attack you."

"She has attacked me," Aimée explained tensely. "Once before. This isn't the first time I've run into her."

"Are you serious? You've seen her before? You're sure?"

Thea could not conceal the doubt in her voice. Watching her, Aimée realized no one was going to believe her story. And the worst of it was, she couldn't blame them. The whole thing sounded preposterous, even to her.

The waiter hovered over them. A plate of grilled mutton, so black it looked like pieces of charcoal, was cooling in his hand.

"You must not mind so much. She is an old woman, just an old woman. We must have kindness in our hearts for the old."

"I know," Aimée agreed contritely. "But she . . . she . . ."

"She is angry for all the changes. Yes, and I think she is afraid, too. The world is not the same anymore. There are foreigners everywhere with their strange clothes. Some of our men even dress like them now. And they sit in the public cafés, these women, with their faces unveiled. How can an old woman accept that?"

"But the same thing happened to me before," Aimée tried to explain, anxious to make him believe her, even though she knew it was impossible. "With the same woman."

"How can this be?" The waiter shook his head doubtfully. "I have not seen this woman before. I think she does not live here."

Aimée did not try to tell him about the church in Cairo. If he found her story hard to believe now, what would he think if she implied that an old woman, frail and penniless, had come all that way just to wreak vengeance on the girl who touched a martyr's painted image?

"It must have been someone else, Aimée," Thea said softly.

The waiter nodded knowingly. "Some other old woman. There are so many."

"You know, I think it was our eyes that frightened her. I got the distinct feeling she was staring at our eyes."

"Ah, yes," the waiter agreed. "It would be the eyes. These old women, these country people, they are terrified of the evil eye. She must have thought you were a jinn. They are awful things the jinns. They leap out at you in the dark and do terrible things. I do not believe such things myself, of course, but the women . . . Why, do you know, if you tell a woman her child is beautiful, she will scream at you. 'No, no,' she will say. 'My child is ugly. He has a wart on the end of his nose. His eyes cross when he looks at you. He is not beautiful.' Always, you see, they are afraid of the jinn. If the child is too beautiful, the jinn will be jealous and take it away."

He stopped for a moment to laugh at his own story. "All the time they are carrying the child, in the months before it is born, they have with them the picture of a beautiful child so their own baby will be beautiful, too. But the minute it is born, and you say, 'What a beautiful child that is, just as you wanted,' they will say, 'No, no, he is ugly.' "

He was still chuckling to himself as he hurried away, pleased that he had managed to calm the foreign lady so easily. Bewildered, Aimée stared after him. Was he right, after all? she wondered. It did seem logical. The deep blue of her eyes had always attracted attention, even in her own land.

"But your eyes are gray, Thea. Surely gray eyes are as unusual in Egypt as blue. Why wasn't she staring at you?"

"I rather think she was. At least, that's how it seemed at first. That's what startled me, you know. When I looked up, there she was, all fiery and fanatical, and staring right at me."

"You could be right." The old woman could have been staring at Thea. She might not even have noticed Aimée until she stood up.

"Of course I'm right. It was some other woman, that's all. In their black veils, they all look alike."

Aimée drew her fingers across her brow, wiping away

damp tendrils of hair. She was beginning to feel foolish. Thea, silly, frivolous Thea, was behaving sensibly, and she was acting like an idiot.

She knew Thea was right. The old woman wasn't the same one she had seen in Cairo. She couldn't possibly be. It had all happened so quickly, she hadn't really had a chance to get a look at her. Dark eyes, an angry gesture, that was all she had seen. Just enough to evoke memories of an experience so frightening it deprived her of her power to reason.

"It's the heat," she murmured awkwardly, reaching in her bag to pull out a lace handkerchief. "I can't stand the heat. Sometimes it's so bad I can't think straight."

Thea agreed. "I know. I can't stand it myself."

"The nights are so cool I almost forget about it. But then in the morning, when it begins to get warm again, when I feel the first morning heat on my skin, it makes me physically sick."

"Sick?" Thea glanced up sharply, her eyes running up and down Aimée's figure. "In the morning?"

"I know it's silly. I suspect it's mostly psychological, but the idea of a whole day's heat ahead is too much to endure. Why, all last week it was so bad, I actually threw up."

"Oh, Aimée . . ." Thea struggled to choke back her laughter. "Oh, my dear, I don't mean to make fun of you, but . . ."

For an instant Aimée could only stare at her, puzzled. Thea might be silly, but she was never unkind. It was a moment before she understood.

"Oh, no . . ."

"Why not? Sick in the morning? Ravenous again two hours after lunch?" Her eyes sparkled as she looked down at the mutton, untouched in front of Aimée.

But it couldn't be, Aimée thought, trying desperately to get her mind to focus on the idea. It just couldn't! All those months with Buffy, those terrible months when her body had refused to respond. She had been so sure she couldn't get pregnant.

"But I'm . . . surely I'm too young."

Thea could control her laughter no longer. "Oh, Aimée, girls far younger than you give birth every day. Don't look so shocked. It's perfectly natural."

She paused for a moment, staring at the stunned expression on Aimée's face. For the first time she remembered what a boor the girl's husband was. The thought of bearing his child might well be a painful one.

"It will be all right. Truly it will. Having a baby is the

most wonderful thing in the world. I can hardly wait until it's my time. A baby can be . . ." She hesitated for a moment, fearing she had gone too far. "A baby can be such a compensation."

A baby? Aimée looked up in surprise. In the shock of realizing she was pregnant, in the midst of all the doubts and apprehensions, she had lost sight of the essence of the thing. A baby. A tiny, delicate creature, loving and dependent. A trial and a joy—a comfort and a responsibility both. A part of the love she could never truly possess, hers to keep forever.

"Raoul." She whispered his name softly, letting it lie on the tip of her tongue. What would Raoul say when he found out? Would he be angry, resenting the burden he had not asked for, or would there be one small, secret corner of his heart that would be pleased? "Don't tell Raoul."

"Raoul? What does Raoul have to do with this?"

Horrified, Aimée pulled herself out of her reverie. The look on Thea's face warned her she had said too much. Frantically she searched her mind for some way to correct her error.

"If you tell Raoul, if he knows I'm pregnant, then he won't let me work in the tomb anymore."

Thea looked bewildered, then burst out laughing. "How surprising you are, Aimée—always doing the unexpected. You've just learned you're going to have a child, and all you're worried about is whether you can work."

Aimée breathed a sigh of relief at the good humor in Thea's tone. Nervously she turned her attention to the grilled mutton, now cold on her plate. She was not hungry anymore, but she wanted some excuse—any excuse—to keep from talking. She didn't dare risk another slip.

"I guess I must be eating for two," she said inanely. She wondered if she looked as uncomfortable as she felt.

Thea did not seem to notice as she sat across the table, chattering with a generous enthusiasm that would have been infectious had Aimée not been so confused and so apprehensive. She barely heard the barrage of words as she struggled to sort things out in her mind.

Pregnant? Was she really pregnant? And would she be strong enough to face it if she was? The experience would be a beautiful one, she knew, beautiful and fulfilling in a way nothing else could ever be—but all that would come later. Now she had only problems to wrestle with, plans to make. Raoul would have to be told. And Edward . . .

Edward! She almost choked on the mutton as she thought of him.

She had told Edward once she was not pregnant, and he had never sent his lover to her again. Would he believe her now when she pretended she had been mistaken?

And how would he feel about it if he did?

She had always known there was a powerful bond between Edward and his lover. A bond as ugly and malignant as it was potent—a kind of perversion that went beyond mere sexual deviation. Edward had been pleased, even smug, to find his lover was little more of a man than he. How would he react when he learned he had been wrong?

No cooling breeze touched the western valleys of the Nile. The sun, reflecting off crystals of sand, scorched the earth. Visible waves of heat blurred the mountains, giving them the effect of shimmering water.

Edward shifted his weight lethargically. Even the shade in front of his tent offered no respite from the heat. Turning uncomfortably, he stared at Buffy, half-asleep as he lounged in his chair.

He felt a growing distaste as he studied his lover. The years had not been kind to Buffy, he told himself maliciously. Not kind at all. His nose, once strong and forceful, had developed a new sharpness, accented by sun-dried skin stretched too tightly across it. Full, sensual lips had slackened, and little pockets of fat nestled under his eyes and in the sagging skin beneath his chin.

He looked, Edward thought, remarkably like himself.

"Must you sit there with your mouth hanging open?" he snapped petulantly. "I'm sorry it's so boring for you here."

Buffy's lids half-opened. "My, my, we are touchy, aren't we? Don't tell me the heat's getting to you, Eddie?"

His eyes were nervous, flitting a little too anxiously toward Edward's face, then darting away again. He knew his lover had been regarding him, and he knew what he had seen.

"It's not the heat that bothers me. It's you. Always sniveling and complaining. Why don't you sit in front of your own tent?"

"And grouchy, too! Now, now, Eddie, don't take it out on me. I can't help it if your pet archaeologist won't jump when you snap your fingers."

"Dammit, I said get out of here! I don't want to look at your face anymore."

Buffy moved with deliberate languor as he eased his body

out of the chair. Edward's anger told him the barb had been a cutting one. The knowledge did not give him the satisfaction it once would have.

"Well, don't give yourself a heart attack, Eddie. I was about to go anyway. Quite frankly, you're right—it is boring here."

He paused just as he reached the edge of the shade. His face was half in sunlight, half in shadow as he turned.

"But I'll be back, you know. After dark, when you're lonely and don't want to turn the light out all by yourself."

He tossed a bright smile over his shoulder, as automatic as it was insincere. It had not yet occurred to him it was no longer pretty.

Edward watched dispassionately as Buffy sauntered away. He had gained weight, Edward noticed, in the months they had been in Egypt. Thighs that were already too large now stretched the expensive fabric of his trousers, and his bottom was as broad as a woman's.

No, he told himself waspishly, he would not invite Buffy to his tent that night. It would give him no pleasure. The act of sex with Buffy had once been an exciting, erotic thing, more stimulating and fulfilling than anything he had ever known. It was as if, with Buffy, he had become a whole person at last, joining the passion of his spirit with the physical beauty that should have been his. But now . . .

Edward shuddered with disgust. The idea of possessing Buffy was now repulsive to him. Buffy was too much like himself, epitomizing the worst of everything that was in him. It would be like making love to himself—the lowest form of masturbation.

"You don't have much time, Buffy," he whispered softly. "Not much time at all." A milk bath for his complexion, a diet for his figure—but he could not hold off the inevitable forever.

Edward felt a little thrill of satisfaction at the thought. He had already begun to imagine the day, not so far in the future, when he would be able to look at the man who had once captivated and tormented him and tell him he no longer needed him. The thought pleased him. He knew he would enjoy it more than he had ever enjoyed the use of his body.

The Nile was lazy in the sunlight. Half a dozen boats drifted on the current; the rest were pulled up on the sand, their low sides forming patches of shade for the boatmen to rest in. Tall sunflowers stood like weary sentinels on the bank, their heads bowed toward the water. An old man in a blue cotton galabiya shuffled through the dust of the road, tugging a small donkey laden with shocks of Indian corn for fuel.

"Hello, ladies. How are you, ladies?"

The singsong tones of the boy Ahmed shattered the stillness of the afternoon. His bare feet barely touched the ground as he skipped toward them.

Aimée smiled as she greeted him. "Hello, Ahmed. Are you going to help us with the boat?"

"Sure, lady, sure." The boy preened with self-importance. The boatman, Aziz, could push the small dahabiya into the water by himself, and Ahmed knew it, but he liked to feel as if he had earned his baksheesh. He was no beggar holding out a bowl for alms.

Thea sighed as she stepped into the boat, sinking onto a shallow, uncomfortable seat. "It's good to sit down again."

Aimée could not disagree. "In this heat, just a short walk is strenuous. I wonder what it's like in the middle of the summer."

The boy grunted loudly, exaggerating the exertion it took to scrape the light boat across the sand. His eyes never left the silver coin in Aimée's fingers.

"Here we go, lady. Okay? Yes?"

Aimée laughed as she watched him leap out of the water, nimbly catching the coin. A soft breeze skimmed the river, easing the sail into a gentle arc. The boat slid smoothly away from the shore.

Leaning down, Aimée let the ripples tease her fingers and splash lightly onto her arm. The creaking of the sail was as rhythmic as the current, lulling her into a quiet contentment.

Everything would be all right, she knew it would. She would tell Raoul about the child, and he would not be angry. How could he mind when that tiny new life would be as much a part of him as of her? As much his flesh as the flesh of the woman who bore it?

She would tell him right away, as soon as they got back to the camp. She would not wait until the thought frightened her again and she was tempted to put it off. The minute she got him away from Thea, she would share her secret with him and he would be glad.

Raoul did not love her, not as she loved him, but there was an excitement in their most casual encounter, an excitement that had not totally vanished even with Thea's coming. Now

220

a part of that excitement would endure forever in tangible, physical form, created in the same Valley of Eternity that was his one great passion in life.

3

Raoul was not with the workmen when the two women returned to the camp, nor were Mohammed and his two oldest sons anywhere in sight. Aimée was surprised. As far as she could remember, all four of them had never been absent from the digging area at once.

Breaking away from Thea, she began to hurry toward the workmen.

"Hassan!"

The young man scowled when he saw her approach. Throwing down his shovel, he took a step toward her.

"Hassan, where is your father? And Daoud and Salem?"

Hassan's scowl deepened as he drew her to the side. "You should not question me in front of the men. You know better than that."

Something in his guarded tones made Aimée uncomfortable. Ignoring Thea, who had hurried to join them, she blurted out, "What is it? What's wrong, Hassan? Where is everyone?"

Hassan threw a quick glance at the workmen to make sure no one was watching. "There has been an accident," he admitted reluctantly. "One of the walls caved in."

"An accident?" Aimée felt as if her heart had stopped beating. All she could think of was thick, heavy walls and massive blocks of stone. "Oh, *mon Dieu!* Is . . . is Raoul all right?"

She did not even wait to hear his answer. Racing away, she dashed toward the workshop, barely aware of Thea's footsteps behind her. Her hands shook as she struggled to light a lantern, coaxing the flame into a bright golden glow. Hiking her skirt up with one hand, she hurried into the stale, musty tunnel.

Bursts of gold leaped out at her when she finally reached the doorway of the tomb. Her eyes, dilated from the darkness of the tunnels, were blinded for a moment. It seemed an eternity before forms and colors began to emerge slowly from the haze.

The place was a shambles. A large section of the side wall

had crumbled away, leaving a pile of stones and debris on the floor. Dust swirled in the air, like a morning mist rising from the earth.

At last she began to pick out figures in the room. Mohammed and his sons were crouched beside the fallen wall, pushing heavy stones out of the way as they scooped sand and chips with their bare hands into canvas sacks. Edward and Buffy stood across the room, silent and immobile, as if they could not figure out what had happened. Raoul was nowhere in sight.

Aimée's nervousness swelled to panic as she searched the room with her eyes.

"Raoul?" Where was he? Why couldn't she find him? "Raoul!"

Then, just as she could bear the tension no longer, a familiar voice boomed out from behind the wall.

"It's about time you got here."

Gasping with relief, Aimée watched Raoul materialize slowly from the darkness. He was covered with sand from head to foot. Even his black hair and white shirt were smudged to a uniformly dirty beige, but he did not seem to be hurt.

"Oh, Raoul, thank God you're all right. I was so afraid."

He brushed aside her anxieties. "Dammit, I need you here. Why did you pick today of all days to go into town?"

For a minute Aimée was stunned. Why was he being so brusque? Didn't he know how frightened she had been?

"What . . . what happened, Raoul?"

He glanced down at her sharply. Then, remembering himself, he began to laugh.

"I'm sorry, *petite*. Of course you don't know what happened. I don't even know myself. I suppose we put too much pressure on the wall, assuming there was solid earth behind it, though God knows, it should have been obvious there was another room there."

"Another room? But there wasn't even a door. Why should there be another room?"

"Think about it, Aimée," he urged. "Remember the way the antechamber looked when we found it."

Aimée shook her head, bewildered. "All bright with gold, that's the first thing I remember. And crowded. Everything piled to the ceiling, until there was only room for a narrow aisle leading . . ."

She broke off abruptly. A narrow aisle leading to a blank wall. But why would an aisle lead nowhere?

"But . . . but you were so sure Ramose's burial chamber was there." She pointed toward the doorway on the far wall, still flanked by a pair of gilt-and-ebony statues.

"I still am. I think the other room—the one we just discovered—is an afterthought. I suspect many of the treasures were originally in there. It must have been cleared out after Ramose was interred, to make room for a second burial."

"A second burial? But why would another man be buried in Ramose's tomb?"

"Not a man—a woman." Raoul drew her attention to the wall beside the entry. "Remember the girl in the painting? The same lovely young woman whose sculpture I brought back from the village? I think perhaps we have found her."

Aimée stared at the graceful figure on the wall. She had sensed sadness in the girl's mien once, a kind of sorrow that went too deep for tears. Now at last she understood it. It was the sadness of her own mortality.

"Who is she, Raoul? Do we know anything about her?"

"Damn little," he admitted. "Being an archaeologist is like being a detective. Don't you remember, you said that once yourself. All you can do is dig up the clues and try to piece them together. Only, in this case I'm afraid we don't have very many clues.

"From the way the girl is depicted in the painting, I would guess she was one of the pharaoh's minor wives, but if she was, why wasn't she buried in the royal tombs? Of course, she could have been the wife of Ramose himself, though she seems young for that, no more than thirteen or fourteen at the time of his death. Ramose's sister then, or his daughter— but why was she pictured in a servile pose behind Akhenaten, as if she belonged to him?"

It was like being a detective, Aimée thought, intrigued as she listened to him. Problems, puzzles, dilemmas—with every clue bringing more questions than it answered. She wondered if they would ever know the truth.

"Come and look." Leaping easily over the debris, Raoul caught Aimée's hand in his own. He barely noticed Thea, hovering wide-eyed in the entryway. "No complete burial has ever been found before. This is a moment unique in history."

As she stepped up to the wall, Aimée saw that a single lantern had been placed on the floor inside. The light, pale and wavering, contrasted with the glowing brightness of the antechamber. It took her eyes a moment to adjust.

She remembered vividly the night they had first broken into the tomb. Treasure heaped upon treasure, crammed so tightly she could not even see the floor. Gold so lustrous and abundant it seemed to shine from within with a light of its own. Sharp-eared jackals and gilded leopards. Graceful winged goddesses standing like guardian angels over the spirits of the dead.

But in this small inner chamber she saw nothing of the grandeur she had expected—or the vanity. The walls were so plain they were stark, with not a single picture, not a touch of color to relieve their monotony. Only a group of hieroglyphs stood black against the dark sand tones, and they were so crude and clumsy they looked as if they had been scrawled in place at the last minute.

In the center of the room, dominating everything else, was a massive stone sarcophagus. Aimée stared at it in wonder. She had never seen anything quite like it. Not a long, narrow case like the others Raoul had shown her, this one was shaped in a cumbersome square, so wide it could have held a pair of coffins. And resting on the center, almost mystic in its simplicity, stood a metal chalice, like a holy vessel on an altar.

More mysteries, Aimée thought, intrigued at the idea. More questions, always more questions—and never any answers.

She let her eyes play around the room, trying to guess what some of the objects were and what they had meant to the woman in the tomb. A crudely carved wooden animal stood alone in a corner, its broad smile making it look like a comical dog, or perhaps a lion. Had it been a cherished toy, treasured even after childhood had been left behind? The silvery chalice was so tarnished it almost looked like steel. Had it belonged to the woman? Had she touched it with her own hands and lips, or was it merely the impersonal residue of an elaborate funeral rite? Boxes inlaid with ivory and ebony were piled against the wall. Did they hold favorite dresses, sheer white linen pleats that half-concealed dark sensuous skin? A tiny carnelian ring perhaps, with a scarab that twisted around to reveal a private seal on the other side? Or a game of sennet, complete with little stone pieces and markers shaped like human fingers with delicately carved nails at the end?

All mysteries. All unsolved. A human life had come and gone, leaving only possessions and not a trace of its essence.

"We know nothing about her," she whispered. "Not who she was or what her life was like. Not even her name."

"Oh, but we do know her name. There was an inscription on one of the boxes."

It seemed to Aimée that Raoul was exceptionally pleased with himself. She had the feeling he was teasing her, though she could not figure out why.

"Well, what was it?"

He paused to make the moment more dramatic. "Her name . . . was Aimée."

For a moment Aimée was confused. Then she burst out laughing.

"Now I know you're teasing me. Come on, truly—what was her name?"

Raoul laughed with her. "I was only half-teasing. Just as Aimée means 'loved' in French, her name, Meryt, or perhaps Meryet, comes from the Egyptian 'Mery,' which means 'beloved.' "

"Mariette," Aimée repeated, giving the name a French sound. It felt comfortable on her lips.

"Or Meryt. We don't know how it was pronounced. The ancient language has been kept alive in modern Coptic, still spoken in church services and in some of the remoter villages, but the pronunciation must have changed through the centuries."

Aimée turned back to the chamber. She was even more intrigued now.

"Are you sure it's all right to go inside?" She picked her way through the rubble that blocked the entryway. "Didn't the ancient kings put a curse on anyone who violates their tombs?"

"The pharaohs, perhaps," Raoul quipped. "But surely not a gentle little princess."

Aimée regretted her flippant words the instant she crossed the threshold. The outer room had been stifling, filled with the sound of footsteps and breathing and the scraping of sand into heavy sacks. The inner room was silent and cold. So cold all the warmth of the desert seemed to have drained out of it.

It had been like this before, she remembered. The first time she had entered the tomb. How could she have forgotten? It had been cold that day, too, bitter cold, and she had been afraid.

For an instant she was tempted to turn and run out of the room. Only stubbornness held her back.

She would not make a fool of herself in front of Raoul. She would not! Besides, she was being ridiculous. Of course the room was cold. It had been sealed off for more than three thousand years. It would take hours, perhaps even days, before the warm air of the tunnels filtered inside.

Raoul stepped beside her. She tried to smile as she looked up at him, but she did not succeed. All she could think of was the lovely, serene face on the sculpture he had rescued from the thieves' village.

"She was so young. So pretty and so young."

Raoul caught the sadness in her voice. Glancing down, he was alarmed at how pale she was. Dammit, why had he forgotten the effect the tomb had had on her that first day? She was too imaginative, too sensitive. He should never have pushed her into the place so suddenly. All he could do now was try to make light of the whole thing.

"Young? She was probably a hundred and twelve. You didn't expect her to pose for a portrait of herself as an old woman, did you? People like to be remembered as they were when they were beautiful."

Aimée took no comfort in his words. Pretty Meryt, young and lovely. It was sad to think of her growing old, as everyone grew old, her face crisscrossed with lines of age. Pretty, beloved Meryt, dying at last, a withered echo of her own beauty.

Beloved Meryt. Beloved of the parents who had given her her name with such hopes and dreams. Beloved of the father who had bragged about her the day she was born. Of the mother who had held her in her arms—just as she would one day hold her own child.

Her hand slipped down to her belly. She was surprised to feel how smooth and flat it was, giving no hint of the secret it held.

She saw Raoul looking down at her, and she pulled her hand away. She could see that her behavior had alarmed him. She tried not to shiver visibly, but that only made it worse.

"It's so cold," she murmured awkwardly.

"Cold?"

Only then did she notice that his hair was plastered damply against his forehead. His shirt was drenched with sweat.

Confused, she turned away. Was she the only one who felt it? This cold that seemed to seep into her bones?

She found herself staring at the chalice on the sarcophagus. Even in the dim light, every detail stood out clearly. Slowly she stretched out her hand. She half-expected Raoul to call out to her, telling her to pull it back again, but there was only silence behind her.

The cup felt alive to Aimée's touch, as if it held secrets she could only guess at. There was a vibrancy in the cool metal surface, a meaning so deep and intense it seemed to cross the barriers of time, if only she had the power to understand it.

Raoul stood behind her, watching helplessly. He longed to pull her into his arms, comforting her in his embrace, but he did not dare. He was acutely conscious of his fiancée, only a few yards away in the next room.

"Perhaps it was part of the funeral rite," he said stiffly, indicating the chalice. "It's hard to tell, since a burial like this has never been found before."

"A last toast?" Aimée could not keep her voice steady. "Like a communion chalice, filled with wine and passed around so everyone could take a sip of it? Only, it would not have been a celebration of faith, but a token of loss."

Raoul did not answer. More than ever he wanted to put his arms around her. He cursed his cowardice when he could not.

Suddenly Aimée felt she could bear the place no longer. This was not the glamour she had expected. Digging through piles and boxes, sketching shrines, and cataloging urns and fans and long brass horns had been exciting in its own way. Violating the privacy of death was not.

"It's stifling in here. So dusty. I can't breathe."

She pushed past him, stumbling on the debris strewn across the floor. Pausing in the doorway, she turned for one last look. The darkened cup seemed to pick up the fire of the lantern, catching reflections of gold and crimson as easily as echoes from the past.

She could almost see them now, a semicircle of mourners, vague in the dim light. White linen, neat and starched, cornflowers and glazed blue beads entwined in tokens of grief. Bronzed hands reaching out to pass the chalice from one mourner to the next.

A last bittersweet farewell. Deep red wine, cool and sweet to the taste. Intimations of eternity built on ashes of the past.

A last gallant toast. Memories of dreams now dead, of pain and longing, love and tears and hope. The cup of the dreamers drained at last, the wine of the dreamers gone. The tomb silent and empty forever.

The wings of the raven were black against the red sky. Aimée sat on the steps of an abandoned tomb, turning her face up to the cool twilight air as she watched it disappear into the enveloping darkness. The desert was quiet and lonely.

Raoul found her there an hour later. Sitting beside her, he reached out to take her hand. He did not try to speak.

Aimée looked up at him, sensing the closeness he could not put into words. His hand was warm against hers.

"I was watching the raven," she said softly. "Do you remember?"

"The raven?"

"You must remember. It was there in the sky the day we opened the tomb. I've seen it almost every evening since then. You told me it was the *ba* of someone who died long ago."

Raoul's eyes crinkled with laughter. "I told you no such thing. I may have said the Egyptians believed the soul took the form of a bird, revisiting places it had known on earth, but I never said it was the truth. Personally, I think any raven hanging around here is just shrewd enough to know the workmen will leave crumbs behind when they finish their noonday break."

"Oh, Raoul, how unromantic you make it sound." She hesitated, glancing up to see if he was still laughing at her. "Don't you see? The princess Meryt was so young and beautiful. I like to think she is beautiful still—as beautiful as a bird in flight."

Raoul ran his hand lightly across her cheek. His lips brushed against her hair.

"You mustn't take it so seriously, *petite*. A raven is only a raven—nothing more. And all those treasures in the tomb, tantalizing as they are, are only clues to a puzzle that does not exist anymore. One day they'll be put in a museum where they belong, so people can pause and stare at them, marveling at the life they represented. But the hands that fashioned them and the people that loved them have all disappeared, as surely as the raven disappears into the night sky, and not all your dreams can call them back again."

Aimée listened to the calm, soothing sound of his voice. Closing her eyes, she could almost believe they were alone in the world. If she leaned toward him now, would he draw her into his arms, telling her with his hands, his lips, the hard pressure of his muscles that he had missed her as much as she missed him? That he needed her as much as she needed him?

The moment was not destined to last. A new voice intruded on their intimacy.

"So there you are. I've been looking for you everywhere."

Thea had changed into a fresh dress, soft blue handkerchief linen trimmed with white eyelet. The bustle flounced coquettishly as she dropped to the steps beside them.

Aimée glared at her resentfully. She knew Thea had a right to be there, far more right than she, but she could not help the rebellion that exploded inside her. It was not fair—not fair at all! She had felt so close to Raoul. Why did Thea have to come along and spoil it all?

Thea seemed to sense her tension. "Really, Aimée," she teased. "You shouldn't hold my fiancé's hand like that. I'm glad you're a married woman—otherwise I'd be quite jealous."

Aimée pulled her hand away. She was glad the darkness covered the flush that burned her cheeks. "It's . . . it's just the tomb. It's upsetting to me. Raoul was trying to comfort—"

"Oh, Aimée," Thea broke in. "I was only joking. Surely you know that. It's just that you looked so solemn. I was trying to make you laugh."

Aimée managed a faint smile. So much for her guilty conscience. Now she was seeing accusations where none existed. "I'm sorry. I guess it's been a rough day."

Raoul rose abruptly, turning away from them to scan the horizon. He did not like seeing them together, these two women of his. They reminded him again what a mess he had made of his life—and there was not a darn thing he could do about it.

Thea ignored his brusqueness. "It has been difficult, hasn't it? Right from the time that dreadful woman barged into the café. Really Raoul, you should have seen her. She was like some kind of terrible avenging Fury. And Aimée thought she had seen her before."

Raoul whirled back to face them. He did not waste words as he crouched beside Aimée, searching her eyes with his own.

"What woman?"

The harshness in his voice made Aimée uncomfortable. "Oh, Raoul, it was nothing. Really nothing." She wished Thea had not brought it up. She felt so foolish about it now. "Please don't laugh at me. It's just that, when I saw her, for a minute at least, I thought it was that old woman in the church in Cairo. But afterward, when she was gone—I mean, when I had a chance to think it over—I realized I must have been wrong."

Raoul leaped to his feet. "Why didn't you tell me this before?"

"It seemed so foolish. Besides, you were busy. You had just discovered the burial chamber, and—"

"Princess Meryt waited three thousand years for us to find her. She could have waited another day."

"Then you think . . ." Aimée could not bring herself to finish the sentence. It couldn't be the same woman. It just couldn't! Why would she have followed them all the way from Cairo?

Raoul saw the alarm in her eyes, and he regretted his rashness. He did not want to upset her any more than he had to.

"No, no, of course not. It would be too much of a coincidence. Still . . ." What could he tell her? That he had known her long enough to know how level-headed she was? That if she thought she had seen the old woman, he was sure she had? "Still, there's no sense taking chances. If she is here—or if someone wants us to think she is—I want to know about it."

Too many things had happened in the past few days. The workshop ransacked, with nothing damaged or missing. A valuable sculpture stolen from the tomb, right under their noses. Ruffians waiting for him in a darkened doorway, when only his closest associates knew where he was going to be.

And now, an old woman from Cairo had suddenly appeared in Luxor—and she had made a point of showing herself to Aimée in a native café.

He didn't like it. He didn't like it at all. He didn't know how it all tied together, but he was going to find out.

4

Aimée stood in the doorway of the tent gazing out into the darkness. Somewhere in the distance a jackal barked, a sharp lonely sound in the night. The silence that followed was so heavy it was unnatural.

It had been an hour since Raoul roused Mohammed and his two oldest sons, taking them with him to the east bank to search for the old woman. Aimée was surprised to realize her hand was trembling as she ran it along the edge of the doorway. Everything had happened so suddenly she did not know what to make of it.

"I'm leaving you here," Raoul had told a startled Hassan.

"Stake out the ghaffirs carefully. I don't expect trouble, but if there is any, I want to be prepared for it."

Hassan's eyes had flashed with excitement. "Sure, sure, you can count on me. If anyone comes here, we'll get them good." He had punctuated his words with a sharp, obvious gesture, making Aimée shiver and Raoul laugh.

Slowly Aimée turned from the doorway, forcing herself back into the tent. She tried to sit down but was too edgy to stay still for more than a minute. Jumping up again, she began to pace back and forth.

Really she was like a caged cat, she told herself, annoyed and amused at the same time. What on earth was she so jumpy about? She had a circle of guards to protect her, and Thea was sleeping in the next tent, with Edward and Buffy just beyond. Surely she couldn't be afraid.

And afraid of what, pray tell? she asked herself scornfully. Afraid of an old woman on the far bank of the river? A woman who was probably nothing more than a figment of her imagination?

That settled it. Impulsively she crossed the room, sinking to her knees beside a large trunk in the corner. Rummaging through it, she found a heavy woolen shawl to wrap around her shoulders.

She might not be able to control her nervousness, but at least she could channel it in a positive direction. She picked up a lantern lying on the bedside table. There was plenty to do in the workshop: records to be written out and cross-referenced, sketches to be drawn, supplies to be organized and prepared. She could keep busy all night if she wanted.

A sudden gust of wind tugged at her hair as she stepped outside, blowing stray curls across her cheek. The tent flap rustled as she tied it behind her. Shivering, she pulled the shawl around her shoulders. The lantern cast a warm, protective circle of gold on the sand as she moved toward the workshop.

The mountains looked deceptively close in the pale moonlight. Aimée paused to stare at them. It always fascinated her to see how changeable they were. In the natural morning light they had been a rich golden beige, streaked with earth tones that bleached to a blinding white in the midday sun. Now, at night, they seemed magical, deep purple rising out of silvery sand and fading into the black of the sky.

Idly Aimée scanned the nearby slopes, picking out shadowy pits that marked entrances to tombs abandoned centuries ago. She half-expected to see the guards, their dark forms elusive against the background of the night, but it did not truly surprise her when she could not find them.

Enthusiastic, predictable Hassan. He had outdone himself. Hoping against hope that the woman would show herself, he had hidden the ghaffirs carefully, dreaming of the glory that would be his when they leaped out and captured her.

She did not see a single guard until she had nearly reached the bottom of the steps that led to the workshop. Even then she sensed rather than saw the man as he crept slowly to the edge of the stairway.

Not wanting to alarm him, Aimée moved up two or three steps, holding the lantern high to illuminate her features. As she glanced up, she caught sight of the hem of his robe.

The men of the desert wore pale robes, she thought, confused and puzzled. Long, flowing robes that deflected the heat of the sun. But the fabric that met her eyes was dull and black.

Like the black malayas that swathed the women from head to toe.

For a moment Aimée caught her breath, afraid to raise her eyes higher. Then at last, steadying one hand with the other, she lifted the lantern, directing the rays upward.

"You!"

The cry was a gasp of shock. Aimée stared at a pair of black eyes, glowing yellow in the light of the lantern. The rest of the woman's face was veiled, her body stooped and undefined as she leaned heavily on her cane, but the eyes were enough to give her away.

Aimée took a cautious step forward, then another. Once she had seen anger in those dark eyes, and hatred. Now she also sensed fear. She held her hand out, as if to tempt a frightened animal.

"Don't be afraid." She knew the woman could not understand the words, but she hoped the tone of her voice would soothe her. "It's all right. I'm not going to hurt you."

She was surprised at how calm and unafraid she was. Not at all like that afternoon in Cairo when she had been terrified half out of her mind. Here, she was not alone Here, she only needed to cry out, and they would be surrounded by guards.

She continued to move slowly up the stairway. The woman took a step backward, like a wary alley cat, then stopped. Reaching up, she gripped her veil in her hand, tearing it away from her face. Aimée watched, fascinated. It was as if she did not want any screen between them.

The light harshly illuminated the woman's skin. Hundreds

of tiny lines and creases gave it the look of brittle parchment. The flesh seemed to have melted from her bones, until her cheeks were sunken hollows, and her lips caved inward, stretching over toothless gums.

She was so old, Aimée thought with a rush of pity. So terribly old. "Please don't be afraid of me. I don't want to hurt you."

Her words had the opposite effect. The woman's face contorted. Her lips moved dryly, as if it were an effort to speak.

"Diable!"

The sound was low and threatening, like the warning hiss of a snake. Aimée recoiled automatically, taking a step backward. It was a moment before she realized the word was in French.

Devil. The woman thought she was the devil. Raoul had been right, after all. Her blue eyes made the woman believe she was an evil jinn. How could she ever convince her she was wrong?

The woman saw her apprehension. It seemed to add to her own courage.

"Diable!" Her voice was stronger now. "You come here like the devil to destroy my son. Now you think to destroy me, too—heh, *diable?"*

"Your son?" Aimée heard the words, but she did not understand them. "I don't even know your son."

"You know." The woman sounded more like a snake then ever. "Ah, yes, *diable*, you know."

Aimée shook her head. She was more bewildered than frightened. She had met few Egyptians, only the workers at the dig, and none of them were Copts. Besides, the woman had never seen her until she wandered into that church in Cairo, the church of Tadrus the Martyr.

Tadrus the Martyr!

What was it Raoul had said? *That was Tadrus' church. His mother kept on going there for years. For all I know, that was her you saw today.*

"Your son . . . is Tadrus?"

So they had been wrong after all. She was not a fanatical old woman, all fired up with religious zeal. She was the mother of the man whose shrine had been violated, and she thought Aimée was the devil incarnate.

Aimée began to inch forward. There was no point trying to reason with the woman. It would do no good. She would have to make a sudden dash past her, luring her out into the open, away from the workshop and its treasures. Then she could scream for the guards.

But the woman blocked her path before she could move. With a surprisingly agile movement she raised the cane in her hand.

Aimée gave it only a cursory glance. She was not afraid of a blunt weapon, not in the hands of an elderly woman. Only when she caught a good look at it did she realize what she was up against.

The thing was not a cane at all, but a scythe. A crude wooden tool, exactly like the scythes she had seen pictured on the walls of the ancient tombs. Only, there was nothing crude about the blade. Honed to a fine edge, it was razor sharp.

"*Mon Dieu!* Are you mad?" Frantically she glanced over her shoulder, gauging her chances for escape. Terrified, she realized she had moved too far up the steps. She would never be able to race down them now, not when she had to expose her back to a sharp blade.

And she had been so sure she could call the guards whenever she wanted. One cry, and she would bring them running. What a fool she had been. One cry would summon them, all right—but it would also bring an attack with the primitive scythe.

"Why do you hate me so much?" She had to keep talking. She had to keep the woman from striking, at least until she could think of something to do. "I am only eighteen, madame. I could not possibly know your son. He has been dead a long time."

"You are the devil—do you think I don't know you? Do you think I don't see you come for my Tadrus, naked and lusting like a whore, tempting him from his faith. You think because he is dead you are safe. But *I* am not dead, *diable*, and you will never be safe."

Oh, God, she had her confused with that other woman. The woman who shared her son's passion—and his shame. She had seen Aimée standing in front of his picture, seen her reach up to touch his face, and she had gotten it all mixed up in her mind. Unconsciously Aimée clutched at the cross around her neck, trying to find in that sacred emblem some power to save her from the evil that confronted her. She did not even feel the sting of the wind as the shawl slipped from her shoulders, dropping to the steps at her feet.

The gesture seemed to anger the woman, as if she sensed in it a superstitious appeal to an alien god. Moving at last, she raised the scythe high above her head. It was so heavy she had to hold it in both hands.

Aimée began to back down the steps. She dared not move quickly, fearing she would hasten the blow that was coming, but she knew she could not stay where she was. Suddenly, without warning, she felt something catch at her ankles. Wrenching treacherously, her feet gave out beneath her. *Nomde nom,* the shawl! Why hadn't she remembered the shawl? All she could do was clutch frantically at the wall to keep from falling.

That was all the woman needed. Lunging forward, she thrust the scythe downward with brutal force. Screaming in terror, Aimée twisted away, but she was too late. A searing pain coursed through her body as the blade grazed her arm.

The woman pulled away, trembling as if the exertion had been too much for her. She swayed for a moment, then got hold of herself. Terrified, Aimée realized she was going to strike again.

She wasted only a second glancing down at her arm. Blood spurted from a long, angry wound in her flesh, but she barely saw it. She could think of nothing, see nothing, but the madness on the steps above her. If she stopped to worry about her pain now, it was the last thing she would ever do.

Cautiously she reached out with her foot, kicking the shawl away. Soon she would have to move again—forward or back, she did not know which—and she wanted nothing in her way.

The cold metal of the lantern bit into her hand. She had forgotten she was holding it. She had to get rid of it, it would only impede her progress—but where? If she set it on the steps, she might trip over it, catching her long skirt on fire in a wild attempt at flight.

Then suddenly she realized what she had to do. The thought was a bold one, the plan even bolder. There was only a chance in a hundred it would work, but it was a chance she had to take.

The woman seemed to read the sudden daring in her expression. Sensing she could wait no longer, she tensed the muscles of her arms, bringing the blade down once again.

This time Aimée was ready for her. The instant she saw the scythe move, she thrust the lantern forward, swinging out with her arms. With a sharp cry she dashed it against the earth at the woman's feet. The sound of shattering glass broke the stillness of the night.

The old woman, caught off guard, stumbled awkwardly.

Her scythe swung wide, crashing against the side of the steps. She did not have a chance to raise it again.

Aimée watched, horrified, as the oil from the lantern spilled into a pool around the woman's feet. It was only a second before a blanket of crimson coated the earth.

Aimée could only stand there, soft whimpers of fear in her throat, as the flames lapped up against the black edges of the woman's robe. The fabric held out for a second, then surrendered, turning into a shroud of fire.

God help her, it was so terrible, so ugly. This was only an old woman. Old and mad. She had never wanted to hurt her.

The woman hurled herself to the earth, rolling over and over in the sand, but the flames defied her agony, catching at new corners of her robe the minute they were exposed to the air again. Her screams were hoarse and penetrating, as inhuman as the cries of an animal in pain.

Aimée could bear it no longer.

Turning, she raced down the stairway. She tripped twice, stumbling painfully on the sharp steps, but she did not stop. Half-running, half-crawling, she fled into the tomb. The sound of screams echoed in her ears, shrill and terrified. She did not even know they were her own.

The workshop was dark as she pushed her way inside. Flailing blindly with her arms, she struggled to pick her way through it, tripping over objects she had not even remembered were there.

Oh, God, why was it so dark? She was completely turned around now, all sense of direction lost, but she did not dare stop. She had to get to the tunnels—she had to! If only she could hide in dark, familiar corridors, clamping her hands over her ears to block out dying screams, perhaps she could feel safe again.

Then suddenly the whole chamber was flooded with light. Blinking in astonishment, Aimée stopped where she was. A lantern seemed to emerge from nowhere in the center of the room, another from the corner, yet another from behind the cupboard that blocked the entrance to the tunnels.

"What on earth . . . ?"

It was then that she saw the condition of the room. Shelves had been torn apart, with all of Raoul's neatly arranged artifacts scattered carelessly on the floor. The gold of the lantern reflected on the brighter gilt of shrines and statues and countless pieces of jewelry.

Aimée did not have time to react. She saw a figure hurtling toward her from the far side of the room, features shaded by the hood of a rough woolen galabiya, but she had no chance to get out of his way. Before she knew what was happening, he had reached out, grabbing her by the arms. Crying out in terror, she tried to pull away from him, but it was no use. The room seemed to be filled with men, and they were all coming at her.

Too late she realized what had happened. What a fool she had been to race into the workshop, the one place she could be easily trapped. She should have known the old woman would not be alone.

A coarse hand clamped over her mouth, pulling her roughly backward. Horrified, Aimée heard her own scream dissolve into a series of sharp, muffled grunts. She struggled desperately, trying to muster strength for one loud cry.

Callused fingers gouged into her cheeks as the man's palm pressed against her mouth and nose, blocking her air. Frantically Aimée realized he did not mean to let her breathe again. She could die in this terrible room. She could die! The guards might come at any minute, but they would be too late.

Redoubling her efforts, she strained every muscle in her body, fighting to push him away from her, kicking, scratching, clawing. Her heels pounded his shins, her nails dug into the hairy backs of his hands, but nothing did any good. More machine than human, he held out against it all, not moving, not reacting, not even seeming to feel.

At last she knew he had won. The light seemed to explode, evaporating into a hundred tiny haloes. It was so beautiful, Aimée thought—so incredibly beautiful. A thousand colors blending into a single burst of gold. She wanted to hold on to it forever.

And then there was only darkness.

When she awoke, she was confused. She thought vaguely that she had not expected to wake, though she could not for the life of her understand why. She knew she should be fighting against something. She knew there was some danger so terrible she could almost taste it on her parched lips, but when she opened her eyes, the eyes staring down at her were warm and concerned.

"Raoul, what . . .?"

Her voice was so hoarse she barely recognized it. As she struggled to pull herself up, a sharp pain raced through her arm, forcing her back again. When she reached up, she could feel it had been covered with a bandage.

"Shhh, *trésor*, don't try to talk." For the first time, Raoul made no effort to hide the affection in his voice. Slipping his hand under her head, he adjusted the pillows to make her more comfortable. "It's all right now. Everything's all right. Thank God, the ghaffirs got to you in time."

"The ghaffirs?" Everything was beginning to come back to her now. "But where were they, Raoul? I screamed and screamed, and no one came."

"One of Hassan's bright ideas, I'm afraid. He thought if he formed his men into a large ring, far from the center of the dig, he could lure the woman inside. It doesn't seem to have occurred to him he left a gap so big an entire army could have gotten through without being seen."

Actually, Raoul had to admit, Hassan had done them a favor. The woman had gotten into the camp, but the woman was dead now, or close to it if his men were right about what they had seen when they raced to Aimée's aid. And thieves had broken in, but the thieves had not gotten away with anything, and now they had tipped their hand.

Aimée felt her eyes begin to close. She fought against the feeling. She was tired, desperately tired, but every time she drifted off to sleep, the same images haunted her nightmares. Little tongues of flame catching at the edge of a long black robe. Dark eyes burning with shock and pain. Hoarse screams that never seemed to end.

"Is . . . is she dead?"

Raoul saw her anguish and her fear. For an instant he was tempted to lie to her, comforting her at least for tonight. But, realizing he could not put it off forever, he shook his head.

"I don't know. We didn't find her."

Ignoring the pain in her arm, Aimée pulled herself up. "You mean she got away?"

"I doubt it. The men said she was pretty badly burned when they got to her, though they didn't stop to check. They were anxious to get to the workshop." He didn't tell her about the living funeral pyre the men had described. He knew it would only bring back memories too painful to face. "She might have crawled off by herself, though it's more likely she was carried away."

Aimée nodded slowly. She had forgotten the men in the workshop. "By her friends?"

"By the men who were afraid she might live long enough to talk."

"You mean . . ." Aimée could hardly believe what he was telling her. "You mean it was all a plot . . . a deliberate plot to steal things from the tomb? And the old woman was part of it? A ruse to lure you away tonight?"

"I mean precisely that. Why the hell do you think she was so anxious to show herself to you in town this afternoon? She found you in that café, remember? You didn't seek her out."

"But what if . . . oh, Raoul, what if they try again?"

"They will," he replied grimly. "Only, this time we'll be ready for them. I'm having iron grilles made for the workshop and the tomb, and I've already arranged to hire extra guards. They won't catch us unaware again."

He could see she was still troubled. Guiltily he realized he was venting his own frustrations at her expense.

"But we don't have to worry about this now. I want you to go to sleep and forget the whole damned mess. Promise me you will."

Aimée did not miss the tenderness in his voice, deeper than she had ever heard before. In that moment, all the terror, all the pain, seemed worthwhile. If only she could be close to him, really close, just one more time before they had to part forever.

"Stay with me."

He was her lover, and she loved him. She was carrying his child in her body, a wonderful secret they would soon share. She could not bear to lose him now.

To Raoul she looked like a little child, staring up at him, hair dark against the white of her pillow, blue eyes wide with trust. He longed to pull her into his arms, protecting her, holding her safe forever. Dammit, if she were his wife, he would never leave her alone again.

But she was not his wife, he reminded himself bitterly. She was only his mistress—and the mistress of every other man who wanted her.

"You need your sleep," he said gruffly. "Besides, what would your husband think if I stayed all night?"

Aimée did not try to argue. She sensed the moment of tenderness was over. She felt helpless as she watched him walk toward the doorway. His voice was gentler as he turned one last time.

"I'll look in on you in the morning."

5

Raoul bent over a makeshift worktable in the corner of the burial chamber. Beneath his fingers, gold and jewels were just beginning to emerge from a blackened crust. The odor of oil and solvents was sharp in his nostrils, but he barely noticed them as the hardened scum dissolved, revealing the details of a magnificent pectoral.

He could barely control the trembling in his hands as he worked to free the piece from the petrified unguents that had hidden it for centuries. Even before he finished, he sensed he had found something so rare and valuable it would pale everything else in the tomb. Similar collars had been common in ancient Egypt, judging by the wall paintings in other tombs, but those neckpieces had always been shaped in the form of a falcon or a vulture. This pectoral was centered around a slender golden image of the goddess Isis, her long, sensuous arms stretching out over turquoise-and-carnelian wings.

Raoul pulled himself upright. Pain ran through cramped muscles as he drew his forearm across his brow, brushing away the dark curls that spilled over his eyes. The beautiful winged Isis was only one of a number of surprises he had found in the princess's burial chamber. The others had not been nearly as pleasant.

It had taken them three days to open the sarcophagus. Rigging a complex system of ropes and pulleys, he and Mohammed, with the aid of Daoud and Salem, had finally managed to inch the heavy lid upward. Even then, it was all they could do to raise it a scant two feet, tying it precariously in place. As he stood beside the open stone shell gazing down at the sight he had dreamed of for years, he found himself half-wishing they had not succeeded.

In all the excitement of discovering the burial chamber, it had never occurred to him that the place might hold a sad secret all its own, and yet he realized now it should have. The pieces of the puzzle had all been there, detective's clues he called them to Aimée—the superb bust of a woman still young and radiant, the comical figure of a toy lion scarred with the marks of tiny teeth, an oversized sarcophagus wide enough to hold a pair of coffins—and only a fool would have misread them so badly. For an instant he was tempted to cut the ropes, slamming the lid back in place forever.

Whirling, he faced the others.

"No one is to know of this, do you understand? Not Lord Edward or his friend. Not even Lady Ellingham."

Especially not Lady Ellingham, he thought grimly. Aimée had already been too deeply affected by the mood of the tomb. He would do everything in his power to keep her from learning its secret now.

In the days that followed, the sarcophagus offered up one disappointment after another. The painted coffin, so tantalizing until he shone his light on its lid, revealed only a dull, amateurish portrait, lifeless beside the vitality of the carved bust, and the mummy itself, blackened and coated with the very preparations that had been intended to preserve it, was badly decomposed.

The thieves of antiquity, he thought ruefully—those same scoundrels who spirited away the corpses of kings and queens, unwinding their wrappings to find the jewels that had been concealed in them—had done their victims a favor in the long run, exposing them to the real "miracle" of the process of mummification: the dry air and arid soil of the desert. And the lovely little princess whose body had been untouched was ravaged at last by time.

Only when he found the pectoral resting on the mummy's breast, so caked with unguents it was barely recognizable, did Raoul realize his luck had changed. The mummy might have deteriorated until it had little value, but its jewels were unique and so perfect that they made everything else worthwhile.

Raoul was so engrossed in his work that he did not notice Aimée slip silently into the doorway. She did not try to speak as she watched him. It seemed to her he had never looked so handsome. Even bent over the worktable he moved with an effortless grace. His dark hair, hanging on his brow, shaded his eyes, accenting the intensity of his concentration. His hands, strong and sure, yet gentle, called back bittersweet memories of the moments her own flesh had responded to that same potent, tender touch.

Irritably she tossed her head, forcing her thoughts away from the past. She had come here for a purpose.

"Raoul . . .?"

She sensed his wariness as he looked up. She had the childish urge to turn and run away. For days she had been trying to work up the courage to tell him about the child she carried in her body, and for days she had found excuses to put it off.

"What do you want?"

Raoul's voice was sharper than he intended as he glanced at the open sarcophagus. Dammit, why hadn't he at least covered it up? He had been so determined she would not learn the secret of the burial chamber. If she stepped over there now, if she saw . . .

"I was curious to see what you were doing."

If Raoul noticed the tension in her voice, he made no allusion to it. Diverting her attention, he drew her toward the worktable. "Come and see what I've found. It's a pectoral, a kind of necklace designed to hang down on the breast. I can't be sure, of course, until I've finished cleaning it, but I suspect it's one of the finest examples of Egyptian art ever discovered."

Aimée cast a tentative eye toward the sarcophagus. "You found it on . . . the body?"

Raoul kept a firm hand on her waist. "We opened the sarcophagus several days ago. I would have preferred to wait until we finished the antechamber, but your husband was impatient."

Aimée sensed the protectiveness in Raoul's gesture, and while she did not understand it, she made no effort to resist. Turning away from the anonymous depths of the open stone case, she let her gaze linger on the wall.

"What are all those funny markings? Those things that look like pictures."

She knew she was stalling for time, and she hated herself for it, but she could not help it. There was no way she could force herself to utter the words she had come to say.

"Those are hieroglyphs—ancient Egyptian writing. They seem to be some kind of poem."

"A poem?" Aimée was intrigued enough to forget her anxiety. "Did they have poetry then, the ancient Egyptians? Love poetry?"

"What a little girl you are," he teased. "Always looking for romance. The Egyptians had all kinds of poetry, and very beautiful poetry at that. Though I must admit, this one does sound like a love poem. It seems to have been written to be sung by a woman to a man."

"Can you read it?"

Raoul shook his head. "The Egyptian language is very complex. It will take weeks, perhaps even months, to decipher it with any kind of accuracy. But I have made out a little of it."

Stepping closer to the wall, Raoul reached up, pointing to a row of hieroglyphs, dark against the drab sand color. "These markings, for instance. They say, 'I am thy first sister.' Egyptians used the words 'brother' and 'sister' to mean 'husband' and 'wife,' or sometimes 'lover.' 'I am thy first sister,' the woman says to the man. Then she goes on to tell him she is like a garden for him. Perhaps we could translate it 'I am unto thee a garden.' A garden of fertile soil, planted with the seeds of flowers and fragrant herbs."

Aimée stared at the wall, fascinated with the sensuous imagery of words she could not even begin to read. Raoul could not take his eyes off her. Watching her, he thought again, as he had so often in the past, how different things might have been if she were a different kind of woman, or he a different kind of man.

"I am unto thee a garden." Aimée repeated the phrase softly, half-whispering it. "How beautiful that sounds."

Raoul slipped to her side, laying a hand on her shoulder. Her eyes were clouded as she looked up at him.

"Did she have a child?"

Raoul stiffened at her words. "What makes you ask that?"

"It just seems . . ." How could she tell him thoughts of a child were very much on her mind? "The words of the poem. I am unto thee a garden."

Raoul laughed at her naiveté. "I think you are taking it too literally," he said gently. "Rich earth laden with the seeds of flowers and sweet-scented herbs. It does sound like a fertility symbol, I admit, but after all, it is a love poem, and fertility is often associated with love—and lovemaking."

Aimée listened to his words, but she barely heard them. Why was it so hard? she asked herself. Why couldn't she just say to this man: I am going to bear your child, and I will love it with all the love that is in my heart?

Her hand brushed against the cold metal of a cup resting carelessly on one of the inlaid boxes. Looking down, she saw the darkened chalice she had first noticed in the center of the sarcophagus. Slowly she lifted it, letting it catch the rays of the lantern. It had seemed vibrant, almost alive, beneath her fingertips once. Now it looked strangely ordinary.

"Is this a valuable piece?"

Still stalling, she scolded herself. Still too much of a coward to say what she had to say.

"Intrinsically, no. It's made of electrum, a natural alloy of silver and gold. Because it was rarer than pure gold, it may have had special importance for the ancients, but that's hardly the case now. As an artifact, of course, it may be more valuable, though I doubt it. It all depends on what it was used for."

"Could I have it, then?"

She could see he was surprised by her request. She was a little surprised herself. She realized she wanted something of this moment to keep forever, not merely a memento of the pretty princess in the tomb, but a remembrance of the one time in her life she had known at least the trappings of love.

"I don't see why not. I'll finish sketching it tonight, then you can have it. All these things will belong to your husband eventually. I doubt if he'll miss one tarnished chalice."

The silence that followed reminded Aimée the time had come at last to speak. Still she could not find the words. Frightened and confused, she turned away, unable to meet his eyes.

"Raoul . . ."

Her voice cracked. Sensing her strain, Raoul lightly caressed her hair. Glancing up, Aimée realized she could expect no help from him. The words that must come were words she alone could speak.

In the end, all she could do was blurt them out. "I am going to have a child."

A child Raoul stared at her blankly, hearing her and not hearing her all at the same time. A child. For a single brief second he felt a surge of hope, as if all the doubt and disillusionment of the past could be erased by the overwhelming potency of her revelation. The emptiness that followed was more intense than anything he had ever known.

"Whose is it?"

Aimée recoiled, as if from a blow. Never, in all the humiliation she had imagined, had she dreamed of anything like this. Closing her eyes, she fought against a wave of faintness.

Raoul felt her pain as sharply as if it were his own. He saw that his cruelty had been deliberate, a retaliation for the emotions she had aroused in him a moment before, and he despised himself for it. He thought he had outgrown the childish need to punish her for wanting other men.

"Well, what's the difference anyhow?"

He had meant the words to be conciliatory, even soothing. He saw now that he had failed. Her eyes, as she opened them, were filled with unhappiness.

"You think it's Edward's?" Aimée could not help remembering the degradation of her wedding night, the only time her husband had ever attempted to touch her. Somehow, she had thought Raoul understood her relationship with Edward. Certainly the way had always been clear to her tent whenever he wanted her. Now she realized he did not.

"Or Montmorency's."

"Buffy?"

Aimée felt the color drain from her face. Raoul knew about Buffy. Oh, God, he *knew*—and yet he didn't know. If he thought she had accepted Buffy willingly in her bed, it was no wonder he treated her like a whore.

Raoul saw her shame, and his heart ached for her. Dammit, what was he doing anyway? he asked himself furiously. Still judging her, still punishing?

He held out his arms, letting one hand drop lightly onto her forearm. Feeling his touch, Aimée pulled away, a quick, convulsive movement, as if the act were physically painful. Raoul's features contorted, but he did not draw his hand back.

"It doesn't matter, Aimée," he said softly. "It doesn't matter. I don't care."

But he did care. He cared desperately. Even as he looked at Aimée, he could see another image, a kind of dazzling, miniature version of the woman he had defied convention and honor to desire. A little Aimée, running by the banks of the Seine, a merry echo of the child-woman he had first seen there. Plump little arms reaching out to pluck a broken blossom from the water.

Raoul had not even thought he wanted children. He had expected them, of course, as every man expected one day to marry and father the children society demanded of him, but he had never carried the thought beyond that. It was a shock to realize now that he wanted to hear that same childish laughter ringing in his ears and see those same small pink lips open to call him "Father." He wanted to love this child, acknowledge her, lavish on her all the warmth and affection he had never been able to give her mother.

Watching him, Aimée saw his longing, and it both frightened and awed her.

Why, he wants this child, she thought. He wants it as desperately as I—and he wants it to be his.

But that was the one thing he could never have.

It tore her apart to watch him and know there was nothing she could do to help him. He could stand in front of her, his eyes haunted with yearning, his arms stretched out to her, and still she could not give him the one thing he needed. No matter what she said, no matter what words she tried to find, there was no way she could make him believe the child she carried in her body was truly a part of him.

And then she was in his arms. She did not know how it happened. She was not even conscious of moving. She only knew his hands were strong as they pressed into her back, his muscles firm against her. It did not matter that he was angry with her. It did not even matter that he would never believe her or love her as she loved him. It was enough to know he needed her.

His lips teased the side of her face, playing against her cheeks and hair, the throbbing veins of her neck. She did not resist as he buried his hands in her thick curls, pulling her head back to receive the thrust of his mouth. She had been so lonely, so empty, without the passion of his body.

She was only vaguely conscious of the pressure of his arms urging her toward the ground. She was far more aware of the reaction of her own body, trembling, yearning, beneath the violence of his touch. She knew she longed to surrender to him, just as she knew she did not dare.

"Raoul, we can't. You know we can't."

He did not seemed surprised by her rejection. Releasing her, he pulled away. The resignation in his eyes hurt Aimée as much as her own pain.

"Oh, my dear, you know I want this . . . long for this . . . as much as you. But it's not right. Someone might come. Edward, or Thea."

Thea. The word was a sharp reproach. Raoul stiffened at the sound of it. Dammit, what a fool he was, what a bastard. If Aimée had not stopped him, he would have dragged her down to the dirt at his feet, not even taking the time to remove her clothing or his own as he stabbed his aching flesh one more time into her body. If she had not stopped him, he would have treated her like the slut he once thought she was.

But she was not a slut. He had tried to convince himself she was, tried to use that as an excuse for his failure to win her completely, but it did not work. Whatever she was—and he had not sorted it out in his mind yet—she was not that. She was lonely, she was passionate, perhaps she had been mercenary in her choice of a marriage partner, but God help them both, she was not a slut. She was with him today for the same reason he was with her, because there was a depth of passion—yes, and a depth of feeling, too—between them. They were the same, he and she, but it was she who had the courage and the decency to break the thing off.

Raoul remained alone long after Aimée had left him, immersed in the one thing that had the power to take his mind off everything else—his work. There was no room for shame in his heart as he bent over the worktable, carefully cleaning each individual stone of the magnificent pectoral. No memories of passion existed, no impossible hopes, no yearnings for dishonor. Here, there was only himself and the long-dead past—and the dreams of a lifetime just starting to come true.

It was dark when he emerged at last into the fresh air, sinking down on the open sand, far from the tents and tombs. The wind was cold as it dried the sweat on his shirt and hair. Thea tried to coax him into the lantern glow in front of her tent, but he put her off, telling her he had to go to work again. He could see as he watched her retreat, all blue and white and lavender in the purple night, that she was disappointed. He knew he was being unfair to her. She had been a good sport to come here with him, and he had given her precious little in return, but he could not bring himself to spend another evening listening to prattle about a shopping expedition in town or an afternoon of gossip with the servants.

I am unto thee a garden.

The words of the ancient poem came back to haunt him. Thea was a garden, a lovely English garden, all primroses and violets peeking out in little rows from behind a tidy picket fence. But Aimée—Aimée was a jungle. Bright tropical blossoms spilling out on overgrown paths. Sweet, heavy perfume intoxicating in its potency. Wild and exotic . . . and exciting.

He could see his life stretching out in front of him, safe and predictable, with not a surprise remaining in it. It was a life he had never questioned. He did not question it now, but he saw it with a new clarity.

There would be another season of digging—a season or two, perhaps even three, for Thea was generous and knew how much it meant to him—and then it would all be over. Then he would be like every other middle-aged adventurer, hanging his hat on a peg in the hall, sitting in a book-lined study in front of a crackling fire, writing up reports on all the dreams he would never dream again. Growing older, always growing older, with days too filled with the past.

It was not a bad life, Raoul had to admit. Not a bad life at all. But it was not the life he wanted.

He was still there, alone in the darkness, when Mohammed found him an hour later.

"I have been looking for you everywhere, *monsieur.*"

"What is it, old friend?" Raoul turned curiously toward Mohammed. Something in the man's voice told him his mission was not a routine one.

"I think you will be pleased to know that Lady Ellingham has nothing to fear now."

Raoul started uncomfortably at his words. He had often

wondered how much Mohammed guessed of his relationship with Aimée. More than a little, he suspected. It seemed to him nothing escaped those dark eyes.

"What do you mean?"

"The old woman, the mother of the Coptic martyr—she is dead."

Raoul drew a deep breath. He nodded slowly. "I thought as much. Where was she found?"

"Two fishermen were pulling in their boat upriver. They dragged it to the shore beside one of the shallow ponds the river leaves when it recedes in the spring. That was where they found her, in a clump of rushes. In a few weeks the river would have flooded again, and the body would have been washed away. Then we would never have known for sure."

The thought troubled Raoul long after Mohammed left him alone. It was all too contrived, too devious. If the old woman had been carried away, and he was sure she had, why would anyone take such pains to hide her body? So they could use her again as a ruse, pretending she was still alive? Well, if that was the case, their plans had been thwarted—at least for the time being.

It was after midnight before Raoul stopped to think what this might mean to Aimée. She had been frightened half out of her wits by the old woman's attack. Though she had never spoken of it, he knew she must still be searching the shadows every time she stepped out of her tent, wondering if she was still there. He would have to tell her everything was all right.

He paused for a moment beside Thea's tent. The sensible, proper thing, he knew, would be to wake his fiancée and ask her to bring the news to Aimée. But that was just the trouble. Thea was too sensible, too proper. God only knew what she would think if he barged in on her at that hour.

Aimée was still awake when he entered her tent. He did not call out even a whispered warning as he slipped inside.

She did not seem surprised to see him. Slowly she rose, her eyes gleaming like dark sapphires against the pallor of her skin.

Still silent, Raoul lowered the flap, tying it carefully behind him. He did not tell her about the old woman. He realized now he had not intended to.

"I cannot stay away from you."

"I know."

She did not try to touch him, pausing instead a few steps away from him. She stood in silence, staring at him with the same helpless longing he felt in his own heart. Then at last she reached up, unfastening the neck of her gown.

Raoul watched the sheer fabric slip from her body, dropping to the floor. He knew now, if he had ever had any doubt, that there was no power in him to turn and walk away from her. Deep pink nipples stretched taut on ivory breasts, and the triangular patch of black that nestled between her thighs accented rounded hips. She had been a child when he had first taken her, a lovely child just on the brink of maturity. Now she was a woman, and his blood ran hot to look at her.

She opened her arms, inviting him to come to her. He did not resist.

The coarse fabric of his shirt felt rough against Aimée's skin and it seemed to her she could feel every fiber of the cloth as it pressed into her flesh. At last she could bear it no longer.

"Oh, Raoul, come to me. Come to me, my love."

"I must always come to you, *mon ange,* as long as you want me."

He did not muffle his cry of longing as he urged her body downward, pressing her onto the narrow bed. His knees separated her thighs, his hips writhed against hers as if he had the power to enter her even through the bulky shield of clothing. His hand was rough as he closed it around his shirt, tugging it from his body. Irritated with his own clumsiness, he pulled away from her, rising to rip off his clothes and scatter them on the floor.

His breath caught in his throat as he gazed down at this woman who was so soon to share his passion again. As always, it amazed him to see how beautiful she was, and how vulnerable.

Even more beautiful now. More vulnerable.

His body ached to look at her, breasts full as they had never been before, belly just beginning to swell with the child that lay inside—the child that might be his.

And he wanted it to be his. He could not deny that now. He did not know why, there was no reason for it, but he wanted it. And he knew he could not have it.

She grew impatient with him, touching his arm with her hand, tempting him back toward the bed. Slowly he shook his head. Tonight, just for one night, he wanted to pretend she was really his. He wanted to feel love between them. No anger, no doubts, no reservations. Tonight he wanted to give her the one gift that asked nothing in return.

"Just lie still."

He ran his hands down her body, touching her breasts, her hips, her legs. He could feel the altered pattern of her breathing as she waited for him to move again. Slipping his hand inside her thighs, he coaxed them apart. Her legs separated easily, rising in eagerness to accept his weight. Gently he pushed them down again.

He wondered at his self-control as he slipped into the space between her legs. Now that he had decided what to do, he wanted only to give.

He did not take the time to play games with her. Shifting his hands under her buttocks, he raised her hips upward. His mouth was hungry as he sank down on her.

At first Aimée thought only that he meant to kiss her, offering her a gentle proof of his passion. Then suddenly his mouth grew demanding, tantalizing her with an impudence that both exhilarated and frightened her. His tongue, bolder and bolder with each passing minute, assaulted her, taking liberties only his fingers had dared before.

"Raoul, what are you doing?"

He did not pull away from her to answer, letting his lips respond instead with mute persuasion. Now teasing, now provoking, he drew her slowly toward the heights of rapture.

Aimée let herself flow with the urges of her body. She did not understand what he was doing to her, but she no longer felt the need to question it. Her legs, moving with an instinct all their own, coiled around his neck, clamping his head in place. Her hands tangled in his hair as she pressed him tighter against her body.

"Oh, Raoul, it is so good. Oh, *mon coeur* . . ."

And then, with a final blinding flash of excitement, it was over. She tried to pull him toward her, longing to share with him the ecstasy that coursed through her flesh, but he eased her gently away. For a minute she lay alone, gasping to catch her breath, clinging to the hand he had placed in hers. When she looked up, she saw that he was gazing down at her.

"You are very beautiful," he whispered softly.

"And you, my love."

For the first time, she let herself study his body openly. Always before, it had been too dark, too hurried. An urgent moment, all too quickly over, and then they had to part again. Now, at last, she could caress him with her eyes.

The strong set of his shoulders gave him more the look of an athlete than a dedicated scientist. Rippling muscles swelled his arms and chest. His hips were lean, his thighs hard and powerful. A thin line of hair ran down his stomach, culminating in a dark mass in that one place her eyes had never dared to linger before.

How foolish it was, she thought, laughing a little at her own modesty. They had been lovers, they had shared all the intimacies of their bodies, and still she was afraid to look at him or touch him. Slowly she raised her hand. He felt hard to her touch, harder than she had imagined.

The quiver that raced through his body told her he was excited by her boldness. Her hand curled around him, grasping him even more firmly.

She remembered her own excitement when he touched her with his lips and tongue, generously giving her the fulfillment that left him unsatisfied. She wondered how he would feel if she did the same thing to him.

Daringly she lowered her lips. The sensation was not an unpleasant one, warm and hard and strangely sensuous. At first she could manage only a few timid kisses. She longed passionately to give him more, but in her naiveté, she could not imagine how to go about it.

Raoul felt the touch of her mouth, but he thought for a moment he must be mistaken. It was a tantalizing sensation, one that had been his only for pay before. He had never expected to know it any other way. God help him, he could not imagine Thea, pretty, gentle, well-bred Thea, who would one day be his wife, giving herself so completely to the lusty needs of her man. This was a gesture that belonged only to a prostitute—or to a woman with a great capacity for giving.

But he was not mistaken. As he reached down with his hands, guiding her, showing her how to please him, he found a willing pupil.

Aimée was aware of an intense thrill of satisfaction as she felt his hands catch for a moment in her hair, sliding down at last to grasp her breasts, while his body twisted compulsively in the rhythm she had set for him. In that instant she sensed he was hers, completely and totally hers, as he had never been before and would never be again.

He drew her head away slowly, satisfied at last. Staring into her eyes, he seemed to be searching for an answer to the question he dared not ask.

At last he spoke.

"Are you sorry?"

Sorry for what? Aimée wondered. Sorry that she had offered him this final proof of her passion? Sorry that she had dared to love him in the first place? Sorry she carried his child within her body?

It did not matter. She already had her answer.

"Yes, I am sorry."

She felt his body go rigid at her words. She did not try to hurry her explanation. She enjoyed teasing him.

"I am sorry you gave me so much pleasure, and I gave you so much pleasure . . . but we could not enjoy the moment of our passion together."

He relaxed instantly. "That can be arranged."

"So soon?" She whispered the words provocatively in his ear. Her hand reached down to touch him, shy no longer. "Are you so virile, my love?"

"It's not that I am so virile. Only that you are so desirable."

This time, he took her tenderly in his arms. He had already grown hard for her again, but he felt no urgency. He could take time to woo her gently, as he never had before.

At last he could acknowledge the one thing he had never dared admit even to himself. He loved this woman, this flawed, imperfect, faithless woman who lay in his arms. Loved her in a way he would never love again.

Funny, love was a word he had never applied to himself. Not even with Thea. For all the polite affection that had prompted him to ask her to be his wife, he had never once thought of himself as a man caught up in the throes of love. Now he was bound by ties he could not understand to a woman who would not even want them if she knew they were there.

That he must lose her was a thing he accepted without question. With the approach of summer, the rigorous climate would soon become unbearable for a woman in her condition. But he knew now that, when she left him, a part of his vitality would go with her.

Aimée stirred in his arms. Leaning forward, she kissed him lightly on the cheek. Understanding his need to draw into himself, she did not try to rush his passion.

Somewhere in his heart, Raoul knew, there would always be an image he could never quite escape. He would see it often in quiet, introspective moments. A miniature likeness of this woman he loved so desperately, but could never have. A tiny creature, dark curls bobbing in the wind, eyes dancing with the same laughter he had once longed to glimpse in other, sadder eyes.

Or worse yet, a likeness of himself. A likeness he could never truly be sure was of him at all.

"Come, my love," Aimée whispered, breaking into his thoughts. "You are too solemn, too far away. Come back to me."

He did not try to fight her. Drawing her into his arms, he shut out both the past and the future. All that existed was the present, and the present was a glowing burst of rapture.

He did not leave her until dawn, but dawn came all too soon. After he had gone, Aimée lay alone, painfully conscious of the emptiness of her body now that he had left her. It was an inescapable sensation, as pervasive and bitter as the emptiness of her life without the promise of love.

It had been good to lie beside him one last time, but it had hurt, too. In a way, it would almost be a relief when the heat grew too intense and she had to go home at last.

Home. The visions the word called to mind were vague and faraway. Paris in the summer. Trees thick with green leaves, and bright red flowers in formal gardens. A graceful house on the edge of town. Three little boys, shouting and shrieking, squabbling with each other at the top of their lungs, until she thought she would scream with exasperation.

And Mama. Gentle Mama, with pale, cool hands. And Papa, with the healing gift of laughter.

She let her hands slip down to her belly, trying to feel the physical traces of a life that showed no signs yet. Soon she would have another love, replacing the love she had lost. A better, purer love.

Yes, it would be good to go home at last.

FOUR

In the Cool of the North Wind

∞ Meryt

Meryt sprawled on the bottom of the slender papyrus boat, her chin pressed against the rough reeds at the edge as she stared into the water. Deep beneath the glassy surface, she caught sight of a heavy undulating form drifting through the luminous play of light and shadow like a mythical monster come to haunt her dreams. Perhaps, she told herself with a smile, it was the enormous fish her lover and her brother were both looking for so expectantly, their eyes searching the dancing reflections. Or perhaps, just perhaps . . .

She almost laughed aloud at the thought. Perhaps it was Sobek, the crocodile god of all dark waters, the fearsome image of her childhood nightmares.

"Be careful, Tuti." Her voice was clear and lilting, carrying easily to the place where her little brother, now nearly five years old, poled his own miniature boat with solemn self-importance through the tall marsh grasses. "Sobek will gobble you up if you don't watch out."

The boy threw her a quick, disdainful glance, then turned back to the water, his fishing spear raised high in his hand. Meryt laughed aloud at the gesture. Already it was apparent her brother came from a far different mold than she. No mysterious, illusive nightmares darkened Tuti's world; no awesome gods hid in the murky waters of his swamps. He would grow to be an independent man, freethinking like his uncle, daring in action like his father.

Behind her, Meryt heard Senmut's laughter, carefully muted so it would not carry to the boy's ears. Pulling herself upright, she tugged her knees to her chin, curling her arms around them as she had since she was a little girl. The tall stalks of papyrus that rose around them seemed to shut them off from the rest of the world.

"Run along, Tuti." The sharp sound of her voice startled the boy as he turned to face her. "Go and play in the pond for a while."

The boy's eyes filled with disappointment, but he did not

try to protest. The determined set to his sister's jaw warned him she had made up her mind. Laying down his fishing spear, he clutched the long pole in both hands, maneuvering his boat slowly through the reeds.

Senmut, standing in the rear of their own craft, looked down at Meryt in surprise. He did not say anything, but watched silently as the child drifted away from them, half-disappearing into the tall, twisting reeds. At last, laying down his own spear, he stepped forward, taking care not to over-turn the boat as he knelt on the floor beside her. Gently he reached forward and gripped her chin, forcing her head up-ward to meet his gaze.

"What is it, Meryt?" His voice was low and concerned. "What's wrong?"

His words cut through her. He knew her so well, this man whose life she had shared for one sweet, enchanted year. There was no way she could hide anything from him.

She was solemn as she gazed at him. "Do you remember your lessons, Senmut?"

The words were crisp, abrupt. Puzzled, Senmut let his hands fall from her face. Even in his confusion he could not keep a hint of laughter from his voice.

"Remember? How could I forget? Oh, the hours of copying maxims over and over on broken shards of pottery, trem-bling for fear I would do it wrong and get a beating."

Meryt turned away from him. "My favorites were the po-ems," she said softly. "The love poems."

Senmut's laughter mellowed. His fingertips traced the naked skin of her shoulders, slipping slowly over her body until they rested on her breast. His breath was hot as he low-ered his lips to her neck.

"I know. How do you think I won you?"

Meryt's body quivered beneath the touch of his lips, the warm caress of his hands. She arched her neck backward, let-ting her head rest against his shoulders. Her breath came in a long, low sigh as he cupped her breasts. It was all she could do to keep from crying out in longing at the sound of the song he hummed in her ears.

Seven days I have not seen my sister . . .

Seven days . . . The same melody the lyre had played as she lay in the shallow water at the shore of a cool lake, let-ting gentle ripples caress her. The same melody that had lin-gered in the air as she looked up slowly, hesitantly, seeing dark eyes smiling down at her.

"My favorite was another poem," she said quickly, breaking into her own reverie. Reluctantly she eased her body away from his fingers. In a slow, steady tone she began to recite:

I am thy first sister.
I am unto thee a garden,
Rich earth planted with flowers and sweet-scented herbs.
There is a lovely channel in my garden,
Hollowed by thine own hand.
In the cool of the North Wind,
It is a lovely place to walk,
With thine hand upon mine, and my body satisfied,
And my heart rejoiced.

Her voice choked on the words, and she could not finish. Rich, sensual images, so lovely once in schoolgirl dreams, now lay like stones on her heart. Turning, she was surprised to see that Senmut was puzzled. She had thought her meaning was so clear.

Slowly she repeated the words:

I am unto thee a garden,
Rich earth planted with flowers and sweet-scented herbs.

Rich, fertile earth. The soil from which life came. Taking Senmut's hand lightly in her own, Meryt pressed it against her belly. She had the uncanny sensation that she could feel a tiny heart beating beneath the warm flesh.

It was an instant before Senmut understood. When he did, he felt his chest contract with a sharp pain.

Reaching out, he drew Meryt tightly, comfortingly into his arms. His hands seemed to move of their own accord as he pressed her head against his chest, stroking the silken strands of her hair with his fingertips.

"It's all right, beloved. It's all right."

The words were mechanical, uttered without conviction. It was not all right, and they both knew it. They had always assumed, right from the beginning, that Meryt would never be able to conceive again. If the fact had grieved them, it had comforted them, too, reminding them it would be easier to conceal their illicit love affair.

"Perhaps we can keep it hidden." Meryt's voice was a tremulous whisper, muffled against his chest. "If I pretended to have a fever, if I stayed inside so no one could see me

. . . Well, afterward, couldn't he just play in the garden with all the other children? Who would know he didn't belong to one of the servants?

She was prattling and she knew it. In her fear, she was trying to avoid the one thing she knew was unavoidable. There was no way she could hope to have the child and keep it hidden—no way at all.

But it was hard. Oh, Isis, it was hard. Even with that other child, the product of a forced union with a man she loathed, the thing she had been forced to do had been agonizing. And this was the child of the man she loved.

Senmut sensed her pain in the tremor that raced through her body, making her quiver against him. He did not mistake its cause. He knew as well as she that there was only one thing they could do.

Idly, almost sightlessly, he let his eyes drift through the dark shadows of the marshland. Always before, the papyrus swamp had been one of his favorite places. Today, for the first time, it no longer looked tantalizing and mysterious to his eyes. Today it seemed only brooding and strangely lonely.

Off in the distance, barely visible through the tall, thick reeds, the boy Tuti pushed his boat playfully back and forth across the shallow pond, singing little snatches of boatman songs to himself as he plunged his pole again and again into the muddy bottom.

Tuti's eyes were black, Senmut reminded himself. Black as the eyes of the man who had fathered him. The mother, the beautiful princess from lands far away, had borne only two children who lived, and one of them had eyes the color of jet. Perhaps Meryt's child too . . .

Bitterly Senmut choked back his own thoughts. He was getting as foolish as the girl he loved. No matter what color the baby's eyes, it was bound to cause gossip—gossip that would sooner or later drift back to the court at Akhet-Aten. Then it would be all over for them. Then they were certain to be discovered.

But they had always known they would be discovered.

The sheer simplicity of the thought took his breath away. Of course they would be discovered. They had known that from the beginning. From the first sultry morning on a shimmering shore when they gave themselves to each other, openly, freely, with no regard for the consequences. The child would make no difference. They would just be discovered a little sooner, that was all.

He was surprised at how light he felt, now that the moment of doubt had passed. His lips were gentle, teasing, as he brushed them against Meryt's hair.

"Perhaps it will be a girl."

And perhaps it would be. A little royal daughter, amidst a flock of other royal daughters, no threat to the pharaoh or the son he still dreamed of giving to the kingdom. When the end came at last, when they were finally discovered, perhaps there would still be enough mercy in Akhenaten's heart to spare one small girl child.

Meryt understood instantly what Senmut was trying to tell her. Her eyes were troubled as she looked up at him. She was keenly aware of the generosity of his gesture, just as she saw the courage that had prompted it, but she knew she could not let him do it. She might risk her own life, even the life of the unborn child within her, but not her lover's. Senmut had been too good to her, too warm and giving. She could not let him throw away his life like this.

"We cannot have the child, Senmut. You know we cannot. We are certain to be caught."

To her surprise, he only laughed. The sound was light, almost giddy. "You are always so frightened, little one. You thought we would be caught before, but we weren't. Don't look for the worst now."

Anxiously she scanned his face. Was he really as rash as he sounded, she wondered, as foolhardy? Could he truly fail to see the deadly peril that lay ahead of them? She did not know if she was frightened or relieved when she saw that his eyes were solemn and steady.

No. Senmut was no fool, no reckless youth laughing away the consequences of his own act. He saw their danger as clearly as she, saw the necessary end of this thing they were beginning, but he was not afraid. The child she carried in her body was as much his as hers. He was ready to pay whatever price he must give it a chance at life.

"You are braver than I," she whispered.

"We must both be brave." His hands caressed her face, reaching up to brush away the wisps of hair that spilled onto her brow. "We will need all the courage we can find."

His arms felt warm, strong, comforting, as he locked her into his embrace. Closing her eyes, Meryt blocked out the light and color of the world around her. Only the sound of the water intruded, soft and soothing as it splashed against the side of the boat, mingling with boyish laughter from the nearby pond. A sudden fluttering of wings broke through the still air as a dark, graceful bird rose from the reeds, soaring into the sky. The sound faded slowly, leaving in its wake only an illusion of peace.

The child was born in the month of Tobi, the rich, fertile season of growth. It was a difficult birth, painful and frightening, leaving Meryt's body so badly torn the physicians swore she would never conceive again, but she did not care. All the suffering, all the anguish, seemed worthwhile the moment she held her baby in her arms.

It was the girl she had prayed for, a tiny, helpless creature, her face red and wrinkled, her dark hair as soft and furry as a little animal. It seemed to Meryt she was the most exquisitely beautiful baby she had ever seen in her life. She named her Teti-Sheri, little Teti, after one of their royal ancestresses. Even if the child was not going to be raised as a princess, she could at least bear the name of one.

Senmut began to make a gift for Meryt the day the child was born. Taking a small, supple sheet of papyrus, he copied out the words of the love poem that meant so much to her, inking in each miniature hieroglyph with painstaking care. He made the paper himself, cutting down tall stalks of papyrus, then peeling off the rind and slicing them into thin strips. After he wove them together, he pounded them into a flat sheet, then rubbed for hours with a small ivory burnisher until the whole thing was smooth and flexible. Even the reed pens were a labor of love, as were the ochre, malachite, and carbon inks he ground and mixed himself. He wanted it to be a gift all his own, untouched by any mortal hands save his.

Meryt's eyes glowed with anticipation as she unrolled the tiny scroll, squinting into the dim light to make out the hieroglyphs inked across its surface.

"I am unto thee a garden." She whispered the words softly, reciting them from memory. The tears that dimmed her eyes blinded her to the markings. "Rich earth planted with flowers and sweet-scented herbs."

Rich earth planted with flowers and sweet-scented herbs. The same words she had chosen to tell him she was to bear his child. It was a gift she would treasure as long as she lived.

When Senmut saw how much the scroll meant to her, he had a case made for it, a scarab carved from a single carnelian and mounted into plain gold. It was the simplest piece of jewelry Meryt had ever owned, and the one she valued most. She placed it on a golden chain around her neck, refusing to take it off, even when the servants bathed her with perfumed water or when she held her baby to her breast.

It seemed to Senmut that the best hours of the day were the ones when he could sit by Meryt's side, marveling again and again at the miracle of life as he watched the woman he loved nurse the child he had helped to create. He did not think he had ever seen anything so beautiful.

Teti-Sheri, her father thought with amazement and paternal pride, was a greedy little creature, grabbing hungrily at her mother's breast the instant it was offered, then smacking her lips with loud satisfaction to let them know she had had enough. Even then, even when she had finished, she seemed to find it hard to turn away, hesitating comically for a moment, as if she thought perhaps she should force down one last mouthful, just to make sure she would not go hungry if the next feeding was a little late.

Senmut laughed aloud as he watched her. As always, the sight amused him.

The sound of his laughter distracted the nursing child. Turning for a moment, she fixed wide, alert eyes on his face. The sight of her made Senmut's heart catch in his throat. Already she was a lovely little girl, exotic and delicate as the mother who had borne her. Thick dark hair provided a perfect frame for the sapphire blue of her eyes.

Meryt caught the expression on her lover's face, and she understood it immediately. Instinctively she tightened her arms around Teti-Sheri, making the child whimper in protest. She knew that Senmut had hoped, just as she had, that the baby's eyes would begin to darken as she grew older, matching at last the eyes of her people. It was obvious now that they were not going to.

Yet it was unfair, she thought rebelliously, brutally unfair. Her brother had dark eyes, as dark as their father's. Why couldn't her eyes have been dark, too?

"Would you have noticed me if my eyes weren't blue?"

She tried to keep the question light, tossing it out as a distraction from their fears. She was angry with herself when she could not keep a tremor from her voice.

"I would have noticed you." Senmut's tone was clear and quiet. "I would have loved you . . . no matter what."

Gently, his fingers brushed away the little fringe of hair that fell onto the baby's forehead. Meryt felt the warmth of his hand as it rested briefly against her breast. Glancing upward, she let her eyes linger on his. The tears on her lashes were not tears of sorrow. That moment came as close to perfection as she would ever know.

Senmut did not fail to see her emotion. It moved him deeply.

"You are happy?" The words were only half a question.

Do you need to ask? she started to say with a smile. Only, the seriousness in his eyes stopped her, reminding her he would not have spoken the words if he did not need to hear the answer.

"Yes, I am happy."

He let himself return her smile.

"And I," he whispered, looking down at his daughter in the arms of the woman who would always be his wife in his heart. "And I."

The seasons passed quickly, fading into a year almost before Meryt knew they were gone, then surprisingly into two, and still the discovery they had feared did not come. Sometimes, especially on bright, sunny days, the thought of it made her want to laugh aloud. Teti-Sheri was a toddler already, her plump little legs carrying her around the gardens so fast her mother could barely keep up with her, and their life had not changed at all. Not a one—not a single one—of all the dark terrors Meryt had conjured up in her mind had come to pass.

But there were other times, times when the shadows of twilight began to lengthen, that Meryt could not help realizing how lucky they had been—she and her lover and the child they shared—how incredibly lucky. And luck was a thing that could not last forever.

It was hardest at night, lying awake in the moon-touched darkness, staring up at a slender crescent glowing through the single window high in the wall. It seemed to Meryt, then, that she was all alone in the world, cut off by the force of her own fear even from her lover. The air was heavy and eerily silent, without so much as a whisper of wind.

Beside her, Senmut stirred restlessly, and the illusion of loneliness was broken. Meryt realized he was awake as she was.

"Isn't the moon pretty?" she said softly, trying to make light of her sleeplessness. "Khons is ferrying souls of the dead across the dark night sky."

"Ummm," Senmut replied carelessly. Meryt smiled when she saw that he was not staring at the moon at all.

"Aren't you sleepy?" she teased. Automatically her arms opened as she felt him move closer to her.

Senmut laughed. "The baby hasn't been so quiet for months. You don't think I'm going to waste all this silence sleeping."

His lips were gentle, coaxing, as he touched them to hers, but his hands explored her body with a hunger he made no effort to control. Meryt sighed as she struggled to relax in his arms, trying to force herself to respond to the passion that always drove her to peaks of ecstasy. Bitterly she realized it was no use.

Senmut was surprised when he felt her pull away. Usually she was so responsive, so eager, her body trembling as violently as his for the union that lay ahead. Reluctantly he let her slip out of his arms. Rolling over on his back, he thrust his hands beneath his head, staring at her as she sat up, her knees tucked under her chin like a little girl. He was careful to say nothing, waiting until she was ready to speak.

"Senmut?"

He could not miss the troubled sound in her voice. Easing his hand from beneath his head, he clasped her fingers. They were cold to his touch.

"Teti-Sheri's eyes are blue, the same blue as mine. Why hasn't anyone noticed?"

So that was what was bothering her. They had never spoken of this, not since the day the child was born, but the question had always been there, lying between them.

Senmut allowed himself a soft laugh. "Of course they have noticed. Everyone in the palace compound must have guessed the truth by now."

"But they can't, Senmut. I mean, if they had—if they were gossiping about it—word would surely have reached my uncle's ears by now."

"I suppose it has." His voice was deceptively cool.

Meryt's eyes widened as she stared at him in the moonlight. "But that's impossible, Senmut, you know it is. Why, if my uncle even guessed what we had done, he would drag us back to Akhet-Aten to disgrace . . . and death."

Senmut's hand tightened around hers. "Your uncle is not a monster, Meryt. Besides, I think the man is genuinely fond of you. As long as we are discreet, as long as the gossip does not get out of hand and make a laughingstock of him, I do not think he will grudge you the happiness you have found."

Meryt began to relax. Leaning down, she brushed her lips against the rough surface of his cheek. "Oh, Senmut, what a fool you must think me, imagining all sorts of awful things all the time."

Senmut wrapped his arms possessively around her shoulders, pulling her down beside him on the bed.

"You are not a fool. But you are wrong to be afraid. Even if it were to end tomorrow, it would all have been worth it."

This time there was no gentleness in his lips as he forced them down on hers. Meryt's low cry was an echo of his own ravenous yearning. Her fingers dug into his dark hair, her mouth parted beneath his as she surrendered at last to her love.

Senmut was hers, she told herself with a sweeping exhilaration, all hers, and she loved him beyond security, beyond comfort, beyond even life. There was nothing she would not do, no price she would not pay, to lie in his arms.

Even if it were to end tomorrow, it would all have been worth it.

Meryt was often to remember those words in the coming months. It did not end tomorrow, or even the tomorrow that followed that, but it was not long in coming, not nearly as long as she had prayed or sometimes even dared to hope. And it came with a swiftness that took her breath away.

There was no hint of warning, not so much as a shadow or scowl, not even little giggled snatches of gossip dying away as she drew near, to prepare her for the moment. Just the sudden approach of a trusted servant at her side.

"Your grandmother wants to see you in her chambers at dusk. You and the scribe Senmut."

And then it was over. Over as they had always known it must be.

There was no doubt in Meryt's mind as she moved beside her lover down the long walkway that led to her grandmother's rooms what they would find when they arrived. One glance at Senmut's profile told her he was thinking the same thing. The woman Meryt had always called "grandmother" shared no blood ties with her, and held the title only because she had been her grandfather's chief wife. She had never before felt a moment's fondness or concern for the issue of her husband's lesser wives. It seemed idle to hope she had suddenly developed an interest in Meryt.

It took only a moment for their worst fears to be confirmed. It seemed to Meryt that her grandmother's face was sharp with malice and amusement as she told them that the gossip, which had indeed reached the court, had finally grown too widespread for Akhenaten to ignore. His soldiers, Meryt's grandmother told them with satisfaction, would arrive at dawn.

And yet it could not have been satisfaction, Meryt thought as they made their way back to their own quarters. For if the woman truly despised her, if she enjoyed watching her pain and fear as much as she seemed to, why had she told them what was coming? Why had she given them the few precious hours they needed to escape?

Senmut took the news with a calmness Meryt envied. Pausing only briefly in the room they had shared since the day they became lovers, he slipped quietly through a doorway into the adjoining chamber. When he returned, he held a sleepy, protesting Teti-Sheri wrapped in a warm blanket in his arms.

Meryt could only stand silently across the room staring at him in bewilderment and disbelief. It seemed to her so final, so terrifyingly irrevocable, this thing they were preparing to do. Yet he looked as casual as if they were only going for a pleasant outing.

Senmut's eyes were understanding and compassionate, but his voice was low and urgent.

"We must hurry."

"But how can we?" She turned around in confusion. "I mean, we haven't even begun to pack."

"We can take nothing with us."

"Nothing?" Her eyes widened in amazement. "Just what we are wearing? Nothing more?" No fresh clothing, no jewelry, no chest of perfumes and cosmetics?

But even as her heart sank, Meryt knew he was right. It would have made no difference if they had had a week's warning or a month's. They still could not bring any of their belongings. Not for them the golden sleighs and massive red oxen that had marked her father's journey to his last home. Their departure must be a secret, stealthy one.

Briskly she nodded. Hurrying to a long, low table at the side of the room, she picked up the jeweled Isis collar her father had had made for her. Her hands were trembling as she lifted it to her neck.

Senmut hid his pain with gruffness.

"Not even that."

Meryt's hands stopped in midair. "Not even the Isis?" Not even the last link she had with her father?

"It is too expensive, too ornate. It would be conspicuous where we are going."

Where we are going.

Slowly she lowered the heavy pectoral to the table, letting it slide from her fingers with regret. It was clear to her that everything had been planned by her lover weeks, months, perhaps even years ago.

"Where are we going, Senmut?"

The muscles in Senmut's face tightened involuntarily. He had hoped she would not ask. He did not want to frighten her any more than he had to.

"To the necropolis."

"The necropolis? But that's . . . that's the city of the dead."

"And the living," Senmut reminded her. "The artisans and priests who serve the dead have lived in their city beside the tombs for centuries. I have made friends among them, good friends who will help us now."

Meryt closed her eyes, feeling her body sway with mounting terror. It suddenly seemed too much to bear, too much to ask anyone to endure. It was bad enough leaving behind every possession she owned, everything she had ever held dear, but to have to go to the city of the dead . . .

A low whimper broke into Meryt's thoughts, pulling her out of the fear that was drowning her. Forcing her eyes open, she focused them on Teti-Sheri's face. The bright blue eyes that stared back at her were wide and sleepless now, their dark lashes glistening with tears.

Belatedly Meryt saw that she had communicated her own fear to her daughter. "It's all right, Teti-Sheri," she said quickly, pinching the girl's cheek teasingly. "We're just going on an adventure, an adventure in the moonlight. Won't that be fun?" She almost made her voice sound convincing, even to herself.

A bulky object dangled from Teti-Sheri's fingers. Gently Meryt pulled away a corner of the blanket so she could see it better. She laughed aloud, a jerky, half-hysterical sound, as the lamplight illuminated a rough, clumsily carved lion with a comical face and an oversized movable jaw that opened and closed with the tug of a short stick. Dozens of baby-tooth marks, gouged into the soft wood, bore witness to the favor it had found in the eyes of the little girl.

Gratefully Meryt glanced up at Senmut. If she had to leave behind every memory, every shred of security she had ever known, every tie to the past, at least her child would have something cherished and familiar to comfort her.

The long covered walkway was strangely silent as they stepped out into deep blue shadows. The night air held a chill, but they barely noticed. Around them, in the courtyard, silver rays of a full moon highlighted sandy paths and vibrant half-tamed vegetation, giving the eerie illusion of dawn's first light.

It seemed to Meryt the palace had never been so quiet. No matter how she strained her ears, she could not pick up a hint of music or laughter or soft whispered gossip from the darkened doorways or the high narrow windows. It was almost as if they had crossed already to the city of the dead, leaving behind them every trace of warmth and vitality.

And yet she knew, even in her fear, that she was only imagining things. The palace must have been just as quiet countless other nights, the dark shadows just as heavy, the moonlight as bright. If she had never noticed before, it was because tonight, for the first time in her life, silence had become her enemy. Tonight the soft sound of her own sandals clattering against the stones made her sick with fear.

Meryt's eyes darted through the shadows that rimmed the garden. This place, so familiar for the past three years of her life, had suddenly become terrifying and alien, hiding the unknown in the inky darkness at the base of its high walls.

Not ten minutes before, she and Senmut had moved confidently down that same walkway, barely noticing the twilight that closed in around them as they hurried toward their rooms. But then they had been an ordinary young couple doing exactly what people expected them to do. Now, they were fugitives, slipping through the night, their two-year-old child clutched furtively in her father's arms.

Meryt's head jerked nervously back and forth as she scanned first one side of the garden, then the other. Out of the corner of her eye she could see Senmut doing the same thing. She knew exactly what he was thinking. If anyone saw them, if an overfriendly servant cried out too loud a greeting or an overzealous guard made his rounds too thoroughly, it would all be over. They could explain their own presence easily enough—a walk in the moonlight beside the river perhaps—but how could they justify a baby wrapped in a blanket against the night air?

"It's so quiet," Meryt whispered. She shivered at the sound of her own voice echoing ominously off the stone of the walk and the mud brick of the walls.

Senmut nodded. His eyes continued to search the shadows. It was quiet—too quiet. He had never seen the gardens quite this deserted. Even on the most uneventful nights, there should have been someone in evidence, a bustling servant

268

perhaps, or an old man, restless and unable to sleep. Someone should have been there to startle them, sending them scurrying deeper into the shadows, their hearts catching painfully in their throats. The silence and the emptiness were unnatural. It was almost as if everyone had avoided the place on purpose, as if they had been ordered to stay away.

The heavy outer wall of the palace compound loomed before them, but Meryt, concentrating on the darkness of the garden, did not even see it until they were almost upon it.

One glance at Senmut confirmed her fears: the most dangerous moment of their flight lay just ahead of them.

There would be a guard at the gate that led to the outside. There had always been a guard there, day and night, as long as Meryt could remember. Luck had been with them so far, but that luck was about to run out.

Meryt felt Senmut stop beside her, shifting the heavy burden in his arms until it looked like a bundle of rags tossed carelessly over his shoulder. The blanket slipped loosely over the child's face. Catching her breath, Meryt waited for the loud howls of protest that did not come. Miraculously, Teti-Sheri, secure in her father's arms seemed to have fallen asleep.

Meryt could only stare at her lover in bewilderment. Then slowly, as she watched his face, she comprehended what he intended to do. The bold simplicity of it took her breath away.

Cautiously, she let her hand slip through his arm, clinging to him with a kind of helpless abandon. As they moved forward, her features contorted into a sly little grin, a conscious imitation of the mockery of laughter she saw on his face. If they were bold enough, quick enough, the plan might just work. When the guard at the gate looked at them, he would see only a high-spirited young couple, bawdy and adventurous, toting a bundle of bedding down to the riverbank for a night of merriment. A lewd wink from Senmut, a subtle smirk from her, and if all went well, an answering wave and a raucous laugh in return.

But the gate was empty!

Meryt paused in the gaping space that cut through the high wall. Her fingers dug into Senmut's arm. Never, in all her memory, had the gate been empty before. Even her grandmother, with all her power, did not have the authority to order the guard to leave. It was inconceivable that he was not here now.

And yet he was not.

Slipping her hand at last from the security of her lover's arm, Meryt forced herself out into the open space that lay beyond the gate. Senmut followed her, his arms closing tighter around Teti-Sheri's body. He moved like a cat, lithe and graceful on the balls of his feet, ready to spring or flee at a second's notice.

The darkness outside the palace seemed even more ominous, more frightening than that in the quiet inner gardens. Imposing sphinxes with heads of men and bodies of jungle beasts lined the long walk that led to the river, casting eerie elongated shadows along the sand. Even the bright rays of the full moon could not penetrate the darkness that lay like a low cloud around their bases.

Meryt moved from one stone figure to the next, trying to ignore the heavy shadows at their bases. Every minute, every second, she expected to see a company of men leap out from behind the sphinxes, their spears raised high in the air as they charged the helpless fugitives. It seemed to her a miracle when they did not.

The way to the river was long and dark. Longer than Meryt had ever remembered, darker than she had ever known. Only a few more steps she kept telling herself. Only a little longer, only one more turn. Then they would be there at last. Then they would be safe and free, standing on the shores of the river that flowed halfway to eternity. But every step they took, every corner they slipped around, seemed to leave them as far away as before. Meryt had to fight to hold back her despair. The river seemed so very far. She could hardly believe they would ever get there.

Then abruptly the path ended, widening into a vast expanse of shoreline. For a moment Meryt could only stand and gape at it, her eyes drinking in the moonlit water as if she had never expected to see it again. Slowly, she began to move forward, following Senmut toward the royal dock. For the first time since they had slipped out into the cool night, Meryt dared to hope.

The dock was quiet and deserted. Only a few vessels, their sides gilded, their masts hung with colored banners, remained to evoke memories of the days when the royal palace had been the center of the living world. Senmut was already carefully assessing the boats as he hurried toward them, choosing the one that would serve their purpose best.

Meryt saw him stop suddenly, shifting the sleeping child in his arms as he turned back toward the shoreline he had just passed. Following his gaze, she glimpsed a small papyrus boat on the sand not far from the walkway. Fascinated, she watched Senmut step toward it, glancing down at the small paddle left carelessly in the bottom. His brow was knit in distrust.

It was not hard to guess what he was thinking. It was too convenient, too easy. Everything had been so simple from the moment her grandmother warned them the soldiers were coming. Any other night, they would never have slipped unnoticed through the gardens, never passed unchallenged by a guardless gate, or found a boat waiting for them when they reached the dock. It was as if some unseen hand had guided them to just that spot at just that moment.

Moving quickly to her lover's side, Meryt reached out, shifting the child's weight from his arms to her own. Silently she watched him as he bent over the boat, running his fingers up and down the long seams where the sheaves of papyrus had been fastened together. It was frighteningly easy to imagine dark water oozing through those same cracks, seeping up around their feet and ankles when they were too far out into the river to do anything about it.

It was a moment before Senmut pulled himself erect. It seemed to Meryt that his shoulders were stooped and weary, as if they bore a weight too heavy even for his strong body. His back was rigid as he stared at the dock.

The choice that faced them now was an impossible one. If they tried to take one of the royal barques, they would have to leave it, gaudy and conspicuous, on the far shore, a clear beacon to mark the path they had taken. But if they decided to trust the simpler craft . . .

"Come on." Senmut's eyes were flashing as he whirled to face her. His lips were set. "There's no time to lose."

Meryt made no protest as she stepped clumsily into the small boat, settling herself uncomfortably on the floor with the baby on her lap. She knew as well as he that there was no other choice. The risk was great, but it was a risk they had to take.

Senmut's tunic was drenched as he pushed the fragile vessel out into the current, but he did not even notice as he climbed hastily aboard, kneeling in the pool that formed around his legs. He paused for a moment, looking at the woman he loved, painfully conscious that this might be the last chance he would ever have to study her face. The quiet courage he saw in her eyes, the trust as she gazed back at him, encouraged him. Picking up the paddle, he dipped it forcefully into the water.

He was careful to stay close to the shore for the first few minutes, warily testing the strength of the boat. Only when it seemed to hold did he head toward the center of the river. Even in his fear, he had to smile a little at his caution. If his suspicions were right, if the thing was indeed a trap, all the prudence in the world could not help them now. At this very minute, soldiers would be slipping through the shadows to line both banks of the river, the sharp points of their spears ready to finish the task if the boat should fail. It might well prove better not to reach the shore. One fate might be kinder than the other.

Meryt's body was tense with fear as she huddled in the bottom of the boat, pressing the child tightly against the warmth of her body. It seemed to her that Senmut, too, was strained, his limbs as stiff as her own as he forced the paddle again and again into the cold water, pushing the small boat closer to the western shore.

Only when they had finally made their way past the middle of the river, only when the boat showed no sign of giving out beneath them, did Senmut at last begin to relax. Drawing in the paddle, he let the current pull them downstream as he leaned his shoulders wearily against the side of the boat. A low, satisfied laugh rose in his throat.

Nervously Meryt glanced over at him, scanning the placid lines of his face with suspicion. For a moment she feared he had cracked under the strain, letting the anxiety and tension affect his reason at last. Her body began to tremble at the thought. Without Senmut, without his cool courage, she did not know how she could face the days that lay ahead.

Senmut saw her fear instantly. Controlling his laughter, he dropped his hand to her shoulder.

"It's all right, little one." His voice was quiet and comforting. "We're safe now. If they had been ordered to follow us, they would have come by now."

If they had been ordered . . . ?

Meryt looked at him in bewilderment. How could anyone have been ordered to follow them, when no one knew they were planning to escape?

With a flash of recognition, she understood. Unveiled warnings from a grandmother who had no love for her, a path free of guards controlled by only one man, a small boat left conveniently on the shore . . . Who had the power to arrange all that?

"Then my uncle . . ."

She left the rest of the sentence unspoken. It seemed too fantastic, too incredible to utter aloud.

Senmut nodded slowly. "I told you once, the man is not a monster. He had to make a public show of retaliation in the face of all that gossip, but I cannot believe he truly intended to hurt you."

Meryt was silent. The image of her uncle, a man she had not even seen for the past three years, suddenly rose before her. So ugly, yet so gentle; so warped and twisted on the outside, so hungry inside for a tenderness he could never show. The thought made her sad.

She reached for the scarab that dangled from her neck and clasped it as if it were a talisman imbued with the power to ward off unwelcome memories. It was a moment before she realized what she was doing.

Senmut laughed gently at her anxiety. "Don't worry, little one, I won't make you toss it into the Nile. It's a simple piece, plain enough to cause no notice. You can keep it."

At last Meryt relaxed enough to smile back at him. Slowly she dropped her hand from the scarab, letting it rest instead in the warmth of Senmut's. All the fear, all the regret, fell from her. They were safe and they were together—and that was all that counted. She had a strong man beside her to lean on, a loving child in her arms to protect. There was not a palace or a jewel in the world she would trade for either.

The moonlight touched the ripples of the water; diamond-bright stars danced in the dark sky. Senmut picked up the paddle again, dipping it soundlessly into the river, bringing their boat to the western shore.

∞ *Aimée*

1

"What a fascinating woman." The count's dark eyes flashed as he looked up at the long tiers of boxes high above the opera floor. Vienna, with the grace of its wide boulevards and the loveliness of its ladies, had long been one of his favorite cities. Now he was enjoying it immensely. "Who is she?"

His companion lounged nonchalantly against a vacant seat. Thin fair hair brushed forward onto his brow, coupled with a small, neatly trimmed beard, gave him the cynical look of a young roué.

"Really, Egon, I should have insisted we go to the theater. Mitzi or Luisa would have been more to your liking. But, no, I forgot. You prefer this type, don't you? What is there about vulgar diamonds set against jet tresses that intrigues you so much? Or is it the virginity of pure white silk fashionably draped over voluptuous curves? I swear, one day you are going to be shot by a jealous husband who doesn't appreciate you nearly as much as you appreciate his wife."

Egon laughed easily. "No doubt, Rudolf, but in the meantime I intend to enjoy myself. Besides, you haven't answered my question. Who is she?"

"Luckily for you, I keep up on all the gossip. She is a newcomer to Vienna, Lady Ellingham."

"English, then?"

"French. She came here a few months ago to give birth to her first child. It's the husband who's English. Lord Richard Ellingham, I think. Lord Edward. Something like that."

"Really?" Egon studied the tall auburn-haired figure barely visible at the back of the box. "I could have sworn he was Austrian."

Rudolf followed his gaze. "Oh, him? Yes, I assure you he is Viennese through and through. The husband, as I understand it, is somewhere in Asia, searching for treasure—or is it Egypt? The man with her now is her cousin. But don't get your hopes up. The family is very religious and very strict."

"Are they?" Egon's voice was calm as he continued to stare at the box. "Well, my friend, we will see about that."

Aimée was not unaware of the sensation she was causing, and it delighted her—as a small child is delighted with a new toy. From the moment she had slipped a tentative, elegantly shod toe out of her carriage in front of the opera house, still unsure of her reception, heads had begun to turn, some discreetly, some openly, like those of the two men on the orchestra floor, as the guardians of Vienna society assessed the new stranger in their midst. To a young woman enjoying her first outing since the birth of her child, the attention was intoxicating.

"Oh, Franz, how exciting it is. Have you ever seen so many lights in your life?"

Franz bent toward her indulgently. It pleased him to see her so happy. He had been alarmed when she arrived from Paris pale and unnaturally quiet, with the look of a lost child. Now she was herself again.

"So you're glad you came to us?"

"Glad? How could I not be? You've been so good to me."

Aimée rested her elbow on the railing, leaning her head against her hand. A flood of memories swept over her, painful memories that would not be held back. The house in Paris, once so gay and full of life, now empty of vitality. Three little boys away at school. A mother pale and distracted. A father so ill he never left his room. It had been a relief, almost the answer to a prayer, when Franz's older sister, Sophie, appeared one day on their doorstep, eager to carry her back to Vienna.

Aimée abruptly pulled her head from her hand, tossing her curls in a gesture of defiance. This was a beautiful evening, dazzling and perfect, and she was not going to spoil it by feeling sorry for herself. Leaning over the rail, she searched the milling crowd for the two men who had been staring up at her only a moment before. She laughed aloud when she saw them.

Franz saw the mercurial changes in her moods, and it fascinated him. She had always been an enchanting creature, this little cousin of his, so childishly exuberant and full of spirit. Only, now, he had to admit, she was a child no longer. Her body, straining against the expensive silk of her dress, reminded him, if he needed reminding, that she had become a woman, and he found himself responding to her with a physical intensity he had not felt for years. If she came to him now, he wondered, as she had come once, lips parted, eyes

275

pleading with him to run away with her, would he still find the strength to resist her?

Glancing up through lowered lashes, Aimée smiled at the ardor her cousin could not conceal. All those years, she thought, filled with dreams of a handsome man who could never be hers. It amused her now to realize the tables had been reversed.

Teasingly, she pointed toward the two men on the floor. "Aren't they good-looking, Franz? The dark one especially. How dashing and romantic he is. And the other one, the fair-haired one, doesn't he look familiar? Have I seen him somewhere before?"

"I doubt it," Franz replied stiffly. "We don't move in the same circles as the archduke. I daresay he wouldn't deign to notice us."

"The archduke? You mean Prince Rudolf?" Aimée forgot her cousin as she gaped at the young crown prince. It did not surprise her that she had not recognized him instantly. In all the portraits she had seen, the heir to the house of Hapsburg had been solemn and self-consciously regal. This man was moody and full of fire, a bold romantic who looked as if he would be more at home in a boudoir or barroom than in the royal salons.

So he wouldn't deign to notice them, would he? Aimée's lips turned up at the thought of the challenge. Well, her cousin was half right, The prince might not notice Franz, but he was most certainly going to notice her.

Impishly she leaned forward, hanging over the railing as her eyes met those of the two men below. She knew she shouldn't, it was foolhardy to flirt with a man so far above her station, but she knew, too, that it was a game she could afford to play. Franz, dear, sweet, courteous Franz, no matter how he disapproved of her frivolity, would always be there to protect her.

Aimée turned away with a laugh. Drawing her attention back to the box, she found herself staring into a pair of vivid blue eyes. For an instant she thought someone had slipped in unnoticed to join them. Then she realized that the girl in the next box, as dazzled by the spectacle as she, had leaned so far over the railing she eluded the partition that separated them. She was hardly more than a child, fifteen or sixteen at most, a pretty little thing with dark brown hair and eyes almost as piercing as Aimée's.

"Hello," Aimée called out, still laughing. "Isn't it lovely?"

The girl dropped her gaze shyly, then looked up again.

"Oh, it is. Truly lovely. "I . . . I've just come from the convent, and I've never seen anything like it before."

Just come from the convent. Aimée was entranced. She could not help remembering another young girl, only a few years before, freed at last from the confines of high walls and eager to drink in all the glamour of the world. Had she looked like this girl then? she wondered. So breathless? So naive? So thirsty for the first awakening of passions she could not even understand?

Impulsively she invited the child to join them at intermission. "My name is Aimée. Lady Ellingham really, but I hate all that formality."

Her shyness gone, the girl let herself smile. "I am the Baroness Marie Vetsera, but everyone calls me Mary."

Aimée stiffened at the name. She glanced over her shoulder to see if Franz had heard. *Mon Dieu,* what had she done? Her cousin would be furious when he found out, and she did not blame him. Franz had always loathed the Vetsera clan. To him they were the crudest kind of social climbers, ambitious beyond their means, and he would not enjoy sharing his box with one of them, even a little girl as charming and unspoiled as Mary seemed to be.

It was a relief when the overture began at last, rich and moody and dramatic. Slowly Aimée relaxed, feeling the power of the music sweep over her until nothing else in the world existed. There was no young girl to distract her in the next box, no handsome prince staring up from the floor below, not even a tall solemn man so close behind her she could almost feel the warmth of his body. There were only the lights and the music and the vivid patterns of color on the stage.

Aimée had always loved *Faust,* feeling in the rhythmic passion of the music a deep primal response. But she had always been a little frightened of it, too, as if even in years past she had recognized in Faust, in this man so ready to sell his soul to the devil for a chance to taste earthly pleasures, something of her own heart. Now she was more intrigued than afraid. Somewhere along the way, the idea of sin had ceased to appall her.

Intermission came all too soon, tearing Aimée out of the magic world the music had spun around her. She caught herself watching the doorway, dreading the moment the curtains would slip open and a timid face peek in. Yet the instant they did, the instant she caught a glimpse of Mary Vetsera she knew she was being foolish. The child was so gentle and innocent, so sweetly diffident, that Franz could not possibly object to sitting with her.

Aimée was so engrossed in her conversation with Mary, and so charmed to find in this child echoes of the young girl she herself had been, she forgot to watch the dark red curtains that screened the box from the hallway. When they parted, she was taken completely by surprise. She realized as she looked up that she had not expected the young archduke to answer her challenge.

And yet he had. He stood on the threshold for a moment, silent and hesitant, as if even princes of the realm could be unsure. Then, without a word of warning he strode arrogantly into the box, as brash and confident as if the invitation issued by her eyes had been firmly engraved on a formal note. Aimée watched him, fascinated, not sure yet whether she was dismayed or exhilarated at this new turn of events. He was already in the box before the curtain opened again and a second figure followed him. As soon as she saw the man, Aimée forgot everything else.

In a way, he was not the man she had seen on the floor below, young and dashing and enigmatic. He was older than she had thought, with barely visible touches of silver in curly chestnut hair. Deep lines had already begun to form around melting brown eyes, but he had a kind of magnetism that would not allow her to take her eyes off him.

Only Mary Vetsera had the presence of mind to remember her manners. Rising swiftly, she dropped a low, graceful curtsy to the archduke. With a flush of embarrassment, Aimée hastened to follow her example. Franz bent slightly in a stiff perfunctory bow that only half-concealed his disapproval.

Rudolf saw Franz's coolness, but he did not bother to acknowledge it. "You will forgive us, I am sure, for bursting in on you like this. Your cousin's beauty has already become legendary, and we could not resist coming up to see her for ourselves."

Aimée wanted to giggle. She knew his words were no more sincere than all the studied flattery she had ever heard, but she loved them all the same. It had been so long since anyone had treated her like a beautiful woman, she had forgotten how good it felt.

"A pretty speech, your Highness," she said easily. "Tell me, is gallantry part of the royal education?"

The prince gave her a sharp glance of appraisal. He had been prepared for a simper or a sigh, tokens of the same fawning sycophancy he was used to from young ladies of quality. He had not expected to be taunted, and it enticed him. He hesitated visibly, as if he could not make up his mind, then, shrugging his shoulders, stepped aside.

"May I present Count Egon Gyori?"

"A Hungarian?" Aimée was intrigued. "They say Hungarians have Gypsy music in their souls. Is that true, Count?"

Egon dipped his head lightly, offering a casual salute. The woman was charming, just as he had known she would be.

"I would gladly bare my soul for you, madame."

He stood in the doorway, safely away from her, but his voice, low and lightly accented, leaped across the space, touching her with a caress. Fleetingly Aimée remembered she had deliberately chosen to play with fire that evening. She had been afraid then only of her own coquettishness, as she dared to toy with a man who had the power to crush her if he willed it. Now she realized it was not the Archduke Rudolf, but the man who stood beside him, Count Egon Gyori, who would prove the most dangerous.

Franz stepped to her side, his hand resting with unconscious possessiveness on her waist.

"How is your wife, Count? I believe my sister, Sophie, has met her. I understand she is an admirable woman. And the children? There are three, are there not?"

Aimée glanced up sharply at the cold reproof in the voice of a man who had never been rude in her hearing before. Why, he's jealous, she thought with a little twinge of excitement. Her proper, stuffy cousin was actually jealous of the attention paid her by another man. It would almost be worth flirting with someone like Egon Gyori if she could pique Franz's interest.

Egon caught the interplay between them, but it did not daunt him. "Eva is doing splendidly, thank you. And the children. But there are four now. The last is the son we have prayed for."

"You must be proud of them. A family like that is a reflection of a man's honor."

The stiffness in Franz's tone was so transparent, Aimée could bear it no longer. She had wanted to tease her cousin, bringing his feelings for her out in the open, but she never intended to make him miserable in the bargain.

"I am a mother myself," she confided. There, that would put an end to the thing once and for all. The man could not possibly be interested in her now.

But Egon was more than a match for her. He saw what

she was doing, and he was not about to let her get away with it.

"You are a mother? But of course, I should have known," he teased. "Here, now, let me guess. You have two children. A boy eighteen—you are looking for a commission for him in the army, but you are so worried, he is so reckless, all that gambling, all those women. And a girl just sixteen, as beautiful as her mother, but she has fallen in love with a Hungarian, handsome but utterly mad, and you are in despair—"

"Enough, enough!" Aimée protested helplessly. She was trying desperately to discourage this man, and all she could do was laugh so hard she could barely speak. "I have one child, a little girl, four months old. Her name is Mariette, and she is very pretty—and if you don't watch out, I will bore you by talking about her for hours and hours."

"I very much doubt, madame, if anything you said would ever bore me."

The words were studied, even flippant, but Egon meant them. This woman was not like any other woman he had met. It occurred to him that a man might spend a lifetime with her and not be bored for a minute.

He bent over her hand in parting, his lips lingering a second longer than propriety allowed, as if defying her to pull away. He was not surprised when she did not.

"We will meet again, madame."

Aimée's hand trembled. The feel of his kiss remained, a searing brand on her skin, long after his lips had released her. She did not underestimate the power of his attraction. There was something about the man that was compelling, something that reminded her every moment she was in his presence that he was a man and she a woman.

She did not look up as the two men left, dreading the reproach she would see in Franz's eyes. She knew only too well she deserved it. She had thought she could play a game with the count, using him to attract her cousin. Now she realized it was Egon who had called all the moves.

The rustle of taffeta behind her reminded her belatedly that Mary Vetsera was still in the box. Guiltily she whirled around, ready to apologize for her neglect. One look was enough to tell her it was not necessary. Mary was still staring at the velvet curtains, watching as the last tremor of movement died away from their deep folds. She was so enrapt she was oblivious to anything else.

She has seen the prince, Aimée thought with a sadness she could not identify, and like every prince in every fairy tale she had known, he was perfect in her eyes. Aimée's heart went out to the girl. How hard it was to be a child and fall under the spell of a man who did not even see her sitting quietly in the corner.

Music filled the hall again, but this time Aimée found it had no power to captivate, but only served as a backdrop for troubled thoughts that would not leave her alone. The encounter with Egon, brief as it had been, forced her to admit the truth about herself. It was a truth she was not ready to face.

Egon Gyori was attractive, there was no denying that, but he was no more attractive than many men Aimée had met. It was not his strongly molded features that appealed to her, nor the dark mystery of his eyes, not even his supple, muscular body. She could have resisted these. What she could not resist was the basic, intangible quality of the man—the bearing that exuded masculine confidence, the teasing hints of sexuality when he looked at her, the warmth in her own body as, against all reason, she began to respond to him.

She turned her head to her cousin's profile, stern and handsome beside her. She had wanted this man as her husband once. Now she realized she wanted something different.

She was a woman. She could admit that at last and understand it. Her heart was a woman's heart, her body governed by a woman's needs. The thought did not shock her as it once had. Her whole life stretched in front of her, long and lonely. It would be a barren life if she could not share at least some part of it with a man.

Only, she didn't want it to be Egon. Dear God, she didn't want that. Not a cheap alliance with a man whose wife had just given him the son he prayed for. When it happened, as she knew it must, she could only hope it would be with someone who was good and kind and honorable.

She was tempted to lay her hand on Franz's arm, but she did not dare. She knew he was attracted to her, deeply attracted, in a way he had never been before, but he was decent enough to be tormented with shame at the thought. He had still not come to terms with his own capacity for sin, as she had. She wondered if she had the right to ask this of him.

Yet, it would be good—so good. It wouldn't be wildly exciting, as it had been with Raoul, but she did not crave excitement again. Raoul had been the first great passion of her life. No one would ever take his place. But Franz was her first love, and love was sweeter than passion.

*　　*　　*

281

Sophie was waiting for them when they got home. She called out from the small salon just off the entry, and they hurried to her. The room was cozy with the glow of half a dozen lamps, which brought out the rich colors of the Brussels tapestries on the walls. A fire in the ceramic stove took the chill from the night air.

Sophie rose stiffly from her chair, setting her needlework aside. She was a tall, large-boned woman, her dark hair liberally flecked with gray.

"I don't need to ask if you enjoyed the opera. I can see by your face that you did."

"Oh, it was wonderful, Cousin Sophie. Everything was beautiful . . . and so exciting. But I did miss my little Mariette. Did she behave while I was gone?"

Sophie laughed good-naturedly. "As well as you can expect a healthy baby to behave. She has a good set of lungs, that little one. I think you might be raising an opera star of your own."

"Then I'd better go to her. If she doesn't get some attention from her mama, I'm afraid she'll keep everyone awake tonight."

Aimée raced up the stairs, taking them two and three at a time, like a child eager for a treat. She paused in her room, discarding her finery and scattering petticoats on the bed for the maids to pick up. The smooth satin of her dressing gown felt cool as she slipped it over her body.

Mariette was still awake when she entered the nursery, but she was no longer fretful. Dismissing the nurse, Aimée hurried over to the baby, leaning down to tease her tiny chin with a finger.

"There, there, *ma petite*. Mama's here, and everything's all right."

She bent over the crib, marveling as she so often did at the sight of her own child. It seemed to Aimée she was a miracle, this little person who was so much a part of her, yet not a part at all. She had expected, before the child was born, an extension of her own flesh. That had been naive. Mariette, small as she was, was an individual in her own right, uniquely herself.

Aimée loved to look at her. Eyes big and blue and solemn, even when she laughed. Hair, once a shock of jet sticking straight out from her head, now just beginning to curl, accenting the baby sweetness of her face. Aimée's heart ached with pride. She had never seen such a perfect creature, so pretty and loving and filled with laughter.

Gently Aimée lifted the child, cradling the soft body against her own as she settled in a comfortable rocking chair. Mariette squirmed in her arms, tugging impatiently at the front of her gown.

"So that's it, is it?" Aimée laughed as she opened her robe, freeing her breast to the child. Mariette, needing no encouragement, closed her mouth noisily over the nipple. "You aren't glad to see your mother at all. You're only hungry, you greedy little thing."

Aimée leaned back in her chair, letting the tensions of the evening fade slowly away. She loved the feel of the child at her breast taking nourishment from her body as she had once taken life. Aimée had known much pain in the past year, and many regrets, but Mariette was not one of them.

Mariette. She smiled to herself at the sound of the name. Mariette. It was like a private secret all her own.

No one had questioned her about it. It was not a family name, but it was a pretty one, and it suited the child. Even Edward, when she cabled him, sent only a polite, indifferent reply, as if the matter was of little import to him. No one seemed to notice a striking resemblance to the name of a pretty princess who had died three thousand years before.

Aimée could not have said herself why she chose the name. She felt a strange closeness to the girl she knew only from portraits, an empathy with the sadness she had sensed in her features, but that was hardly reason enough. Perhaps, she told herself now, Meryt was important to her because the discovery of her tomb was an experience she had shared with Raoul. In those few brief weeks she had been close to him, not just physically, but spiritually, touching his dreams as well as his body. Perhaps Meryt was, for her, not a person of her own, but only a symbol of that closeness.

Raoul. The thought of him was still painful. There was no urgency in the pain, as there had been earlier when another man's touch had reminded her of her passion. But in a different, deeper way, it hurt even more. He had left a void in her heart when he slipped out of her life forever. It was a void she believed would never be filled again, no matter how many men she knew or how many lovers she took.

She was so deep in thought she did not see Sophie slip into the doorway.

"May I come in?"

Aimée looked up. "Of course. You never need to ask." She pulled her robe over her breast as Mariette, satisfied at last, sank contentedly into her arms. A trace of milk still lingered

283

on the baby's lips. Aimée teased her gently as she wiped it away with a soft cloth.

"Let me take her for a minute."

Sophie bent down, lifting the child easily into her arms. Aimée sighed as she nestled back in the chair, closing her eyes sleepily. She had not realized how tired she was.

When she opened her eyes again, she saw that Sophie had moved over to the window. The baby was cuddled in her arms as she stared into the night. Aimée was intrigued by the softness of their image, muted in the dark glass.

Sophie was not a handsome woman. Her features, coarse and blunt, were too stolidly Germanic to be pretty, but she had a warmth that lent her the illusion of timeless beauty. Watching her now, reflected in the glass, Aimée could almost believe she was looking at a medieval Madonna.

"You should have had children of your own, Sophie. You would have made a wonderful mother."

"Nonsense, nonsense." Sophie's voice was gruff, but Aimée could see she was pleased. "Besides, I haven't missed mothering all these years, you know. Franz was so young when our parents died, I almost felt he was my own child."

"And my mother, too." Aimée could not forget that Hélène had been very young when she lost her own parents. She and Franz had been raised together, almost as brother and sister.

"And your mother, too, bless her heart. What a beautiful child she was." Looking at Aimée, Sophie could almost see Hélène, young and vibrant again, still entranced with life and all its golden possibilities.

"And now you have me to take care of, and Mariette."

Sophie studied the girl's face carefully. "Does it hurt you? Having to stay here with us instead of going home?"

Aimée shook her head. "Not now. It did at first, but now . . . well, now I'm happy here."

"But you still don't understand, do you?"

"I suppose not. It all seemed so strange when I went back to Paris. I remember how happy I was, how glad to be going home. But then I got there, and the boys were away at school, even the baby, Edouard . . . Well, the house was so quiet. And Papa was so sick."

"Well, he's better now, thank the Lord," Sophie put in quickly. "Even the doctors are amazed at the way he's rallied. But it's been hard on your mother. It wouldn't be fair for her to have to worry about you, too."

"But that's just it." Aimée could not keep the frustration out of her voice. "I'm not a child anymore. I don't have to be looked after. I wanted to be with my mother, to help her. I thought when I was grown up, I would be closer to my parents. Instead, we seem to have drifted away from each other, living in worlds of our own. Sometimes I feel I don't even have a home anymore."

Sophie was silent for a minute. When she spoke, she tried to keep her voice matter-of-fact and comforting. "The older you get, the more you find that things don't work out the way you expect."

"Oh, I know, I know," Aimée agreed contritely. "I suppose I'm not being reasonable. With the baby, all that crying . . . well, it would be impossible for Papa to get the rest he needs. Mama even had to send the boys away. Still . . ."

Still, she wanted to go to her parents, and she wanted them to want her. It was a thing both she and Sophie knew, but neither of them would speak of again. Sophie's expression was stern, but her eyes were kind as she looked down at her young cousin.

"And I don't ever again want to hear you say you don't have a home."

Aimée sat alone beside Mariette's crib long after the child had gone to sleep. She stared at the dark windowpane, empty save for an echo of light from the room, and she remembered how the glass had looked when it was filled with Sophie's image, warm and soft and serene.

There was so much love in Sophie's heart, she thought, wondering at the enormity of it all. Enough love to fill her whole life. Aimée wanted desperately to be like her.

She knew she had been foolish that evening. She had felt the urgings of her body, and she had been tempted to give in to them. But it would be wrong to take a lover. Wrong for herself and wrong for her child. She could not keep herself from responding to men like Egon Gyori if she let them get close to her, but she could keep them from getting close.

She looked down at her sleeping child. In that face she saw only reflections of herself, no traces of the virile man who had fathered her. She was grateful. In time, with nothing to remind her, she would forget Raoul. Forget the pain and loneliness that swept through her heart whenever she thought of him. Perhaps, in time, she would even forget her need for a man.

Sophie had built a good life loving others. She must learn to do the same thing. There would be many who would need her. Mariette now, grandchildren one day, anyone else who was lonely or hurt or needed a friend—she would devote her life to them. It had been enough for Sophie. It had to be enough for her.

Vienna was a pageant of seasons. The earth, the sky, the trees, even the buildings, seemed to take on new colors as winter burst into spring and spring eased into summer. And every season, with its changing fashions and its changing moods, created a world completely different from the last.

Aimée loved the summer best. Tall pines, black against the limestone cliffs of the Vienna Woods. Boxes and cartons heaped on overloaded carriages as they moved to the hunting lodge, small and cozy and wonderfully warm, with crackling fires on cold nights. Glasses of sweet white wine sipped in a breezy meadow. The scent of the woods in every breath.

Life in the country was slow and mellow. Aimée did not see Egon Gyori again, for she heard he had been sent as an envoy to Berlin, but his family summered nearby and she passed his wife one day on the streets of Baden. The encounter confused her. She had expected a pale, passionless woman. Eva Gyori was tall and striking, not truly beautiful, for her features were too strong, but regal and vital, the kind of woman men squandered fortunes on and fought duels to possess. It had never occurred to Aimée that a man with a wife like that might seek out other women. She was glad now she had not seen him again.

The country air agreed with Mariette. Pink blossomed in her plump cheeks, contrasting becomingly with black curls, and childish giggles were a constant accompaniment to the birdsongs in the garden. It seemed to Aimée the child was growing so fast she could see the difference from day to day. At the beginning of the summer, she carried Mariette with her on long hikes through the woods. By the time the leaves began to turn yellow on the trees, the baby had grown so heavy she had to take the carriage.

Sophie was with them one day when the sound of singing drifted across the fields from a convent high in the hills. They called to the coachman to stop, then sat and listened in silence. The music was hauntingly beautiful.

"How peaceful it sounds."

For the first time in her life Aimée understood the mysterious allure that tempted young girls to dream of convent walls and plain dark robes. In a place like that, safe from the cares of the world, even a poor sinner might come to terms with the conflicts of her heart.

Sophie was lost in her own daydreams. "I was there once,"

she confided softly. "In that same convent. I was going to become a nun, but then my parents died, and Franz was so little. Someone had to take care of him."

Aimée was stunned by her revelation. In all the years she had taken Sophie and her love for granted, she never once stopped to wonder if the woman had wanted a life of her own. It occurred to her now that Sophie had given up more than she ever dreamed to raise other people's children. She could only hope she never looked back with regret.

And then it was fall. Golden lights shimmering on the boulevards on gray afternoons. Orange and brown leaves floating to the earth in a rhapsody of color. One last dying blaze of splendor before the world surrendered to the snows of winter.

The city came alive in the fall. Theaters, operas and concerts, grand balls and intimate soirees—Aimée had never seen anything like it. In Paris, she was only the daughter of a tradesman. Here, she was the wife of a wealthy English nobleman, and the city extended its arms to her. Even Franz, sensing her need for gaiety she had too long missed, set aside his books and his papers long enough to escort her to plays and parties.

It was an exciting life, tinged with all the glamour of her schoolgirl dreams. She waited in vain for a glimpse of the whiskered Franz Josef, older now, but no less powerful and enigmatic than the young emperor he had once been. Or his beautiful Elisabeth, so legendary a recluse even Sophie had not seen her, except in portraits. But the young archduke more than made up for their absence. He seemed to be everywhere· laughing at risqué lines in fashionable comedies or racing his carriage at breakneck speed through the rowdier sections of town, even dancing on rare occasions with his own wife at one of the brightly lit balls.

There were moments, caught up in a whirl of parties and merriment, when Aimée was happy, forgetting the past and the future in the delirium of the present. There were other moments, too, quiet moments, as she held her child in her arms, singing the same lullabies her mother had sung to her, when she was even content. Those moments were almost enough to make her forget how lonely she was. Almost, but not quite.

Sometimes, late at night, she would go into the library. Franz would be alone, reading. When he saw her standing in the doorway, he would look up, slipping a finger in his book to mark the place as he closed it politely.

"Do you think I am pretty, Franz?" she asked him once. She was standing in front of him in nothing but a thin, clinging dressing gown, but she knew he would be too polite—and too embarrassed—to reprimand her.

"Of course you are pretty. But I'm sure you know that already."

Aimée could see that he meant it. But still he kept his finger in the book. "Well, you never tell me so."

"Don't I? I will have to do better in the future."

Aimée watched him silently. This was the man she had once wanted as her lover, not for the passion her body demanded, but for the closeness her heart required. She still wanted him, she would go to him now if he so much as raised a hand and beckoned to her, but she knew he would not move.

"Good night, Franz. I didn't mean to disturb you. Go back to your book."

Winter. Snowcapped mountains in the distance, touched with blue in the twilight. A mantle of white on the earth. Open sleighs with thick blankets of fur, cutting deep scars in the snow. Icicles clinging to the eaves of houses, until the whole city was a fairy-tale dream.

Winter belonged to Mariette. In a world of wonder, everything was happening to her for the first time. Her first snowflake, landing on the tip of her nose, then melting away before she could reach up and capture it in eager fingers. Her first step, bold and confident, as if the world were hers, ending in a tumble on the elegant Persian carpet in the grand salon. Her first birthday, a single candle glowing on the cake that drew more cries of delight than a whole pile of presents from doting relatives. Her first Christmas, spent in the old hunting lodge, nestled in her mother's arms in front of a roaring fire.

Aimée saw Egon Gyori one more time, for he had come to spend the holidays with his family in the woods. He was in an open sleigh with his wife, and he did not try to greet her. Only his eyes spoke, telling her he had not forgotten her. The experience was an unsettling one, and Aimée was glad to return to the city.

Spring. March violets, touching the earth with welcome splashes of blue and white. Pasqueflowers, dark purple against new green grass. Mariette was in heaven. She had never seen flowers before, and she adored them. She would snap the coltsfoot from its stem, watching, fascinated, as it closed up in her hands, then gather primroses in the meadow, and lavender liverwort and shiny yellow globeflowers, clutching clumsy bouquets in chubby green-stained fingers.

The theaters were gay in the spring, the salons sparkling with wit. The Von Werthenheims, Josephine and her daughter, Franzi, presided over lively gatherings on Sunday afternoons, and everyone who was anyone in the cultural life of the city danced attendance on them. Aimée sat with the others on hard, uncomfortable divans, listening to Artur Rubinstein play the piano and sipping wine out of clear Lobmeyer glasses—and wondering why she was so bored with it all.

For the first time, she was beginning to see things she had not noticed before, and they disturbed her. The literary discussions that had once seemed so dazzling now were pretentious and self-serving, the caustic quips a little too cruel, the witty bon mots too self-conscious. Life in Vienna spun at a giddy pace, as if everyone were on a merry-go-round, but all too often the dizzy whirl seemed only an excuse. Don't stop moving, everyone seemed to say. Don't pause for a minute to look at your life. Don't let yourself see how empty it is.

Then suddenly it was summer again, and the world had moved full circle. Aimée sat in a meadow on the hillside watching the tall grasses blow in the breeze and wondering what was happening to her. The seasons had changed, Mariette was a year older and she was a year older, but nothing was different. She had changed on the outside, but inside all that had happened was that she had hardened a little.

"You are unhappy here?"

Aimée glanced up, startled. She had not heard Sophie approach.

"Unhappy? Of course not. How could I be unhappy? Everything is so beautiful."

But Sophie was not to be put off. More than ever the girl reminded her of Hélène, lovely, vivacious, popular, but cursed with a questioning mind and a thirst to find something beyond the pomp and tinsel that made up her world. She had encouraged Hélène in her rebellion. She was not going to make the same mistake with Aimée.

"Beautiful, but not too lively?" she hinted. "It's hard, isn't it? Being young and pretty—and left out of everything."

Once she had thought the girl might find her happiness in the arms of the younger brother she herself had raised. The idea had not shocked her. Franz had been lonely for years, lonelier than he would ever admit, especially to her. He had tried once to force himself into the conventional marriage everyone expected of him, but in the end, it had only made him miserable, and there was at least a measure of relief mingled with the pain when he had laid his wife at last in the cool green earth beside their stillborn son. Sophie would not have grudged him comfort now.

But after a while she had put the thought out of her mind. Franz, like the sister who had taught him, was too rigid, too strict in his values, to accept even his own happiness at such a cost. Weakness, passion, human needs—these were things he could understand in others, but they would have no place in his life.

No, Franz would have to find his solace in other places. And so would Aimée.

"Well, never mind, the season will start soon enough, and then you won't have time for everything you want to do. Even a young mother needs bright lights and gay music now and then, and elegant ball gowns to remind her she is still beautiful."

"Oh, Sophie," Aimée protested wearily, "do you think I care about all that? Balls and ball gowns and boring conversations about things that don't interest me in the least? Honestly, I don't think I care if I never go to a ball again."

Then, regretting her words, she leaned forward, laying her hand on Sophie's arm. She had a thousand reasons to be grateful to this woman who had been so kind to her, and not a single one to cause her such worry.

"Don't mind me. I'm just being contrary today. Of course you're right—it will be good to dance again."

But she was lying, and they both knew it. And they were both troubled.

2

Sitting on the side of a hill, with the scent of pine and wildflowers in the air, Aimée had been certain the world of soirees and balls held no allure for her. But now, standing on the edge of a wide, gilded hall, festive with the lights and gaiety she had nearly forgotten, she was not so sure. Strains of music drifted over the sound of laughter, tempting her to tap a brocaded slipper on the parquet floor. For all her new-found sophistication, she could not forget the childlike delight she always felt when she heard the first notes of a waltz and knew she would turn to find a handsome young man beside her, eager to carry her off in the seductive rhythm of the dance.

Impatiently she turned her head, waiting for Franz to join her. There was an excitement in the air, an excitement she had not felt for months, and she wanted to be a part of it all.

The dancing had already begun when she crossed the threshold. Couples pirouetted gracefully in the center of the room, their images reflected on the polished floor, and hundreds of candles sparkled in crystal chandeliers, until the golden walls seemed alive with fire. The women were a fantasy of color, their ball gowns lavender and pink, white and cherry and hyacinth blue, soft gray-rose and vivid turquoise, and every man looked elegant in his formal court attire.

The music paused, then started up again.

A young man appeared quickly at Aimée's side, and then another, his face a mirror of disappointment when he realized he had come too late. Aimée smiled as she saw them. A year ago she would have been timid and unsure as she stepped into the ballroom, terrified that no one would ask her to dance, and she would stand alone, a wallflower, watching all the other women whirl away with the men who adored them. Now she was more confident. Her hands rested lightly on the stiff fabric of a snowy jacket as she let her partner guide her skillfully into the center of the floor.

The music was intoxicating, the stylized movements of the dance slow and dreamy, and in the arms of a man she barely knew, Aimée felt free at last. Free and light and innocent of care. Closing her eyes, she could make believe she was a bird, a raven dark and majestic against the sunlit brilliance of the sky, soaring into the clouds until the world was far behind. It seemed to her, when she danced, that man had been meant to fly, and only a cruel whim of the ancient gods chained him heavily to the earth.

Franz stood on the sidelines, following her with his eyes. On another night, he would have enjoyed dancing, opening his arms to a series of anonymous partners as he absorbed into his own body the feel of the music. Tonight it was enough to be a spectator, sharing, however vicariously, the triumphs of his lovely young cousin. Watching her, he could almost pretend she belonged to him, and when he took her home that night, all the young men would look at him with envy, knowing those dazzling smiles were his and his alone, that soft white skin a temptation only for one man.

The fantasy was a compelling one. It took him back to other nights and other ballrooms. Hélène had looked like that once, as dazzling and vivacious as her daughter, a colorful little butterfly spinning through the gilt and silver and candlelight of an era now gone. And he had stood at the side then, too, as he was standing now, with the same quiet pride in his eyes.

"She is an uncommonly pretty little thing, isn't she?"

The sound of a voice in his ear was jarring. Turning, Franz saw his host standing next to him.

"Yes, she is," he agreed, watching Aimée slip away from one partner, only to find another waiting for her. "And all the young men seem to think so, too."

"How like Hélène she is. Do you remember? If it weren't for her coloring, I would think I was seeing a ghost."

Franz did not try to answer. Hélène had danced only a season in the ballrooms of Vienna, but no one who had seen her would ever forget. Just as no one would forget Aimée.

It was well into the evening before Franz made his way to his cousin's side. She had just finished a dance, a lively galop, and with a disarming smile put off the next young hopeful who hurried up to her. Now she stood alone, catching her breath beside one of the wide windows that opened onto the garden.

She jumped a little at the touch of a hand on her arm, then smiled as she looked up and saw him.

"Can a cousin claim a dance, or have you promised them all to your young admirers?"

"It wouldn't matter if I had. Any dance you want is yours . . . and you know it."

The music had begun again, a waltz this time, melodic and sensuous as it beckoned her to his arms. Franz had told her once that the waltz created a scandal when it was first introduced. It was easy to see why. Nothing made her quite so aware of her own femininity, or the masculinity of the man who held her in his embrace.

Franz could feel it, too. She was sure of it. He held her rigidly, keeping her at arm's length.

"How stiffly you dance, Franz," she teased. "That's not like you at all. Are you afraid of me?"

She had not spoken so frankly since the day she first came to Vienna. She wondered if he remembered, as she was remembering now, an afternoon long ago when she had begged him to run away with her.

"Only a fool would not be afraid of a woman as beautiful as you. Especially when she is wed to another man."

"Even if he is a man who does not want her and has not seen her for over a year?"

Her audaciousness set up a current of tension between them. Franz flushed, but he did not reply. Aware of the supple movements of her body, only inches from his own, he could find the strength neither to draw her closer nor to push her away.

It was a relief when the music stopped. Franz, with a conservative little bow, turned aside. Aimée felt tired as she watched him walk away from her.

He wanted her, she was sure. And she wanted him, this dear old friend who would have made her such a kind husband. And there was not a thing either of them could do about it.

A sudden flurry of chatter filled the ballroom, growing to a crescendo impossible to ignore. Half-interested, half-irritated, Aimée looked up, turning with the crowd to stare at the doorway. To her surprise, she was rewarded by the sight of the young archduke.

In spite of herself, Aimée could not help being caught up in the excitement. She had seen the man a dozen times before, she had even spoken to him once, but still she could not control the schoolgirl fluttering of her heart when she looked up and saw him there. What was it about royalty? she wondered. What was it that made it impossible to stand in the same room with a handsome young prince and not be awed by his presence?

And Rudolf was handsome, there was no denying that. He stood a little apart, as if he sensed that that aloofness would give his straight slender form an air of power. His dazzling white coat set off his fair hair, and tapered red trousers made his legs long and lean. A red-and-white sash ran across his breast.

Aimée scanned the rest of the royal party to see if his wife was there. The Princess Stephanie, the young Belgian Rudolf had been pressured into marrying, was a plain, unappealing woman, her face already marred by sharp lines of discontent. It was common knowledge that the prince was desperately unhappy with her, and he rarely took her anyplace if he could avoid it. Tonight was no exception.

"So the princeling is preening himself, thriving on the admiration he pretends is so boring."

The words, slow and sarcastic, were pitched just high enough so no one could miss them. Shocked, Aimée turned her head, catching sight of an elderly man, his wizened face touched with humor. She could only suppose he was so old his wits had grown dull. Otherwise he would never have spoken like that.

His companion seemed neither surprised nor appalled. Young and solemn, he adjusted the monocle in his eye. "I take it you don't think he's going to make much of an emperor."

"Bah! How could he? He's had no training. His father has kept all the affairs of state from him. Not that it matters. I don't suppose there'll be much of an empire left by the time he gets a chance at it."

"You don't have much faith in your country."

"Should I have? Be sensible. Look around you. Don't you suppose the last days of the Roman Empire were like this? By God, have you ever seen so many rich, pampered aristocrats parading around like gaudy peacocks, boring themselves and everyone else with their endless galas? And all the while, the people are slaving on farms and in factories just to keep them in silk and champagne."

Aimée was horrified as the two men drifted away, their voices at last becoming inaudible. How could anyone talk about this country like that? Of course, she was bored herself with some of the parties and the prattle—she had to admit that—but that was only because she did not have any purpose in her own life. The Austrian monarchy was a proud, ancient line. The emperor was strong, his son young and vital. With leaders like that, Austria would go on forever.

Aimée did not have time to dwell on her indignation. Almost before she knew it, a partner had come to claim her, whirling her out into the center of the floor, where everyone could see and envy him. Caught up in the mood of the music, she forgot everything else, throwing herself into the intricate steps with a passionate abandon. All the rest of the world seemed to fade away. A gentle cousin, standing alone, watching with longing in his eyes; a sarcastic old man, so warped with age and malice he had to vent his spleen on his betters; even a young archduke already beginning to choose his partners among the wives and daughters of the men who were important at court—none of these mattered to her. She was young, and for a few hours happy, and she did not want to think of anything else.

It was a long time before she noticed the prince again. When she did, she was surprised to see that he had pulled away from his friends, stepping out onto the edge of the dance floor. Waltzing couples spun in wide arcs, working their way around him, but he was oblivious of them. His eyes, solemn against the shimmering gold of the hall, were filled with an intensity Aimée had never seen before.

Intrigued, she turned to follow his gaze. There, at the far end of the room, perfectly posed, as if she had been hired to play Cinderella in some fairy-tale tableau, stood a breathtakingly lovely young woman. Shy and hesitant, she hovered just inside the doorway. Veils of white chiffon floated around her body, accenting the beguiling purity of youth.

It was the little Vetsera girl.

Only, Mary was not a little girl any longer. Looking at her, Aimée could understand what Rudolf was seeing. Wistful blue eyes, bold enough to beg for attention, timid enough to coax protectiveness from the most virile man. Full lips, parted with promises they dared not speak. A ripe young body, already beginning to sway with unconscious sensuality to the music. Cinderella, indeed. Here was a woman created to capture the heart of a prince.

Aimée laughed as she watched them. Once, not so long ago, Rudolf had stood in the same room with Mary Vetsera, and he had not seen her. He saw her now.

"You are amused, madame? I wonder if you are remembering another night."

Aimée recognized the sound of a familiar accent. Apprehensively she turned.

"What . . . what are you doing here? I thought you were in Berlin."

Count Egon Gyori smiled as he bent over her hand. It had made the woman uncomfortable to see him. He liked that. It meant she was not indifferent to him. "So I was. But I am back now. Dare I hope you are glad to see me?"

"I am always glad to see old acquaintances, Count." Aimée was surprised that she was able to keep her voice so cool. "And your wife, is she here? I hope you are going to introduce me to her."

"Nothing would please me more, but I am afraid my wife and children are in Hungary visiting her family. So you see, I am all alone in Vienna . . . and very lonely."

The implication was clear. Aimée searched for a way to put him in his place. She sensed Egon Gyori was not a man who would discourage easily.

"Your wife is a very attractive woman, Count."

He saw her game, and he would not play it. Leaning forward, he peered into her eyes. Aimée had the feeling he was laughing at her.

"Perhaps we had better get one thing clear right now. My wife *is* attractive, and I am deeply attracted to her. She is a proud, passionate woman, and she fills many of my needs. But not all of them."

That was too much for Aimée. She was still naive enough to be disconcerted by a man who could flirt with a woman one minute, then tell her how much he cared for his wife the next.

"You are very frank, sir."

"Sometimes." Egon could control his laughter no longer. It spilled out, clear and uncalculated. "I would have been more coy with you if I had thought it would do me any good. I have been known to trifle with lovely ladies, telling them what they wanted to hear, pleading for their sympathy because my wife doesn't understand me."

"But she does understand you?"

"Oh, she understands me, all right—too well for her own good. She doesn't always like what she sees, but she has come to accept me for what I am. I hope, in time, you will too."

Aimée did not reply. She was confused, and she did not try to hide it from him. The man was far more worldly than she. She could not even begin to deal with him, or with her own reaction to him.

Egon saw her discomfort, and he relented. His voice was soft when he spoke again.

"But I am pushing you too fast, am I not? I don't mean to. It's just that you are so beautiful, I assumed you were more experienced. I'll be gentler with you from now on, I promise. I am a patient man."

Teasingly he held out his arms. The gesture was light and friendly, with no undercurrents of passion.

"Will you at least dance with me? There's no harm in that, you must admit. You'll be in no danger, not in a room full of people."

Aimée was tempted. Egon seemed like a different man now, so kind and understanding. It would be good to feel his arms around her, however casually. But she knew she did not dare. He had told her there would be no danger, but they both knew he was lying. Just the touch of his hands would be danger enough.

"I . . . I think not. It is so hot in here. I don't want to dance again."

The minute the words were out of her mouth, Aimée knew she had made a mistake. Egon was quick to pick up on it.

"You do look flushed. Here I thought you were glad to see

me, and it was only the heat." He seemed his old self again, laughing, daring, challenging. "What you need is a stroll in the garden."

"Oh, no, I . . . I . . ." Aimée was trapped, and she knew it. "I can't. Really, I can't. I . . . I've just remembered, I promised this dance to someone. He'll be coming to find me."

"Well, he'll never look for you in the garden. You'll be safe there."

His hand was strong and possessive as he laid it on her arm, guiding her out of the room. Aimée had the terrifying feeling that he would not let go of her if she tried to pull away.

She was being idiotic, and she knew it. The man was not a fiend. She could stop him easily enough, if she really wanted to. I don't know what you are trying to do, sir—that was all she had to say. It won't work with me, I am not that kind of woman. But she could not bring herself to speak the words. And he knew she could not.

The garden was cool in the moonlight. A long rectangular pool stretched out into the distance, dark and still, like a sheet of glass. Lights poured out of a long row of windows, casting a hazy arc of gold on the ground.

Egon drew her closer. "Now you must give me that dance. You cannot say it is too warm here."

He touched her cautiously, giving her no excuse to pull away. Aimée hesitated, then relaxed into his arms.

As if on cue, the music began again, another waltz, light and lilting. Egon was a superb dancer, moving his body in perfect harmony with hers. She felt strangely at home in his arms, as if she had been there a hundred times before, and would return a thousand times again. Nothing seemed more natural than to feel him draw her nearer, easing her toward him until barely an inch of space separated them. Daringly he lowered his lips to her hair, tantalizing her with all the promises she longed to accept.

He pulled her against him, clasping her tightly as he spun in and out of the luminous circle of light. The music seemed to take on a new sweetness, or perhaps, Aimée thought, as her cheek brushed his chest, it was simply the aching sweetness of feeling a man's lean, muscular body against her own again.

She did not try to protest as the music ended and he took her hand, drawing her slowly into the shadows. All the months of agonizing, all the long months of telling herself what she would or would not do, and in the end, there was no choice at all. Her body had made the decision for her.

He did not try to hurry her, but moved slowly beside her down the long path that flanked the narrow pond. It was enough to be with her now. Enough to savor the moment . . . and the anticipation.

His hand on her waist eased her into a narrow lane branching off the main path. Tall hedges screened them from the house, intensifying the darkness that surrounded them. Dry autumn leaves crackled beneath their feet. The music sounded faint and faraway.

At last he stopped. His hands, gentle no longer, gripped her shoulders, urging her toward him. The moonlight touched her eyes, already bright with desire.

Egon did not speak. No words were needed between them. His lips separated, lowering to hers.

The kiss was strong and tender, generous and greedy, drawing on the hunger that filled both their bodies. It had been so long since Aimée had known the touch of a man. So terribly long.

Egon sensed her abandon. Raising his hands, he pressed them beneath her breasts, cupping the ripe flesh upward to meet his mouth.

He longed to rip the fashionable gown from her body, but he held himself back. He had frightened her once that evening, and he had almost lost her. If he pushed her too savagely now, she might run away from him. And in truth, he did not want it that way himself. He wanted to take time with her, lingering on their lovemaking, showing her gentleness as well as lust. He wanted their union to be beautiful, not just for himself, but for her.

He ran strong hands down her body. His fingers were impatient as they rested on the outside of her thighs, inching her skirt upward.

She felt what he was doing and pulled away from him in an awkward, tentative movement that begged him to coax her back. His hands paused. His lips touched hers, lightly at first, then passionately, pleading his case with an eloquence words could never find. At last her body succumbed, all resistance gone, and he knew she was his. She would not draw back again.

Everything in his body cried out for her. He wanted her desperately, but he knew he could not have her here. There was still time for her to draw away. Time for her to realize that a hasty union in the dirt would be ugly and unsatisfying.

She would hate herself when it was over, and she would hate him. That was something he could not allow. Already he had sensed he would never be satisfied with one coupling with this magnificent woman.

He had to think only of her tonight. He had to guide her toward raptures beyond her dreams, then show her the sweet satisfaction that asked nothing in return. He had to make the experience deep and fulfilling for her. If he did, she would never be able to turn from him again. He would have her whenever and wherever he wanted.

A sudden brittle trill of laughter broke over the garden, echoing off the paths and ponds until it seemed to surround them. Hastily Egon moved back, smoothing the folds of Aimée's skirt. An instant later a young couple appeared, lingering briefly in the narrow space that marked the end of the hedge. Egon took a swift step forward, shielding Aimée with his broad shoulders and powerful back, but the gesture was a needless one. The intruders did not even glance their way as they strolled past, searching for a secluded spot for their own rendezvous.

Egon waited until they were gone. Then, taking Aimée's chin in his fingers, he tilted her head upward. One look at the confusion in her eyes was enough to tell him he had lost her.

Aimée took a slow step backward, shaking his hand clumsily from her face. Her body was trembling badly, and she did not try to control it. Another minute, just another minute, and she would have done anything he wanted. A man she barely knew had walked up to her in a crowded ballroom and led her out into the garden and taken her in his arms and she had not even tried to resist.

She searched hurriedly for a way to summon her indignation. She wanted to tell him how furious she was, how vulgar his behavior had been, but the words stuck in her throat. In the end, all she could do was pick up her skirt and race down the path, fleeing toward the light, as if it could somehow ease the darkness in her heart.

She hesitated at the entrance to the ballroom, struggling to catch her breath. She could only pray there was nothing to give her away. No bruises on bare shoulders where Egon's hands had been too rough, no creases in her skirt from his impatient fingers, no telltale grass stains on her brocade hem. She did not dare look down and check, for fear she would call attention to herself.

Slowly she perceived that something was wrong. The ballroom, so gay and filled with merriment when she had left it, had become strangely subdued. Couples still danced in the middle of the floor, others hovered on the edges, chatting discreetly with each other, but all the frivolity and laughter had drained from the evening. For a minute Aimée felt as if they had all discoverd her secret and were whispering about her. She stood in the doorway, taking slow, deep breaths as she waited for the sensation to pass.

Finally she entered the room, moving toward the edge of the dance floor where she could mingle with the others. A plump woman in a pink faille dress embroidered with red cherries glanced over at her, then turned her attention back to the dancers. Eager to make herself inconspicuous, Aimée followed her example. The instant she did, she saw what had happened.

The young archduke was dancing in the center of the room, weaving gracefully in and out of the other dancers as if he did not even see them. Candlelight glowed on fair hair as a lithe, slender body moved with the music, reminding everyone who watched that the hope of Austria's future was the prince of a fairy-tale dream And in his arms was the lovely Cinderella who had stepped into his life that night.

Aimée held her breath as she watched them. She thought she had never seen anything so beautiful or so vulnerable as this dazzling couple whirling across the floor, so absorbed in themselves and their own feelings they did not see the disapproving stares from the sidelines. Rudolf, bewitched by an innocence he had never known before, stared down at the girl with wonder. Mary, willingly caught in his spell, answered his rapture with all the adoration a young heart could offer.

Poor little Mary Vetsera, Aimée thought, aching with pity. Did she remember that even Cinderella had only a few hours at the ball before midnight came all too soon?

For a young prince with a wife he loathed, flirtations were a way of life. Innocence appealed to him now, with the charm of anything new and untried. but how long would that enchantment last? And when it ended, as she knew it must, what would happen to the mistress he had discarded? No one knew better than Aimée how agonizing it was to love and not be loved in return.

It took her a few minutes to find Franz in the crowded room. He was surprised, for she had never asked to leave early before.

"I . . . I don't feel very well. I must have had too much champagne."

If Franz had noticed her absence, he was too much of a

gentleman to question her about it. He took one look at her flushed face, then hurried off to find her wrap.

The royal party left before Franz returned, gathering their things in a flurry and exiting en masse. Aimée wandered into the hallway after they had gone, enjoying the sound of the music as it drifted out of the ballroom. The air was cool and pleasant.

It was a second before she realized she was not alone. An ethereal figure, garbed all in white, stood in front of the open doorway, staring out into the night. Layers of chiffon caught in the currents of air as Mary Vetsera turned back to the room.

"Oh, Aimée!" Hands extended, she hurried across the hall. "I didn't see you here tonight."

Aimée was not surprised. The girl had had eyes only for the prince.

"But I saw you . . . and you looked very happy."

"Oh, I am—so happy. Isn't this the most beautiful ball, Aimée? Have you ever been any place so beautiful in your life?"

Aimée gazed at the girl in silence. A moment ago, she had felt pity for Mary Vetsera. She felt no pity now, only envy.

She and Mary had done the same thing that night, and yet it had not been the same at all. Mary had spun through the ballroom in the arms of a man who could never be hers, and it had been beautiful. Aimée had danced with such a man in the garden, and it had been a shattering experience. One union was no less unholy than the other, one passion no less sinful. But Mary had looked at Rudolf with love in her eyes, and Aimée felt no love for Egon Gyori. And it was love that made the difference.

3

Aimée was not at home to Egon Gyori when he called the next afternoon. She sat alone in her sitting room on the second floor, watching as he walked slowly toward his waiting carriage. A light rain fell, darkening the dead leaves on the ground.

He came again the next day, as she had known he would, and the day after that. Always the message was the same— "Lady Ellingham is not at home, sir"—but if the rebuff disconcerted him, he did not let it show. Returning to his carriage, he cast a slow, speculative glance back at the house, as if to tell her he knew she was hiding in the shadows, watching him. Aimée could have sworn she saw laughter in his eyes.

On the fourth afternoon, she could stand it no longer. He would come again, she was sure of that, and she was not going to let him catch her like some kind of petty criminal, peeking out from behind lace curtains because she was afraid to show her face. This time, when he heard the words "She is not at home," they would be the truth.

"Come, come, *petite*," she cried, clapping her hands to get Mariette's attention. Bending down, she swung the child up in her arms. "We're going for a ride in the carriage. Won't that be lovely?"

"No!" Mariette squirmed in her arms, forcing Aimée to set her down again. "No rides. Play with Liesel."

Stubbornly the girl clutched at her doll, rescuing it from a corner of the floor. Her lower lip pressed out in the tenative beginnings of a pout.

"We'll bring Liesel with us, darling. She'll enjoy a nice ride in the fresh air. Don't you think so?"

Mariette shook her head vigorously. Her little chin rose in defiance. Aimée laughed as she looked at her. That was the one trait of the father she could see in the daughter, that determined set to her jaw when she had made up her mind about something.

"Really, I think she would. Especially if we asked her nicely."

Mariette continued to shake her head, bouncing dark curls up and down. "No! Liesel wants tea."

"Ah!" Aimée understood at last. "So Liesel wants tea, does she? And maybe a nice sweet, too?"

Mariette, with her wide eyes and black ringlets, was a favorite of the servants. No doubt Cook had promised a special cake for tea. And knowing Mariette, she would wheedle an extra piece for Liesel.

"You are a spoiled little girl," Aimée teased, giving her a quick hug. "But you are too adorable for me to get angry."

And the child *was* spoiled, Aimée thought as she sat alone in the carriage, watching the buildings go by, drab in the gray light of a cloudy afternoon. But she was so winsome, it was impossible to resist her. There would be a special treat from Cook that afternoon, and when Mama returned from her ride, much against her judgment, she would almost certainly bring a sweetmeat from one of the *pâtisseries* in town. Mariette would grow fat as a little dumpling, and still no one would be able to say no to her.

Aimée had always loved the streets of Vienna. Trees lined the curving Ringstrasse, just as they did the boulevards of Paris, and the houses were a whimsical mingling of sturdy elegance and gaudy make-believe. Every second building had a cocky air about it, a kind of *nouveau riche* bravado that defied the pretense of molded concrete ornaments, painted to look like stone and stucco and bronze. It was almost as if the whole city were one enormous stage setting, a kind of operetta *mise en scène* designed to amuse all the people in all the carriages passing by.

Aimée had the coachman stop along the Danube canal. Leaving the carriage, she strolled beside the railing, pausing to stare into the hazy blue-gray of the water. The autumn breeze was exhilarating as it bit into her cheeks. Pulling her collar high around her neck, she slipped her hands deep into warm, fleecy pockets. Soon it would be time to pull out muffs and fluffy little fur hats and sealskin wraps to tuck over her lap in open sleighs.

The sun peeked unexpectedly from behind the clouds, coloring the world with a flood of gold. Turning from the water, Aimée caught sight of a solitary figure scurrying along the promenade, simple yet elegant in a long pearl-gray coat. Dark, intense features were half-hidden beneath a raised hood. The woman had already drawn quite near before Aimée realized it was Mary Vetsera.

She took a step forward, intending to greet her, then paused as she saw Mary stop beside a closed carriage parked at the edge of the promenade. The door swung slowly open, revealing nothing but darkness as she stepped inside.

Aimée watched as the carriage rolled slowly down the banks of the canal. It was plain and black, with nothing but a simple insignia on the side to set it apart from the others, but she did not fail to place it. It was the royal carriage.

Clouds drifted over the sun again, robbing the afternoon of its warmth, as the vehicle disappeared into the distance. Aimée could only stand helplessly at the side of the road staring after it. Barely a few days before, she had dared to envy a pretty girl her single night of dreams. Now she hated herself for the feeling.

She did not want to envy Mary Vetsera. She wanted only to rejoice in her happiness . . . or grieve for her sorrow. She did not want to equate either the pains or the delights of another's heart with her own empty life.

A voice stopped her as she walked back to her carriage.

"So it surprises you, does it? Tell me, are your eyes burning with moral indignation . . . or is it jealousy?"

Glancing up, Aimée recognized the woman instantly. The meeting gave her no pleasure. She had never liked the Countess Marie Larisch, so close to the Vetseras and all their ambitions. She liked her even less now. She had heard that the woman was Mary's chaperon, and she could not help thinking how poorly she filled her charge.

"Neither one, I assure you. I like Mary very much. I just think she deserves better than she is getting."

"Better than an archduke?" Larisch's voice crackled with amusement. "Come, now, you're not such a fool as that."

"Well, if I am, I hope I have better sense than to stand here and discuss it with the likes of you."

The countess's malice broke into open laughter. "So you think you are better than I, simply because you married an old English title. Well, let me tell you, you are a parvenu, just like the rest of us, and all your husband's money will never make you anything else. No, you don't like me, my vain little peacock, but you will stay and talk to me, I think, because you are curious."

"Curious? Whatever for? I saw the carriage as well as you, and I know perfectly well who's in it. What is there to be curious about?"

"Wouldn't you like to know why I'm enjoying myself so much? Doesn't it occur to you that I might know something you haven't even guessed?"

"Don't be ridiculous." Aimée couldn't abide the woman's sly prattle, and she didn't care if she showed it. "I know everything I need to know. All you have to see is a crown, you and that social-climbing Vetsera clan, and you drool to get near it, whatever the price. Do you really think you'll get more for Mary on the marriage market if she's had an affair with the archduke and perhaps borne him a bastard Hapsburg? Or don't you even care? Is it enough just to brag that she's slept with a prince? Doesn't it matter that you'll break her heart in the bargain?"

"Mary would be worth more on the marriage market," Larisch admitted easily. "But that's not what we're after. Our aims are much higher."

"Higher aims? Don't make me laugh. For an ambitious family with a beautiful daughter, there is no higher aim than marrying upward."

"Marrying upward, yes . . . but not bearing bastard

princes. Mary will be the Empress of Austria, and one day her son will sit on the throne."

Aimée gasped at the woman's audacity. "Now I know you're crazy. The Princess Stephanie will be empress. Everyone knows that."

"The Princess Stephanie is a ninny and a bore. Rudolf could never tolerate a bore."

"Bore or not, she is his wife."

"For how long?" Larisch's expression was smug and calculating. "The prince has already petitioned his father to ask for an annulment."

"An annulment?" Aimée was stunned. She had heard of such things, of course, but it was hard to believe they really happened. Surely the proud old emperor would never permit it, even if the pope consented.

Still, she could not forget the look on the face of the young prince as he gazed into the eyes of his Cinderella. If Rudolf had already toyed with the idea of an annulment, even before he had fallen under Mary's spell, what must he be thinking now?"

Larisch was chuckling softly. "So, you are not so sure anymore, are you?"

Aimée looked at the woman in disgust. For a minute she had almost believed her. Now she saw reality.

"You fool! Do you think I give a schilling for you and all your idiotic dreams? I couldn't care less what you did, if you didn't drag Mary down with you."

But they would, Aimée thought sadly. She could see that now. They would play out their stupid, unrealistic games of power, the Vetseras and all their friends, using an innocent girl as their pawn, and they would blame her in the end when things did not work out.

She was still thinking of Mary as she sat alone in her room. Sophie had retired, and Mariette was long since asleep, a single candle burning at her bedside for fear she would wake up and be frightened by the dark. Only the sound of the rain gently tapping against the pane broke the silence of the house.

Mary as empress. It was a pretty idea. She would be everything the people had looked for in their beautiful Elisabeth—and failed to find. Aimée could see her now, stunning in a long white ball gown embroidered with pearls and silver thread, a diamond tiara in her dark hair as she danced the night away. Or smiling in an open carriage, waving spontaneously to adoring crowds as they pelted her with roses and cried out their ecstatic approval.

A pretty idea, but one that would never be. Rudolf was a prince, and he would do as princes do. He would stay with his unloved wife, father a number of anemic children, and continue to give expensive presents to beautiful actresses. And one day he would ascend the throne, but Mary would not be his empress.

And what did it really mean? Aimée wondered. All the love and the dreams . . . and the pain. What would they be in the end, she and Mary Vetsera, but a pair of bitter old women looking back with regret on the ill-fated love that scarred their lives?

But even in her sadness, Aimée knew the truth she had discovered was only a half-truth. Mary would not give up Rudolf now, even if she understood the pain that lay ahead, just as she herself would not change a minute of the time she had shared with Raoul. Love was a gift, a precious echo of eternity, offered only rarely, and it could not be turned away.

She had been hurt by love, but pain was no excuse for pity. She had dared to taste life, savoring it to the fullest, and she would not weep for herself now. For a few fleeting hours, in the embrace of a man now lost, she had known what it was to be a woman. She would be a woman always.

The hallway was dark as she stepped out of her room, moving toward the long curved stairway that led to the first floor. A soft light shone through the library door. She stood on the threshold.

Franz had placed a lamp on the table by his elbow. His brow puckered as he studied the volume in his hand.

How easy it was for a man like Franz, Aimée thought. All he had to do was open a book, and he was in another world. The cares he wrestled there were not his cares, the sufferings belonged to someone else. And all his dreams were only make-believe.

She took a step forward. He did not look up until her shadow crossed the pages of the book.

"So intent, Franz?" she teased. "And where are you now? Back at Austerlitz with the historians . . . or fighting a battle of heaven and hell with the English poets?"

"Actually, I was in Rome," he replied good-naturedly, flipping back the cover of the book. "Watching the empire dissolve."

"*The Decline and Fall of the Roman Empire*—how ghoulish."

"Ghoulish? What a strange way you have of putting things, Aimée."

"Do I? Well, I can't help it. It does sound ghoulish to me, reading about things falling apart and dying. Do you know, the other night I heard two men say Austria was just like the Roman Empire. Can you imagine? Austria? As if this were some decadent society about to disintegrate."

Franz looked at her patiently. "They are right, you know."

"Right? Franz, whatever are you talking about?"

"We are a dying civilization, my dear, though most of us are too blind to see it, or perhaps only too ineffectual to do anything about it. I think perhaps we have been inbred too long. God save us from vacuous aristocrats dancing the night away as if they thought the music would go on forever, or hopeless dreamers staring into the pages of a book because they don't have the courage to look up and see what's coming."

"And what is coming, Franz?" Aimée watched him closely to see if there was a smile behind his solemn expression. "A revolution, like in France?"

"I don't know, Aimée. I'm one of the dreamers, remember?" A lock of auburn hair fell onto his forehead. He reached up with his hand and pushed it back. "That's the difference between you and me. You want to live life. I want to watch it from the sidelines—and at a comfortable distance."

Aimée did not like the turn the conversation was taking. It was too much like the speech he had given her the day he told her he could not marry her. She did not want to hear such things tonight. Dropping to her knees beside his chair, she laid a hand on top of his.

"Don't you ever want to live, too—just once?"

He tried to pull away, but she would not let him.

"Why do you always do that, Franz? Put your finger in the book, as if you wish I'd go away and let you get back to your reading?"

"Do I?" His tone was light, but he did not move.

With a burst of impatience Aimée grabbed the book out of his hands. It had gone on too long, she told herself, the attraction between her and her cousin. They had both tried to hide from it, each in his own way, Franz with his books, she with the dangerous flirtation that had frightened her so badly. It was time to admit the truth to each other—and to themselves.

"Don't you understand I am a woman, Franz?" She clung

to his hand, afraid he would pull back again. "I have a woman's heart. A woman's feelings."

Her touch was insistent. Franz had an almost agonizing sense of her closeness.

"Of course you are a woman, my dear," he replied, trying to cover his discomfort with humor. "I may not look up from my books all that often, but I could hardly have failed to notice that."

"Please . . ." she begged. "Don't make this any harder for me. You know what I am saying to you—you must."

"Aimée, my sweet, innocent child, I think you are mistaking feelings of tenderness for . . . something else."

"Franz, you must understand. I am not a child, and I am not innocent. I am a woman."

She raised his fingers and pressed them to her cheek. Then slowly she eased his hand downward, over her neck, her shoulders, pausing at last on her breast. She could feel him tense, but he did not draw away.

He wanted her now as much as she wanted him. He longed to give in to her, clasping her passionately in his arms, surrendering to the yearning in his body. It was all he could do to hold himself back.

"Did your husband . . . ?" He could barely bring himself to utter the words. He would not have thought the man, clumsy and dispassionate as he seemed, could have touched a woman so deeply. "Did he make you so happy, then?"

Horrified, Aimée realized what she had done. It was too late to retreat, but she would not lie to him. She respected Franz too much for that.

"No," she admitted softly, her cheeks burning with shame. "No, *he* did not make me happy at all."

For a moment Franz could only stare at her in silence, trying to piece together what she was saying.

Then at last he realized.

Of course! What a fool he was. He should have known all along. He had seen the way she looked at Mariette, her face glowing with love and maternal pride. She had found fulfillment in her child, the only true fulfillment a woman could ever know.

Obviously she wanted another baby, and Ellingham, that swine, had denied it to her. She would do anything, stoop to anything, no matter how degrading, to accomplish that end.

"Aimée, *liebchen*, you cannot do this to yourself. You know you excite me—you would excite any man with blood in his viens—but I would never forgive myself if I let this happen. You have Mariette, my dear, and that must be enough for you. You must build your life around her."

"No!" Aimée cried rebelliously. She could not, she *would* not let herself be shunted off in a corner like an old woman, her passions already spent. She loved her daughter with all her heart, but she needed more than that. She would be discreet in her relationship with Franz, she would never bring shame on her child, but she would know love again.

Hands shaking, Franz gripped her by the waist, lifting her away from him. Dammit, he had blundered all the way. How could he have let the thing get so badly out of hand? She wanted a child, and he wanted to satisfy the urges of his body. It was not a fair bargain.

He saw the hurt in her eyes, and it disturbed him. He longed to comfort her.

"You know I would sell my soul to be with you, but I refuse to sell yours, too. I love you too much to do this to you."

It was a long time before Aimée could bring herself to leave the silent room. The fire was already dying in the hearth when she made her way at last to her empty bed. Even when she stretched out between the smooth sheets, she could not force herself to relax. She wondered if Franz was awake too, thrashing in his own bed, kicking the covers away from his body as he dreamed of the joys he himself had cast away. Or had he simply gone back to his book, burying himself once again in a world she could never enter?

Finally she could bear it no longer. Slipping on a plain cashmere wrapper, she tiptoed down to the library again. The lights were out, and she could barely find her way, but the book was gone.

It was almost a relief the next day when the telegram arrived. Edward had not sent it directly to her, addressing it instead to his solicitors. The proper little man in the dark suit was apologetic when he disturbed her dinner.

"I would not have come at such an hour, I assure you, were not time so short. Lord Edward asked me to tell you that he wants you to join him in Luxor, you and the child both, now that she is old enough to travel."

Aimée did not try to conceal her surprise. Edward, who had never even asked about the child, wanted to see her now. But why?

"I don't understand it, sir—you said time was short."

"Lord Edward wants you to come right away. He was most emphatic. I booked passage for you day after tomorrow on the Orient Express. Of course, if that is not convenient . . ."

"No, no . . ." Aimée brushed aside his protests with a wave of her hand. She did not know why Edward wanted to see her after all this time, but it did not truly matter. The excitement that had once been Vienna was exciting no longer. The opening nights had lost their power to dazzle, the salons seemed drained of their wit, and gilded ballrooms were deceptive snares for a lonely young woman with nowhere to turn Besides, she did not think she could live in that house another day and meet her handsome cousin's eyes—and see the reflection of her own humiliation in their depths.

"No, the day after tomorrow will be perfectly convenient. I will be ready by then."

4

The reality of Egypt was not the land Aimée had stored up in her memory. She stood in the shade in front of Edward's tent, staring out at the desert and wondering how the contours of a landscape could remain so perfectly in one's imagination. She remembered every line of the sheer cliffs, white in the midday sun, every dark spot that marked the doorway to an abandoned tomb in the sand, but she had forgotten the effect of the place, the loneliness, the emptiness, the utter desolation of it all.

If only there was something to break the unending monotony. A tree, a shrub, a single blade of grass. The smell of violets in mossy woods, the rippling sound of a mountain stream. a light puff of cloud in the clear blue sky. The welcome kiss of rain.

"I said madame, I hope you had a comfortable journey."

Edward's impatience drew Aimée's attention back to him. He stood in the doorway of his tent. Beside him. Buffy was perched on a wooden table, his legs dangling over the edge.

"Yes, thank you, comfortable enough. though it was very tiring. It would have been better if I had had time to find a nurse for the child."

"Ah, yes, the child." Edward rested incurious eyes on Mariette, curled up like a tired puppy on the carpet that covered the sand. "I would have preferred a son."

"Well, you don't have a son." Aimée felt her patience snap. She was as tired as Mariette, and Edward's childishness was getting on her nerves. "And you're not likely to have—as we both know."

Edward scowled at her impertinence, but Buffy only grinned with amusement. The girl had been an icy bitch the few times he had bedded her. She was showing more spirit now. He liked that.

"Why not a son, my dear?" he asked pointedly. "Why not a dozen more children—if Eddie wants them."

Edward reddened at the mockery in his tone. "Shut up, Buffy." He was not going to let his lover make a fool of him. If Buffy still thought he needed him—for passion or for procreation—he was in for a nasty surprise.

"My, my, what an ugly temper we have." Buffy was more confident than he had been in months. Edward could not handle both the woman's sharp tongue and his own, and he knew it. "Why be so unreasonable? You want a son, and I can give it to you."

Aimée looked from one to the other in disgust. What kind of men were they, these two lovers who knew nothing of love or tenderness or even pity? It only added to her horror to realize that Buffy, for all his lewd insinuations, was staring not at her but at the child he thought was his.

Buffy had aged in the past years, but he had not changed. He had grown fatter, his skin had dried out in the sun, and deep lines marred the prettiness of his face, but the self-absorption she remembered, the petty malice, were as pronounced as ever. Even now, as he looked at Mariette, there was no affection in his eyes, only a gloating kind of curiosity.

Reaching down, Aimée woke the baby, pulling her into protective arms. She could not bear the obscenity of this man's gaze on her child a minute longer.

"Mariette is very tired. If you will excuse me, I'll put her to bed."

She did not wait for her husband's reply. Turning on her heel, she hurried toward her own tent. She was halfway there before she saw Raoul moving toward her from the far side of the site.

Barely daring to breathe, she stopped to watch him. Mariette whimpered softly, protesting the arms that had tensed around her, but Aimée did not notice. All she could feel, all she could see, was the man she thought she had left behind forever.

The sun shimmered brightly on the sand, distorting his image, but she did not need vision to make out his features. Memory was enough. Black eyes flashed a bold challenge, as they had once on the banks of the Seine. Dark hair whipped in the wind, with the savage force of a storm at sea. Strong, passionate lips parted in the lamplight—*I had to come to you.*

She dropped to her knees, letting Mariette wriggle out of her arms. Rising again, she stood to wait for him. She had not known in all the long days of her journey to Egypt how she would react when she saw him again. She did not know now.

He stopped a few feet from her. They faced each other in silence.

The man was not Raoul. Somewhere in the years that separated them, Raoul had slipped away from her, and this man who stood before her now was a stranger. His skin was tanned to a deep brown, forming creases around his eyes; his black hair, hanging carelessly almost to his shoulders, was touched with streaks of gray. Aimée knew she was staring, but she could not help herself. It had never occurred to her that Raoul's hair might turn gray like everyone else's.

He extended his hand. "It's been a long time."

His grip was warm and firm, but it was a stranger's grip.

"How long? Two years? Almost three?"

Raoul felt as awkward as she. He looked at this woman, chic and elegant in her smart traveling suit, with her hair piled stylishly on top of her head, and he barely recognized her. He remembered the day he had first seen her, so pretty and so affected, just beginning to try on the mannerisms of fashion. She had perfected them now. He was not sure he liked her anymore.

"You've changed."

"And you."

They could think of nothing else to say. They stood before each other, silent and uncomfortable, like two strangers who had just been introduced and found they had nothing in common.

It was Aimée who finally broke the silence. "How is Thea? Well, I trust."

"Yes, very well, thank you. She is in Cairo now, visiting cousins in the diplomatic service. I'm afraid it's rather dull for her here."

"I would have thought you'd be married by now." How strange it was, talking to him like this. That question would have cut so deeply once. Now she felt nothing.

"I would have thought so myself, but the excavation has taken longer than I expected. Still, I suppose archaeologists never make reliable fiancés. There always seems to be just one more season ahead."

"The work is going well, then?"

"Reasonably well, I think. We've cleared most of the antechamber already. You'll have to come and see our progress. Maybe you'll decide to help out again."

"Yes, I will. Of course I will."

But she would not, and they both knew it. She could not pick up the pieces again. It was too late. Too many things had been done without her, too much had changed, and the man who would work beside her was a man she did not know.

"That is, I will if I can. But with the child, it's hard, you know."

"Of course. I understand."

They stared at each other mutely, both trying to find a way to end the awkward encounter, neither knowing how. They were spared by a sudden howl of impatience.

"Mama!"

Mariette was tired and irritable. She was hot and the sand was hot, and she hated it all. She couldn't understand why her mother was standing there talking with this strange man, when she wanted her.

Aimée looked at her child, and she laughed with delight. Her lower lip quivered with frustration, and tears welled up in soft blue eyes. She was such a little thing, Aimée thought, and so appealing. It was impossible to resist her. Bending down, she took the child in her arms, brushing away the tears.

Raoul watched Aimée coax Mariette to her feet, brushing sand from a rumpled white skirt. In all the conflicting emotions he felt at seeing the woman again, he had forgotten the child. Now he looked down at her and tried to sort out his feelings, and found he could not.

He had thought he would know when he saw her. Somehow, he had assumed paternity was a thing that could be recognized, however mystically or irrationally. Obviously it was not. He searched the child's face, trying to find something of himself, but there was nothing. Nothing of him, nothing of Edward, nothing of Buffy. Only a perfect little replica of Aimée, with no comfort for the man who had fathered her.

Or would it be comfort? he asked himself coldly. Did he really want this child to be his? Could he really accept a tangible, visible tie to the love that had ended long ago?

"Come, *mon lapin*," Aimée soothed the child. "Come to Mama. You're tired, aren't you? It's time for your nap."

"Not tired!" Mariette pulled away from Aimée, stamping

her foot defiantly. Fascinated at the way it sank into the sand, she stamped it again. "No nap."

Raoul almost laughed aloud. The child was Aimée through and through. She had a mind of her own, all right—just like her mother.

And just like himself. Almost as if she were part of him, too.

Impetuously he bent down. Perhaps if he could see her closer . . .

"Hello, Mariette," he said softly.

The child eyed him warily, as if she could not make up her mind. Then impulsively she threw plump arms around his neck in a natural burst of affection.

The gesture caught Raoul off guard. For a second he hesitated. He longed to return the child's warmth, to catch her up and press her against his body, but he was afraid. It would be so much easier to turn and run away, hiding from emotions he could not handle.

In the end, he compromised. Gripping her firmly, he swung her into the air, tossing her up and down until she shrieked with excitement.

He was conscious of small hands clutching at his shoulders as he settled her down in his arms. For the first time since he had come forward to greet Aimée, he smiled.

"Is she always so spontaneous?"

"No." Aimée was careful to control her face. She did not want him to see how deeply the moment had moved her. "She's usually very cautious with strangers."

Raoul held the child awhile longer. Then, seeing that she was sleepy, no matter how she protested, he handed her back to Aimée. Mariette clung to his shirt for a minute, as if she did not want to let go of him, then relaxed in her mother's arms.

"Shhh, *petite*," Aimée whispered, rocking the child back and forth. "Go to sleep now. Go to sleep."

Petite. The word was a poignant reminder. Did she know what she was saying? Raoul wondered. Did she remember that that had once been his name for her, or was it simply a natural endearment for a French mother to use with her child?

Raoul watched Aimée's face as she cradled Mariette against her breast. Her features were softer now, gentler and sweeter. She was a different woman with her child. This was the woman he had wanted that other Aimée—that wild, captivating girl he had loved—to become.

She was a good woman, he realized as he watched her walk toward her tent, the child secure in her embrace. She had grown superficial and vain, a product of her culture, but beneath it all, she was good at heart. And she would be a good mother to his child.

His child. He realized now that he thought of Mariette as his. It was idiotic—but there it was. He was a bachelor, confronted with a woman he no longer loved, and for some perverse reason he could not understand, he actually wanted the child of that union.

The question of the child remained with him as the days turned into weeks and Mariette and her mother remained in the camp. He and Aimée were careful to stay out of each other's way, as if somehow they could pretend the thing between them had never happened, but there was no way he could avoid the child. Lively and laughing, she was all over the site, brown as a little Arab as she pestered the workmen, coaxing them for the delicious little sweetmeats that had suddenly begun to appear in all their lunches. And every time he looked at her, he wondered.

Sometimes he was tempted to go to Aimée. Just to ask outright, "What are the chances she is mine?" But he already knew what she would say. "Not so good" or "Pretty good"—and that would be that. She could not say "Yes" or "No," and that was all he could accept.

He paused once outside her tent. It had been a hot afternoon, and Aimée had put Mariette's crib in the shade. Now it was twilight, and a lamp rested on the table beside it. He looked down at the child as she slept.

He had never seen anything so pretty. Little curls, moist in the heat, clung to her forehead, and long lashes lay lightly on pink cheeks. Her hand curled around the corner of her pillow, so delicate he could hardly believe it was real.

Once he had loved to look at Aimée when she slept. She had seemed sweetly innocent then, too, and vulnerable. He felt a sudden urge to clasp the child against his body, protecting, cherishing, as he could never protect and cherish Aimée.

He was still there when Aimée slipped out of the tent. She smiled as she saw him.

"I always leave a light burning. Mariette is afraid of the dark."

She looked incredibly young in a white jaconet negligée ruffled up to her chin. Her hair hung loose down her back. For an instant he thought he caught a glimpse of the woman he had fallen in love with.

He reached out as if to touch her, then let his hand fall awkwardly against the crib. It embarrassed him to be caught staring at the child.

"She is so little," he said lamely.

"I know. It makes you want to take her up in your arms and protect her against the world."

He felt a sudden bond between them. Tell me this is my child, he wanted to cry out. Tell me you loved me, and only me. Lie to me if you have to, but tell me, and I will believe you.

But he could not say the words.

"I . . . I had better be going. I have work to do."

Aimée watched him walk away, then pulled up a chair and sat beside her child. She leaned her head against the side of the crib, letting her eyes close wearily.

She had seen her lover's pain. She did not understand it, but she had seen it. She knew he no longer wanted her, but she knew, too, that for some reason she could not fathom, he wanted the child. She wished there were a way she could give him what he needed.

She had been a fool to come back to Egypt. She knew that now. And she was an even bigger fool to stay. She had brought nothing but unhappiness on herself, and on Raoul, too. She didn't know what had prompted Edward to bring her here, but whatever his reasons, he had obviously changed his mind. Perhaps he had just been bored. Edward was always bored. He was bored with her when he had her, bored with her when she was gone, and now that she was back, he was bored again. Well, she was not going to let her husband's whims rule her life anymore. Tomorrow she would tell him she was going home.

She saw Edward sooner than she had expected. Late that night, long after the camp was still, he summoned her to his tent. Aimée had already retired when she heard a serving boy call to her from outside the doorway, telling her that her husband wanted to see her.

Her hands shook as she struggled to light the lantern. Edward rarely sent for her, and never that late. She could not imagine what he wanted, but the thought of it made her nervous. Knotting a blue cashmere wrapper tightly around her waist, she stepped out into the cold.

The instant she caught sight of Edward, she forgot her own anxiety. She had never seen him in such a state before. His waistcoat, usually so tidy, was unbuttoned and his shirttails hung half out of his pants.

"Edward, what's the matter? Are you ill?"

Edward reached out a hand, steadying himself against the edge of the table as he stared at her. He looked surprised, as if he had not expected to see her.

"Ill, my dear? No, I am not ill." His eyes, dilated in the dim light, were almost black. It was a minute before Aimée caught the stale odor of bouza in the air.

"You are drunk," she accused, backing away in disgust. "And on cheap Egyptian beer. You smell foul."

Turning aside, she tugged at the flap of the tent. To her surprise, she found that the boy had fastened it securely when he showed her inside. Bending swiftly, she reached out to pull the knot loose. She did not even hear Edward move up behind her. She was aware of his presence only when she felt his hand brush against her arm. Alarmed, she whirled to face him, but she was too late. His fingers gouged into her flesh as he dragged her to her feet.

"Where the hell do you think you're going? You'll leave when I tell you to, and not a minute before."

With a single furious thrust he flung her across the room. Aimée cried out in pain as the sharp corner of a heavy table jammed into her back. Her fingers clutched the handle of the lantern, clinging to it with all her strength.

It took her a minute to pull herself together. Trembling, she eased the light up to the table, setting it cautiously on the smooth, broad surface. Her eyes were wide with fear and amazement. Edward had always been cruel, but she had never known him to be wantonly violent before.

"Why are you doing this? What do you want of me?"

Edward's breath came in quick, short gasps as he stood in front of this woman who had made a mockery of his life. His own savage force exhilarated him, until he knew he could do anything.

"I want . . . a son."

Aimée felt weak with revulsion. She remembered Buffy's laughter, confident and snide, the day she had returned. It seemed to her she had never loathed anyone so much in her life. Whatever the cost, she could not let him near her again.

"So you're going to hide behind your lover," she taunted. It was a dangerous gambit, but she had no choice. He would never force Buffy on her again. "You're going to use him to cover up your own inadequacy. Tell me, does it make you feel like a big virile man to have someone else father your children?"

"Bitch!" Edward's hand lashed out, swift and powerful as

it hit the side of Aimée's face. Tears of pain stung her eyes, but she did not cry out again. "So you think I'm not a man, do you? I'll show you what a man really is. I intend to have a son, and this one will be mine."

God, how he hated her. When he had first seen her, young and childishly slender, she had almost appealed to him. Now she was a cow, plump and disgusting, with rounded hips and breasts that made him sick just to look at them.

"But you can't . . ." Aimée whispered the words, horrified. "You know you can't. Remember what it was like before."

"Can't I?"

But he could, and he knew he could. He had been practicing with one of the prostitutes from the village. A big, ugly woman, as ugly as Aimée, with breasts that slid down her sides, wallowing on the bed when he lay on top of her, grunting his seed into her.

He waited for Aimée to flinch when he reached out, clutching at the neck of her wrapper. When she did not, he tore it roughly from her shoulders. Her breasts, firm and heavy, looked swollen in the flickering light.

He hated her more than ever now. She was afraid, and he knew she was afraid, and the thought excited him. He was going to enjoy forcing himself on her, humiliating her again and again with angry thrusts of his body, just as he had humiliated the prostitute in the village. It would be worth every cent he had ever spent on her.

Aimée felt him close in until she thought she would scream with despair. Other images tormented her, images she could not drive away. Edward on their wedding night, flushed with champagne and fear. Buffy in the darkened room of a rented house, leering with a bravado he did not feel.

"No!"

She was surprised at the sound of her own voice, strong and sure. All her life, she had let herself be dominated by men. Now it was time to fight back.

Edward glowered at her in amazement. "No?" he shouted furiously. "No to me? Your husband?" His hand was rough on her arm as he pulled her toward him.

Struggling desperately, Aimée worked herself free. Wild with rage and fear, she swung around, raising her hand to strike him a stinging blow on the side of the face. Edward stumbled backward, too stunned to react for a moment. She did not give him time to recover.

"You are a pig, and I loathe you. You married me under

false pretenses, and you have made my life miserable. Do you think I would ever let you touch me?"

Edward's eyes were murderous as he reeled toward her. "And how do you think you're going to stop me?"

Aimée caught her breath with a gasp of terror. She had to do something, and do it quickly.

"Try it, Edward," she called out boldly. "Go ahead and try it, and I'll tell everyone what you are!"

He wavered for a minute. "What . . . what do you mean?"

"You know exactly what I mean. You married me so the world wouldn't know you were a homosexual. Well, my dear husband, everyone will know it if you lay a hand on me again. Can you imagine how they'll laugh at you, all those witty wags who love nothing so much as a good bit of gossip at someone else's expense? And what will they make of it, I wonder, when they find out that even your child had to be sired by another man?"

"Buffy? You'd tell them Buffy was the father?"

"Buffy?" Aimée stared at him in contempt. Really, the man was a fool. He was so afraid his lover would look virile in the eyes of the world, he couldn't think of anything else. "Buffy is no more a man than you are. Do you really think . . . ?"

She broke off abruptly, but it was too late. She could see only too well that Edward had caught her insinuation, and he had not misunderstood it.

"So it wasn't just work?" he said slowly. "All those long hours in the tomb."

"Wasn't it?" Aimée was sure now, surer than she had ever been. "Accuse me of it, Edward—if you dare. I'll deny it, and so will he."

"Damn you, you filthy little whore. Do you really think I'll let you get away with this? I'll cut off your money, you know I will. You'll never get another cent."

"Oh. stop your blustering, Edward. You'll give me everything I want, and Mariette, too. If you don't, I'll shout your perversions from the rooftops—with all the pretty little details."

She did not look back as she walked over to the table, catching the lantern up in her hand. She had been afraid of Edward so long she had forgotten what it was like to live without fear. She did not stop to untie the tent flap, but caught it firmly in her hand, ripping it away from the peg that held it. She did not begin to tremble until she felt the darkness around her.

She was still shaking an hour later when Raoul found her outside her tent. She did not dare go in, for fear Mariette would see her and be frightened. One look at her face was enough to make Raoul forget all his reservations.

"My God, Aimée, what happened? What is it, *mon ange*? What's wrong?"

Aimée tried to speak, but she could not. Her head dropped to her hands. Her breath came in little choking sobs.

"Oh, Raoul, it was terrible . . ." Her voice was barely a whisper. "So terrible."

Raoul touched the side of her face, easing her head toward the light. The beginnings of an angry bruise were already showing on her cheek. Her wrapper was torn where she clutched it over her breast.

"Goddammit," he cursed, anger making his voice low and hoarse. "Who did this to you?"

"Edward," she said slowly. "It was Edward."

"Edward!" That bastard. What kind of a pervert would do this to his own wife? "I'm going to have it out with him once and for all."

"No! Please, you'll . . . you'll only make things worse."

Raoul had a sick feeling in the pit of his stomach. The man owned Aimée, like an animal or a piece of furniture, and there was nothing he could do about it. He had seen the marks of Edward's viciousness tonight. He wondered how many scars of the past were invisible.

Why had he always been so quick to judge her? If she had turned to other men, perhaps she had a reason. To Buffy Montmorency, a foolish popinjay, but a man who understood what it was to be used at Edward's hands. And to himself, cold except in bed, insensitive, thoughtless, but at least a man who did not beat her.

"I'm sorry, Aimée." He drew her tenderly into his arms. "I didn't understand." She felt soft and small against his chest. He held her tightly, soothing, caressing, easing away the pain and the terror.

She was so sweet, so vulnerable, stripped of all her defenses and pretensions. As helpless as Mariette, lying asleep in her crib. And she needed him. He could feel that she needed him.

He knew what she was. It no longer mattered. The die had been cast long ago. As long as she needed him, as long as she trembled in his arms, he could not let go of her. He would throw it all away—his engagement, his career, even the precious honor he had guarded so hypocritically all these years—and he would not give a damn.

Her breast was soft in his hand as he slipped the torn robe from her body. The scent of her perfume lay in his nostrils, rich and fragrant, as his lips dropped to her neck. She was his now, and he would never let another man touch her as long as he lived.

Aimée's body responded to his caress with an awakened longing that tore her heart in two. She had dreamed of this moment so long, yearned for it so passionately, she could not bear to let it go. His hands were stronger than any other hands, his body firmer, his lips the sweetest lips in the world. All she wanted was to catch at this moment of loveliness, clasping it tightly against her breast, holding on to it forever.

But, oh, God help her, she knew she could not.

"No, please, just hold me," she begged. "Just hold me tight."

He seemed to understand her need for tenderness. Containing his own passion, he pulled her lovingly into his embrace. Her head dropped on his shoulder. The closeness of his body was a comfort.

It was a perfect instant, a lovely dream—and it would have to last her a lifetime. There would be nothing more.

Gently, finding the courage at last, she pushed him away from her. She saw the confusion in his eyes, and the hurt, but there was nothing she could do to ease it.

It would be better this way, she told herself as she rose and stepped away from him, staring out into the darkness. It could last for only a little while, and then the pain of parting would be even greater. Besides, the stakes were too high. Edward had learned their secret that night, and Edward was a man who would want his revenge. He would not dare do anything to her, not with all she had to hold over his head, but the minute Thea returned, he was just vindictive enough to make sure she found out about it. Raoul's whole future was wrapped up in a lifetime with Thea. She could not let him throw it away on her.

It was a long time before she turned to face him again. When she did, her face was deceptively calm.

"I have made a life for myself in Vienna."

Raoul felt as if he had been betrayed. For an elusive moment he had found the Aimée he dreamed of long ago, and yearning and tenderness had filled his heart. In that moment, he had been a man capable of love again. Now the moment was gone.

"Is it a good life?"

She wanted to lie to him. She wanted to tell him how happy she was in Vienna, how eager she was to return. But they had played so many games with each other. She wanted their last moment together to be honest.

"No, it is not a good life, but it is all I have. Please don't ruin it for me."

So that was how it was. Raoul nodded his head slightly, letting a brief ironic smile turn up the corners of his mouth. She had made her choice, and they must both live by it. He suddenly felt tired and somehow older as he walked alone to his quarters.

Aimée blew out the lantern and sat alone in the darkness. Her own words echoed in her ears, and she knew she had made the right decision. Her life in Vienna was not a good life, but at least it was *her* life. If she stayed here, she would only be clinging to a corner of Raoul's.

She told Edward the next day that she was going back to Vienna. "The heat is too much for the child," she said. "It is not good for her here."

The words were a blatant lie. Mariette was laughing and squealing outside, tempting one after another of the workmen away from the dig to play with her. But Edward could do nothing about it, and he knew it.

Raoul took them to the station. He had dressed in a suit, dark and immaculately tailored. There was a solemnity about him Aimée had never seen before.

They were both conscious that this would be their last farewell. There were so many things Aimée wanted to tell him, so much she wanted to share, but he had become a stranger again, and she could not find the words.

"Take care of the little princess in the tomb." She tried to make her voice light, but she could not keep it from cracking. The tomb had been so much a part of their lives, a discovery they had made together. It was hard to let go of it now. "And leave some crumbs for the raven if it comes again."

Raoul nodded. He could not bring himself to smile. "And you take care of *this* little princess." He pinched Mariette lightly on the nose. The child giggled with delight. She could not understand why Raoul did not laugh with her.

Raoul helped them into the carriage, then stood beside the track watching the last of the passengers scurry onto the train. He was surprised at how hard it was to part from them. He had never thought of himself as a sentimental man.

Mariette waved at him from the window. He had the strange, uncomfortable feeling that his emotions toward her would never change. He could see himself years from now, he thought wryly, a stooped, graying man, bent over a cane as he peered through the fence of an exclusive girls' school, like some aging roué in a cheap novel, come back for a glimpse of the child he had deserted.

Only, he would be doubly foolish. At least the roué would know the child was his.

The last sight he had of them was Mariette's face pressed against the window as the train pulled out of the station.

5

"Aimée!"

Aimée looked up at the sound of her name. The street, soft with a new blanket of snow, was half-deserted in the early twilight. The spire of St. Stephen's seemed tall and lonely in the distance.

"Why, it's Mary Vetsera." Aimée hurried toward her. Naked trees lined the boulevards, and luminous icicles, brilliant as cut crystal, gave the city a brittle, artificial air. It was like a breath of spring to see someone warm and natural.

The girl was bubbling with enthusiasm. "Isn't everything beautiful—look!" She spun around, throwing her arms out, as if to draw the whole world into her embrace. "Don't you just love winter?"

"It certainly seems to agree with you. Why, you look pretty as a picture." Lacy snowflakes rested on the dark fur of Mary's hat and collar. The ruddy warmth of her cheeks was reflected in voluptuous red lips.

"Do I?" The girl giggled. "I hope so. I've just come from Adele's. I had my picture taken—for *him*."

There was no mistaking her emphasis. Aimée, suddenly conscious of the cold, pressed her hands deep into her muff, but she did not try to speak. Vienna had been giddy with rumors since she had returned, rumors about Mary and the young archduke, but she had tried to ignore them.

Mary did not seem to notice her silence. "Could we have tea?" she suggested impulsively. "Or a pastry at one of the coffeehouses? Oh, Aimée, please say yes! If I can't talk to someone, I think I'll burst."

Aimée hesitated. She had always liked the girl, but she was not sure she wanted to become her confidante.

"Well, I . . . I suppose we could." How could she resist the plea in those wide blue eyes? "Just for a little while."

Mary was uncharacteristically quiet, almost timid, as they settled at the round marble table and wrapped their cold fingers around steaming cups of coffee, rich with cream. She looked as if she were working up the courage to speak.

"I expect you think I'm a silly little thing, carrying on like this. But the truth is, Aimée, I've always felt close to you, ever since that evening at the opera when you were so good to me. Do you remember? That was the first time I saw him."

Aimée nodded slowly. How could she ever forget? "Yes, I remember."

"Look!" Mary could contain herself no longer. Shyly she held out her hand. A dark, slender band stood out against pale skin.

Aimée stared at the ring curiously. It was plain and singularly graceless. A rough piece of iron, strangely out of place on a lady's hand. She did not know what to say.

"It's very . . . interesting."

"*He* gave it to me, as a symbol of our love. I'm supposed to wear it on a chain around my neck, tucked away beneath my dress, but I couldn't bear to keep it hidden like that."

Aimée shook her head doubtfully. Somehow she didn't think, if the ring were hers, she would mind hiding it at all.

"What does your chaperon think of it?" With all their emphasis on wealth and status, the Vetsera clan could hardly have been pleased with Rudolf's choice of a gift.

"Oh, Marie." Mary dismissed the woman with a bored flick of her hand. "Marie says he gave Mitzi Kaspar a house— that's that cheap little actress, you know—and I should have gotten more."

"And you don't feel that way?" Much as she despised Marie Larisch, Aimée had to admit she had a point.

Mary only smiled, half-condescendingly, as if she were years older than Aimée. "What do I need with a house?"

Aimée took a slow sip of her coffee. Poor little Mary, so sweet and so naive. What did she need with a house, indeed!

"A diamond, then . . ."

"Don't you see, Aimée—those things are just vanity. The trappings and pretensions of a society that has forgotten its deeper values. Our love, Rudolf's and mine, is pure and basic, like the simple iron in the matching rings we wear. We don't need tokens to show it off in front of the world."

Aimée listened to Mary, but she knew she was really hearing another, more sophisticated voice, and it surprised her to find such depth beneath the cavalier facade the archduke presented to the world. Rudolf had given gold and diamonds to countless women. It seemed now he had given his heart to Mary Vetsera.

"You love him so much, then?"

"More than life itself. Oh, if only I could tell you . . ." She leaned forward, stretching out her hand. "But I can tell you, can't I, Aimée?"

"Yes." Aimée was surprised at herself. A minute ago, she had not wanted Mary's confidence. Now she almost hungered for it, as if somewhere in a young girl's heart she hoped to find the key to her own lost dreams.

"I was at the palace last week—not at the front door, of course, but I was there. Marie was with me. Do you know, I think she was more nervous than I, poor dear. She wants so desperately to be close to royalty, but when it happens, she gets all frightened about it."

She paused to laugh at her own reflection. Leaning closer, she lowered her voice.

"It was all very secret and mysterious, a clandestine rendezvous. An old servant met us at the door—Rudolf's valet, I think—and led us up a back stairway. Marie was very cynical about it. She kept whispering to me that the man must have done the same thing a thousand times before."

As no doubt he had, Aimée thought, but she had the sense to keep the observation to herself.

"We went up several staircases and through all sorts of different rooms, until I was quite turned around. The last stairway was so dark, I had to grope to feel where I was going. Then the old man opened a door, and we found ourselves on a wide, flat roof. Oh, Aimée, it was so exciting. A cold wind blew in our faces, and there was the most magnificent view in the world.

"Then suddenly we heard a whir of wings, and the most awful croaking sound. Marie screamed and screamed. I thought for sure she was going to faint when she saw it was a raven."

"A raven?"

Mary glanced at her sharply. "You've heard the legend, then?"

Aimée shook her head. She had been thinking about another raven, another time—another pair of lovers searching for a place to be alone.

"What legend?"

"It's a curse, I think, on the house of Hapsburg. They say when you see a raven, it means someone is about to die."

Aimée shivered. "How different beliefs are all over the world. In ancient Egypt, a raven—or a bird—was associated with immortal life."

"I must say I like that better. Eternal life—it sounds so much prettier than curses of death But I don't think you'd get Marie to listen. She was so terrified, she was trembling all over. I was afraid I'd never get her to go on But I just laughed at her. 'It's probably some tame bird,' I told her, and later Rudolf told me I was right. The poor thing lives in the gun room, with the antlers and the trophies. I daresay, with all that screaming, the raven was more afraid of Marie than she was of him."

She paused, as if daring herself to go on. Then, taking a deep breath, she continued.

"Marie waited outside while I went in alone. Rudolf was there, and we . . . we . . . Oh, Aimée, we both lost our heads. Now we belong to each other body and soul."

Aimée looked at her sadly. So, she had taken a lover, this pretty child who was a child no longer. She had known the ecstasy, and she would know the pain.

"I wish you joy, Mary."

Whatever joy you can have, she added silently, but she was kind enough not to speak the words aloud.

We lost our heads. Aimée could still hear Mary's voice as she stood alone on dark, silent streets. The snow was heavier now, catching at the hem of her coat as she tried to walk. *Now we belong to each other.*

Did they belong to each other? she wondered. Mary and Rudolf . . . she and Raoul? Was there an ownership to love, a kind of bond that would endure for all time? They had been a part of each other once, she and this man she loved. Were they a part of each other still? Was there, in the moment of love they had shared, something so eternal it would linger, even after the memories were gone?

Raoul stared blindly into the darkness. It was the night of the new moon, and the sky was an inky pit in which a man could drown himself. Silence was a part of the desert, silence

326

and loneliness. It was a tangible feeling, like the heat and the cold, working its way into his bones.

He had never been drawn to the desert before. It had been a friend, an enemy, a silent, impartial judge, now yielding up the treasures in its depths, now holding them back—but never a part of his soul. Tonight he felt as if he were a grain of sand, mingled with all the other anonymous grains, vulnerable to the force of a wind that would one day pick him up and blow him away, as if he had never existed at all.

Dammit, he had been without a woman too long, he told himself irritably. He had never been moody and mystical before. Seeing Aimée again, holding her, feeling her heart beat one more time against his, had been a potent reminder of needs long unsatisfied. He had retreated too deeply inward, losing the sense of humanity that came from reaching out and touching someone else.

A single sliver of light broke the darkness. Raoul found himself staring at it. Thea, pretty, gentle Thea, was still awake, reading one of the romantic novels she was so fond of or writing a letter to her father or her sisters. The thought made him sad in a way he could not explain. Thea, so near and yet so far. If she were already his wife . . .

He took a tentative step toward the light, and then another. He could not go to her—he knew her innocence would not permit it—but, God, how he longed to lie in the arms of a woman tonight.

"Thea!" His voice was harsh as he called out to her. He did not know why he was there, or what he expected of her. He only knew he was lonely.

He did not wait for her reply, pushing instead through the netting that screened the door. Once inside, he hesitated.

Thea's tent was much like Thea herself, soft and exquisitely feminine. A blue organdy spread covered the bed, and family photos rested in silver frames on the dressing table. Bright little marigolds, carried patiently from town, peeked out of a tall alabaster vase.

Thea had risen to face him. Even in the privacy of her tent she was elaborately garbed. White ribbons trimmed French blue linen, and satin petticoats peeked demurely from a skirt of paisley appliqués. Even in her negligee, Raoul mused, she was protected by as many layers as the most elegant lady of fashion.

Still, she was provocative, he had to admit that. Even more provocative in her own way than Aimée, with all her diaphanous silk. There was an air of untouched innocence about her that stirred him. He yearned to peel away the gowns and petticoats, layer by layer, tenderly at first so he would not frighten her, then faster and faster as his lust consumed him.

"Thea, my sweet, enchanting Thea, do you have any idea how lovely you are? Or how I long to hold your body next to mine, touching you, caressing you . . ."

"Raoul . . ." Thea's voice quavered, her eyes filled with doubt. "Please, I don't understand."

"Dammit, Thea . . ." He caught himself just in time. Everything in her manner told him he had frightened her. "I'm sorry—I know I shouldn't talk to you like this. You are so beautiful, so innocent, and I am such a clumsy fool. I ought to be down on my knees right now, begging you to marry me."

Amusement replaced the confusion in Thea's face. "But, Raoul, you've done all this before. Don't you remember? You did get down on your knees, and quite gallantly, too, and I accepted you."

"I mean, marry me now. Tonight . . . tomorrow if you will. We could go to Cairo. Your cousins could be there if you wanted."

And tomorrow night, after all the years of waiting, they could lie in the same bed at last.

"Cairo?" Thea was not sophisticated enough to hide her dismay. "But we can't be married in Cairo, Raoul. I want to go home—to England. My family is there, all my friends. The church in the little town where I grew up."

Raoul saw her unhappiness. but he could not bring himself to accept it. Slowly he stretched out his hands, offering the mute appeal he knew would never be answered. At last, admitting defeat, he let them drop to his sides.

No, they could not be married in Cairo. Thea was a gentle girl with gentle dreams. She would want a long white gown and a choir of children with sweet soprano voices to guide her down the aisle. The flowers in her bouquet would be English roses, not wild African daisies, and the beaming faces around her comfortable and familar. It would be the wedding she had dreamed of all her life—and deserved to have.

He strode brusquely across the room, reaching up with rough hands to pull the clips out of her hair. He saw that she was frightened again, but he could not stop himself. At last her hair flowed free and golden down her back.

"Why do you twist it up like that, even at night? I like it better down."

She was so pretty, he ached to look on her. He wanted to

wake up and find long pale tresses tangling with the dark hair on his chest. Dammit, it wasn't fair. It wasn't fair at all. He would give her the wedding she wanted—and gladly. Was it too much to ask her to give him something in return?

Thea tensed. She could not comprehend his thoughts, but nonetheless they frightened her.

"You should not be here, Raoul."

"I belong here." He caught her by the wrist, pulling her toward him. "Don't you understand that? I belong with you."

But she did not understand, and he could see that. Reluctantly he let her go. She took a step backward, rubbing her wrist as if he had hurt her, but she did not reproach him.

How much had they told her? he wondered, all the female relatives and advisers who were supposed to prepare a girl for marriage? Had they ever, so much as once, sat down with her and described the things a man would demand of her body? He remembered her mother, a thin, graying woman with pinched lines around her mouth, and he doubted it.

"Do you know what I want of you?" he asked her gently. He wanted her enough to be patient with her. "Do you know what it is when a man needs a woman?"

Thea grew apprehensive. She knew vaguely that a man's body was different from a woman's, and he would sometimes be filled with passions that turned him half into an animal, even in the marriage bed, but these were things women only whispered in secret. She had not expected to hear them now.

"You shouldn't be talking like this, Raoul. It . . . it isn't proper."

"It *is* proper, Thea. You are my fiancée, you are going to be my wife. The love that is between us will be a physical thing, too."

He had never wanted her more. She looked so bewildered as she gazed at him. So helpless. If only he could take her in his arms and teach her to trust him.

"I want you, Thea. Don't make me wait for you."

He did not relent this time as he pulled her toward him. His lips were firm on hers, kissing her with a passion he had never dared express before. He tried to be gentle with her, coaxing her slowly to respond, but his excitement mounted until he could no longer control himself. He forced her lips apart, thrusting his tongue into her mouth. His hands were brutal as they dug into her flesh.

He had to make her want him, he told himself urgently. He had to make her cling to him. He had been lonely so long. He needed to feel a woman's arms around his body, hungry and demanding as his own.

"Raoul . . . no!"

Frightened, Thea pushed him away. Tears streamed down her cheeks, blinding her as she stumbled backward. Hands clutching her breast, she gaped at him in horror.

Damn, Raoul cursed bitterly. What a swine he was. He had thought he could force her passion, crudely, demandingly, as he had with Aimée. Only, he had forgotten one thing. Thea wasn't a lusty bitch who let any man use her for the asking.

"My dearest, forgive me." He took a step forward, arms outstretched to comfort her.

"No!" Thea threw up her hands, frantic to stop him. Her features were distorted with fear and revulsion.

Raoul was sick at heart as he watched her. He knew what he had done, and there was no way he could undo it. He could overcome the fear one day, with tenderness and patience, but the revulsion would always be there.

Thea had seen something in him that night—just as he had seen something in her. They had an understanding of each other now that changed everything.

He had had an image of Thea as a soft, lovely temptress, pale in the white of her bridal gown, untouched by the hand of a man. A beautiful ice maiden waiting only for the handsome prince whose kisses could awaken her passions. It had been a compelling image. His body had wanted the challenge, just as his masculine ego thrived on the scent of victory. Now he knew it was only a fantasy.

Thea was cool with him, not because her innocence demanded it, but because coolness was part of her nature. The prince she dreamed of was not a wildly passionate lover, but a gentle, considerate friend, his kisses filled more with sweet romance than desire.

That was the kind of man she needed. The kind of man who would be tender, almost apologetic when he slipped into her room, driven by needs he could not control. The kind of man who would turn out the light before he lifted her gown, careful not to touch her any more than he had to, as he used her body for his own ends. The kind of man who would leave her alone when he was finished, tactfully giving her time to compose herself again.

But he was not that kind of man, and Thea knew it now. He would demand of her the passion she would never be able to give.

"I'm sorry, Thea. I said I was a clumsy fool. It seems I was right."

The desert was empty when he returned to it. Not even a jackal barked in the distance. He sat alone until dawn.

It was over. He did not try to deceive himself. In the space of a few minutes, he had killed the last of his dreams. There would be no quiet country cottages for him now, no pretty, smiling wife to greet him at the door. No long tramps in rainy English woods. No pipe by the fire. No golden-haired children climbing onto his lap to tease him at the end of a long day.

Now there was nothing. Only the sand and the silence—and the loneliness.

He was part of the desert at last.

Mary Vetsera laughed gaily as she danced into the sitting room. Her eyes sparkled brightly. Aimée hurried toward her, extending her hands in greeting.

"What a lovely surprise!"

Mary tilted her head to the side, contriving to look coy and enigmatic all at the same time. "I've come to say good-bye."

"Good-bye?" Aimée was caught off guard. "But . . . are you going away, then? On a holiday?"

"No, not a holiday. I am going away, but I am not coming back."

Stunned, Aimée looked at the girl in silence. She had always known this would happen one day, but she had not thought it would come so soon. And she never expected Mary to surrender cheerfully.

"But I . . ." She stumbled over the words, not wanting to hurt the girl's feelings. "I mean, you seemed so much in love. I didn't believe you would give up so easily."

Mary's face lit up with an impish smile. "Did you think I was giving up? But I love him more than life itself—I told you that once. I would never give him up. No, I am going away, but I am going with him."

"With . . . Rudolf?" Aimée's eyes widened. Surely the girl didn't mean what she was saying. She must have misunderstood her.

But Mary only laughed. "You look so surprised, Aimée. Did you think he didn't love me enough?"

"But your family—they wanted so much for you to be an empress."

Mary shook her head slowly. "No, I will not be empress,

and Rudolf will never be an emperor. But that doesn't matter. We will be with each other—forever and ever."

"Oh, *mon Dieu* . . ."

Aimée wanted to weep for the child. She was so young, so innocent. She couldn't know what she was doing. All she saw was the glamour of love, and she was ready to fling everything else aside. Not for a minute had she stopped to wonder what life would be like for a man who had been bred to be king and did not know anything else. Or how the world would treat the woman it condemned as his whore.

"How solemn you are, Aimée, and how sad. Come, I don't want you to be sad. Do you remember the raven that flew out at me the first time I went to Rudolf? I told you then that it meant death, but you said it symbolized eternal life. I think now we were both wrong. I think it was eternal love!"

Eternal love? Aimée could only wonder. She could already see Rudolf, balding and plump, growing a little more cynical with each passing year, drinking too much, gambling too heavily, flirting with ambitious young actresses because it had grown to be a habit and there was nothing else to do. And pretty Mary, her beauty painted on with layers of makeup, her hair grotesque with henna, trying desperately to pretend she was not afraid of growing old and undesirable. Could love survive a life like that?

"Be happy for me, Aimée," Mary whispered softly, reaching out to clasp her friend's hand one last time. "I am not afraid. Why should you be afraid for me?"

Aimée longed to hold her back, but she knew there was nothing she could do. And even if there were, she did not have the right. In the end, all she could do was kiss her and wish her well.

Mary would have an empty life, she thought as she sat alone, barely feeling the warmth of the fire in the grate. Empty, and in the end futile, but at least she would have tried. She would not grow old and sit in big cold rooms and know she had never dared.

The servant who appeared at the door was apologetic.

"I'm sorry to disturb you, madam. Count Gyori is here again. Shall I tell him you are not at home."

"Yes, yes," she said shortly, irritated at the interruption. "Tell him . . ."

She caught herself, breaking off abruptly. She did not want to see Egon Gyori, but she did not want to sit alone in that room either. Mary's visit had evoked too many disturbing thoughts.

"Tell him I will see him. Show him into the sitting room."

Sophie would be shocked, she knew, but she would understand when Aimée explained it all to her. After all, they could not have the man coming to the house day after day, creating an embarrassment for everyone. Sooner or later she would have to put him in his place. It might as well be now.

She was standing at the window, her back to the doorway, when Egon entered. He did not speak, but stood silently just inside the room, waiting for her to turn to him.

She took his breath away. The sunlight on the snow, reflected through panes of glass, gave a luminous glow to her features. In a plain afternoon dress, her hair knotted simply behind her head, she was even more beautiful than he had remembered. All the diamonds, all the elaborate gowns and fashionable hairdos, had only detracted from her perfection. He wanted her more than any woman he had ever known.

He did not try to appeal to her senses, as he had before. He took her hands, but held them lightly as he drew her toward him.

"You are very lovely."

Aimée was unprepared for her reaction to the man. She had remembered only arrogance and fire, dazzling wit underscored by brooding intensity. She had forgotten his charm, his warmth, his basic tenderness. He was glib, he was selfish, he was a scoundrel, but he did seem to have a genuine fondness for her, and fondness was a thing she needed now.

"You are very persistent, Count."

"Sometimes."

He raised her fingers to his lips. Aimée found the gesture disturbingly intimate. She had told herself, only a moment before, that she was using him, finding in him a diversion to offset the sadness of Mary's visit. But she had been lying to herself. She had agreed to see him for one reason, and one only. She wanted to.

"If I had an ounce of sense in my head, I would ask you to leave right now."

"But you will not."

But she had to, she knew. It was a dangerous game she was playing, a game she could not win. She dared not let it go on.

"You are so sure of me, then?"

Still she did not ask him to leave. Soon it would be too late.

"I always get what I want."

"And you want me?"

333

"I want you."

She remembered her words to Raoul: "It is not a good life, but it is the only life I have." *Her* life. Not the dream image Franz had of a perfect mother. Not a sad imitation of Sophie, a woman she could never hope to be. But her life, Aimée's, flawed and uncertain as it was.

"We are to be lovers, then?"

The count had expected her to play coy with him, angry one minute, teasing the next, promising, always promising, then taking it back again. Her directness left him speechless.

Aimée was suddenly lightheaded. It was good to feel free at last, to stop pretending all the things she could never be. She burst out in a gale of laughter.

"Come, Egon, I've never seen you at a loss for words before. Is this too much for you? Shall we call it off?"

"Never!" He drew her toward him, stopping only when her body was so close he could feel the warmth of it through his coat. "You are beautiful, and I am never going to let you go again. Come away with me—this very week. Friday."

"Come away with you?" Aimée was appalled. She had made her decision, but she had forgotten the implications. "What would I tell everyone?"

Now it was Egon who laughed. "Did you think I would take you here, in your cousin's house? Why, he would challenge me to a duel if I dared."

"Franz?" Aimée giggled in spite of herself. "I don't think Franz even knows how to shoot."

But he would, Aimée realized, sobering at the thought. If he thought her honor had been insulted, he would defend her, even if he died for it. Egon was right. They could hardly conduct an affair under her family's roof.

"But where . . . where would we go?"

He held her lightly in his arms. "To the Vienna Woods. I have a house there."

Aimée pulled back almost imperceptibly. "Where your family lives?"

Egon knew he had made a mistake. The thought of her own husband did not seem to bother her, and from what he had heard of the man, it was no wonder, but she did not like to think of his wife. He determined not to compound the error by trying to make light of it.

"My family is in Hungary," he reminded her gently. "But no, I am not taking you there. That would dishonor them . . . and you. I have a small lodge I use for . . ." He hesitated. He meant to be frank with her, but not too frank. "For hunting parties."

"And . . . other things?"

He smiled. She had caught him in his hypocritical prudishness easily enough.

"There have been other women there," he admitted. "Many women. You will be the last."

He had intended the words as simple gallantry. They became truth as soon as he uttered them. He had had enough of champagne suppers and coy games, of scheming little actresses and deceitful wives. Enough of lies whispered in dainty ears—and of lies that came back to him. He did not need that any longer. He would have a proud, passionate wife at home, a lusty mistress when he wanted. That would be enough.

"Will I?" she teased. "I wonder." It mattered little to her. She offered this man no claims on her life. She wanted none on his.

"Till Friday, then."

"Till Friday."

6

It was a brisk, windy afternoon, with heavy clouds hanging low in the sky. Mary Vetsera, muffled up in a warm winter coat, stepped out of the train at the Baden station. The ground was icy beneath her feet as she hurried toward a hackney coach.

Rudolf was waiting for her when she arrived at Mayerling. He had come to the hunting lodge the day before, stopping to spend a pleasant hour at a local inn when his carriage broke down on the way. Now he greeted his mistress warmly, teasing her with hints that he had not expected her to come.

Rudolf's hunting companions, Prince Philip of Coburg and Count Josef Hoyos, joined them for the evening. Dinner was a lively affair, with wine flowing freely and the sound of laughter echoing through the corridors until the party broke up at two o'clock. Mary was particularly radiant as she accompanied Rudolf to a simple sleeping chamber on the first floor.

Yet only a short time later, the girl was penning her last words to her mother: "Forgive me for what I do. I cannot resist my love . . . I am happier in death than in life."

Somewhere in the dark hours before the dawn, Rudolf took his mistress in his arms one last time. And Mary, who only a short time before had said she was not afraid, trembled as he made love to her. Then he placed a revolver against her left temple and pulled the trigger.

There was a second bullet in the gun. Rudolf had intended it for himself, but when the moment came, he hesitated. His dark thoughts were his own as he sat in silence beside the body of his beloved, waiting for the first gray light to show at the window.

At six-thirty, Johann Loschek, the same valet who had once shown Mary Vetsera through the back stairways of the Hofburg Palace, answered his master's summons. The man noticed nothing unusual as Rudolf, still in his dressing gown, appeared in the doorway, ordering breakfast for seven-thirty. Loschek recalled later that the prince was whistling softly.

When Loschek returned, there was no response to his knock. He tried the double doors but found they had been bolted from within. Still more puzzled than apprehensive, he put a tentative shoulder to the solid wood, trying to force it, but it did not bulge. He was already alarmed at eight o'clock when Count Hoyos arrived at the main lodge, but the two men, remembering that Mary was in the room, hesitated to act. It was another half-hour before Prince Philip arrived, giving the order to break down the door.

The men, knowing by now that something was seriously wrong, steeled themselves for the worst, but there was no way they could anticipate the grim sight that met their eyes. The young archduke, grotesque in a posture of death, hung over the side of the bed, his head dangling only inches above a pool of blood on the floor. The pillows and bedclothes were stained with a gaudy display of crimson. The nude body of Mary Vetsera was only half-visible beneath a pile of blankets.

The doctor was summoned, but there was little a doctor could do. The room was tidied, and the prince laid out on his bed as if he were asleep. It was a peaceful, almost tranquil scene. A silver crucifix rested on his breast, and tall candelabra stood on either side, as solemn priests and nuns, hastily summoned, chanted prayers for his soul. The body of Mary Vetsera, still nude, had been hidden in a musty storeroom, illuminated only by a single shaft of light from a high window. Gauzy cobwebs stretched across the corners.

Rumors of tragedy spread through the neighboring villages. A crowd gathered on the grounds, and gendarmes were summoned to cordon off the lodge. A policeman, armed with a drawn sword, stood at the door. Aristocrat and peasant alike mingled in the snow, speculating, questioning, still uncertain what had happened.

When at last the door opened, the crowd, tense with anticipation, surged forward. The gendarmes held them back as a long line of servants, clad in somber black, filed out of the lodge, their torches bright in the gray winter air. A hearse waited for them at the edge of the drive.

The coffin was narrow and black, a humble end for a man who had been born to arrogance. A hush fell over the crowd until the only sound that could be heard was the creaking of boots against the snow. Finally the silence was broken and the wheels of the hearse groaned their heavy dirge as the long journey to Vienna began. The Archduke Rudolf, Crown Prince of Austria and Hungary, was going home at last.

There were no ceremonies, no crowds, for Mary Vetsera. The two uncles who claimed her body came in stealth to the Mayerling lodge. It had been decided to keep the girl's part in the sordid affair a secret, not to protect her reputation or that of the Vetsera clan, but simply because an aging emperor could bear no further shame. Franz Josef had publicly admitted his son's suicide. He would admit no more. Mary's uncles were to dress her body, hiding head wounds beneath a veil, then hold her erect between them, walking her out of the lodge so the watching world would never guess she had died with the prince.

The wind was howling through the darkness when they finally reached the Heiligenkreuz monastery. Grim-faced monks, stiff and disapproving, gouged a hole in the frozen earth, providing a last resting place for the unholy suicide in hallowed ground. The uncles watched without a word. Then, silent as they had come, the two men who were Mary's only mourners departed. The grave was unmarked.

7

Sophie paused in the doorway, glancing into the small, dimly lit sitting room. Aimée had pulled a chair up to the ceramic stove in the corner. A soft down quilt, warm and thick, was wrapped around her shoulders, but she could not keep from shivering. She did not look up and see her cousin.

Turning aside, Sophie pulled the door shut, retreating into the chill of the hallway. Her heart grieved for Aimée, but there was nothing she could do. All she could offer was privacy for her pain.

Franz heard Sophie's footsteps as she descended the staircase. Slipping out of the library, he greeted her with a raised eyebrow.

Sophie could only shake her head. "Poor child. She's taken it very hard."

Franz's shoulders sagged with weariness. "I had not realized she was so close to the Vetsera girl. I knew she had befriended her, but . . ."

He hesitated, unable to explain his feelings. The girl's death had been a terrible thing, of course, but Aimée's reaction was all out of proportion.

Sophie put a hand on his arm to comfort him. She recognized the doubt in her brother's voice, and she understood it, but she could not help him. She had seen in Mary Vetsera, as she knew Franz had not, a kind of incubating passion, smoldering into open flames as it struggled to burst free. It was the same passion she had sensed in Aimée, and in her mother before her. Mary Vetsera had been a kind of kindred spirit, a pretty child with dreams and longings that touched the longings in Aimée's heart. Her death, especially by her own hand, had been a cruel shock.

"She has been so lonely," Sophie said slowly, trying to put her thoughts into words. "It is not good for a woman to be that lonely. And now this. . . ."

"I know," Franz agreed. "It was a ghastly thing. The way it happened . . ."

He shook his head, bewildered by it all. They had tried to hush it up, he had heard, but in the end, the mother had talked, and then the uncles, and bit by bit all the ugly pieces had come out. Now it was a favorite topic of gossip in every coffeehouse and salon in the city.

"I am worried about her," Sophie said gravely. "She feels things too much, that little one."

An hour later, Franz found himself in front of Aimée's door. The hallway was so silent he could hear his own heart beat. He hesitated, then pushed the door slowly open. It was the first time he had entered a woman's room without knocking.

Aimée still sat in the same chair beside the small white stove.

Franz felt helpless and inadequate. *She is so lonely*, Sophie had told him. She looked lonely now, huddled up with her quilt beside the stove, as if the room were not already unbearably hot. *It is not good for a woman to be that lonely.*

Was it his fault? he asked himself with unaccustomed bluntness. She had come to him once—he had never forgotten the moment—and he had denied her. He had thought she wanted another child, the one thing that would fulfill her as a woman. Now he wondered if he had oversimplified her emotions. She needed children, yes, but she needed more than that. She needed to feel cherished and protected, as if she belonged to a man, the way other women belonged to their men.

Aimée looked up and saw him watching her. She tried to smile, but it was a weak effort.

"I was thinking of Mary."

"I know." He crossed the room, kneeling beside her chair as he clasped her hand. His touch was the only warmth she had known since they brought her the news.

"She was so pretty . . . so full of life."

Aimée choked on the words, unable to go on. She had been in her room, laying dresses out on the bed, choosing a wardrobe for her tryst with Egon, when they had come to her, Franz and Sophie both. She had listened, tight-lipped and pale, to what they had to say. Then she had taken all the pretty dresses and hung them back in the closet.

She had not gone to Egon. She knew now she never would. Mary's death, with all its attendant pain, had put her own life—and its emptiness—into a new perspective.

Franz comforted her as best he could. "Yes, yes, of course she was pretty, but . . ." The words sounded false. He had never thought Mary was truly pretty. She was too vulgar, too obvious, too blatantly sensual. "But you musn't grieve so much."

"Oh, Franz, she said she wasn't afraid. That very day, when she came to say good-bye to me, she told me she wasn't afraid I should have known then. I should have realized. If only I had been thinking . . ."

All the words came back now. All the little clues she should have recognized right away. *I am going away, but I am not coming back. I don't want you to be sad.*

"Hush, *liebchen.*" Franz sat on the edge of the chair, drawing her into his arms. "You mustn't blame yourself. There was no way you could have known."

"But I should have. Oh, *mon Dieu,* I should have."

And if she had, what then? Would she have stopped the girl? he wondered. Would she have gone to her mother, sent

339

her uncles tearing after her to Mayerling? Or would she have stood aside, trembling with the agony of her own decision, and let the lovers choose their fate?

She remembered the vision of Mary she had had that last day. A foolish old woman, gaudy crimson lines painted where red lips used to be. A vain, aging courtesan, head tilted coyly as she danced and flirted, trying desperately to hold on to a man whose soul had dissipated long ago. She wondered if the lovers, too, had seen that same vision.

No, she would not have stopped the girl, she realized now. Life held few choices for Mary Vetsera, and none of them were happy ones. She had the right to her own destiny.

Pulling away from Franz, she leaned back in her chair. "It's all so futile, so meaningless."

Franz's heart ached as he listened to her. *She is so lonely. So lonely.*

And it was all because of him.

She had needed him, and he had turned away from her. And why? Because he was too prudish to understand a woman's heart.

He dropped his hand to her shoulder, caressing her lightly, tentatively through the sheer fabric of her robe. She raised her eyes to look at him. He answered the question she was afraid to ask.

"I failed you once. I will not fail you again."

"Oh, Franz."

She watched him silently for a moment, hesitant and unsure. Then at last she dared to raise her hands, resting them softly against his cheeks. She knew what he was saying to her, this dear friend she had loved so long, and she was grateful. She needed his comfort now. Slowly she drew his face toward hers.

His lips were cool, but she could feel them trembling. His hands tantalized her shoulders. Tonight, more than any other night, she needed the strength of a warm body enveloping hers through the long hours of darkness.

"Oh, my dear, I will love you," she whispered. "I will love you so much."

He lifted her up in his arms. "I would do anything for you, *liebchen*—anything."

She let herself relax in his embrace, clinging to his shoulders as he carried her into the adjoining bedroom. Slowly he lowered her to the bed. Too many nights, too many long, sleepless nights, she had lain alone in that same empty bed. Now she would lie alone no longer.

Franz's face was filled with tenderness as he bent over her. The lamplight caught the red of his hair. Single strands of white stood out against the color. Aimée had never noticed that Franz's hair was graying. Raoul had gray hair now, too, she thought. When he came to her, when he looked down at her, as Franz was looking now, his hair would be streaked with gray in the lamplight.

She pushed the thought aside. Raoul was not going to come to her. She would never see him again. She belonged to another man now. A man she had loved before she laid eyes on Raoul.

Franz left her side, stepping over to the lamp. Cupping his hand around the flame, he bent toward it.

"Please . . . leave the light on." She wanted to see him as he returned to her arms. She wanted a strong visual memory of their first moments together.

"Leave it on?"

She could see that she had shocked him. "Perhaps I am afraid of the dark," she teased.

"You don't have to be afraid of anything. I am with you now."

Gently he blew out the lamp.

He could barely see in the dim light that drifted through the half-closed door. She seemed so little to him, so frightened, lying in her pretty white robe on top of the coverlet. He felt a sudden urge to rip the thing from her, gazing at last at the body he had touched a thousand times in his dreams. Fighting his own impulse, he clenched his fists at his sides. She was already giving him enough as it was. He would not add to her humiliation by subjecting her to unbridled lust.

She seemed to sense his longing. She laid her own fingers on the laces of her robe, as if she would untie them for him.

"Oh, no, my love." He would not let her do that. "It is not necessary. Believe me, I do not ask this of you."

He took her hands in his, coaxing her away from her own generosity. Still holding them tightly, he pressed them against the bed as he eased his weight on top of her. His lips were soft on hers, telling her without words that he loved her and would be tender with her. He hated to take her with his clothes on, like a cheap whore in some second-rate bordello, but he did not want to frighten her with his nakedness.

Aimée could not understand his restraint. Frustrated, her body cried out for the passionate lovemaking she had come to expect. She longed to feel rough, impatient hands tearing away her clothes, caressing her, urging her own hands to explore him.

At last she could stand it no longer. She wanted him as a strong virile lover, not a tender suppliant. Clasping her arms around his neck, she drew his head downward and kissed him passionately.

Her efforts revolted him. Firmly he pushed her away. She was trying desperately to give him the things she thought he needed, even though it had to be sickening for her. What a beast that husband of hers must have been.

"It's all right, darling. It's all right. You don't have to do these things for me." Did she really think he required that of her? If only she knew. It was exciting just to be with her.

Aimée still did not understand. She only knew that whatever it was he wanted of her, it was not the same thing she wanted of him. What would he say now, she wondered, if she asked him to get up and slip away in the darkness, leaving her alone with her thoughts. But she could not bring herself to speak the words.

He was gentle as he entered her. He knew he had already destroyed her sense of dignity. He did not want to hurt her as well. Aimée lay still beneath him, as he had known she would, feeling the rhythmic motions of his body up and down inside her and wondering how it was possible to feel so untouched in her heart. It was all over in a minute.

Franz let his weight collapse on top of her. Spent and satisfied, he longed to pull her into his arms, holding her tightly against his body, touching her with a thousand tender kisses to tell her how grateful he was. He knew he could not. She had already been generous enough with him. With an effort he forced himself to rise, turning his back as he adjusted his clothes.

Aimée pulled her robe down, covering her thighs, as Franz stepped into the other room. It was all so pointless, she thought, so hideously, frighteningly pointless. She had been filled with a man tonight . . . and still she was empty.

She watched as he carried a small lamp into the room. He set it on the dresser before he moved back to the bed.

Aimée had thought it would be a shabby thing to take Egon Gyori as a lover. She realized now it was even shabbier with Franz. It was Raoul she wanted, and only Raoul. No one else could give the slightest meaning to her life.

Franz sat gingerly on the edge of the bed. He wished he knew more about women. Did she want him to stay with her now, holding her hand and soothing her, or would she be more comfortable if he left her?

He could think of only one thing to say. He did not try to touch her as he bent forward, whispering, "I love you."

Aimée turned her head away. She could not bear to see his face. There would be tenderness in his eyes, she knew—tenderness and quiet possessiveness—and it would break her heart. He was thinking she was his now, his mistress to cherish and enjoy. How could she find the words to tell him she would never lie with him again?

Her rejection hurt him deeply; he knew, in some way he could not even understand, that he had disappointed her. Or perhaps she had disappointed herself. All the pretty daydreams she had spun in her head, all that magic sweetness that was to have been hers when she lay in the arms of a man she loved. She could not believe this was all there was to it.

"It's all right, *liebchen*," he said softly. "Everything is going to be all right. I'll take care of you. And if there is a child—*when* there is a child—I'll take care of you both."

"A child?" Aimée glanced at him sharply. In all the longings that had racked her body, all the doubts and indecisions she had struggled with, she had never let herself dwell on that one thing. Now, suddenly, it was a very real possibility.

"I know how much you want another child."

"Of course I do. It would be heaven to hold a baby in my arms again. But I cannot, my dear—you know I cannot. Edward would be beside himself if he found out."

"Edward can do nothing to us. Except refuse to give you a divorce, and truly that does not matter, since we cannot be married in the eyes of the church anyway. We will be ostracized, of course, but we can endure that."

Aimée stared at him in amazement. How could he be so calm?

"But . . . Mariette." Didn't he understand? Edward was rich and powerful. Money could buy anything. "Oh, Franz, he . . . he could take Mariette away from me."

Franz looked at her with pity. He had appreciated the reality of the situation long ago. He had hoped she would not have to see it so soon.

"Perhaps it will not come to that. And if it does, that is the price you will have to pay to bear more children."

"How can you say that, Franz?" Aimée's fear began to mount. Edward wouldn't dare do that to her, she was sure he wouldn't. Still, if she made a public fool of him . . . "I

343

couldn't bear to be parted from Mariette. You know I . . ."

She stopped suddenly, realizing for the first time what she was saying. This was the excuse she had been looking for, if only she had had the sense to see it. This was the one way she could break off with Franz without hurting his feelings.

"*Mon Dieu*, what a fool I've been—but perhaps it is not too late. Surely I can't be pregnant yet. Oh, my dear, hard as it is to say, I . . . I fear we cannot do this again."

She was more transparent than she had hoped. The veins in Franz's temples throbbed with tension as he looked down at her.

She did not want him. He had disappointed her, and she did not want him anymore. It was not his fault. It was her own unrealistic hopes, but that did not make the pain any less.

She saw his hurt, and she was sick at heart. She had used him, trying desperately to assuage her own loneliness and pain, and she had failed. Who now would ease his suffering?

"I think it's best that I leave. Perhaps I could go back to Paris."

"No . . ." Franz could not let her do that. With Etienne ill and brooding again, the house in Paris would be a prison for her. "You could have the hunting lodge, if you want. You always liked it there. Or perhaps I should go, and you could stay here with Sophie. Yes, I think that would be best."

He was being generous, far more generous than she deserved, and she could not bear it. It would have been so much easier if he had slapped her and called her the whore she was.

"The hunting lodge is a good idea," she admitted. "But it would be easier to explain if I went. Sophie will understand why I want to be by myself. Besides, I think it would be good for me. I need some time alone to think things out."

He started to pat her hand clumsily, then pulled away. He felt awkward with this woman now, as he never had before.

"Do you want me to blow out the light?" he asked on his way to the door. It was inane, but he had to say something, and it was the only thing he could think of.

"No, leave it on." Aimée tried to force another quip about being afraid of the dark, but could not.

Franz paused in the doorway, turning to gaze at her one last time. She looked sad and very beautiful. He realized now what he had not been able to admit in the midst of all his hurt pride. He had gone to bed with her, not to give her the child she longed for, not because of the closeness she needed, but simply because he wanted her. He had brought out all the excuses, all the rationalizations, but in the end, he could not hide the truth from himself.

He had done the one thing he had promised himself he would never do. He had taken a woman he loved and made her an accommodation for his own lust. He was a complete blackguard, and he deserved everything he got. He had never felt so vile in his life.

Aimée could not sleep that night. She had seen the confusion and pain in Franz's face, and she knew he blamed himself for what had happened. Dear Franz, so good and selfless. No matter what she did, no matter how foully she behaved, he would always be ready to take the guilt on his own shoulders.

She had been so busy playing games with her own heart, she had not stopped to realize she might hurt the one man who had always been kind to her. Now it was done, and she could not erase the act—and she knew it was a thing she would have to live with for the rest of her life.

Yes, it would be good to go to the woods. The woods would be open and free and clean. There would be none of the taint of Vienna there. None of the garish, pretentious soirees. None of the ambitious social climbers, ready to sell their souls—or the souls of their daughters—for a moment's flirtation with greatness.

And none of the reminders of her own shame.

FIVE

I Am Thy Fate . . .

⦾ Meryt

"Tell me the story of the doomed prince and the crocodile."

Meryt looked up from her loom, smiling at the sound of her daughter's voice as it drifted through the open doorway. Teti-Sheri, barely three years old, knew she dared not disturb her mother at work, but that did not keep her from cornering everyone who happened to pass by.

"Not the story about the doomed prince and the dog?" a man replied. Meryt did not recognize his voice.

"No!" Teti-Sheri squealed. "The prince and the *crocodile*."

Meryt laughed aloud at her daughter's determination. The tale was the child's favorite, and she would tolerate no substitutions. The prince had been doomed to meet his fate at the hands of a dog or a snake or a crocodile, but Teti-Sheri was not the least bit interested in the first two creatures. Only the story of the crocodile appealed to her, and she could listen to it a dozen times a day, her eyes wide and rapt, as if she were hearing it for the first time.

"Not the doomed prince and the snake?" The man's voice was low and teasing. Meryt still could not place it.

"No, no, no!" Teti-Sheri had heard all the ploys before, and she was tired of them.

"Well, then, the story of the prince and the crocodile," the man conceded, laughing good-naturedly. "One day, the prince went out for a walk, and he took his dog with him."

"The dog he had raised from a puppy." Teti-Sheri knew the story by heart. She was not going to let him get away with anything.

"Yes, yes, the dog he had raised from a puppy. But then suddenly, almost before the prince knew what was happening, the dog turned on him and tried to take a bite out of him. 'I am thy fate!' the dog cried." The man shouted out the words of the dog's threat, imitating them so ferociously the child shrieked with laughter. "So the prince turned and fled, running into the water to escape him."

348

Meryt's hands were idle, resting on her weaving as she listened to the tale she had heard a thousand times before. Something in the man's voice made her uneasy. She was certain now he was a stranger. It was a long time since a stranger had wandered into their half-deserted village.

The thought made her nervous, though she knew she was being unreasonable. At least half a dozen strangers had passed through the necropolis in the year they had lived there, and not a one of them posed the slightest threat to their security. Surely, by now, Meryt reminded herself, irritated by the rapid fluttering of her heart, she should have been able to feel safe in their new home.

And it was a home, she told herself, smiling a little as she forced her fingers back to her weaving. She had been frightened of the place at first, but she had to admit Senmut was right. The necropolis was as much a city of the living as the dead. The workers who tended the tombs—the artists and goldsmiths and weavers, the carpenters and jewelers, even the *ka* priests and the white-robed priests of Amon—were a remarkably friendly, fun-loving lot. Their beer was as pungent as the beer brewed in royal households and their wine as sweet, and even the musicians of the pharaoh could not rival the haunting loveliness of their melodies.

If times had been hard since the capital was moved upriver to Akhet-Aten, the dwellers of the necropolis did not show it. Opening their homes and hearts to the refugees from across the river, they willingly shared everything they had. The newcomers found it easy to fit in. Cautiously submerging his own identity, Senmut became Khai, the scribe who inked hieroglyphs on the walls of tombs, and Meryt, as Teti, his wife, learned to weave, creating sheer lengths of linen to be embroidered later by more skillful fingers.

"Then the crocodile said to the prince, 'I am thy fate that has been pursuing thee!' And the prince was frightened, but there was no place he could run. 'But, lo,' the crocodile said to him, 'for these three months past I have been battling a water demon that has kept me prisoner. If you would have me to spare your life, you must help me kill him.' "

Meryt gave up trying to work. The stranger's voice was too distracting. Smiling a little at her fears, she rose and went to the door. The sun was bright as she stepped outside.

The man looked up instantly, rising from the dusty earth where he had been seated next to a laughing Teti-Sheri. He was older than his voice had sounded. His deeply lined face had a sensitive quality, and his thinning hair had turned nearly white. His eyes were filled with undisguised admiration as he stared at Meryt.

The child glanced up at her mother, her full lips forming a tentative pout at the unwelcome interruption. Then, seeing that Meryt was paying no attention to her, she turned to her favorite toy, a carved wooden lion, lying neglected in the dust beside her.

Meryt greeted the man. In the bright sunlight that caressed the deep creases of his face, her fears suddenly seemed foolish and unfounded.

"I am Teti the weaver." Her lips formed easily around the false name. "This is little Teti, Teti-Sheri. I hope she hasn't been pestering you too badly."

"On the contrary," the man assured her, his tone warm and sincere. "She is a charming child—a delight to talk to. But actually, I was waiting to see you. Teti-Sheri told me you could not be disturbed while you were working."

"To see me?" Meryt tried to keep her voice steady, but there was a tremor in its depths. "Did you want something woven? I am far from the most skilled weaver here."

Her nervousness made him uncomfortable. "No, no, let me assure you . . ."

He broke off awkwardly, turning to stare at the tall, bronzed figure approaching them. Following his gaze, Meryt was relieved to see Senmut hurrying down the walk.

"My husband, Khai," she said with forced brightness, laughing as she extended her hand. "This man has come to see me, my dear. My fame as a weaver seems to be spreading. Perhaps I am improving faster than I thought."

The stranger joined in her laughter. "No, lovely lady, I promise you. Though I have no doubt your weaving is as exquisite as your face, I have no intention of imposing on you. I was drawn here only by tales of your beauty."

"My beauty?" Meryt raised her hand, running it lightly along her cheek. It had been a long time since she had thought of herself as beautiful. The idea was strangely threatening now.

"Where did you hear of my wife's beauty?" Senmut could not keep a sharp edge out of his voice.

The man realized he had said something wrong. He took an awkward step backward before he continued.

"I am only a poor artist, Opi by name, assistant to the great Bek at the pharaoh's court. For many months we have heard tales of a beautiful weaver in the old city of the dead.

Her loveliness, they say, outshines the stars, and her blue eyes put the midnight sky to shame."

Meryt drew in a deep breath, fighting the sickening faintness that swept over her. If this man had heard of her—this man who lived in her uncle's court—how long would it be before the news reached the ears of Akhenaten himself? How long would it be before the pharaoh learned that her infidelities had once again made a laughingstock of him?

Teti-Sheri looked up, her eyes wide and solemn at the turn the conversation had taken. The toy lion slipped unnoticed from her fingers.

"My eyes are blue, too."

"Why, so they are," the man retorted kindly. "Do you know how rare that is? Usually only princesses have blue eyes. Foreign princesses from lands far away."

"Really?" The idea seemed to appeal to her. "Are we princesses, Mama? Are we?"

No! Meryt wanted to shriek, crying out the false denial with all the pain and terror in her heart. It was all she could do to hold herself back. Realizing how suspicious her panic must look to the stranger, she tried to turn the whole thing into a joke.

"Of course we are," she teased. "We are captive princesses from far away. One day perhaps we will be rescued, and tall ships will bring us back to our own land. Then we will sit on golden thrones and wear rich robes and splendid jewels."

Senmut laughed at her words, as if he were genuinely amused by the fantasy she was spinning for their daughter. Only the tension in his voice gave him away.

"As you can see, my wife is not a princess, only a humble weaver. I cannot imagine why you have sought her out."

"I am an artist, sir. Beauty is my business, my trade in life. What does an artist have to do with princesses, or care to?"

Meryt shivered at the emphasis of his words. They were too pointed, too obvious. She had the uncomfortable feeling he had guessed her secret and was trying to tell her she had nothing to fear from him.

"But I don't understand," she said softly. "I mean, what do you want from me?"

"I am an old man." His voice was low and quiet. "There is so little beauty in the court, so little to appeal to the soul of an artist. If I might be permitted to paint you, perhaps to fashion a small bust, it would brighten my days greatly. I have come a long way to ask nothing else of you."

For a minute Meryt could only gape at him. Then slowly she shook her head.

"I am sorry, but I cannot—"

Senmut interrupted her. "What harm would it do, little one?" His voice was deceptively casual. He did not even seem to notice the artist Opi as he scrambled for his tools.

"But Sen . . ." How hard it was to remember that strange name. "But, Khai, don't you think—?"

"Let the man make his sketches if it will please him." There was a quiet finality in his voice that warned her not to argue further. Taking her arm, he led her away, seating her on a low brick wall that lined the narrow street. He bent over as he took his place behind her, making sure their heads were only inches apart.

"Are you mad, Senmut?" she hissed, careful to keep the words low. "What if those pictures get back to court?"

If Opi noticed the intensity of their conversation, he paid little heed. Pulling out his ink and brushes, he began to make quick, deft strokes on a handful of broken pottery shards. He worked swiftly, as if he were afraid they might change their minds at any minute.

"What difference does it make?" Senmut replied coolly. "A picture or a description, it's all the same thing. They have already heard of a woman with dark blue eyes living with a man who claims to be her husband. How long do you think it will be before everyone guesses the truth?"

The logic of it was indisputable. Turning her head, Meryt let her eyes linger on the long, low valley and the mountains beyond. The mud-brick huts of the town faded into the sand of the desert, providing a golden-ocher background for dark shapes moving slowly through hot midday streets. It surprised her to realize how deeply she had grown to love this place.

"Then we must leave."

Silently Senmut nodded.

"Tonight?" She bit her lip to keep from crying. She knew she was being unreasonable. Wherever they went, whatever happened to them, at least they would be together. As long as she had that, she had no right to complain.

Senmut did not fail to see her pain. Ignoring the curious eyes of the artist, he drew her into his arms. His lips were comforting against her cheek.

"It won't be like the last time," he promised. "We'll have a few days to plan—to pack the things we need. We can't take much, only what I can carry on my back, but at least we won't have to steal out into the night with nothing but a blanket and a wooden lion."

Meryt forced a weak smile to her lips as she fought back her tears. Whatever lay ahead would be hard enough as it was. She would only make it worse by weeping now.

Twilight brought only uneasiness. Meryt stood in the doorway of their small house, watching as the late-afternoon shadows faded slowly into darkness. One by one the outlines of the surrounding buildings evaporated into a heavy veil of black, until only the closest were visible. Soon they, too, would disappear from sight. She had the eerie feeling that she would never see them again.

Turning at last from the darkness, she began to make her way into the house. Only at the last moment, only when she was nearly ready to step into the room, did she catch a movement out of the corner of her eye. Turning back, she saw two figures making their way up the path that led to the house.

"Senmut . . ."

She could not keep the apprehension from her voice. Even the child, playing quietly with her lion on the floor, heard it. Her small blue eyes were puzzled as she watched her father hurry toward the door.

Senmut's arm was tight around Meryt's waist as he stood beside her, waiting for the men to move closer so he could make out their features. When they did, he stepped forward to greet them. Even in the dim light Meryt could see that his face was drawn and tense.

"Paneb. Iry. What brings you here?"

One of the men, the older of the pair, turned to Meryt briefly, giving her a quick nod of acknowledgment. His face was as grim as Senmut's.

Abruptly, as if he had just remembered she was there, Senmut faced her.

"Go in to the child."

Meryt opened her lips to protest, but the words died away before she could form them. This was no time to quarrel, no time to weaken their sense of unity, especially in front of strangers. She slipped into the house.

The room was cool and lonely as she stood in the center of the floor, waiting for Senmut to return. The child was absorbed in a low, giggling dialogue with her lion. Not another sound broke the silence that drifted through the open door and windows.

It was only a few minutes before Senmut reappeared, but

the time seemed an eternity to Meryt. The instant she saw him, her heart sank with despair. His face was devoid of color, his lips set.

"The older man is Paneb," he told her. "A good man from a farming village up the river. The younger is his nephew Iry. They will take you and the child home with them. Paneb's sister will make you welcome."

You and the child.

Meryt heard the words only dimly, as if they did not apply to her. She was conscious that there was a question she needed to ask, an important question that must not go unspoken, but she could not bring herself to form the words, even in her mind.

Senmut could not hide his own pain. "I promised you more than a blanket and a lion. It seems I was wrong."

At last, even the child picked up the tension. Dropping her toy, she looked up at him.

"Father . . .?" Her voice was low and quizzical.

Senmut hesitated for a moment, unable to bear the bewilderment in his daughter's eyes. Then, squaring his shoulders with a determination he dared not lose, he snatched up a heavy woolen blanket lying on a table in the corner. Dropping to his knees, he threw it over Teti-Sheri's shoulders, wrapping her securely in it. His arms were strong and possessive as he held her. Then reluctantly he forced himself to pull away.

"We are going on a trip, little one." He was careful to keep his voice cool, deliberately soothing. "It's a long, cold trip, so you will need the blanket to keep you warm. You must be very grown-up and very brave and help your mama so she won't be afraid."

Meryt's heart caught in her throat as she stood in the center of the room staring down at them.

"Aren't you coming with us?"

At last, the question she had been afraid to ask, on her child's lips rather than her own. She did not breathe as she awaited his reply.

"Not right away. I have to go ahead and prepare things for you. But I'll come soon, you know that. I would never leave you alone for long."

Gently, with a tenderness that tore at Meryt's heart, he lifted the child in his arms, pausing only long enough to let her clutch her lion with anxious fingers. A shadow filled the doorway, marking the bulky presence of a man on the threshold. Moving quickly, as if he were afraid he might change his mind, Senmut hurried toward him.

"You must go with Paneb now, Teti-Sheri. That's a good girl. See, Paneb has big, strong arms, just like mine. He will take good care of my little dove."

The little girl's eyes were wide and frightened as she relinquished her hold on her father's neck, but she did not protest. Paneb tightened his arms around her, then slipped tactfully back into the night, allowing Senmut a moment of privacy with the woman he loved.

Senmut stood quietly in the doorway, staring out at the darkness. It was a moment before he could bring himself to turn. When he did, Meryt's eyes were glistening with unshed tears.

She had never looked so lovely to him. He could still remember as if it were only yesterday, his first vision of her, a dazzling little child of thirteen, exotic and exquisitely beautiful. She was even more beautiful now that she was a woman. He did not regret a moment of loving her.

He had always known that one day he must pay for his passion with his life. He had never been afraid before. He was not going to begin now.

"We have less time than we thought," he told her quietly. He did not try to play games with her. His last words to his child had been a lie. He would not part that way from Meryt. "Columns of soldiers are approaching the village. They will be here within an hour."

"Oh, Isis, help us. What . . . what can we do?"

"We have only one hope. If I can trick them, if I can lead them in a false direction, there might still be time to escape."

Meryt stared at him, her eyes clouded with bewilderment. Taking a deep breath, Senmut forced himself to continue. He knew that what he had to say would hurt her more, but there was no way he could avoid it.

"I will have to show myself to them. If they see me, if they follow me, it will give you and the child a chance to flee."

At last she understood. "But you—what will happen to you? How will you get away?"

How could he answer her? How could he tell her that he did not expect to get away? That in a perverse way he did not even want to? The pride of the pharaoh could only be assuaged with blood. Let him be satisfied then with the death of the lover, leaving the woman and child alone.

He forced a teasing tone into his voice. "Still frightened, little one? You don't have enough faith in me. I am young, and I am quick. Without you and the child to slow me down, I will elude them easily."

"No!"

She could not let him go, not now. They had gone through too much together. How could she leave him to face the danger alone?

"You must find the courage. If not for yourself, then for the child. The child is our love—my love for you. She must have a chance to live."

Senmut saw her pain and he knew he had won. It was a victory that had no taste of sweetness. Turning away from her, he slipped into the darkness. He knew she would follow.

The night air had never seemed so black to Meryt, so heavy and impenetrable. She could barely see the faces of the two strangers, though they were no more than a few paces away. Glancing upward, she stared at the slender, useless crescent of silver high in the sky. She wanted to weep at the sight of it. Darkness, she knew, would only make her lover's mission more dangerous. Before he could lure the soldiers away, he would have to draw near enough to show himself in the glow of their torches.

The streets that had once seemed so familiar were alien and frightening in the dark. Meryt groped along the walls that lined the narrow lanes. She longed for the comforting strength of Senmut's hand in hers, but he had taken the child again and was moving surefootedly ahead of her. She was tempted to call out to him, begging him to help her, but she forced the words back in her throat. It was important for him, desperately important, to carry the child in his arms one last time.

The buildings stopped abruptly, dropping away into a sudden pit of inky darkness. Terrified, Meryt realized they had reached the edge of town, and with it, the edge of everything known and familiar to her. She had the illusion that she was a blind beggar groping her way through open hills and ever-steepening paths with no one to help her, nothing to guide her way.

And then suddenly it was over. Suddenly the men ahead of her stopped, pausing to let her catch up with them. At first, resting beside them, catching her breath, Meryt felt only a deep relief, as if somehow, with the comforting presence of the men, so close she could see their outlines again, she could make herself believe the worst of the ordeal was over. It was only after a moment that her frightened mind began to grasp the truth. The sickening terror increased as she turned to face her lover again.

Already he was handing the child into Paneb's keeping. Meryt's heart caught in her throat as she watched him. The moment of parting had come at last.

Senmut's eyes shone not with fear, but pain, as he turned to gaze at her in the faint moonlight that touched the mountain path. He had not realized how hard it would be to part from her. Death lay ahead of him in the valley below, but it was not death that rested on his heart at that moment. All he could think of, all he could feel, was the loneliness of an eternity spent without even a glimpse of her beauty.

How could he say good-bye to her? he asked himself with despair. How could he find the words? His love for her was a potent, tangible force, running so deep it was a physical presence, as much a part of him as his heart or his body. How could a man be expected to end a passion like that in a few tidy words of parting?

At last he did the only thing he could. He took her hand in his, clasping it tightly for one brief moment. He let his fingers speak for his lips, filling that single gesture with all the tenderness in his heart. Then, releasing the love that had dominated his life, he let his fingers ease away from hers. Turning at last, he slipped into the darkness.

Meryt could only watch helplessly as her lover disappeared one last time into the void that swallowed up the earth. Tears of protest sprang to her eyes, but they were tears she could not shed, just as she could not allow her lips to open, crying out in her weakness for him to come back to her. There were so many things she wanted to say to him, so many words of love and longing and gratitude. So many things and so little time. Images of golden afternoons floated through her memory, long, lazy afternoons on the shores of the lake behind the old palace or drifting idly through papyrus swamps, afternoons when they had been content with the languor and the silence, knowing there would always be tomorrow and yet another tomorrow for all the things they wanted to say to each other. But now, the last tomorrow had come, and still the words were unspoken.

She whirled at the touch of a hand on her arm. Iry's tense features, only inches from her own, reflected his pity.

But why should he pity her? she asked herself. Senmut was strong, and he was clever. He had a chance to outwit the soldiers—a good chance. It was not time for pity yet.

"We must hurry." Even his voice was heavy with pity. Meryt hated the sound.

She could not force her feet to move. She did not know if she would ever move again; she belonged here, in this place where she had last known the touch of her lover's hand. She could not leave it now.

"Mama . . ."

The cry was soft and low, barely carrying on the cool night wind. Slowly, instinctively, Meryt turned her head.

The child is our love—my love for you.

But it hurt. Oh, how it hurt to leave him behind.

The child must have a chance to live.

At last she moved, slipping quickly to her daughter's side. Gently she laid her fingers on silken curls. The little head was trembling as she cradled it in her hands.

"Shhh, little dove," she murmured, bending down to kiss away tears on baby cheeks. "It's all right. Father has just gone away for a little while. Be a good girl, good and brave, and he will come back soon."

Teti-Sheri's eyes were wary, hesitant, but she did not cry out again. Her knuckles were white as she gripped the toy lion in her fingers.

The path was eerily silent as they pushed forward. Only the shrill cries of the jackals, howling their lust for carrion in the distant reaches of the desert, mingled with the sound of their own breathing. The rest of the world was deathly still.

Meryt did not know when she first became aware that the silence had been broken. She only knew that somewhere in her consciousness a new sound had penetrated, a sound more chilling and ominous than any she had ever heard. An ugly sound, penetrating, bizarrely unreal.

At first she thought it was the cry of a man, low and hoarse, mingling with the wails of the jackals. But then she realized it was a series of cries, echoing and blending with each other, as if they had been deliberately orchestrated, forming in the end a single entity, a sound more animal than human.

The soldiers.

The soldiers were in the valley below, their ranks swelling out until they filled it from mountain to river. And they were close—so close she could hear their voices.

Meryt's feet grew heavy beneath her, pulling her slowly to a stop, as if they did not have the strength to carry her farther. Her body was trembling violently, whether from fear or exhaustion, she did not know. Ahead of her, Iry paused, then turned back, stepping swiftly to her side.

They had already climbed high, she knew. So high that if she turned she would be able to see into the valley below. The temptation was as compelling as it was frightening.

Even in the darkness, Iry seemed to read her thoughts.

"Don't turn around."

He was right. Meryt knew the act could only cause her pain, but she could not help herself. Senmut was down there somewhere, submerged in that jungle of animal sounds. She could not walk away from him.

She turned her head.

She could not believe the sight that met her eyes. It was a nightmare, a dark, hideous dream that could not possibly be real.

There on the valley floor, stretching out so far she could barely see the end, was a long line of flickering lights, already beginning to fan out in a methodical pattern of search. There must have been hundreds of them. Her uncle had sent a whole army. A king's army to subdue one small runaway wife and the scribe who was her lover.

At last, without thinking, without even putting her fears into words, Meryt understood. For the first time since she had begun her ill-fated affair with Senmut, the image of death was a tangible presence in her heart.

Quietly, with a weariness new to her, she forced her eyes from the valley floor, turning instead toward the dark, rocky path, searching for the kindly peasant who held her child in his arms. A stab of panic cut through her when she realized he had moved too far ahead to see. Pushing past the startled Iry, she stumbled after him.

There was nothing she could do for Senmut. No way she could help him or even share his pain. All she could do was go on. All she could do was make sure the child was safe.

The path grew steeper, climbing up into the hills at a sharp, terrifying angle. Meryt felt like an animal, half-lunging, half-crawling into the darkness, clawing and clutching with her fingers at the rocks and sand, trying desperately to keep from sliding back again. Tensely she strained her ears, searching for the sound of footsteps that would tell her she was close to her child at last.

But there was nothing. Only the harsh scratching of her own feet against the stony path. Not a trace of Paneb ahead of her, not even an echo of Iry, moving up stealthily behind. She might as well have been alone, blindly, helplessly groping toward the illusion of security that always lay just beyond her reach.

Pain shot through her ankle as she slipped on loose rocks she could not even see in the darkness. She bit her lip to keep from crying out in pain, terrified that her voice might drift downward, sounding as loud and bold to the soldiers' ears as their ominous shouts and cries did to hers. She had to get away from them, she had to, she and the child both. That was what Senmut wanted. That was what he had risked his life for. She could not let his sacrifice be in vain.

If only she could see Paneb. If only she knew her child was still safe in his arms, perhaps she would not be so afraid.

The sounds that echoed up from the valley began to change, growing more forceful, tinged with an animation and excitement she could almost see through the darkness. One minute they had been random, confused, more chaotic than coherent; the next minute they were fused into a single, reverberating clap of thunder, growing and intensifying to deafening power.

Terrified, she stopped to listen. Even before she turned her head, she knew what she would see.

The flickering torchlights dotting the valley had changed as dramatically as the sounds that accompanied them, centralizing into a forceful pattern. Meryt almost cried out with fear as she looked down on them. Already the golden flares had formed into a sweeping arc, cutting through the marshland and opening out to the river beyond. Almost immediately the semicircle began to tighten, drawing slowly, surely toward a single space in the center.

They had seen him. Meryt stood silent, immobile, not daring to breathe. They had seen her lover, and they were closing in on him.

But that was what he wanted, she told herself, trying to calm the rapid beating of her heart. That was what he had planned. He knew what he was doing.

He could still escape. She was a fool to feel so frightened, so despairing. Senmut was bolder than her uncle's soldiers, and cleverer. They thought they had him on the run, working him into a snare of their own making, while in reality it was he who was maneuvering them, leading them into the trap he himself had set. If his luck held out, he might still outwit them.

If only there were not so many of them. Her blood ran cold at the thought. If only there were not so many.

"Run, Senmut!" she whispered. "Run!"

But she knew he was running already, running like the cornered animal he was. He was leading them deeper and deeper into the marshes, twisting with the shrewdness of a hunted beast, evading the sharp tips of their spears.

And then, terrifyingly, incredibly, the cries of pursuit seemed to explode, shattering the air like the savage roar of an enraged lion. Meryt did not for an instant mistake the bestial excitement in that collective cry of triumph. She had lived with the threat of death too long to fail to recognize it now. Silently, still not moving, she stared down, hypnotized by the circle of light as it formed into a small, tight ring. The tears that glistened on her lashes gave the torches a blurred, softened quality, melting them into a single shimmering halo.

It was only a moment before the savage violence peaked at last, leaving the brutish shouts to die away, evaporating until they were nothing more than a series of staccato bursts like the grunting of a satisfied animal finished with its prey. Meryt twisted with agony at the sound. Helplessly she sank to her knees. She did not feel the razor-sharp rocks as they scarred into her flesh.

Seven days I have not seen my sister . . .

The remembered sweetness of the lyre was incongruous and bitter amidst the dying sounds of slaughter. Meryt thought her heart would break as the melody echoed, haunting and illusory, in her ears.

Seven days she would not see the beloved brother who had been so good to her. Seven days and seven—and seven yet again. Her uncle's soldiers were brutal and efficient. There would not be a scrap of flesh left whole, a single bone unbroken. Nothing for the priests to dress and protect, no trace of a physical essence to be guided by the *ka* through the hazardous journeys of the underworld. She would not see Senmut again, not in this life, nor in the long, dark life that followed. Seven times eternity she would not see her brother. The love that ended today had died forever.

"The child." Iry's hand was impatient on her arm. "We endanger the child if we linger."

Meryt shook her head. She understood now what Senmut had known from the beginning. The soldiers, already dispersing, would not follow them into the hills. Their blood lust had been satisfied. They had killed the lover of the young queen. Their orders went no further than that.

Senmut had won the gamble he had chosen for himself. He had won, but Meryt had lost. In his victory, she had given up the happiness that should have been hers for eternity.

She was barely conscious of her body as she finally rose, slipping past the worried Iry to work her way up the path to the spot where Paneb had stopped, his eyes mesmerized by the lights in the valley. Her arms were surprisingly steady as the baby's weight was transferred to her own embrace. She could feel her trembling through the thickness of the blanket.

"It's all right, little one," she soothed, listening with a detached awe to the sound of her own voice, so cool and controlled now that it was over at last, now that there was nothing to hope for, nothing to pray for. Her feet were sure and confident as she moved sightlessly up the path. "Shall I tell you about the doomed prince and the crocodile?"

But this time her favorite story was not enough to divert the frightened child. Even in the dim light, Meryt could see her eyes wide and glowing with tears. Forcing laughter into her voice, she bounced Teti-Sheri up and down in her arms.

"What did the crocodile say to the prince when he caught him?" she teased. "Do you remember?"

Still the child was silent.

"Come on, you remember. The crocodile caught the prince when he fled into the water, and he said, 'I am thy fate that has been pursuing thee.'"

Her voice broke as she lowered it, trying to make it sound deep and menacing like the crocodile.

I am thy fate that has been pursuing thee.

She had always been afraid of crocodiles. Even when she was a little girl, she had been afraid. Dark, fearsome creatures lingering in murky depths beneath the surface of the water. Stern, forbidding gods of all the lost, unseen eternities.

And the crocodile had won that day. The prince had met his doom.

"You don't tell it right." The child's voice broke sharply into her thoughts. "You don't sound like the crocodile. I want Father to tell me the story."

For an instant, Meryt thought her heart would break. She stumbled awkwardly, barely catching herself as she struggled to keep from falling to her knees again. Her arms gripped the child.

"He will come soon." The words were a strangled whisper, but Teti-Sheri did not notice. "Maybe tomorrow, maybe the next day. But soon . . . soon."

To her relief, the child seemed to believe her. Gently Meryt eased the little head down on her shoulder.

How long would it be, she wondered, before Teti-Sheri

stopped asking when her father was coming back? How long before she realized she would never see him again?

And would it hurt her then, or would her young heart already have begun to forget?

The child was warm and still in her arms. Meryt closed her embrace around her. Teti-Sheri was all she had left of a man who had been both her happiness and her hope. All she had of a love that was more beautiful than the sun and the stars and the sweet, cool touch of the North Wind.

But she was the best of that love, Meryt reminded herself slowly. She was everything that was good and pure in their lives. As long as she could be saved, it would all have been worthwhile.

Meryt turned for one last glance into the valley. The torches were going out one by one, vanishing silently and invisibly in the darkness that stretched out into eternity. Nothing was left of the brutality and carnage, no hint of the ugliness of man to mar the starlit world that belonged to the gods alone. Her eyes were clear and tearless as she turned away, daring to move forward at last.

∞ Aimée

1

"Hah! The devil is no match for a mother-in-law."

Mohammed threw an amused glance at his wife as she darted back to the kitchen, answering shrill complaints that poured out from behind a plastered wall. She moved quickly, but not quickly enough to satisfy the strident voice.

"Two generations of women under the same roof?" Raoul raised a quizzical brow. "Is that wise?"

"Three." Mohammed nodded proudly toward the wives of his two oldest sons. "But Saadia is used to my mother after all these years. That's an old saying I just told you—the devil is no match for a mother-in-law. I sometimes think women stay up late at night figuring out ways to live up to it."

The harried Saadia reappeared in the doorway, a heavy platter steaming in her hands. In deference to her husband's wishes, she had served the dinner herself instead of sending a trusted servant from the kitchen, but Raoul could see she was uncomfortable in his presence. A dark veil hid her features, and the few quick glances that came his way were shy and nervous.

Mohammed's two daughters-in-law, both named Laila, seemed more at ease in front of him. Salem's Laila, still childless, though she had been married over a year, sat quietly in a corner of the room, churning cream into butter as she listened idly to the men's conversation. Although she still wore a veil, she had pulled it down beneath her chin, letting it form a decorative bib against drab Arab robes. A bulky goatskin swung rhythmically between the legs of a bamboo tripod braced sturdily on the floor beside her. Callused fingers reached out with infinite patience, pushing the primitive container back and forth, back and forth again, as the cream solidified slowly into butter.

Daoud's Laila, bolder than her sister-in-law, discarded her own veil as she played with the younger of her two sons, tempting him with a choice piece of sugarcane. She laughed with obvious pride when the boy smacked plump lips around it.

"That's a fine grandson you have," Raoul remarked politely. "You must be very proud of him."

Daoud and Salem burst out laughing. Puzzled, Raoul looked from one to another, then back to Mohammed, trying to figure out what he had said. Hassan was not with them. As the youngest son, and the only one still unmarried, he had been excused from the family gathering to supervise the guards at the dig.

"Don't let my mother hear you say that," Mohammed warned. "She and Laila are always quarreling about that very thing. Laila loves to show her boys off, brushing their hair until it shines and dressing them in pretty clothes. If my mother had her way, they would run around in rags so the evil jinns would not see them and be jealous."

Raoul shook his head ruefully. He had forgotten how threatening the simplest compliment could be to an Egyptian parent. "I must apologize. I'm afraid I didn't stop to think that even a modern man could still harbor ancient beliefs in his home."

"Beliefs? Bah, superstitions, my friend—and we both know it. But they are only for my mother, and perhaps my wife, too, though she wouldn't dare admit it in front of me. Myself, I don't believe in the jinns—and if I refuse to whistle after dark, well, perhaps that is for my own amusement. Though sometimes, mind you, when no one is around, I do catch myself whispering, 'With your permission, blessed ones,' when I go out at night, so the spirits will hear me and get out of my way. It wouldn't do to step on one by accident."

Raoul laughed as hard as Mohammed's sons. "I suppose I have been known to steer clear of a black cat myself," he admitted. "Not that I believe in it, of course."

"Of course, of course—no more do we. Old habits are hard to break. But come, you've hardly eaten anything at all. Is the food not well prepared? Is it not to your taste?"

"The food is excellent, and you know it. I've already had more than I should."

The meal had been superb. Thick soup, pungent with Eastern spices, filled a single large tureen, into which each man had dipped his own coarse wooden spoon. Round, flat loaves of peasant bread, fresh from the oven, formed scoops for dishes of pickled turnips and sharp, salty cheese. Mutton, richly seasoned with onion, garlic, and green peppercorns, was an exotic contrast to the raw carrots and tomatoes and cucumbers. To Raoul, used to dipping a fork into tins of cold food as he worked, it was nothing short of a feast. He had already loosened his belt twice, but he knew Mohammed would be insulted if he did not at least sample the small roasted chicken Saadia had just carried in.

Mohammed tore off a piece of the succulent flesh with his own hand, offering it to his guest. He nodded approval as Raoul, careful to let only his right hand touch the food, took it from him. To an Egyptian, steeped in the traditions of the past, the distinction between the right hand and the left was an important one. A man would be as appalled to see another eat with his left hand as he would be to have it extended in greeting. The guardian angel of the Copts, the Egyptian Christians, always sat at their right hand. While the Muslims allowed themselves two such spirits, it was the one on the right who recorded their good deeds, the one on the left their bad deeds.

It was nearly an hour before Mohammed, agreeing at last that Raoul had done sufficient honor to the pastries, layered with sesame and honey, and the sweet melon and tender white grapes, beckoned to his daughter-in-law. Laila rose from her churn, moving toward the kitchen. When she returned, she carried a pitcher of warm water.

Holding the vessel high, Laila tilted it, letting the water spill into a shallow basin on the floor. Like the ancients, modern Egyptians found it repugnant to wash in stagnant water. Raoul, conscious of the custom, kept his hands well above the basin as he held them in the steady stream, rinsing away the grease of the meal. When he had finished, he wiped his hands on the large white serviette Saadia held out to him.

The minutes that followed were pleasant ones. Leaning his elbow against the carpet, Raoul stretched stocking feet out in front of him as he watched the women clear away the meal. It was good to sit on the floor, relaxing among friends, with none of the furnishings and utensils and pretensions that dominated the Western world.

Most of the homes on the west bank of the Nile were nowhere as inviting. A majority of the dwellings were nothing more than reconverted tombs, with mud-brick partitions separating families from cows and camels, sheep and goats and dogs. But Mohammed had insisted on building a proper house of sun-baked brick, whitewashed to show he was a man of standing, with a broad, flat roof to store his fuel and his livestock, and even to sleep on during hot summer nights. Inside, the walls were plastered but unpainted; the floors, the same packed earth of the poorest peasant huts, were immaculately clean and covered with richly patterned rugs.

Furnishings were sparse. A narrow table against the wall, a handful of lower tables throughout, colorful cushions scattered across the floor. Nothing more. The walls themselves were unadorned. Only a long row of knives, their blades sharpened until razor edges shone in the lamplight, filled a single space above the table. Raoul smiled as he looked at them. It surprised him a little to think of Mohammed, otherwise so cultivated and westernized, standing with a sharp blade in his fingers, poised to throw a knife with the shrewdest of the desert bandits.

Mohammed saw Raoul glancing around, and he sensed the other man was admiring his house.

"It is good for a man to live with his sons," he said quietly. "A house without sons is not a home."

Raoul nodded slowly. He envied Mohammed the peace of his home and the warmth of his family. They were things he knew he would never have. It was at moments like these that he missed them most.

A rich aroma filled the air as Saadia brought a tray of coffee to the men. The women had roasted fresh beans in an iron ladle over the fire, grinding them by hand until the mixture was fine enough to brew. Now they served it in demitasses, with huge lumps of sugar.

Mohammed passed strong Egyptian cigarettes, and the men sat in silence, enjoying the tobacco and the coffee. It was Mohammed who finally spoke.

"It is not good for a man to live without sons."

Raoul had to smile. The remark was too pointed to be misunderstood. He knew that Mohammed disapproved of his bachelor life, although he had never been so frank before. A glass of wine, a cigarette among friends—and a man grew bolder.

There was no stopping Mohammed now. "We have a saying in our country. A man without brothers is a man with a left arm, but no right. But I say to you, a man without sons is a man with no arms at all. He is a man without a life. My sons are my life."

Raoul was touched by his quiet passion. "I know what you are telling me, old friend," he said softly. "I, too, would rejoice in sons. But the woman I was to marry has gone back to England."

It had been over a year since Thea left him. He had barely thought of her in all that time, yet in a strange way he missed her. He had heard from friends that she had married, an older country squire with a comfortable estate and a reputation for kindness. He was happy for her, he wanted her to make a good life, but he could not help feeling bereft all the same. Thea had been a part of his dreams for so long. It left an empty space in his life to be without her.

Mohammed bobbed his head up and down, acknowledging the solemnity of the situation. "The woman is gone," he agreed. "A man must accept the things that are. But there are other women."

Raoul smiled to himself, wondering if Mohammed had ever really approved of Thea. To him, she must have seemed lightheaded and frivolous, the kind of woman who would be nothing but a useless decoration in a man's life. Sometimes Raoul had the feeling that Mohammed thought he should throw it all up and marry Aimée instead.

The fact that Aimée was already married would not have concerned Mohammed in the least. The husband did not care for her, that was clear. So why should he not say to the woman, "I divorce you," three times, and they would both be free? It was all simple logic. Then she could marry Raoul and make him a good wife—a good mother for his sons.

Life had a childish simplicity for a man like Mohammed. Raoul often wondered why it wasn't as simple for him.

It was well after midnight when Raoul rose at last to take his leave. Mohammed protested vehemently, partly because hospitality demanded it, but more because he was genuinely sorry to see the evening come to an end.

"But why should you leave us now, my friend? The flight of hours matters not. I have had the clock stopped for you."

Raoul knew the man's words were literally true. One of the few European possessions in his home, a bulky table clock in which he took great pride, stood at the side of the room, its pendulum motionless, as if to remind them all that in the presence of a friend, time stood still.

"I would stay all night, and gladly, but I have to rise early—and so do you."

For Mohammed and his sons, the day would begin even earlier than it did for him. There would be an hour of labor in the fields, perhaps even two, before they left at dawn to supervise the workmen at the dig. Their women would toil beside them, bending over the earth until their backs ached with exhaustion. The sun would already be high in the sky when they turned at last to their own chores—cooking food and gathering fuel, fetching water in large earthenware pots and sifting wheat, winding thread and churning butter.

The night air was cool as Raoul rode back to the camp. The horse was restless, straining at the bit, as if even a light rein defied the freedom of his spirit. Spurring him impulsively, Raoul gave the stallion his head, letting him soar across the sandy soil until he left a film of dust in the moonlight.

Raoul had always loved to ride. The cold wind against his face was the purest kind of exhilaration, the supple warmth of the horse's muscles beneath his legs an extension of his own strength. It had been too long since he had given himself up to sheer pleasure. When he returned home, the first thing he wanted was to saddle a swift horse and race across country fields, letting buttercups blur into a dizzying swirl of yellow as he leaped fence after fence, daring to pretend he was part of the earth and the sun and the wind.

He reined in the horse on a low bluff overlooking the camp. Pausing to gaze down at the desert floor, he reminded himself for the first time in months how incomparably beautiful this desolate land could be. He had been there so long, he had come to take it for granted.

The place had an untouched air about it, as if man had not violated its soil since the last pharaoh laid his dead in the valley thousands of years before. The workmen's tools had been hidden away for the night, the scars in the earth that marked their labor softened by the deceptive rays of the moon. Even the place where a trio of tents once stood was only an eerie void in the vast expanse of sand.

Raoul had been surprised, at the beginning of the summer, when Edward announced he was going to Berlin, taking Buffy with him. He had not expected the man to leave him alone at the dig, even with the threat of another long, searing season looming up ahead. He had been even more surprised when the first cooling hints of autumn came, and still Edward did not return.

Perhaps they had finally come to terms, he thought, he and this man he despised so much. They hated each other, they distrusted each other, but they were caught in a web neither of them could escape. All it would take was a word to the authorities, and Raoul could write an end to Edward's dreams forever; but Edward could do the same thing to him. Like it or not, they needed each other, and in their need, even mortal enemies could become temporary allies.

How long had he been in that camp? Four years? No, five—five long years. He had thought, when he first came, he would be there only two seasons, three at most. Now it looked more like six or seven. He had almost turned into an Arab himself, learning to exist with the heat and the sand and the loneliness. He wondered if he would still know how to live among men when the time came for him to return.

Hassan was waiting when he arrived at the edge of the camp. He watched as Raoul swung out of the saddle.

"You have had a pleasant dinner with my family?"

"Very pleasant. I'm sorry you couldn't have been there."

Hassan's teeth flashed white against dark skin. "Better for me I was not. I would have shamed my father in front of his guest. 'It is not good that a man should have no wife,' he would say to me. 'A man should not live without sons.'"

Raoul laughed as he handed over the horse's reins. "You're probably right, Hassan—but then you would have spared me the same lecture."

Hassan slipped a wineskin from his shoulder, catching it deftly in his hand. "We will enjoy a drink of wine before you go."

Raoul glanced at him sharply. He did not allow drinking on the dig, and Hassan knew it.

But the young man was undaunted. "A sip of wine among friends. Will this do any harm? We are not drunk—either of us."

Raoul relaxed. The lad was right. There was nothing wrong with a sip of wine. Besides, for all his show of bravado, Hassan could not help feeling left out that night. The least Raoul could do was enjoy a drink with him. Taking the skin, he raised it high above his head.

The wine had a strong taste, pungent and sweet, as it slid down his throat, sending a warm glow through his limbs. He took another deep swallow, then wiped his mouth on the back of his hand, tossing the wineskin to Hassan.

The young man held it to his own lips, tilting his head as he drank. A little stream of red trickled down the side of his chin, staining his robe, before he lowered the bag again. He extended it one last time to Raoul, but did not press when he refused. Shaking hands, the two men bid each other good night.

Raoul felt strangely tired as his feet sank into the drifting sand that blew across the site. Was the heat getting him down, he wondered, or the long days—or was it just age catching up with him at last? His hair was heavily flecked with gray now as he looked in the mirror each morning to shave. The temples were almost white against the tan of his skin. It surprised him in a vague way to realize he was mortal like everyone else.

Mud-brick platforms that had once supported tents still rested on the sand, halfway between the workshop and the tomb he was using as his own quarters. They looked lonely and futile as he passed them, like so many gravestones marking the memory of everything he had loved and hated in the past five years.

Why was he so hostile to Edward? he asked himself. The man was a prig and a fool, belligerent and cowardly all at the same time, but he had known other prigs before, other fools, and he had always managed to get along with them.

Why was he being so stubborn, so deliberately stubborn, about the disposition of the artifacts? The exquisite little bust Edward had paid such an exorbitant sum for—why was it still resting on the shelves in his workshop, years after he had finished cataloging and photographing it? And the winged Isis collar, the single piece that Edward, like himself, coveted beyond anything else in the entire collection—why couldn't he let the man hoard it away in his own private vaults, where it would be even safer than it was now?

Was it just the natural pigheadedness of a man grown inflexible from too many years in the desert? Or was it spite, as cheap and petty in its own way as Edward's? Did he hate the man, not because of what he was, but because of what he had? Because he was the one man in the world with the acknowledged right to enter the bedroom of a woman he had once loved. The one man who could take a pretty little child on his lap and demand that she call him Father.

He was aware of a peculiar dizzy sensation as he reached the top of the staircase that led to his room. He hesitated, bracing his feet against the sand to steady himself, but he could not shake a queasy feeling in the pit of his stomach. His body felt hot, even in the cold night air, as if he were coming down with a fever. He put an anxious hand to his brow, but he could feel nothing.

371

Irritably he shook his head, trying to drive away the sensation. What the hell was the matter with him anyhow? He was reeling like a drunk after a night of carousing.

Slowly he forced himself to move, running a hand awkwardly along the wall as he struggled to negotiate the steep stone steps. For a single horrifying second he had the feeling he was going to lunge forward, plummeting headlong into the darkness. His throat was dry with tension as he clung to the wall.

Was he drunk? But that was incredible. He had had a good deal to drink, of course—bouza with Mohammed and his sons, wine with dinner, more wine with Hassan when he returned to the dig—but he had always been a man with a capacity for drink.

Damn, he hoped he wasn't getting sick. He had been so lucky all these years. He had seen it happen often enough to other men. A devastating illness, then months—even years—of recovery. But he couldn't afford months now. He couldn't even afford weeks. There was so much to be done.

He barely made it to his bed, groping with his hands as he eased his body down on the hard mattress. His head seemed to be spinning on his shoulders, rotating with a force all its own. He thought he was going to vomit, but he didn't have the strength to get up and search for a basin. Then mercifully, just as the nausea grew unbearable, darkness settled over him, and he was conscious of nothing else.

When he woke, his whole body was cold and clammy, as if he had sweated the night away, but at least the sickening dizziness had passed. Whatever it was, a surfeit of wine or a lightning-quick illness, at least it was over now. Groggily he dragged himself to his feet. Making his way to the doorway, he pushed aside the dark brown blanket that served as a drape.

"What the hell . . . ?"

Amazed, he stared at golden sunlight streaming down the steps. Even ill—or drunk—it was hard to believe he had overslept so badly. And where was Mohammed? Surely they had missed him at the dig. Why hadn't someone come to see where he was?

Alert now, Raoul raced up the steps, taking them in a few quick leaps. The instant he reached the top, he realized something was wrong.

The place was quiet, so deathly quiet not even the ring of a pick or the faraway chant of a solitary workman could be heard. Nervously Raoul scanned the area. It took him only a second to spot Mohammed.

He stood alone, a slim silent figure pale against the glare of the sand. His head was bowed, his shoulders stooped, as if he had aged in a single night. His two oldest sons stood a few paces behind him, one on either side, like a pair of sentinels assigned to guard him.

Raoul covered the ground between them in a dozen brisk strides. The nearer he drew, the more alarmed he became.

"What the devil's going on? Why didn't you wake me?"

Mohammed stared at him with dark, burning eyes, but he did not try to speak. Turning slowly, he faced the workshop steps.

Raoul did not know what was happening, but he knew it could not be good. Tensely he hurried toward the stairway, standing at the top to peer down into the shadows. He could not believe what he saw.

The heavy iron gate—that same gate he had locked himself the evening before—was standing wide open.

But that was impossible, he told himself slowly, too stunned to feel anything but surprise. Even from that distance it was obvious that the gate had not been forced. But he had the only key. It was right there on his key ring.

Reaching down to his belt, he pulled up a heavy ring, jangling with keys to all the gates in the tunnels and the workshop. He counted them to make sure.

They were all there—all but one.

He counted again. This time, there could be no doubt. One of the keys was missing. It was obvious which one it was.

With a cry of rage he bolted down the steps, stopping abruptly when he reached the open gate. For a moment he could only stare into the room, trying to comprehend what he was seeing.

The workshop had been ransacked before, but never like this. Even on the night Aimée was attacked, only a few artifacts were harmed. But tonight everything had been pulled from the shelves and hurled to the floor with a force so savage it looked as if the malice were deliberate. Alabaster vases that had survived the centuries lay with deep cracks on the ground, and delicately carved ushabti figures, once so charming and whimsical, were splintered beyond recognition. Virtually nothing had escaped damage.

The work of years undone in a single night. A bridge

through the centuries broken, perhaps beyond repair. Raoul wanted to weep as he looked at it.

There was no way to assess the damage now, he realized with a quick glance around the room. It would take weeks, even months of carefully searching through the pieces, marking everything off against meticulous lists. Only then could he tell what was missing or totally destroyed. Grim and silent, he climbed the steps again.

Dammit, he could see Edward's hand in this. The man had rummaged through the workshop before, he was sure of that. He had not dared take anything then—he was too much of a coward to risk a confrontation with Raoul—but there was nothing to keep him from making lists of his own, careful catalogs that would provide a blueprint for hired thieves in the future.

And the beauty of it was, he couldn't do a thing about it. There was nothing he could prove, and without proof, he could not risk retaliation.

But Berlin! Goddammit, Berlin? It was perfect. Not only a foolproof alibi for an absentee thief, but the ideal place to fence the pieces he did not plan to keep. Sooner or later, everyone who was interested in antiquities passed through Berlin, and Edward would have no trouble gaining an introduction to the least scrupulous of them.

It was a sober Raoul who stopped at the head of the stairs, facing Mohammed and his sons.

"How did this happen?"

Even as he spoke, he knew the question was pointless. He was the only one who could possibly know anything, yet he had no answers at all. The key ring had been on his belt every minute since the gate was locked. He had not even taken it off when he slept. No one could have touched it without his knowing.

Unless . . .

Unless he had slept so deeply he felt nothing. Unless his unnatural dizziness the night before was neither sudden illness nor a reaction to too much wine.

Unless he had been drugged.

Sensory memories bombarded him. Pungent, salty cheese, the taste lingering in his mouth. Rice heavy with exotic spices, strong coffee rich with sugar.

But the drug had acted quickly, and it was easily an hour from the time he finished dinner until the dizziness struck.

Sweet, warm wine, then, strong against his tongue. A last drink before retiring.

But Hassan had drunk from the same wineskin. He had seen the trail of red, trickling like blood down his chin. And Hassan—

Daoud interrupted his thoughts. "They did not have time to do much, *monsieur*."

Raoul glanced at Mohammed, but the man did not meet his eyes. It was Salem who continued.

"My brother came here in the early morning, before it was time to work in the fields. He thought the responsibility was heavy for one so young as Hassan, and he wanted to make sure everything was all right. He surprised the thieves in the act. There were only three of them. Two were so frightened they dropped the bag they were carrying between them."

For the first time Raoul noticed a heap of canvas lying on the ground beside the stairway. It was big and bulging, like a bag of Christmas toys dropped from the hands of a hasty Santa Claus.

"Then perhaps nothing was taken." He spoke slowly, trying to pull his thoughts together. It was possible the damage was not as extensive as he had thought. And if nothing was missing . . .

Salem was quick to dash his hopes. "We know there was one thing. Daoud saw it in . . . in the third man's hands."

"What was it?"

There was a moment's hesitation, just enough to make Raoul dread the answer. "The Isis collar."

"The winged Isis?" Raoul felt a wave of anger flood his body. The beautiful Isis pectoral, the prize of all the treasures. More than any other piece, that was the one thing he had planned to stake his reputation on. Now if it couldn't be exhibited . . .

He choked back his bitterness. Dammit, he was thinking only of himself, and that wasn't fair. One look at Mohammed's face was enough to tell him the man was as heartsick as he.

"Well, there's no use crying over the Isis," he said gruffly. His head felt as if it were ready to split open. He did not know if it was from shock or anger—or simply an aftereffect of the drug. "Let's get this mess cleaned up. Where's Hassan? With the men?"

The brothers glanced at each other. "I sent the men home," Daoud replied warily. "I told them you were ill and there would be no work today. I did not want them to see this."

"Then where is . . . ?"

Raoul broke off, too shocked to continue. Hassan had drunk from the wineskin, too—and he would have taken more than a swallow or two.

"Where is he, Mohammed?"

Dammit, if anything had happened to Hassan, it was all his fault. If he hadn't been so stubborn, if he had let Edward have just a few of the treasures . . .

"Answer me, Mohammed. Where is he?"

Mohammed opened his lips. They moved slowly, as if it were an effort to form the words.

"He is gone."

Gone? What a strange way to put it. But at least he had said "gone," not "ill." Or "dead."

"Don't worry, old friend. We'll find him." He must have crawled into one of the tunnels, or perhaps a cool abandoned tomb, searching for a place to sleep off the drug. "He'll be all right."

"You do not understand, *monsieur*. Hassan is gone . . . and the Isis collar is gone."

Raoul stared at him, trying to understand what he was saying. There was that strange choice of words again. "Gone." Not "missing," but "gone. " And the winged Isis was gone.

"You cannot mean . . ."

But he did mean it. And Raoul knew he was right.

A sudden vision flashed across his brain, as sharp as a photograph, indelibly imprinted on his memory. Hassan, a red stream of wine running down his chin. Hassan, holding the skin up to his lips, stopping the wine with his tongue, letting the little that seeped through trickle down his chin so the poison would not affect him.

All the gold and the treasure. Too much temptation for a young man who was going to be poor all his life.

At last he recognized the look in Mohammed's eyes. It was a look of shame.

"You are too hard on yourself, my friend," he told him quietly. "Do not blame yourself. I do not hold you responsible for this."

But it was no good, and he knew it. This was the man who had told him, "My sons are my life." His sons were his honor, too. And a proud old man could not live without his honor.

Furiously Raoul whirled to face the two younger men. "I want a new gate put up—a new gate with a new key. And I want it today. See to it, Daoud. And you, Salem, help your father get that sack inside. Leave everything else where it is. We'll clean it up when I get back."

Daoud had already started to move away. Now he turned back.

"You are going someplace?"

"I am going to Berlin." Lord Edward Ellingham had ruined more than a single life with his work that day. He had destroyed not just an archaeologist's dream, but the faith of a good man in his sons. "I'm not going to let him get away with this."

2

Berlin was not what Raoul had expected. He had not been in the Prussian capital since he was a small boy, and he found his memory had played tricks on him. He had thought only of wide avenues and broad expanses of green, stately Unter den Linden with its constant parade of carriages and charming little parks gay with flower-decked shrubs and pretty ladies twisting parasols over their heads. He had forgotten the narrower, seamier streets of the slums, where the houses were so close together there was not an inch of space between them, and open garbage littered the gutters. That was the Berlin he had come to now.

He pressed back into a shallow doorway, lifting his hands to block his face as a stealthy figure slipped past him, hurrying down the twisting lane. The man's form was gray and indistinct in the hazy light of a rainy afternoon, but Raoul recognized him instantly.

In the four weeks he had been in the city, he had had no luck trying to locate Lord Edward Ellingham. All his efforts—all the discreet inquiries he had made in the salons of the fashionable and the back rooms of those who trafficked in stolen goods—had told him only that the man was clever enough to cover his tracks. But a swarthy Arab, uncomfortable in poorly fitting Western clothes, handicapped by only a few words of broken German, had not found it so easy to hide.

Cautiously Raoul eased his way out of the doorway, following the man down the narrow street. He did not know what he expected to find. Three times in the last three days, Hassan had left his quarters. Each time, Raoul had followed him, and each time the man led him nowhere.

The soft sound of a slow footstep, cautious in the mud behind him, caught Raoul's ear. Nervously he whirled around. The rain had stopped, leaving stagnant puddles in the deep ruts that ran along the street. There was not a trace of motion anywhere.

Angry with himself, Raoul turned back to his quarry. He was just in time to see Hassan vanishing around a distant corner. Stepping up his own pace, he hurried after him. He would have to be more careful in the future. He was getting so jumpy, he had begun to imagine he was being followed himself. And in the process, he had nearly lost his man.

It was twenty minutes before Hassan finally paused, stopping in front of a dark, solidly built house in the center of a long, drab block. Constructed of the same shabby bricks as its neighbors, there was an air of substance about it that set it subtly apart from the others. Hassan hesitated, staring at a sturdy metal gate in the high wall that surrounded the place, then stepped up to it, raising a tentative hand to push it slowly inward. It was open.

Raoul stood on the opposite side of the street, watching as Hassan slid the gate cautiously shut behind him. For the first time in days he dared to hope his luck was changing. If Edward had scoured the area for years, searching for the perfect place to hide, he could have found nothing more ideal.

Impulsively, Raoul hurried toward the side of the house, raising his arms to catch a grip on the top of the wall. Agilely he swung his body upward.

Perching tensely on the top, he let his eyes scan the house. It took him only a second to see what he wanted. Thick green vines, already darkening to an earthy red in the cool autumn air, climbed with showy boldness toward the roof. And stout branches, solid against a solid wall, formed the perfect toehold for a man.

Raoul wasted no time. Leaping to the ground, he covered the space to the house in a few broad steps. As he had hoped, the vines proved strong, easily supporting his weight as he pulled himself upward. Sharp edges cut into his hands until his palms were torn and bleeding, but he did not let that slow him down. He had to get to the roof before anyone spotted him. From there it would be a simple matter to find a high window or a skylight leading into an unused storeroom.

He had nearly reached the top when the sound of voices stopped him. Inching carefully along the face of the building, testing each new foothold as he caught his toe in it, he eased himself toward a second-floor window. Cautiously he reached out with one hand, brushing leaves back from the glass. The window had been poorly hung, leaving a wide gap between the sash and the outer frame. A small pool of water had already begun to form on the wooden flooring.

One glance at the room was enough to whet Raoul's anticipation. The furnishings, dramatically at odds with the austerity of the building, were fashionable and opulent. Walls covered with red damask set off the elegance of walnut tables topped with Florentine marble mosaics. A rosewood screen with tapestry embroideries stood against one wall, forming a backdrop for Louis XVI chairs upholstered in cream-white brocade. On a simple reading desk in the center of the room, a dainty little Meissen clock rested beside a heavy antique candelabrum, its silver arms bright with a pair of blazing candles.

Leaning forward, Raoul strained to see better. He felt like a fool, hanging on to vines in front of the house, in full view of anyone who happened by, but there was nothing he could do about it. He had to know what was going on.

There were two men in the room. One of them, lounging at the side, just out of range of his vision, was only a shadow cast by flickering candlelight on the polished floor. But the other, standing with his back to the window, was fully visible in the center of the room. Raoul felt a surge of satisfaction as he caught sight of dark hair curling onto a soft pink neck, and sloping shoulders too narrow for the thickening waistline beneath them.

So he had found Edward Ellingham at last. And if Edward was there, the Isis could not be far away. He pressed his face even closer to the glass.

The man at the side of the room began to step forward, moving slowly. Raoul glanced incuriously at the motion, catching sight of a stranger.

He had assumed the anonymous figure was Buffy Montmorency. In the five years he had known Edward, he had rarely seen him without his sycophantic shadow. But this man was no Buffy, although he bore a resemblance to him.

Taller and younger, so much younger he was barely more

than a boy, he reminded Raoul of the way Buffy had looked the first time he saw him. He had the same nose, a trifle too sharp, but strong enough to appear aristocratic; the same chin, bold, but softened with the fat that would one day grow loose; the same sensuous, brooding lips. Only his hair was different, so pale it was almost white. And his eyes were the light blue-gray of winter ice.

The young man turned to speak to Edward, but his voice was so low Raoul could make out only a few scattered words. He spoke in English, with a slight German accent, giving the impression of a soft, barely perceptible lisp.

Edward threw back his head, giggling at the remark that seemed to please him. "So you like it here, do you, Christian?"

Christian's lips twisted into a calculated smile as he drawled a slow reply. Again Raoul could not make out the words, but he knew they were smug and sure. The man's garb marked him as a servant, but there was nothing servile about his manner.

"Come here, boy. Come, come." Edward's hand rested on Christian's shoulder, friendly and demanding, as he led him toward one of the marble-topped tables. "I have something pretty to show you. You like pretty things, don't you?"

He stepped toward the window, pausing only when his face was inches from the glass. Raoul pulled back, snapping the branch sharply against the pane. He held his breath at the sound, praying that no one inside would hear. One false move, and it would all be over for him.

It began to rain again, softly at first, then more heavily. Moisture soaked his hair, dripping down the side of his face and running into his collar. Afternoon darkened slowly into twilight. A cold wind began to howl.

Finally, lulled by the silence inside the room, Raoul dared to lean forward, slipping the vine one more time from the window. He moved slowly, easing the leaves a scant inch apart as he peeked discreetly between them.

A large black jeweler's box lay on the table. Raoul had not seen it before. He knew Edward must have pulled it from one of the cabinets of a tall secretaire, or perhaps drawn it out of a secret hiding place beneath the floorboards while he wasn't watching.

Christian was staring at the box with frank curiosity. Edward paused to pat him on the shoulder, deliberately increasing the suspense. He smiled as the youth bent forward, resting pale fingers inches from the lid, as if he longed to pull it open himself. Watching from outside, Raoul was as tense as Christian, but he had an advantage over the younger man. He already knew what he would see when Edward raised the lid.

Neither of them was disappointed. Gold and semiprecious stones flashed with a pure brilliance against deep velvet as Edward held the case up for the boy to admire. Christian gasped with amazement, but Raoul, clinging to damp vines outside the window, was silent. He was aware of a deep sense of vindication. The long month that had passed, all the doubts and the uncertainty, had not been in vain.

He longed to smash the glass with his bare hands, leaping into the room in a single daring bound, but he knew he would be a fool to stake everything on one impetuous charge. His fingers clenched the vines, letting jagged edges dig into his skin as he held himself back.

The Isis was there, and it would be his, but he had to be patient. Sooner or later they would snap the lid shut again and put the case back where it belonged, slipping away to enjoy other diversions in other rooms. Then he would have his chance. An isolated second-floor study, a window so loose a simple shove would push it from its frame—it would all be over in a minute. He would be halfway to Constantinople before they even discovered it was gone.

He was so intent on the Isis, he had forgotten the two men in the room. He was startled now to see Edward move, lifting a hand to lay it lightly on Christian's cheek. There was a strange impertinence to the gesture, a kind of intimacy Raoul found embarrassing between a man and his servant. He was surprised when Christian did not pull away.

None of them noticed a third man standing in the doorway. He must have made a slight noise, something Raoul could not hear, for Edward and Christian both looked up at the same time. The boy was confident, almost defiant, but Edward could not keep from flushing.

"What . . . what do you want?"

Buffy Montmorency did not answer. He stood beyond the light of the candles, barely visible in the gloom. He was not looking at Edward, but at the pretty youth beside him. As he took a slow step into the room, Raoul could see his eyes. They were blazing with hatred and pain.

In that sudden instant of recognition, Raoul understood at last. He wondered why he had not seen it long ago.

Edward and Buffy. Always Edward and Buffy. Sitting in front of the tent. Going off on jaunts into town. Giggling through the late hours of the night, their voices blending with the jackals' howls. He had seen their closeness, he had even wondered at it, but he had never understood. Edward and Buffy.

Only, now it looked like it was going to be Edward and Christian.

"I said, what do you want?"

Buffy had regained his composure. Raoul had to give the man credit. He was holding a losing hand, but no one would know it by his face.

"My, my, Eddie, how touchy we are all of a sudden. You have a visitor. I didn't think you'd want me to send him up all by himself."

Raoul cast an anxious eye toward the door. There, in the darkness of the hallway, was a slender black-clad form.

Dammit, he had forgotten all about Hassan. He had followed him there himself, he knew the man had to be in the house, but in all the excitement, he hadn't given him a second thought. Now, as Hassan moved coolly into the room, he knew he had been a fool to dismiss him so lightly.

Edward gave the man a casual glance, then turned toward the doorway.

"That will be all, Buffy. You may leave now."

Buffy blanched at the curtness in his lover's tone, but he did not speak. He stood for a moment, just inside the threshold, studying his rival. Without a word, he slipped into the darkness.

Edward waited until Buffy had gone, then whirled to face Hassan. His expression, so placid an instant before, was livid with rage.

"What the hell are you doing? I told you never to come here. What if someone saw you?"

Raoul was taken aback by the sudden change in Edward's manner. But Hassan, as if he had expected it, stood his ground.

"You told me not to come here—bah!" He spat on the floor to punctuate his words. "You told me not to come, but you also told me you would pay me if I stole the Isis collar. 'You will be a rich man, Hassan,' you told me. 'A very rich man.'"

"I told you no such thing. I said you would be rich if you stole *all* the things on my list. But you got only one."

So the thieves were falling out already, Raoul thought. Well, so much the better for him.

"Sure, sure, I only got one thing, but it was the Isis collar."

"And I paid you for that."

"Fifty English pounds! Do you think that is enough? You are a rich man. You have a home. I, Hassan—I have no home. My father and my brothers, they will kill me if I try to go back. Do you think I did that for fifty English pounds?"

Edward fidgeted uncomfortably. Behind him, Christian stepped closer, as if to support him.

"If you hadn't bungled it so badly, I would have paid you more. You've botched things right from the beginning, you know—right from that stupid, amateurish raid when you let a crazy old woman get into the camp. You don't even deserve fifty pounds. I gave it to you only because I felt sorry for you."

Right from that stupid, amateurish raid . . .

So Raoul had been right after all. Edward had been in on the thing from the very beginning—Edward and his hired thieves.

"You paid two thousand pounds for the painted wooden head."

"That . . . that was different." Edward looked surprised, as if he had not expected Hassan to know about the other piece. "That was art—I can sell that to a museum. But who's going to want an overdone necklace with a bunch of carnelians and turquoise and little bits of colored glass? Diamonds, that's what everyone wants—diamonds and rubies and emeralds. Why, I'll be lucky if I get my fifty pounds back when I finally unload the thing."

He was lying, and Raoul knew it. He had no intention of selling the Isis. Not for fifty pounds, not for fifty thousand. He wanted to keep it for himself, and he didn't want to pay for it.

And he was a fool if he thought Hassan didn't know it, too.

Hassan took a step toward him, and then another. There was no mistaking the tone of his voice.

"If you do not want the thing, then you will give it to me."

Christian did not wait for him to move again. Leaping out from behind Edward, he hurled himself at Hassan, gripping the man's arms as he struggled to pin them against his back. Hassan managed to twist himself free, slamming his attacker violently against the wall, but he knew he had stopped him only for an instant. Out of the corner of his eyes he saw Edward make a frantic dash for the desk.

Hassan took only a second to gauge the situation. Christian was strong, much stronger than he had guessed, and he was determined. And Edward would not be racing toward the desk if he did not keep a gun in one of the drawers.

Hassan wanted the Isis, but he valued his neck even more. With a last raging glance at Christian, he fled into the hallway.

Christian took a step after him, then stopped in the center of the room, breathing heavily as he stared at the empty doorway. Edward stood beside the desk, his hand poised over an open drawer. Then slowly he slid it shut. He laughed quietly as he looked up.

"They are all cowards, these bullies. Every last one of them. Don't tell me he had you frightened."

His voice was teasing, his hands coaxing as he held them out. Christian went to him.

Raoul did not stay to watch them. He did not dare. Any minute now, an irate Hassan would come tearing out of the house, and when he did, he might pause for a last glance at the second-story window.

Raoul huddled on the roof, pressing his body tightly against the eaves. The rain had stopped, and the clouds began to break up, drifting away from the face of the moon. Deep blue light bathed the earth with an eerie clarity.

He waited five minutes, then ten, but still there was no sign of Hassan. Slowly it occurred to him that the man was not going to appear. It was unsettling to have no idea what was going on inside the house. Had Edward, thinking better of his nonchalance, sent Christian after the man? Or had Hassan, recovering his boldness, decided to have one last stab at the Isis?

The room was strangely quiet as Raoul made his way back to the window. Edward was alone, standing beside the table. The jeweler's box, tightly closed, still rested in front of him. Raoul could see no evidence of tension in his bearing.

He had almost begun to think he was imagining things when a sudden bold figure appeared in the doorway. The ill-fitting black suit made him look like an angry crow as he lunged at Edward's back.

Edward whirled toward the sound.

"Damn you!" he shrieked. He turned to run, but it was too late. Hassan already had an arm around his neck, pulling him back against his own body. Tense with strain, the Arab tightened his hold until Edward's face was crimson with terror. The only sound that escaped his lips was a harsh, gasping rale.

Raoul had just spread his hand against the window, ready to send it crashing into the room, when Edward managed to wrench himself free. Whimpering with fear, he ran toward the desk, tugging at a drawer to pull it open. Hassan did not give him a chance. He was at his side in a second, raising the heavy candelabrum menacingly in his hand. The lights flickered, then went out as he crushed it against Edward's skull. A sharp cry mingled with the sound of shuffling footsteps in the darkness.

Raoul did not wait to see what had happened. This time he knew Hassan would come flying out of the house, and he meant to be ready for him. Swinging to the earth, he pushed the metal gate aside. He wanted to be far from Edward—and the range of his gun—when he confronted Hassan.

Once in the street, Raoul hesitated, then began to run lightly along the course he remembered. He knew he was taking a chance, but he had no choice. Besides, he was sure Hassan would go back the way he had come. He had no reason to believe he was being followed.

He found the perfect spot less than a block away. A tall, narrow building jutted out into the street, half-blocking the road. And the doorway was deep enough for a man to hide in.

He waited only a few seconds. The sound of approaching footsteps, half-running, half-stumbling, told him he had not lost his gamble. He braced himself, waiting until the sound had almost reached him. Then he thrust out his foot.

Hassan gave an astonished cry as he tripped over Raoul's leg. The sound ended in a hoarse grunt, as if the fall had knocked all the air out of his lungs. Raoul did not pause for a second. Reaching down, he grabbed the man by his lapels, pulling him upward. He did not even notice a black case lying in the gutter on the side of the road.

"You bastard!" All he could see was Mohammed's face, weary and defeated, robbed of the last vestige of his pride. "You swine!"

Angrily he hurled him against a rough brick wall. Hassan's head cracked audibly, but his expression held more astonishment than pain. Disgusted, Raoul backed away from him, his eyes searching the road for the jeweler's case. He could do nothing to Hassan—he was hardly in a position to go to the police—but he didn't really care. The man had sold everything he held dear for fifty English pounds. Let him live with that.

He spotted the case and stooped to pick it up. Watching him warily, Hassan slipped a cautious hand into his pocket. Raoul saw him, but he was not quick enough to stop him. Hassan's hand, as he drew it out of the pocket, was not empty.

Raoul did not try to move as he stared down the barrel of a small silver revolver.

Edward's gun. Dammit, of course it was Edward's gun. Why hadn't he thought of that before? Naturally Hassan had it. Only a fool would have left it behind.

"Are you sure it has a bullet in it?" Raoul raised an ironic eyebrow, as if he were more amused than afraid. He had hoped to catch Hassan off guard. He did not succeed.

"We will see, won't we?"

"I should have taken it away from you when I knocked you down."

One mistake. One stupid mistake, made in a moment of stress. Surely a man couldn't give his life for something like that.

"But you did not."

"Well, then, it seems you have won." He took a step back, bending down to pick up the case. "This is yours, then. You can take it with you."

"Leave it!"

Raoul straightened quickly. He did not try to speak again, sensing he would only antagonize the man. He did not have to wait long for Hassan to break the silence.

"You think I will just take the collar and walk away from here? With you behind me?"

"Well, you could run," Raoul offered helpfully. He was in a tight spot, but couldn't afford to let the other man sense his fear.

"I cannot leave you here. You know that."

"You left Lord Edward and his friends." Raoul was bluffing. He had no idea what had happened to Edward in the minutes after he fled the house. He could only hope he was still alive.

"I was in a hurry. Besides, I was not afraid of him."

So he was right after all. Hassan was a thief and a scoundrel, but he was not a killer—not yet.

"Don't be a fool, Hassan. Theft is one thing—but you know what they do to murderers."

"If they catch them."

"Oh, they'll catch you, all right." That was the hell of it, he was telling the truth. "You've botched everything up so far. You heard Edward say so. You'll botch this, too."

He hoped to provoke the man into a quarrel. An angry spate of words, a volatile gesture—anything that would lure him into pointing the gun off center, even for a second.

But the plan backfired. The gun was cool and steady as he aimed it. Raoul felt his chest tighten with fear.

"I did not botch anything. Lord Edward is a fool. I have the collar now. He has nothing."

"That's true," Raoul admitted. Conciliate—that was the key. Agree, flatter. "Lord Edward must have been wrong to say you made a mess of things. Still, there was that night the old woman attacked Aimée . . . ?"

A hint of question in his voice. Not enough to anger. Just enough to coax him into explaining himself.

"That was not my fault. How was I supposed to know the woman was there? Anyway, we were almost through. A few minutes more and we would have been safe."

That's right, Raoul thought. Keep talking. Just keep talking, and sooner or later, I'll catch you off guard.

"But you knew about the woman, of course. You and Edward both. When you planned—"

"Not Edward," Hassan broke in angrily. "Why do you always say Edward? Edward had nothing to do with it. It was all my plan—mine!"

Raoul was beginning to see. He had thought he was dealing with one plot all the time. Actually, there were two. Hassan, young, arrogant, naive—daring everything for the dazzling wealth he hungered to possess. Edward, aging and greedy, endlessly writing out surreptitious lists of all the treasures he would never have the courage to steal. It was inevitable they should find each other.

"He found out what you were doing, didn't he? What happened? Did he come out that night when he heard Aimée scream? Did he see you running away? I suppose he threatened to expose you unless you went along with him."

"Threatened me?" Hassan snorted his contempt. "No one threatens Hassan. No, he *begged* me to help him. I did not need him. I had already stolen the carved head right out from under your nose, one day when you were working with

Lady Ellingham in another part of the tomb. I smuggled it out in a filthy sack. I would have gotten more, too. Bah, what did I need with Edward? He needed me."

The pieces were all beginning to fit together. Raoul could see it clearly now. The petty pilfering. The one bold raid that did not work. Hassan was determined and ambitious, but he lacked the organization to pull his plans off. And organization was a thing Edward could supply.

"So it was Edward who brought the old woman from Cairo."

"Edward again. Always Edward. Why must you be so stupid, *monsieur?* Edward did not plan anything. The old woman was just there. Don't you understand that? She was just there.

She was just there. Raoul shook his head slowly. So much for all his theories. Just an old woman, a pathetic old woman, warped by the violence of her own life. Why hadn't he been able to see that the one piece that never fit into the puzzle was just coincidence after all?

Why must you be so stupid, monsieur? Why indeed?

Everything made sense now. "And the attack on me? That was you, too. You wanted to get me out of the way."

Hassan laughed. The sound was too easy, too careless.

"You are taking it all too personally. I assure you, I had no wish to kill you. You were just carrying the carved head, and I wanted it back—to sell again."

To sell to whom? Raoul wondered. To Edward? Obviously they were not partners on that little caper. But if they weren't working together . . .

"Why did you let Edward get away with all that cash?"

Hassan grinned. "I did not know Edward had all that cash, or he would not have gotten away. I would not have minded killing him."

The cool dispassion in his voice chilled Raoul. He had tried to convince himself before that Hassan was not a killer. Now he was not so sure. Only a man who had already killed could be so comfortable with the idea.

Hassan raised the gun, leveling it in a steady hand. "You were a strong fighter that night. I am sure you are strong tonight also. I am glad I have this. I would not like to meet you hand to hand again."

A light drizzle blew into Raoul's face. His flesh felt clammy against his fingers as he reached up and brushed the hair back from his brow. He had to keep the man talking. He had to hold his interest somehow.

"And the wine you gave me. Obviously, that's how you drugged—"

But Hassan would have none of it. "I am not a fool. You think I am, but I am not. I see what you are doing, and I am tired of it."

"But surely—"

"Not surely, *monsieur*. Not surely at all. The only thing that is sure is that I am going to pick up that box and walk away from here, and you are not going to follow me."

A cold sweat coated the palms of Raoul's hands, but he would not let himself wipe them against the side of his coat. Dammit, this was a stupid way to die. Standing in a dingy alleyway in a cold rain. Squabbling over a thing that had not belonged to anyone for three thousand years.

He forced himself to meet Hassan's eyes. He had heard once that they gave a blindfold to a condemned man. He wondered now if it was for the man himself or for his executioners. Hassan would kill him, he could not stop him, but he would have to look into his eyes as he did it.

Raoul felt a cold, detached curiosity as he watched Hassan's face. What was it that gave a man the will to kill another in cold blood? What would he see in Hassan's expression that marked the change of a human being into a murderer?

But when it came, it was not the expression he had expected. There was no anger in it, no regret, not even a show of grim determination. Instead, it almost seemed to him the man was surprised. Dark eyes widened with the look of an ingenuous child. Lips opened as if to whisper a secret.

Only the words never came.

Raoul stood and watched as his form, so sinister only a moment before, slid slowly to the earth, like a puppet whose strings had been cut. He felt as if he were caught in a dream, imagining the evaporation of all his fears because he did not have the courage to face the idea of his own death. At last he forced himself to look down.

He had imagined nothing. Hassan was lying at his feet, face down in a shallow pool of water. Dark hair floated out from his head. Gentle ripples splashed against his body, caressing his jacket, his skin, the shiny black of his shoes, before they faded into glassy stillness again. The dull, metallic gleam of a knife hilt showed between his shoulder blades.

Raoul raised his eyes. He could barely make out a dim form in the darkness, only a few yards away, but he did not need the man's features to recognize him.

"My friend . . ."

He held out a hand, then dropped it to his side. He could not ask the man to touch him now.

Unlike his son, Mohammed still wore his native robes. His figure looked short against the tall buildings, as if he had shrunk in stature when he stepped out of his own world.

"My son has brought enough dishonor upon himself. I could not allow him this shame, too."

Raoul saw the bitter choice that had been Mohammed's, and it appalled him. To take the life of his own son . . . or to stand aside and watch that son kill another man. He must have hovered alone in the darkness, the blade of the knife cold in his fingers, ready to throw if he had to, waiting, praying, even as Raoul had prayed for the miracle that would stay Hassan's hand. The miracle had not come.

My sons are my life, Mohammed had told him once. What was left of his life now?

"But how . . . ?"

He stopped. He had started to say, How did you get here? but he already knew. If it had been easy for him to find Hassan, it must have been just as easy for Mohammed. He would have wanted to recover the Isis himself, salvaging with the ancient collar at least a part of his pride. Perhaps he hoped, too, as only a father could hope, that he would be able to bring a repentant Hassan home to his mother. Now Hassan would never go home again.

Mohammed was silent as he turned away. Raoul did not try to stop him, but watched the man walk slowly down the street. His shoulders were bent, but his spine was still straight. He did not look back.

Raoul stood in the darkness, listening as the last echoes of footsteps died away and he was alone. He still had one thing to do, but it was a long time before he could face it.

Hassan was only a shadow in the dark path, like a bundle of rags discarded with the rest of the trash. Raoul squatted beside him, watching as the mud soaked into his jacket.

It was a stupid way to die. His own words came back to him now. A dingy alleyway in a cold rain. A thing that had not belonged to anyone for three thousand years.

Raoul could not leave him like that. Putting his hands under lifeless arms, he dragged the body to the side of the road.

He was breathing hard when he finished, but he managed to prop it against the wall. Bending one last time, he forced cold hands into a mud-stained lap, folding them around each other in one last, ludicrous attempt to make a corpse look natural. It was all he could do.

He had always liked this young man, with his vitality and his bright laughter. He could not hate him now.

Dammit, what had he expected? The temptation had been too great. A young man, poor all his life, with no expectations ahead of him. One European clock as the whole measure of a family's wealth, and the tombs of the pharaohs held gold beyond imagining.

He bent slowly, picking up the black case from the mud. And what was it all for? he asked himself bitterly. All the cost in human life and heartbreak.

He snapped the case open. The collar, dark in the faint light of a rising moon, seemed to be mocking him. Maybe there was a curse on the pharaoh's treasures after all. A curse on the greed of the men who tried to steal them.

His greed. He could deny it no longer. If he had tried harder, if he had even offered to share the treasures with Edward, he would not be standing in the filth of a foreign road looking down at a man who used to be a friend.

He had told himself it was all scientific integrity. The need to excavate the past ranked above human considerations. Scientific integrity, hell! It was greed. Plain old-fashioned greed, no better or purer than Edward's. He had wanted the discovery all to himself, not to be divided among millionaire backers or other archaeologists, just as Edward wanted the treasure for his own. And now, between the two of them, they had killed a young man and shattered the last years of an old one.

Well, there was nothing he could do about it now. Nothing but learn to live with his regrets. But he could see to it that it didn't happen again.

Hassan was beyond temptation. But as long as Raoul kept on digging, as long as he stole wealth from the earth and hid it away again, other young men would learn a lust for gold, and other fathers would die of a broken heart.

It was time to pack it all in. Time to admit that he, Raoul Villière, was not above the laws of God and man. Time to give up dreams of the past and glories of the future, if the past and the future were going to make a wreck of the present.

The treasures belonged to Egypt. Not to a grasping English gold-seeker or a French archaeologist who wanted them only to build his own reputation. The time had come to give them back.

He paused one last time, glancing over his shoulder as he prepared to leave. Hassan looked sad and silly, like a doll all dressed up in the wrong-size clothes. He should not have worn a Western suit, with sleeves a little too short and the fabric rumpled where it did not fit. At least in his own robes he could have had a measure of dignity in death.

3

"*A* is for apple."

Aimée held the book open on her lap. A big blue *A* stood out against the white of the paper. Mariette barely glanced at it as she swept her hand through a pile of dead leaves, scattering them in a flurry of color across the hillside.

"I don't like apples." She picked up a dark red leaf, dry but perfectly formed. Fascinated, she watched it crumple in her fingers, leaving only a lacy skeleton of veins.

Aimée sighed as she drew the child's attention back to the book. Already Mariette was beginning to develop a logic of her own that defied her.

"Then *A* is for . . ." For what? Ambrosia, aardvark, aspidistra? Why did *A* have to be such a hard letter?

Mariette looked up solemnly. "I like apple torte."

"Of course you do." Aimée gave the child a little squeeze, pinching pink cheeks with teasing fingers. Mariette liked cookies and plump little cakes with thick icing and candies from the store in town. "All right, then, *A* is for apple torte."

Mariette repeated the words dutifully, but she was more interested in what was left of the leaf. Already the skeleton was vanishing as she pulled the veins off one by one. Aimée turned the page.

"And this is *B*. *B* is for boy."

"I don't like boys either."

"How do you know, you silly little goose? You've hardly even seen one."

Aimée felt a twinge of conscience at the thought. Mariette was already four years old. She wondered if she had been selfish, keeping the child in an isolated cottage, with only servants to play with and an occasional visit from a doting Cousin Sophie to provide distraction. Soon she would need companions her own age.

"What else is *B* for?"

"Well, *B* is for ball, and bread . . . and butter."

There, that was good. Mariette liked rich, sweet butter spread on thick peasant bread with a dollop of jam on top.

"*B* is for bread and butter," the girl parroted, making no effort to hide the boredom in her voice. The game was much too simple for her. Swishing her hand through the leaves again, she churned them round and round, making a loud rustling sound. She liked that. It was far too quiet on the hillside. "Why aren't the nuns singing today?"

"It's not time yet. Later, when we're going home, perhaps we'll hear them."

Music had always been an integral part of the hills for Aimée, as essential as the sun and the breeze and the gently blowing grasses. It intrigued her now to realize that her daughter loved it as much as she. She could not forget another afternoon, long ago, when she and Sophie had stopped the carriage to sit and wonder at the beauty of it all. Mariette was only a baby then. How quickly they grew.

"And this is *C*. What do you think *C* is for?"

"Sea lions?"

Sea lions? Good heavens, where did she pick that up?

"No, that comes later." She had not realized anything so simple could be so complicated. How was she ever going to explain the different sounds of *C* and *S* to the child? "Listen for a 'ke' sound. Like cat."

"Or cookie?" Mariette asked hopefully. "Could *C* be for cookie?"

For the first time since the game began, the child seemed interested. "Why not?" Aimée agreed good-naturedly. "*C* could certainly be for cookie—and if you're a good girl and learn the lesson quickly, we'll see if we can find you a cookie when we get home."

Mariette brushed the leaves away with an impatient hand. Suddenly she was intent on the book in her mother's lap. Turning the pages quickly, she pointed to the gaily colored letters, repeating them aloud.

"*A* is for apple torte. And *B* is for bread . . . no, *B* is for bread and butter. And *C* is for *cookie!*"

She looked up expectantly.

Aimée could not help smiling. How quickly the child

learned when she wanted to. Soon ABC's on a hillside in cooling autumn breezes would not be enough for her. Soon she would need a proper school and proper teachers.

"Just one more now. This is *D*. Do you know what *D* is for?"

Mariette wrinkled up her nose. It was obvious she had hoped the lesson was over. "*D* is for . . . Daddy."

Aimée froze into position. For a minute she did not even breathe. "For Daddy?"

She had always known the subject would come up, but she had hoped it would not be so soon. Mariette had never even played with other youngsters and their families. Where could she have heard the word?

"Yes, of course, it could be for Daddy," she admitted, faltering. God help her, what was she to tell the child? "But it is for other things, too. *D* is for darkness and dewdrops and . . . draperies."

Why was it so hard? She knew she was a coward. She ought to take Mariette in her arms and explain to her, as best she could, what the word Daddy would mean to her, but she could not bring herself to do it.

"I know," she said, forcing an artificial brightness into her voice. "Let's find something good to eat, like we did for *A* and *B* and *C*. How about this? *D* is for dumplings."

Mariette ran through the four letters, repeating them again and again until they were perfect, but Aimée barely heard her. D *is for Daddy . . . Daddy . . . Daddy.* A little childish voice, just beginning to question the things other children took for granted.

But Mariette would have no Daddy.

Edward? How could she tell the child Edward was her father? A hard man, grasping, petty, self-centered, and totally unloving. Raoul then? But she could not tell Mariette about Raoul. Not without making her the heir to her mother's shame.

"Come on, *petite*. That's enough for now." And it was enough. Four letters in one afternoon. That was all a little mind could handle.

She held out her hand, but Mariette pulled away, skipping ahead down the path. Dry leaves crackled beneath her feet, making her shriek with delight as she disappeared around a bend in the road. She did not even look back to see if her mother was there.

Aimée's heart caught in her throat as she watched her. She

had grown so big. Where had all the years gone? Only yesterday she was a baby in her arms. Now she was running on ahead.

She picked up her skirts as she hurried after her. "Don't go so fast, Mariette. Wait for Mama."

Edward fidgeted in his chair. It was a stiff, uncomfortable contrivance, one of those old-fashioned decorative things with half a cushion and a little curlicue for an arm. He had always hated chairs like that.

Irritably he glanced toward the clock. Dammit, where was Buffy? Impatient fingers beat a brisk tattoo on the inlaid surface of the table. Why the hell wasn't he here? He wanted to get the thing over with once and for all.

Buffy had been magnificent the day he found him. He could still remember it as if it were yesterday. A pretty, impish street urchin, barely more than a child, trying so transparently to pretend he was a young gentleman of quality. Edward had pulled his carriage to the side of the road and watched, enchanted, as the boy tried to con a wealthy matron out of a few shillings. He had known then he had to have him.

The woman had been enchanted, too—every bit as enchanted as he—but Edward had won. He had often wondered if he touched on Buffy's natural preferences, or if his clothes and his carriage had simply looked more expensive than hers.

He had almost loved Buffy, in his own way. It had been a vital, stimulating, incredibly exciting relationship. The physical satisfaction had been intense, more compelling than anything he had known before or would ever know again. Yes, and the emotional satisfaction, too, the tremendous ego thrill that came from looking at something so beautiful and knowing it belonged to him.

It was a pity Buffy was not beautiful anymore. Edward could never forget the first time he had looked at that boyish face and seen thin lines sinking into the skin around his eyes. He felt as if he had been betrayed.

He should have gotten rid of the man then, that day or the next, before unpleasantness turned to ugliness, but he had needed him too much. Buffy was shrewd, he had to admit that. All those schemes in Egypt, the lists, the plots, the use of mercenaries to commit their crimes for them—they seemed so clever and foolproof. And he had wanted them to work so desperately.

Well, it was over now. He pulled himself out of the chair and walked to the window. It was all over, and it was all for nothing.

He rested his hand on the sill as he leaned forward. There was an uncomfortable feeling in the pit of his stomach. That irritated him. He took it as a form of weakness, and weakness was a thing he could not accept.

Dammit, he had been looking forward to this moment for years. Every quarrel he had ever had, every caustic quip he'd endured, every day when hatred seemed stronger than passion—they had all been stored up, neatly boxed and tied away in a private corner of his soul, waiting for this moment. Why was he dreading it now?

The sound of a discreet cough made him jump. Glancing up, he caught sight of a slender form in the doorway.

"What are you doing here? Didn't I tell you to stay away?"

Christian's expression did not change. If he even noticed the rebuff, it did not bother him. In spite of himself, Edward had to smile. Buffy had been like that once, sure and arrogant and unafraid. It was one of the things that had excited him most.

"I thought you might have changed your mind. I thought you might want me here when you tell him. In case he gets violent."

Edward laughed shortly. "Violent? Buffy?" No, Buffy would not be violent. Waspish, yes. Petty, vitriolic—but violent? That was not in his nature. "Just run along now. I'll call you when I want you."

Christian hesitated. "You haven't changed your mind? About going to Paris?"

If he were in a better mood, Edward would have teased the boy. He was so wonderfully transparent. "No, don't worry. I haven't changed my mind."

There was no point staying in Berlin. If it were only the Arab, he would have been willing to fight it out. But he had heard about the body in the alleyway, and he knew what it meant. It was better to cut his losses while he still could. He would think of some way to recover later.

Christian's shoulders were strong and supple as he turned, twisting with an animal grace. His hips were provocatively slim, his thighs muscular beneath tight pants. It made Edward feel young again to look at him.

Perhaps he had been too short with the boy. "We'll go to the theater tonight, you'll like that, won't you? And then a champagne supper, and after that . . . a glass of brandy before the fire in my room."

Edward was restless after Christian had left. He went to his chair, but he could not force himself to sit. He paced to the window, then back again. Dammit, Buffy was doing this on purpose, making him cool his heels just because he knew he hated it.

He had just turned back to the window when his ears picked up a footstep in the hall. The sound was annoying. Buffy used to walk like a cat, creeping into a room so silently no one would know he was there. Now he had developed a clumsy, loping gait.

Edward's suit felt tight and uncomfortable, pinching his neck until it was hard to breathe. He tried to remember when he had felt like that before. Then it came to him. A spring afternoon in Paris. A superbly beautiful Aimée, poised and motionless. Hot tea spilling against his skin as she told him she would not marry him. Raising his hand, he ran a finger inside his shirt collar. It was damp with sweat.

It was a long time before he could bring himself to turn. When he did, he saw Buffy was leaning casually against the doorjamb.

"You sent for me?"

Buffy's voice was dry and impersonal. If Edward was going to treat him like a servant, he was going to act like one. But he was damned if he was going to be gracious about it.

"You took your own sweet time getting here."

"Well, I'm here now. What do you want, Edward?"

Edward. He had called him Edward—not Eddie. It was a small slip, but a telling one.

Edward eased his body back into the chair. "You haven't taken very good care of yourself, Buffy. The bags under your eyes are getting worse, and you've developed quite a pot."

Buffy was careful to show no reaction. "Yes, I suppose we've both outgrown the clothes we wore when we met. Could it be that middle age is catching up with us?"

It was a subtle reminder that Buffy was nearly twenty years younger than his patron, and Edward hated him for it. For the first time that afternoon, he began to bristle with anger. It was a comfortable feeling. He tried to hold on to it.

"I'm sorry to hear you're aging so badly. I suppose that means you're in no shape for the little trip I have planned for you."

"Trip?" Buffy was puzzled. Edward was teasing him, actu-

397

ally teasing him, the way he used to. Could it be that Christian had made a mess of things already? "Are we going back to Egypt?"

Edward stared at him in disgust. Buffy had never been dense before.

"Egypt? Hardly. I'm afraid Egypt is out of the question." With Villière out for blood, it would be insane to go there, at least until he had some kind of plan. "*I* am going to Paris for a few weeks. Then I'll decide what to do."

The emphasis was unmistakable. Buffy's skin crawled as he listened. "So *you* are going to Paris? And what do you have in mind for me?"

"I thought perhaps the south of France. You always liked that. Or Italy, if you prefer. They say it's a good place for aging . . . roués."

He did not mean roués, and they both knew it. He meant pretty young boys who were neither pretty nor young anymore and who had lost everything they sold their souls to buy.

Buffy stood absolutely still, too stunned even for sarcasm. He had been waiting for this for years, bracing himself against it, fighting the humiliation and the fear, but in the end, he found he was not prepared at all. He had been so young when he met Edward. Young and gullible, trusting even in his shrewdness. He had known no other closeness in his life, no other dependency. There had never been anything but Edward. He did not think he could live now if he had to go to the south of France and paint subtle lines around his eyes and pretend he loved to giggle the night away in tipsy revels.

Edward could not meet his eyes. The thing was more humiliating than he had expected.

"Well, don't get so upset about it. I'm not going to cast you out on the streets, though God knows I should, after all the sarcasm I had to put up with. I'll give you a nice little pension so you won't starve."

He had learned his lesson with Aimée. He was vulnerable, more vulnerable than he cared to admit. If she, his wife, could blackmail him, what could his former lover do? No, it would be better to give him something. Not too much, of course—he didn't want to set him up in a life of style. Just enough so he'd be afraid to lose it.

"A pension? You want to give me . . . a pension?" Buffy's voice cracked on the words. He had given Edward everything he possessed. His youth, his devotion, his manhood—even the love Edward disdained. "Goddammit, do you think I'd touch a cent of your money that way? What do you think I am? A servant? A lackey? Someone to lick your boots, then crawl off in the gutter and wait for you to toss a few pathetic coins? You've done a lot to me, Edward, and I've taken it because I wanted to, but I'll be damned if I'll let you do this!"

Edward stared at him in astonishment. This was the Buffy he remembered, eyes flashing, nostrils flaring with arrogance and rage. This was the Buffy he had first seen, scrapping for shillings in a London slum. This was the Buffy he had wanted. He felt his body respond, as it had responded years ago, to the power he could only sense in others, never feel himself. He was tempted to reach out, touching the other man, pulling him onto his lap, forcing angry lips down on his. It would be exciting to tame that wild fury again, subjugating it to his own will, as helpless flesh quivered in his arms.

But, no, that was disgusting. Underneath those expensive clothes, there was nothing but flab. White, naked flab, hanging on an aging body. It would be ludicrous to make love to something like that. Christian had no vitality, no passion, he did not cry out with excitement to have his body used again and again—but at least he could look at Christian.

"What fire, Buffy, what temperament . . . and what lunacy. Come, now, you don't seriously intend to refuse my offer? You've lived in slums before. Think about it. Do you really want to go back there?"

"Goddammit, you bastard!" Buffy grabbed the front of Edward's shirt, hauling him roughly to his feet. He longed to smash his fist in that soft face. "I've earned more than a pension. I deserve more."

He held on to Edward for a moment, then with a burst of rage shoved him back in his chair. He could see everything now.

"You used me, the way you use everyone. You needed me to steal the Isis. But when you got it, you thought you could cast me off like some poor filthy Arab. Don't think for a minute I believed that cock-and-bull story of yours. The Isis stolen? By an unarmed man, when you had a gun in the room? Bullshit, Edward! You wanted it all for yourself, and you didn't care who you stepped on to get it. Now you think you can keep me quiet by pensioning me off like some arthritic housemaid. Well, you can take your fucking pension and shove it up your ass!"

Edward sat rigidly in the chair, feeling the sharp wooden frame dig into his shoulders. At first he could not figure out what Buffy was talking about. Then slowly it began to dawn on him. Tilting his head back, he let himself laugh, softly for a minute, then louder and louder.

"You are an idiot, Buffy." He had almost been killed by that damned Arab, and Buffy thought *he* had been robbed. "You are an absolute idiot."

But, oh, God, he was a glorious idiot. This was the way he wanted to remember him. This was the way he had dreamed it would end. The exhilaration of one last battle with his lover, and the heady knowledge that he had won.

Buffy looked down at him with loathing. The man was laughing at him, he was actually laughing! Once he had lain all night in his arms, and now he was laughing. He could kill him. He could put his hands around that white throat and squeeze until his face bloated up and his eyes bulged with fear. Trembling, he held himself back.

"I'm not going to kill you, you bastard. Killing's too good for you. But when I get done with you, you'll wish I had."

He did not look back as he rushed out of the room. He knew Edward was still laughing at him, but he didn't give a damn. He could laugh all he wanted now. He wouldn't be laughing later. Grabbing up a heavy coat, he hurried down the stairs, flinging open the outside door, then slamming it shut again.

Dammit, the swine. The filthy swine. Who did he think he was? Jump, he had said, and Buffy had jumped, like the obedient little lapdog he was. Bark, and he had barked. Beg. Roll over and play dead. And what was his reward? Pensioned off like an old servant.

Well, he wasn't going to roll over anymore.

The sky was overcast, the wind cold, but Buffy did not feel it. The streets were nearly deserted as he hurried down them, turning one corner, then the next, not even knowing where he was going.

So Edward wanted to declare war, did he? All right, let him find out who his opponent was. He had underestimated Buffy once that day. He would not make the same mistake again.

Buffy slowed down as he reached a wide boulevard. The sun broke out from behind a heavy layer of clouds, but the air was still cold. Turning up the collar of his coat, he tucked it tightly around his neck.

There were two things in the world Edward cared about. The way men looked at him, and the way they envied his possessions.

And there was no possession he valued more than the Isis.

The boulevard was crowded. Buffy paused at the corner, watching as people scurried by, like so many busy little ants on their way to nowhere.

Edward's reputation . . . and the Isis. It was an intriguing idea.

A man jostled against him, glowering when he did not move. A woman turned to peer curiously into his face, then looked away again. The steady stream of traffic flowed down the street, but he was not a part of it.

Edward's reputation and the Isis.

He had found his revenge.

Aimée looked up from her needlework. The hands on the wall clock had just touched four. The sound of chimes was melodious against the silence of the room.

"Mariette." She was not surprised when she received no answer. Her daughter was usually absorbed in some make-believe game of her own and rarely heard the first call. "Mariette!"

She glanced in the hallway, then began to move toward the kitchen, certain she would find the child there. A cold draft caught at her ankles, warning her that the outer door was open. She had just reached out to pull it shut when she saw Mariette in the distance, romping through the yard with a pair of dogs from the stable.

Exasperated, she stepped outside. "Mariette, come here this instant. You know it's too cold to go out without your jacket."

As usual, the child did not hear her. Sighing, Aimée picked up the jacket. Throwing a woolen shawl over her shoulders, she began to hurry across the yard. Mariette was a sweet child, lovable and happy, but she could be a trial at times.

Aimée barely noticed a solitary carriage in the road that ran past the house. Only when it slowed, turning in at the drive, did she pause to stare at it. No one ever came to visit them except Sophie, and Sophie always rode in her own coach, never a hired hackney from the station.

Aimée hurried forward, curious to see who their visitor

might be. She was halfway to the drive when the door swung slowly open and a man emerged from the interior.

She did not recognize him at first. Cold autumn light was harsh on features that had aged and sharpened. It was not until she had covered the last steps to the coach that she realized who it was.

"Buffy!"

"You don't sound pleased to see me, my dear. Don't tell me you've forgotten all those lovely times we shared together."

Forgotten? Aimée felt sick at the sound of his voice. Did he think she could ever forget those terrible nights?

"Surely you didn't expect me to be pleased. You couldn't possibly imagine you would ever be welcome in my home."

Buffy leaped down, slamming the door of the hackney. The woman had courage, he had to give her that. She had been horrified to see him, but she was determined not to let him know it. He remembered how amused he had been with her once. Amused and intrigued. She could intrigue him again if she played her cards right.

"You've changed since Edward married you. You've filled out, and quite spectacularly, too."

She had been a scrawny little thing when Edward found her, slender and flat-chested as a boy. Edward had liked that, but he had not. He had been with women before he met his lover, buxom, heavy-chested creatures all of them, and he loved to smother himself in their flesh. He wondered if that would still excite him.

"You've filled out yourself," she said tartly. "Tell me, does it bother you to be fat? You were always so vain about your figure."

Buffy sucked in his breath audibly. God, she had fire. He loved that. It would be like sparring with Eddie again, only this time it would be even better. This time he would have the upper hand.

"I've come to bring you to Berlin."

"Berlin?" Aimée felt as if the air had been knocked out of her. She thought she had come to terms with her husband long ago. Why would he send for her now?

"Doesn't the idea excite you? It should. Berlin is a lively city. You must be bored here."

Aimée fought to regain her calm. "I'm perfectly content, thank you. I have no intention of leaving."

"Had no intention. You're leaving, all right, and you're leaving now."

"I don't think I made myself clear. I am not coming with you. Not now . . . and not ever. And you can tell Edward that."

Edward? Buffy could not figure out what she was talking about. Then slowly he began to understand. Edward—she assumed Edward had sent him. Well, so much the better. It would make her more docile if she thought he was only doing her husband's bidding.

"I don't think I made *myself* clear."

Calmly, as if he were reaching for a cigarette or a pocket handkerchief, he slipped his hand inside his coat. When he brought it out again, he was holding a small, deadly revolver.

"What . . . what are you doing?" Aimée recognized the gun instantly. It was one of a pair Edward prized highly.

Buffy shifted it in his hands, as if he were uncomfortable. "What does it look like I'm doing?"

"You're mad, Buffy. You know you are."

And he was mad, he and Edward both. She didn't know why her husband wanted to see her, but she knew now that his hatred had gone beyond sanity. Somehow, she had to get away. If only she could find something to distract Buffy, something to take his attention off her, just for a second.

"Mama!"

Horrified, Aimée whirled around. She had forgotten Mariette. Now she saw the child racing toward her. Her face was bright with curiosity.

"No, Mariette, no!" She took a step forward, then caught herself. "Go into the house. Now. Run!"

"No!" Buffy's voice rang sharply in her ear. "The child stays here."

Mariette hesitated, looking at her mother. Aimée allowed herself one quick glance over her shoulder. Buffy had slipped the gun back in his pocket, but an angry bulge reminded her it was pointed directly at her. Stretching out her hand, she watched helplessly as Mariette ran to her.

Buffy was fascinated with the child, and he made no attempt to hide it. He had not seen Mariette for two years, and then she was just a baby. It had not occurred to him she would grow into such a well-defined little person. It amused him to search her face, trying to pick out traces of himself.

Mariette was staring back at him just as frankly. Aimée

put her hands on the child's shoulders, pulling her protectively against her body.

"This is a . . . a friend of your father's."

"My father?" The eagerness in her voice tore at Aimée's heart. "You know my father?"

Buffy began to laugh. He tried to stop himself, but he could not. Tears of amusement sparkled in the corners of his eyes. "Do I know your father? Oh, dear, dear—that's a good one. Do I know your father, indeed?"

Aimée tightened her arms around the child. Her eyes flashed as she faced Buffy.

"Edward is her father. Do you hear me? Edward is her father . . . and you know Edward."

"You're a protective little bitch, aren't you?"

So the child didn't know the shame of her birth, and the mother was determined to shield her from it. Well, that was all right. Buffy liked that. He wanted the mother of his child to be protective.

She had a blazing beauty about her as she challenged him. All fire and fury. He had never had a woman like that before. Oh, the others had been pretty enough, all of them pretty, and they had come to him willingly because he was even comelier than they, but none of them had been fertile enough to bear him a child.

"The child is coming, too."

He hadn't thought about it before. It was not part of his plan. But after all, why not? Why shouldn't he have the child *and* the woman?

"No, please . . . please. Do what you want with me, but leave Mariette alone."

There was passion in her. He could see that as she fought for her child. He would teach her to unleash it in his bed. Then he would have everything. Edward's reputation, Edward's possessions, and Edward's wife. And his body would writhe in her embrace with an excitement that had once been only Edward's.

"The child comes."

Mariette sensed their tension. "What's wrong, Mama? Where are we going?"

"To Berlin," Aimée answered mechanically. Her mind was spinning, caught up in the terror of the situation. She had to do something, she had to get away from him. But how? I'll . . . I'll just pack a few things, and then we'll be ready."

If only she could get inside the house . . . if she could just get to the servants. Even if she couldn't speak to them, perhaps she could leave a note someplace where they'd be sure to find it.

"You take me for a fool, madame. That's a dangerous thing to do. You'll go as you are."

"A coat—at least a coat . . ."

"I said you'll go as you are. Now, get into the carriage."

"Mama." Mariette was tugging at her skirts. "Mama, why are we going to Berlin?"

Aimée could see the child was frightened. "It's all right, *petite*," she soothed, dropping to her knees beside her. She tried not to let her fingers tremble as she helped Mariette into the light jacket, buttoning it over her chest. "It's all right. We're just going to . . . to see your father."

"Father?" Mariette's fears dissolved instantly. Her whole face lit up. "We're really going to see my father?"

Aimée wanted to weep as she watched her. So little and so full of hope. And there was no way she could protect her. All too soon she'd see the father she'd been dreaming of—and then her dreams would be all over.

4

The rain was a constant drumming against the window. Raoul's breath formed a frosty pattern on the glass as he stared down at the street in front of the hotel. A solitary carriage rolled past. Two men hugged the walls, collars turned up, heads lowered, as they pushed through the gusty torrent. Then the street was still again. The only movement was the rush of water as it overflowed the gutters, forming a river of rain.

Raoul turned back to the half-empty suitcase lying open on the bed. He picked up a pair of soiled shirts, not even bothering to fold them as he stuffed them inside. It would be good to get away from here. He had not intended to remain so long, but there had been things to arrange, supplies to order. If he was going to turn the tomb over to the Egyptians, at least he could repair the damage the thieves had done first.

The heavy beating of the rain throbbed in his head as he finished packing. Snapping the suitcase shut, he placed it beside the door. In a few hours, just a few short hours, he would be out of this place. The wind howled through cracks in the window, setting the panes rattling against the frame.

Berlin. What a romantic sound the name had. An imperial city. Vital, teeming, alive. But there had been no romance here for him. No life. Only gray autumn streets, cold with rain. Only deceit and disappointment—and death.

He picked up his coat, tossing it impatiently on the bed. The rain was heavier now, a solid sheet pouring down the window. The world outside had grown invisible, as if it no longer existed.

Buffy shook the water off his coat. It was a futile gesture. He was already drenched to the skin, but he enjoyed watching little puddles form on Edward's expensive Persian rug.

"You seem surprised to see me."

Edward glowered back at him. He was standing alone next to the window in his study on the second floor.

"How the devil did you get in?"

He looked, Buffy thought, more irritated than apprehensive. That was too bad. He had wanted him to be apprehensive.

"You should tell that new playmate of yours not to leave the windows open, especially in the rain. Or isn't he here? Don't tell me you've quarreled already. That would be a pity, wouldn't it?"

"Oh, Christian's still here—as you'll find to your regret." Edward moved toward the bell cord at the far side of the room.

"I wouldn't do that if I were you, Eddie."

Edward hesitated, his hand only inches from the cord. Something in Buffy's tone, quiet but sure, held him back.

Buffy laughed softly. "I have something to tell you—something very interesting. I don't think you'll want your little friend to hear."

Edward scowled, but Buffy knew he would not move. Pointedly, he turned his back. With a slow, deliberate movement he drew his fingers along the surface of a polished rosewood table, so smooth it felt like glass. Bending down, he peeked into a heavy crate on the floor beside it. He recognized a blue-and-white K'ang Hsi vase.

"Packing all your favorite things?"

"I told you I was going to Paris."

"But not that you weren't coming back." Edward always

kept a house once he had bought it. He liked to string them out behind him, like so many monuments to his wealth. "Could it be that darling Christian doesn't want to come home again?"

"I don't think that's any of your business. If you have something to say, say it . . . then get out. You're making me impatient, and I don't like to be impatient. You wouldn't want me to change my mind about that pension I offered you."

Buffy sat down slowly. It amused him to think that his wet coat was staining the upholstery.

"Pension, Eddie? I told you once before I didn't want your charity. I want what you owe me—and I mean to get it."

"And what the hell do you think I owe you?"

Buffy did not answer. Rising again, he stepped over to the desk. The Meissen clock had not been packed. Picking it up, he held it lightly in his hands.

"You have lovely things, Eddie. Very lovely. I think it would be nice if you shared them, don't you? Especially with someone who's shared so much with you—if you know what I mean."

Edward's scowl darkened. Wasn't that just like Buffy? Whatever he offered him, he always wanted more. A nice Norfolk jacket with pleats to the hem? But Buffy wanted a silk waistcoat and striped trousers, complete with top hat and cane. A cozy room apart from the servants' quarters? Only a suite of his own would do, with a white ceramic stove and gilded limewood furnishings. Now he was ready to give him a modest pension, and how did Buffy react? He had the nerve to stand there and demand a share of his possessions, as if their relationship gave him some kind of claim.

"I'll be damned if I'll give you a thing, you weasel!"

"Won't you? Oh, I think you will."

Edward began to sweat. He watched his former lover turn the fragile clock over in his hands, and he wanted to run up to him, tearing it out of his grasp.

"What do you want?"

What *did* he want? Buffy asked himself. He had come with only one idea, but now his horizons were expanding. He wanted to live like Edward, enjoy the things Edward enjoyed, without having to grovel for them.

"A little of everything, Eddie . . . a little of everything." And he would get it, too, bit by bit, finding new ways to bleed him over the years. "Right now, I want the Isis."

"The Isis?" Edward choked on the word. He had been nervous, almost afraid, as he listened to the confidence in Buffy's voice. Now he knew he had overestimated the man. "You damn fool. Do you think I'd give you the Isis, even if I had it?"

Edward's choice of words was unfortunate. *If* I had it. . . . Buffy was sure he was on the right track now. That trumped-up robbery. So childish, and so obvious.

"You have it, all right, and you're going to give it to me."

He reached into his inside pocket, pulling out a sheet of paper. It was soaked with rain, but the writing was still legible. Without a word, he handed it to Edward.

Edward's hand shook slightly as he reached out to take it. Slowly he lowered his body into the chair. The upholstery was still wet from Buffy's coat, but he could not get up and move. He did not want him to know he had noticed.

Buffy smiled as he watched him open the paper, unfolding it carefully so he would not tear it. Aimée's handwriting was distinctive. Edward could not fail to recognize it.

He remembered the look on the woman's face when he dictated the note to her. Amazement, disbelief, then sheer, utter horror. Until that moment, she had still, stupidly, clung to the belief that he was acting for Edward. Even when she saw the miserable hovel he dragged them to, even when he locked them inside, without food, without water, without blankets to protect them from the cold, she tried to pretend to herself it was all a whim of her husband's and everything would be all right in the end.

Well, now she knew where she stood. In another minute Edward would know, too.

Edward's lips moved as he read. He struggled to make out the words, blurred against the damp paper, but he couldn't seem to piece them together. No matter what he came up with, it didn't make any sense.

"What's the matter, Eddie? Can't you read?" Buffy was tempted to laugh out loud. Poor Edward, poor simple Edward. The whole thing was so diabolically clever, his slow mind could not follow it.

Reaching forward, he pulled the paper out of his hands, holding it up to the light. He did not falter, even when the words had been smeared beyond recognition. He knew it all by heart.

" 'Dearest Edward'—That's a nice touch, don't you think, as if the woman really loves you. 'Dearest Edward, We are being held prisoner, your daughter and I. Do not try to find us, and do not call the police. If you value our lives, give him whatever he wants. He will kill us if you do not. He means what he says.' "

Buffy looked up expectantly when he finished. Edward could only stare at him dully.

Of all the things Buffy could have done, all the threats he could have made, why did he chose this one?

"What the hell do I care what you do to them? I don't even like the woman. As for that snivelling brat, she isn't mine."

"Yes, but *they* don't know that. That's the beauty of it all."

"They?"

"*They*—all the people out there who are always judging you . . . and laughing at you. What will they say, I wonder, if you let your wife and child be killed because you can't bear to give up a piece of jewelry—and a stolen one at that? How many soigné little dinner parties will you be invited to then?"

His eyes narrowed as he studied Edward's face. "You know, I think it's going to be amusing . . . very amusing. Of course, I'll have to help the gossip along, but then, I have such juicy tidbits to add, don't you agree? Can't you just hear them, Eddie, all those snobbish matrons at their snobbish matinées? 'Such a greedy little man,' they'll say. 'So nasty and unappealing. And did you know, he's a . . .' And then they'll lean forward, because 'homosexual' is not a thing one says out loud. And they'll whisper the word—but everyone will know what they're saying. And they'll laugh, Eddie. Oh, yes, they will laugh."

Edward was sweating again. He hated the way Buffy was looking at him, leering, smirking, as if he had begun to tell people already. He wanted to take out his handkerchief and wipe his face, but he knew he couldn't.

"Really, Buffy, I'm bored with all this. I don't give a damn what you do, or what people choose to laugh at. I'll tell you what. Why don't you just take the two of them and tie stones around their necks and drown them in the river?"

Sweat dripped into his eyes, but still he could not wipe it away. Buffy stood and watched as he blinked uncomfortably.

"Maybe I will. That's not a bad idea. I can see the headlines already: 'WOMAN AND CHILD DROWNED LIKE KITTENS WHILE MILLIONAIRE FAGGOT STANDS BY.' Maybe I'll kill the woman first—just to show you I mean business. After all, I'd hate to have to drown my own child."

"Your child?" Edward meant the words as brittle sarcasm, but they came out in a shriek of rage. Damn the man, he had forced him to sit there with sweat dripping down in his eyes, and there was nothing he could do about it. "What makes you think it's yours?"

He had kept the information to himself for two years, harboring it, nourishing it in secret, waiting for the day he threw Buffy out at last. It was meant to be the final blow to an arrogance that had grown unbearable, but when the time came, he hadn't been able to do it. He had looked at Buffy and seen a broken, defeated man, and he simply couldn't say the words. He had pitied him too much.

He did not pity him now.

"Did you really think you were man enough to father a child?"

Buffy stiffened, but he was careful not to let the other man see it. He did not want Edward to think he believed him.

"I suppose you're going to tell me you're the father? Come, now, Eddie, do you seriously expect me to believe you bedded your wife? Don't forget, I was in the next room on your wedding night."

Edward's eyes burned with rage as he stared at him. Even after all these years, the wound was still open.

"No, the child is not mine, any more than it's yours."

"You don't know that." The words were brusque—too brusque. Edward picked up his tension.

"Of course I know, you fool. I know because she told me—Aimée."

"Aimée?" Buffy faltered, unsure now. Aimée had told Edward . . . what? That Buffy was not the father of her child? But that was impossible. He had to be.

Or did he? He stared at Edward, and he knew he was telling the truth. Edward was always so transparent when he lied.

Damn her, that filthy bitch. He had been ready to offer her devotion, the same devotion Edward tossed away. He had even wanted to teach her the passion of his body, and all the time . . .

"But who . . . ?"

He did not need to finish the question. He already knew who the man was. Villière, that bastard, always so ready to look down his nose at him. Villière, cool and businesslike, and all the time he was screwing Aimée behind his back. God, how he hated the man.

Edward's face relaxed as he watched him. "Now I suppose you really will drown them. Just out of spite."

And he probably would, too, Edward thought wryly, but it didn't matter anymore. Buffy had had all the wind knocked out of him. He would take the modest little pension his lover offered him, with all the humiliations that went along with it, and he would be grateful for it.

"I'm going to ring for Christian now. I think it's time you were leaving."

But he had misjudged the man he once knew so well. Buffy reached the bell cord before he did, slamming it into the wall with his fist.

"Do you think this changes anything?"

Dammit, he was more determined than ever. He had been bluffing before when he threatened to kill them. Now he was ready to go through with it. The bitch had double-crossed him, and she deserved to die. As for the child—why should he worry about another man's brat?

Edward stared at him in mild surprise. "I think it changes everything. Think it over, Buffy. If they'll laugh at me, a greedy little faggot trying to hold on to his fortune, what do you think they'll make of you—a faggot who thought he could father a child?"

"Damn you." Buffy's hand closed tightly around the bell cord. Then suddenly he released it, dashing it violently against the wall. "Ring for your little ass-kisser if you want. It doesn't matter now. But the deal still stands. The Isis . . . or I'll kill them both. And frankly, Eddie, I hope you choose the Isis. I'd like nothing better than to see you ruined—even if I go down with you."

He was shaking with anger when he turned toward the door. Edward's voice stopped him before he could leave.

"You *are* a fool, Buffy." He waited, patient and amused, for the man to face him again. "You've miscalculated badly. I really don't have the Isis."

"The devil you don't."

"You should keep up with things, you know. The body of an Arab was found in an alleyway only a block from here the same day the Isis was stolen. It could be a coincidence, of course, but I doubt it. I think I know who the man was, and I think I know who killed him."

Buffy studied Edward's face, trying to figure out if he was lying. But it would be such a stupid lie, he thought. A body in an alleyway. What could be easier to check?

So the Arab had stolen the Isis after all. And now Villièr had it back.

Edward touched his hand to the bell cord, then pulled i away. He would not need help now. He handed the not back to Buffy.

"You might rip off that 'Dearest Edward.' It had a phon sound to it anyway. Then you could see if it works better o Villière.

Buffy seethed as he reached out to take it from him. Villièr again, always Villière. Whenever he wanted anything, Villièr was always there. Still . . .

"I might just do that." His hand was steady as he slippe the note into his pocket.

After all, what did it matter who had the Isis now?

Edward was beginning to enjoy himself. "I wouldn't hol my breath if I were you. The only thing Villière cares about i his work. You could kill a dozen women and a dozen chil dren, and I doubt if he'd even look up and notice."

Perhaps, Buffy thought. Perhaps. But archaeologists wer human, too, and archaeologists had reputations to protect just like millionaires. Everyone had an Achilles' heel, eve Raoul Villière. It was merely a matter of finding it.

He wanted the Isis, and he was going to have it. It was a simple as that. He wanted to open that elegant, understate jeweler's box right in front of Edward's eyes and hear hin gasp with envy. He wanted him to know, once and for all, that everything he had ever loved or possessed—o coveted—was going to be taken away from him, piece b piece, until he was as poor as Buffy the day he found him.

"*Au revoir*, Eddie," he said softly. "And won't worry—we will meet again."

Christian came out of a side room just as he was bolting down the stairs. He paused to grin at the startled expression on his face.

"You're an asshole, Christian. Do stop gaping. You look like a dying fish. Edward loathes that. You're going to have to develop some personality if you want to keep him."

It was a childish taunt, but it gave him an enormous amount of satisfaction. He glanced over his shoulder one last time as he opened the door.

"And do remember to keep the windows closed, that's a good boy."

He was strangely pleased with himself as he strode out into the street. He had taken all his anger and channeled it in one direction, and it gave an electric excitement to his life. He had not felt so alive in years.

Aimée paced nervously across the narrow room. Six steps. Six steps across, and six back again. It was so small, so very small, like the cage for an animal at the zoo.

She shuddered at the image. The place *was* a cage, she thought. Small and square and dark, and there was no way out of it.

Stopping tensely, she drew her forearm across her brow, brushing back the hair that had fallen into her eyes. Even in the cold night air, her face was damp with sweat. A heavy rain beat steadily on the roof, hammering at thick tiles with a dull, relentless monotony.

No way out, it seemed to say. *No way out. There's no way out of here*.

Wearily she looked around her. The place seemed to be a storage shed, or perhaps a farm outbuilding, in some isolated area. The walls were high and thick, with row upon row of bricks firmly cemented with mortar. The door, sturdy wood reinforced with metal plates, had resisted all her efforts to jolt it from its hinges, and the only window, if it could even be called that, was a narrow horizontal slit high in the wall. Even that was covered with a metal grating.

"Oh, *mon Dieu*, it's hopeless."

And yet it couldn't be, she thought desperately. It just couldn't. Somehow, there had to be a way to escape, if only she were clever enough to see it. Buffy had left them an hour ago, or perhaps two. He could come back at any minute. And when he did, they couldn't afford to be here.

Anxiously she turned toward Mariette. The child was seated on a straight wooden chair at the side of the room.

"Oh, *petite*." Her voice was heavy with discouragement. Mariette was tired, she could see that, but she had taken off her jacket and let it fall to the floor. "Why did you do that? You know you have to wear your jacket."

"But I'm hot, Mama."

Hot? How could she be? Even with a woolen shawl wrapped around her shoulders, Aimée was shivering. Exhausted, she leaned down, picking up the jacket and tossing it to Mariette.

"I'm too tired to argue with you now. Just put it on."

"But, Mama, I'm—"

"I said put it on."

She could see that the child was near tears, but she had neither the time nor the energy to comfort her. She had barely slept on the long train journey, and she did not dare take even a few minutes to nap now. Somehow, hopeless as it seemed, she had to think of something to do.

She could still see the look on Buffy's face when he had left them. So gloating, so sure—and so utterly mad. She wondered what he would look like when he returned.

Oh, God, why had she ever been fool enough to let Edward find out about the child? Now he would tell Buffy. She knew he would. He would sit back in his chair, smug and sarcastic, and he would drawl out the words. And he would laugh in his face.

If Buffy teetered on the brink of madness now, what would happen when he learned he was no more a man than the lover who had cast him out?

Exhausted and frightened, Aimée began to pace again. She knew she had to do something, but what? Why—*why*—was it so hard to find a way out of there?

"If only it weren't such a pigsty!"

She stared around her in disgust. Pigsty was the word for it. The floor was covered with matted straw, slimy and foul-smelling, as if the place had been used to shelter livestock. A plain wooden chair, crude but sturdy, rested against the wall. Across from it, a rough-hewn table, dotted with flecks of paint, teetered precariously on three legs that still supported a rotting plank. A single candle, half burned away, flickered in a wooden holder on the floor. There was only one other object in the room, a massive iron bedstead, so heavy Aimée could not drag it. It was covered with linen, but the sheets were so dirty they looked as if they had not been cleaned in years.

"Oh, Mariette . . ."

Aimée was so tired she was tempted to give up. She had told the child to stay on the chair, she had begged her to be good, and now Mariette had crawled onto the bed, resting her face on those vile sheets.

"Mariette, get up at once. Why are you being so naughty? I know you're tired, but it will be just a little while and then we will be out of here. I don't want you lying on that filthy thing."

Mariette only looked up at her. She made no attempt to move. "I don't feel well, Mama."

"Oh, no."

414

Alarmed, Aimée hurried to the child, bending over the bed. Mariette couldn't be sick, she told herself, half-frantic at the idea. She just couldn't.

She laid her hand on Mariette's brow, praying it would be cool. It was not.

"Oh, *petite,* I'm sorry." No wonder she had thrown off her jacket. And Aimée had only snapped at her. "Does it hurt anywhere? Tell Mama where it hurts."

"I just don't feel good. Please don't make me sit on the chair again."

"No, baby, no. I'm sorry," Aimée picked her up tenderly, cradling the fragile body in her arms. She could feel the warmth of Mariette's flesh against her breast. The little jacket was drenched with sweat.

That horrible train station, she thought bitterly. So crowded and stifling. God only knows what she picked up there. And nothing but a thin jacket to shield her from the rain. No wonder she was sick.

Aimée took off her shawl, spreading it over the bed. It was caked with dust from the journey, but at least it was cleaner than the sheets. "Here, *mon lapin,* lie on this."

She unbuttoned the jacket, pulling it gently from feverish limbs. Mariette did not resist, but she was too weak to lift her arms to help. Her whole body was hot, Aimée thought with despair. Her chest, her arms, even her hands. It was as if there were a fire raging inside her, struggling to get out.

She laid the jacket over the child, tucking it around her, but Mariette pushed it away, shrugging it off as if it were an irritation. Again Aimée wrapped her in it, and again Mariette threw it off. Sighing, Aimée folded it tidily, laying it on the edge of the bed. Perhaps it was better that way, she told herself wearily. The jacket would only hold in Mariette's body heat. At least the air would be cooling. Perhaps it would bring down the fever.

She rested her hand on the child's forehead again. She was alarmed to find it was even hotter than before. A few minutes, just a few minutes, and the fever had already gone up. All Aimée could do was sit at her side, brushing damp hair from her flushed face, and pray everything would be all right. It was an agonizing, helpless feeling. Mariette was so little—so very little—and there was nothing she could do for her.

They had to get out of there, she thought desperately. Somehow they had to get free. Mariette needed a doctor, a hospital, medication. A sick little girl didn't belong on filthy sheets in a bitter cold room, with rain blowing in from the window.

Aimée ran her hand one last time over Mariette's brow, then forced herself to stand up. She didn't know what she was going to do, but she had to do something. They couldn't stay in that place.

Anxiously she scanned the room one more time, searching for something she'd overlooked. The door? But she'd already tried the door, and it held against her assault. The window? But the window was too high to reach, and she had nothing to stand on. And the walls were thick and strong.

The floor, then. She fell to her knees. The floor was her only hope. Somewhere beneath all that matted straw and dirt, there had to be a weakness, some single flaw she could exploit to get out of here. Groping with her hands, she crawled along every inch of the space, searching for something—*anything*—she could use. Filth caked her fingers, moldy straw clung to her skin, vermin scurried out of the way as she disturbed their hiding places, but she did not let herself think about that. She was fighting for her child, and that was all that mattered.

But the floor proved agonizingly solid. There was not a single soft, decaying spot, not so much as a chink she could break through in a desperate attempt to tunnel into the earth with her bare hands. There was not even a mouse hole at the base of one of the walls to give her a ray of hope. She wanted to put her head in her hands and give up, but they were so filthy she could not touch them to her face.

The sound of a whimper across the room jolted her out of her despair. Pulling herself together, she sat on the edge of the bed.

"Are you all right, *ma petite chère*? Are you feeling better?"

But Mariette did not answer. Frantically Aimée tried to wipe her hands on her skirt, but she could not get them clean. She wanted to take the child in her arms, but she did not dare.

"Mariette, open your eyes. Please open your eyes for Mama. Wake up now, Mama's here."

The child looked up at last, but she did not see Aimée. Her eyes were glassy and dark.

"It's all right, Mariette. Tell Mama how you feel. Does it hurt anywhere?"

"I have a kitten," the girl murmured softly. "A kitten with a cookie."

Her voice was so low Aimée had to bend to hear it.

"There's no kitten. You must have been dreaming."

"No, I have a kitten. I do. Don't you see him?"

Oh, God, Aimée thought, terrified. Mariette was delirious. The fever had gotten worse, and there was nothing she could do about it.

"Oh, my poor *petite*." Aimée could bear it no longer. Rubbing her hand one last time on her skirt, she laid it on the child's brow.

The heat seemed to sear through her fingers. Aimée wanted to cry when she felt it. She had never known anything like it. Mariette had always been such a healthy child, with no more than a few sniffles or an occasional sore throat. There was nothing to prepare her for this.

"Oh, *petite*." She pulled her up in her arms, pressing her tightly against her own flesh, as if somehow a mother's closeness could provide a protective shield. "What can I do? What can I do?"

She wanted so much to help her child, she wanted to ease the fever and the pain; but she did not know how. She needed someone, she realized desperately, someone with experience, someone who knew about these things. Always before, all her life, whenever she had been afraid, there was someone there. Her mother, her father, Sophie. Now she was alone.

"Oh, please, help me," she cried out. "Please . . . someone . . . help me."

But there was no one to hear. She was completely alone. No one was there, and no one would come. It was all up to her now. If she was going to help Mariette, if she was going to get her to a doctor, she would have to do it by herself.

Buffy sat quietly in a chair by the window in the small hotel room. He ran his hands slowly up and down the damp edge of his lapel. He was beginning to feel calmer now, more sure of himself. If Edward had disappointed him, Raoul Villière was all he could hope for.

Raoul flicked the note carelessly across the table. His features were set and expressionless.

"What makes you think I'd be interested in this?"

The man was good, Buffy had to admit. He knew how to

play the game. Well, that was all right. Buffy did not mind. In a way, it was amusing.

"I thought—that is, we thought . . ." Yes, that was a nice touch. Let Raoul assume he was Edward's messenger. Then, if anything went wrong, Edward would get the blame. "We thought you might care what happens to your mistress."

"My mistress?" Raoul tried not to let his surprise show. How the hell could Edward know about that? He had been so careful.

"Don't play innocent with me." Buffy decided it was time to get tough. "We know about that . . . uh . . . shall we call it romance? The woman told Eddie all about it."

Dammit, Raoul thought, what kind of a perverted relationship did those two have, anyway? Edward with his pretty boys on the side, Aimée with her lovers. Looking at Buffy now, it occurred to him that they had even shared one of those lovers. What did they do, sit around and compare notes?

"So now you think you can blackmail me. Just because I shared her favors with . . . with everyone else in town."

Buffy sucked his lip between his teeth. Damn! That time Villière had seen him outside Aimée's room. It had made him feel good then, self-satisfied and superior. Now he was sorry it had happened.

"If you don't care about the woman, surely you must have some feeling for your child."

"My child?" Raoul's laughter was bitter. "You know damn well the child could as well be yours . . . or Edward's."

"Edward's?" Buffy did not know why the thought struck him so funny. He tried not to giggle, but he couldn't help himself. The whole thing was so ludicrous. "Edward's Oh, dear, dear—you don't think it's Edward's?"

"Aimée's his wife. It's logical."

"It may be logical, but good Lord, man! Why, Edward couldn't sire a child if his life depended on it. He couldn't even fuck a woman. He said he did it once, but I don't believe it—do you?"

Raoul winced at his words. He was used to gutter language, but coming from someone as effeminate as Buffy, it sounded grotesque.

"Yours, then. Yours or mine. I'll tell you what, Buffy. We'll flip a coin. Heads it's yours, tails it's mine. Only, if it turns up heads, you pay the ransom."

Buffy squirmed in his chair. He did not like the way things were going.

"It has to be tails, Villière." He hated doing this. He hated exposing his weakness to the other man, but he wanted the Isis. "I only touched her a few times—long before the child was conceived. You see, Eddie thought it would be amusing to have a son—he really wanted a son, you know—so he sent me in to do the job he couldn't handle himself. We would have kept it up, but quite frankly, I found the woman unappealing. So sluttish, don't you think? I prefer more of a lady. Naturally, I had to ask Eddie to release me from such unpleasantness. You may have noticed, Eddie can deny me nothing."

He broke off, waiting for Raoul's reaction. The man was staring at him as if he could not believe what he was hearing.

"You mean to tell me Aimée's husband forced her to take you into her bed?"

"Oh, I wouldn't say 'forced.' " Even for gain, even for revenge, Buffy could not humiliate himself so intensely. "Let's just say 'suggested.' She was willing enough, after the initial shock. I am not unskilled as a lover, even with a woman."

"You son of a bitch!" Raoul lunged forward, grabbing Buffy by the lapels. He knew Aimée well enough to know the pig was lying. She might surrender to her passions, but only with the man of her choice. "You force yourself on Aimée, then you have the gall to come here and tell me about it."

Buffy barely had time for a startled gasp before Raoul pulled him out of his chair. He threw his arms up to protect himself, but he was too late. With a single swift thrust Raoul flung him across the room. The wall shuddered as his body slammed into it.

Stumbling, he clutched at the bedpost to keep from falling. He thought Raoul would charge at him again, tearing into him with his bare fists, but at the last minute he held back.

Good, Buffy thought, exhilarated. Villière was no fool. He was an arrogant bastard, but not a fool. He knew Buffy still held the woman and the child.

And Villière had made the mistake of showing he cared about them.

"The child is yours," he taunted slowly. "Whether you like it or not."

Raoul did not answer. He stood across the room, eyes black with rage, but he did not speak.

Buffy grew bolder.

419

"Which of them do you care about most? The female or the child? I'll save that one for last. We can kill the other one first. Eddie wants to tie a stone around its neck and drown it like an unwanted kitten."

"Shut up." Raoul could feel a nervous tic tugging at the corner of his mouth. He knew Buffy was aware of it, too. "I don't have the thing here."

It was a lie. He had gotten it that morning out of the vault where he kept it, but he needed time to think. He needed time to decide what to do.

"Well, that's simple enough." Buffy reached up, straightening his collar. "Go and get it. I'll wait."

"Like hell you will. I've had enough of you. Get out of here."

Buffy tensed for a minute, then relaxed. The man was angry, but he was only blustering.

"All right, I'll go."

After all, what could Villière do? Go to the police? But the police would never find Aimée and the child in time.

"But I'll be back in two hours. And when I get here, you'd better have the Isis. If you don't, they're both as good as dead."

He closed the door quietly behind him.

5

Raoul stared down at the open case in his hands, trying to figure out what there was about a silent, enigmatic remnant of the past that could be so compelling. Broad wings swept in a graceful arc beneath golden arms, and deep red and blue stones picked up fiery highlights from the candle flame, but grace and fire alone were not enough to explain the appeal. The Isis was beautiful, but she was passionless—an inanimate accumulation of metal and minerals, nothing more. He wondered why it was so hard to give her up. Flipping the cover shut, he tossed the box on the bed, then glanced out the window.

Did it always rain in this city? he asked himself bitterly. In the month he had been there, it seemed to him he had known only a few hours of sunlight, and even those had been followed by dark, threatening clouds. He began to resent the steady, monotonous battering of raindrops against cold glass.

If you don't care about the woman, at least you must have some feeling for your child.

He wished he could stop hearing the words. The image of Buffy's face was smug and gloating in his memory.

His child? The man was a liar, it was obvious he was a liar—he would say anything to get the Isis. And yet, there had been a ring of truth in his tone.

His child? He remembered the girl. A pretty little thing, with black curls all over her head, and bright blue eyes. She had been barely a toddler then. Now she would be a little lady, with vanities and caprices all her own. He wondered if she would still run up to him and throw her arms around his neck.

He wanted to believe she was his. He did not try to deny that now. He had already admitted there would be no other children for him. No pretty fiancées, no plans for weddings and country homes and big family gatherings at Christmas in front of the fire. He was a loner, and he knew it. This child was his only chance, his last private, secret stake in immorality. And still . . .

And still . . . Yes, that was the problem, wasn't it? Still, ultimately, no matter what they told him, no matter how many assurances they gave him, he could never be sure she was his. He sat in a chair by the window and stretched his long legs out in front of him.

His child—or not his child? How many men had asked themselves that same question? And which of them could be sure of the answer?

And did it matter?

He was surprised at the simplicity of the thought. It was so basic and so obvious, yet it had eluded him all this time. Did it really matter what man's seed had created this child? She was her own being now, separate and apart from them all. He cared for her, and that was all there was to it. Somewhere in the years that followed her birth, he had come to love her and think of her as his. And in all that was essential, she was.

He walked over to the bed, picking up the case again. He held it unopened in his hands. This child—*his* child—had to be protected, no matter what the cost.

And so did her mother.

Raoul moved restlessly back to the window. He could see nothing through the heavy rain, but he knew that Buffy must already be somewhere just beneath him, pushing his way across storm-swept pavements to the hotel entrance.

Aimée. Even now it was hard to think of her. Aimée. He had been so unfair to her, and she had never said a word. He could still see her stepping out into the lamplight in front of her tent, her eyes turning to black in the twilight as she looked down at her sleeping child.

Mariette is afraid of the dark.

And Aimée? Was she ever afraid? Was she afraid now?

He lifted the box in his hands. He was tempted to open it again, looking one last time at the Isis, but he held himself back. He had seen it often enough, studied it, memorized it with his eyes. It was time to let go of it now.

He set it slowly on the table.

"It's all right, *petite*," he whispered. "I won't let anyone hurt you."

Aimée stood in the center of the room and looked around her. She was frightened, desperately frightened, but she did not stop to listen to the rapid beating of her own heart. Panic was a luxury she could not afford.

Buffy had been gone at least three hours. She calculated the timing in her mind. An hour jostling over country roads to get into town, perhaps an hour and a half . . . another hour to locate Edward. That was all it would take. He had to have arrived by now.

And he had to know the truth.

She threw an anxious glance at Mariette, so little and defenseless on the bed, her arm thrust out as if to reach for the help her mother could not give her. Only an hour ago, in Buffy's mind at least, she had been his child, and she had had a hold, however tenuous, on his vanity. Now there was nothing to protect her.

Edward would not give his lover the Isis, Aimée was sure of that. He would agonize over the decision, he would sit and think of the scandal he was creating until sweat poured in little streams down the creases in his cheeks, but in the end, he would hang on to his possessions with the same grip of a dying man, and Buffy would be thwarted again. When he returned, if he returned . . .

If he returned. Aimée shuddered at the thought. He could as well leave them in that hellhole to die. He was perfectly capable of that. And even if he came back . . .

If, if . . . if. Aimée forced the word from her mind. There were a dozen ifs, and each more unpleasant than the last.

Only one if counted. *If* Buffy returned, he had to find that dim, stinking cell empty.

She scanned the room again, this time more carefully.

"The door is out."

She spoke the words aloud, making them as crisp and efficient as she could. Her voice was hoarse with tension, but she did not care. Anything that broke the incessant pounding of the rain on the roof was welcome.

Yes, the door was definitely out. It was strong enough to hold against the harshest battering, and the metal plates that covered its surface were too thick to scratch or break away. She had already searched it carefully, running her fingers along the frame to try to get at the hinges, but even that was no good. The thing was as invincible as a prison gate.

The floor was just as bad. She had groveled over every inch of it with no better luck. And the window, set high against the ceiling, was so unattainable it might as well have been a painted prop on a theater backdrop.

"Well, that leaves the walls."

She said the words boldly, as if she were confident, but she could not fool herself. She knew she would be able to break through the walls eventually if she had the time and the tools. But time was a limited commodity, and there was not so much as a single rusty hammer or rotting wedge lying unnoticed in a corner.

Shoulders bent with weariness, she forced herself over to the wall. It was hopeless, she knew, but no more hopeless than standing idly in the center of the floor. The least she could do was try.

She chose the wall beneath the window, picking it arbitrarily, for no other reason than that it was there. Sinking to her knees, she laid her palm against the rough surface, shivering at the icy slime that seeped down from the high open window. Her hand was tentative as she pushed it against the bricks, expecting nothing more than the solid resistance that met her effort. With little more hope, she scratched long fingernails into the mortar, scraping and clawing as if she dared to believe she could work through it. To her surprise, it crumbled beneath her touch.

Pausing, she looked up at the wall. Broad dark streaks ran down its length, marking the course of rain from countless storms. And wherever the wall was stained, the concrete was soft and rotting.

For the first time she let herself hope. The bricks themselves were solid, but if the settings had deteriorated enough she might be able to pry them loose, one at a time, until she made a hole big enough to crawl through. A few bricks, that was all it would take. Eight or ten—twelve at most—and then they would be free.

She fell on the wall with an energy that amazed her. She was exhausted from fear and lack of sleep, she had not eaten for forty-eight hours, but if she was weak, she no longer noticed. Her fingers gouged at the mortar until they were torn and bleeding.

At first it was an easy task. Scrape and brush away, scrape and brush again, and the space grew deeper and deeper. Only as she dug farther into the wall did she finally see the one thing she had not let herself think about before. The line of concrete between the bricks was a thin one, so thin even the slimmest fingers could not slip into the crack. The decaying surface was easy to get at, but there was no way she could reach the more solid material that lay beneath.

She wanted to scream with frustration. She had found the way out—it was so simple and so close—yet she could not get at it. She tried one last time to claw through the sharp stubborn edges of the bricks, then gave up at last. Trembling with despair, she slid to the floor.

If only she could find something to use, she thought, searching the room with her eyes. If only there was some simple, obvious thing she had overlooked. But what? A sliver of wood from the table leg perhaps? Only, the wood was rotten, it would never be strong enough. The candleholder, then? No, that would be too thick, and besides, she needed it to hold the burning taper erect. It was the only light she had and night was already falling. The bed? But that was ridiculous. The bed was solid iron, and she would never be able to pull it apart.

Damn him, the bastard! If only he had not forced them to come away so quickly. If only she had had time to bring at least a handbag with her. A comb, a manicure set, even a broken piece of mirror, might have been enough.

If again, she thought bitterly. Always *if*. Only you couldn't build a life around ifs. She didn't have a handbag, and that was that. All she had was the clothes on her back.

The clothes on her back. . . .

The words sank slowly into her consciousness. Glancing down, she let her eyes appraise those same clothes she had just disdained; there had to be something she could use.

She studied the heel of her shoe, then dismissed that quickly, knowing it would never be thin enough for her purposes. She was tempted to tear a strip of leather from the sole, rolling it into a stiff wand, but she knew that would be a waste of time. She needed something hard, something hard and firm, like a band of metal or a sharp, narrow flint. Something that would be strong enough not to break under pressure.

And then she had it. It was so simple she wondered why she had not seen it right away. Clumsily she tore at the fastenings of her dress, eager to pull it off her body. A cold draft stung her skin as she stripped to her underlinen, but the icy touch was exhilarating. She had a plan at last, and it was a good one.

Why did women have to wear such idiotic clothes? she thought, struggling to loosen the ties that bound her corset tightly around a slender waist. Why did it take so long to get out of them? She giggled out loud, a half-hysterical sound, as she realized what she was thinking. If women's clothes weren't so idiotic, they wouldn't have stiff, uncomfortable stays in them—and she might still be sitting in the filth and refuse of the floor, ready to weep at the hopelessness of her situation.

It took her only a minute to climb back into her dress. It was a strange sensation, pulling clothes over her body without the rigid restraint of a corset underneath, but it was not an unpleasant one. The waist of her skirt was too tight, binding into loosened flesh, but she did not mind. She had not felt so free in years. She knew she would move faster, more efficiently now.

She paused to bend over the sleeping child. Mariette's brow was hotter than ever as she let her lips brush against it, offering comfort she knew the delirious girl could not feel. She was such a sweet little thing, Aimée thought, her heart aching as she watched her. So sweet and so vulnerable—and she wanted desperately to help her.

Impulsively she reached up, catching at the clasp of the crucifix she wore around her neck. She had had it since she was a little girl, and it had always been a comfort to her, a kind of implicit promise of help in need. Now she surrendered it gladly, tying it around another, smaller neck. She no longer asked God's protection for herself, only for her child.

"Soon, *petite*," she whispered, kissing the tiny flushed

cheek. "Soon Mama will take you out of here, and then everything will be all right."

Picking up the corset where she had tossed it on the floor, Aimée began to work at it with a new determination, tearing the seams with her teeth until she finally forced a single long stay out of the fabric that held it captive. With a cry of triumph she turned back to the wall.

The task proved even easier than she had hoped. The mortar, softer than it looked, crumbled quickly into tiny chunks, so small they barely made a pattering sound as she brushed them onto the floor. It took her no more than a few minutes to work her way around the brick. At last she was ready to reach up with eager fingers and pull it out of the wall.

One brick down, she thought with a rush of excitement and relief. One brick down and only a handful to go. "Soon" she had promised her daughter, and soon it would be. Soon a doctor, soon a hospital, soon help for a feverish body.

But the brick, when she curled her fingers around it, refused to budge. Surprised and angry, Aimée wedged her hand into the shallow space, then, gripping the brick tightly, pulled again. Still it did not move. She felt a sudden moment of helpless fury. This was not the way it was supposed to be—not the way at all. She was certain she had dug through the mortar. All it should have taken was a simple push, a little tug one way or another, and the thing should have broken free.

Slowly she began to realize she had been naive to assume it would be so easy. Something lay behind that brick, and whatever that something was, the brick was fastened to it with concrete.

But it would be the same concrete, Aimée reminded herself firmly, determined not to give up. It would be the same decaying concrete, and if she had broken away part of it, she could break away the rest. Grimly she tightened her hold, pulling at the brick until she could almost feel it move, rocking it up and down, up and down again, back and forth, until at last it weakened enough to snap away from whatever held it. Cautiously she slipped it out of the wall.

She reached for the candle, but she reached hesitantly, barely daring to move. She wanted to know what lay beyond the space she had made, and yet she dreaded it. If there was nothing there, if the brick had just caught on the stronger outside facing, they would be all right. If not . . .

Slowly she held up the candle.

She wanted to cry out as a weak flickering light touched the darkness, but she could not. There was no strength left in her, even for despair. All she could see as she stared into the space that had once held a brick was a solid expanse of gray.

So it was just a facade after all. All those bricks lining the wall. They were just a facade. And behind them was a layer of concrete, perhaps even another row of bricks.

She felt as if she had been betrayed. Deliberately, cruelly betrayed. It was all so unfair. She had dared to hope. She had slipped a crucifix like a talisman around her daughter's neck, and God had let her hope. Now there was no hope left.

She sat in the center of the room and stared at the hole she had made in the wall, and she hated it more than she had hated anything else in her life.

Why—*why*—had she been such a fool? Why had she only antagonized Buffy when she should have been sweet and cajoling? And why had she ever let him go to Edward, where he had to learn the truth? Buffy was the only person in the world who could help them now, and he was the one person who was certain to turn against them.

The dark, rectangular hole seemed to stare back at her like a reproach. You should have done something, it accused her. You should have been cleverer, bolder, stronger. You should have been able to save your child.

It was a long time before Aimée could focus her mind enough to realize what she was looking at. When she did, she was surprised at the image.

A deep hole in a sturdy wall. Not a hole to the outside, but still a hole.

Nom de nom, she'd been a fool more than once that day. And she was ten times a fool now if she was ready to give up. All she had to do was pull out one more brick, a foot and a half, perhaps two feet above the first, and then another the same distance above that. She would have to work in a zigzag pattern, taking care not to weaken the structure of the wall, but if she was skillful enough, she could form a makeshift ladder to the ceiling.

Standing back, she studied the window. The bars seemed strong, but then, the bricks had seemed strong, too, until she had examined them closely. And the same mortar fastened them both. If it had been weakened in the walls, where the rain only poured down periodically, what would have happened at the window, open to the full force of all the elements?

She worked now with a new purpose. Buffy might not come back, but if he did, he could be there at any moment. She did not have so much as a second to spare. Working frantically, she forced out brick after brick. At last she reached her goal.

It was a simple matter to climb up the wall. The holes she had made were deep and strong. It was not as simple to force herself to raise her hand to the grating. She had already pushed her body to the limits of her endurance. She knew if this plan did not work, she would never find the courage to try again.

Unconsciously, her hand slipped to her neck, feeling for a cross that was no longer there.

"Please, God, let it be all right," she prayed. "Please let the grating be loose."

Her fingers were numb with cold as she touched them to the metal.

The wagon balked in the muddy road, sliding as the wheels spun through the mire. Buffy pulled deftly on the reins, guiding the horse back onto coarse, stony soil. He liked the idea of driving a crude peasant vehicle. It gave him an earthy, robust feeling. Besides, anyone who saw him, a solitary man, anonymous in plain dark clothing, would simply think he was a local farmer caught out on a miserable night.

The rain had eased, turning into a light drizzle. Buffy threw back his head, tilting his face into the mist. Reaching down, he groped with his hand, making sure a broad, square box was still tied securely beneath the seat.

He had outwitted them all. They thought they were so clever. Villière with his arrogance, Edward with his smugness. Well, now they knew who was clever.

It couldn't have turned out better. Buffy could still see the look on Villière's face when he handed the Isis over to him. As if he wanted to break every bone in his body, and hated himself because he couldn't.

And Edward . . .

He turned the thought over and over in his mind. The more he dwelled on it, the more he liked it. Edward would have gone to Paris, but that was all right. He did not mind following him. He was a patient man—if he knew he was going to get what he wanted.

As for that two-timing little bitch . . .

He had told Villière he was going to release the woman,

and the fool believed him. But the woman was the only one who knew the plot was his and not Edward's—the woman and the child. Only an idiot or a madman would leave two witnesses behind him.

But he would not kill them now, not the woman at least. The child could stay behind and starve, for all he cared. But he still needed the woman.

Aimée clenched her fingers around cold bars. They had to give, she knew they had to give, and yet she was terrified they would not. She held her breath for a minute, then, forcing a last show of will, pulled as hard as she could. They did not move.

She wanted to scream with frustration. *Break away, dammit—break!* The concrete was loose and crumbling until she could almost brush it off with bare hands. How could the grating cling to that?

Drawing her strength together, Aimée pressed both hands on the bars, balancing as best she could against the unyielding wall. It was her last chance. With a little grunt of concentration, she shoved firmly outward.

The grating held for a long, sickening second. Then, with a sharp rasping sound, it slipped out of its moorings. Aimée barely had time to clutch at the ledge with frantic fingers, to keep from being thrown to the ground. She listened, unbelieving, as the grating crashed to the earth outside.

Her breath came in short gasps as she looked up. The window was free and open. The night air was dark, so dark she could not catch even the vague outline of a tree or shrub outside.

"Come on, Mariette," she urged, hurrying back to the bed. Pulling the child up in her arms, she coaxed the limp body into the thin woolen jacket. "Wake up, *petite*. It's time to go now."

Her heart sank when the child did not respond. She knew she was being unreasonable. She had expected nothing else. The fever was so intense Mariette was not even conscious of her surroundings, but still she had hoped against all reason that somehow the delirium would ease, at least long enough for the girl to clasp trusting arms around her mother's neck while she carried her piggyback up the steep wall. Now she knew that would be impossible.

"It's all right," she whispered. "Don't be afraid. Mama's here. Mama will take care of you."

She knew the child could not hear her, but she spoke the words anyway, as much in a vain attempt to soothe herself as in the hope that Mariette would sense a familiar voice and be comforted by it. She began to wind her shawl around the child's feverish limbs, forming a tight cocoon. Tugging it sharply with her hands, she tested to make sure it was secure. Then, sitting on the edge of the bed, she eased Mariette upward, forcing her firmly against her back. With a quick sure movement she caught at the ends of the shawl, knotting them around her own body.

Gingerly she pulled herself to a standing position. The shawl, heavy with Mariette's weight, dug excruciatingly into her shoulders, dragging her back until she was afraid she would fall on the bed. Struggling to hold herself upright, she cast a nervous eye toward the wall. The steps she had made for herself were deep and even, but their surface too smooth to provide more than a tentative hold for her hands. She did not know if she could make it to the top with the pressure of Mariette's body pulling her backward.

She wondered if she had the right to try. Perhaps the best thing—the most sensible thing—would be to wait until morning. By then Mariette's fever was sure to have broken, and she could climb up the wall herself with her mother's help.

Aimée stood, hesitant and undecided, in the dim light of the squalid room, listening as the rain began again. *Clop-clop, clop-clop, clop-clop.* A dull, repetitious sound against the earth.

Mon Dieu, she had been so sure the rain had stopped. How could she take Mariette out now? The child was much too ill for that. The wind was bad enough, but the rain too? Even a pigsty was better than a cold wind in the rain.

Clop-clop, clop-clop, clop-clop. The sound seemed to grow louder and louder, as if the rain had been far away and was slowly drawing near. *Clop-clop, clop-clop, clop-clop.*

Aimée was fascinated by the monotonous rhythm. Heavy and slow, and strangely plodding. Not like the rain at all. Not light and free. More like . . .

More like the slow, sure pace of a draft horse's hooves.

A horse? Aimée strained her ears, listening through the darkness for a sound that was barely audible. A horse on an isolated road, deep in the country? On a night no farmer or wayfarer would be abroad?

He was coming back. She did not merely guess, she knew.

He was coming back for them, and his heart would be black with hate.

Anxiously she glanced around the room. Traces of activity were everywhere. Loose bricks lay haphazardly against the wall, and dust from crumbled mortar was strewn across the floor. Helpless and frightened, Aimée realized she had burned her last bridges behind her. Even if she had been tempted to throw herself on his mercy, begging his charity at least for the child, she would never dare do it now. He was angry enough as it was. When he saw what she had done, he would be ready to kill them on the spot.

She hesitated only a fraction of a second. The wall, so steep an instant before, seemed perilous no longer. Escape was their only chance, and she had to take it.

Fear lent her strength as arms and legs responded to the summons of a determined will. She reached the top swiftly, clutching at the windowsill to pull herself the last few inches upward. Reaching out, she caught a firm hold on the edge of the eaves, twisting her body through the open slit until she finally managed to crouch on a narrow ledge outside.

Her hands and arms ached with exertion as she clung to the eaves, her legs throbbed so badly she was terrified they would give beneath her, but she could not force herself to move. A sharp wind whipped through the trees, catching at the branches with a low whine. The icy spray that touched her skin was so fine it felt like fog.

It was so dark. God help her, it was so terribly dark. She had not known it would be like this. All through the long, agonizing hours, even in the worst of her fear, she had been sure everything would be all right if only she could get outside. But now she was out, and she could not even see her hand in front of her.

She knew she could not stay where she was. Only a fool would remain on a slippery ledge, a sick child on her back, waiting for a man who wanted to kill her.

But only a fool would jump to the ground when she could not even see where the ground was.

Frantically she peered into a heavy veil of black, trying to get her bearings. The grating that had blocked the window. Where was it now? She had thrust it forward with all her strength. Had it flown out from the house, falling far beyond the wall? Or did it lie just beneath, ready to catch her ankle or tear into her skin when she landed painfully on top of it?

431

And what else was hidden in that unfathomable darkness? Sharp stones? Broken logs with jagged edges?

The hoofbeats were louder now. Aimée strained her eyes in the darkness. She could see nothing. Not a shadow of movement, not even the faint glow of a lantern beam far in the distance, picking out the path for a patient horse. But she knew he was there. She could not see him, but he was there.

And he was close.

It gave her a sick feeling in the pit of her stomach to realize she had no choice. She had to jump from her clumsy perch, and she had to do it now. Another minute and he might be close enough to hear her land. Reaching down, she caught a firm hold on the corner of the ledge.

She hesitated a second, but only a second, then swung her body over the side, clinging as tightly as she could. The ledge gave a single loud crack, as if it would break away. Then, miraculously, it held, and she and Mariette dangled safely only a few feet from the ground.

She held on a second longer, knowing she could not maintain her grip, but terrified to release it. She did not know what lay beneath her. She could not even guess. She only knew there was nothing else she could do.

Taking a deep breath, she let go.

SIX

From the Dawn of
the World

∞ Meryt

Not a breath of wind touched the earth, not a hint of moisture filtered into the air from the drying canals. Searing heat rose in visible waves from the soil, turning the valley into a fiery furnace. The Nile was a languid strip of brown, threading through golden fields, and the hot yellow ocher of the dusty sky blended into desert hills until the world seemed an endless stretch of sand.

Sighing, Meryt pulled **herself upright, drawing her arms** out behind her to relieve the stiffness in her back and shoulders. The harvest season was the hardest time in the small village where she had taken refuge. The sun baked the earth until it was parched and cracked, and crude wooden scythes formed painful blisters on hands that reached down hour after hour into a sea of grain and flax.

Beside her, the widow Nebut stooped over the tall grasses, her scythe slicing through them with long, rhythmic motions. Meryt paused to watch her. She had shared a hut with Nebut for several months now, and in all that time she had never once seen her bend to weariness or privation. Always, as now, her back was strong, her face calm and expressionless, her passive spirit as constant and enduring as the soil itself.

To Meryt, the woman even looked as if she had been carved out of the earth. Her skin, dark brown from years of exposure, was lined with creases until it seemed as dry and brittle as the land in the days before the flooding came to renew it. It was hard for Meryt to remember that Nebut was only a year or two older than she was. She wondered if she, too, would look aged and haggard in a few years, when the sun had had a chance to ruin her skin and the heavy work taken its toll. The thought held no horror for her. Beauty was a need that no longer touched her heart.

It had been a long time since she had remembered the man whose eyes once reflected her loveliness in their depths. She had not dared to think of him in the long nights that had followed their parting. She would not let herself think of him now. Senmut was dead, not just for this life, but for all eternity. It would only bring her pain to let her heart dwell on him.

Reaching up, she wiped the sweat from her brow with her arm. As she tilted her head backward, she caught sight of a pair of dark eyes across the field, staring at her with undisguised curiosity. She cast her gaze hastily back toward the ground.

When she had first arrived in the village, it had been easy to keep her eyes averted, allowing no one, not even the most trusted of Nebut's friends and neighbors, a glimpse of midnight blue. Now, with the passing months—with the dullness that seemed a constant partner to heat and hunger and exhaustion—it had grown harder to remember.

Not that it really mattered, she reminded herself wearily. Leaning on her scythe, she did not even bother to screen her eyes as she looked toward the edges of the field, searching the clusters of small naked bodies that romped in the sun.

She found what she was looking for instantly. Teti-Sheri, lively and vivacious, stood out from the other children. Her laughter sparkled across the fields as she darted mischievously into tall grasses, waiting for a nearby adult to chase her out. Little Taharet, Nebut's daughter, though nearly a year older, was slow and clumsy as she struggled to keep up with her.

And Teti-Sheri's eyes were even bluer than her mother's!

Meryt despaired at the thought. She could keep her own head lowered, reminding herself over and over again of the deadly consequences of carelessness, but she could do nothing to inhibit the natural exuberance of her child. One day, perhaps one day soon, Teti-Sheri's striking beauty would cause a little too much gossip, spreading to the next village down the river and then to the village past that.

And then it would be all over for them.

Meryt's heart was still heavy as she shouldered her scythe at last and began to follow a sandy path that led through the fields. Every muscle in her body ached from the brutal exertion she had forced on it, but for once she did not notice her exhaustion. Today there was room in her consciousness only for a single image: the vision of a long line of soldiers moving slowly up the river, their shields and spears glittering in the sun.

Hordes of flies buzzed in the dusk, stinging her skin and landing on her eyelids. Irritably she reached up, trying to brush them away. They clung so tightly, it almost seemed as if they had been glued in place. She had to scoop them off, gouging at them with her fingers, before she could tear them away. The instant she dropped her hand, they were back again.

What a fool she was, conjuring up specters of faraway armies when she had more dangerous enemies close at hand. The pharaoh, for all his wealth and power, could never be as threatening as the hunger and disease and filth that were a part of her daily life. Every month, another child went blind from the flies clustering on its lashes; every week, a dozen others fell to the fever that raged up and down the river during the hot harvest season, killing, maiming, crippling, leaving even those it spared with shortened, twisted legs and lifeless arms.

"These cursed flies," she muttered later, careful to keep the words under her breath as she helped Nebut clear the last traces of lentils and onions from the single bowl they owned. Teti-Sheri was playing quietly on the pallet that served as her bed on the other side of the room.

Nebut agreed gruffly. "The flies . . . and the fever."

Meryt caught an uncharacteristic sharpness in the woman's voice. Glancing up, she looked at Taharet, curled listlessly on her own pallet. Her mother's instinct told her what Nebut was thinking.

"She's all right," she assured her. "It's been a long day. It's no wonder she's tired."

She did not add that Taharet always seemed to be tired. She did not have to. It was a thing Nebut already knew and feared.

Gratefully she cast her eyes toward her own child, plump and giggling as she worked the jaw of her wooden lion up and down so vigorously it nearly fell off in her hands. At least Teti-Sheri was healthy. She did not have to feel cold inside every time she looked at her.

But other children had been plump and healthy, too, she reminded herself with icy objectivity. Other children who belonged to Osiris now.

"Come on," she said softly, trying to reassure herself as much as Nebut. "Let's get the children to bed. They'll be fine as long as they get their sleep."

Meryt had nearly forgotten her fears in the morning. She was so tired she could barely drag her protesting body out of bed, much less worry about vague premonitions from the night before. Taharet was still listless and cranky, but Meryt paid her little heed as she hurried about her chores, setting

ut the bread and beer that would serve as their breakfast,
hen turning to wake her own daughter. If she thought about
t at all, it was only to wish that Nebut's child was a little
unnier, a little pleasanter to live with.

She did not notice anything wrong until she had stepped
across the room, and even then she was not sure. Nebut was
bent over Taharet's pallet, as she had been every morning
since Meryt had known her, but this time there was something different about the scene. For the first time, Nebut's
shoulders were bowed with a weariness she could not control.
Her hand trembled as she laid callused fingers on her daughter's brow. Meryt's heart caught in her throat as she watched.

The fever. The thing she had dreaded, the thing every
mother in the village dreaded. Only, now it was inside the
walls of their hut.

Anxiously Meryt dropped to her knees by her daughter's
side. Teti-Sheri seemed unusually fretful as she awakened her.
She was almost afraid to raise her hand, laying it on the
small sun-browned forehead. It was all she could do to keep
from sobbing with relief when it felt cool to her touch.

"Run along and play," she told the child, trying to keep
the tension out of her tone." See if any of the other children
are out yet."

"But I haven't had my bread," Teti-Sheri argued, pouting
deeply. "I'm hungry."

"I said run along!" Meryt's hands were rougher than she
intended as she pulled the child out of bed, giving her a pat
on the fanny to shove her toward the door. She thought her
heart would stop beating when the girl paused on the threshold, throwing one last puzzled glance over her shoulder before she disappeared outside.

Finally Meryt found the strength to rise and cross the
room to the spot where Nebut still crouched beside her ailing
child. As she stared down at them, she had the urge to take
Teti-Sheri and run as far away from this place as she could
get. But there was nowhere else she could go.

Nebut looked up, "I'll take Taharet to the other room," she
said softly. Her back was rigid as she wrapped the child in a
coarse sheet, lifting her in her arms. "Keep Teti-Sheri away,
and stay away yourself. There's nothing you can do."

Meryt did not go to the fields that day. Although she was
careful to keep Teti-Sheri out of the house, she herself remained inside, stepping often into the doorway that led to the
small inner room. She had never felt so useless in her life.
She could fetch heavy buckets of water for the child whose

437

burning body did not feel the moisture, she could offer crusts of bread or tempting morsels of dried fish to the mother who had no appetite, but try as she would, she could think of nothing that would help—nothing. There was no way she could stop the fever, no way she could ease Nebut's pain.

And no way she could protect her own child from the same fate.

They had been so lucky, she thought. So lucky all these years. She and her lover, defying pharaoh and the gods to clutch at a few moments of joy.

Now it seemed the luck had run out.

When Teti-Sheri peeked through the doorway a few minutes later, she was startled by the sudden force of her mother's embrace. The arms that locked her in their grasp were so tight she could hardly breathe.

"You're hurting me," she protested, wriggling free. "Can't I come in now? I'm hungry."

Meryt laughed at her own possessiveness as she loosened her hold on the child. Still, it was hard to let go. She had the terrifying feeling as she watched Teti-Sheri slip away from her that she would never hold her child in her arms again.

Meryt did not sleep that night or the night that followed. She sat silent and immobile in the darkness, her arms coiled around her legs, her knees tucked up to her chin. Senmut used to laugh at her when she sat like that, she remembered. He said it made her look like a little girl, helpless and innocent, begging for someone to look after her. She wished she could feel like a little girl now.

Memories of Senmut were heavy in her heart that night. He had not been a part of her life for so long. She had not expected to feel him so intensely now. She could not help thinking it was a bad omen.

The sound that broke into her thoughts was a fragile sigh too soft for any but a mother's ears to pick up. Meryt heard it instantly. Scrambling to her feet, she hurried to her daughter's bedside.

She bent over the sleeping child, waiting for the sound to be repeated. At first, as she stood in the darkness, pressing her hand against her breast to still the rapid beating of her heart, she thought she had imagined it. Then, just as she dared to let herself hope, she heard it again.

This time, there was no mistaking it. She recognized instantly the pain in that low, hoarse cry. With a cry of her own, she dropped to her knees.

"It's all right, little dove," she whispered soothingly. "It's
t a bad dream. Wake up, now. Mama's here."

But even as she spoke, Meryt knew it was no use.
aching down to gather up the sheet Teti-Sheri had kicked
, she tucked it around her. The instant she touched her
nder arms and shoulders, she could feel they were burning
th heat.

"Oh, Isis help me," she cried. Teti-Sheri was hot, so unbe-
vably hot. Hotter than the desert sand in the midday sun.
)w could any small, vulnerable body endure such blazing
at?

She dared not let herself give up.

"Wake up, Teti-Sheri," she urged frantically, pinching the
ddened cheeks to coax the child to stir. "Please try to wake
."

But the child's only response was a dull whimper. Trem-
ng with fear, Meryt wrapped her arms around the burning
dy, drawing it to her breast. The sting of tears was hot
ainst her cheeks.

Nebut glanced up when Meryt stepped through the door-
ay of the inner chamber. Her eyes were filled with compas-
)n as she watched her make up a pallet in the corner, but
e did not speak. After a moment she turned away, re-
:ating into her own pain. When she did, the silence and
neliness were complete.

The hours that followed were the most agonizing of
eryt's life. She could see her daughter's suffering, but she
uld do nothing to ease it. She could lay her hands on fever-
a flesh, but she could not make Teti-Sheri feel the coolness
her touch. The child did not even know she was there.

There was little she could do. A damp rag dipped over and
er in a bucket of water, a crude fan woven from papyrus,
at was all she could find. Neither did the least bit of good,
t she had nothing else to offer. No priests or doctors with
eir drugs and incantations. No scented perfumes to cool her
in, if only for a second. No sweet, tempting drinks to coax
wn her throat. She could have wept with despair.

All through the night, the dark night that seemed to close
around her, dense and stifling, Meryt had a mystical sense
the closeness of the man she had left behind forever. At
nes, his presence was so real, so tangible, she felt as if he
ere standing beside her, his hand resting on her shoulder.
he thought was not always a comfortable one.

The child is our love—my love for you.

She was filled with shame at the memory. Teti-Sheri was

Senmut's love, and he had entrusted that love to her. She ha failed him.

The child is our love.

And when the child died, all that was left of a love th had been good and beautiful, and in the end even selfles would die with her.

In the still, hot hours of the afternoon, Taharet died. It wa a quiet moment, slow and sultry, with nothing to mark i passing.

Nebut sat silently beside her child, not even noticing th shadows that drifted through the doorway, lengthened slow into twilight. At last she raised her hand, laying it on th brow that was cool at last, brushing away strands of hair th clung to still-moist skin. Taharet could not feel her comfo now, but she could think of nothing else to do.

Meryt, absorbed in her own fears, did not see Nebut pain. If she recognized anything at all, it was that the silenc had grown deeper, more oppressive. Tilting her head bacl she listened for a sound in the void that surrounded her, bu there was nothing—nothing at all. Not a whimper from Ta haret's bed, not a rustle of movement or cool splash of wate not even a cry from her own feverish child. Nothing bu silence.

When at last the stillness was broken, the sound tha touched Meryt's ears was one she had not expected to hea She pulled herself to her knees, straining to see through th darkened doorway that divided their room from the oute chamber.

Footsteps. She was sure she had heard footsteps. But wh could have entered their house, and why? Surely by now ev eryone in the village had heard of their misfortune. No on would come willingly to a house where the fever had struck.

Anxiously she glanced toward Nebut, but Nebut had nc heard the sound. Rising, her hand mechanically caressing he daughter's brow, Meryt cast a glance at the fitfully sleepin child on the pallet beneath her, then stepped into the othe room.

A tall, sun-darkened man stood in the outer doorway. A fine linen tunic fell in crisp white pleats beneath a muscula chest and firm belly.

Meryt stepped forward nervously. She had just opened he lips to ask the man who he was and what he was doing here when she saw an unexpected blur of motion outside the doo Squinting into the shadows, she made out the indistinct form

440

at least a dozen other men. They were all dressed like the
st, and they all seemed to be watching the doorway of her
use.

Soldiers!

Of course they were soldiers. Everything about them—their
anner, their garb, the casual arrogance of their bearing—
oclaimed their calling. What a fool she had been to forget,
en in the midst of other, more absorbing fears, the single
rvasive danger that hung over their heads.

She whirled around, casting a quick glance into the room
hind her. She was trapped. Even if there were another way
t of the hut, even if she were foolhardy enough to think
e could outrun or outwit the soldiers, Teti-Sheri was too ill
flee. She turned back to the man in the doorway, her dark
ue eyes wide with fear.

The captain of the pharaoh's guard was a young man. He
d been well trained in the ways of war, but he had never
d to face a helpless woman before. It was a task that did
t appeal to him.

"We have not come to harm you." His voice was gruff, un-
re. In some strange way that he could not explain, even to
mself, the woman's terror put him at a disadvantage. "We
e here to bring you back to Akhet-Aten—you and the
ild."

Meryt sensed his hesitance. For one desperate moment she
t herself hope. She could not escape the soldiers, either by
uile or by force, but she could appeal to their mercy.

Slowly she stepped forward, her hands stretched out in
ont of her.

"The child is ill." She made no effort to disguise her fear.
She has the fever. It would kill her to travel now."

The young captain wavered, unable to conceal his pity.
e had seen the fever that raged through the poorer villages,
aving in its wake hundreds of children dead or cruelly
rippled.

"I'm sorry." His voice was softer than he had intended.
My orders are to bring you both—immediately."

"But she will die." Meryt was filled as much with anger as
nguish. "Don't you understand? She will die!"

The captain shifted his weight awkwardly from one foot to
e other. He could only repeat the words that were all too
adequate.

"I'm sorry."

He *was* sorry, desperately sorry, but there was nothing he
ould do. He was a soldier and he had his orders. Besides, it

441

might well prove best this way. The child would die on trip, he knew that as well as the mother, but what would fate be if it lived? The pharaoh's position was already sha his rule threatened on every side. It would make him lc weak, fatally weak, to show too much mercy to a waywa wife or to the child of her illicit union.

This time his voice was firm, "You will have to get t child. Now!"

Neither of them noticed a slender figure slip into the inr doorway.

"It makes no difference now."

Meryt saw Nebut standing on the threshold. A bu bundle, swathed in blankets, was clutched in her arms. Me stared at her, puzzled.

Had the woman packed her belongings for her? she wc dered. But she did not own enough to make a bundle th size.

"Take the child if you must," Nebut held out the burden her arms. "She is dead."

Dead?

At first the word meant nothing to Meryt. *Dead*, Neb had said. *The child is dead*. But the child was Teti-Sheri, a Teti-Sheri could not possibly be dead. Meryt had not ev been there, her arms wrapped protectively around the ti body, her hands soothing the feverish brow. How could t child die when her mother was not there?

Bewildered, she turned toward the young captain, searc ing for a confirmation of her own doubt. But the captai face was red, uncomfortable. His eyes were cast downwar as if he could not meet her gaze.

At last she understood.

Teti-Sheri *was* dead. The child she had borne in pain a sacrificed her love to raise had been taken from her. Th punishment of the gods was complete. Somewhere in the la few minutes, in the light of a flickering oil lamp, she ha passed from the world of the living, and her mother had n even been there to ease her pain.

Anger coursed through Meryt's veins. She felt cheated, b trayed. Her child had needed her, and she had not bee there.

It was all Nebut's fault, she told herself bitterly. All he doing. If Nebut had not sat selfishly beside her own child, r fusing even to listen to the sound of footsteps in the out room, she would never have left Teti-Sheri. Her child woul not have died alone and frightened.

She was being irrational, but she could not help herself. It hurt so much . . . so much. Suddenly she could not bear the thought of Teti-Sheri lying limp in Nebut's arms another instant. Stretching out her own arms, she hurried across the room.

"Give her to me."

"No!"

The word was a strangled cry in Nebut's throat. Meryt stopped, gaping in shock and amazement.

She could have sworn she saw rage flashing out of Nebut's eyes. Rage—or was it fear? But what right did Nebut have to rage at the gods? It was not her child, dead and still, wrapped in a blanket in her arms. What did she have to fear? Her child was warm and alive, lying on a pallet in the other room.

"Give her to me."

But the young captain sided with Nebut. Pulling Meryt back, he forced her into a corner.

"It is better this way. You are only making it harder on yourself."

His back was rigid as he turned away from her, stepping toward Nebut to pull the pathetic bundle into his own arms. He had to steel himself to touch it, pretending he did not feel the cold moisture of a blanket still drenched with dying sweat. He had seen death many times, on far-flung battlefields at frontier posts, but it had never seemed so real before. He was glad to relinquish his burden into the waiting hands of one of the soldiers outside the door.

Meryt was immobile as she watched a stranger carry her child out of her life forever. A tiny, barely defined form muffled in the thick folds of a blanket. Bronzed, muscular arms, so strong and sure, clasping her in a tight embrace.

Senmut.

Once Senmut had held their child like that. Once he had cradled her, comforted her, soothed away the fears of a desperate flight through the darkness.

Who would soothe her now?

At least we won't have to steal out into the night with nothing but a blanket and a wooden lion.

But Senmut had been wrong. There was nothing else. Nothing then . . . and nothing now.

Nothing for a child's last journey but an old blanket and . . .

"The wooden lion."

Meryt whispered the words. Slowly she turned toward N
but.

"Get me Teti-Sheri's lion."

She saw a glimmer of defiance in Nebut's eyes. It seem
to her a dark, sly thing. At first she did not understand. Th
she realized.

The woman expected to keep the lion for herself. S
wanted to give the toy to her own child when Meryt a
Teti-Sheri were far away. In her greed, she was even willi
to steal from the dead.

Meryt moved furiously toward the doorway, grateful
have found a purpose at last. She was not going to let Neb
get away with her selfish plans. The lion had been Teti-Sher
only consolation in long, dark journeys of the past. Sl
would not let her begin the darkest journey without it.

"No!" Nebut's cry was a little too fast, a little too shar
but neither Meryt nor the captain seemed to notice. "I'll g
it."

She darted into the sickroom, pausing only when she cou
no longer be seen through the doorway. She hated the thir
she was about to do, but she had no choice. At all costs, sl
dared not let Meryt come into that room.

Kneeling silently, she coaxed the wooden lion fron
clenched fingers. It seemed to her the child clung to the to
tightening her hands around it as if she knew she was abou
to lose it. Nebut barely managed to force her fingers oper
pulling the toy out of their grasp.

The young captain had already left the room when Nebu
returned, but his shadow was still visible in the doorway
Meryt stood alone, her eyes staring straight ahead, but unsee
ing. As she turned to face Nebut, her hands were stretche
out in front of her. Reluctantly Nebut laid the lion in them.

Meryt's fingers closed around it as tightly as the child'
ever had. She pulled it toward her breast, as if she were try
ing to draw some kind of strength from it. In that instant Ne
but realized Meryt needed its comfort even more than th
child did. She was glad she had given it to her.

Meryt's back was straight, her shoulders squared as sh
moved toward the door. Nebut thought her heart woul
break as she watched her. She was a mother, too. She knev
the pain that was hers at that moment.

She felt an overpowering urge to call her back. To tell he
to take one last glimpse into that little room where sh
thought her heart had broken.

"Meryt . . ."

Meryt's eyes were filled with questions as she turned.

But Nebut could not tell her. She dared not. If Meryt knew, if she betrayed by so much as a sound, a fleeting gesture of recognition . . .

"May Isis grant you peace."

They were not the words she wanted, but she could find nothing else. She watched Meryt turn again, drifting at last into darkness.

The room was still and lonely as she stood in the twilight shadows. Meryt would have understood, she consoled herself. Meryt would have wanted it this way. She had already sacrificed everything for her child—security, comfort, even happiness. She would willingly have given the last of her dreams if the choice had been hers to make.

A low, childish cry reached Nebut's ears, drawing her back to the sickroom. She was careful not to look at the empty pallet in the corner.

She dropped to her knees beside the child. The tiny brow was still hot to her touch, the bright blue eyes closed in delirium and pain.

Nebut did not know if the girl would live or die. It was a thing she did not truly question. Teti-Sheri's fate was in the hands of the gods. All she could do was give her a chance to live.

The dying sun flooded the sky with crimson. Meryt stood apart from the others, her back turned toward the small wool-swathed bundle in an anonymous soldier's arms. Her face was tilted upward, catching the last rays of the sun as it descended into the west.

Sunset. She liked the feel of it on her cheeks. Warm and soothing.

The soldiers stirred impatiently, glancing toward their young leader. He raised his hand, stilling their unspoken protests with a single gesture.

Sunset. The whitewashed walls of Akhet-Aten red with echoes of blood. A hundred faces, a thousand, all staring upward. Eyes glowing in the shimmering light. Lips parted to cheer a pharaoh's unwilling bride.

And somewhere in all those faces, one face rigid with strain. Somewhere in all those eyes, one pair of eyes naked with the pain of parting. Would that that had been their only parting. Their only pain.

The captain stood a few paces away. He could not help staring at the beautiful young queen he had been sent to capture. Deep flames of sunset glowed against her skin, highlighting dark eyes bright with pain. Her head was proud, her chin tilted upward even in defeat. It seemed to him there was a nobility about the woman, a kind of majesty he had never seen before, even in the pharaoh's court.

Sunset. A breath of fire against the doorway of her father's tomb, about to be sealed off forever from the touch of human hands. Darkness easing away the twilight, leaving only silvery reflections of the faraway moon on the Nile. The voice of the blind harper echoing in her ears as she crossed the river to her destiny:

Generations pass away, others come in their place; yea, from the dawn of the world. Re rises in the morning and sets in the west. Men beget, women bear, and every life draws breath, but in the dawning, their children come in their place.

But there were no children now. No children to stand in their stead in the dawn of time. Her child had died today. Her father's would die tomorrow.

The young captain, eyeing his men's restlessness, reacted at last. Slowly, taking care not to startle the woman, he moved toward her, laying his hand on her arm. She pulled away, telling him wordlessly his touch was unwelcome.

Sunset. The hills of the necropolis, bathed one last time in a blaze of color. Dusk shifting their outline subtly into the darkness until they were no longer visible to her eyes. A final moment of turning. A final glimpse of features, loving and beloved, in the flickering light of an oil lamp.

The child is our love—my love for you.

But now that love was gone.

The captain's hand was firm, as he laid it once again on her arm. This time, she did not resist. She needed his strength to guide her over the rough path. Her eyes were blinded by graying twilight and a golden haze of tears, and she could not see.

∞ Aimée

1

Aimée pressed against the side of the rough brick hut, shivering in the cold wind that swept through the clearing. The child in her arms shuddered, a convulsive movement that racked her entire body. Aching with exhaustion and fear, Aimée cradled her against her breast.

She had been incredibly lucky. Five minutes—only five minutes more—and she would have been trapped inside that godforsaken hovel with no hope of escape. Even her last frantic leap from the roof had ended on a soft patch of dying grass, without so much as a wrenched ankle to show for her desperate gamble. She could only hope her luck would hold.

The sound of hoofbeats grew closer and closer, until at last Aimée could hear the creaking of wagon wheels above the patter of rain on autumn leaves. It stopped suddenly. The moment she had dreaded was here.

She stiffened her back against the wall, peering into the darkness. She did not know what she expected to see, only that she expected something. She did not have to wait long.

A single shaft of gold, scintillating as it touched drifting raindrops, pierced the black of the night. Closing her embrace around Mariette, Aimée took a slow, unconscious step backward. The light was brighter than she had expected.

A lantern. Of course he had a lantern in his hand. What a fool she had been not to think of it. And now it was too late to hide. Even if she knew what to do, even if she could guess where she might find a fallen tree or a pile of dead leaves to crouch behind, she could not risk it in the dark. One misstep, one clumsy stumble, and he would know where she was.

And then, just as the tension grew unbearable, the beam of light vanished around the corner, and they were safe again, if only for a minute, in the darkness that followed.

She had only sounds to guide her now, but sounds were enough. She knew where he was every second of the time, and what he was doing. Heavy, sloshing footsteps, slow and cumbersome in the mud, told her he was working his way around the front of the hut. Jangling keys warned her he had already reached the door. Now he was inserting the key in the lock, cursing softly as he struggled to find an unfamiliar keyhole in the dark. And now he was drawing a heavy bolt steadily back.

And any minute, any second, the door would slide slowly open.

Mariette whimpered in her arms. Aimée pressed the girl's head onto her shoulder, lowering her lips to offer what comfort she could to a feverish brow. The child relaxed again. Even the rain had stopped, and the silence was complete.

When the stillness was broken at last, the cry that tore through the night was wild with fury. Aimée sucked in her breath, drawing Mariette closer in her arms as she listened. She heard the madness in that single thwarted cry, and pain, and she knew what it meant. The thirst for vengeance was complete.

Hypnotized with terror, she watched the lantern reappear suddenly, careening though the clearing as if it had been caught in a violent wind. She could only stare at it, horrified. If he stopped for a minute, even a minute, shining it methodically around the hut, trying to pick up their tracks . . .

But he did not stop. Reeling a little, as if he were drunk, he clambered onto the seat of the wagon, pausing only long enough to tie the light securely on a post. Aimée wanted to sob with relief as she watched him, but she did not dare. Even with the wind wailing through the trees, she was afraid he would hear her. At last the horse plodded slowly forward, and the light faded into the night.

Now the darkness was total. Aimée stood in the center of it, alone except for her unconscious child, and she wondered why she was trembling. Always before, the darkness had been her friend, offering a private warmth just beyond the comforting glow of a light in the hall. Tonight, for the first time, she was afraid of it.

Gripping Mariette tightly in her arms, she forced herself to move. She did not know where she was going, she could not see a thing in front of her, but she had to trust her instincts, heading always toward the last place she had seen the lantern. Her progress was awkward. She dared not slide her feet more than an inch or two at a time, but she faltered only occasionally, pausing now and then to duck as a low branch brushed her cheek. Gasping with relief, she finally felt firm soil beneath her feet, telling her she had reached the road at last.

She stopped for a moment, staring into the emptiness. The sound of hoofbeats still echoed in the distance.

It was an ominous sound, she thought, shivering as she listened to the unrelieved tramping of horse's hooves against the earth. And yet comforting, too. She knew Buffy was searching the road, stopping every few feet to shine a lantern into the woods on either side, but she knew, too, as long as he stayed in the wagon, she would be safe. As long as she could hear the sound of hoofbeats ahead of her on the path, she would know where he was—and he could only guess at her presence.

At last she began to move forward, walking as she had walked before, inch by inch, groping with her feet in front of her. It began to rain again, almost imperceptibly at first, then more and more heavily with each clumsy step she took. Desperately she tried to shield Mariette with her arms, but there was nothing she could do to protect her. A minute ago she had been terrified that the fever would never break, growing hotter and hotter until the child's body could bear it no longer. Now she was even more afraid it would abate suddenly, leaving her cold and shivering in the night. And there was no place Aimée could find shelter for her, no dry clothes to warm her body, no blanket to wrap around her.

Aimée felt as if she were a blind woman, running her foot along the edge of the road, feeling for the ruts and stones and heavy clumps of grass that would tell her where she was. She was tired, desperately tired. Her feet were swollen and blistered from shoes that had been made only to look pretty, and her arms ached with the burden she was not strong enough to carry. She did not know how long she had been walking. She only knew it was a long time—and she had gotten almost nowhere.

Her eyes scanned the ground automatically, staring tensely at each step she took, as if she thought she had the power to see through the darkness. After a while, she almost imagined she could visualize a dainty toe slipping cautiously between the stones and puddles that threatened to catch it unawares. It was a strangely unsettling illusion, so vivid it was eerie. It was several minutes before she realized it was not an illusion at all.

Surprised, she stopped to look around her. The woods, anonymous and menacing only a moment before, were

449

bathed in a deep fairy-tale blue, and elfin figures seemed to dart in and out among the shadows that intertwined the trees. Glancing up, she realized for the first time that rain no longer touched her cheeks, pelting her with tiny drops of cold. The clouds were still heavy, but they had begun to drift into clusters, and a round white moon stood free and bold against the sky.

Aimée did not know whether to be dismayed or relieved. Bright moonlight made it easier for her to walk, and she would make better time, but the same light would also make it possible for Buffy to see her long before she could hear him coming. Racked by doubt, she stopped to ponder her problem. The sensible thing, she knew, would be to move back among the trees, slipping from trunk to trunk like one of the elves she had imagined, always careful to keep the road in sight, even though she herself could not be seen. But if she did, she realized with despair, she would lose whatever advantage the moonlight had given her, and her progress would be even slower than before.

Wearily she stood in the cold mud, so tired she did not have the strength to make even a simple decision. Then slowly, almost without being aware of it, she let her eyes pick up a faint image from across the road. Puzzled at first, then curious, she stepped toward it, bending as far as she could with the child in her arms to examine it. When she straightened again, she was no longer tired.

There was a second road. A narrow, barely noticeable path, leading off the first. It was only a country lane—scarcely more than a pair of wagon ruts in the earth—but it was deep and clearly formed, as if it had been there for years.

And where there were wagon ruts, there had to be a wagon.

Aimée felt her heart lighten for the first time since she had loosened her grip on the high ledge and felt soft earth beneath her feet. The thing was perfect—absolutely perfect! Now she could find help, miles closer than town, and she would be safe while she was searching for it. Buffy would never look for her there.

But the path that had seemed so perfect no longer looked promising when she paused beneath the shadow of the trees, daring for the first time to study it closely. The ruts were still there, just as she had noticed before, but now she saw other things, too. Thick weeds, growing so deep in long trails of water they barely stuck their tips out into the air. Long grasses bent across the path until they were firmly mired in mud. Heavy stones settling into the earth where wagon wheels should have turned.

Wagons had used that path once, but it looked as if they had not been there for months.

Discouraged, Aimée was tempted to give up. Only despair drove her on. She could not turn back now. There was nothing for her there. Nothing but a long road she dared not follow, and a long hike she did not have the stamina to complete. More from habit than will, her feet began to move, each following the other in a narrow, obedient line along the side of the road.

The path led a quarter of a mile into the woods, twisting through the forest, then a quarter of a mile again, and still it showed no signs of stopping. Every time Aimée rounded a bend in the road, she prayed she had reached the end at last, but every time, the path continued to meander into the trees, winding toward yet another bend just ahead.

And then she rounded one last bend and saw, not a single track stretching ahead of her, but two, as the path forked out to the left and right.

She could only stop and gape in dismay. Two roads. Two roads to follow—and she did not have the strength for even one.

She stood for a long time looking at them. She knew she had to choose one, making the reasonless, arbitrary judgment that would leave her praying she had picked the road with a house at the end, but she could not force herself to make the decision. She tightened her hold around her child and thought only that her arms ached with exhaustion and her feet were so numb she could not feel the pain anymore.

Then she looked down and saw flushed cheeks and a tiny head resting against her shoulder, helpless and dependent, and she knew she could not give up.

"We'll go to the right." She forced an artificial brightness into her tone. "We'll go to the right, and it will be the *right* way." She giggled at her own silliness, a sharp, brittle sound bordering on hysteria.

Pushing herself forward, she bounced the child in her arms as she struggled to readjust an increasingly heavy weight one more time on her hip. When Mariette did not respond, Aimée lowered her head, resting her face lightly on the little brow. Giggles nearly dissolved into tears as she felt the heat against her skin.

"It will be all right, *petite trésor*," she promised. "It will be all right." There would be a house at the end of the road, and there would be people in it, good, kind people who would hitch up their wagon and take her into town. Then she would get Mariette to a doctor and everything would be all right.

She did not have to wait long for the house she had promised herself, but one look was enough to tell her that her hopes were in vain. She did not even want to cry as she stood silently and stared at it. She was so exhausted she was beyond feeling.

It stood in the center of a broad, circular clearing, well away from the trees, as if it had once been proud and strong. There was no pride in it now. It was only a skeleton, barely fleshed out with the rotting boards that still clung to its sides. The roof was half torn away, and the windows were only a few jagged pieces of broken glass, with cobwebs catching the silver of the moon. A single shutter, half torn from its hinges, surrendered to the wind, swinging with a steady *slap-slap, slap-slap, slap-slap* against the boards, hollow and empty, as if the place were deliberately mocking its own loneliness.

Slowly Aimée turned and began to retrace her steps. She knew what she had to do, but it was getting harder and harder all the time. She had to find that other path, the one she had rejected, and she had to follow it to the end, just as she had followed this one. She knew it would do her no good. She knew she would find nothing more than she had found this time, but she had to try all the same. There was nothing else.

She saw the fork ahead of her in the moonlight. Turning off the road, she cut through the shrubs and undergrowth that divided one set of ruts from the other. She was already exhausted, almost beyond endurance. She could not afford to waste an ounce of strength taking the long way around.

Stumbling awkwardly, she felt a thorny branch catch at her skirt. The sound of ripping fabric was harsh in her ears as she struggled to keep from falling. Tensing her arms around Mariette, she glanced down at her dress. The skirt was badly torn, with one side hanging in tatters from the knee. Looking over her shoulder, she caught sight of a long strip of cloth waving like a jaunty streamer from the branches of a low shrub.

She started to go back for it, then caught herself abruptly. She was too tired to worry about it, and besides, the thing could do her no good now. She was not about to stop and mend her skirt, even had she had a needle and thread to work with. The dress was ruined. It was best to let it go.

The second road was even less promising than the first. The weeds that filled the ruts were taller and stouter, scratching against her knee through the rent in her dress, as if to remind her with each step she took that she was a fool to go on. The instant she reached the end and saw the house she had used all her strength to find, she knew her instincts had been right.

She should have turned back, she told herself bitterly. The first time she paused in the woods and looked down and saw weeds in the ruts, she should have turned back. Now she was too tired.

The house was almost a twin of the first abandoned hut she had seen. The same circular rim of trees, dense and untamed, encroached on the clearing, the same rough gray boards formed an uneven pattern across its surface, and the same aura of emptiness hung over it like a low-lying cloud that would never go away. Aimée stood beneath the thick branches of a sheltering pine tree and stared at the house, and she knew it was all over. She had gambled everything on a lonely road that led into the woods, and she had lost.

She longed to sit down and feel the strength of the pine over her and hold her child in her arms. And the night would enfold her in a dark blue blanket, and she could sleep at last.

Slowly, mechanically, Aimée urged her feet toward the house. She knew there was nothing there she cared to see, but she knew, too, she could not stay beneath the trees, listening to the elusive lullabies that whispered through their branches. If she let herself sit down now, she would never get up again. She had nearly reached the house before she realized there was something wrong, something that did not fit in with the image she had of the place.

Pausing, she studied it closely. It was in better condition than the first house she had seen, as if it had been abandoned only recently. The roof was still intact, and glass, so filthy it was opaque, sent back reflections of moonlight from the windows. Curiously she scanned the yard. At last she realized what had caught her eye.

A long strip of iron, the last broken remnant of some tool she did not recognize, lay not far from the front wall. Even in the pouring rain, it was barely touched with rust. And beside it, strewn carelessly around the yard, as if even cleanliness were too great an effort, scattered bits of garbage had just begun to mold and rot.

Excited now, Aimée glanced around the clearing. There were no low, broad outbuildings to shelter wagons or carriages, no sturdy horses tied beneath the trees, but at least there were people in that house—and where there were people, she could find help. Rallying her strength, she marched up to the door.

The sound of her own fist was loud and ominously hollow as she pounded it again and again against the solid wood. She paused to listen, but she could hear nothing from within. Only the last fading echoes of her own urgent summons bouncing off of empty walls.

What if she had read the signals wrong? she asked herself in despair. What if she had let her hopes rise one last time, only to be dashed again?

"Please be there," she cried out, ramming her hand against the door until her knuckles were bruised and aching. "Please, please, come and help me."

But the only answer was silence. Admitting defeat, Aimée let herself lean against the door, her cheek resting on the rough cold grain of the wood. She had just laid her hand on the hard surface, ready to push herself back, when she caught a faint sound from inside.

It was only a soft rustle, perhaps no more than a startled rat scurrying across the floor. But perhaps . . .

Anxiously she grasped the handle, pulling it back and forth. "Please," she cried again. "Please open the door."

Again there was no voice, no footsteps, not even a whisper from within. But Aimée's ears picked up another sound—and this time she knew what it was.

Surreptitiously, as if afraid she could see through the door, someone was drawing a heavy bolt across the lock.

Of course! Aimée was amazed she had not thought of it before. A lonely house, a dark, rainy night—and then the sudden pounding that must have terrified them half out of their wits. What had she expected? Cautiously she moved back, stepping out in front of the window so they could see she was a woman alone, with only a child in her arms.

She could not see anyone at the window, but she could sense a presence. Somewhere, behind that mirror of moonlight, eyes were staring out at her, studying her face, scanning the shawl-wrapped burden in her arms.

At last the door slid open, a slow, tentative crack. A man's voice came out of the darkness.

"What do you want?"

Aimée took a step forward, then stopped. The man opened the door the rest of the way, letting moonlight spill into the house. He was short and stocky, with a heavy belly protruding over grimy workpants. Long gray underwear looked as if it had not been washed in years.

"I need help. Please . . . I have to get to town."

A woman stepped out from behind the man, staring at Aimée suspiciously. Thin hair had been pulled into an untidy bun at the back of her neck, and even an oversized nightdress gave no substance to a scraggly form.

"We have no horses here, nor fancy carriages."

Aimée felt her heart sink as she looked at her. The man was slovenly, but at least he did not seem unkind. She could sense no warmth in the woman.

"I can pay you," she said tentatively. "I have no money with me, but my husband is very rich. He will give you as much as you want if you help me."

The woman hesitated, bony fingers playing with the neck of her gown. Aimée thought she would speak again, but the man stopped her.

"I am sorry." It seemed to Aimée his eyes were filled with regret. She wondered if it was for her or for the money she had offered them. "We are only poor people. We have nothing. We cannot help you."

"At least you can tell me how to get to the nearest village. Or perhaps the house of a neighbor. Someone around here must have a horse."

"There is no one. This is rough land. Everyone else has given up."

The woman threw him a harsh look. "Everyone except you. You're the only one fool enough to stay."

He did not seem to notice her sharpness. "Where would I go?"

Her face darkened with impatience. She opened her lips as if to snap at him again, then closed them abruptly. Tugging at his sleeve, she nodded toward Aimée.

"Close the door, Wilhelm."

"Wait!" Aimée was desperate. These people were her only hope. She could not let them slip away from her.

Wilhelm paused, his hand on the door. The woman reached out, trying to pull it from him, but he held her back.

"My child. I have my child with me. If you won't help me, at least help the child."

The woman was hard, but she was, after all, a woman. Perhaps she was a mother, too.

"She's so sick." Aimée pulled the shawl back so the woman could see the pink cheeks and sweating brow. If she had any heart at all, surely that would melt it. "I don't know what to do. If I can't get help for her, I'm afraid she'll die."

At first it seemed to work. The woman crept forward, slipping curiously through the door to gape at the child in Aimée's arms. But the instant she got a close look at Mariette, her face contorted with horror.

"Get her out of here!" she screamed, stumbling into the house. "Get her out!"

Aimée realized she had made a mistake. She had meant to win the woman's sympathy. Instead, she had only roused her fear.

"It's just the cold. The cold and the rain. She caught a bad chill in the rain."

But it was not the rain, and the woman knew it.

"There are children here. Do you hear me? There are children. You can't bring her in here."

Aimée stood and watched her, and she felt her heart tighten with despair. And the worst of it was, she couldn't even blame the woman. She wondered what she would do, frightened and isolated in the woods, if someone came to her in the middle of the night and threatened to contaminate her children.

"If you won't help me, at least go for the police. I'll go away, I promise you. I won't come near the house again, but please, please, go for the police. Tell them I've been kidnapped. A man was holding me for a great deal of ransom."

The woman's eyes widened at that, as if curiosity had gotten the better of her fear. Aimée dared to hope she had at least piqued her interest.

"Listen, there's an old house near here. An abandoned shack on the other fork of the road. You must know it. Tell the police I'll be there. And tell them to bring a doctor."

She could still see regret in Wilhelm's eyes as he swung the door shut. The same regret that had punctuated his words only minutes before.

I am sorry.

It could not be a good sign, she knew. Regret was a futile, empty emotion. Regret was only for when there was no help.

A light rain was falling as she reached the fork again, lingering a moment in silence before turning up the other path. She knew it was a dangerous thing she was doing, a foolhardy thing, but she could see no other way. She had found Wilhelm's house easily enough. Buffy could find it, too. And Buffy would have at least a spare coin or two to tempt them.

She did not know about the man, but she sensed the woman would sell at least one of those children she was so anxious to protect if the price were offered in gold.

Well, that didn't matter anymore, she told herself fatalistically. She was tired and cold and totally drained of will. She could go no farther.

They would tell Buffy, or they wouldn't. That was all there was to it. They would go for the police, or they wouldn't. Or perhaps they would simply go back to bed and pull warm blankets over their heads and forget she had ever existed. And she would sit in an empty house and listen to the sound of the rain and wait . . . and wait.

And wait.

2

It had stopped raining when Aimée reached the abandoned house. The moonlight was a pale, iridescent presence, lending unreality to the lonely setting. Black trees sent out twisting leafless branches against the sky, and matted grasses soaked into the mud. In the center stood the ramshackle hut, so gray and shadowy it looked like a ghost that would disappear with the first pink glow of dawn.

Warily Aimée moved toward the entrance, urging the door open with her foot. Faint rays of light filtered through openings in the roof, highlighting corners of the deserted room as she stepped inside. A foul, heavy smell, stale and rank, sweet and rotting, spoke more eloquently of decay than all the piles of trash festering in the corners.

Aimée forced herself to look around, studying the place as carefully as she could in the dim light. She had never seen anything less promising. Wind howled through the open doorway, mingling with cold air from broken windows, and stagnant pools of water seeped slowly into the wooden flooring.

Little that was usable remained in the hut. A primitive table standing against one of the walls was nothing more than four long pegs pressed into the bottom of a wide, uneven plank, and the two straight-back chairs beside it were so cracked and wobbly they would not support even the lightest weight. Otherwise, there was nothing. No beds, no blankets, not even a moldy heap of straw to wrap around their bodies for warmth.

Aimée touched her foot tentatively to a pile of trash in the corner. A single tap was enough to do it. The rustling that met her ears told her the place was alive with things she did not want to think about. Discouraged, she turned back to the table.

It was a crude piece of furniture, so rough she could almost see the sharp splinters sticking out of it, but it was all they had. Slowly she lowered Mariette to the hard surface, careful to keep at least a single thickness of the shawl beneath her. Her arms clung to the child a last lingering second, resisting the need to let go.

Her body ached as she pulled herself up, standing straight for the first time in hours. Tense muscles burned in rebellion. Sharp pains shot through her back and shoulders.

At least the child would be safe, she thought wearily. The table was not comfortable, it was not even clean, but Mariette would be elevated from the floor, away from things that crawled through the darkness.

What would it be like in the morning, she wondered, when they were still alone and the police had not come? Could muscles so stiff they quivered with exhaustion pick up their burden again? And could a heart so tired it had no feeling find the courage to go on?

Or would she simply give up, sinking to the ground with the rats and the trash? Waiting and praying . . . and wondering if she had really seen regret in a woodsman's eyes?

It would be so easy, she realized. So frighteningly easy.

The sound of water dripped on dead leaves outside. The darkness grew heavier, oozing into the room so slowly Aimée did not even recognize the moment her hand disappeared on the table in front of her. She no longer tried to question the whims of the storm. All she could do was stand beside her child, too tired to move or care.

And she *was* tired. All she wanted was sleep—all she needed was sleep—but she could not lie on the floor, not with the vermin, and she could not go outside and leave the child alone. And there was no place else.

But she was tired. Oh, God, she was tired.

A faint sound caught her ears, jolting her into awareness. Her head snapped up, and she clutched the edge of the table to keep from stumbling. Terrified, she realized she had nearly fallen asleep. She could not let that happen again.

Her body tensed as she strained to listen. She had heard something, she was sure she had heard something, but there was nothing now. Not a drop of rain, not a low moan of wind, not even the scurry of rats' feet or the screech of an owl in a nearby tree.

And no hoofbeats in the distance.

Then the sound was repeated. Bending down, Aimée realized it was a soft murmur from her daughter's lips.

"Mariette." She laid her hand on the child's cheek. "Mariette, can you hear me? Are you awake, darling?"

Was it only her imagination, or was the child actually better? She was still feverish, but the heat in her brow did not seem so intense now.

Or was she just tired? Aimée asked herself wearily. So tired she could not tell the difference anymore?

"Mama . . ."

Mama! It was only a soft cry, barely loud enough to hear, but it was there.

"Yes, *petite*, I'm here. Mama's here."

She *was* getting better. Her brow still burned with fever, she was still delirious, but at least she could speak now. Aimée pulled her up in her arms, pressing the little body as tightly as she could against her own. If Mariette was conscious—if she could feel anything at all—she would sense her mother's presence and it would comfort her.

She held the child for a long time, soothing her, whispering to her, lulling away the pain and the fever. When at last she released her, easing her back on the table, she felt suddenly light and buoyant, as if a weight had been lifted from her shoulders.

She could barely keep her eyes open. She was so sleepy, so desperately sleepy, she didn't think she could fight it anymore.

But it didn't matter now, she told herself with relief. Mariette was better. The fever would break soon and everything would be all right. She could fall asleep if she wanted.

The fever would break soon.

459

But the fever couldn't break—not now. She didn't know why, she couldn't remember why, but she knew the thought made her afraid. If only she were not so tired. If only she could force herself to concentrate.

Why didn't she want the fever to break? But that was absurd, of course she wanted it to break. That was what she had been hoping for, praying for, all those long, terrifying hours. The fever had to break, easing the heat and the sweat that drenched a helpless body.

The heat . . . and the sweat.

Aimée willed her eyes to stay open. She had to think. She had to focus her mind.

The sweat. Cold sweat. Cold rain. Clothes and covers saturated. If the fever broke now, what would protect Mariette from the cold?

Aimée realized she had to do something. In an hour, two hours, perhaps only a few minutes, Mariette's temperature would drop drastically, and then she would need something to keep her warm.

But what? Frantically Aimée turned around, trying to search the darkness with her eyes. There had to be something in that room, something that would cover a sleeping child, but *what*? Everything was as wet as the shawl that swathed her now. Aimée would gladly have stripped off her own clothes, standing naked in the cold, if it would protect Mariette, but they were no drier than anything else.

She clutched at her petticoat, tugging it awkwardly to her ankles so she could step out of it. Her hands were strong as they gripped it, twisting it in a helpless attempt to wring away the moisture.

Glancing down, she visualized the object she could not see. The fabric was wet, but it was sturdy. If she could find something to fill it with, perhaps she could fashion it into a kind of quilt.

That was it. If she could gather something outside—straw perhaps, grass, pine needles—she could tie it up in the petticoat. It would be wet, but at least it would be thick. Thick enough to hold in body heat when the fever broke.

She found she was clinging to the table edge. She tried to let go but could not force her hand to move. Her legs were so weak she did not think they would support her weight any longer. Her eyes began to close.

If she could only lean against the wall. Just for a minute,

that was all. A single minute of rest. Then she would find the strength to go on.

The wall was hard against her cheek, rough and masculine, like a forgotten embrace. It would be good to let herself go at last. Good to sink into a deep, dreamless sleep.

Her mind sent out frantic signals, but she could not understand them. *Don't fall asleep. You can't fall asleep. You still have something to do.* But no matter how she tried, she couldn't remember what that something was.

Escape? Was that it? But she had already escaped. She was out of that terrible place now, and she was safe. In a minute she would wake up, and Sophie would be leaning over her, her hand warm on her brow. And Papa would laugh and draw her into his arms with a great bear hug, and he would say, "I'll always take care of my brave little soldier." And Mariette . . .

"Mariette!"

Aimée pounded her fist into the wall to pull herself out of her stupor. Mariette needed her. She had to remember that. Her child needed her. She had nearly fallen asleep once. She could not let it happen again. Not yet.

She had to take the petticoat in her hand and go outside, bending to the ground as she scooped up needles and grass and cracked pieces of leaves to make a cover for a fragile body. Then she could sleep if she wanted. Then she could come back inside and sink down on a filthy floor and let the rats and the insects crawl all over her, and she would know her child was safe.

But not yet . . . not yet.

The rain was falling in heavy sheets when Aimée stepped out into the night. Icy torrents drove against her face. She had been so sure the rain had stopped. When could it have started again?

Everything was dark and still. So still even the rain seemed silent. Aimée thrust her hands out in front of her to feel the way, and she realized she was afraid. She puckered her lips, trying to whistle away the unnatural quiet, but the shrill sound of her own bravado seemed more a travesty of despair. It was easier to surrender to the silence.

She stopped abruptly as her hand brushed against a solid object just ahead of her. The thing startled her. She knew it should not be there, not so close to the house, but it was. Cautiously she groped with her fingers, trying to make out contours and textures in the dark. She felt her skin crawl with horror.

It was warm. Not cold like the rain, but warm.

She ran her hands over it again. Hair, she could feel hair, wet and curling beneath her fingers. And a cheek rough with whiskers, and a nose. And teeth.

At last she could stand it no longer. The sound of her screams, harsh and piercing, penetrated the silence until the woods echoed with her fears.

Rough hands clutched her arms, pulling her forward, shaking her until her teeth rattled and her hair fell out of the clips that held it up, but still she could not stop screaming. Terror held her in its grip, pure animal terror, and her own anguished cries were her only release.

The sharp sting of a blow on the side of her face finally cut into her screams, breaking them into a single gasp of pain. Aimée felt her body swing backward, saved from falling only by the hand that clamped her wrist in a painful vise.

"Bitch!"

Aimée could hide from the truth no longer. Even a single angry cry was enough to reveal a voice she could never forget.

"Buffy?"

It couldn't be Buffy. She would have heard him coming. Hoofbeats in the distance. The wagon groaning into the yard.

But she had not heard the rain. The rain had begun again, and she had not even known it was there.

Buffy tightened his hold. The sound of her voice, weak and frightened, rekindled the rage inside him. Sharp fingers dug into her skin as he pulled her back, dragging her, half-stumbling, through the mud. He did not stop until he had flung her against the coarse slats that formed the side of his wagon.

Struggling to catch her breath, Aimée looked up at him. She could see him clearly now in the light of a lantern balanced unsteadily on the high wooden seat. His eyes burned two dark holes in his face. His skin was unnaturally flushed.

For a long time they stood and stared at each other in silence. It was Aimée who finally spoke.

"How did you find me?"

He raised his hand as if to strike her again, then dropped it slowly to his side. His face was rigid with self-control.

"Does it matter?"

No, it did not matter. A woodsman with kind eyes and a

grasping heart. Footprints in the mire where a narrow path turned off the main road. A scrap of cloth dangling in the chance beam of a lantern. None of these mattered now.

"What . . . what are you going to do?"

Self-control snapped in a burst of fury. His hand swung out, pinning her tightly to the wagon as he leaned forward. His breath was hot in her face. "What the hell did you think you were doing, running out on me like that? Am I really so disgusting you couldn't bear to lay eyes on me again?"

Instinctively Aimée raised her hand, ready to ward off a blow. "I was afraid. Can't you understand that? I was afraid."

"Afraid of what? That I would kill you? But I didn't kill you, did I? I had you in my power and I didn't even touch you."

Aimée was silent. She knew only too well what she feared, but she didn't dare put it into words. She didn't have to. Buffy did it for her.

"Shall I tell you what you were really afraid of? You were afraid I would go to Edward, and Edward would tell me the truth."

"The . . . the truth?"

Buffy exploded with anger. "Dammit, what kind of a fool do you think I am? I know the child isn't mine. I know you were only playing games with me."

"Games?" Aimée studied his face, trying to figure out what he meant. "But I never played games with you."

"Didn't you? What do you call it, then, sharing a bed with one man and slipping off to another on the side? Pretending you belong only to him, when all the time you really belong to everyone."

Aimée could hardly believe her ears. Could he seriously, even for a minute, believe she had ever belonged to him?

"I only did what Edward told me."

"Edward? I suppose Edward forced you to go to Villière. I suppose he insisted you wallow in the pleasures of his bed."

Aimée could hardly believe what she was hearing. She struggled to choke back the hysterical giggles that rose to her throat. "Of course he did. Doesn't that sound just like Edward? And afterward he wanted to know every detail—just like he did with you."

She meant the words as the most blatant form of sarcasm. It amazed her when he took them seriously.

"Edward *wanted* you to go to Villière?"

Slowly Aimée realized she had stumbled on the one thing that might save them. If only she could take his hatred for her and turn it against Edward . . .

"Edward wanted a child, you know that. When you didn't get me pregnant right away, he decided to look for another man."

Buffy eyed her suspiciously. He was sure she was lying, she had to be, and yet there was a germ of truth in what she said. It was just like Edward to be impatient with a stud who didn't succeed in the first month. And it would give him malicious satisfaction to double-cross his own lover.

Aimée sensed she was winning him over. "I hated it with him, Buffy. You know I did. You remember how it was with you. It was even worse with him. You know I would never let a man lay his hands on me if I weren't so afraid of Edward."

That was true, Buffy had to admit. The girl hated to be touched, that was obvious. So it was Edward all the time!

"Get in the wagon!"

He had more than one score to settle with Edward. And the woman, if she really hated him, might be willing to help. He was glad now he had come back for her. He was beginning to think she might be worth more alive than dead.

He began to tie the lantern back on the wagon. He was irritated when he turned around and saw that Aimée had not moved.

"Get in the wagon, dammit!"

"But Mariette . . . what about Mariette?"

Hell, he had forgotten the child. He glanced over his shoulder impatiently. It was so dark he couldn't see the hut.

"Leave her there. She's better off anyway. What kind of mother would bring a child out on a night like this? In the morning, when the rain stops, she can find her way out to the main road. Someone is bound to pick her up."

"Have you no decency?" Aimée's eyes snapped with anger. "You can't leave a child alone in that place. She'll . . . she'll be frightened, and besides . . ." She lowered her voice to a whisper. "Besides, she's sick."

Buffy was instantly wary. "What's wrong with her?"

"She has a fever," Aimée said quickly. "Children often have little fevers. She'll be fine once I get her someplace warm and comfortable."

Buffy hesitated. The last thing he needed was a sick child on his hands. Still, if she really did have a fever . . .

"This better not be one of your tricks."

"No, I swear it's not. Please, just help Mariette and I'll do anything you want." She forced herself to lay a provocative hand on his arm. "Anything."

Buffy tensed at her touch. "Why should I care, when the child isn't even mine?"

Aimée tried to make her voice low and sultry as she replied. "She could have been your child—if Edward hadn't gotten in the way."

Buffy pulled his arm back slowly. She was telling the truth now. He could not deny that. Perhaps she had been telling the truth all along. Reluctantly he pulled the lantern down and began to move toward the house. He could hear the woman hurrying anxiously behind him.

Furiously he whirled around. "Go back to the wagon, and stay there! I don't need you pestering me every minute of the time."

She had already confused things enough with her lies and her prattle. He had been so sure of himself when he pulled the wagon into the clearing. Revenge and greed had marched in neat little rows through a clear-cut path in his mind. Now he was not sure of anything.

Aimée watched, dismayed, as he slipped into the darkness. Angry retorts rose to her lips, but she choked them back. She could not bear leaving her child alone with him, but reason warned her she had no choice. She had already tried to save Mariette herself, and she had failed. Now she would have to rely on the mercy of a man who had never shown a generous emotion in his life.

Buffy was gloating as he stepped into the doorway of the hut. He sensed Aimée's tension, as an animal scents fear, and he found it peculiarly exciting. She was afraid, deathly afraid—and she was afraid of him.

He did not worry that she would try to escape. She would long to leap into the wagon, feeling the sharp bite of leather against her palms as she pulled the reins in her hands—she would long for it desperately, but she would never be able to do it. She was a mother, and she would have to hover outside, drifting toward the house, peeking into the windows perhaps, in a desperate attempt to get close to her child, like a lioness separated from her cubs.

He liked the way it had all turned out. Villière, his face angry but resigned as he handed over the Isis. Aimée, so

frightened of his power she would never defy him again. An
Edward ...

Yes, Edward. He had something very special planned fo
Edward.

The child lay quietly on a table against the wall. Buffy wa
apprehensive as he approached her. For all the mother's pro
testations, she had not even managed to make the girl com
fortable. He began to wonder if Aimée was really as devote
to her daughter as she claimed.

His footsteps creaked on the wet boards as he stepped u
to her. She was lying on her side, dangerously close to th
edge of the rough plank. Automatically Buffy reached ou
pushing her back toward the wall. He was surprised at th
heat of her skin against his fingers.

Buffy was no stranger to fevers. He had grown up in th
worst kind of slum, with a dozen people crowded into
single small room. Every season, a new fever had rage
through the area, and every season hosts of children fell vic
tim to it. The strong survived, the weak did not—that was a
there was to it. And he had never known a child with a feve
like Mariette's to live.

But then, he reminded himself wryly, he had never know
a child whose family could afford medical attention.

For the first time, he remembered that Aimée had bee
outside the house when he found her. And she had been mov
ing away from the doorway, not toward it.

Not that he blamed her. He had to admit that. Not afte
he got a look at Mariette. He had seen many a mother hold
dying child in her arms, and he knew more than one of the
would have run away if she could.

Still, it did complicate things. He glanced toward the doo
He had counted on the power of mother love. It was the onl
hold he had over Aimée.

He was not really nervous. Even if she tried to get away
there was nowhere she could go, not in the dark without
lantern. The horse would balk if she tried to force him, an
she could not get far on foot.

The child was flushed, restless in unnatural sleep. He ha
not noticed before how dark her lashes were as they reste
against her cheeks. He had studied that face often enough
looking for something of himself. Now he searched for re
minders of Raoul Villière. It surprised him to find none.

He could still see Villière's face in front of him, a kind o
counterbalance to the child's innocence. Dark, angry eye

466

impotent with rage, lips set with disgust. Dammit, the man was arrogant. Even when he had lost, even when it was clear he had been outwitted, he still looked down his nose at him. It was too bad, Buffy thought, that he would not see Villière's face when he learned his child was dead.

For the child would die, there was no doubt of that. Without a doctor, she could not last the night, and a doctor was out of the question. The night train to Paris left in just over an hour, and he intended to be on it. There was no time to stop at a hospital along the way, even had he been willing to risk the questions certain to be asked.

He found the idea strangely stimulating. It was not a clever plan, or a daring one, as he would have liked. And it was certainly not amusing. But it was satisfying in a way he had never expected. If he could not touch the man who mocked and rivaled him, perhaps he could reach him through his child.

Mariette thrashed restlessly on the plank, rolling toward the edge again. Lifting her up, Buffy eased her against the wall. He was impatient as he glanced around the room. He was already late. He couldn't waste his time taking care of a sick child. Aimée was the girl's mother. Why the hell hadn't she left her in better shape?

His eyes lit on the pair of straight-backed chairs beside the wall. Grabbing them hastily, he forced them against the tabletop. The tall backs were cracked and rotting, but at least they were heavy. They would form an effective rail for a little girl.

He paused one last time in the doorway. The setting was perfect, almost as if he had planned it that way. He could see it all through Villière's eyes as the police ushered him in to identify his dead child. A tiny body in a makeshift cradle, tight against a rat-infested wall. Tenderness and brutality all at once. It was enough to rend even a hard man's heart.

He found it hard to leave. He didn't want to look at the child again, but for some reason, he couldn't tear his eyes away from her.

She could have been your child, if . . .

Buffy had never dwelled on ifs. They had had no place in his life. He did not know how to deal with them now.

She could have been your child, if . . .

Oh, hell, she was only a child, after all. What did she have to do with Villière or Edward, or even Aimée? She was just a little girl, caught in other people's traps. It would give him no satisfaction to kill a child.

Aimée was hysterical when he returned without Mariette. She had stood alone in a deep pit of black, halfway between the house and the wagon, clenching and unclenching her skirt in tense fingers and praying he would hurry. When at last she caught sight of a faint beam in the darkness ahead, she began to stumble toward it, arms outstretched to draw her ailing child against her breast. The instant she saw that his hands were empty, she fell on him with a cry of rage.

"You bastard! You goddamned bastard!"

She had trusted him—she had actually dared to trust this foul swine of a man—and now he had come back without her child. She would kill him with her bare hands if she had to. He would not keep her from Mariette.

Buffy barely had time to draw up his hands, protecting his face from the fury of sharp nails as she flew toward him. Instinctively he thrust out his arms, hurling her back. Mud spattered against his coat as she crashed to the earth.

He knew he had stopped her for only a second. She would be back, and when she was, she would be a wildcat again, all claws and teeth as she attacked him with a madness he did not know how to handle. Fingers grasped clumsily for the comfort of cold metal. He was sure of himself again as he pointed the gun at her.

Aimée crawled to her knees, her eyes flashing with fire. "Do you think that will stop me, you son of a bitch? I don't care what you do to me now. I'm going to my child."

"Go ahead, but you won't get three steps. I'll shoot you down like a mad dog. And who'll help your precious child then?"

Aimée rose slowly. Every muscle in her body urged her to defy him, but reason held her back.

"And who'll help her if I don't try?"

Buffy dared to smile. For a moment he had doubted her maternal instincts.

"We'll send someone back from town—if you behave."

Aimée watched him tensely. She did not want to trust him again, but she could not afford to anger him.

"Why can't we take her with us?"

"We haven't got time. Besides, she'll be better off in the house, miserable as it is, than in an open wagon in the pouring rain."

"But not alone." Oh, God, what if she woke up and was

468

frightened, all alone with the dark and the rats? "Oh, please, not alone."

Buffy was losing his patience. Dammit, it was irritating. All that bitching and whining. He wondered how a man ever managed to live with a woman.

"We'll send word from the station—if there's time."

But there was no time. The train was already pulling out of the station as they raced across the platform. Buffy was sorry, genuinely sorry. He had not meant it to end that way.

Aimée gave a soft cry of fear as tight fingers gripped her arm, dragging her onto the moving train. She longed to turn back, leaning out of the open doorway, screaming for someone to help her child, but she did not even know where the deserted hovel was, and she was not sure how many words she could get out of her mouth before he shot her down, leaving her crumpled and defeated on the platform as the train vanished into the night. Then suddenly they were in a private compartment, and Buffy was locking the door behind them, and it was too late.

She felt like an old rag doll, with no form or substance left to her body, as she sank into a corner of the wide seat. All through the hours of her terror, pushing blindly into the rain with her child in her arms, watching as the only door that had been opened was slammed in her face, clinging to the rough seat of a swaying wagon with a madman by her side, there had at least been hope. What could she hope for now?

Buffy fidgeted in the seat opposite her. He did not know why the woman made him feel awkward, but she did.

"We'll send a telegram from Paris."

They wouldn't, of course. By the time they got to Paris, the child would already be dead. But it was easier than speaking the truth.

"Paris?" Aimée whispered the word so softly he did not hear her. Paris was far away, and Mariette was alone.

She wanted to close her eyes, but she couldn't. Once she had been tired, so desperately tired she could barely hold them open. Now there was no sleep left in her.

Paris. So far away. So very far. And yet it was all she had. A tiny shred of hope again. She would cling to that. Her eyes were dull with fear as she stared vacantly at the colors and lights and forms she could not even see.

Buffy turned away from her, picking up the motion of his own face against the glass. He wished the woman would stop looking at him like that, as if she were accusing him with her eyes. Buffy had always hated accusations. They made him feel guilty, even when he hadn't done anything.

"I said we'd send a telegram from Paris. What the hell do you want?"

It was too bad about the child. He never really meant to kill the child.

Dammit, why didn't the woman stop staring at him like that? And why did he feel so uncomfortable? It wasn't his fault. If the bitch hadn't run away from him like that, the whole thing would never have happened.

Still, it was too bad.

3

The house in Paris recalled only painful memories. Aimée had been a young girl, barely more than a child, when she first crossed the threshold five years before. Had she known then the things that lay ahead, she wondered if she would have had the courage to face her fears that night.

The wind cut through the thin fabric of her dress as she stepped out of a hired carriage onto the stones of the courtyard. The sky was clear, but it was nearly twilight and the air was cold. She shivered as she turned toward the house.

It was all she could do to force her hand through the arm of the man who walked beside her. Even the feel of his flesh beneath the rumpled fabric of his coat disgusted her, but she dared not let her revulsion show. Buffy Montmorency, much as she loathed him, was all that stood between her daughter and death.

She listened to the slow, dull clatter of the horses' hooves as the coachman guided the hackney out of the yard. Closing her eyes, she tried to remember the feel of Mariette's brow beneath her fingers the last time she touched her. Cooler, surely it was cooler—she couldn't have imagined it. The memory was all that kept her going.

She stumbled as Buffy tugged at her arm, pulling her impatiently toward the door. She realized she had almost forgotten he was there.

"Please . . . couldn't we send the telegram now?" It would take minutes, just minutes, for the word to reach Berlin. And then her child would be safe.

Buffy glanced down at her sharply. There was no point sending the telegram, and he thought the woman knew it.

"Later," he said abruptly. Might as well encourage her in her delusions. It would make her easier to handle. "When we're through here."

Aimée pulled back, as if to protest again, but he did not give her a chance. He rapped on the door.

The footsteps that responded to his knock were slow and shuffling. Buffy leaned forward, tensing with anticipation as the door eased slowly open. He did not try to conceal his surprise when he caught sight of a familiar figure.

"Well, Eddie . . ." He had never expected to see Lord Edward Ellingham opening his own door.

"What . . . what do you want?"

Buffy's contrived smile widened into a natural grin. He had expected something more like: What the hell do you think you're doing here? It seemed to him it was a good sign.

"Aren't you going to ask us in?" Pushing Aimée ahead of him, he forced his way through the door. "Where are your manners, Eddie? Your charming wife and I have come a long way to chat with you. Haven't we, my pet?"

Aimée tilted her head to look up at him. "Yes, of course, my dear."

She was amazingly cool, Buffy thought as he watched her turn calmly toward the drawing room, as if they had merely come to pay a social call. Her gown was torn and disheveled, her hair so untidy it hung down her back, but she walked like a princess, carrying herself with regal pride. And underneath it all, she was so frightened, she could not keep her hand from trembling. Who would have dreamed she'd turn out to be such a superb little actress?

Edward followed them to the door of the drawing room, but he did not step inside. "State your business and get out."

Buffy ignored him as he moved to the center of the room, turning slowly to look around him. He remembered it as a rich, extravagant hall, with gilt and rosewood standing out against red carpeting, and rock-crystal cherubs catching sunbeams from the chandeliers. Now all the valuables were packed away, and grayed sheeting shrouded the furnishings, as if no one had bothered to tell the servants Edward was coming home.

"I thought you were planning to stay in Paris. Didn't Christian have his heart set on the place?"

He strolled over to the windows, careful to keep the light

471

behind him. He liked the idea that Edward would have to squint into the sun to look at him. It would put him at a disadvantage.

"By the way, where is darling Christian?"

Edward glowered as he stepped into the room. "I don't see that that's any of your business."

"In other words, you have no intention of telling me. Well, never mind, you don't have to." The petulant set of Edward's lower lip made it all too clear what had happened. "I must say I'm surprised. Christian always seemed like an opportunistic little brat to me. I never thought he'd leave you so soon."

"No one leaves me Buffy—as you know only too well."

Edward's show of bravado was painfully obvious. Buffy snickered, then began to laugh outright. "I know, you found him too, too tiresome, didn't you? So demanding, and so greedy. You had to get rid of him. Come off it, Eddie, who do you think you're fooling? I can see right through you."

Edward would never have discarded one lover if he wasn't sure he had another on the string. He was too afraid of being alone. How he must hate the nights now, all those long nights when he blew out the candles in his big, empty house and went upstairs alone.

"Come on, tell the truth, Eddie?" he coaxed. "Did little Christian find a better pigeon, is that it? A man even richer than you?" Something in Edward's furious gaze told him he was missing the point. "Don't tell me he left you for a *woman*?"

Edward took a quick step forward, his hands doubled into fists at his side, then stopped abruptly. He looked pale and drained, as if he had aged in a single week. "Dammit, Buffy, say what you have to say and get the hell out of here."

So it was a woman. "By God, Eddie, that's priceless! Come on, now, even you have to admit that. Here you are, so afraid of women you have to send me in to your own wife—and now your pampered lover has run off with one. I hope at least she's rich. I'd hate to think the boy gave up you *and* your money for a little trollop of a chorus girl. What was she, Eddie? A countess? A baroness?"

"Oh, cut it out, Buffy." Edward was too tired to fight back. "Aren't we both a little old for this kind of thing? If you must know, she was the widow of a wealthy American industrialist."

"An industrialist?" Buffy tried to make his smirk cutting,

ut he did not quite succeed. Edward had found a new dignity that was disconcerting. He was taking the fun out of everything. "How common, Eddie. That's a little play on
words—get it? A commoner . . . so common. But you're not
laughing."

Edward stepped up to the windows. Now he wasn't looking
into the sun anymore. "No, I'm not laughing."

Buffy seethed slowly. He had never seen Edward so cool.
No anger, no regrets. No feeling. All those years—and then
nothing. Not even a pat on the cheek and a perfunctory:
Sorry, Buffy, I'll miss you, really I will, in my own shallow
way.

"Does it upset you, Eddie? Thinking of pretty Christian in
someone else's arms? I wonder if he writhes and cries out
with pleasure, the way he never did with you. Imagine, all
that soft young skin wasted on a wrinkled old bitch."

Aimée caught her breath as she stood at the side of the
room and listened to the vindictiveness in his voice. If there
had been any doubt in her mind, it was gone now. Buffy's
malice had destroyed his reason.

Cautiously she glanced toward the doorway. He was so
wrapped up in Edward—and in his own bitterness—he did
not even see her. Perhaps if she was stealthy enough, she
could slip out into the hallway without being noticed. If only
she could make it to the street before he realized she was
gone . . .

But she was not quick enough. Buffy caught the movement
out of the corner of his eye.

"Come and join us, my dear."

Aimée knew she had no choice. She held her back straight
as she forced herself to cross the room, sitting on the edge of
one of the chairs. Buffy barely glanced down at her.

"I was about to tell your husband a nice little story—a sort
of fairy tale, you might say. I'm sure it will amuse you, too."

He leaned back against the windowsill as he turned to Edward.

"It's really a pretty story, Eddie, a once-upon-a-time story,
the kind that should have ended with 'And then they lived
happily ever after.' Once upon a time, there was a little boy
who lived in a slum in the big city. He was a beautiful boy
with soft brown curls and huge, liquid eyes. Does that sound
familiar, Eddie?

"Now, this little boy—shall we call him Bobbie, just for
the fun of it?—Bobbie may have looked like an angel, but he

473

wasn't one at all. He was tough enough to survive on the streets, and that means tough in a way you never imagined. He was an accomplished thief, the smoothest pickpocket you would ever hope to see, without a qualm or a scruple in his body.

"Shall I tell you about little Bobbie? He killed a man once, in a street brawl. Not by accident, mind you, not with a careless smash of the fist, but with a fruit knife, buried deliberately in the side of his throat. Does that shock you, Eddie? Does it make you nervous to sit and chat with a man who can kill with no more compunction than sticking a knife into a ripe, juicy peach?

"But I'm boring you. You want the pretty part of the story. The part where Bobbie met the nice man who rode through the slums in his carriage, handing out candy to little boys. You have to see it from Bobbie's point of view. Fifteen, sixteen years old, naive and impressionable—and along comes a man, smiling and elegant, who seems to offer him everything in the world.

"Oh, Bobbie had prostituted himself before, but never with a man. Only older women with a few coins to toss his way, much as your Christian is doing now—only of course Christian expects more than a tuppence or two. He had never even been with a man—or wanted to—but this man seemed to him the epitome of everything that was perfect and unattainable.

"I wish you could see it the way Bobbie saw it. I can, you know—I still can. A shiny black brougham with a crest painted ostentatiously on the door, and then—ah, the height of ostentation, Eddie—white satin upholstery. And the man himself. Tapered legs and pointed toes. A silk cravat knotted against a velvet collar. A top hat brushing the roof of the coach. And ugly . . .? Oh, God, yes, he was ugly, but so arrogant he looked like a prince. Bobbie would have laid down his life for him then. All he wanted was to be like him someday."

Buffy paused to watch his former lover. Edward was quiet, as if he were saddened in some way by the memory, but he did not look uncomfortable. That was not the way Buffy had planned it.

"It occurs to me," he said softly, "I'm almost the same age you were when you picked me out of the slums. Maybe I can be like you after all—exactly like you. What do you think,

ddie? Is it time for me to ride through the streets and try
y luck with a new generation of urchins?"

"And do what, Buffy?" Edward's voice was irritatingly
lm. "Dazzle them with fancy carriages and expensive
othes? With diamonds sparkling on your fingers?"

"Why not?"

"For a very good reason. You don't have them."

"Don't I? I told you once that I wanted nothing more than
be like you. Well, now I'm going to have that. Only, I'm
ot going to be *like* you—I'm going to *be* you."

His tone was too serious to misinterpret. Edward took a
ep back as he stared at him. "You're mad, you know. Ut-
rly mad."

"Am I? I suppose I must be. But you know, my dear, it's
ally quite a lot of fun. You should try it sometime."

"And how do you propose to do this? Take over my iden-
ty?"

"I've already begun. You see, Eddie, I have you all figured
ut by now. Your identity is nothing more—and nothing
ss—than a sum total of your possessions. When I have them
l, I'll have all of you."

"And you think I'll just hand them over to you?" Edward
aned against the wall, a calm, casual gesture. Buffy could
ave sworn he saw his lips turn up.

"You like being smug, don't you? You think you're so safe,
ou and all the things you've accumulated and held on to so
ghtly. Well, for all your caution and your stinginess, I've
anaged to acquire the two prizes of your collection al-
eady."

He bent toward Aimée, resting a possessive hand on her
air. "Do you remember the day you married her, Eddie?
ou thought all of Europe would fall at your feet with envy.
ow do you think they'll react now when they find out she's
ving openly with another man—and your former lover at
at?"

Buffy watched Edward closely. He wanted to see sweat
listen on his forehead. Edward always sweated when he was
ervous.

"Or don't you think she'll do it? Do you think she'll refuse
e, too, as tartly as she refused you. Come on, Eddie, look at
er. She was proud and arrogant when you had her. Where is
ll that fire now? That's the difference between you and me. I
now how to handle women."

He drew his hand back from Aimée's hair, slipping beneath his coat to pull out a long black case.

"Women . . . and goddesses."

Slowly he flipped it open.

Edward's breath was an audible hiss as he gaped at t' thing. Damn! He had gotten it. He had actually gotten it. E ward had been wrong after all. He thought there was no w to get to Villière, but there was.

He began to look at Buffy with new eyes.

"You are clever, Buffy, I have to admit that. I wonder if didn't make a mistake about you."

Maybe he had been wrong to dismiss Buffy so hastily. least he could be sure of Buffy, not like that ingrate Chri tian, running off with someone else the minute his back w turned. Buffy was getting older, of course, he was not pretty as he used to be, but prettiness was a thing that va ished all too quickly when the lights were turned out. Mayl he ought to take him back, at least for a while.

"Were you really so taken with me, Buffy—all those yea back? Was it really me you wanted—and not my money?"

Buffy felt his stomach turn as he watched the man he ha once adored. Edward was actually being coy with him, ju like he was when they met.

"Do you think I'm such a fool, Eddie? Do you real think, after all you've done, that you only have to snap yo fingers and I'll come running?"

"If you want me enough you will—and I think you do."

The idea was becoming more and more appealing. The fir time he took Buffy in, he was a penniless orphan. At least th time he brought a dowry—the Isis.

Buffy's nausea rose to his throat. Edward was teasing, flir ing, almost groveling in front of him. He was getting to l an old man, and he was pathetic in the years when he shoul have had dignity.

"I don't want you anymore, Eddie, and I don't need yo You see, I intend to have everything you own, piece by piec I think I'll start with this house. I've always had a fondne for it. What do you think I'll have to do to persuade you t part with it?"

Edward saw what was happening. He was in a corner, an there was no way he could get out of it. Even if he agreed Buffy's demands, even if he paid the blackmail that woul grow more and more exorbitant each month, Buffy woul

476

still ruin him with malicious gossip. He was too vindictive for anything else.

"I'll see you in hell first!"

"Will you, Eddie? Will you really? I don't think you've considered all the possibilities."

But Edward had considered them only too well. He could see himself reflected in Buffy's eyes, and he knew the picture was an accurate one. He was an ugly man, gawky for all the expensive tailoring of his clothes. Ugly and foolish—and old. He was only in his fifties but he was old. He could not climb a flight of steps without feeling a tightness in his chest. And now every time he went outside, he would make a laughing-stock of himself.

And there was not a thing in the world he could do about it.

"You scum. You filthy scum. I took you out of the gutter and gave you everything you have, and I can throw you right back in. Spread all the rotten little stories you want. I'll shut myself up with my fortune, afraid to face the world, but I'll be thinking about you every minute of the time, and I'll know you're back on the streets with the rest of the waste from the sewers. What will keep you warm then, Buffy? Your revenge? I think, in the end, I'll have the most satisfaction."

"Do you really think so, Eddie?" Buffy was calm as he drew his hand out of his pocket. He waited for the first sign of alarm when Edward recognized his own gun. "Did you really think I'd let you sit in one of your big houses and enjoy your money?"

Edward stared at him coldly for a minute. Then, to Buffy's irritation, he burst out laughing.

"Don't be melodramatic, Buffy. You always were such a child."

A child, was he? Buffy tensed at the mockery in Edward's tone. As long as he could remember, his lover had made fun of him, belittling everything he did—or tried to do. Straightening his arm, he adjusted the handle of the gun comfortably against his palm. He aimed it at the deep crease that divided Edward's forehead.

He understood at last that this was what he had wanted all along. He had told himself he had plans for Edward, but he had not realized until this moment what they were. He thought he wanted his lover's house, his carriage, his jewels, even his wife. Now he knew those things would never be enough.

"You have to die, Eddie."

He waited for the beads of sweat to roll down Edward's forehead. He wanted to see fear in dark eyes as he sank to his knees in front of him, whining and begging for his life.

But Edward held his ground.

"Do you want money, Buffy? Is that it? I never keep much in the safe, you know that."

"Beg, dammit!" Where was the fear? He needed to see fear—the same fear he had known all these years while he waited for Edward to get tired of him and toss him back in the slums.

"Beg? Really, you are an ass, Buffy." Edward turned his back as he walked calmly toward the door.

"Turn around."

He didn't want to shoot him in the back. It wasn't fair. He had waited so long for this moment. He didn't want to be cheated of the fear in Edward's eyes.

But Edward did not turn. When Buffy saw him reach the door, he knew the moment had come.

He leveled the gun automatically. The trigger slid easily beneath his finger. Edward stopped, then staggered a moment. A bright stain spread across the back of his jacket.

At last Edward turned. His eyes, as he focused them on Buffy, still held no fear. He almost seemed to be irritated, peeved with the childish lover whose immaturity had annoyed him one last time.

Buffy felt betrayed as he squeezed the trigger again, and then a third time. Even in death, his lover had eluded him. It might as well have been a stranger crumpling into a heap of skin and blood and expensive velvet at his feet.

"Oh, my God!"

Aimée's cry was a shrill wail in the sudden stillness. Stumbling, she hurried toward her husband's body, sinking to her knees beside him. Once she had hated this man so much she thought she could never touch him again. Now she cradled his lifeless head in her lap.

"Get up!"

Buffy's voice was demanding. Aimée's eyes were glazed with horror as she looked up at him.

"But why . . . why?"

"I said, get up." Her whining was beginning to get on his nerves.

Numbly Aimée obeyed. "Hadn't you done enough already?

His whole life was falling apart. Why did you have to kill him?"

"Why?" He stared at her coldly. "Because I wanted to, that's why."

Shall I tell you about little Bobbie? He buried a fruit knife in the side of a man's throat.

"Oh, please—" Aimée's hand clutched at her throat. Killing meant nothing to him—nothing. And this was the man who held her daughter's life in his hands. "Mariette . . . You promised to get help to Mariette."

Buffy was getting tired of the woman. He had thought it would be amusing to have her around. Now he knew it would not. He could understand why Eddie never wanted to have anything to do with women.

"No one can help the child now. She's dead."

"Dead?" Aimée backed away from him. "But . . . but you can't *know* that."

Buffy took a step toward her. He liked the look in her eyes. It was the look he had wanted to see in Edward's.

"Oh, but I can, you know. She was dead when I left the hut."

Aimée searched his face, trying to find something that would tell her it was only a malicious joke. There was nothing.

"She . . . she was dead?"

Buffy almost smiled as he watched her. She was so pale even her lips had lost their color. That was the way Edward should have looked when he fell on his knees and begged.

"Of course she was dead, I saw to that." He couldn't resist twisting the knife a little deeper. "I wouldn't leave a sick dog like that. I had to put her out of her misery."

"You killed her?" Aimée whispered the words in sheer horror. She didn't believe him. She could not let herself believe him. And yet she had just seen him shoot a man in the back.

Like a knife in a ripe, juicy peach.

"Damn you!"

All the rage and terror in her heart broke in one torrential flood as she lunged at him. She did not even see the gun in his hand. It didn't matter what he did to her now. Nothing mattered anymore. This was the man who had murdered her child, and she wanted to dig her nails into his flesh until he screamed with pain.

She flew at him like a crazed Fury, seeking an outlet for vengeance and grief alike. New strength flowed into her limbs as she remembered the agonies she had endured. The terror when she struggled to shield her child's burning body from the rain . . . the hope that kept her alive on the train ride to Paris, long after Mariette was dead. She beat at him wildly with her fists.

Buffy was too stunned to react quickly. He tried to push her away, but the savage force of her assault was too much for him. He was conscious of the gun, cold against his palm, but he could not manage to aim it. Inching it forward, he tried to bury the muzzle in her flesh.

Aimée felt hard metal press into her side, and she sensed her danger instantly. Groping with her hand, she clutched at the gun, struggling to turn it away. Buffy fought fiercely, but she was more than a match for him. Rage had given her a power beyond her native strength—rage and despair.

They grappled across the floor, pulling and turning, twisting in the last frantic embrace that was sure to end in death for one of them. Aimée's hand curled around his, clasping it so tightly she could feel the shape of the gun. Her finger slipped slowly forward. She did not know what drove her now, she only knew she had to get at the trigger.

A violent explosion burst in her ears. It was a bewildering sound, deafening her for a second. The smell of smoke burned in her nostrils.

Aimée pulled back, tensing for the searing pain that would follow. She felt nothing. Buffy seemed to do the same thing, retreating into a rigid stance, listening, waiting, expecting the thing that did not come. Then slowly he began to heave forward, sliding against her as his body sank to the floor. The gun fell with a dull thud on the carpet beside him.

His eyes looked up at her. Open and dark with pain. And in their depths, if only he could have known it, was exactly the look he had longed to see.

Aimée stood and stared down at him. He was dying, but she could not feel anything. No horror, no remorse, no relief. Only a passive curiosity at the fleeting transition of life into nothingness.

I wouldn't leave a sick dog like that. I had to put her out of her misery.

And her finger had slipped forward, groping toward the trigger, moving as if it had a will of its own.

Must I spell it out for you? I am here to make up for the aborted ecstasy of your wedding night.

And she had pulled the trigger.

But it was an accident. Only an accident. She was not a killer. Buffy was a killer, but she was not. Not for vindictiveness, not for grief, not even for five years torn out of her life.

Like a knife in a ripe, juicy peach.

And then there was no more fear, no more pain, and the eyes that looked up at her were dull with death. And still she felt nothing.

Aimée was still there, her head buried in her hands, when the gendarmes arrived an hour later. They had to break through a window to get in, smashing brittle fragments of glass against the marble floor of the entryway. They did not truly expect to find anything. The telegram from the authorities in Berlin was too vague—and too fantastic.

The younger of the two men, Louis Duval, had been a policeman for less than a year. Nothing in his experience had prepared him for the brutality that now met his eyes. Lord Edward Ellingham, a man he knew by sight, was sprawled face-up on the carpet, blood seeping into a dark circle around him. Half of his chest was blown away. The man who lay across the room was a stranger. His coat had fallen over his body, half-hiding the wound in his side, but his head was twisted up until he seemed to be gaping at the policeman.

"Dieu, what a mess!"

Duval's face was ashen as he stared at them. He knew he was supposed to do something—examine the bodies perhaps, make sure they were dead—but he could not make himself go near them. He tried to swallow the lump in his throat.

Beside him, Robert Gautier assessed the situation with a practiced eye. Glancing at his partner, he chuckled softly.

"I told you you'd be sorry if you put a second éclair on top of those fried potatoes."

Duval's skin took on a greenish pallor, but he did not try to speak. Relenting, Gautier patted him clumsily on the arm. He liked this boy they had given him to train. He just needed a little hardening, that was all. Besides, he had thrown up himself when he saw his first violent murder—and he hadn't even had a second éclair.

"Let's get to work. You take care of the woman. I'll see about those two."

Turning slowly, Duval was surprised to see a woman crouched on the floor beside the doorway. He had not even noticed her when he stepped into the room. He felt clumsy

481

and inept as he squatted beside her, trying to urge her to look up at him, but anything was better than dealing with those two corpses. When she finally pulled her hands down from her face, he saw that her eyes were dry. She had been trembling so badly, he thought she was weeping.

Aimée was stunned when she looked up and saw a policeman staring at her. All she could think of was what she had done.

"It was an accident," she whispered desperately. And it *was* an accident. It was. Not her finger slipping against the trigger. "Oh, please, you must believe me. We were struggling, and the gun ... the gun just went off."

Duval was puzzled at first. Then slowly he began to understand. He had assumed the two men shot each other. Now he realized the woman must have killed at least one of them.

"Of course it was an accident." He tried to make his voice comforting, not stiff and embarrassed. "Of course. It was self-defense. We know that."

The poor woman. She was on the edge of hysteria. Not that he blamed her. She must have been through hell. Kidnapped—if the telegram was right—by her own husband. And now this.

Gautier had already tidied the room when Duval finally coaxed Aimée to her feet. Dust covers, hastily pulled from the furniture, lay across the bodies, tucking them out of sight. The only visible traces of death were the bloodstains drying on Aimée's skirt.

She stood at the side of the room, bewildered, and tried to take it all in. The bodies looked so still, so innocent, beneath their gray-white shrouds, like a pair of overstuffed chairs that had melted away in the center of the room.

Slowly she turned toward Gautier.

"My child—he killed my child."

"But, madame, the child is all right."

Aimée stared at him, confused. She tried to study his face, but she could not bring it into focus. Everything in the room seemed to be a blur.

"You don't understand. He told me he killed her."

"No, no, madame." The poor woman had been so frightened it affected her reason. "I promise you the child is all right. The police found her in an abandoned hut. The telegram said a woodsman led the authorities to her."

"The woodsman?"

A flicker of regret in a man's eyes. A moment of daring to trust.

"Then . . . she is all right? You are sure?"

Gautier hesitated. The telegram had said something about an illness, but there was no point worrying the woman now. She had already been through enough.

"Did I not promise you? Of course the child is all right."

"But she was so sick when I left her, she had a terrible fever. Oh, please . . ."

She was so pale Gautier was alarmed.

"You will make yourself ill, madame." He pulled her toward one of the chairs, but he could not force her to sit down. "You must not worry so, every time a child's temperature goes up. This is a thing that happens all the time. Haven't I raised six children myself? I should know. The child may have been sick, but most assuredly she is well now."

"Then . . ." Then it was a joke all the time. A petty, spiteful joke. How like Buffy to be so cruel. "Then it was all for nothing."

And her finger had slipped on the trigger. And it was all for nothing.

"Madame . . . ?"

Aimée pulled herself together. Her face was stricken as she turned to him. "But she is alone. She is so little—she'll be frightened."

"No, no she is not alone. The telegram said most specifically . . ." Gautier paused awkwardly. "The telegram said the child was with her father, but of course . . ."

"Her father?" But Raoul was the child's father, and Raoul was in Egypt. "That's impossible."

Gautier glanced uncomfortably at the sheet on the floor. "Yes, yes, it cannot be the father. Perhaps some other male relative?"

"Franz?" Of course. That was it. The authorities would have sent word to Vienna. "It must be my cousin Franz."

"Your cousin? Yes, that must be it."

Aimée closed her eyes, shaking with relief. Mariette was all right. She had been afraid, so desperately afraid, but it was all over now. Mariette was all right, and she was not alone.

Tomorrow she would take the train to Vienna. Franz would already have brought her child home, and Mariette would be safe and happy. Tomorrow she would feel little arms around her neck again. But tonight . . .

Tonight she was so tired.

"Please . . ." She turned to the two policemen. "Could you take me to my father's house?"

4

She looked so little lying there. A corner of the long ward had been sectioned off, with a pair of wrinkled sheets draped hastily from the ceiling, giving Raoul the illusion that he and the child were alone in the world. They had cropped off her long black hair, leaving the ends to jut out dark and uneven against the pillow.

"Mariette?" He knew it was no use, but he tried anyway. "Mariette, can you hear me?"

He ran his fingers lightly along the side of her face. He had never realized how small a child could be. Her whole head was not as big as his own callused hand.

She stirred slightly, as if to pull away from the roughness of his touch. He cursed softly under his breath. Dammit, the child needed a woman now, tender and instinctively maternal, not a man with big clumsy hands and a voice too gruff to soothe.

Where was Aimée anyway? He rose impatiently, stepping over to the window, as if he expected to see her hurrying across the gray stones of the courtyard below. The police had sent a telegram to Paris the instant they found the child; he had seen to that himself. She had had plenty of time to get here.

"Nurse." He pulled aside the makeshift curtain, calling out to a stocky young woman at the far end of the room. There were other people in the rows of beds that lined the walls, but he barely saw them.

The nurse's voice showed irritation as she strode toward him. "Must I tell you again to keep your voice down, Herr Villière? This is a hospital, not a common barroom. Your little girl isn't the only one who's sick here."

She's the only one sick enough to have her bed screened off, he wanted to shout back. The only one you're afraid to let the others see.

But he could not bring himself to utter the words. Instead he said only, "Hasn't Lady Ellingham arrived yet?"

"If she had, I would have sent her to you. Is this what you waste my time for? Foolish questions? I am very busy, *mein Herr*. I have many patients to attend to."

Raoul stood and watched her walk off, speechless with frustration. Mariette needed a woman's touch, but there was no woman here to comfort her. Only one brisk, efficient nurse, whose hands were even more callused than his own.

He pulled the sheets together, clinging to the curtained privacy as he stepped back into the alcove. Mariette's eyes were still closed, her cheeks even redder than before. He rested his hand on her brow. It was burning with heat.

Nothing—was there nothing he could do? It was infuriating to feel so helpless. He was a man, a grown man, but he felt awkward and inept, like a little child in the face of something it could not understand.

Bring the fever down, they had told him. Try to bring it down. He reached for a bottle of alcohol on the bedside table, soaking it into a soft cloth. He had already spent hours with the same cool cloth in his hand, trying desperately to tempt the heat from a tiny chest and limbs, but it had done no good. He knew he would spend hours more if he had to—and still he would accomplish nothing.

It was all strangely unreal. He sat at the side of a hospital bed, lifting a limp, slender arm off the sweat of the sheets, and he could not make himself believe it was happening. This was not Mariette lying in front of him, so weak she could not move or whimper. It was not Mariette at all. It was only a little rubber doll, lifeless and rouged, like some kind of prize at a cheap honky-tonk carnival, and he was a man playing with children's toys and making himself sick over a thing that did not exist.

He drew back for a moment, feeling a pain he could not express or understand. He remembered how important it had been once to know whether this was his child or not. It was important no longer. She was a child he loved, and he could do nothing to help her.

A footstep on the other side of the curtain made him turn his head. He thought at first it was the nurse, and he tensed automatically, dreading the impersonal efficiency that seemed so out of place beside the sickbed of a child. Then he realized it was the doctor.

He had met the man only briefly, when they first brought

Mariette into the hospital. Now he was almost pathetically grateful to see him again.

"She is better, I think, doctor. Quiet now, not so restless. She seems much better."

It was ridiculous, and he knew it. The child was no better than she had been before. He knew he was playing a game with the doctor, trying to coax him to agree. Then, when he said Mariette was better, Raoul could believe it, too.

The doctor did not reply. Stepping over to the bed, he laid his hand on Mariette's forehead, then examined her briefly. When he looked up, his face was grave.

"I am afraid you must understand, Herr Villière. The child's condition has not improved. Not yet."

Raoul felt as if he had been kicked in the stomach, with all the air knocked out of him. He sank heavily into the chair beside the bed. He had expected so much from the doctor. Promises, cures, even miracles. Now he knew there would be no miracles.

"Dammit, why can't you do anything for her? What kind of doctor are you? All you do is lean over her and pat her a little here and there and look solemn. Surely there must be something you can give her, something that will make her better."

"I am a doctor. I am not God."

Raoul let his head drop into his hands. *I am a doctor. I am not God.* Were they all callous, all these people who worked in a hospital? Had they grown so inured to sickness and death they no longer understood the need of the human heart for comfort or illusions?

"Do you even know what's wrong with her?"

The doctor seemed tired, as if he had not slept for days. "Oh, yes, we know what it is, but that does not help us. We can put a name to it, we can describe the symptoms and the risks, but we cannot do a thing to cure it or even change its course."

"And the name?"

"It has a scientific name, of course—everything seems to have a scientific name nowadays—but that would mean little to you. We call it infantile paralysis, because it often strikes children."

Infantile paralysis. Even the words made Raoul's blood run cold. Infantile paralysis. It was an ancient disease, as old as time. He could remember hearing other archaeologists talk about it. They had found burials, they said. Burials of children who had died of that same disease.

They had died of it.

At last he forced himself to admit the thing he could not face. He had known when they set a curtain around Mariette's bed what they feared, but he had not been able to accept it. Now he could hide from it no longer.

"Then she is going to die?"

"I have said to you already, I am not God. I cannot tell you. Sometimes these children recover, but even then . . ." He hesitated uncomfortably, finding it painful, as he always did, to bring even a strong man to grips with reality. "I think you must be ready for the worst. Even when they recover, they are often crippled or . . . deformed. It is a rare child who escapes without at least a twisted leg or a useless arm."

"But they do recover?"

The doctor glanced sharply at Mariette. She had been sick for a long time, and he knew she was at the end of her resources. But to take a man's hope away entirely—that was a thing he could not do.

"We must trust in God."

Raoul sat quietly after he left, watching the child, so still on the bed. *We must trust in God.* But the man was a doctor, and Raoul had always been taught to believe in doctors. He did not know if he had enough trust left for God.

He caught sight of a small gold crucifix, half-hidden beneath a heavy chain on the table. The nurse must have taken it off when they placed Mariette on the bed, grumbling that it got in the way. Raoul picked it up now, fastening it around the child's neck. The cross had been Aimée's. It was all there was of the mother to comfort the child.

We must trust in God. How many fathers had sat by the bedsides of their children, how many mothers, and said those same words since the dawn of time? Had Egyptian parents prayed, as he was praying now, to Ra and Isis and Horus to give them back their child, whole and healthy again? Thousands of years—*thousands* of years—and in all that time, no one, not one doctor, not one scientist, had found a way to stop it.

Mariette's condition remained stable for the next hour, but even stability was a thing Raoul had come to dread. She lived through the hour, and he was grateful at least for that, but he knew she could not endure the fever much longer. He leaned

487

back in his chair, rubbing his hands against his temples in a vain attempt to ease the tension.

When he looked up again, he was surprised to see that Mariette was awake. She did not seem to notice him as she stared at the dull glow of the windowpanes. Her eyes were dark with fever.

Raoul leaned over her, brushing damp curls off her forehead. He was careful not to frighten her. For the first time since the doctor had told him the truth, he let himself hope.

"Hello, Mariette," he said softly. "Do you remember me? You were a very little girl when we met."

Still the child did not see him. Her eyes turned in the direction of his voice, but she could not pick out his face. Her lips were moving, as if she were trying to speak, but the sound was so soft it was inaudible.

Raoul bent lower, his ear toward her mouth. "What is it, Mariette? What do you want?"

"Mama . . ." Her voice was so soft he could barely hear it. "Mama . . ."

It was a plaintive little cry, and it tore his heart. He longed to draw her protectively into strong arms, but he knew his were not the arms she needed. The child wanted her mother, and her mother was not there.

Dammit, where was Aimée? What kind of a woman tied a cross around her child's neck, then just abandoned her? He knew what she'd been through—it must have been agonizing for her, too—but how could she have left Mariette like that? If it had been him, they would have had to kill him before they could drag him away from his child.

The light that filtered through the window was dim and gray. It was still early afternoon, but the sky was heavy with clouds and it was already so dark it seemed like twilight. The walls were as gray as the air, gray and scarred with peeling strips of paint. Why were hospitals always so ugly? he wondered. Was everyone afraid—or ashamed—to touch on beauty in the face of death?

The nurse came in with an oil lamp, setting it on the table by the bed.

"Another cloudy day. Looks like we'll have rain before nightfall." She laid her hand on Mariette's brow, then checked her pulse quickly and mechanically, just as the doctor had done before.

So brisk, Raoul thought as he watched her. So cool. More like a machine than a woman of flesh and blood. He followed

488

her with his eyes as she disappeared. In a way he envied her the very coolness he pretended to despise. It would be so much easier now if he could only be like her.

The child stirred again. This time, as her eyes opened, they stared directly at Raoul.

He could see her more clearly now that the nurse had brought a lamp. Her eyes were still unnaturally bright, but at least she was able to focus.

"How do you feel, Mariette? Are you better now?"

The child did not hear him. She studied him closely, as if she were trying to make out who he was, but she did not seem puzzled or apprehensive.

"Do you know my father?"

"What?" The words were so clear, so distinct, they startled him. At first he did not realize what she had said.

"Do you know my father?"

"Yes, Mariette." How easily the words slipped out. "Yes, I know your father."

He had avoided the issue for so long. Now he wondered why. *I am her father*, he had told the police when they asked who he was. They had looked at him strangely, knowing he was not the mother's husband, but they had not questioned him further.

I am her father. It was all so simple now.

"My father is a very big man."

"What, *petite*?" How solemn her eyes were as she looked up at him.

"My father has a horse. A big white horse. When I am five years old he is going to give it to me. Then it will be mine."

Raoul studied her face, trying to figure out whom she was talking about. Then slowly he understood that she was lost somewhere in a delirious fantasy of her own. He rested his hand on her cheek and found it even hotter than ever.

But she had sounded so lucid. Only a second before, she had looked up at him and spoken, and he had been so sure. It was hard to believe that anyone who could speak so clearly was desperately ill.

He rose from the chair, standing for a moment by the window, trying to escape realities too painful to face. The glass was cold against his brow.

There was a faint whimper from the bed behind him. Turning quickly, he saw the child thrashing awkwardly, as if trying to pull away from invisible ties that bound her. He hurried to her side.

He could feel the sharp convulsions in her limbs the instant he put his arms around her. It was not a simple trembling, but a series of spasms, twitching and pulling until they threatened to tear her muscles apart.

"Oh, God, Mariette."

He wanted to cry out for the nurse, but he could not. He could hear her already—*I am too busy for this. How many times do I have to tell you not to call me?*—and he could not stand it. If he had to listen just one more time to her voice, he would never be able to control the rage and fear building up inside him.

The child tried to speak but could not. Raoul drew her up in his arms, holding her, coaxing her, but she could not force the words out. It did not matter. He knew what she was trying to say.

Mama, those silent lips were pleading. *I am afraid and I want my mama.*

And he could not get her mama for her. He loved her so much. He would do anything for her, but he could not give her her mother.

The child's lips moved again. This time a sound came out, but it was not the sound he had expected. It was a harsh, strangled rale, as if she were trying to breathe but could not.

"Nurse." Now he could cry out. Now when he sensed it was too late. "Nurse!"

The woman did not scold as he had expected. She took one look at the child in convulsions in his arms, and she stopped where she was.

"Help me with her. For God's sake, help me!"

She did not answer. She stood at the end of the bed, and she was silent as she stared down at them. For the first time, Raoul saw emotion in her eyes, and he knew she pitied him.

"I will get the doctor."

And then she was gone, and he was alone with his child again.

He pulled her tightly into his arms, clasping her against his chest, trying to find some way to drive the strength of his own body into hers. She was so little, so fragile, it frightened him to hold her.

He had held a bird in his hands once, long ago, when he was just a boy. A poor wounded bird with a broken wing. It had surprised him to feel how small it was, all fluff and feathers, shrinking away to nothing when he closed his hand around it, feeling the pulsating body against his palm. It had

490

given one quick, unexpected convulsion, almost like a sigh, and then it had died.

"It's all right, Mariette. It's all right." Mariette would not die like a wounded bird in his hands. "Daddy's here. Daddy will take care of you."

He had thought once there must be some kind of instinct, strong and undeniable, that would tell a man when a child was his. He felt that instinct now. This child in his arms was his child, as much an extension of his body as his hands or his legs. He knew that now, with a certainty that went beyond belief, just as he knew he was going to lose her.

By the time the doctor arrived, she was already still in his arms, a quiet little figure, trembling no longer. The fever that tormented her body was cool at last.

The doctor hesitated for a moment, a big clumsy man uncomfortable in the presence of death. When he finally stepped forward, he was ready to ease the child away from Raoul.

"No!"

Goddammit, he would not let them take her. This child was his, a part of his flesh, and he had never even known her. When she had taken her first step, said her first word, when she had laughed and cried and learned to love, he had not been there. He had had so little of her life. He was not going to let go of her now.

The nurse was brusque and matter-of-fact as she supported the doctor. "You must be sensible. You are only making it harder on yourself."

Raoul listened to her words, but he did not understand them. He could not let himself. When they took his child away, he knew he would never be able to hold her again, and he was not ready for that.

The nurse moved toward him, impatient hands prepared to pry the child from his grasp, but the doctor held her back. He seemed to understand, for Raoul could hear his voice, low and urgent as he argued with her, somewhere just beyond the sheet that screened them off. At last even their whispers faded away, and Raoul knew he had won.

He eased his hold, but he did not try to put the child down again. He had loved a woman once, with an intensity he had not understood until she was gone. Now he loved a child, and once again it was too late.

He touched her hair with his hand, feeling each strand between his fingertips. This was his immortality. This child—

and not all the treasures he longed to exhibit before a dazzled world. And now she had slipped away from him.

When the doctor returned, he had a clean sheet folded over his arm. He paused, then spoke softly.

"There is a time to let go."

Raoul nodded heavily. He knew the man was right. He knew he could not sit there forever, holding onto the shell of what had once been his child, but it was hard to give her up. He laid her slowly on the bed.

The doctor unfolded the sheet. Horrified, Raoul realized what he was going to do.

"No—not that." He could not let him throw a cover over his child as if she were some sort of obscenity that had to be hidden out of sight.

"Not over her face," the doctor promised, pulling the sheet across the bed. "We don't have to cover her face if you don't want. Just let me lay it over her. It is better that way."

Raoul sat beside his daughter throughout the night. She looked so pretty, with short, dark curls framing the pallor of her cheeks and a clean white sheet pulled up to her chin. So pretty and so peaceful, like a little angel tucked in for the night.

The ward outside was silent, as if even in sleep an impersonal hospital sensed grief in that screened-off corner and was reluctant to disturb it. A snore from somewhere far away, a muffled cough, a whimper like a sleeping animal, and then there was nothing.

There should have been tears, he told himself bitterly. When a man lost his only child, he should be able to weep. But he was too empty to cry.

He left her at last at dawn, pausing at the end of the bed to look down at her. He could not forget he was alone.

"Aimée . . ."

The word was a soft reproach. Aimée. It was her child as well as his he said good-bye to now, and she was not there to share the grief with him—or let him share it with her. Mariette had called out for her mother. She had been afraid in the moment of dying, and she had called out.

And Aimée had not cared enough to come.

He bent over the light as he left the room. He knew they would blow it out when he was gone, and he preferred to do it himself. At least it was not dark anymore.

It was hard to believe her father was dying. Aimée sat in the big empty drawing room and stared at the geometric pattern the sun made as it streamed through leaded glass windows. Once the house had echoed with the sound of childish shrieks, and servants laughed and scolded three young boys as they wiped away all the muddy footprints and plumped up rumpled cushions. But now the boys were away at school and the sofas and fauteuils were tidy—and the servants only dared to tiptoe and whisper as they passed the open doorway.

Etienne LeClare had been seriously ill for five years. Aimée had known all that time that one day he must die, but even five years was not long enough to prepare her for it. She wondered if the death of a parent was always like that. A fact of life, a reality that was inevitable, but in the end a concept too alien to accept. Perhaps one day Mariette, too, would sit alone in a silent house and feel as bewildered as she did now.

Hélène slipped into the doorway so softly Aimée almost did not hear her. Only the rustle of silk gave her away. Aimée looked up slowly.

"How . . . how is he?"

The question was a mechanical one. Routine, polite words she knew were expected.

Hélène did not try to hide the gravity of her husband's condition. "The doctors did not think he would live through the night, but he did."

"Then perhaps . . ."

Hélène shook her head quickly. "He survived one night. He will not survive another."

Aimée sat quietly, her hands folded in her lap. It was so final, this death of a man who had always comforted and protected her. She did not know if she was strong enough to face it.

"I want to see him."

"I thought you would. But are you sure . . . ?" Hélène hesitated almost imperceptibly, as if she were not sure what to say. "Are you sure you are rested enough?"

No! Aimée wanted to cry out. No, she was not sure at all. She had slept through the night and halfway into the day, but still she was drained and desperately weak. She longed to put it off, begging for an hour, a night, even a few minutes of healing and rest. But she knew if she did, she would never have the chance again.

"Yes, I am all right. I want to go to him now."

The first step was the hardest. After that, Aimée's feet moved easily as she followed her mother up the stairs and along the second-floor hallway. She hesitated only when she reached the threshold of her father's room. Then she forced herself inside.

One glance at his face was enough to tell her Hélène had not been wrong. Etienne LeClare would not live through another night.

"Papa . . ." She knelt beside the bed, clasping a limp, lifeless hand in her own. Her father had always been such a vital man, dynamic and full of a zest for life. It frightened her to see him now, ashen and still, as if he were already lying in his coffin. "Papa, I am here with you."

One more day. She would stay in this house where she had been so happy one more day. Mariette did not need her. She would have Sophie and Franz to fuss over her, tempting her with little cakes and whimsical gingerbread men, bright with colored icing, and she would barely notice her mother was gone. Besides, Etienne would need her such a short time longer.

She sat beside her father in a darkened room, with all the shades drawn and his hand held tightly in hers. He was too weak to respond, but she kept on talking, hoping that the sound of her voice would remind him she was there and soothe him. She knew she was prattling, but she knew, too, he would not mind.

It was hard to find things to talk about. She could not tell him about Edward. Her father did not know she was a widow, and there was no need to trouble him with that now. Nor could she chatter frivolously about Vienna, not when Vienna was Mary Vetsera's lonely grave and the shame in her own heart as she struggled to come to terms with the needs of her body. In the end she settled on Egypt.

"Do you remember how frightened we all were when I went there?" she teased. "You and Mama both. Yes, and me, too, though I was too stubborn to admit it."

And she had been afraid, terribly afraid in her own naive way, although she had not admitted it at the time. Now she knew how foolish she had been. The months spent in Egypt, for all their pain, had brought a richness to her life she would never know again.

Her voice was soft as she described the Egypt she had come to love, sharing with her father the hundred little details that made up the sum total of the place in her mind. The tomb she and Raoul had discovered, a sealed, airless chamber packed to the ceiling with all the hopes and longings that had once been a human life. The ruins of ancient temples, tall and grand no longer, lying scattered and broken beneath the same sands that covered the streets of timeless peasant villages. The colorful bazaars in Cairo and Luxor, crowded with row upon row of silversmiths and tin workers, bakers and carpenters and jaunty hucksters of fruits and flowers, just as they had been in the days when Etienne himself was young and saw it all with his own eyes.

She even told him about the old woman who had caught her, unveiled, in front of a Coptic shrine. Not about the violence of her attack, of course, nor the fiery death she met months later, for that would only upset him, but about the superstition and fear that had marked her first sight of Aimée.

"Isn't it funny?" she mused, trying to put it all into perspective. "She was so angry, so filled with hate, as if somehow by lashing out at me she could make up for her son's death. You know, they say he was a saint. Perhaps you have heard of him. They call him the Martyr. Tadrus the Martyr."

She glanced down at her father, half-expecting a flicker of recognition in his eyes. Instead she saw that he was struggling painfully, opening and closing his mouth, as if he were trying to gulp in breaths of air. His face, so pale only seconds before, was unnaturally flushed.

"Oh, Papa, forgive me. I am tiring you."

Hélène hurried to her husband's side. "This is too much for him, Aimée. You must go now."

But Etienne's hand closed around his daughter's wrist.

"No." It was an effort to speak, but he drove himself on. "No, I do not want her to go."

Hélène's face was tense with anxiety. "But Etienne—"

"No!"

Etienne held his grip on Aimée's arm, but he did not seem to see her. He lay back against his pillow, a gaunt, worn man with only his eyes alive as he stared at his wife. It was a long time before he found his voice again.

"A man can live with a lie, Hélène. He cannot die with one."

Hélène opened her lips to protest again, then closed them slowly. She was gray and still, as if she had been carved from ice. Aimée stood between the two of them, feeling the tension of her father's hand against her arm, and she could not make herself meet their eyes. She did not understand why, but she knew they frightened her.

"Tell her." Etienne's voice was low and intense.

"No, Etienne . . ."

"Tell her!"

At last Aimée looked up. Her mother seemed to fade before her eyes, like a brief candle that flickered and went out in the darkness. Nothing was left but a shadow. She stood by the bed and studied her husband's face as if she dared to hope he would change his mind, even when she knew he would not. Then slowly, without a word, she slipped through the doorway.

Aimée remained behind, bewildered by the sudden silence that filled the room. Her father's eyes were closed, his face so rigid and waxen she would have been frightened had not the heavy, rhythmic movements of his chest beneath thick blankets told her he was still alive. At last she realized he would not speak again.

The garden was cold in the autumn air, but Hélène did not shiver as she stood in a thin silk dress staring down at her reflection in the small lake. Pale and mystical, the lonely image seemed a ghost of all her memories.

Sensing her daughter's presence behind her, she turned around.

"I should have told you long ago, but I would not have hurt him for the world." She sank down on the grassy shore, tucking her skirt neatly around her legs as she waited for Aimée to sit beside her. "No, that's not true. I did not tell you because I was a coward. I was afraid of hurting myself."

"Oh, Mama." Dear, gentle Mama. It broke Aimée's heart to see her pain. "Whatever it is, surely it can wait."

But Hélène seemed to regain her strength, taking refuge in the quiet dignity that had sheltered her all her life. She let her gaze linger on the dark water, broken only by a single dry leaf drifting idly across the surface.

"He was right, you know. You cannot die with a lie. But he was wrong about one thing. You can't live with one, either."

Her eyes were clear as she looked up at her daughter.
"It is time you knew the truth."

The Vienna Hélène had known as a young girl was the same city her daughter took refuge in two decades later, but there were subtle, almost intangible differences that gave it a quality all its own. The turmoil that was changing the face of Europe touched Austria in the Revolution of 1848, but the last death rattle of a dynasty that had endured half a millennium was still too faint to be audible in the gilded ballrooms of the rich and royal. Ferdinand I abdicated in favor of his young nephew Franz Josef, and the musicians raised their bows again, drawing them across their strings with an age-old sweetness that mocked the fury of the outside world. Even the battle of Sadowa in 1866, the crushing defeat that left Austria victim to Bismarck's rising star in Prussia, gave the dancers only a moment's pause as they drifted, light and carefree, through the elegant halls of palaces that had been built to last forever. To a beautiful young girl, dazzled by the gilt and satin and candlelight of an era, life must have seemed little more than a stirring waltz that would never end.

And Hélène was beautiful. Seated on a straight-backed chair at the side of the ballroom, watching all the other matrons point to their daughters and crow with pride, Sophie could not help remembering the day the girl had first come to her. Barely seven years old, a tiny, trembling figure, unable to comprehend the tragedy that had taken her parents, she stared up at Sophie with pale, enormous eyes. Even then, even terrified and unsure, she was the most beautiful child Sophie had ever seen.

She was even more beautiful now. The silver-blond hair that had streamed down her back was arranged in soft curls around her face, and wide, wistful eyes seemed to melt as she glanced upward, letting long lashes flutter against flushed cheeks. Hélène had never quite lost her shyness, and it was that quality as much as her beauty that drew young men toward her, reminding each in his own way that masculine strength was a perfect foil for fragile femininity. Tonight, slender and ethereal in wisps of white chiffon, she seemed almost more elfin than real.

Glancing across the room, Sophie caught sight of her young brother, Franz, standing quietly at the edge of the dance floor. Like his sister, he, too, was watching Hélène, but unlike Sophie, there was no objectivity in his gaze.

497

From the day Hélène had come to live with them, Franz had taken her as his own special charge. The girl's shyness, coupled with an innate gentleness and delicate beauty, brought out a strong streak of protectiveness in the youngster barely two years her senior. As he grew, Franz found that his need to shield and cherish his cousin had grown with him, until at last feelings that began as innocent and brotherly changed slowly into emotions he could not understand or control. With adolescence came sexual awakening, and with the strange new stirrings of his body, a host of unfamiliar dreams, all the more terrifying because they were directed toward the one person he was determined to protect—his beautiful young cousin.

At first Sophie was amused by her brother's infatuation, and perhaps, she reminded herself guiltily later, she had even encouraged it. Hélène's beauty was not merely a physical thing. The girl had a warmth and spirituality about her that every mother longed for in the woman who would one day marry her son, and Sophie was, by nature if not by circumstance, above everything a mother. She could not help looking at the two young people she loved more than anyone on earth and thinking what it would be like if they could be together forever, a family in the end as they had been in the beginning.

But the years passed quickly, and Sophie was too wise to cling to her dreams. She watched her brother with the lovely cousin he adored and she knew it would never work out. Hélène was a gentle, serious girl, so mystical sometimes she seemed to have withdrawn into a world of her own, and she and Franz could sit on the hillside for hours and talk of the Greeks or the saints or the stars, and then they would be happy. But there was a wildness in her, too, a kind of unfettered passion that made her leap up suddenly, without warning, and race across the fields, letting her hair blow out in the wind behind her, and that was a part of her spirit Franz could never share.

And the girl knew it, too, Sophie thought sadly as she watched Hélène turn with natural coquetry in the arms of her partner, teasing him shyly until he blushed with pleasure. Franz would ask her to be his wife, and she would refuse him, just as she had refused all the others, because she could never live with a man who would be a stranger to her soul.

Sophie did not have to wait long to learn she was right. Franz picked a cool, starry evening, barely a month later, to ask Hélène to marry him, and then he sat alone through a long, empty night, staring out of the study window and wondering what he was going to do now that his dreams were gone. In the morning, without so much as a word, Sophie realized the inevitable had happened, and she knew there was nothing she could do about it.

Franz's was not the only heart Hélène broke that season. A young Polish count terrified her by threatening suicide, and a hotheaded Viennese youth would have fought a duel to the death in her name had not his opponent, older and more skilled in arms, had the confidence to laugh the whole thing off. A prince of the realm, handsome and moody, retired for months to the seclusion of his hunting lodge when she refused to see him again, and one of the richest men in Europe asked for her hand. It was the makings of a fairy tale—every girl's dream come true—and Hélène did not even seem to notice it was happening.

The girl's coolness would have disturbed Sophie if she had not understood it so well. Hélène was enchanted by the attention she was receiving, she was even intrigued by it, but she took it all for granted. She had always been beautiful. It was a thing that had been part of her life since the day she was born. It simply did not occur to her that other young women were not enjoying the same dizzying experiences.

She wept for only one of her suitors, her handsome young cousin on the day he finally gave up his hopes and vowed his devotion to another. Even then, her tears were not for herself or the promises of love she had left behind, but only for a fond childhood companion who deserved more than the grief a hasty ill-advised marriage was certain to bring him. For all the others, there was not so much as a backward glance or a moment of regret.

Hélène sensed there was something wrong about her reactions. When one of her friends received a proposal of marriage, the girl could hardly wait to brag about it, embellishing every detail until everyone was agog with envy. But when the same thing happened to her, she felt only embarrassment, as if she had been caught playing games with someone else's heart.

She tried to figure it out sometimes. She did not know if there was something wrong with her or something wrong with the world she was living in. She only knew she did not belong there, and if she tried to force herself to fit in, she would be desperately unhappy. She pondered it for a long time, pulling back from the whirl of balls and parties and picnics until Sophie began to worry about her. When she finally came up with the answer, it was so simple she wondered why she hadn't realized it all along.

Even now, a quarter of a century later in a chilly autumn garden in Paris, she could still remember the feel of the sun on her face as she sat on a grassy slope in the Vienna Woods and told Sophie her decision.

"You have been good to me, very good, and I don't want you to think I'm not grateful, but I don't belong in Vienna. I've decided to enter the convent."

Sophie studied her carefully. It was true, there had always been a mysticism about her young ward, but it was not a mysticism she usually associated with the cloister.

"No more parties? No pretty dresses? No young men to flatter you and steal kisses in the garden?"

Hélène smiled, shaking her head. She had enjoyed the complex stirrings of her body as she drifted into the arms of a handsome man on the dance floor or let him brush lips against hers in a private corner of the lawn, but no man had yet found the key to awaken longings that could not be stilled again.

"No ... no young men."

Sophie was still skeptical. She had been happy enough without a man of her own, a child of her own, but she wondered if it would be right for Hélène.

"I can understand how the convent would appeal to an idealistic young girl, especially after the superficiality of Vienna, but . . ." How could she find the words? She had sensed the deep vein of passion that was the core of Hélène's essence, but she could not find a way to express it. "But it's too important a decision to be made so hastily."

"Hastily? Oh, Cousin Sophie, I've been thinking about it for weeks."

Weeks? Sophie had to smile. Weeks—and the girl thought it was a long time. In the end, she compromised.

"Take a year to think about it. Get away from Vienna. See a little of the world. And when you get back, if you still want to go into the convent, I will give my permission."

It was a compromise they were both to question in the years that lay ahead, but it seemed an ideal solution at the time. After her initial disappointment, Hélène found she was actually looking forward to the idea. It had begun to occur to her that she was young and very pretty—and there was a whole world out there she had not even seen.

Much as she coaxed, she could not persuade Sophie to come with her. Even had the woman been willing to leave her home, there was Franz to consider. His young wife, never in the sturdiest health, was already pregnant, and without a mother of her own to look after her, she would need Sophie's care in the months to come. The difficult task of finding a suitable chaperon for a high-spirited young girl led to a second compromise—Cousin Elisabeth.

Elisabeth was a distant cousin, barely entitled to the name, but a lifetime of genteel poverty had taught her family loyalty, especially if a year's living went along with it. She was an elderly lady, fussy and vain, kindhearted enough when she remembered, but too absentminded most of the time to worry about anything more pressing than the foolish little curls she trained so carefully around her finger each morning, despairing as the heat and humidity dissolved them into chaos by midafternoon. Hélène was soon to discover she made a delightfully negligent chaperon.

They went first to Italy, staying in a small, elegant villa near Rome, where Elisabeth amused herself at her dressing table and Hélène was left to her own devices for the first time in her life. When the girl tired of that, it was a simple matter to persuade her cousin to move on to Egypt. Elisabeth would be happy anywhere, as long as the house had plenty of mirrors and a full staff of clever little maids used to making an old lady look attractive.

Egypt. Even the name had a mysterious, exotic sound. The land of pharaohs long dead, of emirs and caliphs, of naked peasants tilling the soil with the tools their ancestors had used thousands of years before, and veiled, black-robed women peeking out from the lacy lattices of their harems. It was, Hélène thought as she stood at the base of the tallest pyramid and stared up the timeworn steps that seemed to lead to the sky itself, every fantasy come true.

Had Cousin Elisabeth been a different kind of chaperon, Hélène would have been confined to mingling with her own kind, calling at the houses of diplomats' wives and dancing at teas and soirees with all the proper young officers whose dreams and aspirations were exactly the same as the proper young officers' she danced with in Vienna, and she would quickly have been disappointed in Egypt. But Cousin Elisabeth was not that kind of woman, and left alone, Hélène dared to discover a Cairo that few young girls of her background were privileged to see.

Like her daughter twenty years later, Hélène explored the raucous covered markets and the dark twisting streets that led past crowded hovels, fascinated by the sights and sounds and smells that were like nothing she had ever known before. But unlike Aimée, she did not have to content herself with a few hours of casual sightseeing. She stayed her year in Egypt, and then a second, learning Arabic and slipping into native costume to talk to people in the shops and streets, until at last she had an understanding of the land that was rare for a European of that era.

Her absence did not go unnoticed in Vienna. Sophie's anxiety turned to alarm as time passed and Hélène showed no signs of returning, but the girl's letters no longer spoke of the convent, and her guardian decided to say nothing, at least for the time being.

Another compromise, she was to tell herself later. Another weak decision. Another time she failed the young woman who had been left in her care.

By the time Cousin Elisabeth, ailing and no longer able to cope with the heat, decided to return to Austria, it was too late to do anything with Hélène. She had had a sample of independence, and she was not about to give it up. She brought Elisabeth to Alexandria, kissing her with genuine gratitude as she helped her up the gangplank, then waved good-bye until the ship pulled out of sight.

She stood alone on the shore long after the crowds had dispersed, and wondered what it was going to be like to feel free. One day she knew she would return to Vienna—whether to the convent or a husband, she had not decided—and on that day she would no longer belong to herself. Fate had given her, a woman, an unexpected respite, offering a day, a week, perhaps a year to taste the freedom that was usually reserved for men. She knew she would be a fool if she did not take advantage of it.

She did not return to Cairo. She had already explored the city, and it was enough for her. Now she longed to see more of life. She stayed a few days in Alexandria, commissioning a dressmaker to fashion a pair of long, loose-fitting robes for her, then made her way into the countryside, stopping at one of the loneliest outposts of the desert.

Here, for the first time in her life, Hélène began to understand the mystical needs of her own soul. An old man in

airo, an Egyptian Christian, had once told her the Copts
puld soon be extinct because all their people, men and
omen alike, yearned for the solitary cell of a religious rec-
se. Now, seeing the barren, empty sands stretch out as far
her eyes could see, Hélène understood at last what he was
ying to tell her. She, too, could have been content with the
e of a desert nun. She was closer to God here—her God—
an she could ever have been in a convent in the comfort-
le hills of Vienna.

She loved to saddle a horse while it was still dark, riding
to the lonely gray light that foreshadowed the pink of
wn. It was the perfect moment of the day. The wind, still
ld from the night, whipped her gown out behind her, biting
to her cheeks and forehead with a challenge she dared to
fy. Reining in her horse, she would pause on the highest
ne, watching as the misty gray of the earth faded into the
ay of the sky and wondering at the vastness of an eternity
e had never even imagined.

And she was a part of it all. For the first time, as long as
e could remember, she had found a place she belonged.

It was on one of her early-morning rides that she first saw
e man who was destined to change her life. She did not see
im as Fate, of course. She saw him only as a man, dark and
litary, his black robes blowing into the wind, but she was
trigued enough to stop and look at him. A lonely mud-brick
ovel, half-hidden behind him, blended so perfectly into the
nd it was almost invisible.

He must be a Coptic monk, she thought, staring openly at
e long robes and black beard that made him look exotic
nd forbidding all at the same time. She had thought often
nough of the many cells that dotted the desert, and she had
ondered about the men and women who chose to live in
em, but she never expected to stumble on one by accident.
elatedly she realized that curiosity might well seem rudeness
 a man who had come to the desert for solitude. Raising
er hand, she gave him a quick wave as she spurred her
orse. He did not wave back.

She was surprised, as she threw one last glance over her
houlder, to realize she was hurt by his coldness. She knew
hat she must look like to the man, a hoyden with her skirts
ulled up to her knees and her hair flowing down her back,
rofaning a place that was holy to him, but she could not
elp her reaction. He was so different from any man she had
ver met, so quiet and self-contained in his dignity, she could

not help wishing he would let her stop and talk to him, only for a while.

As the weeks passed, the Coptic monk became almost a obsession with Hélène. She saw him a score of times, dark an rigid against the gray-gold sand, as she rode by his cell, som times in the last cool minutes of the dawn, sometimes late the afternoon when twilight had already eased the heat fro the earth. Each time she passed, she would pause for a m ment, waiting for a word, a gesture, even a nod, that wou tell her she was welcome to stop. And each time, there w nothing.

At last she began to despair. It seemed to her so hopele and so unfair. This man, whoever he was, this Coptic mor without a name in her thoughts, was her only clue to a wa of life that had grown increasingly important to her. Th desert had become her private convent, the sanctuary she ha longed for since she was a little girl and the security of h parents had been taken from her. She needed someone nov someone to help her put her feelings into perspective, som one who could teach her to understand her hunger for th sand and the wind and the searing heat of the sun.

It was only after weeks of agonizing that she realized wha she had to do. The thought was so simple it amazed her. I the man would not reach out to her, if he would not call t her to stop, then she would have to reach to him. That wa all there was to it. She would go to him, she would tell hi what was in her heart, and if he was really a holy man, h would not be able to deny her. And if he was not . . .

Well, if he was not, it would not matter anyway.

She left earlier than usual the next morning. The man wa not there when she arrived. Undaunted, she guided her hors slowly toward the small hut, stopping only when she was few yards away. She was surprised to feel how calm she wa She had been certain her heart would be beating wildly.

It was nearly half an hour before he emerged from th doorway. If he was surprised to see her sitting high on he horse only a short distance from his sanctuary, he gave n sign of it. Slowly he began to walk toward her.

As she saw him approach, Hélène felt her courage falter The man was younger than she had expected, much younger and there was an earthy masculinity about him that was more provocative than anything she had encountered in the hand somely tailored men of Europe. For the first time she dare to ask herself if she had come to him because she needed to

lk to a man of God, or simply to talk to a man. The
ought both excited and unnerved her. She did not attempt
 speak as he drew near.

He stopped beside her, silent and patient. Hélène looked
own at him, studying his face. He was not handsome, she
ecided. His features were too coarse, the dark beard that
alf-masked his swarthy skin too thick and unkempt, but he
as vital and exciting—and strangely frightening. He had
aunting eyes, a deep, piercing blue that gave her the
ncanny feeling he had the power to see through to her soul.
he wondered, if she asked him, if he would tell her what he
aw there.

At last she found her voice.

"I have wanted to talk to you."

She waited for him to reject her, raising his hand in an an-
ry gesture of defiance. Instead, his features softened.

"And I have wanted to talk to you."

Hélène dismounted slowly. She was surprised, as she stood
eside him, to realize he was barely taller than herself. He
ad seemed such a commanding figure, alone in the desert.

"My name is Hélène."

"Men call me Tadrus."

She went to him every day after that, sitting beside him in
he shade of the shallow wall, and they talked of all the
hings she had dreamed about. Of God, and man's need to
ind an image of God in his own faith. Of the desert and
oneliness and the spiritual essence of the wind and the sand.
Of vanity and hypocrisy, of birth and death, and of the hun-
er in the human heart to feel—for a single instant in
ime—completely free and unfettered. And nowhere in their
housands of words was there anything about bravery in war
nd promotion on the battlefield, or perfectly tended rose
gardens and expensive blue-and-white Chinese vases, or gay
alls and sparkling soirees and who was having an affair with
hom.

They did not touch each other in all the days they spent
ogether. They sat a foot or two apart, each careful not to
nove too close, as if they had drawn an invisible line in the
and and knew they dared not cross it. It was a tacit under-
tanding, a kind of unspoken pact that would have taken as
nuch courage to acknowledge as break.

And yet they both knew how they felt. When Hélène looked
at this man, once so alien, now sweetly familiar, she saw not
he perfect soulmate she had yearned for, but a compelling

physical presence with the power to awaken her dormant sexuality. And Tadrus, as he fell under the spell of her gentle warmth, understood at last what it was to want to be a man.

When it happened, it happened simply, without warning. This time it was Tadrus who reached out to her, and she did not pull back from him. A light touch of a hand on her arm, the caress of warm fingers against her skin—and that was enough.

Wordlessly she was in his arms and they were closing around her. Her own nakedness seemed natural in the desert where the wind swept across the sands, baring the earth to the heat of the sun and the bitter chill of the night. Pain and longing mingled until she could not tell one from the other as he entered her at last, joining his body to hers with the same passion that had already joined their souls. Now she was his and he was hers for all eternity.

They lay in each other's arms through the long cold night and all the nights that followed, enjoying the wonder of their passion with an exhilaration that was as unquestioning as it was instinctive. They knew what they were doing was a sin, an affront to the church Tadrus served as well as the society that would judge them both, but they neither thought nor cared about the consequences. In that one moment—the single moment they had both longed for—their hearts were truly free.

Hélène lived with her lover for six months in the isolated desert cell that was lonely no longer, and they were happy, with the happiness of small children too naive to understand the complexities of the future. They were safe enough from discovery, for travelers almost never passed that lonely area, and discovery was all they feared. Things might have gone on indefinitely if Hélène had not discovered she was pregnant.

When she felt the first signs of life within her body, she hesitated to say anything, telling herself she wanted to be sure before she pressed that burden on the man she loved. But even later, when she could hide from the truth no longer, she still found herself holding back, waiting until the first magic glow of their passion had begun to fade and they were ready to face their responsibilities. At last, when all her excuses were gone, she had to admit she was afraid, and the only thing that forced her to be honest in the end was a burgeoning body that would not let her keep her secret any longer.

He reacted exactly the way she had known he would. Dark blue eyes widened with shock as he turned away from her,

ying to hide the emotions he did not want her to see. He
as not quick enough. She caught his pain and understood it
nly too well. Tadrus was afraid—not for the immortal soul
e had pledged to his God, but for the tarnishing of his
mage in the eyes of the world. It was a weakness, and he
ated himself for it almost as much as he hated her for bring-
ng it out in him. She fell asleep in his arms that night, but
hen she woke in the morning he was gone.

Hélène wept for a week, then packed her cotton robes and
moved back to Cairo, taking a simple room in one of the
poorer sections of town. She wrote a long letter to Sophie,
ying as best she could to explain what she had done, but she
made no excuses for herself. It was hard to expose her own
name, but it would have been even harder to lie to a woman
who had never shown her anything but warmth and kindness.
ut when Sophie's reply came, generous and forgiving as she
ad known it would be, she refused to return home. She
anted her child to be born in the land of its father.

The child was a girl, born in the hot summer months, and
Hélène named her Aimée, a reminder of the love that had
created her life. It was a long, agonizing birth, but the pain
nd the heat and the exhaustion were almost a relief, as if
omehow through them Hélène hoped to atone for her sins,
icking up the pieces of her life again. Later, she realized it
ould never be that simple.

She would have returned to Vienna, her head held high,
ven with the child she refused to hide, if she had not
umbled across a little Coptic church, only a few streets
way from where she lived. She did not know what drew her
oward it, a hunger for the simple faith she had known in the
esert perhaps, or only a need to feel close once again to a
ern, loving God. She only knew that she did not expect to
 e a slender, dark-robed priest. And he did not expect to see
er.

Tadrus was in Cairo. She felt weak with surprise as she
ood before him, her baby in her arms. Slowly she dropped
o her knees, not from the need for piety, or even an appeal
o a man she had loved, but simply because she did not have
e strength to stand any longer. She saw his pain and his
onfusion as he took a slow step back from her, but she saw
omething else, too, something she had never seen before—
e essential vulnerability of the man.

Tadrus was still afraid, desperately afraid. He had fled
om the desert he loved to the city he hated to be among

men, but even then, even when he walked beside them a...
felt their sleeves brush against his arm, he could not be a pa...
of their world. Hélène knew in that moment she would nev...
be able to leave him. No matter how many times he turne...
away from her, no matter how often he passed her in t...
street and pretended not to know her, she could not dese...
him. If she left him now, she knew he would be alone—a...
if he felt alone, he would die.

She went often to the little church in the narrow si...
street, taking the child with her so Aimée could share, ho...
ever vaguely, in a sense of closeness to the man who had f...
thered her. She was careful to remain discreetly in t...
background, not wanting him to feel threatened or pressur...
by her presence, but she sensed the day would come when...
would need her, and she wanted him to know she was ther...
Strangely, she was not unhappy, for she had a purpose in h...
life, and she had never had that before she met Tadrus.

She knew the day her lover was going to die. She knew
almost before he was aware of it himself. She had shared
complete, almost perfect communion once with this man, an...
even coldness and despair had not been enough to sever
completely. It did not fail her now. She stepped out of t...
house early in the afternoon and stared up at the clear blu...
of a winter sky and knew that was the last day she wou...
ever see her lover.

Aimée was well over three by then, old enough to fus...
when her mother left her unexpectedly with a neighbor, b...
for once Hélène paid no heed to her tears. She could not le...
the child come with her that day. "I'll be back in an hour,...
she told the neighbor. What she did not tell her was that he...
face would be ashen and her eyes red from weeping.

She was not surprised to see the soldiers gathering at th...
end of the street that led to the church. Trouble had bee...
brewing in the city for months, with angry Copts, weary...
the restrictions of Turkish rule, growing openly rebelliou...
and none but the most naive discounted the possibility...
open violence at any moment. Now it seemed it had come.

Tadrus stood on the steps of his church, a stern, imposin...
figure, the cross of his faith high in his hands. Small cluster...
of people milled around the corners, pushing back into dar...
doorways as they watched the soldiers, fifteen or twenty a...
most, huddling nervously at the entrance to the street. Th...
polished metal of their rifles picked up the gold of the after...
noon sun. Only two people dared to venture out from th...

crowd, two slender, solitary women: one a beautiful girl with silvery hair slipping carelessly from beneath a hooded robe; the other dressed in the somber black of her country. They did not acknowledge each other, but each knew the other was there—and each knew what was going to happen.

Death was not necessary that afternoon. Tadrus had enflamed the crowd with his own zeal, and he could call them off just as easily, but he would not do it. Death was not necessary, but Tadrus had decided to die.

"Suicide" was a word that would have been alien to him, but the will to die was the only way to describe the passion that engulfed his heart. Shame, guilt, dishonor—they were all pains that could be borne no longer. Tadrus, soon to be the Martyr, had found his destiny.

He was magnificent in his last moments. He was not tall, but he looked tall in the twilight as he strode down the street, his long robes flowing out behind him, his dark hair floating to his shoulders. He held the cross in front of him, a last defiant gesture, as he bore down on the Turkish soldiers who were already forming into a hasty, crooked line at the end of the road.

The soldiers were young, barely more than boys, as incapable of understanding what was happening as the crowds that watched with solemn eyes. Their bodies were stiff, their hands cold and sweaty as they dropped to their knees, rifles at the ready, waiting for the order they could not disobey.

The captain called out to Tadrus to stop, he even begged him to stop, but there was no holding him back now. He was a man whose moment had come—his single moment of vindication and glory. Boldly, his eyes blazing with blue fire, he moved forward until at last the soldiers had no choice but to shoot him or lose face with the crowd. They did not lose face.

Hélène stood alone in the darkness, even after the streets had been cleared, tears streaming down her face. She did not notice a solitary man leaning against the wall of a nearby building. Etienne LeClare had seen the whole sickening thing, and he did not know which appalled him most, the sloppy discipline of soldiers who could find no better way to handle an unarmed man, or the naked pain he had seen in a lovely woman's eyes.

He approached her now, holding out a comforting hand as he addressed her tentatively in French. The instant she turned toward him, helpless and lost like a little child, he felt the last traces of his caution vanish. Reaching out, he pulled her into strong, protective arms. She did not resist.

They stopped only briefly at the home of the neighbor, picking up the little girl whose deep blue eyes, a miniature of her father's, answered Etienne's last questions. Then, reluctant to leave them alone and not knowing what else to do, he brought them back with him to his hotel.

He held Hélène in his arms all night long, daring only to touch her brow with the most innocent kisses he had ever known, but she did not even feel his touch. She was weeping for other lips, other arms, other nights. In the morning, when she pulled away from him, smoothing the rumpled cotton of her robe with an automatic gesture, her eyes were dry. The battles that had torn her heart were fought and won, the violent passions that tormented her spirit quelled at last, and Etienne LeClare, like so many men before him, knew that he was hopelessly in love with her.

Sophie sailed to Egypt on the first boat. It was a rough, unpleasant crossing. To the day she died, she would always remember standing at the rail watching an angry sea and asking herself again and again what she could have done to prevent this tragedy. She had hoped, with Franz a widower now, that Hélène might look to him at last, but one glimpse of her young brother's face when she had been forced to tell him the truth warned her he would never feel the same about his beautiful cousin again.

When she got to Cairo, she realized all her speculations had been in vain. Hélène understood her handsome cousin far better than the sister who had raised him, and she knew there would be no choices for her when she returned to Vienna. She had already married the French merchant who found her on the street the day her lover died.

Sophie looked at Etienne LeClare, and she felt herself relax for the first time in weeks. He was older than Hélène, old enough to be her father, but he was a kind man. He would be good to her and the child who would bear his name if not his blood. That was all she asked for her young ward.

Etienne did not feel as warmly toward her. "I do not ask for your blessing, madame, Hélène and I are already married. Besides, I do not consider that you have been a proper guardian, and you have no right to question her decisions."

Sophie was hurt by his coldness, but she understood it. Etienne might have been able to forgive her for failing Hélène, even if she could not forgive herself, but he would never stop being afraid of her. Sophie was part of Hélène's past, and the past would always be a threat to her new husband.

She kissed Hélène one last time on a crowded train platform in Cairo, finding it surprisingly hard to let go of the young woman who would always be her only daughter. She wondered, as she watched her slip away, if it was as hard for the girl to part with her. But Hélène's eyes were already veiled over, and no one would see into her heart again.

Hélène paused as she finished. She did not look up to meet her daughter's gaze. She had spared herself nothing, not even the pain she had shared with no one since a night long ago when she wept in her husband's arms.

Aimée stared at the dark waters of the lake. So many things were falling into place now. "So that's why Papa always hated your family. Because he blamed them for what happened."

"Perhaps," Hélène admitted softly. "But I think it's more because he was afraid of them."

"Afraid? But what could they do to him? Or to you?"

"He was not worried about himself . . . or me. He was worried about you."

"Me?" Aimée could not understand.

"Don't you see, my dear? Etienne always said he would never let you go to them, especially as a bride, because the same lack of discipline that scarred my life might ruin yours. But I think he was not being honest with himself. I think he was really afraid if you went to live with them, especially if you married Franz, that one day they would decide you had a right to know the truth."

"But why should he mind so much? About me, I mean? After all, I am not . . ." She stumbled on the words. "I am not really his daughter."

"Oh, but you are—don't you understand? From the moment he first picked you up and carried you through the streets of Cairo, you have been a part of his life. He held me in his arms that night and felt the depth of my grief, and he knew a part of me was dying, a part that could never belong to him. In you, he found a substitute. He could tease you and pamper you, lavishing on you all the open affection he was afraid to offer me. You became his daughter, and he lived in dread of the day he would lose you."

Aimée could understand that. She remembered the look on Raoul's face as he gazed down at Mariette in her crib, and she knew a man could feel a desperate hunger for the child

511

he wanted to be his. She sat alone in the gathering dusk after her mother had left her and tried to sort things out in her mind. The pieces all began to fit together, like a giant jigsaw puzzle.

It all made sense now. All the smells of Cairo, the dust and the sweat, the cinnamon and sandalwood, at once so strange and so familiar, like a half-forgotten childhood dream. The street she had walked on before, the church that seemed more real than all the cathedrals of her formal faith. Even an old woman, superstitious and alone, unable to accept a haunting image from the past, eerily shaded in with the striking coloring of her own lost son.

Tadrus the Martyr.

She tried to form a mental picture of the man who was her father, but she could not focus on him. Where there should have been a depth of sympathy, the first stirrings perhaps of an instinctive love, she was conscious only of emptiness. All she could see was a young Turkish soldier, beads of sweat glistening on baby fat as he raised his gun. He would be middle-aged now, that same young boy. She wondered if he still saw a cross in the darkness, closing in on dreams that never seemed to end. She did not think she liked him very much, this man who made a killer out of children because he did not have the courage to face a life he had made for himself.

And yet he was her father. The word came hard to her. Father was not this priest whose painted image she had seen only once in her life. Father was the man who had always been there for her, picking her up when she got hurt, lifting her onto strong shoulders, laughing with her when she only wanted to cry.

And then she realized. She wondered why they hadn't seen it, too, her mother, her father, even Sophie, all so much older, so much wiser than she.

It was all a matter of putting things in their place. He was only a stranger, this man who had died in a desert land, and he would never be anything else. He had no claims on her heart.

She tiptoed quietly into her father's room, bending down to take hold of his hand. Her voice was soft as she spoke.

"*You* are my father."

All the years, all the love, could not be wiped out by a whim of fate. Father was the man who was father in her heart.

Etienne did not answer, but he seemed to understand, for his hand tightened around hers. She sat beside him in the long hours of the night, clinging, comforting, soothing him through the darkness they both knew would be his last.

He died in the first light of dawn. Hélène stood away from the bed, a slim silent shadow in the background. She wanted to go to him, drawing him close into arms that had never reached out before, telling him in those last minutes that generosity and devotion had won her love in the end, but she knew it was too late. They had been reticent with each other too long. The time for words was past. She felt like a stranger in her own life as she watched her daughter ease her husband into death.

It was raining when they buried him on a green hillside in the outskirts of Paris. Aimée tilted her umbrella back, letting cold raindrops slide down her cheeks as she listened to the monotonous sound of the priest's last prayers. She remembered how she had loved to climb on her father's lap when she was a little girl, watching streams of water run down the study window and feeling warm and cozy and safe in arms that would never let her go.

She stood alone beside the grave after the others had left. It all seemed so empty now. So pointless. All the lies, all the fears, all the needless years of separation—and for what? They could have told her sooner. She would have understood.

She raised the umbrella again as she turned at last to leave. She could do nothing about the past, but the future was still hers. She would catch the evening train for Vienna, and when she got there, she would take her daughter on her lap and tell her the truth about everything. Her parents had not been honest with her, and in the end, they had paid for it. She would not make the same mistake with Mariette.

She caught up with her mother, slipping an arm around her waist. "I'm going home tonight, Mama."

Going home.

She liked the sound of the words. Warm and comforting. *Going home.*

For a long time she had not known where home was. Now at last she understood. She was a mother. Home was where her child was. It was as simple as that.

6

Aimée was already at the door as the train pulled into the Vienna station. Catching her skirt in her hand, she hurried down the steps, scanning the crowd. It took her only a second to pick out her cousin.

"Oh, Franz, it is good to see you." Impulsively she held out her hands, drawing him toward her for an affectionate kiss on the cheek. Franz had aged in the years she had not seen him, his hair graying until it held barely a trace of auburn. It was hard to remember that this kindly older man would have been her husband had not fate—and her father—decided differently.

Franz stared down at her solemnly. She had never looked so beautiful. The black of her mourning became her, setting off pale features until she looked like a little girl again. He longed to pull her into his arms, a warm, safe refuge against the pain to come. It made him feel clumsy when he did not know how.

Aimée barely noticed his tension. "Where is Sophie? I hoped she would be with you."

"No, Sophie . . . Sophie isn't well. Sometimes her arthritis bothers her so much she can hardly walk."

It would have been so much easier, he thought, if Sophie were beside him now. Women understood these things better than men. Sophie would never shift her weight from one foot to the other, hemming and hawing because she could not think of what to say.

"And Mariette?" Aimée glanced toward the carriage, half-hoping to see a little nose pressed against the glass. "I thought you might bring her with you."

Franz had expected the question, but that did not make it any easier. He looked at Aimée's face, and all he could see was Mariette, so pretty and innocent in the white dress Sophie had bought as a surprise for her birthday. How could he tell this woman that the last glimpse he had of her child was when they closed the lid on a tiny coffin?

"Aimée, I . . . There is so much I must tell you. Oh, my dear, I don't know how to begin."

"Oh, Franz . . ." Aimée bit her lower lip to keep from smiling. Franz was so sweet and awkward—and so delight-

514

fully prudish, even after all these years. "Darling Franz, must we still be uncomfortable together? After all this time, surely we have learned to forgive each other—and ourselves—for our one moment of foolishness."

"I . . . Of course we can, Aimée. Of course."

He couldn't tell her. That was all there was to it. He was a coward, and he despised himself for it, but he simply couldn't do it. He would bring her home to Sophie, and somehow Sophie would find the words that had failed him.

Sophie was standing in the doorway as the carriage pulled into the yard. She took a step forward when she saw them, then stopped, leaning heavily on her cane. It made Aimée sad to look at her, bent and tired, as if the burden of age had grown too much for her. Angrily she brushed the thought aside. This was her homecoming. She was not going to let anything spoil it.

"Sophie! Oh, Sophie, I'm back!" She waved brightly from the window, barely controlling her impatience as the coachman pulled open the door and helped her down. She did not even see a man standing at the edge of the drive until she had already started toward the house. When she did, she stopped abruptly.

He was tall and straight, a dark figure in a plain dark suit. Sun-bronzed skin stood out against the white of his collar. Even with a three-day growth of beard, he was as handsome as she had remembered.

"Raoul . . . ?"

What on earth was he doing here? He was supposed to be in Egypt, working in the tomb. Delighted, she stretched out her hands, laughing as she welcomed him to her home.

Raoul did not respond. Arms stiff at his sides, he stood in front of her, and all he could see was laughter on pretty pink lips. A dying child had called for Mama and Mama had been too tired to come.

But Mama was not too tired to laugh.

"Bitch!"

"Raoul . . .? Her warmth had been impetuous, an indiscretion that forgot the constraint between them, but surely that was no reason to treat her so harshly. "Why . . . why are you angry with me?"

He stared at her, and he could not believe what he saw. So beautiful . . . and so fashionable. Black silk styled to accent graceful curves. A coquettish little hat with just a hint of veil.

A shiny onyx brooch adding sparkle at her throat. He could have stood anything but the brooch.

"You don't give a damn, do you? You never did. All those hours I held your child in my arms and prayed for you to come, and where were you? Someplace safe and comfortable, recovering from your ordeal. What did you care for her pain . . . or mine?"

"Your pain? I don't understand." What could she know about his pain? She hadn't even realized he was in Europe. She knew nothing about his life now.

Raoul watched her face, eyes widened with surprise, lips parted as if to question him again, and he wanted to reach out and slap her. Once her innocence had seemed so beguiling, even when he knew it wasn't real. Now it sickened him to look at her.

"She was my child, wasn't she?"

"Mariette?" Was that what this was all about? Was that why he was so angry? Had he found out the truth about the child?

"Was she mine?"

Was she mine? Why did he say "was"? What a funny way to talk.

"Yes, she is yours."

He did not need words to confirm what he already knew. He hated her doubly now. It was not only her child she had abandoned, it was his child, too.

"What kind of a woman are you? How could you walk out on your own child? Does it matter to you that she was afraid? She called out for her mama—and you weren't there."

But I was there, she wanted to cry out. *I was with her until he forced me away.* Only, he looked so hard and uncompromising, she was afraid to speak.

"No excuses?" His voice was cold. "Or don't you need any? Maybe you think it's enough to dress in black so you'll look sad and pale and everyone will weep for you, even when your own eyes are dry. Well, it won't work on me. You see, I was there, and I know your child was crying for you when she died in my arms."

Died? Aimée stood and watched him, and she could not figure out what he was talking about. For a minute she thought he said "died," but of course that was ridiculous. Mariette was not dead. The telegram from Berlin said she was all right.

"Franz?" She turned toward her cousin. Franz would straighten everything out. He had been in Berlin with Mariette—the policemen told her so. Franz would tell Raoul that Mariette was all right.

But Franz did not reply.

For the first time Aimée began to feel apprehensive. She turned back to Raoul, searching his face carefully. His expression did not change. And in those dark, brooding features she finally saw a reality she could no longer escape.

Raoul had not lied to her. Mariette was dead.

The enormity of it overwhelmed her. Death, even the death of her father, was a thing she could not truly believe, but the death of her child was unthinkable. Only a moment ago she had been happy and excited, waving to Sophie in the doorway, waiting for a little black-haired whirlwind to come racing into her mother's arms. Now suddenly the whole world had changed and she could not understand it anymore.

She wanted to cry. She wanted desperately to cry. But all those years she had never learned how. Now it was too late.

Raoul watched her face, blank and emotionless, and his anger intensified into bitter sarcasm.

"By God, madam, I envy you your composure. Not a trembling hand, not even a discreet dab at the corner of your eye with a lacy handkerchief. You are a cool bitch, aren't you?"

"Am I?" She turned toward him dully, as if she were seeing him for the first time. "Well, perhaps you are right." There had been too much pain, too many losses. Humiliation, brutality, death. All powerful anesthetics that took away the power to feel. "If you will excuse me, I will go upstairs now. I am very tired from my journey."

Her room was cool and empty as she stepped inside, drawing the bolt across the door. The silence, even the loneliness, was welcome. Bright rays of late sunlight drifted in an open window, touching the tarnished electrum of an ancient chalice set on a table against the wall.

The electrum chalice. She remembered the day she had asked Raoul if she could have it. She had gone to tell him she carried his child in her body, and all he had said was: *Whose is it?*

She ran her hand along the surface of the cup. It was warm from the sun. She had wanted it desperately once. An empty keepsake of an empty love. It meant so little now.

She could barely remember her dreams anymore. They

seemed so faraway and unreal. She had loved once, but love was gone and would not come again. Raoul had touched her once, letting his longing merge with hers, but he did not long for her now. And Mariette had thrown baby arms around her neck, giggling as she begged to be lifted up, but Mariette . . .

"Oh, God, Mariette . . ."

Mariette had cried out for her mama—and she had not been there.

Raoul was right. He hated her now, and he should hate her. But he could never hate her as much as she hated herself.

And what did it mean in the end? she asked herself bitterly. Her eyes lingered on the cup in front of the window. Pretty Meryt, dead for three thousand years, and little Mariette, her namesake, new in a child-sized grave. What did it all mean? All the pain and the grief and the loneliness. All the tears that would not come.

I am not afraid. Why should you be afraid for me?

Mary Vetsera. She had not thought of her for months. Mary, with eyes nearly as blue as her own. And a beautiful blue-eyed princess, silent among the treasures of the ages. But Mary lay in an unmarked grave with no gilded shrines for her worship, no funny carved ushabti figures to guide her through eternity.

Only, Mary had died with her lover, while she and Meryt . . .

Meryt? Why was she thinking of Meryt now? Meryt was not like Mary. She was a hundred and twelve when she died. Raoul had told her so.

But Raoul's voice had been strained when he said it. Little things began to creep into her memory, things she would rather forget. A love poem painted on a drab brown wall: *I am unto thee a garden, rich earth planted with flowers and sweet-scented herbs.* A carved lion, scarred with the marks of tiny teeth, a favorite plaything of a beloved child. A wide stone sarcophagus twice the size it should have been. Slowly she began to understand.

A sarcophagus wide enough to hold a pair of coffins could only have been built for two.

And a child's toy was never meant for an adult's eternity.

She lifted the electrum chalice gently in her fingers. Three thousand years ago. Three thousand years—and the pain was still the same. A princess and a merchant's daughter, both

518

weeping for the loss that could never be replaced. A common bond that spanned the centuries.

She cradled the cup, warm against her fingers. Once it had seemed alive with secrets of its own. Now it held no mysteries for her. She had seen into another woman's heart, and she had understood.

The pain, the despair, the emptiness. The longing to escape. At last she knew what the cup had meant to the Princess Meryt.

And she knew what it would mean to her.